Lonewood

The Domino Effect

For the people of North Dakota, from someone who's been away too long <3

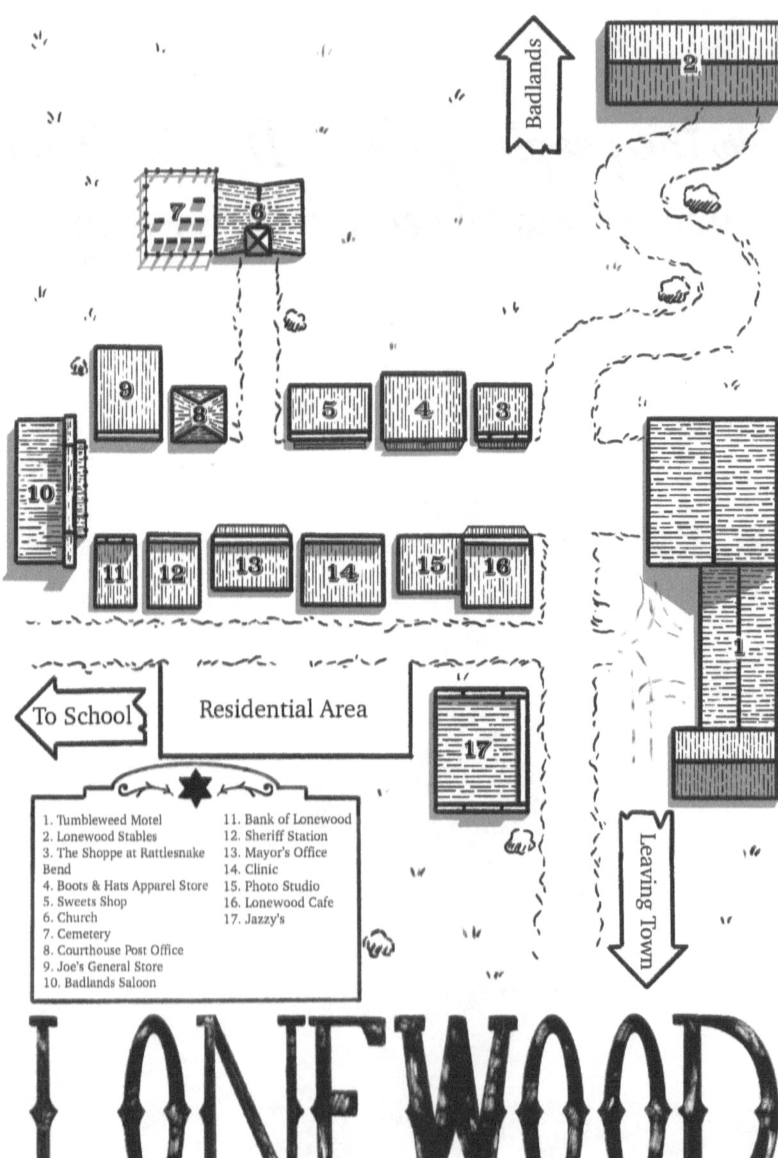

Badlands
Leaving Town
To School
Residential Area
1. Tumbleweed Motel
2. Lonewood Stables
3. The Shoppe at Rattlesnake Bend
4. Boots & Hats Apparel Store
5. Sweets Shop
6. Church
7. Cemetery
8. Courthouse Post Office
9. Joe's General Store
10. Badlands Saloon
11. Bank of Lonewood
12. Sheriff Station
13. Mayor's Office
14. Clinic
15. Photo Studio
16. Lonewood Cafe
17. Jazzy's
LONEWOOD

Chapter 1

"Everything is going to change tonight. I can feel it."

Scarlett Jacobs took a long breath in through her nose and let it out through pursed lips as her younger sister curled up her deep cherry hair. Alexandra hummed as her nimble fingers pulled back a few strands to keep them out of Scarlett's face. She raised one manicured brow. "Yeah? You think Mason's gonna propose, huh?"

"I hope so," Scarlett admitted as she stared at her reflection in the mirror. Her hands trembled in her lap as she held still, not willing to tempt fate and bump into the curling iron. She'd made that mistake more than once over the years and the last thing she needed was a burn mark when her boyfriend of four years finally popped the question.

Alexandra responded with another hum as she moved from Scarlett's hair to her makeup. It was an old tradition between the two of them: ever since they were teenagers Alexandra would do Scarlett's hair and makeup for important events. From high school graduation to her interview at Thomas and Co. Marketing, Alexandra had always been there to help Scarlett look perfect.

"What makes you think he's gonna propose tonight?"

Scarlett shrugged as Alexandra carefully lined her emerald eyes. "I mean, it's the perfect night to propose. I've worked so hard to become a marketing director... I feel like- like he'd want to reward that?"

"With a ring?" Alexandra scoffed.

Scarlett narrowed her gaze at her sister's reflection "I love him. We've been together a long time. This feels like the right time."

"It didn't feel right before your promotion?"

Scarlett breathed out heavily through her nose and explained as calmly as she could, "Well, I was really focused on getting it, and now I have, so now I'm ready for the next step."

"More like the next box to check off on your five-year plan."

Scarlett glared at her sister in the mirror as Alexandra's thin lips twisted to the side in a grin she was attempting to hide. Since she'd spent the past several years bouncing around Broadway shows as a dancer, Alexandra should have been better at hiding her emotions, but she wore her thoughts clearly on her face. Scarlett, much to her chagrin, often did the same.

Despite their matching poor poker faces, sometimes it was hard to believe they were related.

While Scarlett was petite with an hourglass figure, her little sister was all long limbs and sharp angles. Scarlett couldn't remember a time when Alexandra didn't have bright colors in her hair and lipstick in hues that would never be allowed in Scarlett's workplace. Alexandra wanted to be seen and adored, and her high heels and short dresses usually did the trick. Unfortunately for both of them, Scarlett got the better boobs of the two of them. They were, according to Alexandra, "wasted on someone who dresses like a boring secretary". Scarlett often wished she could trade for her sister's B cups so the men at her office didn't spend so much time leering at her chest.

They sat in comfortable silence for a while as Alexandra contoured Scarlett's round face. After applying fake lashes carefully, Alexandra pulled Scarlett's heap of curls over her shoulder and took a step back. "Damn. You look great. I did a fantastic job!"

"Thank you. Looks like years of stage makeup are finally paying off," Scarlett retorted dryly as Alexandra shooed her out of the chair to start her own makeup. Scarlett watched as her little sister pulled her long ebony hair into a sleek, high ponytail. Bright blue streaks poked out, and to Scarlett's horror, Alexandra made sure to wear a lipstick blue enough to match her hair.

She smirked at Scarlett, who gaped at her, but neither of them said anything. Scarlett didn't say anything when her little sister managed to wiggle her way into a skin-tight bodycon dress. Alexandra didn't seem to note that Scarlett chose to wear a one- shouldered, floor-length black dress with a slit up to her thigh. The sisters looked as though they belonged to different worlds, but they didn't mention it to the other as they got ready together.

"Can you grab my clutch?" Scarlett asked as she sat down to pull on her red stilettos. Alexandra handed over the Chanel bag and she slung it over her bare shoulder as she pulled on the other shoe. When she looked up at Alexandra, she found her little sister smiling sadly. "What? What is it?"

"You're just... all grown up. It's kinda weird." She sighed and took a seat on Scarlett's bed. "We're both grown up, obviously, but this feels different. This feels like you're stepping off into a different kind of unknown- and I'm happy for you, but I don't know where I'm gonna fit into the life you're trying to move towards."

Scarlett stood and pulled her sister against her chest, murmuring, "It's me and you. Just like it's always been. Nothing is changing, except my last name. But I'll always make sure you're taken care of. I promise."

Alexandra pulled away with a little nod. She checked her blue lipstick in the mirror and motioned towards the door. "We, uh, don't want to keep Mason waiting." Scarlett beamed as she headed for the door, towards the life she'd always dreamed of. When she reached for the knob, Alexandra asked bluntly, "He's paying for this, right? Because I sure as hell don't have money."

Scarlett laughed and nodded, locking the door behind them before ushering her sister towards the stairs.

The cab ride through Manhattan was quiet. Alexandra scrolled through her phone, clearly anxious because she was doing that nervous thing where she ground her teeth together. Scarlett was doubly nervous. She breathed in through her nose and out through pursed lips, being cautious not to smear her lipstick.

She was nervous about the potential proposal. She was also nervous about Alexandra embarrassing her. If anyone could find a way to inadvertently ruin the best day of Scarlett's life, it was her well-meaning little sister.

When the car stopped, Alexandra leaned over Scarlett's lap and gawked up at the skyscraper. "This is where the restaurant is?"

"Apparently. He just gave me an address. Said he'd meet us outside," Scarlett explained as she paid the cab driver and slid out of the car after Alexandra. A smile broke across her features when she saw Mason waving from the steps of the building with a massive smile on his face.

He pulled Alexandra in for a polite hug, then grabbed Scarlett's hand and spun her around slowly. "My God, you are stunning."

"Thank you, I did all the work," Alexandra deadpanned, but Mason just gazed down at Scarlett with a proud smile. He leaned in and kissed her cheek lightly, lingering a little longer than usual. It sent her stomach churning with excitement and nerves.

When he pulled away, Scarlett gestured towards the building. "Where are we exactly?"

"An old friend of mine is opening a restaurant in June, but he offered to let us in early for a sampling of the menu. Some of his investors will be dining here tonight and when I told him what a special night it was, he insisted we join." Mason took Scarlett's hand and led her towards the glass doors.

She felt like she was floating as one doorman held open the door for her and another escorted the three of them to a private elevator down the hall. Scarlett looked back at Alexandra and gave her a grin, but Alexandra was too busy fixing the hem of her too-short dress to notice.

When the elevator doors slid open, they revealed glass panes reaching from the floor to the ceiling all around the room, looking out over New York City from the highest floor. Another two-dozen people sat at little tables around the restaurant, but when Mason gave his name, the waiter ushered them to the far corner overlooking the bay with the Statue of Liberty in the distance.

Mason pulled out Scarlett's chair, and she sank into the plush, ivory covered cushion as he did the same for Alexandra. Her little sister looked positively out of place in her skimpy dress and colorful hair and makeup, but she raised her chin proudly and took it in stride. If anything, she was acting the part, pretending she belonged. Scarlett would never admit it aloud, but she was doing the same.

This wasn't the first time Mason had treated her to dinner at an upscale restaurant. Far from it; it was their favorite pastime as a couple, but this was the first time he'd gone out of his way to do something this extravagant. It was the first time he'd used connections to get them somewhere they couldn't go on their own, and it made Scarlett feel both important and incredibly unprepared.

"Mr. Cardoza, I'm so happy you could join us this evening," an older man in an Armani suit called as he approached their table. Mason stood quickly to shake the man's hand before they turned their attention to the sisters. "And who might these stunning women be?"

"My girlfriend, Scarlett Jacobs, and her sister Alexandra," Mason explained as the restaurant owner reached down to shake Scarlett's hand. "Scarlett was just promoted to marketing director at Thomas and Co. I know you've parted ways with your old marketing firm and thought it would be a disservice to not introduce you. Scarlett is the best in her field and hopes to open her own firm in the near future."

"Oh really?" the man said, and Scarlett wondered if Mason would introduce him or if she was supposed to already know who he was. "After you dine tonight, I'd love to hear your thoughts from a marketing perspective. I trust Mason. He's never steered me wrong with my finances, and I know he only keeps the best company. If he thinks you'd be a good fit, I'm inclined to trust his judgment."

Scarlett's eyes widened and she cleared her throat, standing quickly to shake his hand again. "Of course. I'd be honored."

"I look forward to hearing your thoughts about your dinner tonight as well. Please wave me over if you need anything. This evening is on the house of course, so order anything and everything you'd like to try. I want all the critiques I can get before we open."

As he walked away, Scarlett practically collapsed into Mason's arms as he laughed. "I assumed he'd wine and dine you a little before throwing out the offer, but it appears I still have quite a bit of pull with him. You'll love working with Richard, and when you eventually start your own firm, I'm confident he'll come with you."

"Did you just get me my first client?" Scarlett gasped as Mason pulled her into a quick kiss. "I can't believe this, thank you. Thank you so much."

"I hope this isn't the only reason we're here," Alexandra mumbled under her breath. Scarlett shot her a warning glare, but Alexandra ignored her in favor of perusing the menu. Scarlett sat back down between her sister and Mason with her back to the bay. The setting April sun washed the skyline with an orange and pink glow, making Manhattan look otherworldly from every angle.

Mason studied the wine list before waving over the sommelier and ordering an expensive bottle of champagne. Alexandra eyed Scarlett before clearing her throat and setting down her menu. "So, Mason, what's new with you? How are the stocks?"

He chuckled. "Stocks are fine. Nothing new. Just excited for Scarlett's new job. We've been talking about it for a long time and it's finally happening."

Alexandra nodded as the sommelier poured them each a glass of champagne. To Scarlett's horror, Alexandra took two huge gulps and held out her glass for another, causing Mason to laugh a little louder than he had before. "How are you? How's your show doing?"

"Oh, I'm between shows at the moment," Alexandra confessed as she sat down her glass.

Scarlett snapped her head towards Alexandra, eyes wide in question. This was the first she'd heard about Alexandra being let go. The younger woman flinched and explained quickly, "I'm looking for new employment until I get my next role. I spoke with my agent today and she's got a handful of auditions for me to go to in the next two weeks."

"What are you thinking for dinner?" Scarlett asked Mason, stealing the attention away from her sister. They could talk about her lack of employment when they got home. Scarlett just wanted this *one night* to go smoothly with her two favorite people.

Mason lifted his lips to kiss the corner of Scarlett's mouth quickly. "I'll just get whatever Richard recommends. And another bottle of champagne.

We're celebrating new beginnings tonight. Let's celebrate with the best New York has to offer."

Alexandra tossed back the rest of her second glass and said a little too loudly, "I'll try whatever the chef recommends, too. Since it's free."

Mason chuckled politely at Alexandra's comment, then shot Scarlett an unimpressed expression. When he'd extended the invitation to Alexandra, he'd hinted that she'd need to be on her best behavior if she joined them. Perhaps Scarlett shouldn't have brushed off his concerns.

Although she'd promised she would always be there for Alexandra, Scarlett knew she would move in with Mason once she had a ring on her finger. Alexandra could either pay rent herself for once or move back in with their parents. Maybe what she needed was a heavy dose of reality in the form of starting over. Maybe then she'd finally grow up instead of partying her life away.

After twenty-seven years together, minus a few where they were in college and off on tour, Scarlett and Alexandra Jacobs needed a little space. Scarlett thought it might be the best thing to ever happen to either of them.

"Before dinner comes, I want to do something," Mason started and Scarlett swore her heart stopped beating for a moment. Her worries about Alexandra fell away when he pushed his chair back and stood, and one of the waiters scurried over with a large gift bag. He sat back down and held out the bag for Scarlett to take. "You've worked so hard for so long for this day. You've put in countless hours working towards your goals, and I couldn't be prouder of you. You are a phenomenal businesswoman, and I can't wait to see where life takes you."

She carefully pulled apart the black and white tissue paper to reveal a brand-new Italian leather laptop bag. "I know how much you love your old one, and what it represents for you. I wanted to help bring you to your next step. I'm excited to see what you'll do next with this new job."

She ran her fingers over the smooth black leather before studying the clasp. Where there might normally be a brand label, there was a gold plate with her initials. Mason obviously had the bag designed specifically for her.

It was beautiful. It was wonderful and it was generous, and it was very, very sweet, but it wasn't a ring. It was a bag. He'd gotten her a work bag because that's what she needed. She didn't need a husband; she needed a bag to carry her work around in because her work was her life.

It felt like something inside of Scarlett broke, like all her hard work and dedication had been for the wrong thing. Like she'd won a game, but not *the* game.

When her gaze landed on Alexandra, she looked absolutely shell shocked. Her green eyes sparkled mischievously, even as her mouth sat agape. Then, because Scarlett needed to be broken from her spell, Alexandra whispered under her breath, "You got Elle Woods'ed."

That was precisely what had happened. She'd planned on a proposal and would leave without a ring.

This was supposed to be a new start professionally and personally. Scarlett wanted Mason to propose because she was riding high, but suddenly, she remembered that Mason was business first, pleasure later. Of course, he would think a proposal on the day she got promoted would be almost an insult, like proposing at somebody else's wedding.

Scarlett didn't want him to think she was ungrateful though. He meant well. He understood her better than anybody, and they would get engaged. Just not... today. So, she looked Mason in the eye and cooed, "It's perfect. I love it."

She convinced herself she meant every word.

Alexandra's face dropped when Scarlett leaned forward to kiss Mason. The sound of a chair scraping caught Scarlett's attention and she looked up to see Alexandra looming over her. "I need to use the restroom. Could you actually join me? My zipper is kind of stuck."

"Thank you again," Scarlett told Mason sincerely as he tucked the bag into its plastic pouch to keep it safe. "I'll be right back."

Her sister practically dragged her to the bathroom, and once they were alone, she turned on her. "What the hell was that?"

"Excuse me?" Scarlett snapped back. "You're asking me that? You're the one who chose my celebration dinner to confess you're unemployed! Did you quit? Or did you get fired?"

"This isn't about me-"

"Bullshit, everything is always about you. This one day couldn't be about me, could it? And for the record, I'm happy with how this evening turned out. We're not ready for an engagement right now, especially since I gotta stay with you and make sure you don't end up living on the street."

Alexandra gave an overdramatic scowl. "Are you kidding me? You're just gonna roll over and pretend to be happy?"

Scarlett shrugged. "Listen, I got my dream job. This doesn't mean a proposal isn't coming, it just reminded me that there are more important things right now."

"More important than love?" Alexandra's voice was laden with sadness, as if she truly believed nothing could be above love. Love was important, sure, but right now Scarlett's priority was her job. Mason knew and understood that.

Alexandra shook her head, an incredulous expression on her face as she sighed. "You deserve better than him, Scarlett. I know you think he's the one, but you two don't have any spark-"

"There's more to life than finding that magical spark you always talk about," Scarlett droned loudly. "Grow up. Maybe that's why you can't stay with a show for more than six months. You have potential Alex, you're just not applying yourself."

Alexandra scowled down at Scarlett and spat, "I wish you'd get your head out of your ass and care about more than work! It's just a stupid job."

"At least I have a job. You couldn't even afford to keep your life here if it weren't for me and my *stupid* job. You'd be back home with Mom and Dad, not performing, not drinking the night away with your friends. Clearly, you're a sucky actress, otherwise you'd be able to keep a role!"

The words were meant to sting, but Scarlett was startled by how horrible they sounded coming from her lips. Alexandra clamped her jaw shut, pursing her lips together tightly as her nostrils flared. She looked around the bathroom, shaking her head as her fury built. "I'm sorry that I don't want you to end up some miserable workaholic who marries a man she doesn't love because she doesn't even know what love is. But if that's what you want, who am I to stand in your way? Enjoy your dinner."

Without another word, Alexandra stormed out of the bathroom. Scarlett clenched the edges of the sink and simmered. She took a deep breath through her mouth and pulled her curls back over her shoulder before straightening the neckline of her one-sleeved gown. She smoothed out the edges of her lipstick before heading back to the table.

"Did she have to take off?" Mason asked casually, not alarmed but not unhappy either. That made two of them happy to see her leave.

"Yeah, she wasn't feeling well. She's gonna head home, but says thank you for the champagne." Scarlett clinked her glass against Mason's before taking a long drink. He watched her, studied her, like she really was stunning. Like he really did love her.

They'd said those three little words time and time again over the years, and never once did Scarlett doubt them. Even though Alexandra thought he wasn't sincere, Scarlett believed every word and passing glance he shot her way.

Despite what Alexandra thought, Scarlett was happy. She was sure of it. After all, she had everything she'd ever wanted.

Chapter 2

ALEXANDRA STORMED OUT OF the skyscraper, but she didn't call for a cab. The night was still young and she was far too restless to go home and wallow in her frustrations alone.

This neighborhood was a little too high brow for her tastes, so she wandered a few blocks north until she came across a neon sign flashing BAR. She moved towards it like a moth to a flame.

Pool balls smacked against each other over the sound of an old jukebox. The dive bar wasn't nice by any means, but the clientele looked decent enough for Alexandra's purposes. She wanted to drink- nothing more. She just wanted to forget for a moment what a failure she was compared to her older sister, and this place seemed perfect to drown her sorrows in booze and drunken dancing.

After she carefully pushed her way past a couple of older men to get to the bar, she wiggled her way between two curvy blonde women and called to the bartender, "Whiskey sour, please. Make it a double." She lowered her voice and added, "It's been a hell of a night."

"Put her on my tab, Gail."

Alexandra looked up to see a tall, lean man resting against the bar a few stools down from her. He leaned forward and waved, and she called back, "Thank you, but I don't take drinks from men whose names I don't know. If you wanna pay, you're gonna have to introduce yourself."

Alexandra bit at her bottom lip as she waited for the man to come over or leave her alone. She knew she should enjoy a drink by herself and go home, but she was lonely. A handsome distraction might be exactly what she needed for a few hours. He looked her up and down for a long moment, then got off his stool to stand beside her.

When he reached her, she realized he had piercing gray eyes that rolled over her features like a wave over the sand. Her stomach fluttered under his scrutiny, but there was no judgment in his gaze. He studied her for a long moment, as if trying to decide whether or not he wanted to take her back with him into the depths of the ocean. "Tell me a secret, something nobody knows, and I'll tell you my name."

"Hmm, but how will you know if my secret is true or not? You don't know me. Not even a little bit," Alexandra challenged back, perplexed that he'd asked her for something she wasn't prepared to give. She had to lean back to see his face since he was standing so close to her. Almost six feet tall, definitely. Short, black hair as dark as her own. So shiny it almost looked blue, as if they matched. As if they were meant to be seen together.

And he seemed to like her challenge. His feline smile widened as he leaned against the counter to get even closer. When the bartender handed over her whiskey sour, the cut muscles in his upper arm flexed. This man did hard physical work, or at least spent some time in the gym instead of slaving away behind a computer screen. Alexandra noticed a tattoo she couldn't make out on his forearm, but she wasn't ready to ask. They were circling each other now, waiting to see who'd make the first move.

She took a slow sip of her drink as the stranger shamelessly swept his eyes over her chest to her thighs in the short little dress. He lingered a moment on her neck, then her lips before meeting her eyes again with a small, confident smile. "Tell me two lies and one truth, and if I can figure out what's real, you'll give me your name."

"Yet you won't have told me yours. That doesn't seem fair."

"Landon," he answered quietly, sincerely. It seemed he was willing to give a little more than he'd intended to keep her in his reach. "Now tell me three things, mystery girl. You've piqued my interest."

"Is that all I'm good for? Piquing your interest?" Alexandra challenged, taking a slow sip of her drink. "I'm flattered, Landon, but I have my drink and your name. You've given me everything I need. Why should I play this game with you when I could just as easily run up your tab and leave without so much as a goodbye?"

His piercing eyes sparkled in the dim lights of the bar as he ran them from her eyes to her lips, then back up again. There was a wildness there that Alexandra didn't often see, but it was intoxicating. She thought she'd get more drunk from his eyes than the whiskey sour she'd barely touched.

He smiled. "Most women take the drink and ask to be taken home. But not you. You're more difficult than that, and I mean that in a good way. I like a challenge, and I'm not leaving until I know your name."

"A bit presumptuous, aren't we?"

"And you're lookin' a little promiscuous this evening for wanting to be left alone," the man bit back with a sly grin. "You came walking into this bar looking like that without knowing anybody. It means you're coming from somewhere else. You looked around cautiously when you entered, meaning you haven't been here before. You ordered a whiskey sour, something easy, meaning you aren't familiar with what they offer. When I offered to buy you a drink, you refuted me, meaning you want to vet your men before you get too deep in with them. I respect that. So, I want to know your name, and what sorry excuse of a man ruined your night enough to leave in favor of this shithole."

"I was on a horrible date. I was let go from my job. My brother is a condescending asshole." She raised her brows, daring him to guess which was the truth.

Landon studied her for a long moment, leaning against his fist as he considered the snippets of information she'd given him. He raised his head and smiled sadly, as if he felt sorry for her. "You got let go."

Alexandra furrowed her brows and huffed. She was a professional actress; she shouldn't be that easy to read. Maybe Scarlett was right. Maybe she wasn't any good after all. "How did you know?"

"You started with the horrible date. It rolled off your tongue so quickly it didn't feel genuine, but that could also be because you assumed I'd guess that no matter what you said after. The lilt of your voice was sad when you said you'd been let go, though, and the last one was so aggressive that

I think it's a half truth. Maybe your mother, or a sister, or friend. But not your brother. That part you faltered, because it isn't true."

Alexandra felt her cheeks heat up at his accurate evaluation of her. She cleared her throat and ducked her head, nodding a little as she raised her whiskey sour back to her lips. "Sister. Older sister. We got in a fight. And I was let go yesterday. Haven't been on a bad date in months, so it definitely isn't that."

"Well," Landon said gently as he drifted his fingers over her arm, causing her to shiver. His deep, honeyed voice partnered with his steely eyes had Alexandra hooked on every word he said. "I don't intend on being a bad date. But I will buy you another drink if it'll bring a smile to that pretty face of yours."

"You still haven't gotten my name. You said you weren't leaving until you got it. Does that mean you're in it for the long haul until you get what you want? You're that sure I'll follow through on my end of the bargain?"

"You'll tell me if you want to," Landon murmured, watching her with those piercing eyes. "I've got time. I'll do whatever it takes to make your night better, and if at the end I don't get your name, I'll know I did everything in my power to earn it."

She scratched at her scalp, feeling a headache coming on from the tight ponytail. Deciding to throw caution to the wind for a moment, she pulled out the scrunchie and shook out her hair, pulling it over her shoulder as she attempted to smooth down the bump. She laughed a little too loudly, feeling the alcohol beginning to fog her senses. She took another long drink and shrugged. "I'm a mess."

"A beautiful mess." Those silver eyes locked onto hers as he grabbed her hand and kissed it gently, the way the restaurant owner had done to Scarlett earlier. Alexandra stared at him curiously as his smile grew. "There's nothing wrong with a little mess here or there. It gives us character."

"Thank you!" Alexandra exclaimed gratefully as she motioned to Landon. She scoffed and shook her head before tossing back the last of her drink. "You should tell that to my sister. She's so proper and shallow and-she's not the same. She's got this big fancy job and her big fancy boyfriend, living in this big fancy city. And I'm drowning. She doesn't even realize

I'm barely staying above water." Landon ran his thumb over her knuckles and used his other hand to wave over the bartender, allowing Alexandra to order another drink. Then she looked back at him and confessed softly, "I miss her. I miss the way we used to be, before work became everything. I want more out of life, but she's so stuck in her own little bubble that she doesn't care what anyone else needs. And her boyfriend, Mason, he's the worst. Tonight... tonight she thought he was gonna propose, but instead he bought her a bag. I don't think he has a clue what she wants from him. I don't think *she* has a clue what she wants from him."

She expected Landon to politely nod and change the subject, but he didn't. He urged her on, letting her know her feelings were valid and he was listening. Nobody had *listened* to Alexandra in a really long time.

For the next two hours, Landon listened as Alexandra rambled on about her problems as she tossed back a few more drinks. She complained about how her parents favored her older sister and how her older sister favored her job. About the roles she lost out on and the dreams she'd given up on. He held her hand and smiled comfortingly, as if he really cared.

Around eleven, when the bar was beginning to get too loud to talk, Landon slid off the stool and held his hand out. "C'mon, Love. I want to see you dance."

Alexandra nodded, too drunk to think better of it, and allowed him to twirl her around the dance floor while she laughed loudly. She felt weightless, like they were floating above the ground. She hadn't felt this way in a long time, as if she was finally dancing for herself instead of people who didn't care about her. She laughed and danced with Landon for another hour until he looked at his watch and smiled at her sadly.

"I have to go, Love. This has been a wonderful night. Thank you for sharing your heart with me." He kissed her on the cheek, but when he tried to pull away, Alexandra grabbed the collar of his leather jacket and pulled him back, kissing him passionately. He kissed her back, sliding his hand down her dress to rest at the small of her back, holding her close to him as she allowed his tongue into her mouth.

When she pulled away quickly, she gasped, "Alexandra Jacobs. That's my name. Give me your phone. I'll give you my number so you can call me. I want to see you again."

Landon handed her his cell phone, and she somehow managed to punch her number in and save it before turning the camera towards herself to take a selfie, saving it as her contact photo.

"Alexandra Jacobs. I'll see you again, soon," Landon promised, pulling her close for one more kiss before disappearing into the crowd.

She stood in the middle of the crowded dive bar, panting. There it was: the spark. That magical chemistry people found in stories that Alexandra wanted more than anything in life. She'd felt it before, and maybe she'd feel it again, but she felt it for Landon *right now*. Looking around the bar, she knew her time here had come to an end, but she wasn't ready to go home.

She wanted to find him. She wanted to stay with him a little longer.

Quickly pushing through the crowded bar towards the exit, Alexandra looked around, trying to figure out which direction he would have gone. She started stumbling down the street, looking each way for the man she'd spent the past three hours with.

Maybe it was the whiskey that clouded her judgment or her deep-seated need to prove to Scarlett that love was more than a business transaction, but Alexandra was determined to not let Landon go.

The bright lights dotting the soaring buildings around her did nothing to help her cause, but the brisk April air did clear her head a bit as she slowed down and looked at her phone. She hoped maybe he'd text her, tell her he had a great evening. Then she'd have his number at least. At the moment, she didn't have the slightest clue how to find him if he didn't reach out. The idea of one magical night wasn't horrible, but Alexandra wanted more. She was tired of being on the cusp of something good, she wanted it squarely in her palm, where she could hold onto it and not lose it again.

It occurred to her as she continued to wander down the pavement that this was a wild goose chase. She didn't have a clue where he was going or how to find him. She didn't even know his last name. But his kiss lingered on her lips and his beautiful eyes were burned into her mind. Above all that, though, it was the way he spoke to her and listened. When she spoke, she felt like he really heard her, and understood her. She hadn't felt like anybody understood her in a long time.

Alexandra leaned down and pulled off her heels, choosing to instead walk barefoot down the street. The farther she got from the bar, the quieter the streets became, and she realized she'd made a mistake. She pulled out her phone, finding it close to dead. The best thing she could do was try to retrace her steps, maybe even find the restaurant and go home with Scarlett and Mason.

She sure as hell shouldn't be out here all by herself.

A clang and a crash was heard from an alleyway up ahead, and she startled, backing up a few steps until she saw a small cat sprint out of the alley. She took a deep breath and kept walking, pausing only when she heard hushed voices coming from the dark corridor.

She was about to turn around and go back the way she came when a voice she'd recently become familiar with spoke up in the darkness.

"We had a deal."

"And the deal is evolving. I know what's on these records, and it's worth more than the original price. If you want the files, you're gonna need to give me a little incentive not to report you to the cops. We both know they're closing in on you."

There was a silence, and Alexandra looked up, seeing it really was Landon at the far edge of the dead end. He was facing off with a man twice his size, holding a cheap briefcase in one hand and his phone in the other.

Landon's gaze was steady, uncaring even. He looked bored with the conversation and sighed, "You're not gonna go to the cops."

"Wanna bet? Two million or you get nothing."

Landon reached behind himself and removed a small dagger from his belt, hidden beneath the waistband of his jeans. Alexandra swallowed hard. Had he carried that all night? Had her hands just barely missed the hilt he'd kept hidden?

Now the knife was being held to the man's neck, and Alexandra knelt behind a trash bin, too afraid to move. She watched as Landon whispered in the man's ear, never touching him with the knife until the guy spat in his face.

The move was swift, borderline graceful. Landon sliced deep and fast, and the man yanked his neck back a moment too late. Alexandra watched the blood start slipping from his skin, and he crumpled to the ground, eyes wide as he watched Landon in horror.

Landon knelt down, grabbed the briefcase with his other hand, then plunged the knife into the man's chest. He stilled, and Alexandra gasped.

Her hands flew to her mouth, but the noise could have been a scream. It felt like it echoed down the alleyway, and Landon looked up as he stood slowly. He met her distant gaze with his piercing gray eyes, and Alexandra's chest shook as she pushed herself to her feet.

For a moment, they stared at each other, but then instinct took over, and she began to run. She dropped her heels and ran as fast as she could, sprinting blindly down the street until she knocked into an older man taking his dog out in front of an apartment building.

"Help! Please help, I just saw somebody get stabbed! Somebody- I need help, he saw me! Please- please help me!"

The man quickly ushered Alexandra into the lobby of his old apartment building, and she whipped around to look through the glass. In the distance, she saw movement, and let out a sob as she started registering what had happened.

Landon killed that man. Sliced open his neck and stabbed him in the chest and Alexandra *saw* it. He'd held her all night, he'd listened to all her problems... he knew all about her family, her friends, her life. He knew her name. And he knew that she'd seen him.

She vaguely heard the old man calling the police, but when he addressed her, she barely heard him. Everything echoed as she slid down the wall and sat on the floor. He'd looked right at her. There was no doubt in her mind that Landon knew what she'd seen. He killed that man so effortlessly- as effortlessly as he'd danced with her less than an hour ago. He'd held her hand and kissed her. She'd told him all about Scarlett and Mason and her job. She'd told him about her parents vacationing in Greece and her friends at the theater. She'd told him far too much.

"I think she's in shock."

A slight buzzing emanated from Alexandra's phone, and she swallowed, hoping it was Scarlett asking where she was.

It wasn't.

There was a text from an unknown number, and there was no name attached to the message, but she knew exactly who it was.

I know who you are Alexandra Jacobs, and I know where to find you. I'll be seeing you soon.

Chapter 3

It was a little after one in the morning when Scarlett and Mason finally made their way back to Scarlett's place. She held his hand tightly and leaned against his arm as they slowly clunked up the stairs to her apartment. She shushed him when they got to the second level, saying, "We don't wanna wake her up!"

"I mean, we could be quiet," Mason chuckled. She hummed and leaned forward to kiss him hungrily. Mason pulled away after a minute and smiled down at her, pushing a curl away from her cheek. "Did you have a good night?"

"I had a perfect night. Thank you for everything," Scarlett told him, rubbing her thumb across his cheek. She straightened up and tugged him towards her apartment.

Scarlett reached into her little purse to grab her key, but Mason grabbed her wrist softly. She looked up at him, and he nodded towards the door. She followed his gaze, finding it cracked open.

"What the hell..." she mumbled to herself as she dropped her key back into her purse, pulling out her phone to dial 911. She held her finger over the button as she used her other hand to grab the knob, carefully pushing the door to the apartment. She peeked around the corner, not seeing Alexandra anywhere. "Alexandra? Are you here?"

She pushed the door open all the way, Mason lingering in the doorway as she cleared her phone and started calling her sister instead of the police. The apartment had been ransacked. There was glass shattered in the kitchen, and their bookshelves had been knocked over. The worn leather couch had been ripped to shreds and a knife was planted squarely in the television screen, causing the glass to crack and shatter into little twisted webs.

The phone line clicked open, and Scarlett could hear her sister crying softly on the other side. She didn't even greet Scarlett, which scared the shit out of her. "What happened? Are you okay?" Scarlett asked quickly as she whipped around to Mason when he crept into the apartment behind her.

"Something's happened. I- I-"

Scarlett flipped on the light and looked around again. With the light, she realized there was blood on the floor. The sight caused her stomach to roil as she became aware of the smell in their apartment coming from Alexandra's bedroom. Alexandra was sobbing so hard she couldn't get words out, so Scarlett snapped, "What happened? Talk to me!"

"Where are you?"

"I'm at home, where are you?"

"I'm at the police station," Alexandra cried softly. Scarlett pushed her way into her bedroom, dropping off her new bag and looking around, but her stuff was untouched. It didn't bring her any comfort. "Scarlett, I'm scared."

"What the hell is going on?" Where her bedroom had been untouched, everything that had been Scarlett's in the living room was in pieces. Her diploma that had once been hung on the wall was in pieces on the ground. The books she'd carefully curated to make their living space look the perfect balance of organized yet lived-in were blood splattered and strewn across the carpet. The framed photo of their family was shattered on the coffee table. "This place is trashed!"

"The apartment?" Alexandra's voice shook as she asked the question quietly.

Scarlett strode across what was left of their living room to the other side of the small apartment, swinging open the door to Alexandra's room and letting out an ear-piercing scream when her eyes landed on a body on the floor. She dropped the phone and stumbled back into Mason's chest as he appeared behind her, sobbing into her palm.

This isn't happening. This can't *be happening.*

Leaning against the edge of her sister's bed was the security guard who watched the building. His neck was slit open and written in blood on the far wall, a horrible contrast against the soft yellow paint, were the worlds *You Talk, You Die.*

The police arrived at 1:26, and Scarlett and Mason were escorted to the police station at 1:52. By 2:11, Scarlett was reunited with her little sister, who could hardly breathe through her sobs.

"I- I told the police everything I knew, and they think... they think it's really bad Scarlett," she managed to finally get out.

Scarlett pulled away from her tight embrace to study her sister, finding her eyes bloodshot from crying and her pupils were still huge. Her hair was messy, and her skin was covered in a gross, sticky layer of sweat. Scarlett was scared to ask what had happened that led to all of this, but she didn't have time to pry before a lean man with a detective badge hanging from his neck and an exhausted-looking redhead wearing a U.S. Marshal's jacket came in to collect Alexandra for questioning.

"I'm not going without her," Alexandra told them firmly as she clenched Scarlett's hand. "I already told the police everything."

"We need to speak to you alone," the detective stated, but the woman with him leaned over and muttered something in his ear. He shot her an annoyed look, but relented, "Fine. She can come. This affects her, too."

Alexandra and Scarlett shared a nervous look as they were led into a windowless room with a small metal table and two chairs on either side.

"Miss Jacobs, I'm Detective Shields," the man introduced himself, then gestured to the redhead, "This is Marshal Masterson. I know you're having a difficult time processing what you saw, but we're gonna need you to answer a few more questions. You told a man in SoHo that you witnessed a murder."

"You witnessed a murder?" Scarlett squeaked as she turned to Alexandra, who just clenched her eyes closed and nodded. Scarlett looked up at the detective and stammered, "I found someone dead in our apartment. Our security guard."

"Miss Jacobs," Detective Shields said to Alexandra, completely ignoring Scarlett. He gestured toward the chair and ordered, "Take a seat. Start at the beginning."

Alexandra did as she was told, sitting slowly, and looking up at Scarlett with tear-filled eyes. Scarlett slung her arm around her sister's shoulder and squeezed her, nodding a little to encourage Alexandra to explain what she knew.

"I went to a bar. I ordered a drink and this random guy offered to put it on his tab. We started talking- he said his name was Landon."

At that, the detective let out a hushed swear and turned to his colleague, but the female Marshal gestured for Alexandra to continue.

"Tall, black hair. Muscular build. He had a tattoo on his arm, but I didn't get a good look at what it was..." she trailed off. She stared at the far wall, eyes wide and unseeing before blinking her way out of her daze and adding meekly, "I already told the cops everything I knew."

Detective Shields leaned his forearms against the metal table between them, offering Alexandra a weak smile. "I understand that, but we need to hear it again. I just examined both of the bodies and I want to hear exactly what you know about the man you saw in the alley."

"We drank together. We danced for a while. We kissed... he left. Around midnight I think," Alexandra rambled, trailing off towards the end as she massaged her head. She looked like she was still tipsy, like she couldn't quite see straight. Scarlett rubbed her shoulder, but stiffened when Alexandra confessed to her, not the detective, "I complained a lot in the beginning. I told him about you, and Mason. I told him about my job. I told him so much... At the time he didn't even know my name, it felt harmless enough. But we ended up having such a good time... I gave him my name and number before he left. I really liked him."

Scarlett looked up, finding Detective Shields watching the two of them curiously while Marshal Masterson leaned against the door with her hands in her pockets, nodding as she chewed her bottom lip. Her pretty blue eyes seemed to consider them both, as if it would help her piece together the puzzle of what had happened over the past couple of hours.

Scarlett looked down at Alexandra as her little sister whispered, "I went looking for him. I was so drunk, and I really liked him. When I found him, he was with this guy. Really big guy, and they were talking about files or something... I don't know."

"What happened then? What did Landon do?" Marshal Masterson asked from her place near the wall. "He killed the other man?"

"The other guy wanted more money. Landon slit his throat, and then stabbed his chest. He took the briefcase, but I gasped, and he... he saw me."

Scarlett's heart plummeted at that. It wasn't from what Alexandra confessed, but from the way the Marshal and the Detective shared a long look of resignation. Scarlett understood that this was what they'd been worried about.

After a moment, Detective Shields slowly asked, "You're sure?"

"Yes. He texted me after. He knows who I am."

"He's the one who was in our apartment?"

"Maybe. I- I don't know." Alexandra dropped her forehead into her palm. "I'm so sorry."

"Who is this guy?" Scarlett pulled away from Alexandra to address the detective. "Who did she meet?"

"We believe the man she met was Landon Maddox. We've been tailing him for a long time, but he's impossible to get close to. He's smart. He's lethal, as you've seen. And very..." he trailed off, with a slight disgusted twist of his lips, "...distinctive. I took one look at the body and knew who killed him."

Alexandra swallowed hard and Scarlett felt all the energy drain from her body. Detective Shields rubbed a hand down his face and sighed loudly. "He has a lot of dangerous people working for him. People with very specific, very deadly skill sets." Shields rubbed his brow before adding, "I guess I'd say he's mob adjacent, but mostly self-serving. He's former CIA, so he knows how to get his hands on government secrets. What you witnessed tonight is just another Friday night for him."

"But," Marshal Masterson cut in with a surprising amount of optimism in her voice, "This is the first time he's gotten close to someone and left them alive. It's surprising that he let you go. You'd be a great asset to our efforts to lock him up."

Alexandra sniffled and pointed at herself. "Me? You want me to help you catch him? I don't really know him-"

"But you witnessed him commit a murder. That's enough to put him away for life," Detective Shields explained. "If we can keep you safe long enough to get him in custody, and get a trial underway, you'd be crucial to getting a guilty verdict. You could save a lot of people, Miss Jacobs."

"If you can keep her safe?" Scarlett parroted. "How do you plan on keeping her safe?"

"Well, there's the Witness Protection Program," Marshal Masterson started, taking the seat across from Alexandra as Detective Shields stood. "We can relocate you. Give you a new identity. Once we get Maddox, we'll bring you back for the trial and go from there. We just have to keep you safe until then. You won't be safe here, I can guarantee that. He doesn't leave loose ends."

The room felt like it was spinning. Scarlett felt her knees buckle and Detective Shields quickly grabbed her elbow and guided her towards the door as Marshal Masterson began to give Alexandra a rundown about what would happen next.

They were going to take Alexandra away. They were gonna wipe her away and send her somewhere nobody could find her. Scarlett didn't know if she'd ever see her sister again. If their parents would ever see her again. She'd disappear into the abyss, becoming nothing but a government pawn to take down someone more important. Of all the men in Manhattan, Alexandra found the one man who the NYPD and US Marshals were actively trying to capture. And he knew her name. And her face. And where she lived.

Where Scarlett lived.

"Miss Jacobs," Detective Shields started as he hauled her to her feet and ushered her into another windowless room to wait. He didn't let go until she fell into the chair, grabbing her stomach with one hand and her scalp with the other, holding her head as her mind tried to catch up with what was happening to her. "Miss Jacobs, can I get you some water?"

"Are they going to send me away?" Scarlett choked out. She looked up, searching the man's dark eyes for any sign of deceit. "Do I have to go into Witness Protection, too?"

The detective had a good poker face. Scarlett couldn't tell what he was thinking when he replied with a simple, "Marshal Masterson will be here soon."

Scarlett sat in shock for a long time after Detective Shields left. Gruesome scenarios played out across the backs of her tightly closed eyes: Alexandra's fear at seeing a man die, thinking she was next. Their poor security guard at the edge of Alexandra's bed, with his blood strewn across the carpets and the walls. If Scarlett and Alexandra stayed in Manhattan, they'd almost certainly suffer the same fate.

Scarlett could stay and risk her life or let herself be wiped away. Both options were horrible, and she felt like she was suffocating.

Marshal Masterson came in and closed the door with a sigh, then took the seat across from Scarlett. Scarlett saw exhaustion in the woman's blue eyes. Her wiry red curls were pulled back away from her face in a messy bun, her skin devoid of makeup. Scarlett wondered if she'd been woken up to come in for this.

Then she thrust her hand towards Scarlett for a formal greeting, and Scarlett felt a tiny bit of her tension ease at the gesture. "Bridget Masterson."

"Scarlett Jacobs," she replied quietly as she shook the woman's pale hand.

"So, here's where we're at," Bridget started as she settled into her seat. "Landon Maddox will kill your sister if he finds her. She's fortunate to be alive now, and I want to keep her that way. She's opted to do the Witness Protection Program, and I think you should, too"

Scarlett swallowed, feeling her stomach drop. Bridget smiled grimly, giving a little nod obviously understanding Scarlett's apprehension.

"If you choose to enter the program, you're able to go alone, or with Alexandra. We can send you two away together, but you'll need to cut off contact with everyone. Your parents. Your friends. Your coworkers."

"My boyfriend?" Scarlett questioned, looking towards the door. "What happens to Mason? The man I came here with?"

"He's being given the option to join you, since he was closely affiliated with you. If he wants, he can go under cover with just you, or you and your sister. If he chooses not to, you'll need to cut contact with him as well. Since you aren't married, it's a simple yes or no from him." She watched Scarlett for a moment, like she was under a microscope. "What are your thoughts? Do you have any questions?"

Scarlett felt tears brimming in her eyes. "I don't want to do this. I don't want to do any of this. I want to stay here and live my life. I want everything to be okay."

The other woman smiled sadly and nodded. "I know. I wish it was that easy, but it isn't. The only way that's even a slight possibility is if Landon gets put away for life and the people he works with are incarcerated. You can get out of the program after a while but staying here in New York and going on with your life is incredibly dangerous."

"I didn't do anything wrong," Scarlett croaked, feeling the tears finally spill over her cheeks.

"No, you didn't. But neither did Alexandra. She met a nice guy at a bar. She stumbled upon a situation that she shouldn't have. It was a one in a million coincidence, and honestly, I'm just so amazed he let her go. I've had this conversation with many people, Scarlett, and it's usually very different. The siblings, the parents, the friends of…of the people he's crossed paths with, well, they're usually dead. If I were you, I'd feel very fortunate that your sister is alive. It's my job to keep it that way, and I want to offer you that same kind of opportunity."

Scarlett stared up at the fluorescent lights. "I just want to sleep. I want to go home. I want so, so many things, but none of it matters anymore because my sister met a bad guy. Oh sure, it might not have been Alexandra's fault, but if she'd gone home instead of to some bar to get shit-faced maybe we wouldn't be in this mess." She put her head back in her hands. "I'm just so angry."

Bridget sighed as she leaned back into her chair. The woman was trying to be patient, but she was obviously exhausted. Scarlett could relate. "I know. But we don't have time to waste. We need an answer because we need to put things into motion. What do you want to do?"

Scarlett wanted to go back to her life. She wanted to go back to her apartment and her promotion and the social status she was fighting to build in Manhattan. But that was gone. Everything Scarlett had worked for was gone. At least she could still have her sister and Mason. Maybe she could salvage what little was left of her dreams somewhere new. They seemed incredibly certain that she wouldn't live long enough to do much else if she stayed here.

Scarlett looked at the Marshal, chewing the inside of her cheek thoughtfully. She knew what she needed to do, she just didn't want to accept it. She didn't want to be wiped away, but it was better than having her throat slit. "I'd like to join the program with Alexandra. I want to stay with her. Then at least I'll know she's okay."

Bridget offered a smile, one that told Scarlett she'd made the right choice, even if it made her sick to her stomach.

"We'll get you and Alexandra to a secure facility and begin the orientation process. You should be heading to a new home in about a week or so once we've got you acclimated to your new identities."

Scarlett thought she might throw up at the idea of having to become somebody new. She sucked in a sharp breath and asked, "Do we get to go home and pack?"

"No, but I'll head over there with my team to gather up what we can. It won't be much. If there's anything sentimental, let me know, and I'll do my best to grab it." She stood and opened the door. "We're getting transport prepared now to take you to a secure facility. I'll give you a few minutes alone with Alexandra while I speak to your boyfriend."

"Okay," Scarlett murmured. She was so tired. She wished she wasn't still wearing her heels. Her dress had once felt classy, but now it was a prison garment. It was the last remnant of everything she'd worked for all these years.

When the Marshal opened the door to the room Alexandra was in, the younger sister sprang to her feet and engulfed Scarlett in a tight hug. She sobbed into her shoulder as Scarlett rubbed her back, shushing her softly.

"I'm so sorry. I didn't mean for this to happen. I wish I could take it back. I wish- I wish-"

"It doesn't matter now. We just have to figure it out." Scarlett closed her eyes to hold back her tears. She heard Alexandra murmur that she loved her. Scarlett was too angry to reciprocate the sentiment.

About twenty minutes later, Bridget returned.

"Time to go."

She led them to a black, windowless van and herded them into the backseat before following them and sliding the door closed.

"Where's Mason?" Scarlett asked slowly as they began to drive away from the police station.

Bridget's soft smile dropped like a ton of lead. She ducked her chin, keeping her eyes locked onto Scarlett. "He declined our protection. He asked to return home... and cut off contact."

Her head pounded loudly in her ears as Bridget's words played over and over like a broken record. He'd chosen to return home. To cut off contact. To never speak to Scarlett again.

"I'm very sorry," Bridget added softly. Scarlett felt the tears brimming in her eyes, and was suddenly very aware that she was still wearing that one-shouldered black dress that she'd worn specifically for Mason, hoping he'd ask her to be his wife. He'd chosen his social life and career over his safety. He'd chosen it over *her*.

She cleared her throat and lifted her chin, trying to appear brave and unmoved. "What did he say?"

Bridget's face somehow paled, as if it had any color to begin with. "We told him that you'd opted to join your sister. We gave him the option to join, but he declined."

"Did he think about it?"

Bridget hesitated a moment before answering Scarlett. "I wish I could say he did, but no. He didn't." Bridget murmured. Even she sounded a little disappointed. "I offered to let him say goodbye, but he said he didn't want to make this harder than it already was."

Scarlett shook her head rapidly, disbelieving. Alexandra tried to hold her hand, but she ripped it away. Alexandra whispered, "I'm so sorry."

Without thinking, Scarlett snapped, "Please just leave me alone! You fucked up everything, and now our lives aren't even ours anymore. Don't apologize, because I don't forgive you. I don't know if I ever will, but I'm going to make this work, because I want to live. Just- stop telling me how sorry you are. It isn't going to bring our lives back."

Alexandra leaned away, settling her head against the side of the van as they drove. "Okay." Her voice wavered on the word, but Scarlett wouldn't take back what she'd said.

When Scarlett's green eyes landed on Bridget, the U.S. Marshal didn't say anything. She kept her expression neutral as her asset lost her temper. Scarlett was impressed by her ability to keep it together in such a stressful situation. Clearly, she didn't possess that same skill.

She couldn't pretend she was okay. She couldn't forgive Alexandra right now. Everything Scarlett had worked for was gone. Everything she loved and was would be wiped away and she'd be forced to become somebody new because her sister made a bad decision.

She wondered who she'd become next.

Chapter 4

Ten Days Later

"SIENNA?"

At first, the redhead didn't respond, but then she remembered Sienna Jade was her name now, and she needed to start responding to it.

Perhaps Alex Jade would be an evil genius in this new life, because she'd found a way to make her older sister finally speak to her.

"Yes?" Sienna looked up from where she was reading over her notebook, making sure she had Sienna's life story straight before they left for their new home. No, not Sienna's life story, she reminded herself again. Her life story. Bridget would be there to collect them any minute now.

Alex grinned. Sienna rolled her eyes. She'd done a decent job of ignoring Alex over the past ten days, despite Bridget's perfunctory attempts to get them to make up.

Sienna was upset. The therapist at the facility told her she was allowed to be upset about her circumstances, but taking out her frustrations on Alex wouldn't bring her the closure she needed to succeed in her new life.

Alex. Their mother had hated when people shortened Alexandra's name. "Alex is a boy's name, and you are *not* a boy," she'd told them time and time again in their youth.

As soon as Bridget had given the parameters about picking a new name, Alexandra had asked if she could go by Alex. Perhaps it was an olive branch, because Alex was what Scarlett had called her when they were kids.

It seemed counterproductive to go by a shortened version of her real name, but Bridget approved it. Scarlett told Bridget to pick something for her. She didn't have the heart to pick out a new name, her mother had loved the name Scarlett. Bridget picked Sienna Jade. "You can at least keep your initials, right?" Bridget had offered. Sienna had smiled weakly and shrugged. It was a nice gesture by the Marshal regardless.

Although Alex had been told she could keep some semblance of her name, keeping her recognizable hair was out of the question. Sienna had watched them hack off Alex's long black hair to her shoulders and dye it blonde with dark roots. Sienna's appearance was mostly intact, aside from some thick bangs that she'd grown to tolerate over the past four days.

"Is there something you wanted?" Sienna asked Alex as she went back to her notes. Bridget had them practice together: practice their signatures, practice their life stories, recite the rules they had to follow to stay in the program.

Try to fit in. Find a job. Don't tell anyone who they used to be. Make a new life.

Sienna raised her eyes to Alex, seeing her sister grinning hopefully down at her. Her blonde hair was pulled back in a high ponytail and her face was devoid of bold makeup. Instead Alex had applied blush and mascara, basically a bare face to the former actress.

"I wanted to see how you're doing. We're leaving for our new home today."

"I'm aware," Sienna answered quietly. As angry as she wanted to be at Alex, the therapy sessions hadn't been for nothing. She sighed and closed her notebook to give Alex her full attention. "I made the decision to come with you. I'm pissed at you for causing this shit show, but I know you didn't do it on purpose. That said, I'm not ready to pretend everything is great."

Alex's hopeful expression fell and she heaved a sigh. "Fair enough. But you can't blame me for trying."

"I'm trying too, just in my own way," Sienna mumbled, pushing a chunk of hair behind her ear as she turned back to her notes. She could feel Alex looming over her, but she stayed silent. They'd have plenty of time to talk when they were dropped off in their mysterious new home.

Bridget had told them that nobody could know where they were going, even the other members of her team. Landon Maddox had endless resources and likely still had contacts within the government.

She was sending them somewhere safe, somewhere she had an old friend who used to be with the Marshals who could keep an eye on them without knowing the real reason they were there.

When they heard a steady knock on their door, Alex shuffled over to open it, finding Bridget standing on the other side with two large suitcases behind her.

"You two ready to go?"

"Ready as we'll ever be," Sienna replied. She stood and left her notebook on the kitchen counter. She met Alex's nervous gaze and reached out her hand. An olive branch.

Alex took it and they followed Bridget out the door.

After another trip in a windowless van, they arrived at an undisclosed airstrip to board a private military plane with Bridget. Throughout the ride, they sat in silence. Sienna couldn't tell which direction they were even flying. Bridget didn't supply their destination. Neither did the pilot.

It wasn't until they were off the plane that Bridget explained where they were for the first time.

"Welcome to Bismarck!" She gestured around, and Sienna looked around the barren place they'd landed. In the distance, on a small hill, was one mildly tall building. Not a skyscraper by any means, but the only tall building around. Everything else was flat.

"Bismarck... that's the capital of... uh..." Alex trailed off, wracking her brain for where the hell they were.

Sienna whipped around to glare at Bridget as the Marshal supplied, "North Dakota."

"North Dakota? You're sending us to *North Dakota*?" Sienna sneered as she crossed her arms. The temperature was hot, but the breeze was cool. Since there were no trees and few buildings around to block the wind, Sienna's hair flew wildly around her face as they stood on the tarmac. She ground her teeth together before she barked, "You're sure there's nowhere else we can go?'

"Try living here for a while, and we'll go from there. If you hate it that much we can move you later. First we have to find Maddox." Bridget called over the roaring of the plane engine as she led them away from the airstrip to their transport. Sienna looked to Alex, who looked around curiously. There was no frustration, anger, or disappointment in her face, only curiosity. A new adventure.

But Sienna didn't know what to do with herself.

She'd traveled. She'd been to different places around the U.S. and beyond, but she didn't know the first thing about North Dakota. She was impressed that Alex remembered Bismarck was its capital. She'd never met anyone from here and she'd never heard anything about the state. It was quite literally the middle of nowhere.

Landon would most likely look everywhere else on the planet before considering this place.

Bridget slid open the back door of a black van. She smiled grimly at Sienna, but her smile brightened a little at Alex when she climbed in. Sienna grunted and slid in beside her sister before Bridget climbed into the driver's seat. The door slammed, she clicked her seatbelt, then looked in the rearview mirror. "You two ready to go?"

"Let's do it," Alex said confidently. Sienna scowled out the window, ignoring Alex and Bridget as they started to drive away from the airstrip.

For miles and miles, they passed nothing. Flat fields as far as they could see. Sienna saw cows and hay bales, but they barely saw other cars as they cruised down the four lane highway. Occasionally they'd drive past the outskirts of little towns. Past humble football fields and gas stations. They passed random homes miles from the nearest town.

The van's clock showed eight-thirty but the sun was still trying to set. Sienna was thankful it was early May. She prayed they'd be long gone by winter. If the summer days lasted until nine at night, she was terrified to find out how long the night would last in the winter time.

"How much further?" Sienna asked quietly, and Bridget perked up at the sound of her voice. It was the first thing anyone had said since they left the airport.

"I think about a half hour. We're almost there." Bridget looked at her phone quickly, frowned, then changed the van's clock to seven-thirty. They'd switched time zones.

Alex caught it too, because she asked, "What timezone are we in?"

"Mountain time. We crossed over a little bit ago. They are two hours behind Eastern time so it's nine-thirty back on the coast."

"No wonder I'm exhausted," Sienna mumbled to herself. She didn't want to seem crabby, but she hadn't slept well. With only a half hour left to go, she knew it wasn't worth trying to sleep now. "Since we're so close, can I ask where we're going?"

Through the rearview mirror, Sienna saw Bridget's lip turn up into a small smile. "Lonewood. It's a little tourist town on the edge of the Theodore Roosevelt National Park. There's another town called Medora that's similar, but more popular. Lonewood is more... immersive... from what I've gathered. Skylar will be able to explain it better. She's my friend who lives there."

"She was in the Marshals, right?" Alex asked. She leaned forward on her knees, staring through the center console at the road ahead as they drew closer to their destination.

"She was my roommate in basic training. We were stationed together for a long time in Manhattan before she moved home to take care of her mom. She's good at what she does, and she'll look after you guys. If there's any trouble, she'll put an end to it." Bridget explained, clicking her turn signal to get off the highway.

They passed a large, old sign on the side of the road. "Lonewood- Six Miles Ahead". Sienna rolled down her window, getting a good look at her surroundings. Grassy plains disappeared quickly, and bare, rolling hills of tan and orange scooped into deep valleys. Sienna looked back at Alex, finding her surprised by the abrupt change of scenery. Even Bridget seemed distracted by the view, slowing down and rolling down her own passenger's window to get a better view.

For six miles, they drove down a smooth road, admiring the view until they came upon another sign reading "Lonewood". As soon as they passed the sign, Bridget turned right, and the road turned to gravel. Sienna coughed a little as the tires kicked up dust and rolled up the window at the same time as Bridget.

The dust created a cloud as the sun finally dipped below the horizon, stealing away whatever good view the women had of the small town ahead of them.

Bridget slowed down at a stop sign, allowing the dust to settle. To the left, loud pop music blared from an old bar. Alex leaned against the window to try and get a better view through the tinted glass, but it was just music in an abyss. Bridget turned right, taking them down another short road until they reached a sprawling single-floor motel.

She pulled into the parking lot and stopped, then turned off the van and looked between the seats at Sienna and Alex. "We're here." Sienna raised her brows in question. She wasn't under the impression they'd be living in a rundown hotel. Bridget sighed and explained, "Obviously we don't want you to live in a hotel forever, but we wanted to get you somewhere safe quickly. If you need help finding a more permanent place to live, let me know. Let Skylar know, she'll help. Or if you'd rather figure something out on your own, you're welcome to do that, too. Don't forget about the stipend you've got, but use it wisely please."

Alex popped open the door first, sliding out and looking around. Sienna took a long breath through her nose, told herself she could do this, and let it out through pursed lips.

The motel looked old. The building was made of wood with cracked numbers carved into every door. The curtains looked dirty beyond spotty windows, and the pathway was nothing but rocks and dirt. Hopefully it was meant to look rundown on the outside, and it would be decent enough on the inside. If not, Sienna wasn't against sleeping outside if the conditions were better.

She accepted that this would be her bed for the night, and slowly opened the door and climbed out of the van. As she wandered over to the other side of the vehicle, she saw a small woman with jet-black hair pulled back into a ponytail jogging towards them with a beaming smile.

"Bridget!" she shrieked as she tackled the redhead in a fond embrace. When she backed away, she looked Bridget up and down before gasping, "You look amazing! How are you? It's been so long!"

"It's so good to see you!" Bridget answered as she pulled Skylar in for another quick hug, then turned and gestured to Alex and Sienna. "Skylar, these are my friends! Alex and Sienna Jade. From California. They're looking for a change, and I remember you talking about this place and I told them about it and they thought it could give them the change of pace they needed..."

Skylar narrowed her eyes at Sienna and Alex. She looked them up and down, nodding a little as her knowing smirk grew. She knew full well they weren't here by choice; that was obvious by the way her eyes twinkled mischievously. "It's pretty different from California here. Sure you two can hack it?"

"We're just looking for fresh air and a chance to try something new. Based on what you told Bridget, we decided to take a leap of faith," Alex told her evenly. Sienna was impressed that Alex was able to conjure such a bold lie. Bridget hadn't told them anything about Lonewood until thirty minutes ago.

That seemed to please Skylar enough, because she gave a single nod and turned to Bridget. "What about you? Are you gonna stay the night? Catch up?"

Bridget looked down at her watch, then smiled grimly and shook her head. "Unfortunately I have a plane to catch. I want to see them get settled, but then I really gotta go."

"You sure? After all this time you come to visit and you don't even stay?" Skylar teased. She wore old ripped jeans and a three-quarters sleeve green shirt that was cuffed around her forearms. Sienna noticed her worn boots. They were cowboy boots.

Bridget had said the town was immersive. Suddenly, Sienna found herself worrying about what she'd meant by that.

"I wish I could stay and see your home, but I really gotta go. Big case back home..." she trailed off. Her gaze fell on Alex and Sienna and she asked Skylar, "Who do I have to talk to to get these two a room?"

Skylar reached into the back pocket and pulled out a key. A literal, metal key for a lock. She handed it over to Sienna, but spoke to Bridget. "I already took care of it. First night's on me."

"You sure?" Bridget asked, but Skylar just waved her off.

"Of course. Least I can do for friends of a friend." She looked between Alex and Sienna with an amused expression, her bottom lip between her pearly teeth in the golden light of the hotel lamps. "How about I stop by tomorrow morning around nine and take you two out for breakfast? I know it's a little early California time, but hopefully it'll give you enough time to rest. I'll give you a tour of the town. Introduce you to some people. I know it can be hard in a new place... meeting good people makes all the difference in the world."

It was the most genuine thing Skylar had said. Her last sentence was clearly directed at Bridget, and the Marshal smiled a little when she realized it, too. Skylar pulled Bridget in for another hug, then nodded her goodbyes to Sienna and Alex. She gave one last wave to Bridget before she disappeared around the corner to head home.

"She seems nice!" Alex chirped. She plucked the key from Sienna's hand and read the tag, then looked at the door numbers to find the right one. Bridget silently tugged their suitcases from the back of the van, handing Sienna's over while dragging Alex's herself.

Alex reached one of the farthest doors in the block of rooms and shoved the key into the hole. She fiddled with the lock for a bit before getting it to pop open, then turned and smiled brightly at Bridget and Sienna. "I don't remember the last time I've used a real key in a hotel room."

"Well, this place is pretty old fashioned," Bridget mumbled as she pushed open the door to drag Alex's bag inside. She flipped on the light switch, causing a lamp to illuminate on the bedside table. There were two full beds with a table between them, and a small table and chairs near an old television.

Sienna's eyes darted around the dimly- illuminated room, but she kept her expression neutral. She wasn't a hotel connoisseur, but she wouldn't even give this place two stars.

"It'll do for a few nights. You've got plenty of money to rent a nicer place, or even buy once you get jobs. Skylar will help. I'll be in touch with her, but I'll try not to reach out to you two unless I really need to. Please feel free to call or text if you need anything though, and let me know if you notice anything suspicious," Bridget warned as she placed Alex's bag at the bed near the door. Sienna pulled her suitcase over to that bed though, placing herself between her little sister and the point of entry. She slung her heavy suitcase up on the mattress, wincing when she heard the springs creak. Bridget gritted her teeth, trying to hide her grimace behind a weak smile. "I think you two will have fun. An adventure to say the least."

"Mmhmm," Sienna hummed, unimpressed. At least the likelihood of Landon finding them was slim to none. If it were her, she'd scour the oceans before she considered looking for someone in Lonewood, North Dakota.

Bridget stood there awkwardly, waiting for one of them to say something, ask something, or give some sign they needed her or not. The temptation to ask to come back with Bridget was strong, but Sienna swallowed down her frustrations when she remembered that Landon would be looking for them.

She hoped she'd never have the displeasure of meeting the man who'd stolen her life. She didn't even know what he looked like, and she hoped she never would.

"Thank you for everything," Alex finally told Bridget. She pulled the shorter woman into a hug. "We'll be okay if you want to go. I know it's a long drive back."

"I can be here quickly if I need to be. There are closer airports, but I didn't want to leave a trail-"

"We'll be okay," Sienna repeated, wanting to assure Bridget they could handle this. "Thank you."

Bridget pulled Sienna in for a hug, then waved a little and disappeared out the wooden hotel door.

Once it clicked, the silence was deafening.

Alex sat on the bed near the bathroom, perched on the edge of the mattress as she looked around. The walls looked like they were built out of logs, as if they were in a cabin. Sienna wandered further into the room, twisting the handle to the room she assumed was the bathroom. It didn't open easily, so she smashed her hip against it, causing it to pop open and reveal a wooden counter with an old iron basin. Across from the small counter and sink was a bathtub, but a shower curtain had been installed to create a shower option. Sienna was surprised they had that much for amenities.

"I think it's cute. Rustic. Like Bridget said, it could be fun!" Alex's voice was strained. She didn't believe what she was saying either. There was a pause as Sienna left the bathroom, opening a small closet across from the bathroom door. "It's like camping."

"Well, if our electronics spark in these old-ass outlets, we'll have one hell of a campfire," Sienna mumbled as she pushed against the dull-colored, loosely screwed outlet near the floor by the closet. So much for needing a curling iron, she'd be lucky to charge her phone.

She turned around when she heard Alex grunt as she swung her suitcase up onto the bed. She watched the way the mattress dipped, wondering if they'd be able to feel the metal screws that struggled under the weight of their few belongings. "I'm tired. I'm glad Skylar isn't coming until nine, that'll be eleven Eastern time."

"Maybe we'll wake up and it'll all have been a horrible dream," Sienna chuckled. Wishful thinking.

Sienna chewed the inside of her cheek as she unzipped her suitcase, flipping it open to reveal all her new things. Part of her wanted to unpack, because they wouldn't have a new home by tomorrow, but the other part of her didn't want to accept that she was stuck here. She shifted the neatly folded clothes around until she found a t-shirt and a pair of purple sleep shorts tucked beneath a white lace dress that Bridget picked out. She zipped the suitcase back up roughly and dropped it back to the floor. The decision of whether to unpack or not could wait till tomorrow.

From the corner of her eye, Sienna watched as Alex locked herself in the bathroom to get ready for bed. Sienna knew she should brush her teeth and wash her face, maybe even shower, but she was exhausted. Tonight, she'd crash, and maybe tomorrow she'd pull herself together.

It took everything in her weary bones just to change into her pajamas.

As Alex reappeared, Sienna padlocked the motel door. She dragged her suitcase in front of it to create an extra barrier. She'd never been a paranoid traveler, but she was in a strange place. Also, there was the man who wanted to kill them.

She looked up when Alex dragged her suitcase over and leaned it against the door too, giving Sienna a firm nod. "It's a good idea."

"Was the rest of this, though?" Sienna whispered. She pulled the old white curtain to the side, seeing the parking lot dark. There were only a half dozen cars, even though there seemed to be at least a hundred motel rooms around the sprawling single-story building. Clearly the motel wasn't busy. Sienna wondered if Skylar even paid, or just told them she had guests staying for the night and they gave her a key. This seemed like the type of place to take favors as payment in lieu of money. "I somehow feel less safe here than in Manhattan."

"It's just because it's new. I'm sure it's perfectly safe," Alex argued as she sidled up next to Sienna at the window. They looked past the parking lot towards the road. Beyond it, there were lights, and faint music that echoed through the dark night. Although the hotel was quiet, whatever was happening across the street wasn't.

Alex grabbed the curtain and pulled it closed, turning to look down at Sienna. "You'll feel better once we get the lay of the land tomorrow. Everything is creepier at night when you don't know where you are. Nobody is coming for us."

A high-pitched yelp, followed by a howl came from outside the motel room. Somewhere in the distance, but not nearly far enough. Sienna glared up at Alex and she shrugged. "I'm sure whatever that is doesn't have the ability to break through a door."

"What if there are bears?"

"So what if there's bears? We aren't in a tent. Let's get some sleep. Set an alarm for eight so we can be ready when Skylar gets here to pick us up." Alex popped open her little brown purse and pulled out her phone charger to plug in her phone into the outlet near the little table. Sienna groaned and pulled her charger out of the front of her suitcase, kneeling down to inspect the underside of their bedside table for an outlet.

Alex scoffed, "What? You think the place is bugged?"

"Literally just looking for a plug. And I'm much more worried about actual bugs than listening devices."

Alex shivered a little at that, shaking her arms out as if she could feel the creepy crawlies on her arms. "We got this. It's an adventure. We've had plenty of adventures."

"The last time I camped we were in a motorhome overlooking a crystal clear lake. We're out of our depth here," Sienna grumbled. She pulled back the sheet and crawled into her bed, causing the springs to creak. She groaned angrily, then pointed at the light switch. "Can you shut that off?"

Alex did as she was asked, and the room was plunged into darkness. Sienna laid on her back, glaring at the ceiling. The faint music blaring across the street brought a little comfort, because if it was silent, Sienna didn't think she'd sleep. She missed the white noise of the big city. The muffled pop music was more familiar than whatever four-legged creature lurked in the wilderness of their new home.

She heard Alex crawl into bed, her mattress shifting loudly as she tried to get comfortable. Sienna slammed her eyes closed, hoping she got some sleep. She was too exhausted for another sleepless night, and no amount of coffee would wake her from this living nightmare.

"I'm sorry I got us into this mess."

"We're already here. There's no going back now," Sienna grunted, rolling over to face away from Alex. She stared at that wooden door with resentment. She was tired of being angry, but her whole body was wound up, like she could snap like the springs in her shitty mattress.

"Will you try to be open minded?"

It was a reasonable request. Alex hadn't asked Sienna to join her. Not even once. Sienna agreed without ever considering whether or not her little sister would rather endure her second chance at life alone. All Sienna had done since meeting Bridget was ignore and blame Alex for ruining her life, but she could have done her own thing. She could have gone into hiding alone or stayed in Manhattan. She'd asked to stay with Alex, meaning Alex was just as stuck with her as she was with her little sister.

Since she was here now, Sienna knew she owed it to Alex to at least try and make the best of it. That needed to start with them opening up to each other again.

"Yeah," Sienna murmured. She rolled over, groaning as the bed squealed in agony at her movement. "But we need to find somewhere else to live. I'll never sleep again at this rate."

Alex shifted and laughed loudly when a slight crack was heard from the wooden base of the bed. "Deal."

Chapter 5

When Sienna's alarm went off at eight a.m., she was already wide awake. She never slept past eight at home, and right about now it was ten at home, meaning she should already be up and productive. Today, though, she stared at the ceiling until her alarm summoned her.

She rolled over, causing the bed to screech as she reached for her phone. Alex groaned a little at the noise and pulled the pillow over her face.

"It didn't charge," Sienna mumbled as she pulled her phone from the cord. She flopped onto her back, staring up at her new phone. She wished there were photos, or texts, or some sort of semblance of personality. It was a husk. Exactly how she felt right now.

Alex pushed herself out of bed, stumbling toward the bathroom. When the door slammed closed, Sienna closed her eyes and sat her phone down. She breathed slowly through her nose, then blew the air out through her pursed lips. She counted to ten.

Outside their motel room, Sienna heard whooping and yipping, followed by the sound of thundering hooves. She opened her eyes, furrowed her brows, and sat up. The sound got closer before fading away, and she slowly stood to pull open the curtain. A cloud of dust wafted through the parking lot of the motel, hiding whatever had caused the ruckus.

She pulled Alex's suitcase away from the door, followed by her own as her sister emerged from the bathroom. When she popped open the door, she saw a family with two little kids coming out of another motel room nearby. The kids were wearing little cowboy hats and boots, while their mother wore a plaid button up shirt and jeans. Dad wore a t-shirt, but watched his son and daughter with pride as they sprinted down the dirt road away from the motel.

"C'mon, we should get ready. Do you wanna shower?" Alex asked. Her voice was groggy and her eyes looked tired. She had a mark across her cheek where the pillow had creased in the night.

Sienna shook her head, then looked back at the parking lot. "No, I'm good. I'll just pull my hair back for breakfast."

"Suit yourself. I'm gonna shower," Alex grumbled and tugged her suitcase into the bathroom with her. Sienna closed the door and pulled the curtain open a little wider to bring more light into the room.

In the daylight, the run-down motel was almost charming. The wooden furniture had intricate details carved into it, and there was a card on the table that had been ignored in favor of sleep.

Picking it up, Sienna read it to herself, "We hope you enjoy your stay at the Tumbleweed Motel. If you have any issues, please feel free to reach out to the front desk, located across from Main Street. Kennedy and Trevor Stone." She put the note down, exploring the room a little more. She pulled open the drawer between the beds, finding a worn Bible inside of it. She picked it up and ran her finger over the leather cover before replacing it and turning her attention to the dresser drawers under the small television against the far wall.

Sienna didn't quite understand where they were yet, but she understood that she and Alex would be here for the foreseeable future. Although the beds were creaky and the dust made Sienna's nose itch, hiding in this hotel was suddenly more appealing than forming the relationships needed to find a more permanent housing. If she accepted this motel was her home for now, maybe she could convince herself they wouldn't be in Lonewood for long.

So she unpacked.

Sienna carefully placed all of her belongings in the three drawers on the left. She managed to shove the suitcase along the wall near the door, knowing it would continue to be a barricade for them at night. She found another outlet, testing it to make sure it worked before leaving her phone to charge. The battery hadn't run down much, but she needed to know which outlets actually worked. She needed to know what she was working with.

Alex returned from the bathroom once again, this time dressed in a button down plaid shirt similar to the one the mother outside was wearing. The tennis shoes and skinny jeans clashed a little with the red plaid, but Alex didn't seem to care as she ran a brush through her wet hair to detangle it. She'd applied mascara and blush, looking perfectly presentable yet casual.

Sienna grabbed her own makeup bag to get ready in the bathroom. She emerged five minutes later with mascara-covered lashes, blush on her cheeks and a dark plum lipstick. Her long, deep red hair was pulled up into a high ponytail, and she fluffed out her bangs to give them some body.

It was already 8:45. She didn't need fifteen minutes to get dressed, but it might take that long to pick something to wear. Sienna didn't want to dress up like the little family and her sister, but Alex held out a green plaid shirt that matched hers. Sienna scoffed and shook her head, pushing past Alex to dig through her organized drawers.

She settled on a short-sleeved button up blouse in dark purple, almost matching her lipstick. She tucked it into the waistband of her black slacks and wore a pair of wedge sandals with it. It was the closest thing to heels Bridget had packed for her.

Her sister smirked down at her, finding her outfit as ridiculous as Sienna found hers. "Really?"

"Really. I'm trying to make a good first impression. We live here now, this isn't a vacation."

"We should be trying to fit in, not stick out like a sore thumb," Alex shot back playfully and Sienna glared at her.

"I'm not going to pretend I'm from here. I just moved here, there's no reason for me to look like a local."

Before Alex could argue her point, there was a knock on the door. Looking at the clock, Sienna realized it was 9:00 on the nose. She appreciated a prompt arrival, especially when it gave her the last word.

Alex opened the door and Skylar was on the other side with her thumbs slung through her belt loops. She wore a pair of high-waisted jeans held up by a leather belt and shiny belt buckle. Tucked into the shorts was a loose cream blouse that cuffed around her wrists, even though the top was open and flowy, revealing the white lace tank top she wore as an undershirt. Once again, Skylar wore her cowboy boots.

"Good morning!" Alex chirped, taking a step back and motioning for Skylar to enter. "Thanks for taking us to breakfast!"

Skylar looked around, taking note of the few belongings strewn across the room before answering, "My pleasure. Any friend of Bridget's is a friend of mine." Skylar's sharp eyes snagged on Sienna's shoes. "You sure you wanna wear that? Everyone here is pretty casual."

The sound of Alex trying to hide her snort wasn't lost on Sienna, and she huffed. "I want to make a good first impression. I'm comfortable in this."

Skylar shrugged, unphased by Sienna's fashion choices. "You're more than welcome to wear whatever you want. It's just kinda dusty. Your clothes might get dirty."

"Aren't we taking your car?"

"No," Skylar laughed. "It's just across the street. We'll walk. So if your shoes aren't comfortable, I recommend changing them."

"I'll be fine, but thank you. I practically lived in heels at the office in California," Sienna said firmly, and Skylar looked like she was holding back laughter.

Alex grabbed her tiny brown purse and pulled it across her shoulder. "I'm ready, lead the way," she told Skylar brightly. Sparing one more look down at Sienna's wedges, Skylar held open the door for them, allowing them their first good look at their new home.

There were a handful of cars parked in the lot, but they were spread out. As quiet as it was last night, Sienna assumed the motel was mostly empty. The walls definitely weren't thick enough to hide the noise if they had immediate neighbors.

Skylar led them along the edge of the wooden building, pausing when she got to the main office. "If you need anything, let Kennedy know. If there's anything wrong with the room, she'll send Trevor out to fix it. If it gets too loud at Jazzy's, go join in because they aren't turning down the music. Trust me, I've asked." She chuckled at her own explanation and continued walking down the dirt road away from the motel.

When they got to the street, she pointed up to the right at a long, winding road. "That'll take you to the riding stables. Lyle cares for about two dozen horses up there, half of them are his for trail rides and such. He'll happily give you lessons if you're interested."

Alex shook her head rapidly, looking down the road with fear in her eyes. "I don't do horses."

One dark brow rose on Skylar's pale face. "Oh. Okay. Good to know."

Sienna stepped closer to Alex and threw her arm around her middle to squeeze her into her side. "C'mon, Alex! Where's your sense of *adventure*?"

Her sister glared down at her, but Sienna kept her smile wide and taunting. A dare. Alexandra had been nineteen in Mexico when they went horseback riding along the beach, and her horse spooked and dropped her into the ocean. Scarlett teased her for the next two days while she massaged her aching tailbone.

Seeing Alex quivering atop a horse in the place she'd gotten them stuck in might just make Sienna forgive her faster. Alex must have realized this too, because she narrowed her green eyes at her sister and huffed, continuing to follow Skylar across the road.

After a long moment, Alex muttered, "Maybe. I'll consider it."

Skylar led them towards a small, old restaurant with the words "Lonewood Cafe" written across the wooden paneling over the door.

Inside, Sienna's eyes widened in surprise. Although the motel was virtually empty, the cafe was packed with wall-to-wall people. There were wooden booths on the far wall of windows, and smaller tables scattered along the main floor. The kitchen was situated in the far corner behind a counter, and a pair of older women scurried around with trays packed full of food.

Alex chuckled, smiling down at Sienna when her sister looked over at her. She nodded towards a bulletin board next to the door, seeing dozens of pinned up photos of families wearing cowboy hats and saloon girl outfits. The walls of the cafe itself were lined with framed photos of cowboys with little plaques underneath stating their names.

"Table for three please," Skylar told one of the waitresses, and a woman with curly gray hair nodded frantically and motioned with her chin towards a booth by the far window. Alex slid in first, then stiffened, causing Sienna to lean around her to see what had bothered her.

Two horses were tied up to a hitching post outside the window, drinking water out of a trough while another two horses sprinted past behind them, being urged on by two men in hats and boots.

"This place is wild," Sienna murmured as she settled in beside Alex. She felt her breath hitch when she looked past the horses, seeing several storefronts across the street. They all looked vintage, like they were from a different time. Perhaps they'd gone through a time machine while they slept on the squeaky springs of the old motel's beds.

"Welcome to Lonewood," Skylar said under her breath, turning to beam up at the waitress when she approached them. "Morning Brenda. How's it going?"

"Busy. Does nobody work in this town on a Saturday morning?" she yelled loudly over her shoulder, causing several patrons at other tables to laugh. She shook her head and looked back to Skylar before glancing at Sienna and Alex. She looked to be in her sixties, maybe early seventies. Although her hair had lost its color and her skin had begun to sag, there was a light in her eyes that was much more youthful than her weathered exterior. She studied Sienna with mild amusement, lingering on her outfit before sliding her gaze to Alex. She quickly turned back to Skylar and asked, "Where are your friends visiting from?"

"Oh, they're actually friends of a friend I know from New York. They're from California."

Brenda's eyes widened to match her smile. "California! That's so exciting! What brings you here to Lonewood?"

Sienna and Alex shared a quick look and Alex leaned her elbows on the table to see Brenda better. She opened her mouth to answer, but somebody called Brenda's name across the diner, asking for another coffee. She glared over her shoulder at the man and sighed, "Give me a minute, darling, I'll be right back to take your order. Then we'll talk some more."

Alex nodded as the woman cruised through the diner to scold the man for being so rude. Sienna scanned the menu, starving but not wanting anything too heavy. Everything looked heavy and hardy. Every meal came with hash browns, sausage, and eggs. Sienna smoothed back her hair and decided she'd start with coffee. Her sister pursed her lips as she perused her options, occasionally looking up when she caught a glimpse of one of the horses snorting outside the window.

"Sorry about that. That man is such a nuisance," Brenda grumbled once she returned to their booth.

Skylar whispered, "That's her husband."

"Doesn't make him any less of a nuisance. Now, where were we?" Brenda asked and Sienna's stomach tightened. She forced a smile that came off more nervous than she'd hoped, but Brenda pretended not to notice and changed her question. "What can I get for you ladies this morning?"

"I'd love a coffee. Two creams please," Sienna said quickly. Coffee was familiar. It was safe. She knew they had coffee here.

Alex leaned past Sienna to ask Brenda, "What's a caramel roll?"

Brenda's electric eyes widened and she turned to Skylar in surprise, who just shrugged. "Listen, I tried to make them popular in New York, but I guess my hard work hasn't reached California yet." When Alex looked between Skylar and Brenda questioningly, Skylar explained, "It's like a cinnamon roll, but with caramel. They are phenomenal, and I haven't been able to find one anywhere but around here."

"I'll try one of those. And a coffee. Three creams please," Alex said happily. She sat her menu on top of Sienna's as Skylar ordered waffles with bacon instead of sausage and scrambled eggs on the side. Sienna passed the menus over to Brenda and she disappeared from their booth to check on the people behind them. Sienna realized it was the family from the motel, except they'd finished eating and the children were excitedly pointing at the horses outside the window, wanting to leave the diner to go see them.

As the family left the restaurant, Sienna looked around at the patrons, trying to decide if anyone else were visitors or if they were locals. Brenda's husband sat at a two-person table near the door, chatting with another man wearing a worn leather jacket over a dirty button up. They both wore boots that were covered in mud, but beneath the muck Sienna could tell they were high quality. These men weren't poor by any means, but whatever they did for work they clearly got their hands dirty.

She hoped there was something in this town for her and Alex to do that didn't involve being covered in dirt.

There was a group of women in their late fifties, early sixties sitting in a corner booth, sipping coffee and talking quietly among themselves. Occasionally their eyes would dart around the room, and Sienna made eye contact with one woman before Brenda reappeared with their coffees.

"Here ya go," she said as she sat the mugs in front of Alex and Sienna. "The food should be up shortly. It's a mad house this morning." She gestured around the room before beaming down at the women. "What do you have planned for the day? Is Miss Skylar gonna take you around the town?"

"I'll give 'em the tour, then let them explore for themselves. I have to head to work in a bit," Skylar interrupted.

She looked like she was going to say something else, but the door to the diner swung open dramatically and smashed against the wall, causing the bulletin board to shake. Brenda shook her head and let out a sigh that shook her whole body. She shot Skylar a knowing look, then wandered away as the whole restaurant looked towards the door.

Alex looked up and over Sienna's head, chortling as Sienna turned to see who'd arrived. A stocky man in his mid-fifties sauntered into the diner with his hand lightly dancing over the gun in his holster. Spurs jingled against his cowboy boots as he walked through the restaurant, and there was mud smeared across his black chaps. His shirt was clean though, black with a swirly white stitching around the top. He looked like a cowboy from a movie, and he tipped his hat to the women in the back booth as he meandered past them.

"You've got to be shitting me," Sienna murmured as she watched. From the corner of her eye, she saw Alex beaming with unbridled excitement. Skylar leaned her mouth against her fist, hiding her grin and watching Sienna and Alex as the cowboy got closer to their table. Sienna groaned and closed her eyes, furrowing her brows as she asked, "Please tell me we didn't move to one of those historical reenactment towns?"

"I'd say we're a... historical interpretation town..." Skylar trailed off with a shit-eating grin. "This place isn't based on reality, but rather, what people imagine the wild west was. It's the wild west people want to have been real."

Sienna opened her eyes when the spurs came to a stop next to their table, and Alex whacked her arm to get her attention. With a deep breath, Sienna turned to the man, finding him staring down at them with a million dollar smile.

"Ma'am," he greeted as he tipped his hat. Sienna raised her brows, but she was saved from more of an awkward introduction when another cowboy entered the diner. He made a beeline for the first man, coming to stand beside him at their booth.

"You harassin' these pretty ladies, Hank?" The second man was much younger, maybe his late twenties. He was tall and lean. Clean shaven and pale while the first man had scruff growing all over his sun-kissed face. The younger cowboy pulled off his hat and bowed his head a little, revealing a head of thick brown hair smushed from the tight band of his cowboy hat. "Jesse Jameson."

"Alex Jade," Alex greeted as she reached over Sienna to shake the man's hand. Sienna cleared her throat and Alex added, "This is Sienna. My sister."

The older cowboy looked between Skylar and the two curiously before asking gruffly, "What brings you two to Lonewood?"

Alex shrugged, meeting Sienna's gaze before answering slowly. "I guess we're looking for a change. This seems pretty different."

Jesse returned his hat to his head as the corner of his mouth slid up into a shy smile. "Well, perhaps we'll see you two around. Keep outta trouble though. Hank's been locking people up left and right this weekend. You'd hate to end up behind bars."

"Good for nothin' son of a bitch knows better than to bother the girls at the saloon. Maude woulda shot him if I hadn't arrested him," Hank muttered.

Sienna's eyes practically bulged from her head and she looked between Skylar, Hank, and Jesse, unsure what to think. She wanted to assume this was all part of the act until Skylar sighed and asked, "Who'd you lock up this time, Hank?"

"None of your business."

"As an actual cop in this town, it *is* my business to know when you're arresting people, even if it's in fake jail. You can't lock up any more tourists."

Hank huffed, looking over his shoulder at the women in the back corner. "This is my town. If I don't keep the riff raff out, who will?"

Alex leaned over to Sienna and whispered, "I'm obsessed with this place."

Sienna should have taken her chances with Landon in Manhattan.

"You two stay out of trouble, ya hear?" Hank called, trying and failing to hang on to the authoritarian tone while Jesse guided him away by the shoulders.

"Or if trouble sounds like something you're interested in, I'll be at the Badlands Saloon at 9:00 tonight. I hope to see you there." Jesse winked, but Hank wasn't done bothering Skylar and her guests.

"Where are you two from, anyway?"

"California," Sienna deadpanned, wanting this conversation to end. Hank's eyes narrowed at her and she sighed, "What's wrong with that?"

"City folk," Hank grumbled and Jesse smirked. Their good-cop bad-cop routine might work well with children and tourists who came to this town on purpose, but Sienna wasn't amused. Alex, on the other hand, was infatuated.

She leaned on her elbow, gazing up at Jesse with a flirty smile as she purred with the slightest country drawl, "Honestly, I'm not sure I'll ever go back. Y'all seem like much better company."

The young man's smile grew bigger, but Hank scoffed and rolled his eyes. "Young people."

"You're so embarrassing," Sienna hissed at Alex as she drained the last of her coffee. She shot Skylar a pleading look, wanting to leave. The diner, the town, the state... all of the above.

Brenda shoved her way past Hank and Jesse with their plates in each hand. She sat down Skylar's big breakfast before placing a warm, gooey pastry dripping in caramel in front of Alex. She shooed Hank away, then slung her arm around Jesse's middle and squeezed him tightly against her side. "You treating these young ladies well, Mr. Jameson?"

"Yes, ma'am. Hank isn't being very welcoming, though."

She shot Hank a warning look and he grunted. "I have the right to know who is wandering around my town."

"You aren't a real deputy, Hank," Skylar droned, leaning back against the wooden seat and shaking her head. He clearly didn't appreciate her spoiling his act. "If you don't keep out of trouble, you'll be the one handcuffed in fake jail."

Hank's grin returned, but it was equal parts threatening and excited. This felt less forced, less of an act. It was a friendly game between two people who knew each other well. "By who? You?"

Skylar rolled her eyes and grabbed her fork, scooping up a chunk of eggs. She looked to her left out the window as she chewed and smirked at what she saw. Lolling her head to the side, she motioned towards the horses and said, "I'm having breakfast, but maybe you'd like to answer to the sheriff."

Jesse and Hank both looked up, and Sienna followed their gaze to see another horse tied up at the hitching post. It was black and white with light blue eyes. It was taller, more stocky, and its saddle was more worn than the other horses. It stomped its foot and nickered, causing Alex to lean into Sienna's arm.

"It's outside, it can't hurt you."

"It's eyes are creepy," she muttered. Sienna tilted her head, causing her ponytail to fall over her shoulder as she studied the horse. She thought it was beautiful with its splattered body and too-blue eyes. Like a work of art.

Hank pulled his hat a little lower over his head, finally content to bid the women goodbye. "We'll be seeing you around."

"Mmhhmm," Skylar hummed back as the door to the diner opened and another cowboy walked in. Sienna rolled her eyes and looked back at the horse, finding it more interesting than the town's obnoxious entertainment, but Alex elbowed her and nodded towards the newcomer.

When Sienna looked over her shoulder, she took a good, long look at the cowboy in the entryway. He wore an easy smile as he spoke to Brenda. The sleeves of his button down cream shirt were rolled to his elbows, looking more casual than Hank and Jesse. His light-brown vest was unbuttoned and his jeans were worn, but clean. He didn't have chaps or spurs, but he did have a gun holstered to his hip. His hat was old and faded from the sun, but even beneath the brim, Sienna could see his russet brown eyes watching her and her sister with interest.

For a brief moment their eyes met, and Sienna felt her breath hitch when he gave her a nod and a little smile.

She turned away, snatching Alex's fork that she twirled between her fingers to cut a bite of her caramel roll. She focused on how delicious it was and not the nervous feeling in her stomach at catching the cowboy's gaze. Alex chuckled lightly at her reaction, leaning her elbow against the back of the booth as the man strode towards them.

"Hank, why the hell was Bill locked up in the jail this morning?"

Sienna chewed through her snort, covering her mouth and nose as she looked up at the man. He stood close to them now, towering over her at easily six feet tall. He smelled like horses, dirt, and cologne. Upon closer inspection, she realized the gun on his left side wasn't fake.

Hank looked over at the women in the corner, seeing them staring at him with bright teeth all on show. "He was messing around at the saloon late last night."

Those brown eyes slid to Skylar and she just shrugged. "Don't look at me. I have company."

"You can't be locking people up if it's not part of the show. Even Bill. If there's no audience, you leave him alone, you hear me?" The frustrated tinge in the man's voice told Sienna he wasn't part of their act and wasn't amused by Hank's infringement on his actual job. He turned to Skylar, then Sienna and Alex with a gentle smile that made Alex clench Sienna's forearm in excitement. "Nice to meet you two. If you need anything, or if Hank gives you any trouble, let Skylar or me know."

He turned to walk away, and Alex leaned so far over the table that the ends of her blonde hair fell into the sticky caramel roll. Once he was far enough away to talk about him, Alex hissed to Skylar, "Who is *that*?"

"Don't sound so excited. You'll offend your boyfriend, Jesse," Sienna grumbled sarcastically. She cut another small piece of Alex's roll to eat. If she wasn't worried about dancing girls swarming the diner to serenade them, she'd ask if she could order one for herself.

Skylar laughed through a mouthful of food, grabbing her napkin to wipe her mouth before answering. "That's my boss. He's the sheriff. The real one. Nice guy, but he won't flirt with you like Jesse. If you're looking for a good time, I suggest the saloon, not the sheriff's station. Unless you want to hang out with me."

"If that's where he'll be, I'll consider it," Alex murmured quietly before snatching her fork back to finish her own breakfast. Sienna watched as Brenda passed off a white to-go cup to the sheriff and he handed her a ten dollar bill. Hank watched him from the far end of the diner, while Jesse was busy entertaining a man and woman who didn't look to be locals.

The sheriff almost made it through the door when a tall, lean woman in her mid-thirties walked in with a megawatt smile and her thick blonde hair pulled up into a high ponytail. It cascaded down the back of her pink blouse towards the waistband of her light wash jeans. Although casual, she was infinitely more put together than the other people in the diner, and Sienna assumed she was a tourist until she grabbed the sheriff's wrist and tugged him close, leaning up in her shiny black cowboy boots to whisper in his ear.

He rolled his eyes at whatever she said and they looked over at Hank and Jesse together, but when she saw that they were entertaining some guests, she shook her head a little and went back to her conversation with the sheriff.

Her lips were painted a soft pink that matched her blouse, and she wore light makeup over her pale skin. When she shifted from foot to foot, Sienna could see the muscles in her calves tightening beneath the denim. When her gaze landed on their booth, her bright amber eyes lit up and she trotted over to them.

"Skylar! I didn't know you had friends coming," she cooed when she reached them. Brenda approached from the side, asking if she wanted anything, but the blonde shook her head and smiled. As Brenda left, the woman placed her hand on the back of the booth behind Skylar and leaned, kicking one boot behind the other as she greeted Alex and Sienna. "Where are you visiting from?"

"California," Alex said quickly, with much less confidence than she had with Jesse and Hank. Alex was tall and impressive with her dancer's legs and sharp features, but she didn't hold a candle to this woman. Confidence oozed from her every pore as she hovered over them. From this brief interaction, Sienna could tell she was a force of nature, and she hadn't even given them her name yet.

"Alex, Sienna," Skyla gestured to the pair, "this is Mayor Wyatt."

"You can call me Dakota." She pushed off of the booth to shake Sienna and Alex's hands. "What brought you two to Lonewood? From California, no less. I've always wanted to go." She tilted her head, causing her mass of blonde hair to spill over her shoulder and cover her blouse. Sienna was stunned that the mayor of this town was somebody so young and beautiful, but she had a commanding presence that must have leant itself to her profession. The sheriff sure seemed to think so.

He lingered by the door, sipping his to-go cup occasionally. Sienna caught him watching the blonde, but his expression was hard to read. Something between uneasy and unsurprised. When he caught Sienna staring at him, that tight expression eased up, but instead of leaving or coming back to join their conversation, he wandered over to the table with Brenda's husband. The entire time however, he kept his gaze on the mayor.

Since Sienna had decided to let Alex lie her way through their predicament for the two of them, the younger sister stumbled over her words to explain their presence to the mayor. "We know a friend of Skylar's. California is... well it's rough. The cost of living is high, crime is high. The fires, don't get me started on the fires. I really wanted a change. I wanted some fresh air and wide open space, and our friend Bridget told us about Skylar and Lonewood and I wanted to check it out. Sienna offered to tag along. She's between jobs at the moment."

Mayor Wyatt's brows shot up as she turned her attention to Sienna with a sweet smile. Sienna couldn't understand how this woman could be so genuinely nice to people she'd just met. Sure, she was the mayor and this was her town, but it wasn't necessary to introduce herself to everybody who passed through. She seemed to legitimately enjoy it, though.

"What did you do in California?" Dakota asked, and Skylar cocked her head in a way that told Sienna she wanted to hear the answer, too. Bridget couldn't tell her that they were in Witness Protection Program and that they'd been sent here to hide, but Skylar wasn't stupid. She knew that whatever came out of Sienna's mouth wouldn't be the truth, and she was waiting to hear how well Sienna lied. This was most likely the reason she hadn't bothered to ask them anything personal. Since they'd left the hotel, Skylar had told them about Lonewood, and given them information to help them during their stay, but she'd never asked anything about themselves.

She knew they couldn't tell her the truth.

Sienna cleared her throat, torn between wanting to build herself up and wanting to set the bar low. Mayor Wyatt didn't know who she'd been or what she'd accomplished and she really didn't need to. She wouldn't care one way or another, but Sienna wanted Dakota to think she was impressive and potentially useful. She wanted to be useful to this powerful woman. "I used to own my own marketing firm."

Alex's brows furrowed, and Skylar shot her a look that told her to watch herself. Sienna quickly beamed up at Dakota, nodding her head as the blonde gaped in excitement. "Really? A marketing firm, that's wonderful! Gosh, I'd love to have someone like you work for the town. We are in desperate need of some good marketing, that's for sure." She paused, looking out the window with a thoughtful expression. After a moment, she asked softly, "How long are you here for? Maybe... if you have some free time during your visit, I could bounce some ideas off of you?"

Having clearly been eavesdropping, the sheriff sauntered over to stand beside the mayor, shoving his hands in his pockets. Skylar looked up at him with a nervous expression that made Sienna regret taking liberties with her story. Maybe he'd sweep the mayor away before she had to admit they weren't on vacation.

"You trying to talk business with our guests?" he drawled in a country accent that hadn't been there before. As if he knew how to act around the locals and how to *act* with the town's visitors. Suddenly, he'd deemed them the latter. The smile he shot the mayor reached his eyes, but it was a taunting smile, daring her to continue her conversation. It was lighthearted, not vicious. Playful in a way that made Sienna's heart echo in her chest. She shoved down the brief and sudden desire to have him look at her like that. Nobody ever had, not even Mason.

Mason had been a good boyfriend. He'd opened doors for her and paid for meals and taken her on nice trips. He'd made sure she was pleased in the bedroom and that she knew she had his full support in all her professional endeavors. They didn't play, though. They weren't spontaneous, and more often than not, they weren't romantic either. At the time Sienna thought they were too mature for that kind of relationship, but now she wondered if it was because she and Mason were *boring* and that there hadn't been much chemistry between them to begin with.

Or maybe it was just easier to tell herself that than to believe that he took thirty seconds to decide his job was more important than making sure his girlfriend wasn't murdered.

The mayor waved off the sheriff, dismissing him as she turned back to Sienna. He lingered close though, and Sienna noticed him fidget a little, as if he was prepared to pull Dakota away if she tried to ask Sienna for help again. "If you're busy, it's fine. Please don't feel obligated-"

"Oh, I'm definitely not busy," Sienna said quickly. Despite Skylars warning glances and the sheriff's anxious behavior, Sienna *wanted* to help the mayor. She wanted to get back to work. "We aren't on vacation. We've moved here. We haven't really seen the town, but we aren't just passing through."

The diner fell silent at her confession, and Sienna looked around to see everyone staring at her with wide eyes and mouth's agape in a mixture of shock, confusion, and excitement. It seemed everybody had been listening in on their conversation with the mayor and their arrival was infinitely more fascinating now that everyone realized they weren't leaving. Alex grabbed her arm, holding her tightly. Skylar looked mildly amused, but she probably expected this reaction.

Sienna cleared her throat, sitting up a little straighter as Brenda hustled over with their bill. She handed the slip to Skylar but addressed the women excitedly, "You're staying? That's wonderful! Oh, let me get you some things to take back to your motel! Do you need lunch? Let me get you something to eat for lunch, or you're welcome to come back! It'll be on the house of course, my husband will treat!"

"Thank you, but you don't have to do that..." Alex tried to say, but Brenda had already disappeared to gather something up for them, leaving Alex to gape at Sienna. "That's so nice!"

The mayor beamed at Sienna and Alex, looking over at the sheriff excitedly. From the scowl on his face, he clearly didn't share her enthusiasm but it didn't damper hers one bit. "It's so wonderful to have some new faces in town. Once you're more settled, please reach out. Skylar has my information- or just stop by my office, I'm there pretty much every day. I'm so excited to hear your thoughts about the town. Let me know if there's anything we can do to make you two feel more comfortable here. Where are you living?" She smacked the back of her hand against the sheriff's broad chest and he stared down at it with contempt. "If you need anything please let us know. We can round up the boys if you need help moving," she said with a smirk.

"Dakota, give them a chance to breathe," the sheriff told the blonde through clenched teeth. It was clear his patience was running thin as he looked out the window at the horses, then slid Dakota's hand from his chest and pulled off his hat to run his fingers through his ashy brown hair. After he'd pushed the strands away from his sweaty forehead, he replaced his hat and asked Sienna and Alex, "When did you arrive?"

"Late last night. They literally have only seen the motel and the diner." Skylar leaned against the wooden back of the booth, a content smile playing across her features. "They're staying at the motel for now."

"Oh, yeah, that won't do." Dakota pulled out her cell phone, then quickly shoved it back into her jeans pocket and sighed as she looked up at the sheriff with a pout, "I have a meeting that I need to head to." She paused and he shot her a warning look, so she looked back at Sienna and said, "Once you're a little more settled, I'd love to catch up to see how you're enjoying Lonewood. If you need anything- anything at all- don't hesitate to reach out. We're always around."

Sienna nodded and smiled graciously. "Thank you so much. It was wonderful meeting you."

"Yes, thank you for such a warm welcome to your town," Alex added.

The sheriff tipped his hat and backed away without another word. The mayor grinned from ear to ear though, and Sienna swore her amber eyes sparkled with excitement. "I hope we continue to impress you. I'll see you both again soon."

She said goodbye and strode towards the exit, where the sheriff held open the door for her. Once they were gone, everyone in the restaurant seemed to go back to their own business. Clearly, Dakota was the shining sun that all of Lonewood rotated around, and even Sienna found herself getting caught in the mayor's orbit.

Chapter 6

EVERYONE IN THE DINER watched them when they thought the sisters weren't looking, but Sienna caught their less-than-subtle gazes. The first rule was to try to blend in, but she'd made one hell of a first impression.

"So, you only have a little while before you work?" Alex asked Skylar quietly, as if she felt all the eyes on her, too. "If you need to go home, we can find our way around."

Skylar shook her head, dismissing the idea as she climbed out of the booth. "I have a little time. I can at least show you Main Street, after that you'll be fine on your own. Main Street has pretty much everything you'll need to know."

Motion outside the window drew Sienna's attention as she stood. She turned to see the sheriff mounting the black and white horse, tugging the reins sharply to turn it around. He looked up and accidentally met Sienna's stare. He studied the redhead for a moment, sizing her up. Then he gave her that same taunting smile he'd given the mayor earlier, as if he'd come to some conclusion that he liked. Sienna felt her stomach drop nervously at whatever that smile meant for her future in Lonewood.

He kicked his heels into the horse's sides and it snorted as they slowly left the hitching post.

"For you two, a little something to munch on in your hotel room." Brenda handed Alex a brown paper bag. She peeked inside and grinned, then passed it to Sienna to hold as she thanked Brenda. The waitress pulled Alex into a light hug, then threw her arm around Sienna. She tried not to stiffen, but Sienna wasn't used to strangers being so friendly. If this happened in New York, Sienna would assume they were trying to pickpocket her.

Alex welcomed it though. She was practically glowing from all the attention Brenda showered her with.

They started to leave, but Jesse came jogging between the tables to stop them. "Hey! I didn't realize you two lived here... I hope Hank and I didn't scare you too much. It's all part of the act, you know-"

"I found it endearing," Alex told him sweetly, and he ducked his head and blushed. "I will be honest, though, I don't know if I'll be visiting any saloons tonight. Maybe another time?"

He looked up with wide eyes, as if he suddenly realized what he'd insinuated earlier, and that she wasn't just some tourist for him to entertain and never see again. "Yeah. Anytime. Or not at all, if you'd rather. I don't want you to think I'm an ass. It's my job to flirt with people."

Alex chuckled a little and shrugged. She gave him the most sincere smile Sienna had seen on her sister's face since they'd left Manhattan. "I used to be an actress, so I get it." She turned to leave, but first she said, "See you around, Jesse."

It felt like they'd been in that diner for days, but Sienna pulled out her phone to find it was only 10:15. The blank background of her phone taunted her, reminding her that she wasn't just in an unfamiliar place. She was in an unfamiliar life.

Skylar led them around the corner of the diner, and when they came around to the other side they were faced with a wide, dirt street that ran for about half a mile. At the far end was a two-story wooden saloon, and smaller old-fashioned buildings lined both sides of the road leading up to it.

To Sienna's right, Alex laughed brightly, looking down the empty street as the sun rose higher in the sky. It was warm but not hot, although considering there were hardly any trees it would most likely be hell in the heat of the summer. Alex spun around at the sound of whinnying, practically jumping back a step to bump into Sienna. Jesse and Hank approached the two horses tied up to the hitching post and she tried to put as much distance between her and them as possible.

"They're everywhere."

"The cowboys?"

"The horses," she mumbled, watching as the men mounted the horses and started wandering down the dirt road.

Sienna turned to Skylar, who watched the women patiently as they took in their surroundings. "Are there no cars?"

"Nope. Everyone has to park in the motel parking lot. Tourists and locals alike aren't allowed to drive on Main Street, but we all have cars at home. This street is the attraction, the rest of the town is mostly residential."

The couple from the diner walked past them, then the woman pulled him to look closer at the building next door before crossing the street. Sienna slowly took a few steps towards it too, looking up to read a sign that read 'Portrait Studio'. She nodded a little as she continued, careful not to twist her ankle on the rough ground. "It's kind of nice. Weirdly quiet though."

The sound of a gunshot shattered her theory, and Alex ducked, holding her head down as she quivered behind Skylar. The woman didn't even flinch though, instead motioning down the road to where Hank and Jesse had ridden. "It's all just part of the show."

Sienna grabbed Alex's quivering hand and led her past the portrait studio to stand behind the family from earlier. The little girl held her hands to her ears, looking up at her mom with a nervous expression as she motioned for her to look ahead.

Hank meandered into the middle of the road, his fingers dancing over his gun. About thirty feet away, another man stared him down. He was short and round, with a thick handlebar mustache that made him look like a cartoon villain. His eyes were narrowed at Hank as he held his smoking gun in the air.

"I told you what would happen if I caught you in these parts again, Bill Cassidy!" Hank yelled loud enough for everyone to hear, even from behind. Sienna looked around, realizing there was nobody else there to watch the show. Just them and the little family.

Bill Cassidy cracked his neck back and forth, lowering his gun to aim it at Hank. "You're not in a position to be making threats, Hank. Your deputy's a little tied up. Your horse has run off, you don't have anyone left to save you now."

Sienna wasn't an actress or a writer or even vaguely familiar with live theater, but she didn't think this was very good. Sparing a quick look at Alex, she found her sister's head cocked to the side, watching with confusion written on her face.

Hank drew his weapon and the kids in front of them gasped. "You came into my town, and I heard you was harassin' my woman last night. I won't stand for that. You come near her again, and it'll be the last thing you ever do."

"I can't tell if they're acting or if this really happened," Alex whispered loudly to Skylar, who sighed and shrugged.

"With these two, it's hard to tell."

Beyond the stand off, Jesse had been tied to the front pillar of a building across the street. It was the nicest building on the strip, made of white stone instead of wood. Jesse squirmed and called for Hank to help, but the older man kept his eye on his enemy. With guns pointed directly at each other, it wasn't exactly a quick draw.

"They don't even know how to hold a real gun," Skylar mumbled. "I gotta head to work. They'll do this for another ten minutes or so if you wanna stay and watch. End of the street is the Badlands Saloon. Joe's General Store is next to it, and the building Jesse is tied to is the Court House. If you need a post office, you'll find it in there. The Bank of Lonewood is across from the general store, but if you have actual business I recommend you come in through the back entrance on 1st Street. Same with the Sheriff's Station. Everything else is pretty clearly labeled out front." She held out her hand to Alex and said, "Gimme your phone. I'll put my number in, so if you need anything you can shoot me a text or call me. Or just stop by, we're pretty casual. You'll hear a lot of gunshots but these idiots don't have real guns, so don't worry about it."

Alex took back her phone, holding it close to her chest as Hank took a bold step towards his opponent. Bill Cassidy waved his gun around wildly, yelling, "Take another step closer and Old Joe Ferris will be building you a casket!"

"Joe Ferris is in the town south, we have Joe Grocer here!" Hank yelled back angrily, clearly not acting, but correcting his nemesis in the middle of their scene. He took another step and Bill fired his weapon, but Hank sidestepped dramatically, then shot back twice.

Bill stumbled a few steps backward, holding his shoulder tightly before collapsing to his knees. Hank sauntered over, pulling a pair of handcuffs out of his chaps. "I told you what would happen, Bill Cassidy. It's back in the slammer for you."

Skylar looked down at her phone and nodded her approval. "Six minutes. That's a new record for them."

The family in front of them clapped wildly as Hank shoved Bill to the side of the road. Jesse managed to wiggle free and bounded over to his scene partner, handing him a cartoonishly massive key to lock Bill Cassidy up with.

Alex jogged forward a few steps to see better, and Sienna stumbled behind with Skylar. She saw Hank pull open a metal door, shove Bill into it, and slam the cell closed. The prison cell faced the street, so everybody could see that he'd caught his villain.

He turned to his audience with that big, cheesy smile he'd given them earlier and threw his arms out. The mother of the children motioned for them to run up and grab a picture, but Sienna turned to Alex and gave a firm shake of her head to tell her they weren't doing that.

Jesse waved awkwardly as they passed him, but he didn't stop to talk to them. Instead, he knelt down to speak with the little boy dressed up with his boots and hat. Jesse pulled the badge from his vest and pinned it to the boy, causing him to whoop loudly. It wasn't lost on Sienna that the little girl looked disappointed she didn't get a badge, too.

Skylar led them past the incarcerated actor, who growled menacingly as they walked by.

"Oh, put a cork in it Bill." Skylar winked at the older man. He was younger than Hank, but not by much, and up close it was clear they had similar facial features. Sienna looked back to Hank, then to Bill again. They had to be related.

To the left of the jail, that black and white horse was tied up to another hitching post, this one in the shade. Alex gave the animal a wide berth, but Sienna took a step forward, reaching her hand out to pet its nose until Skylar stopped her. "I wouldn't do that if I were you. He isn't very friendly."

Sienna quickly retracted her hand and caught up with the others, stumbling a step until Alex grabbed her arm. Skylar made a big show of looking down at her wedges, then up at her eyes. Sienna cleared her throat and asked, "Does he bite?"

"Domino? Oh- no. I was talking about Gentry. He doesn't like people near his horse."

Gentry. The sheriff.

Dread filled Sienna at the idea of running into the massive sheriff again as Skylar held open the door. It wasn't that he was rude by any means, but Sienna got the idea he wasn't a fan of their presence. The last thing she needed was to make an enemy of the person whose job was to keep them safe.

Although Bill's jail cell was nothing but a covered cage, the inside of the sheriff's station was a legitimate operation. There was a petite receptionist at a desk near the wall who smiled up at them when they entered, and she motioned towards another door leading farther into the building and said, "Sheriff's in the back."

"Didn't ask. Don't care." Skylar walked over to a file cabinet and pulled open the second to last drawer. She used a small key to unlock it and reached in to grab a badge and a gun that she strapped to herself before turning to Sienna and Alex. "This is where I work. I'm a deputy. One of four. It's a small team, but the town's only five streets, so we cover enough ground."

Alex smiled as she looked around, walking past the desks and looking at everyone's knick-knacks. Sienna stayed put, because she didn't want to be nosy and her feet hurt. When Alex tilted her head to get a better look at a framed photo on a desk, the receptionist cleared her throat and called, "I take it you two are Skylar's friends? Where are you visiting us from?"

"We're friends of a friend from California," Sienna answered. Alex shuffled away from the desk to stand next to her sister. She clutched her paper to-go bag tightly, as if she was protective of whatever was inside. Sienna's little sister was fun-loving and bold, but she seemed almost childlike in this new environment. Maybe this was her pretending to be somebody else, but Sienna hadn't quite gotten the hang of pretending yet.

The receptionist nodded slowly, then smiled. "Well, welcome to Lonewood. I hope you enjoy your stay with us."

"Oh, they've moved here. They aren't here for the weekend," Skylar laughed and the receptionist furrowed her brows. She looked confused, but not angry.

After a long moment, the mousy woman asked, "But... why?"

Skylar raised her dark brow, and waited for Sienna and Alex to explain. Alex smiled weakly, running her fingers through her shoulder-length hair. "California's been tough on us. I really wanted a change, and I convinced my sister to join. A friend of ours knows Skylar and she told us about this place." The look Alex gave Sienna was hopeful, but Sienna couldn't muster one in response. "We're taking a leap of faith."

"Well, if you need any extra help in that department, the church is just north of here, up the road." The receptionist pointed out the door towards Main Street where they could hear Bill and Hank yelling at each other. The receptionist sighed and told them, "Try to stay out of trouble."

"Cecily has to say that since we're the police department," Skylar teased. "Have fun. Text me if you need anything."

Sienna managed a grateful tip of her head as Alex took another good look around the station. "Thanks for breakfast. We really appreciate you taking us under your wing."

Skylar held her hand out towards the door and Sienna confidently took the lead, more than ready to have a little time away from people. Alex was lucky she allowed *her* to stick around.

Once outside, Sienna squinted into the sun. She scrunched her nose, smelling horse manure nearby. Shaking her head, she turned to Alex, who stared around with a wonderstruck expression.

When Alex realized Sienna was watching her, she cleared her throat. She looked over her shoulder at the sheriff's station with a look of slight resignation on her face. "I'm disappointed we didn't get to see the hot sheriff again."

"I'm not. He doesn't seem too excited that we're here." Sienna looked towards the saloon at the end of the street and added under her breath, "That makes two of us."

Alex ignored her comment and took a few steps towards the saloon, but when Sienna started to follow, her wedge slipped on the gravel and twisted sideways. She let out a shriek as she lost her footing and fell to her knees in the middle of Main Street. Alex squatted down to help her, gasping as she tried to dust off of Sienna's black dress pants. "Are you okay?"

"I'm fine!" Sienna spat back, wiping her hands on her slacks. Sienna groaned loudly as she stood, wanting to go back to the motel.

But Alex had a sad look in her eyes as she gazed at the saloon, clearly wanting to go in. Sienna groaned, "Let's see if I can get cleaned up in there."

Chapter 7

Alex followed Sienna towards the two story building, walking up the three wooden steps to the double doors. Alex tentatively pushed the door open and was greeted by a massive dance hall with a stage on the far end. On the left side was a bar at least fifteen feet long, lined with round wooden stools. A handful of circular dining tables sat closer to the stage and an upper level was open with a balcony that curved around the edges, giving extra space for people to watch the shows on the stage. The acoustics in this room would be incredible if there was anyone there to enjoy it.

"Can I help you ladies with something?"

Alex and Sienna turned to the left, finding a woman in her late sixties watching them while wiping out a glass beer mug. Her hair was faintly red, thick, and curled around her round face. Her smile was lazy, unbothered. She didn't seem too eager to harass them, and Alex knew Sienna was thankful for the quiet of the empty saloon.

Sienna raised her hand, showing off her cut palm. "I, uh, took a bit of a tumble. I was wondering if you had a restroom I could use?"

"Of course, sweetie. 'Round the corner on the left. You need a bandage or anything?" The woman sat down the mug and draped the washcloth over her shoulder. She leaned against the bar with one elbow and used her free hand to grab a clean wine glass from under the counter. "I'm guessing wine. Or mixed drinks, but I don't do that fruity shit here."

"Excuse me?" Sienna blurted, which caused the woman to laugh and shake her head.

"I'm guessing you don't drink beer. So I have red or white wine. Maybe an old bottle of bubbly if I look hard enough. I can make you a mixed drink, but it won't be no margarita. I've seen a lot of city girls come through here, and they don't usually like what I'm pourin'. Unless it's wine."

Alex raised her hand to stop the woman, shaking her head and rejecting her sweetly. "Oh, no, we're fine. She really just needs the bathroom, and I wanted to look around-"

The woman poured a glass of red wine and sipped it slowly, watching as Sienna wobbled back and forth in her wedges. Finally, the woman scolded her, "Go clean up. It'll get infected if you don't wash it out."

Alex watched Sienna amble towards the edge of the saloon until the woman caught her attention with a thoughtful hum.

"I think you drink something stronger."

Alex raised her brows to the woman, who pulled a bottle of whiskey from below the counter. She poured it into a glass, then grabbed an ice cube with a pair of tongs and popped it in before sliding it down the bar towards Alex.

Her stomach roiled nervously as she approached. When she got to the glass, she sat on the stool, setting down her purse and to-go bag to pick up the drink. She stared down into the liquid and sniffed it, then swallowed down the tears that threatened to brim in her eyes.

It reminded her of the bar. And the dancing. And the drinking. And Landon. And the knife slicing along a man's throat.

Setting down the drink, she pushed it away and shook her head, sucking in a sharp breath to hold back her tears. She closed her eyes, trying to push away the memory of that night, but the whiskey brought it all back in startling detail, as if it transported her back to that dive bar into Landon's arms.

Another glass hit the wood, and Alex looked up. A glass of water sat in front of her, and the bartender was drinking the whiskey herself. Her dark eyes stayed locked on Alex, but she didn't say anything as she sipped her drink until Alex downed half of her water and her breathing evened out.

Then she asked that popular question: "Why are you here, sweetheart?"

Every person they'd encountered wanted to know the same thing. Alex could act and lie until she was blue in the face, but honestly, she didn't know. She didn't know why she was left alive, let alone sent to this little town where outsiders were gawked at like a shiny new penny. She had wanted a change, but not like this.

Because she was tired of lying, and because this woman made Alex want to trust her, she whispered, "I don't even know anymore."

The woman nodded, finishing the whiskey and running the sink to clean out the glass. She glanced past Alex with a look that said Sienna was returning. She had to pull herself together or Sienna would be mad that she'd made them look suspicious. She was mad enough as it was.

"Well, maybe we're just what you need to heal whatever's hurtin' ya."

Sienna climbed up on the stool beside Alex, but she didn't look over at her. Sienna was blissfully ignorant of Alex's trauma, and Alex wanted to keep it that way.

"So, red or white?" The woman leaned close to Sienna, and she furrowed her brows at the smell of whiskey on the woman's breath. The bartender laughed. "It's my saloon, darlin. And as you can see, it's pretty lonely here. I can eat and drink and dance and sing all I want and nobody will notice. Not until Memorial Day."

After a moment, Sienna surprised Alex and told the woman, "Red please." She finally spared her little sister a glance, and Alex was thankful she'd wiped away her tears. Sienna leaned her arm on the bar and looked up, letting out a long whistle that echoed off the rafters. "How many people can you get in here? A hundred? Two?"

"Three-fifty if we pack the place," she answered, setting down a glass filled to the brim with Sienna's red wine. "Which isn't often, if I'm being honest." She looked at Alex, then added, "You two just passing through?"

"Nope," Sienna answered before tipping back her wine and downing it. Alex widened her eyes, surprised to see Sienna act with such abandon. Sienna stared into her empty glass as she sat it down and muttered, "We're here for a change."

That was for certain.

"I'm Alex, this is Sienna. We got here last night. From California." Alex didn't mean for her voice to break, and the sound caught Sienna's attention. As quickly as her brows furrowed in question, the bartender had another glass of red wine in front of her. To distract her from Alex.

Sienna thanked her, sipping this one slowly, but the frustration in her expression told Alex it might not be her last glass. If Sienna wanted to drink herself into a stupor, at least they only had to walk down the street to get home.

Home. This was their home now. A little town full of friendly people with big hearts and people who acted, even if they weren't very good. It felt like Alex had stepped into a living show, and her soul was begging for her to find a part in it.

But she couldn't. If she drew attention to herself, Landon could find her. Skylar said it herself, there were only four cops in this town. They might be able to cover their five streets, but they wouldn't stand a chance against Landon and however many men worked for him.

Her breath turned shaky at the thought, and she drank some more of her water. If the woman had said anything about their move from California, Alex hadn't heard it. When she made eye contact though, the woman said, "I'm Maude Rivers. I run this saloon. I manage the bartenders and the talent when we have it. We're running on a short staff right now. I'm down to four dancers and one guy who plays the piano when he's not busy running the stable. The ladies are getting up there, but they get the job done. I'd invite you to come tonight, but if you're stickin' around, I suggest you wait until the end of May. Once the tourists come, this place will come alive." She gestured around the massive room, and Alex imagined it full of life and music. The part of her that she'd been told to lock away wanted to be set free here.

Maude tilted her head, studying Alex's wistful look as if she could decipher it. Maybe she could. She seemed to have a good read on people.

"How much do I owe you?" Sienna asked bluntly as she finished her wine.

With a shake of her head, Maude waved them off. "This round is on the house. Just promise you'll come back and visit." She smiled between the two, then grabbed Alex's hand with her worn one. "Water's as good a medicine as whiskey, as long as you know what you're trying to heal. Have one of the boys take you out into the Badlands. It's cured everything that's ever ailed me."

Alex didn't understand what Maude was trying to tell her, but she nodded and thanked her anyway. Maude chuckled and shooed them away. Alex grabbed her purse and to-go bag. As they reached the main doors, Maude called after them, "Get her some sensible shoes or I'm not serving her any more alcohol!"

Sienna snorted, glaring over her shoulder which only caused Maude to laugh harder as the big double doors slammed closed.

They carefully walked down the stairs and Sienna smoothed down her dark blouse as she looked to the left. The general store looked inviting, and they had nothing at the motel as far as sustenance besides the two caramel rolls Brenda had packed up for them. The fact that these didn't exist in Manhattan was a crime.

"You wanna get some things for the motel?" Sienna asked quietly. Alex realized she'd stopped in front of the store and opened her mouth to answer, but Sienna blurted, "Let's get some snacks or something. I don't feel like facing the diner for breakfast, lunch, and dinner."

The reality was, they didn't have much of a choice. They didn't have a microwave, or even a mini fridge. It wasn't like they could cook, and there weren't any other food options from what Alex could tell. She could text Skylar and ask what she recommended, but Alex didn't want to bother her. It wasn't like they were actually friends. They weren't even actually friends with Bridget, which Skylar probably knew. They were just two women who got sucked into a horrible situation and now had to live a different life.

Alex wondered what would happen if she spoke to Skylar about their situation. If she admitted to being in Witness Protection, would they have to leave? Or would Skylar be a sounding board for them while keeping a watchful eye out for Bridget? Alex didn't know how much she knew, but she knew she shouldn't ask.

The general store was small, but it was clearly the town's grocery store. There were freezers in the back, next to refrigerators full of food. Meat, milk, cheese, and other perishables were kept tightly packed together, while everything else lined the many shelves. Near the front was a large man with a beard, ringing up a tall gentleman in a button up shirt.

When he turned to leave, he almost knocked into Sienna and Alex. He looked annoyed until he realized he didn't know the women and started apologizing profusely. "I'm so sorry, ladies! I should watch where I'm going-"

"It's fine! We're fine." Alex assured him. Sienna offered a weak smile before stalking off to find snacks without a word, leaving Alex to have a conversation with the man. A small price to pay for ripping her sister from her life.

The man adjusted his black tie over his white shirt and thrust his hand out for Alex to shake. "I'm Doctor Brad Thompson. Chief medical physician of Lonewood." He glanced over at Sienna in the next aisle and added under his breath, "I'm the town doctor. I'm also a barber, unfortunately. Gotta make a living somehow in a small town."

This man couldn't have been younger than forty, but his gaze kept finding Sienna as she perused the shelves. Alex wondered if her sister would be upset if she told Doctor Thompson Sienna was too young for him.

"I'm Alex Jade, that's my sister Sienna. We just moved here from California." Alex blurted quickly, thinking maybe he'd stop ogling her sister if he realized they weren't leaving in a few days.

His smile didn't drop, but his eyes widened and the man behind the counter looked at her curiously. She shrugged a little and said, "We've gotten that reaction a lot today."

"Two city girls in Lonewood. Who woulda thought?" the man behind the counter said to himself. He picked up a newspaper and chuckled. "I expect to see you two on the front page within the week."

"We don't actually have a newspaper here, that's from the next town over," Doctor Thompson drawled under his breath with thinly veiled annoyance. Alex watched the store owner's eyes peek out above the paper before hiding again, trying to stay out of their conversation.

Doctor Thompson took another step towards the door until Sienna reappeared with two bags of potato chips and a box of glazed donuts. The man's eyes raked over her quickly, but Sienna just responded with a soft smile. It was something she'd offer a child or a dog, but definitely not a man she wanted to give the impression of interest.

"Welcome to Lonewood. If you're ever in need of medical assistance, I'm located next to the mayor's office. Don't be strangers." He gave Sienna a wink and Alex fought the urge to grimace. Doctor Thompson was the first person in this town Alex was thankful to say goodbye to.

"Did you find everything alright, city girl?" The man's eyes slid from Alex to Sienna, but the redhead was clearly unamused. Alex held her breath, waiting for Sienna to say something snarky in return, but instead she just handed over her debit card for him to ring up her snacks.

Scarlett had been even tempered for as long as Alex could remember. Hard working, logical, and a lifelong people-pleaser. Sienna seemed a bit more volatile here though, as if she decided her new Lonewood persona wouldn't bother trying to pretend to be demure to get ahead. If Scarlett had always been this strong, Alex had never seen it. All she'd seen was a girl married to her work, who wouldn't see her sister at all if she didn't live in the same apartment.

The general store owner packed up their groceries and handed Sienna her card back. "Thanks for stopping in. Hope to see you both soon."

From the general store they made their way back towards the motel. Alex looked up at the Court House, then up a long road into the hills. The Badlands were what Maude had called them. They were pretty, like a painting made real.

"I think that's where the church is."

Alex followed Sienna's train of thought up the path, realizing she was probably right. It was the direction Cecily had pointed to at the sheriff's station.

"Well," Alex said quietly, "we might need all the help we can get."

They passed by another couple of storefronts, one containing an ice cream shop, a store aptly called Boots and Hats, and finally a smaller two story building with a wooden plaque reading 'The Shoppe at Rattlesnake Bend'.

Alex paused at the steps of the porch for a moment to read the sign, murmuring to herself, "I wonder why they call it Rattlesnake Bend?"

"Cuz of the rattlers that live beneath the porch!"

Sienna screeched and bolted up the steps, cowering against the wooden pillar with their groceries dangling from her arms. Alex moved slowly, looking around as a woman who'd spoken laughed behind Sienna. "If you don't bother them, they won't bother you. Just keep an eye out." She looked down at Sienna's feet, her expression a mix of confusion and displeasure. "Maybe wear closed-toed shoes."

Sienna blushed profusely and leaned against the pole, looking up at the wooden building to give herself something to do while Alex introduced them. "Sorry, we're new in town... I'm Alex, this is Sienna. We just checked into the motel last night."

The woman was tall, but thin as a beanstalk. She had fine blonde hair, bright blue eyes, and a little pink on her nose from the sun. Her lips were pale and her fingers were long as she played thoughtlessly with the edge of her side braid. "You said you checked in last night..." she trailed off, looking past them towards the motel across the street. "But you're new in town? Like, you're staying?"

"Yeah, we moved here. For reasons I no longer remember," Sienna spat. Whatever patience she'd had for Lonewood had slithered away with the rattlesnakes beneath the porch.

The blonde chuckled and thrust her hand forward for Alex to shake. She was completely unphased by Sienna's rude words as she introduced herself. "It's nice to meet you both! I'm Kitty Cassidy. This is my pride and joy." She gestured to the storefront, beaming with pride. "My fiancé is inside, but I can go get him real quick! You'll love Beau, he's a hoot! He helps me with the store, but sometimes he works at the saloon during the summer. He was a bartender in Bismarck for a while."

Alex nodded along with the information, storing it away for later, but it was Sienna who asked, "You aren't related to Bill Cassidy, are you? The desperado guy?"

Kitty's big, sparkling teeth broke through her lips and she gave a firm nod. "Yep! That's my daddy! Him and Uncle Hank are the big draw here in Lonewood. Aside from the Badlands of course." She took a couple of steps towards the edge of the porch, as if she was gonna go around back and see. She must have thought better of it, because she whipped back around and exclaimed, "So you two just moved here? Have you met anyone yet? Do you need a guide?"

The look Sienna shot Alex froze her from the inside. Alex smiled gently and nodded, trying to find the delicate words needed to reject Kitty's offer. "We know Skylar, actually. We're friends of one of her friends, so she's been showing us around."

Kitty stuck her lip out in a thoughtful pout, humming to herself for a few moments. "That would make sense. Skylar Hyde spent a lot of time in New York. Although, you two probably get along well with her. If you want someone who isn't trying to escape town, though, you know where to find us."

That was the most information they'd gotten about Skylar since they arrived, and it broke Alex's heart.

"Well, thank you for the warm welcome," Sienna said coolly, but Kitty seemed too aloof to notice. "We should really get going. We have to unpack at the motel."

Eyebrows as pale as her hair shot up to her forehead as Kitty gasped, "You're living at the motel? The Tumbleweed Motel?" She pointed across the street and Alex nodded. Kitty tsked and shook her head. "If you two plan on sticking around, you're gonna need somewhere better than that. Kennedy has Trevor running rampant and they still can't keep the place in one piece. Once you're more settled, you let me know and I'll help you find a place to live."

That was the second time today somebody said the motel wasn't fit for living. Alex didn't necessarily disagree, but putting down roots felt a little too real.

Sienna bid Kitty goodbye, and the blonde waved excitedly as they carefully made their way down the steps. Alex noticed the way Sienna looked back at the stairs worriedly before picking up the pace and practically dragging Alex back to the motel.

Chapter 8

The next day was Sunday, and seeing as it was a day of rest, Sienna and Alex decided not to leave the motel. They munched on potato chips and donuts and finished off the caramel rolls Brenda had packed up for them. They played games on Alex's phone and watched anything that would play on the limited cable tv.

Monday found the girls with no food, which brought a need to go back into town. Sienna swore she'd buy half the general store if it meant she could spend the foreseeable future holed up in this motel.

Although, the Lonewood Cafe had caramel rolls, and Joe's General Store did not.

Around eleven, Alex emerged from the bathroom with her hair up into a ponytail and some face-framing fringe left loose on either side of her cheeks. She pulled on her jeans and tennis shoes again, but instead of another plaid button-down, Alex wore a flowered tank top. She tucked in the front and threw her arms to the side. "Whatcha think?"

"Less obvious than Saturday," Sienna answered. Then she lowered her head to continue reading an article about Lonewood on her cell phone.

"The town was formed in 1885 as a cattle ranch town. It's located just north of the South Unit of the Theodore Roosevelt National Park. The most recent census stated the population of Lonewood as ninety-eight people. During the summer months, the town becomes an immersive experience, featuring shoot outs, dancing saloon girls, and trail rides through the Badlands led by real cowboys. Every April and August the town holds its annual cattle drive, where the local ranchers move their livestock through the town. Located in a small, flat pocket amongst the

Badlands, the town has striven to keep the western lifestyle alive and give an immersive experience for its visitors."

Sienna wasn't able to find much more information beyond the Wikipedia site, and a town website that left quite a bit to be desired. If she was looking to vacation here, she wouldn't.

"You gonna get dressed? Or am I getting food and bringing it back?"

"Would you?" Sienna snapped her head up. "That would be great!"

Alex pursed her lips to show her displeasure, giving a sharp shake of her head to tell Sienna no. She groaned loudly and stood to get dressed. Sienna had given up on her desire to make a good impression, and had opted to wear jeans and a baggy black t-shirt that she tied at the bottom to make a little more fashionable. Ditching the wedges in favor of some black high-top Converse, she felt a little safer braving the dirt roads and rattlesnakes.

She pulled her black purse strap over her shoulder and fluffed out her bangs before opening the door and gesturing for Alex to take the lead. "After you."

Clearly breakfast was rush hour for the Lonewood Cafe, because there were only a handful of local patrons when Alex and Sienna arrived at eleven-fifteen. The little bell above the door announced their arrival, and Brenda rushed over to greet them.

"Welcome! Welcome back! How were your caramel rolls?" Brenda pulled Alex into a tight hug. When she pulled away, she looked towards Sienna and beamed. She gestured towards an open booth by the window. "Take a seat and I'll be right with you two."

They did as she said, taking a seat at a booth overlooking Main Street. Brenda appeared with two menus, placing one in front of each of them. "Do you two want to start with coffee? Or would you prefer something else since it's almost noon?"

"Coffee would be great," Sienna told her. She massaged her right temple and leaned her elbow on the table to look up at Brenda. "And two caramel rolls please. We're gonna take lunch to go if you don't mind."

Surprised by her request, Brenda opened her mouth, then quickly closed it and nodded. She hustled away and Alex watched her go, twisting her mouth to the side thoughtfully. Knowing Alex, she probably wanted to stay and socialize all day and night. Sienna, on the other hand, wanted to return to their motel room as quickly as possible for some solitude.

A pair of gunshots sounded from outside, followed by hooves thundering down the dirt road. Sienna lolled her head towards the window, watching as Hank and Jesse sped by on their brown horses. They swerved and started up the road towards the Badlands.

Bill Cassidy rode up to the hitching post outside the window and dismounted with a thud. He tied up his horse, a beautiful black creature with white socks above its hooves. Bill strode away without so much as a look at his steed, and Sienna wondered if it wasn't actually his horse.

"I heard there were new faces in town!" Bill bellowed as he stomped into the diner. Alex's eyes burst open in surprise as he strode over to them, his heavy steps echoing across the tile. When he stood at their table, he tipped his large cowboy hat in greeting, then smiled brightly. "Kitty told me she met two new girls from California the other day. She was tickled pink to make some new friends and then that numbskull Hank was talking up a storm about you to Jesse, who was blushin' like a tomato at the mention of your name. I had to come meet you two lovely ladies myself and welcome you to town."

Kitty said Bill Cassidy was her dad and Hank was her uncle, which meant the two actors were brothers. Hank hadn't dropped the act around them on Saturday, but Sienna was thankful that Bill was attempting to have a real conversation.

"Sienna Jade." She thrust her hand up to shake his.

"I'm Alex." The blonde tilted her head a little and grinned. "It's nice to meet you. You and your brother are both actors here, right? How exactly does that work?" When Bill's brows rose in surprise, Alex added quickly, "I was an actress in Cali."

Sienna's focus zeroed in on her sister. "Do you want to do that here?"

Looking between the cowboy and her sister, Alex shrugged meekly. "I-I don't know. Maybe. Gotta pay the bills somehow. I'm curious about how the entertainment works... if you don't mind me asking, of course!"

Bill reached behind himself and grabbed a chair, dragging it across the tile to sit at the edge of their booth. Brenda appeared with three mugs and a coffee pot, leaning over Bill without so much as a greeting. She poured the coffee into each and told Sienna, "I'll be right back with those rolls."

"We'll pick out some lunch by the time you come back!" Sienna called.

Bill picked up his mug to drink his coffee, leaning his weight against the chair back and causing it to groan. He wore a long brown jacket over his matching vest and chaps. Despite the menacing mustache and stature, his smile was warm and welcoming. Ironic that he played the villain while his gruff brother played the hero.

"So you're considering joining the Lonewood act," Bill said thoughtfully, more of a statement than a question.

"Considering is the key word here," Sienna interjected. As much as Alex would love to be up on stage performing again- even in a small capacity- becoming any sort of public figure could make it easier for Landon to find them.

Alex slumped against the back of the booth, looking out the window at the horse. "Considering. I just miss it."

"It's a decent living. We're paid by the city through Maude's LLC," he explained. When Brenda arrived with their caramel rolls, he leaned to the side to make sure she had enough room to put them down. "Since we're part of the town experience, the other businesses put a percentage of their profits towards our salary. Maude runs the shows in town. Mayor Wyatt runs everything else."

"So Maude's the person to talk to?" Alex clarified, and Sienna shot her a warning look. She snapped her mouth shut, pursing her lips into a thin line.

Bill groaned as he stood, causing the chair to buckle a little under his weight until he released his grip on the back. "Maude's a good person to talk to in general. If you're looking for any sort of work that is. Unless you want to work for the city, in which case you'll want to speak to Mayor Wyatt. I hear she's quite excited about your arrival."

"Why?" Sienna asked softly. Bill shifted his belt buckle and looked out the window, seeing Hank and Jesse sprint past on two different horses than they'd had earlier.

Sienna and Alex didn't want attention. They didn't want excitement, and they definitely didn't want to cause any waves. They had to keep their heads down and survive. Maybe once Landon was incarcerated and Alex testified in the trial, they could be located somewhere that made more sense.

Bill placed his hands on his hips and leaned backward to crack his shoulders, then rolled them back before answering. "It's no secret that Lonewood isn't doing as well as we used to and as well as we'd like. The mayor is under a lot of pressure to keep this town up and running, but to be honest, I don't think she has a clue how. Between you and me, I think we should have re-elected our last mayor, but I think the accident a couple years ago got people feeling bad for Dakota."

Sienna nodded slowly. She hoped he would elaborate on whatever accident got Dakota elected, but she knew it would be rude to press him about it.

He supplied nothing else though, so Sienna said, "Good to know. We'll definitely keep it all in mind." She shared a look with Alex, seeing the same curiosity etched across her face. "We're just trying to lay low. Find ourselves, if you will. We aren't here to cause a big fuss, otherwise we would have stayed in California."

"Well, if you need anything, don't be a stranger. And stop by Kitty's shop again if you get a chance, she wants you two to meet Beau." Bill smiled fondly, nodding to himself as he started ambling away. "I remember when she used to think I was the most special man in this town."

Within moments of Bill's departure, Brenda reappeared to take their lunch orders. Sienna realized his coffee was still here, and she reached into her purse to grab some money, but Brenda stopped her. "It's fine. It'll just come out of his pay. I keep a tab of what they eat here and give that much less to the actor's fund."

"So you're expected to pay for them to work?" Sienna wasn't quite sure how this whole arrangement benefitted any of them. Bill and Hank wandered around shooting fake guns at each other and taking turns taking over the town while the people who actually worked hard had to pay for them to do shows for nobody. Perhaps if the town was bustling with people and they were the main entertainment, but the little family was gone, as was the couple. The only people currently in Lonewood who hadn't been in Lonewood last week were Sienna and Alex.

Brenda shrugged off her question, gesturing towards Bill as he mounted his horse. "We're a team here. There really isn't enough income for everyone to survive, so we make it work. We give a little to them, because they bring in the people who spend the money at the diner and the shops. There's hardly any of us here, so it's not really a huge deal. As long as we all have food on the table, everything else falls into place."

That seemed a little unrealistic, but Sienna was still trying to grasp how this town worked. "Okay, umm, could I get a cheeseburger and fries to go please? With a coke?"

"I'd love to try your chocolate milkshake. And the cheeseburger. I'd like pickles though, she wouldn't," Alex rattled immediately after. Brenda scribbled down their order, grabbed their menus, and swept away to gather their food. "You know," Alex started, "we could just eat here. We could go shopping and come back for lunch."

"Or, and hear me out," Sienna countered, "we can get our food to go, get more snacks from the general store, and hide for the next three days."

Alex huffed, turning her gaze away from Sienna to watch out the window. With seemingly no one to perform for, the Main Street was quiet. It felt more like a ghost town than a tourist locale.

Their to-go lunches were dropped off and Alex handed Brenda her debit card to pay while Sienna continued to stare out the window. The wooden boardwalks of the three businesses across the street could be spread down Main Street for a more consistent effect. They could put extra horses outside of the buildings to give the appearance of being busier, as if there were more people living here than the three cowboys who wandered the street every hour. With a few tweaks, Lonewood could be bustling with business.

"It's so quiet," Alex mumbled to herself.

Sienna's chest clenched, knowing she could help bring in more business, but knowing she shouldn't. "I know."

With their lunch in hand, Sienna led Alex back to the motel. Looking back over her shoulder, she saw there wasn't a soul on Main Street. Even Hank, Bill, and Jesse were nowhere to be found. This was the solitude she'd expected from a small town, but now that she had it, Sienna hated it.

Suddenly, though, from the winding road leading to the stables, a large, speckled gray horse came galloping towards them. Alex pushed Sienna in front of her, holding her shoulders tightly as the horse slid to a stop. Sienna glared at her sister over her shoulder as boots hit the ground.

"Hi!" Dakota greeted excitedly. She wiped her hands on her jeans as she beamed at the sisters. Sienna tried to meet her eyes, but Dakota's legs were so long and muscular beneath the denim that Sienna couldn't help but stare. If the mayor noticed the way Sienna gawked at her, she didn't mention it. "How are you two? How was the rest of your weekend?"

Her long blonde hair was unbound, flowing over her shoulders and white tank top with lace details around the neckline. Her smile was as electric as her stature was intimidating, but she had the kindest, most sincere look in her eyes that put Sienna at ease.

"We're good! Still acclimating. It's... different!" Alex replied brightly. She stayed behind Sienna to keep away from Dakota's horse, eyeing it warily when Dakota scratched its nose and caused it to snort. "Your horse is very pretty... very big."

Dakota breamed at that, resting her cheek against the horse's neck, and it leaned into her. "Aww, thanks. He's my big baby," she cooed as she patted his neck roughly. The look she gave him was adoration, the way someone would look at their own child. Sienna found it precious.

"What's his name?" Sienna asked, reaching out to pet him tentatively. Dakota didn't stop her, so she decided it was okay, and he stood patiently as she scratched down his long face.

"Bandit," Dakota purred lovingly. She dug her nails deep into his coat, and he swung his head towards her to nudge her. "Cuz he stole my heart the moment I met him."

Sienna turned to Alex and cooed, "He's so sweet, Alex! Look at him!"

Alex shook her head rapidly and Dakota let out an "ahh" as she grabbed his bridle to hold him a little tighter. "You scared of horses?"

"Got tossed off of one. Wasn't a fun experience."

"I mean, that's where the saying comes from. You gotta get back up on the horse." Dakota smiled reassuringly and backed Bandit up a step. "You don't have to get near him if you don't want to. But if you do want to conquer your fears, Bandit's a good one. He's a big puppy dog. Even if you don't ride, he likes to cuddle. If you wanna try and pet him, I'll hold him tightly so he doesn't move."

Sienna motioned towards the horse and Alex took a tentative step forward. Bandit tried to toss his head, but Dakota held him tightly, shushing him when he blew air through his lips. Alex nervously raised her hand and laid it on his face. When nothing happened, she started stroking him slowly. He kicked his foot against the road, and she stiffened, but Sienna urged her on. "See, I told you he was sweet." Sienna stroked his cheek, and his eye shifted to look at her. "Sweet Bandit."

Alex dropped her hand and took a step back, content enough having pet the horse. Dakota could see that this small step was enough for today and loosened her grip on Bandit's bridle to hold his reins loosely again. Sienna continued to administer affection and Bandit tried to bump himself into her, causing her to laugh a little.

"Bandit! Don't knock her over," Dakota scolded lightly, but the horse continued to turn his head towards Sienna so she could keep scratching him. "He likes you. I take it you don't mind them?"

"I actually really like them. I liked riding. I was riding on the beach though, not in a place like this."

"Aww, you'd love the Badlands then," Dakota gestured towards the multicolored hills in the distance. "If you want, I'll take you riding. Or Lyle will, he runs the stables. Visit anytime and he'll get you set up with a horse. Take a guide though, it's easy to get lost and a couple of these horses used to be feral."

Sienna leaned past Bandit to look at Dakota. "Feral? Wild horses?"

"Yeah, there's tons of them in the national park. We're at the edge. Our entrance is up past the stables." She nodded down the road she'd come from. "The herds get too big, and sometimes they're captured. It's all on the up and up, and we'd prefer to keep them here than send them off somewhere far away. So we've given some a home here in Lonewood. But give 'em the chance, they might just take off with their old herds."

"Was Bandit wild?"

"He was! He was actually injured when he was a baby, so that's why he was captured. He went to auction with a couple others from his herd, but nobody wanted him. He had a bad foot. He was expected to be put down, but I took one look at him and knew he was mine. And when we met, oh..." she ran her fingers through his coarse mane with a sad smile on her face. "If he never walked again, I knew I'd sit in the stable with him until his dying day. Lyle helped me nurse him back to health and he's been the best boy I could ever ask for..." Dakota trailed off, then seemed to catch herself reminiscing and straightened up. "As I was saying, if you want to ride, the stables are open until five. Lyle will set you up. I'm free most days after one, so if you ever want to take a ride, I'd love to join. Have you gotten to experience any more of Lonewood since I saw you?"

"Well, Skylar took us to the sheriff's station after brunch," Alex detailed, "and we saw the showdown between Bill Cassidy and Hank. We stopped by the saloon, which was fun. I mean, it was empty, but it was fun to see. We bought some snacks at the general store and met Kitty outside her shop. Yesterday we just hung back at the motel. It's been a long couple of days of traveling."

"Oh, of course, I'm sure you two are exhausted!" Dakota answered. Bandit huffed, blowing snot onto her shoulder and she wiped it off and shot him an annoyed look. "I'm sure you'll find the town much more lively after Memorial Day. That's when business picks up. I'd love to keep the town busy year round, but we really only get people who've been here before. And they come in the summer when school's out. The college kids will come back home for the summer, and there's a few seniors who will work after they graduate, which is awesome. We'll be rockin' and rollin' come June."

Sienna thought her tone sounded a little nervous, tinged with disbelief. She wasn't convincing them the town would get busier, perhaps she was trying to convince herself. Being the mayor had to be difficult, especially when they were a tourist destination with no tourists. Bill had made a comment about people feeling bad for Dakota, but Sienna didn't know the woman well enough to pry.

"Hopefully business will pick up. I'm hoping there will be something here in this town for us... work wise. We can't live in the motel forever."

Although if they tried, maybe it would be easier to leave the first chance they got.

"Yeah, about that- Kennedy called down to the sheriff's station this morning and said she had some guests who were squatting in one of their rooms. Is there any chance she's talking about you two?" Dakota raised her brow and Sienna's stomach dropped.

They'd been so busy hiding that they hadn't bothered to visit the front office to extend their stay. "That's totally us. We'll take care of it right away."

Dakota nodded, looking towards the motel before sucking in a sharp breath, as if she remembered something important. "Do you want me to come with you? Explain what happened?"

"I think we can handle it, but thank you." Sienna gave Bandit one last scratch and Alex bolted away. She would take any excuse to put some space between herself and the massive animal.

When Sienna started to pick up her pace, though, Dakota called, "Before you go, let me give you my cell number. Just in case there's any issues at the motel."

"Thank you, I really appreciate it," Sienna said as she pulled out her cell phone and handed it to Dakota. She typed in her number and handed it back. "I'm sure we'll get it all sorted out. It's just a misunderstanding."

"I know. Just in case," Dakota repeated. She smiled weakly, and Sienna had a sneaking suspicion she knew something they didn't.

When they reached the motel office, Sienna took the lead. She waltzed up to the front desk and pulled out her wallet quickly, even before introducing herself. "I am so sorry, we're the ones living in room eighty-seven. Skylar Hyde paid for the first night and we were so tired from traveling we completely forgot to put down a card for more!"

The tiny brunette behind the counter looked stunned by the rapid and blunt introduction and took Sienna's card tentatively. "Yeah, no worries! I just didn't know what the situation was since there wasn't a name on the reservation or anything. I would have reached out myself, but when I knocked nobody answered." She inserted Sienna's card into a card reader, then smiled. "I'm Kennedy. My husband and I run the motel. How has your stay been? How many nights do you want to pay for?"

"Well," Alex started, stepping up to the counter. "We've actually moved here. We need to find a more permanent place to live, but until then we'll probably be renting one of your rooms."

"If that's alright, of course," Sienna interjected.

Kennedy's blue eyes widened and she nodded enthusiastically. "Of course! You can stay as long as you want! Honestly, business has been so slow, we are thankful to have you here at all. Please stay as long as you need to... I know it'll get expensive eventually, but I'll talk to Trevor, see if we can give you a discount-"

"No need, we'll happily pay full price." Sienna wasn't going to let these people take a pay cut to save the government some money. "Thank you for your hospitality and understanding. We really appreciate it. Please continue putting our room on that card."

"You got it!" Kennedy chirped as she handed Sienna's card back. Having one room rented lit up her whole demeanor. Sienna began dreaming again, wondering what kind of life sweet Kennedy could have if all their rooms were filled.

Alex thanked the woman and they started to leave, but Kennedy called after them. "Hey! Umm, if there's any issues, please let me know. I can iron everything out if need be."

It was that same guilty tone that Dakota had, and Sienna's mind started rolling through reasons for their worry.

When they came around the side of the building to their room, she finally understood.

Leaning against the wall next to their door was the Sheriff of Lonewood. Boots, hat, the whole nine yards. He even wore a badge today on his brown suede vest, looking like a cowboy at a Halloween party. It took everything in Sienna not to chortle at the sight, especially when he stopped swiping against his cell phone with a dirty thumb to look up at them with an annoyed expression.

"I got a call that somebody was living in a room without paying."

He'd been mildly pleasant at the diner on Saturday, but what little politeness he'd shown was long gone now. He looked between Sienna and Alex as he waited for one of them to say something. Sienna thought he didn't look to be in the mood for listening though.

"We're so sorry, it was a misunderstanding! It's all been sorted out, though. We just talked to Kennedy and made sure she got payment for the nights we missed," Alex explained. She was trying to be pleasant, but the sheriff wasn't having it.

He grunted and stood up straighter, shoving his phone into his jean's pocket. "By staying here without paying, you've been stealing a room from the owners. In this town you'll be arrested for less."

Sienna rolled her eyes and pulled the key out from her purse, handing it over to Alex to let them in. She had to assume he was joking, because there was no way the head of law enforcement could be such an arrogant prick to the town's guests. "It was an accident. Skylar paid the first night and we were exhausted. We forgot to pay for the past two, but it's been taken care of now. Kennedy isn't mad-"

"Doesn't matter, you come to my town and cause trouble, you pay the consequences."

"Are you really going to arrest us for accidentally not paying for a hotel room?" Sienna was seething as she took a step closer. She wrinkled her nose at the smell of sweat and dirt. It was a travesty that everyone in this town couldn't help but be filthy. She swung her arm out to the empty parking lot. "There's literally nobody else here. She was ecstatic that they'd have customers."

The sheriff narrowed his eyes, crossing his arms and staring down at Sienna. He was a good nine or ten inches taller than her. His head almost reached the top of the door and his shoulders were so broad she didn't know if he'd be able to make it inside if he tried. He'd be handsome if he wiped that scowl off his face and took a shower once in a while.

"My town. My rules. If you break them, you deal with me."

And then he smiled. That devious, heart stopping smile that filled Sienna with rage because it was clearly a sign of aggression. She had to assume that he was having a fiery, passionate affair with Mayor Wyatt, because only a woman of her caliber could tame such a frustrating, volatile individual.

Alex popped open the door and went inside the old motel room, but Sienna didn't follow her. She glared up at the sheriff with furrowed brows, not about to give him the satisfaction of intimidating her. Alex looked between the two, then hissed, "Sienna."

"Do you want to come in, Sheriff..." Sienna trailed off, gesturing for him to introduce himself. Although she guessed this was the Gentry that Skylar had mentioned owning the black and white horse, she wanted him to tell her his name. Sienna wasn't about to run scared from some self-righteous, podunk-town sheriff.

He made a huffing noise that almost sounded like a horse, and Sienna couldn't contain her amusement. Her smile started to grow until she couldn't hold it back, and then she chuckled. And he glared at her like she was the most wretched being he'd ever laid his russet brown eyes on.

She half expected him to handcuff her and carry her to the jail over the back of his splattered horse, but instead he looked over his shoulder at the empty parking lot with a defeated, frustrated look in his eyes. "Gentry," he grunted. "Sheriff Gentry."

"Do you have a first name?"

"Sheriff," he deadpanned without missing a beat. "Now if I hear about you causing any more trouble, the next time we'll be having this conversation at the station. Do I make myself clear?"

Sienna's lip curled up in a taunting grin and she nodded slightly. "I don't expect there to be any more trouble, Sheriff Gentry. With any luck, this will be the last interaction we ever have."

He scoffed at that and turned away, mumbling under his breath, "If only I could be so lucky."

With the sheriff gone, Sienna closed the door and leaned against it, finding Alex sitting at the table scarfing her cheeseburger. "I think that went well."

"As much as I don't want to ask questions about this weird little town, I'd love to hear about why he's got such a stick up his ass," Sienna hissed at the door as she joined Alex. She took a bite of her own cheeseburger that Alex had set out and hummed. "I feel bad for Mayor Wyatt. She probably has to work closely with that asshole."

"I don't think she minds. They seem rather fond of each other."

"Glad to know you see it, too," Sienna took another bite, thinking about the gorgeous blonde mayor and the irritable sheriff and this odd little town they had to hide in.

Chapter 9

Tuesday morning, Sienna decided she wanted a notebook. It was an oddly specific request, but Alex didn't question it. She followed Sienna across the road to Kitty's little store, the Shoppe at Rattlesnake Bend, and waited patiently while her sister perused Kitty's wares.

Alex picked up an arrowhead, turning it over to read the price tag before putting it back in the bowl. A wall was lined with a dozen different magnets, most of them North Dakota themed but a few reading Lonewood. She studied the Lonewood ones, finding them cheaply made and giving her a pretty good indication that Kitty herself created them.

"Do you like this?" Sienna asked as she held up a blue notebook with chevron arrows running along the bottom. Alex shrugged and grabbed it, flipping through it before handing it back.

"It's a notebook. I have no feelings about it one way or another."

Sienna went back to browsing the shelves, looking for notebooks or pens or whatever. While her sister wandered away, Alex noticed a small paperback book about Lonewood displayed prominently on the shelf.

She flipped through it slowly, studying the black and white photos on the first page. After a brief history of the town, the photos began to appear in color, and Alex smiled when she saw a photo of cattle running down Main Street. The sidewalk was packed with people, most of them wearing cowboy boots and beaming as the cattle stampeded by. Alex wondered if Lonewood got this busy in the summers today, or if this type of popularity was long forgotten.

When she reached the back of the book, there was a photo of three women sitting atop horses facing the other way, gazing at the sunset over the Badlands. The one in the middle was clearly Dakota, because of the long blonde hair that flowed down her back and the speckled coat of Bandit. To her left was a small woman with jet black hair tied into a loose braid. Her hands pressed against the back of her saddle to hold her upright as she leaned back. Her posture was confident, casual. She wasn't worried about losing her balance or her horse taking off from under her. To Dakota's right was the third woman, another blonde. Her hair was pulled back with a bright red bow, and she was turned slightly towards the other two women, just enough for the photo to capture a joyous smile.

In small, white lettering on the bottom, their names were written: Jasmine Lee, Dakota Wyatt, Kenzie Wyatt.

"Huh." Alex flipped the page, but there was nothing more. It was an interesting way to end the book. She looked over her shoulder, noticing that Sienna had moved on to the jewelry, and Kitty had joined her.

Alex decided $12.99 was a decent enough price for the book, and she wanted to look at it again later. She held it to her chest and made her way over to Kitty and Sienna.

Sienna held up a pewter ring, inspecting it before putting it back. Kitty gasped happily when she saw Alex, but her excitement turned to surprise when she noticed what she held. "Oh! Do you like the book? I made it myself."

"Really?" Alex asked, holding it out to get another look at it. "I thought it would be fun to learn a little more history of the town. And the photos are beautiful."

She considered asking Kitty about why she'd chosen to put the photo of the mayor and her friends in the back of the book, but Kitty turned her attention to Sienna as she picked up a long silver chain with a beautiful blue stone in it. "That's one of my favorite pieces. I went to a craft fair in Bismarck last fall and came back with a bunch of them."

"May I ask you a rather personal question, Kitty?" Alex started, and the blonde nodded without hesitation. "Do you get a lot of business here? In the store? In the town?"

Her smile fell a little, and she shrugged. "We get enough to get by. Summers are busy. Not as busy as I remember them as a kid, but busy enough."

From the corner of her eye, Alex saw Sienna lift her gaze to Kitty. It was clear that Sienna was antsy to work, and she had the skills to bring in business for Lonewood. She had that hungry look in her eyes, the one that said she was gunning for a promotion or a big account. If she set her mind to it, she could market the hell out of Lonewood, and it could be a bustling boomtown once more. But the people who lived here maybe wouldn't want that.

"Do you wish it were busier?" Sienna asked and Alex clenched her teeth. She gnawed her molars a little, wanting Kitty to say she liked things the way they were.

Tell her no.

Kitty tilted her head to the side, staring at the wall with wide eyes, as if thinking through her answer. "I think we got a good thing going here. I wish people would come and see it."

Careful what you wish for.

"Hmm," Sienna hummed, holding the necklace up to her collarbone. Alex turned around to look at the raccoon skin hats. She picked one up, staring at it before showing it to Sienna. The redhead turned to Kitty with a questioning expression. "What exactly is the aesthetic of this town? Like, is it the old west? Modern west? The frontier? Should we expect an Indian attack?"

"They actually prefer to be called Native Americans," Kitty explained carefully.

Sienna furrowed her brows, gesturing over her shoulder as she countered, "You sell teepee paperweights."

Kitty snorted, covering her nose and shrugging. "I sell what I find. I've had those since I opened the store. Don't think I've ever sold one."

"How long have you had the store?"

"Oh..." Kitty trailed off as she counted in her head. "Seven years? Seven years this June."

Alex looked around the store, wondering how much of this stuff had been here for seven years. There were little carved horses with a slight covering of dust, and a couple of bison plushies near the window that looked almost faded from the sunshine.

"Well," Sienna said bluntly as she placed the necklace on top of her notebook and pens to purchase. "I used to work in marketing and I think with a little work, this place could be buzzing with life again."

"Really?" Kitty gasped. "You really think so? I mean, Daddy used to always tell me about the good ole' days, but I don't know if people want to do the whole western vacation thing anymore. Especially with Medora down the road. They are just a bigger draw for tourists and locals. We get return visitors but that's about it. People who remember it as kids, but... they don't come back as often anymore."

Since they were done with their shopping, Sienna and Alex followed Kitty to the cash register. Sienna placed all her stuff down first, then reached over and grabbed the book from her sister.

"I can get it."

"It's all the same money, might as well make her job a little easier."

Ever since the Landon incident, Alex had been patient with Sienna. She was having a hard time adjusting to something Alex caused, so she'd kept her mouth shut and her feelings to herself. But this was her home now. Alex was ready to be her own person again.

"So, Kitty, what do you all do for fun around here?" Alex asked, desperately needing to be around people who weren't Sienna. "Like, where does everyone hang out? The young people?"

Kitty's whole countenance brightened at the question and she flipped her hair over her shoulder and leaned on the counter after handing Sienna her bag. "Well, if you're wanting to get the full Lonewood experience, I recommend the Badlands Saloon. They do shows on the weekends if people show up, and all through the summer. If you need a break from all the country, Jazzy's is the place to go, but it gets a little rowdy there sometimes. I personally prefer the saloon since my mom performs there. If you go during the week, you can grab a drink and enjoy the quiet. Sometimes Lyle plays the piano in the evenings if he finishes up early at the stables. Once summer hits, this place will come alive, though. It's only a few more weeks. We should start seeing people arrive pretty soon, just you wait."

"Can't wait!" Sienna squeaked in an attempt to sound excited that fell flat. "We'll see you soon, Kitty!"

Alex followed Sienna out the door to the wooden porch, then stopped as her sister started to go down the stairs. She glanced at the apparel shop next door and called, "You head on back. I'm gonna check out the boot store!"

There was a long moment of silence where Sienna just stared at Alex, then finally asked, "Why? If you aren't going to get near the horses, why would you need cowboy boots?"

"For fun?"

"You know, the money isn't endless. If you want to buy stuff, you're gonna need a job."

Lucky for Alex, she was looking up at the building, so Sienna didn't see her roll her eyes. "That's the plan. Always was." She looked back at Sienna and added, "I just wanna look."

Sienna twisted her lips to the side and looked back at the motel. It was only two o'clock. The day was young. She had plenty of time to work on whatever she wanted the notebook for, and maybe she'd enjoy being alone for a little while. Maybe that solitude was worth whatever Alex would spend at the boot shop.

"Fine. While you're at it, can you pick up something for dinner?"

A happy compromise. Alex could explore on her own and Sienna could hide until she was ready to face Lonewood again. "Of course. I'll see you tonight."

Sienna turned to leave and Alex practically jogged into the apparel store. The inside smelled like leather. Boots lined the left wall, hats lined the right, but the center had a half dozen racks of clothes. This was where the tourists came to dress the part.

"Can I help you?" A feminine voice called and when she came around the corner, Alex realized it was Kennedy from the motel. She paused when she recognized Alex, giving a little wave. "Hi."

"Do you run this, too?" Alex asked gently. She didn't want to offend the woman, but she looked exhausted. She nodded, and Alex asked, "How do you keep up with both?"

"Well, we don't own the store, we just run it in the off season. Trevor and I alternate between here and the motel during the day and then Cecily from the sheriff station watches it in the evening until closing time." Kennedy looked around, almost as if she was overwhelmed. "Usually some of the college kids run it when they come back for the summer. Doesn't see a lot of business during the year so somebody just has to watch it. We do our best to keep it open, just in case..."

Alex wondered if their arrival was reason to keep it open. Clearly she and Sienna were in need of appropriate clothing, be it to act as locals or just to exist in the environment. Kennedy had been ecstatic to have someone staying long term in their motel. It was then that Alex realized Kennedy was wearing the same shirt as yesterday, either from exhaustion, or because she didn't have much else.

"So here's my dilemma." Alex took a few bold steps farther into the store and looked around, pushing some of the shirts aside on the rack to get a closer look. "I'm terrified of horses, so my sister says I don't need boots. That said, I'd like to apply to be one of the actors here. I've been told to talk to Maude, and I want to impress her, but I look like a tourist. I'm assuming she doesn't run a costume department, so I'm gonna need a few things of my own if I get a part."

Kennedy seemed surprised by this confession. She turned around to look at a rack of dresses, then asked, "What size are you?"

"I don't know, a six? A medium? Depends on what it is."

The woman grabbed a dress with a red corset top and black lacing that moved down to a piece of black ruching over a red skirt. A saloon girl dress.

Alex looked up at Kennedy from the dress. "Really?"

Kennedy grimaced and admitted, "Yeah. There aren't any cowgirls. There's the showgirls who work in the saloon, but that's about it for women. If you want to work for Maude, this is the best you're gonna get."

"Hmm," Alex grabbed the dress and held it up to her chest, looking down at the flowing fabric. It was beautifully made. Every stitch was perfectly placed and the boning on the corset was thick. Alex wasn't sure if she had the boobs to fill out this kind of dress, but it might just make her long, lean body look like a lady's. Although she wasn't sure she wanted to look like this type of lady.

"I mean, you could try to bartend. She might let you help during the busy season. I'm assuming you're old enough to drink, meaning you're old enough to serve." Kennedy led Alex towards the boots, gesturing to them broadly. "Even if you aren't big on horses, boots are easy on the feet on the dirt roads. Get a nice pair and they'll last you for years." She took the showgirl dress and put it back and grabbed a mid-length flowing dress in a subtle beige color. "If you really want to impress Maude, be yourself. She doesn't take anybody's bullshit, and she'll see right through you if you try too hard."

Alex didn't have a clue who she was at the moment. She was trying to get back to some semblance of the career she knew and loved, the same way Sienna was. She wanted to act, because if she was focused on pretending to be a character, she didn't have to dwell on who she wanted to be. That was something she'd struggled with for years.

She grabbed a pair of brown boots in her size and sat to try them on. They had swirly designs stitched up the boot, giving them a little feminine touch. When she slipped them on, she understood what Kennedy meant about being easy on the feet. They were thick and padded, and even taking a few steps around the shop was more comfortable than her tennis shoes. She pulled them off and checked the tag, paling a little at the price.

But if that was the price to belong here, it was worth it to Alex.

"I'll take these!" Alex called. She held onto her boots fondly, excited to have her first personal thing from Lonewood. It made it feel a little more like home.

Kennedy came over with a small stack of cowboy hats, setting them out on one of the counters and gesturing to them. "Can't be a cowgirl without a hat."

Alex picked up a dark brown one that sat a little too low on her forehead. She shook her head to dismiss it, then tried a black one, but it made her look a little stiff. Finally, she placed a brownish-gray hat on her head. It was a little more fedora than cowboy hat, but Alex liked the way it made her look. It would look nice with her dress and her boots. It made her want to go out and be around people again.

"I'll take it."

Chapter 10

"Do you wanna go to the saloon tonight?"

Alex raised her brow to question it, seeming to think Sienna had lost her mind. "You want to go to the saloon? On a Friday night? I think this is when they do their shows."

"Well," Sienna started, "I thought maybe you'd enjoy it. You could wear your new dress and boots. You could get to see a performance, which you'd love."

"And you can get a better grasp on how to market this town."

Sienna rolled her eyes and tossed her big red curls over her shoulder. "No. Maybe I just want to have a good time? Is that a crime?"

She'd put in extra effort today, curling up her long red hair and lining her big green eyes to make them pop. She'd even painted her lips deep red and worn the green plaid shirt Alex had wanted her to try.

It was clear that Alex didn't believe Sienna's claim about not having ulterior motives, but she sighed anyway and said, "It could be fun. Let me get ready and we can head out."

"Great! I'm excited," Sienna said honestly. It had been exactly a week since their arrival in Lonewood. She needed to figure out how to make a life in this little town. That had to start with leaving their motel room.

At a little after six, Sienna and Alex strode down the dirt street of Lonewood. It dawned on Sienna that there were actual homes here and people actually lived here, but they'd never gone beyond Main Street. They hadn't needed to yet.

She looked over at her little sister, noting how beautiful she was. She'd curled ringlets around her face and pulled the rest up into a messy bun on top of her head. Her dress was belted at her waist, which only accentuated the high-low effect of the fabric that showed off her expensive boots. She had opted not to wear her cowboy hat, and Sienna had almost asked if she could borrow it, but she wasn't quite ready to fully give into Lonewood yet.

Sheriff Gentry's black and white horse was tied to the hitching post in front of the sheriff's station, but the man was leaned up against a wooden railing lining the porch of the mayor's office. When Sienna got a little closer, she noticed Dakota standing outside her door with her hand clenched into a fist at her side. Her lips were pulled into a tight line, and she looked up at the sheriff from under her thick lashes. Whatever they were talking about wasn't pleasant, and Sienna picked up her pace to try to get past quicker.

Their presence wasn't unnoticed though, and she heard Dakota call weakly, "Hi! Where are you two off to?"

It was an easy question. Friendly, but not demanding. If it weren't for the large man looming over Dakota, her clenched fist, or the uncomfortable way she looked at the sisters like it pained her, Sienna wouldn't have thought anything of it. She pointed towards the Badlands Saloon. "We're gonna go to Maude's place. We were told there'd be a show tonight or something? Figured we'd check it out."

Dakota nodded, relaxing her fist and putting forth her best smile. It wasn't as bright or sincere as it usually was, but it tried. "That's great! I hope you enjoy it."

Alex grabbed Sienna's wrist and tugged a little, giving Dakota a wave to say goodbye, but Sienna didn't move. She locked eyes with the sheriff and called, "I don't mean to intrude, but is everything okay here?"

"Mind your own business, everything's fine," the sheriff grunted and Sienna took another step towards them. His harsh tone made her even more determined to stay until she knew Dakota was okay.

Dakota placed her hand on his upper arm and shook her head. "We're okay," she told him. Her words seemed to ease whatever bothered him, because his shoulders relaxed. Her smile grew until it reached her eyes, and she added to Sienna, "He's just being a pain in the ass." Dakota turned and locked up her office, shooting him a taunting look that had the sheriff shifting uncomfortably. Sienna realized she'd upset him, not the other way around. "And I was just leaving for the evening. Perhaps I'll join you at the saloon."

"Oh, maybe then I'll come too." Gentry started to follow, but Dakota waved him off to tell him he wasn't welcome before trotting down the stairs to join Sienna and Alex. He crossed his arms and leaned against the banister. "So this conversation's been put to rest, then?"

"Just for tonight," she warned. "I'll see you tomorrow."

He smirked as she walked away, leading Sienna and Alex towards the saloon.

Sienna dared to tap Dakota's shoulder, getting her to slow her long strides and give Sienna her attention. "Are you sure you're okay?"

"Psh, yes. He's fine. Just cranky. He'll go home and drink and be fine in the morning."

"Are you sure?" Sienna looked to Alex, but she gave a sharp shake of her head, telling Sienna to drop it.

As they walked, Dakota reached behind her head to pull out the scrunchie holding her hair in a tight braid. She shook out the messy waves from the braid, then stopped walking to flip her hair over her head and shake it out some more. When she stood upright, her big hair flowed wildly around the shoulders of her baby blue dress. The look on her face was one of contentment, as if she'd shed the heavy weight of being mayor and could finally just be herself after a long day.

She pushed open the doors to the saloon, and the small group sitting near the stage whooped at her appearance. She laughed and waved, striding through the empty tables and chairs to take a seat near everybody else. Sienna and Alex kept their distance, unsure if Dakota meant for them to *join* her, or just be in the same building as her.

"Oh, my girls are back!" Maude yelled from the bar. Alex looked up and beamed at the woman, practically jogging over to her, but Sienna just gave a casual wave.

Since Alex was preoccupied with Maude, Sienna wandered a little closer to the stage, looking at the people in attendance until Dakota pulled out the chair next to her. She pointed at it and ordered, "Sit."

Doing as she was told, Sienna slung her purse over the chair back and looked around as Dakota began pointing to the people sitting around them. "Sienna, this is Cecily, she's the receptionist for the sheriff's station and my office. That's Joe, he owns the general store and that's his wife Sadie May. Jesse you know, he's one of our cowboys, and this is Wayne and Leah. They work at the school. He's the principal and she teaches the high school kids. Their son is graduating." She turned to them, laying her palm flat on the old wooden table to lean against. "That's crazy right? Can you believe he's already heading to college?"

"No, I can't," Wayne answered quietly. He leaned against the table, looking at his wife fondly. "It'll be weird being empty nesters. He's not sure if he's coming back next summer though. Might wanna warn Lyle that he's gonna be a little short on help."

Dakota nodded, taking a deep breath and looking up at the stage as a lanky man in his early thirties sat down at the piano. "Annie should be coming home for graduation. She said she was gonna try to come back this summer."

"That doesn't mean she'll come back next year. That girl is going places. Sooner or later she's going to leave Lonewood in the dust," Leah answered wearily.

Sienna could feel the tension between them, like there was a conversation happening beneath the words. It wasn't the same type of tension between Dakota and the sheriff, but rather apprehension over something that they were all aware of, but didn't want to talk about. Maybe they didn't want to talk about it in front of Sienna.

"So how's your first week been, City Girl?" Joe asked. He gave her a toothy grin, showing off a golden tooth and the smell of tobacco. Sienna wondered if these people chose to be living caricatures, or if their sense of self faded into what they were supposed to be after so many years of pretending.

"It's been fine." Sienna adjusted the buttoned cuff of her plaid shirt. She looked over her shoulder, seeing Alex on a barstool talking to Maude, not about to save Sienna from this conversation. "We've really just been settling in. Haven't done much, so we're excited to be here tonight."

The lights went down and Dakota whooped loudly as the curtains rose. The guy at the piano began playing, and the lights came up on four women facing away from the audience, long ruched skirts in hand. Alex appeared and sat beside Sienna, looking up at the dancers excitedly.

However, while the piano player was clearly skilled, the dancers left a lot to be desired. As they turned around one by one, it became very apparent that they were all in their fifties, maybe older. These were the women they'd seen in the corner booth of the diner that first morning in Lonewood.

They danced with ease, but their routine was safe, easy. Sienna imagined it had once been harder and more impressive, but these women couldn't pass for young, excitable saloon girls anymore. It was sad, but it was an effort.

When she turned to Alex, she saw her sister's head tilted to the side, causing her curls to fall away from her face. Her eyes followed the dancers, nodding occasionally but furrowing her brows when they did a move badly. It must have killed her to watch these amateurs struggle through the number when last month she'd been on Broadway.

The number ended with the four women raising their hands to the balcony, even though it stood empty. Sienna and Alex clapped, but Dakota hollered loudly, showing her support along with the other patrons. The dancers ran offstage and the lights came up, but the man at the piano continued to play. Everyone except Jesse and Dakota got up to go to the bathroom or the bar, and the young man shuffled from his chair to take a seat next to Alex.

"You made it! How have you been?" He beamed at her, looking her up and down before stammering, "You look beautiful by the way."

"Thank you! It's all new from the store. I'm trying out a new look. Do I look like I belong in Lonewood?"

Jesse smiled shyly and nodded. "I'd say so."

While Jesse entertained Alex, Dakota sighed and turned to Sienna. Her expression was hard to read, but it leaned towards sadness. Disappointment. It definitely wasn't pride.

"It's pretty rough," Dakota murmured quietly so Jesse couldn't hear. "But they're all we've got. At least Maude makes the drinks strong. We open the bar a good hour before the show, hoping the people won't realize that half of our showgirls have grandchildren."

Sienna didn't even know what to say. She didn't want to offend Mayor Wyatt, but Lonewood *was* in rough shape. They were acting to a non-existent crowd, sharing money that half of them didn't even earn, and their talent left a lot to be desired. Even if this place was packed with people, they'd be disappointed. And probably wouldn't come back.

Dakota leaned her cheek against her fist, looking the most downtrodden Sienna had seen her. "You're in marketing. You know how to make things popular and how to make things sell, right? My town is dying. Nobody is coming to visit. There's no revenue, and there's so little life left here. Every year more kids graduate high school, and when they leave, less come back than the year before. Sure, loss of business is a problem, but loss of residents is a bigger one..." She massaged her temples, staring at the empty stage. "Nobody wants to change. They don't want to change the way we work and live, because it's all they've ever known. I get it. I grew up here, but at some point, there will be nobody left. I would have never run for mayor, except the horse wasn't doing any good."

Sienna furrowed her brows and cocked her head. "The horse?"

"Yeah, General Grant. He was named after a pony that Theodore Roosevelt had."

"That's super random."

"I mean, Theodore Roosevelt came here once... He was lost, but he did spend the night."

"So, what about the horse?" Sienna questioned, legitimately confused as to what Dakota was talking about.

The tall blonde leaned back in her chair and nodded. "Yeah. He was mayor for, like, fifteen years. He did nothing helpful." She chuckled, but Sienna didn't laugh.

"The horse… was the mayor?" Sienna asked, trying to comprehend what kind of town elected a horse instead of a person.

"Everyone thought it would be cute! He had a special stall built next to the mayor's office and we'd have 'Meet the Mayor' events; kids loved it!" Sienna continued to stare at her in disbelief, so Dakota cleared her throat and continued, "Things had gotten rough. The town was losing hope and I decided that we needed to make a change. So I ran, and I won….barely, but I won. Good thing, too, because the horse died about three months later. That was last May. Things have only gotten worse since."

Sienna took a deep breath, carefully considering her words before speaking the truth anyways. "Please don't take this the wrong way, but this place is bonkers. I have no idea what's happening and I think the longer I stay here the more I lose my mind."

Dakota snorted, then tossed her head back and laughed. Her hair spilled over the back of the chair, and her chest shook with laughter until she sniffled and wiped the tears from the edge of her eyes. "God, I totally get that. It's mind numbing at times. I work so hard and nothing happens. I'm so bored; my town is five streets. I shoulda let the horse win."

From the moment they met her, Sienna thought of Dakota as an unstoppable force of nature. Watching her crumble and admit that her efforts were in vain was heartbreaking. Sienna didn't think she deserved this kind of honesty from a woman she barely knew.

"What can I do?" Sienna whispered just loud enough for Dakota to hear.

She smiled sadly, her shoulders slumped. "Tell me what I need to do to make this town more appealing. I want more people to move here…and visit here. I think we need to work on both, but I don't know where to start. I don't know what to do anymore. I'm from here. I don't know anything different than what you see. But everything I love and understand is failing and I need help." She swallowed and looked back at the door, as if worried someone would show up. Or wishing somebody would. "We used to all be so close, but… God had other plans. So I'm trying to finish what we started, but I can't do it alone. Not anymore."

This was the moment Sienna prayed for and dreaded all at the same time. If she played this right, she could help Lonewood, build a new reputation, and get her life back on track.

"I can help you. I can figure something out to boost business and hopefully then people will want to move here. It won't be easy, though. A lot of this is going to have to change."

Dakota considered her offer, staring at Sienna like she was about to make a deal with the devil. By accepting Sienna's help, she'd be putting the good of Lonewood above everyone's opinion of her. For someone so well-liked and personable, Sienna wondered how Dakota would react to her citizens resenting her.

The mayor thrust her hand forward for Sienna to shake, raising her chin proudly as she smiled. "Meet me at my office Monday. One o'clock. Bring your ideas and we'll get started."

Chapter 11

Sienna Jade was outside the mayor's office at 12:55 Monday afternoon.

As they reached the middle of May, the temperature in western North Dakota was growing warmer. There was no humidity, which meant Sienna's makeup stayed as precise as she intended it to be. Although Dakota wouldn't care if she showed up in jeans and a t-shirt, Sienna felt like herself again in a forest green sheath dress. She'd even dared to wear her wedges again to appear more put together for this meeting.

She took a deep breath through her nose, then blew it out through her lips. After smoothing down her dress, Sienna pulled open the door to the mayor's office, greeted by pale violet walls and a couple of small sofas. A waiting room.

Sienna assumed Dakota would open her office door when she was ready for her, so she carefully sat on a loveseat and stared at the walls, taking in the framed photos. Several of them were featured in Alex's book, the one Kitty made. On the far wall, though, above a small glass table with a candy dish, was a photo of a slim woman with honey blonde hair. She was looking at the camera, smiling brightly as the sun set behind her, painting the sky brilliant shades of pink and purple and orange. Sienna didn't know what was more beautiful, the photo or the woman it showcased.

Suddenly, the door to the mayor's personal office swung open and Sheriff Gentry appeared in the doorway. When he saw Sienna, he narrowed his gaze and called over his shoulder, "What the hell is she doing here?"

There was a loud sigh, then Dakota's voice saying, "I asked her to come. I want to hear her ideas."

Sienna cautiously approached the doorway, keeping her eyes on the towering man who glared down at her. His gaze briefly slid down to her shoes before he asked, "What kind of ideas?"

"I ran a marketing firm in California and I have some ideas to help boost business."

The sheriff shifted slightly, just enough to stare at the mayor. Sienna tried to sneak past his massive frame to enter the room, careful not to bump into him as he ignored her. It wasn't difficult for him; he easily looked right over Sienna's head. "You can't be serious."

"I'm very serious," Dakota answered casually. "We're in trouble and I think she can help."

"She doesn't know the first thing about our town. How is she going to help?" His words were laced with venom, and Sienna steeled her jaw when his fury landed on her once again. He'd been annoyed the last couple times they'd met, but he looked *angry* now. "We don't need you. We can take care of this town on our own."

"No, we can't. If we could, we would have done it by now. We need fresh blood, and fresh insight. You know how far that can go-"

Gentry cut her off, pointing an accusatory finger at Sienna. "Not from her. I've seen the way she looks at us all, like we're a bunch of backwoods simpletons. Like we're less than what her big city ideals can comprehend," he hissed with a quiet intensity that gave Sienna goosebumps. He took a swift step towards Sienna and she stumbled back a little, her body reacting before her mind could tell her to toughen up and stand up to him. The logical part of her knew this law enforcement officer wasn't going to beat her in front of the town's mayor, but her instincts told her to give him his space. He grinned wickedly when he saw the trepidation in her eyes, and warned in a deep baritone that made Sienna shiver, "This is my town, and I'm not going to let you ruin it."

"No," Dakota spat. She stood from her chair and leaned over her desk, glaring up at him. "This is *my* town. I am the mayor. You work for me. And I suggest you get back to your station, Sheriff. We're done here."

He huffed loudly, clenching his jaw so tightly Sienna thought it could come unhinged. He shook his head as he stormed out of the room, and when the door slammed closed, Dakota relaxed.

"I'm so sorry about him. He just... he's wary of outside opinions," Dakota explained weakly. She sat back down and gestured for Sienna to take a seat across from her. "I swear he's all bark and no bite. Please don't let him intimidate you, that's all it is, intimidation. He knows he can scare you with his size and his snark, but he's really not so bad. He's a great guy. He's just... scared of change."

Sienna needed to tread carefully around the subject. She had a lot of grave concerns regarding the mayor and the sheriff, but Sienna really wanted to work with Dakota. Accusing her of being in an abusive relationship probably wouldn't get her very far.

So instead, she nodded and forced a weak smile. "I trust you. If you say everything's okay, I believe you."

Dakota let out a sharp laugh and leaned back in her chair. She pulled open one of her desk drawers and pulled out a silver flask, unscrewing the cap and taking a quick swig before putting it away. "It's fine. He'll get over it."

"I just don't want to cause any issues at home..."

"We don't live together, we aren't that close," Dakota said quickly, furrowing her brows before sighing and folding her hands together. "Tell me your ideas. What would you do to help Lonewood?"

Sienna took a deep breath through her nose, holding it as she flipped open her notebook on Dakota's desk. It was beautiful oak, smooth, but not professionally made. This desk was probably made by someone right here in this town. "You want more people to live here, right? In order to get people to relocate to the town, we need to make the town desirable. Nobody looks into a place they've never heard of, so we need people to visit first. Let me ask you this, how do you usually attract business?"

Dakota pursed her lips, looking at some framed photos on the wall. When Sienna looked, she saw a horse framed up next to her photo. "Honestly, we just kind of rely on people remembering us. We used to be really popular in the eighties and nineties. Before social media became big, everyone just came back every summer. It was a tradition for a lot of people. And some people wanted to be a part of that. For instance, Hank and Bill came when they were little kids, then when they became adults they moved here. Bill met his wife here and raised Kitty here. Jesse's family brought him as a child, and he wants to be an actor, so he thought he'd get his feet wet here before trying somewhere else..." Her voice trailed off. Another person who'd leave eventually. All she had were people who were leaving, and nobody coming in.

"You said the college kids come back for the summer? People who grew up here?"

"Yeah, they don't really like it though. It's more an obligation to their parents than a desire to live here. I know a couple people said they'd only pay for their kids' tuition if they came back between semesters. We try to make it worth their while, but they aren't happy here."

Sienna wasn't surprised. She'd never been to a place that had so little to do. Even if you liked riding horses or watching the reenactments, you couldn't do that for the entirety of your life. Sienna had lived in Lonewood less than two weeks and was already bored out of her mind. "I think our first step is building business. We can't really control who lives here, but we can make revenue for those who decide to stay. That'll definitely help create an environment that people will want to be a part of."

Dakota nodded slowly. "Okay... what do you have in mind?"

Sienna put forth her best business smile and smoothed down the soft fabric of her dress. "Well, advertising is a good start. Social media can be very easy." The slight bob of Dakota's head showed Sienna she was considering the idea, so she continued with a few more. "Now, once we get the word out, we need to make sure we deliver an exceptional experience. I think the shows could use a revamp. To be honest, the shootout doesn't make a lot of sense-"

"Well, that's because Bill and Hank just do whatever they want," Dakota grumbled. "Unfortunately I have no sway as far as the actors are concerned. Maude's in charge of all that, so if you want something different from the entertainment, you'll have to go through her."

That was unexpected, but Sienna didn't expect this to be easy. "Alright, so we'll put a pin in the shows. Alex did theater for a long time, maybe she could talk to Maude."

She could market this town as phenomenal, but nothing could be worse for Lonewood than failing to meet expectations. If she couldn't make the entertainment better, she'd have to focus her efforts on something she could control *now*. "What is there for people to do in Lonewood? Like, activities?"

"Well, it's meant to be immersive. That's why we have the saloon girls and the shoot outs and such."

"But what is there to *do*?" Sienna asked again and Dakota swallowed. She didn't look upset, but she was clearly uneasy. Sienna realized it was because she didn't have an answer. "So there's nothing for people to do? They just come, walk around and watch things, and then leave?"

"They can shop. And eat. They can ride horses at the stables. If someone's available we sometimes do trail rides and we used to have the portrait studio open for old-timey photos. We haven't had it open the past couple of years, though."

"If it's supposed to be immersive, you need to immerse the people. This town is part reenactment, part hometown charm, with a little bit of tourist trap sprinkled in. I don't really understand what we're trying to achieve here."

Dakota tapped her fingernails against the oak desk, staring at it thoughtfully. "I just don't know how to immerse people in the old west without feeling cheap. All people want to do is snap photos and post to their Instagrams and make YouTube videos. They tend to not be impressed by our hometown values."

Sienna already knew this. She'd watched half a dozen YouTube videos on Lonewood on her phone. Not a single one of them were good. "We can change that. There's so much potential here, we just have to figure out what our angle is. People want to visit beautiful and captivating places." Sienna pulled out her phone, then asked, "Does the town have an email for inquiries? I want to set up an Instagram account for the town."

Without hesitation, Dakota scribbled an email and password on a sticky note and slid it across the table to Sienna. "Here's our official email address and password. You're welcome to use it for whatever you need, I rarely check it anyway. We don't get a ton of inquiries."

"Well, once the website is updated, I think that'll change," Sienna told her firmly. She downloaded the Instagram app on her phone, rejecting the urge to log into her old account. She wasn't even allowed to search for herself, because she could be tracked by Landon. And it probably wouldn't matter anyway, because the Marshals had most likely deleted all their social media accounts.

When Sienna glanced up, Dakota looked weary, as if she wasn't so sure she wanted to do this. Sienna tentatively stated, "You can pull the plug on this, you know. You don't have to hire me at all if this isn't what you're looking for."

"No- no this is what I'm looking for. It's what we need. I'm just nervous. You have lots of good ideas, they are just... different from anything we've tried before. But if you want a job, you have one here. Give me a day to write up a contract. I can't pay you what you were paid in California, though."

Sienna shook her head quickly, assuring Dakota she wasn't expecting that. "No, of course not! I'd be happy with anything, honestly. I want to try a few things until Memorial Day. We'll see how they work and then we can modify our plans from there. I'd like to get that motel full by the Fourth."

Dakota stared back at her with surprise. "Of July? You think you'll be able to garner that kind of business by then?"

"That's the goal anyway." Sienna grabbed the sticky note with the email and placed it in the front cover of her notebook. "I'll get to work right away. I want to get a little more familiar with the town and do some brainstorming. Could you squeeze me in on Thursday or Friday to hear a bigger pitch?"

"Friday would work great! I have a meeting at eleven thirty, but I'll be done by one if you want to swing by after lunch?"

"Perfect! Thank you so much for the opportunity," Sienna sprang to her feet and shoved her hand forward for Dakota to shake. "I won't let you down."

Dakota's hopeful smile lit up the entire room. "Of course! Happy to have you! Text me if you need anything."

Sienna beamed from ear to ear as she held her notebook to her chest. She pushed open the door to the porch, holding back her desire to cheer at her little victory. The only thing that dampened her excitement was Sheriff Gentry untying his horse from the hitching post next door.

He didn't speak to her, but he stared at her as he gripped the saddle, situating his left foot into the stirrup before swinging himself up and over his horse. Sienna raised her chin defiantly, and he scoffed and rolled his eyes, pulling the reins to turn his horse around and slowly walk down Main Street towards the motel.

As he rode away, Sienna walked into the middle of the street, raising her phone to take a picture. With the sun bright overhead, the photo turned out sharp and Sienna studied the image of the cowboy riding down the empty dirt road. She was no photographer, but it was a statement. It would have intrigued her if she'd seen it in a magazine or online.

She had this job in the bag. As small and inconsequential as it might seem to anyone else, Sienna felt like she was piecing herself back together. This was more than something to keep her busy, this was an outlet for all the anxious energy Sienna had building inside. She'd been stolen from her life and dropped into a place she didn't belong. Getting back to work gave Sienna purpose and direction when she felt like her world was spiraling out of control.

Deep down, Sienna knew this was a bad idea. Bringing attention to the place she and Alex were hiding was a *bad idea*. But she couldn't sit back and watch this place struggle when she could help, and she definitely couldn't twiddle her thumbs when she could work.

So she strolled down Main Street, snapping quick photos of all the buildings and imagining everything this little town could be.

Chapter 12

"I'M EXCITED TO WATCH you break your neck the day before your big pitch."

Sienna rolled her eyes, adjusting the waistband of her skinny jeans. She'd finally splurged and purchased a pair of cowboy boots. They were stiff, and Sienna stumbled a little as she and Alex walked the road towards the stables.

She popped the top button of her sleeveless denim button up, fanning herself as they walked down the dirt road. Although Alex had no intention of getting on a horse today, she'd worn her boots with ripped jean shorts and a pink halter top that dipped all the way to her lower back. It seemed she was intending on getting a nice tan while Sienna re-learned how to ride.

"Listen, I'm not joining a rodeo. I just want to get back up on the horse so I can go riding with Dakota. I think this could be something to market for the town, and I need to get a sense of how the stables work. It's literally the only thing for people to do here."

Alex shrugged as the stables came into view. "I just feel like you're giving yourself a little too much credit. When we rode horses in Mexico, you came in acting like you were Annie Oakley."

Sienna scoffed as they walked under a big metal sign over the road, reading "Lonewood Ranch" with two wrought iron horses carved on either side of the words. "It wasn't my first time on a horse-"

"Riding ponies at the circus doesn't count as horseback riding."

"Well, I didn't wipe out into the Pacific, so I'm feeling confident enough," Sienna grumbled.

The ranch was more modern than most of Lonewood. Although everything was wood, it didn't look old. There was a massive stable with big barn doors leading inside. On either side of the two story building, there were big corrals with horses grazing. Beyond the building, there was a larger fenced area that spread as far as Sienna could see, giving the horses room to roam all the way up to the Badlands that acted as a backdrop for the area.

Sienna and Alex reached the first corral and Sienna stepped up on the lowest rung of the fence, leaning against the top and scanning the area beyond the stable. She could see a small ranger's station to the far right, and what looked to be some sort of cattle guard in a break of a taller, more prominent fence. That must have been the edge of the national park. Farther left of the ranger's station she could see a gate in the corral fence, allowing people to ride their horses into the hills beyond their borders. A chance for guests to experience the Badlands as Teddy Roosevelt and his cowboy companions did over a hundred years ago.

This was what Sienna wanted to sell to the public. This was what would bring people to Lonewood.

"My God, this place is gorgeous," Sienna breathed, loving the fresh air. Although the horses didn't smell great, the grass had a strong earthy aroma that made her feel alive. This was much more relaxing than the old, dank buildings of Lonewood.

Alex leaned against the fence, the same height as Sienna when she kept her boots in the dirt. "Maybe eventually I'll get back up on the horse. I would like to go and see it."

"I'm assuming you can take cars through the national park. That's clearly what that road is for," Sienna said. She gestured to the cattle guard over the road and added, "Horses can't go over that, but I like that there's a special entrance for the Lonewood Stables. I wonder if entry is free."

"I guess we're about to find out." Alex nodded towards a lean blonde man walking towards them from the open stable doors. It was the same guy who'd played the piano at the saloon last Friday night and Sienna remembered his name was Lyle. He was surprisingly tan, clearly from time in the sun because his features looked like they were naturally pale. His smile was warm, but there was a mischievous look in his brown eyes that Sienna couldn't quite pin down.

Although they hadn't met yet, Sienna assumed he already knew who they were. Maybe he knew that they were from the city and depending on who he'd talked to over the past two weeks, maybe he knew that Alex was afraid of horses. Either way, Sienna hoped he'd give her a fair shot.

"Welcome to Lonewood Ranch," he greeted happily as he reached them. He reached out and shook Alex's hand first, then Sienna's. "I'm Lyle. Dakota said I might see you around. I hear one of you isn't as fond of horses, though."

Alex threw her hand up above her head, stating firmly, "That's me. I was tossed off and don't want to experience that again. Sienna likes horses, though. She wants to ride."

Lyle nodded a little, taking in the information silently. Sienna looked towards a couple of horses grazing in the left corral, wondering if he'd let her ride today. "I want to get the full Lonewood experience. I'm helping the mayor try to bring in more business, and I think this could be a lucrative opportunity. I'd like to understand your operation."

"Operation?" Lyle snickered. He took a deep breath, pulled off his black cowboy hat and shoved his hair back before settling it onto his head again. "I care for twenty-three horses. Twelve are mine for lessons and trail rides and the other eleven are boarded here by people in the town. I shovel shit and occasionally take two or three people for an hour-long ride through the hills. If it weren't for Preston and Owen out at the Circle W, I wouldn't be able to afford feed for the winter."

"Well, if you had more business, would you?" Sienna asked.

He shrugged, wiping his hands on the back of his old jeans. He looked over his shoulder at the horses longingly, but his answer surprised Sienna. "Honestly, it might be time to start selling off mine. Even if I could have a person for every horse I own, I wouldn't be able to keep up with the demand. I don't think the girl who helps me in the summer is gonna come back much anymore and I know the kid who helps during the school year is leaving in the fall. I'd need a staff to keep up with that kind of business. Might just keep one or two and take the profit from the others to keep the roof over my head." He gestured up to the second floor of the stable, and Sienna's jaw dropped open as she realized that he *lived* in the barn.

Lyle chuckled and motioned towards the stable with his head. "I see what you're thinking, and it's not as bad as it sounds. This place is state of the art. Air conditioning, electricity. I even have decent Wifi upstairs. It smells a little funky, but I'm happy here. The horses I board are treated like my own, and my horses are like my kids. As long as people are willing to pay, I'm happy to care for them."

"So let me get this straight..." Sienna started as he led them through the open sliding doors into the stable. Her words died on her lips as she got a good look around. The inside was beautiful. All red wood with little name plates above each of the stalls. She counted twelve stalls on each end of the foyer, six on each side facing the other six. The foyer had a long counter along the wall lined with stools, and a fridge at the end with a coffee machine next to it. Another four-person table sat nearby with comfortable chairs. Right inside the main doors was a beautifully made desk, similar to the one Dakota had in her office. There was a file cabinet behind it and on top was a photo of a dozen horses and riders, all lined up in a row. When Sienna looked a little closer, she made out Dakota, the sheriff, and that same blonde from the photo in the mayor's office. She also saw Lyle riding the horse whose photo hung next to Dakota's in her private office. The horse that had been mayor.

"General Grant, right?" Sienna asked as she pointed at the horse at the end, and Lyle nodded. "Was he yours?"

"Yeah. I loved that horse so much. He was treated like a king while he was the mayor," Lyle said gently, as if everyone in the world knew his horse had once been in charge of this town. "I miss him."

Sienna turned away from the photo, noticing a tight spiral staircase leading up to the second level of the stable. As much as she wanted to tour Lyle's private residence, she knew that request was far too inappropriate from a nosy stranger.

"So," Lyle said as he pulled open one of the drawers of the cabinet and grabbed a piece of paper. "If you want to ride, you gotta fill out the waiver. Read it carefully so you know you're signing your life away."

If that was meant to be a joke, it wasn't funny, but Alex snorted and cleared her throat, pretending she hadn't been laughing. Her toothy grin caused Sienna to roll her eyes and she snatched the waiver from the desk to read it quickly.

"I've ridden before. I just need a refresher."

"Have you actually ridden, or done a trail ride? They're different," Lyle stated and Sienna scoffed, grabbing a pen from the desk and signing her name quickly. Lyle studied the waiver and asked, "So you're an intermediate rider?"

"You are *definitely* a beginner-" Alex started but Sienna cut her off by arguing, "I feel pretty confident in what I'm doing."

Lyle looked between the two, a mischevious smile growing on his lips. "Well, I'll get someone saddled up for you then. Give me about ten minutes. You can look around until then if you want." He spared a quick look at Alex and added a little more gently, "If you get bit or kicked, I'm not liable." He gestured to an official sign by the door stating it, and Alex nodded a little.

As Lyle walked away to prepare the horse, Sienna followed him down the hallway to the left, reading the plaques above the stalls. Several of them were empty, but a couple had horses in them who stuck their heads out as Lyle passed. Alex stayed close to Sienna as a large black horse snickered, causing Alex to flinch away from it. Lyle looked over his shoulder when she let out a little gasp, and asked, "So you got bucked off?"

"Yeah. In Mexico. Dropped me right into the ocean."

"That's not fun," Lyle answered casually, as if he wasn't really listening. He walked past an empty stall, then unlocked one of the doors to go inside. "Horses can sense fear. They get a read on their riders, and if you're nervous, they could get skittish. But riding is a lot of fun. If you want I can help you get over your fears. You're welcome to stop by any time."

Great, another boyfriend for Alex.

Sienna rolled her eyes and followed close behind Lyle, getting a good look at the horse whose stall he'd unlocked. The horse was beautiful. It was almost a muted yellow, with a shiny black mane and tail. The horse snorted when Lyle entered the stall, then tossed its head to the side, sending its long mane flying away from its face. It side-eyed Lyle, but didn't even flinch when he clipped a lead to its halter.

"This is Cheyanne." Lyle led her out of the stall and Alex leaned up against the empty one next to it as they passed by her.

Sienna reached out to ghost her fingers along the horse's neck as Lyle led her past. "She's beautiful."

"I'll get her all saddled up," Lyle said as he walked her around to the main doors, then took a right to go to the corral.

Suddenly, a large gray horse stuck its head out of the stall beside Alex, causing her to shriek. The horse whinnied, swinging his head towards Alex, but Sienna quickly recognized the horse as Bandit. She reached forward, petting down his long face as she shushed him, "Hey Bandit. It's okay. You're okay." Sienna shot Alex a dirty look and chastised, "You scared him!"

"He scared me," Alex hissed back. She looked up, reading the nameplate above his stall.

Sienna followed her gaze to read the horse's names. Bandit, Domino, and Cheyanne called the back corner of the stable home. Across the hall, another empty stall with a framed photo on the door and the name Grant on the nameplate above. It made Sienna sad that Lyle's horse died, and that he thought he needed to sell more of them. "Hey Alex?"

"Yeah?"

"Do you ever feel guilty that we had such easy lives? Growing up, and even in Manhattan?" Sienna scratched Bandit's neck, but looked back at Alex as she grabbed her bare arms, goosebumps forming in the air conditioned stable. "These people can't possibly enjoy living like this and there's not really anything they can do about it unless they leave. I want them to have a chance at a better life here."

To her surprise, Alex reached up and dared to stroke Bandit's neck. Her emerald eyes slid over to Sienna and she challenged, "You want them to have a chance? Or you?"

Looking down at her phone, Sienna took a sharp breath and whipped around, looking around the rest of the stable. She wasn't going to dignify Alex's cruel question with a response. Sienna didn't believe she was that selfish. She was allowed to want to do nice things for this town, even if those efforts helped her in the end.

She ambled past the other stalls, exploring the other end of the stable as Alex took a seat at the small table. Sienna noticed most of the horses on the other side weren't in their stalls, but she studied all their names anyway.

After about ten minutes, she came over to Alex in the foyer, meeting her gaze and pursing her lips. She didn't want to fight with Alex. With a sigh, Sienna asked, "You gonna come watch?"

"Yeah, I think I will," she laughed airily as she followed Sienna out the big double doors. They circled around to see Lyle tying Cheyanne up to the fence by a little step stool.

Blowing air out through her lips to calm her nerves, Sienna strode over to the gate that he opened for her. She stood face-to-face with the horse, holding out her hand for her to sniff. "Hey, Cheyanne."

Cheyanne sniffed Sienna's hand, then snorted, tossing her head to the side in an effort to get away from the place she was tied up. Lyle held her reins tightly as Sienna moved around to the little step stool, using it to get closer to the stirrup.

"You know how to mount?"

"More or less," Sienna grumbled as she situated her boot in the stirrup, grabbing the horn of the saddle with one hand and the back with the other. She took a deep breath and swung her leg over, and Cheyanne shifted beneath her, tossing her head a little as Lyle shushed her.

He untied the reins and led Cheyanne away from the step stool into the middle of the corral. Two other horses grazing near the far edge of the fence raised their heads, then went back to their grass. Alex stepped up on the bottom rung of the wooden fence to get a better view, watching as Sienna was led around like a child on a pony.

"We're gonna start with this, get you two comfortable with each other."

Sienna reached down to pat Cheyanne's neck, and the horse tossed her head, causing her mane to fly away from her face. "Is she skittish?"

"Not particularly, just free-spirited." Lyle spun them around and started walking them towards Alex. "You gotta keep a pretty tight grip on her, or she'll take off from under you. Definitely a horse for a rider with more experience."

The remark was said close enough to Alex for her to hear, and Sienna wasn't amused. She couldn't tell if he was being sarcastic because the horse was actually for children or if he was making fun of her because he didn't actually believe she had any experience.

"I'm feeling pretty good. Can I try by myself?"

Lyle raised his brows, but his smile remained. "You sure?"

"Yeah. I got this." Sienna allowed Lyle to hand her the reins, and Cheyanne backed up a step once he didn't have a hold on her anymore. Sienna held the reins tightly, pulling them back a little. "Whoa, there. Easy, easy."

She loosened her grip on the reins and Cheyanne started walking forward, going wherever she wanted to go. Sienna allowed it, too proud to admit the horse was in control. Once they'd built some trust, she could decide where she wanted Cheyanne to take her.

"Can you take my picture?" Sienna called and Alex pulled out her cell phone. She raised it, tapping the image of her sister on the horse to focus it, then snapped a couple shots in quick succession. She gave a thumbs up and Sienna smiled, pulling the reins to the right to turn the horse.

"Does she actually know what she's doing?" Lyle asked as he leaned his back against the fence beside Alex.

He looked up at her with a smart-ass grin and she shrugged. "She thinks she does. That's half the battle, isn't it?"

Lyle let out a little sigh, turning to watch Sienna and Cheyanne again. They watched Sienna walk around the pen for about twenty minutes until she gave the horse a little kick to pick up the pace. Alex narrowed her gaze, then leaned closer to Lyle and asked, "Should she be doing that?"

"If she wants to go faster, Cheyanne is pretty fast."

The horse picked up her pace, not quite a run but definitely not the slow gait she'd been going. Lyle looked over his shoulder, then stiffened and called, "Hey Dakota! How's it going?"

Alex turned to see the mayor walking up to them with a beaming grin. "Came to take Bandit for a ride. How's it going here?" She stopped talking abruptly when she saw Sienna riding around the ring. She pulled the reins to slow down the horse, having gotten going a little too fast. "Is she riding Cheyanne?"

Lyle averted his gaze when Dakota stared at him, and Alex felt her stomach drop. She looked back to Sienna, seeing the horse begin to back up, tossing her head over and over again as Sienna tried to regain control.

"Whoa, it's okay. We're okay."

She kicked the heels of her boots into Cheyanne's sides, but she didn't move, instead backing up a few more steps. She was backing up towards the fence, and Lyle looked like he was ready to intervene when a pair of gunshots went off close behind them.

Alex instinctively ducked, looking over her shoulder quickly before turning back to see Cheyanne rearing up, kicking at the air wildly until Sienna tumbled off her back.

Cheyanne bolted once Sienna was off, and Lyle sprinted after her as Dakota opened up the gate to run inside the corral while Alex kept a safe distance away. The thundering sound of hooves approaching caused Sienna to stiffen and clench her eyes closed, prepared to be trampled until they slid to a stop a few feet away from her.

When she peeled open her eyes, she saw Dakota past the legs of the horse, frozen about fifteen feet away with a horrified look on her face. Then Sienna looked up and saw Sheriff Gentry looming over her with a look in his eyes that could freeze over Hell. He dismounted his horse and landed a foot from Sienna as she leaned on her elbows, feeling a shock of pain radiating down her lower back.

"What the hell do you think you're doing?"

"Riding. I got bucked off, obviously. Something startled the horse," she huffed. She expected him to offer his hand to help her up, or ask if she was okay, but instead he just shifted his jaw and kept her gaze. His nostrils flared and his hand curled into a fist. As much as Sienna wanted to accuse him of firing the gun, she legitimately thought he might pummel her into the ground.

After an uncomfortably long moment, Gentry finally spoke. His voice was so full of quiet fury that Sienna believed his threat- "If you hurt her, I'll bury you so deep that God Himself won't be able to find you."

He grabbed his horse's reins and turned to walk away, leaving Sienna in the dirt. Dakota sprinted to Sienna's side, kneeling down and cupping her elbow. "Are you okay? Can you stand?"

"Yeah, I think so. Just a little tumble."

That was a lie. Everything hurt. Sienna had never been in so much pain in her entire life, but she wasn't about to admit that. She allowed Dakota to slowly help her to her feet and turned when Lyle approached, leading Cheyanne by the bridle.

Sheriff Gentry strode towards them and Lyle *cowered*. "Why the fuck was she riding my horse?"

"You pay me to take care of the horses. I'm trying to take care of her. She needs to be ridden, Gentry! Nobody's ridden her since Annie went back to college-"

"Annie will be back soon."

Lyle let out a long sigh. "Yeah, maybe, but who says she'll stay? Cheyanne needs to be ridden regularly. If you aren't gonna ride her, you might as well set her free to go back to her herd."

Gentry handed over his black and white horse to Lyle, then quickly swung himself up and over Cheyanne. He ripped the reins to the side, causing her to snort and back up a little as she turned. "Fine. You happy? Open the gate."

"Gentry..." Dakota warned, but he ignored her.

"I said open the damn gate so I can ride the damn horse!"

Lyle reached into his pocket and pulled out what looked like a garage door opener. He hit the button and Sienna saw the gate at the far end of the corral slide open. Gentry kicked Cheyanne's sides, leaning forward as she took off sprinting towards the gate.

Sienna watched them until they disappeared into the Badlands.

Dakota turned to Lyle with a scowl and he ducked his head. "What the hell were you thinking, Lyle? Do you have a death wish?"

"I was thinking that Cheyanne needed to be ridden and she might actually ride her." He gestured to Sienna, who massaged her tailbone as Dakota and Lyle slowly led her back to the gate. When they got there, Dakota let Sienna out, but locked Lyle in with the horses. He sighed, "She needs to be ridden. Annie isn't sticking around, we all know that."

"You have horses that are yours to do what you want, please don't be renting out ours," Dakota told him firmly, then turned her attention to Sienna. Her expression became a worried one and she gently touched Sienna's arm, causing her to wince. "Do you need to go to the hospital? I can drive you to the town over, or you can visit the doctor here."

Sienna knew going to the doctor would be smart, but she was seething. Her tailbone ached and her pride was bruised, but there was a bigger issue here that Dakota was ignoring.

"I'm fine," Sienna said evenly, trying to keep her temper in check. "I'm going home. Honestly, let's just cancel our meeting tomorrow. I'm reconsidering whether or not I want to work for you after seeing the company you keep."

Dakota's jaw clenched and her head tilted slightly, like she wanted to look over her shoulder but decided not to. She knew exactly who Sienna was talking about. "I'll talk to him."

"He threatened my life! You think talking to him is gonna make that better? You need to get your boyfriend under control." Sienna swallowed hard as Dakota's brows furrowed. She knew she was throwing away her chance to work for the mayor, but she felt too defeated to give in to her deep-seeded tendency to please everyone. She wanted to scream and throw things and weep for the life she had to give up and couldn't seem to find here, but all of that would hurt too badly. Tears began to well in her eyes as she got out, "This was a mistake. I wish we'd never come here."

The comment seemed to wound Dakota, but Sienna couldn't bring herself to care. She stormed away before Dakota could respond, limping down the dirt road. Alex chased after her, eventually throwing her arm around Sienna's shoulders to help her back to the motel.

Chapter 13

SIENNA LAID ON HER back, staring up at the dusty ceiling fan that rotated overhead. Moving was excruciating, but nothing seemed broken at least. She'd definitely have bruises tomorrow, but her pride took the brunt of the fall.

She wondered if this was cause enough to be moved. Part of Sienna wanted to march down to the mayor's office and confess that she was in the Witness Protection Program, then give out her former identity to anyone who would listen. Maybe Sheriff Gentry would call Landon Maddox personally to get rid of her. Sienna and Alex could be whisked away to never suffer another night in Lonewood and they could try again somewhere else.

She groaned, closing her eyes as she shifted a little. "I don't think I've ever met a more vile man in my life. Words cannot describe my hatred for him."

Alex chuckled from the bed next to Sienna, and the sound of the creaky mattress warned that she was getting up. "You know, you're giving him exactly what he wants, right?"

"And what's that?"

"He wants to get under your skin so you give up."

Sienna groaned loudly and slammed her eyelids closed. "You're right."

"Now, I'm not saying you should do it," Alex said slowly, "but you have some good ideas for the town. I think you should still talk to the mayor. Maybe she'll fire him?"

"Doubt it, then she'd have to get out from underneath him first," Sienna scoffed and Alex laughed. Sienna sat up slowly and pulled her hair over her shoulder, twisting her lips thoughtfully. "He'd be so annoyed if Dakota hired me."

"I mean, maybe don't do it because of him, but you're not a quitter. You said you wanted to give these people a chance. You've never given up because it was hard and you've never given up because somebody bet against you."

Sienna hated that Alex knew exactly what to say to convince Sienna not to give up on this town. She'd decided to make Lonewood a boomtown again, and nobody, especially not some ignorant hick, was going to stop her.

A half hour later, Sienna was at the mayor's office with her notebook in hand. She twisted the knob, finding the office still open, but once in the waiting room, Sienna heard yelling coming from Dakota's office.

"Are you out of your damn mind? You discharged a real gun in a non-emergency situation!" Dakota screamed. "You could have gotten her killed."

"She was fine!" Gentry yelled back and Sienna froze when she realized that he had scared her horse on purpose.

"You didn't know that. Do you have any idea what would have happened to *you* if she had died? You can't do this, Gentry! You can't keep lashing out at them, they haven't done anything wrong-"

"Being in this town is doing something wrong. They don't belong here!"

"Neither of them have done a single thing to bother anybody since they arrived," Dakota argued loudly. "This isn't your town!"

"It isn't yours either," he screamed back. "I got you this job! The only reason you're mayor is because of me!"

"No, it's because of Kenzie!" Her voice softened and it sounded like she was crying. "You think this isn't hard for me? You think I want to do this alone? She wanted this town to succeed so badly. Sienna knows how to bring in business. She's an expert in her field and she wants to help and you're standing in the way. You're standing in the way of Kenzie's legacy. You're the one stopping us from finishing what she started."

There was silence after that, and Sienna started tiptoeing towards the front door. She didn't want to be caught eavesdropping on this incredibly personal conversation. She quietly pulled open the door, then heard the sheriff's voice break when he said, "It's just hard."

Sienna turned to look over her shoulder at the office door. She knew she needed to leave but she wanted to hear if they'd say anything else.

The doorknob to Dakota's office twisted and Sienna realized somebody was about to come out into the waiting room. She didn't have enough time to pretend she hadn't been there, so she quickly slammed the door closed, warning them of her presence.

It worked, because Dakota opened her door and popped her head through to see who'd arrived. When her amber eyes found Sienna, they burst open in surprise and she gaped at her, stammering, "Sienna! Are you alright? Umm," she looked over her shoulder, but there wasn't a peep from her office, "What can I do for you?"

"I wanted to apologize for snapping at you earlier." Sienna wouldn't apologize for what she'd said about the sheriff though, especially because he would hear it. "I was hurt. Physically, but also my pride." She chuckled and Dakota smiled weakly. Then Sienna said something she really didn't mean, but her desire to patch up her relationship with the mayor was stronger than her hatred for the woman's boyfriend. "I'm sorry if I've caused any trouble. I really didn't know I was doing anything wrong."

"Oh, you did *nothing* wrong," Dakota said quickly. She swung open the door and looked over her shoulder obviously, nodding towards Sienna. "In fact, I was hoping I'd get a chance to talk to you about some things that were said today."

Sheriff Gentry appeared in the doorway to slide past Dakota into the waiting room. He bumped her shoulder lightly, but neither of them reacted. It was just another tell of how comfortable they were with each other. Once he got past Dakota though, he crossed his arms and set his gaze on Sienna.

Maybe he'd convinced Dakota that working with Sienna was a waste of time. Or maybe she'd given him some ultimatum, which had sparked their fight. God forbid, if Sienna caused them to split up she'd actually feel sorry for the poor bastard.

"Gentry."

"What?"

Dakota's bright eyes slid from Gentry to Sienna, then back to him again. She raised her brows expectedly and he sighed. Defeated. "I'm sorry for earlier. I overreacted and you did nothing wrong."

"And?" Dakota prodded.

"And Lyle's been arrested for unrelated reasons."

The mayor's eyes burst open in surprise and she gaped at her sheriff, trying to find her words through her disbelief. "Damn it, Gentry! No! That-" Dakota massaged the bridge of her nose. "We'll have a conversation about that later."

Gentry smiled knowingly, and Sienna could only imagine what kind of conversation that would be. He lolled his head to the side and took a deep breath, letting its release heave his chest. "If you have ideas to help Lonewood, you'll have my support. I'm sorry I've been..."

"An asshole?" Dakota supplied.

"A pill," he settled on instead, causing Dakota to shake her head at him. "I'll be better, and I'm sorry."

Sienna wasn't expecting an apology from the man, but she wasn't about to turn her nose up at it. She blinked back her surprise and nodded a little as her big eyes stared up at him from beneath her lashes. "Thank you. I really appreciate that."

"Now that we've settled that..." Dakota trailed off, gesturing towards the door for Gentry to leave. "Sienna and I have a few things to talk about that don't concern you. I'll see you tomorrow morning."

He nodded at Sienna, reaching his hand up to tip his hat instinctively, even though he wasn't wearing one. It made her smile a little as she gave an awkward wave and watched him leave.

Once the door clicked closed, Dakota beamed at Sienna. She seemed to be trying to hold back a laugh as she motioned for Sienna to take a seat in the waiting room instead of her office. A more casual setting.

"I wanted him to leave before we had this conversation, because it would make him vomit."

Sienna cocked her head and furrowed her brows. That was a weird way to start. "Okay?"

"Gentry isn't my boyfriend. He's my little brother."

Sienna blinked a couple times as her mind raced. Brother. Little brother. They weren't close because they were sleeping together, they were close because they were *siblings*.

"Oh."

"Yeah."

The reason they were so comfortable with each other was because they were family. Of course they'd be close. Of course he'd hold doors open and have lunch with his sister. Of course they'd fight and of course she would brush it off as nothing. In hindsight, he'd never touched her in a way that should give the idea of intimacy. Sienna hadn't considered, even for a moment, that two people in this incredibly small town could be related.

"I feel like an idiot," Sienna got out and Dakota laughed loudly.

"No! No, you're fine! That's my fault, I should have said something. I didn't realize you didn't know- everybody knows. We're kind of a family town. You knew Kitty was Bill's daughter, I assumed you knew about Gentry and I. And when you said something earlier I understood why you've been so alarmed about him... he's legitimately just cranky because his big sister is his boss. I never considered how it looked from the outside."

Sienna laughed lightly and waved off Dakota, relaxing for the first time since she'd fallen off the horse earlier. "I shouldn't have assumed. You two were clearly close and I jumped straight to-"

"Yeah, no, let's not talk about it, it's really weird." Dakota folded her hands and sat them in her lap, raising her chin as her smile shifted from friendly to professional. "I know you said moving here was a mistake, but I'd like to try to prove you wrong. I think with your help we could make Lonewood somewhere you could be really happy, but I don't want your pitch yet. After Memorial Day - after you've had a little more time to settle in here - I'll do whatever you suggest. That's two weeks for you to get a feel for how we run in the summer, give you a chance to get to know everybody a little more. Then we'll try your ideas until the Fourth. Does that sound like a plan you can get behind?"

It sounded like two more weeks of not getting paid, but she had accused the mayor of sleeping with her brother, so Sienna figured she should take what she'd been offered and put this disaster behind her. "I think that sounds like a great plan."

"Great. Glad to hear it." Dakota stood, and Sienna's gaze fell on that photo of the blonde in the sunset. The photo in the back of Alex's book captioned this woman as Kenzie Wyatt. It stood to reason that if Gentry was Dakota's brother, maybe Kenzie was their sister. Either way, she was very clearly not around anymore.

Dakota caught her staring and Sienna sucked in a sharp breath and apologized, "Sorry. There's a photo of her in this book Alex bought. It said her name is Kenzie Wyatt."

The mayor's countenance fell and she gave a little nod. "Yeah, it was."

Was. Sienna knew better than to ask what happened, but she dared to question, "Was she your sister?"

Dakota raised her chin, sniffling at the same time she gave a firm nod, probably an attempt to hide how upset she was. "Yeah. She passed away a couple years ago."

"I don't mean to pry," Sienna whispered, walking towards the door. "I'm very sorry for your loss."

The corner of Dakota's mouth tugged up into a sad smile. "Yeah, me too. But she loved our home, and she'd be excited to see what's in store for it. Once you're feeling a little better, text me and we'll go riding. I'll make sure you get a horse that Gentry won't bury you over. Or if you want to continue annoying him, I'll saddle you up on Domino just to piss him off."

Sienna snorted, laughing a little. "I want nothing to do with your brother or his horses, but thanks for the offer."

Dakota laughed as Sienna passed her, slowly shuffling down the steps of the porch. The mayor looked content after their conversation, and Sienna felt the same. Memorial Day would be here before she knew it, so she wouldn't have too much time to kill before she was busy. At least she knew she'd find less interference now.

Chapter 14

For the next several days, Sienna Jade and Gentry Wyatt managed to avoid each other. Alex spent her afternoons watching Hank and Bill circle each other on Main Street, usually performing for her alone. In the evenings, she hung out with Maude at the saloon. From what Sienna had gathered, Alex hadn't gotten up the nerve to ask for a job yet.

While her sister kept busy with Maude and her acting troupe, Sienna spent her time sitting on the various wooden porches of Lonewood, jotting down ideas and taking photos on the rare occasion that something caught her eye. Although their talent left much to be desired, Bill Cassidy and Sheriff Hank made for an amazing photo series. Their drawn weapons and well-worn outfits gave Lonewood an authentically Western feel, something Sienna wanted to explore beyond the pair's random spats in front of the Bank of Lonewood. Occasionally, even though Sienna kept them to herself, she was able to capture adorable photos of Jesse looking over at Alex with a shy smile while Hank and Bill yelled nonsense at each other.

A week after she was thrown from Cheyanne, Sienna found herself sitting on the bench outside of Dakota's office. She knew Dakota was at the diner, because the effervescent blonde was easy to keep tabs on. Wherever she went, eyes followed her stunning figure and vivacious personality. She wondered if Gentry's cantankerous demeanor was a direct result of working beneath his bubbly sister or if he became difficult to spite his older sibling when they were much younger. Sienna couldn't imagine he'd always been this quarrelsome, because Dakota spoke so highly of him despite everything he said and did. Everyone who saw him or spoke about him did so with a big smile, as if he was the best thing since sliced bread.

The small, guilty voice in the back of Sienna's mind reminded her that he'd suffered a loss, but it didn't excuse his behavior. Sienna didn't know the details about what had happened to Kenzie Wyatt, but she was confident it wasn't *her* fault.

While she sat with her notebook open on her lap, Domino was tied up outside the sheriff's station, meaning Gentry was inside. Even if he was going two buildings down the street to the diner, he took his horse with him. Sienna had seen him lead the horse across the street just to tie him up again outside the general store.

Sienna watched the horse as he stood at the hitching post. Very purposely placed beneath the biggest, greenest tree in Lonewood, Domino would occasionally take a drink from the water trough before staring ahead, one back hoof tipped up as he rested.

He turned his head, blue eyes catching a lazy glimpse of Sienna. She picked up her phone and adjusted her settings to take a photo of him while she had his attention. Domino was the most beautiful horse she'd ever seen, and she wished she knew how to draw or paint, so she could capture his likeness in a masterpiece worthy of him.

Skylar's warning from their first day played in the back of Sienna's mind, but knowing it would annoy Gentry made her desire to approach the horse that much stronger. She stood slowly, peeking through the window of the sheriff's office. She saw the shadow of Cecily at her desk, but couldn't get a good view farther into the building.

Deciding she could pet the horse quickly and mosey on her way, Sienna held her notebook tightly and trotted down the steps. Hank hadn't locked up his brother yet today, but they could start their daily routine at any moment, so Sienna had to be fast. She looked up at the door as she paused, waiting to see if Gentry would burst through and arrest her. When he didn't, she approached Domino, reaching up to stroke his long face.

"Hey handsome," she cooed and he lowered his head a little so she could reach him. He wanted to be petted. He probably didn't get enough of this kind of affection from his owner. "Does the big, mean sheriff leave you outside alone all day? You're such a sweet boy. I'm sorry you have the misfortune of being owned by him."

"If you want to experience time in the fake jail, you could have just asked."

Sienna jumped, whipping around to see Skylar at the top of the stairs. Her smile was broad, even if she kept her lips tightly closed in an attempt to appear serious. Sienna pulled her hand away from Domino and scuttled a few steps away. "I- couldn't help myself."

"I see that," Skylar hummed, taking the few steps down and shoving her hands in her pockets. "I'm gonna take a walk around town on patrol. Would you like to join me?"

Looking around the empty street, Sienna nodded. Clearly Skylar wanted to talk, because Lonewood definitely didn't need one of its cops on patrol. "Alright."

Sparing one last look at Domino, Sienna followed Skylar towards the saloon. She waited for Skylar to say what she wanted, and the former Marshal seemed to understand that, because she said under her breath, "I've heard that you're working for Mayor Wyatt. Thought the sheriff was gonna punch through the wall after she made him apologize to you."

"He tried to break my back, so it was warranted." Skylar raised her brow curiously and Sienna stammered, "He shot off his gun and scared my horse." Skylar ducked her head and smirked, nodding a little.

They paused outside the saloon when they heard off-key singing coming from inside. Sienna cringed when the female voice struggled to reach the high note she was aiming for, voice cracking instead.

Skylar turned towards Sienna, dark eyes looking sad as she sighed, "You might be able to help this town, Sienna, but at what cost? If you fail, the people will resent you. If you succeed, they still might resent you, but your chances of being found go up exponentially. I never worked with WitSec, but I understood enough about it to know what you're doing is dangerous."

"I'm supposed to make a life for myself here. I'm supposed to find a job and-"

"And normally that would be fine, but this place is an unsuccessful tourist trap. The people who run this town take it very seriously, and they don't want to change." Skylar paused, licking her dry lip before continuing.

"It's not that we don't want business. It's not that we don't want people to come and enjoy our town, but they don't want it to change. They just want people to come and like it the way they used to, but they don't anymore. Nobody wants to make it better, they just want people to like it more."

Sienna looked towards the saloon, gazing up at the large building. It was terribly old and run down, but massive. It could hold shows and parties and classes and meetings. A new coat of paint, a slight restoration, and it could be the crown jewel of Lonewood. But if the tone-deaf woman was determined to sing, the audience wouldn't enjoy it just because she wanted them to. Skylar was right, these people didn't want Lonewood to change, but it wasn't going to get any better without some serious upgrades. People would need to lose their jobs. The cost of success would be hard, and Sienna couldn't make that decision for them. Neither could Dakota, because even her own brother didn't want Sienna's help. Maybe the town wasn't hopeless, but it was as reluctant to change as its sheriff.

"Bridget sent us here because she thought we'd be safe with you," Sienna admitted quietly. She hadn't spoken to Skylar since their first day a couple weeks ago. As much as Bridget trusted Skylar, she'd shown no sign of caring what happened to Alex and Sienna. "Maybe we should ask to go somewhere else if we aren't wanted here."

Skylar considered this for a moment, looking down the long dirt road towards the motel. She smiled sadly, then met Sienna's eyes. "Just because I don't want to be here doesn't mean you two can't enjoy it. I wanted to get out so badly, and I did. I loved my life in New York. I'd give anything to go back now that Mom's gone..." Sienna felt bad for bringing up such painful memories, and opened her mouth to apologize, but Skylar cut her off. "I know I haven't really been around. I have been, I just wanted to give you two space to make your own lives. But I have been keeping an eye on you. I'm worried that you could succeed in what Mayor Wyatt wants, and I don't want you and Alex to get hurt if this town actually draws attention."

"I get that, but I could make a difference here. Alex could make such a big difference if Maude gave her a chance. We could bring life back to Lonewood!"

"You make it sound like it ever had much life to begin with," Skylar chuckled, shaking her head. "If this is what you want to do, I'm not gonna stop you. The town needs help and you're the first person in years to have the balls to try anything new."

Sienna nodded a little as they continued walking, but Skylar continued, "You gotta stay away from the sheriff, though, Sienna. If he catches you messing with Domino, he'll blow a gasket."

Rolling her eyes, Sienna turned to give Skylar a blank stare. "He already threatened to, and I quote, bury me so deep God Himself couldn't find me." Skylar snorted and Sienna added, "If I never see him again, it'll be too soon."

"That'll be hard working with Dakota. Those two are attached at the hip. They were never this close before the accident, but now..." Skylar stopped and closed her mouth. She looked ahead and Sienna had never wanted someone to continue speaking more. The mysterious third Wyatt was a looming presence over Lonewood and Sienna wanted to understand why she was so important. Skylar, though, obviously didn't feel like elaborating, so Sienna changed the subject to something else that was harmless enough but useful to her understanding of the town.

"How old is Dakota? She's so pretty and young... not what I'd picture as a mayor of a small town. I'm trying to understand how she won."

"Well, the horse wasn't getting anything done," Skylar huffed. It was the same thing Dakota had said, but Skylar sounded miffed about it. While Dakota saw her predecessor as a gimmick, Skylar saw it as an annoyance. "Listen, I grew up in this weird little town and I still don't understand these people's thought process. I remember when Lyle's horse got elected- he nominated Grant right out of high school as a joke and everyone thought it was cute. The thing won because nobody wanted Hank in charge of the town, and it kept winning until about a year ago when the state threatened to merge our school with the town next door. Dakota's only thirty-five, but she ran with Gentry's support to keep the school open, and it was just enough to win."

Sienna nodded at the information as they reached the ice cream parlor next to the apparel store. She'd been meaning to visit but didn't want to go by herself. Not that she couldn't, but Sienna thought going for ice cream alone made her seem even more lonely and dejected than she actually felt.

"So how old's the sheriff?"

"He's thirty-three. He went to the police academy right after high school at eighteen. He was sheriff by twenty-seven because the one before him died at ninety-two. There was nobody else who wanted it."

"What about you?" Sienna asked quietly. She didn't know if Skylar would want to talk about herself, but she felt bad knowing nothing about Bridget's friend. She and Alex had been so caught up in their own lives that they hadn't even tried to reach out to the first friend in Lonewood.

Skylar shrugged, gazing up at Kitty's shop with a forlorn look. "I wanted out, so I left. Wasn't super welcome when I came back from the Marshals. I felt like I didn't belong anymore, but Gentry told me I had a job if I wanted it. I had the training... more than him, and he's smart enough to know that's worth something. If I wanted to be sheriff, I could probably take the title from him, but I don't want to play cowboy for the rest of my life. That's why I stay holed up in the sheriff's station as much as possible. If they need me, I'm there."

"If you aren't happy, why don't you leave?" Sienna questioned.

"Because even though Mom's gone, these people still need me. There's four of us. Four cops in a town that draws rowdy, drunk tourists every summer. Three of us have rotating schedules, but the sheriff rarely gets a day off. The only saving grace is that nothing happens here during the off-season, so it's pretty quiet for me and the other two deputies. Gentry plays the role of sheriff in front of the tourists, wandering down the road back and forth on Domino. He'll stop to take pictures with people, and if he's in a good mood, he'll let them pet his horse."

Sienna stopped dead in her tracks and whipped around to Skylar. "What did you just say?"

"I said Gentry plays the sheriff-"

"No, I mean about Domino. You said he lets the tourists pet his horse, but I'm not allowed to?"

Skylar smirked, trying to hide her grin, but she let out a dry chuckle anyway. "I'd say it isn't personal, but it definitely is." Sienna's lips dropped into a scowl. Skylar shrugged. "He hasn't been in a very good mood since you arrived. The moment his sister realized you were in marketing, I could see he put a target on your back. The townspeople want the kids to move back after college, not have strangers move in from the city to change things."

Sienna narrowed her green eyes at Skylar. "Maybe he shouldn't be so closed minded."

"He's from a small town in North Dakota. It's not his fault that he doesn't know any better." Skylar shifted from foot to foot before letting out a sigh. "I gotta get back to the station. If you need anything, don't be a stranger." She started to leave, but not before turning back around and calling, "If you want Domino to love you forever, sneak him sugar cubes. They're his favorite but if Gentry catches you, he will absolutely throw you in jail."

"The real one or the fake one?"

"Depends on his mood," Skylar called, waving before turning around to head back to work.

Sienna, on the other hand, marched right back to the general store to buy a box of sugar cubes.

Chapter 15

The Sunday before Memorial Day weekend, all of Lonewood was abuzz with excitement. Sienna hadn't seen anything like it- it was as if a jolt of electricity had been pumped into the town.

The Lonewood Cafe was full to the brim with people chatting excitedly, and for the first time since that first weekend they'd arrived, there were people in attendance who didn't live in town.

Sienna quickly realized that they weren't tourists, though. The people she didn't recognize spoke to Lonewood's residents like they'd known each other forever. These people were clearly family or old friends, but she still didn't understand why they were all here right now.

Brenda was rushing by with a full coffee pot when Sienna tried to stop her. "Hey, what's happening? Who are all these people?"

Brenda threw up her index finger, telling Sienna to give her a moment, and hurried over to one of the booths. Since the diner was exceptionally busy, Sienna and Alex weren't able to get their usual booth by the hitching post, which was oddly lacking horses this morning.

"Do you think this is for Memorial Day?" Alex asked as she popped the last bite of caramel roll into her mouth.

"I don't know," Sienna trailed off when Brenda appeared and started pouring coffee into Sienna's Coke glass. "Brenda. Are you okay?"

"I'm swamped. Colleen is running late because she's gotta get the spare room ready for her granddaughter. What is it you need?" She suddenly realized what she'd done and huffed. "I'm sorry. Let me get you another one."

"I'd settle for what's going on," Sienna answered, not needing any more soda or coffee or whatever Brenda accidentally brought her next.

The waitress pushed back her hair, taking a deep breath as Hank, Bill, Kitty, and Beau erupted into laughter with one of the dancers from the saloon show. Alex had come to learn the singer was Bill's wife, Kitty's mom, and that she was so tone-deaf she'd accidentally broken glass once. Sienna asked Alex why they let her sing, and Alex just stared at her blankly, as if the answer was obvious: they didn't want anything to change.

Brenda thoughtlessly passed off the coffee pot to Jesse, who looked down at it in confusion before noticing there was coffee in Sienna's soda. He carefully made his way towards the kitchen to pass off the pot to the cook without Brenda realizing it, and Alex gave him a happy little wave before he left.

"It's graduation day at the high school," she explained quickly. "We have four seniors graduating this year. Everybody is gonna be there. Graduation, if there is one, marks the beginning of summer. It's when most of the college kids come back to prepare for Memorial Day and then we're in full swing until Labor Day. All of these people are families of the four seniors."

Sienna looked around the room after learning the new information, starting to see similiarities. Wayne and Leah, who worked at the school, were talking to a man who was identical to Wayne and his wife while a young boy played on a bright yellow Nintendo Switch. Three young women who appeared to be in their late teens or early twenties sat together by the window, chatting excitedly as if they hadn't seen each other in a long time. Occasionally they'd look over at a group of five guys, ranging from teens to mid-twenties, hanging out by the counter. They'd laugh loudly when one of them realized their friend had caught the girls' eyes, and Sienna realized she'd never seen so many young people here.

These were the college kids, and maybe the high schoolers. They breathed life into the sleepy town, because their families seemed to understand that their presence meant change was coming. This was the first change the town of Lonewood seemed to accept, and Sienna realized why Dakota wanted to make life better here for these young people. If they brought this much excitement to return for the summer, imagine what would happen if they didn't move away for good.

When Skylar moved away, the people turned on her for abandoning them. According to Alex, Maude casually mentioned that Skylar moved away at a time when everybody felt the responsibility to come back. Nowadays, everyone followed Skylar's lead, leaving for college and finding a greater purpose beyond Lonewood.

It was no wonder Skylar was bitter. They hadn't forgiven her for leaving, but they now did everything in their power to stop others from following in her footsteps.

"Looks like one hell of a party," Alex chuckled as she handed Brenda her debit card. "At least business is up!"

"And thank goodness the girls are back to help out," Brenda gestured towards the three girls by the windows. "Maddie and Jewel, the two blondes, are a Godsend in the summertime. They are cousins, but they're going to different schools so they haven't seen each other since last summer. Maddie wasn't able to make it home for the holidays because her parents were with her mom's family in Montana." Brenda then motioned to a tall brunette whose hair was chopped into a pixie cut. She blew a kiss to the boys and giggled as the other two girls hissed at her to stop it. "Jolene is our tomboy. Never afraid to get her hands dirty. She's old enough to serve alcohol now, so I've heard she's thinking about asking Maude to bartend, but she'll miss hanging out with her friends here. Sometimes she helps Lyle out at the ranch, but I think it'll all come down to what happens with Annie."

Sienna watched as one of the boys slid off his stool to wander over to the three girls, and one of the blondes smacked his upper arm playfully when he reached them. Brenda smiled and dropped her voice so only Alex and Sienna could hear. "Jewel and Colton dated all through high school, graduated last year. I've heard he broke her heart when he broke things off, but he's been at her feet like a puppy dog ever since Christmas. Maddie says he wants her back, and she's gonna let him marry her once he's learned his lesson."

"How do you know all this?" Alex asked quietly, not wanting the teens to hear the strangers gossiping about them. Brenda didn't seem to care, though, chuckling when Jewel turned away from Colton to continue her conversation with Maddie and Jolene.

Brenda leaned in closely between Sienna and Alex, and said, "Gossip is wildfire in a town this size. Us old folks aren't doing anything too interesting these days, so we live vicariously through you young people. Everyone knows everything and everybody knows it. Just because I didn't mention your little spat out at Lyle's with the sheriff doesn't mean we don't all know it happened."

Sienna's eyes burst open wide and she stared up at Brenda with an open mouth, trying to come up with some way to defend herself, but the waitress was already pushing her way through the crowd to take their payment so they could clear the table for another customer.

Alex poked Sienna's shoulder, then motioned towards the entrance of the diner. Gentry was holding open the door, a sure sign Dakota would follow right behind. Sure enough, the blonde appeared wearing a beautiful green flowered dress that reached all the way to the toes of her black cowboy boots. Her hair was curled and brushed out, cascading around her in wild waves as she beamed at the cafe patrons.

Gentry didn't appear nearly as excited to see the place so busy, but he did manage a genuine smile to everyone who greeted him as they bustled from table to table to catch up with each other. His brown eyes scanned the room, taking in all the people before gazing back at Dakota with a look of disappointment. She was too busy greeting Wayne's twin brother to notice.

To Sienna's immense surprise, Sheriff Gentry started walking towards them, stopping at their table and shoving his hands in the pockets of his jeans. Like his sister, he'd dressed up today- wearing black jeans, black boots, and a dark green button up shirt with white embroidery at the top. His hat was black, stark and clean, clearly meant for dressier occasions such as this. An even bigger surprise was that he smelt like cologne and shaving cream, but there was a hint of Domino there, meaning he'd clearly made time for his horse despite the busy morning.

"Miss Alex," he greeted Alex with a tip of his hat. His eyes slid to Sienna and he grunted, "Miss Jade."

"Oh, so you two are on a first name basis but we aren't. I see how it is," Sienna mocked, unsure if she was insulted or disappointed. She didn't want to be disappointed in his blatant rejection of her, but it crept into her bones anyway when he winked at Alex. "What are you doing here?"

"Getting brunch."

"No, I mean here. At our table. Bothering us." Sienna reached behind her head to split her hair, pulling it over her shoulders. While the mayor and the sheriff were dressed in their best, Sienna was wearing yoga pants and a baggy t-shirt with no makeup, looking pathetic compared to the naturally beautiful people all around her. Over the past couple weeks, Alex and Sienna had learned that Sunday mornings were for church, and if they wanted some solitude, this was a good time to find it at the diner. Today though, the service had been canceled, rescheduled, or moved to the diner for all she knew, as crowded as it was. She wanted to sneak out once Brenda returned Alex's card, but now that the sheriff was looming over them like a beacon, it was only a matter of time before Dakota floated over to greet them, too.

Gentry shrugged, pursing his lips and looking around the room. "Haven't bothered you in a few days. Thought it was the opportune time." He smiled and shifted to stand a little closer to Alex, smiling down at Sienna as sarcasm dripped from his velvety voice. "You look great by the way."

Sienna gasped up at him, furrowing her brows. Being an asshole because he didn't appreciate her ambition was one thing, but insulting the way she *looked* was another. "I loathe you."

"That's cute," Gentry said quietly, his attention already caught on a pretty woman talking to Kitty and Beau across the room.

Sienna rolled her eyes as Brenda handed Alex her card back. Finally able to leave, Sienna pushed back her chair quickly, bolting up from her seat and immediately smacking into Gentry's broad chest.

He looked just as startled as she did at the contact, clearly not realizing how close he'd been standing to her. Those russet eyes widened when they met Sienna's, and he accidentally backed up onto Alex's foot, causing her to yelp. He turned from Sienna to her sister and worriedly asked, "Are you okay? I'm so sorry!"

Sienna was already wiggling her way towards the door, not about to stick around and hear her sister's answer. Most of the people in the cafe looked up at her as she fled. Those Sienna knew went back to their conversations when they saw it was just her, but the people who she hadn't met stared in surprise when they understood she wasn't some early-arriving tourist. As if realizing there was an outsider among them in this safe and quiet place.

She slipped along the side of the building until she was past the windows, then rested her back against the siding to catch her breath.

"Sienna!"

The redhead looked up to see Dakota striding towards her with a worried look on her face. She studied Sienna before asking sharply, "What did he do?"

As amusing as Dakota's lack of faith in her brother was, Sienna didn't want to make a bigger deal out of what had actually happened. Explaining that a brief moment of accidental physical contact with Gentry had caused Sienna panic might give the wrong impression.

Sienna shook her head, waving her off. "He didn't do anything. He was actually friendly... ish. More so than usual." She smiled as Alex came to stand beside Dakota. "We got through a conversation without needing to be broken apart, so I consider that a win."

"Then why did you run?" Dakota's voice was strained. Sienna realized how much Dakota was banking on her to help her town. She hadn't even given a pitch yet and Dakota was ready to bite her brother's head off just for insulting Sienna.

She looked towards the door when it opened to see Gentry emerge with a worried look that melted into frustration. Sienna turned back to Dakota and answered, "It just got really loud and crowded and I needed some air. It was nothing, really. I'm fine. We're all fine."

Dakota shot Gentry a dirty look, but he just shoved his hands in his jeans pockets, sticking his lower lip out ever so slightly. He was waiting to see how much trouble he'd get into for bothering the Jade sisters in the first place.

When Dakota turned back to Sienna though, her smile was easy, unstrained. She looked at Alex, then down at her watch. "Well, I suppose I should let you two get ready. I'll pick you up at three."

The sisters shared a confused look, but Alex was the one to ask, "Ready for what? Where are we going?"

"Graduation. The whole town will be there," Dakota answered, as if it were obvious.

"But," Sienna started, sparing a quick glance at Gentry to see him take a tentative step towards them, then stop when he met her eyes. "We don't know anybody graduating."

Dakota nodded, as if that were obvious, too. "I know, but this is an opportunity to meet them. You might end up working with them this summer, and if nothing else, it's good to get to know their parents. Besides, it's a big party. You don't want to miss it, do you?"

"I don't know if I want to go if everyone is going to look at us like aliens," Sienna admitted under her breath. Alex gave a nod, telling Dakota she felt the same way, but the mayor "pff'd" and waved away their worries.

"They won't! It'll be fun, and I think it'll be good for you to see past Main Street. Have you even been through the residential area?" Alex shook her head and Dakota beamed at them. "Please come tonight! If you come, it makes a statement that you want to be part of this town. If you don't, they'll keep looking at you like you're outsiders."

Alex bobbed her head side to side, considering it for a moment before looking to Sienna for her opinion. "I guess it won't hurt," Sienna replied. She looked towards the door when the young people came charging out. Colton chased after Jewel, scooping her up from behind and lifting her off the ground as she giggled wildly, tossing her head back in pure joy. Sienna wondered if that joy would spread through the town. "You said you'll come by at three?"

"Graduation is at three-thirty. Wear whatever's comfortable. We like to dress up a little, since we don't have much reason to otherwise," Dakota grabbed each of their hands and gave them a squeeze. "It'll be great. You'll see."

They watched Dakota rejoin her brother, but Gentry leaned down to say something close to her ear and she shoved him away, causing him to chuckle. She looked over her shoulder to Sienna and Alex, giving a little wave and an awkward smile. Whatever he'd said was obviously about them, or, more specifically, about Sienna.

Chapter 16

AT EXACTLY THREE, DAKOTA was standing outside their motel room door. She wore the same dress she had earlier, but her hair had been tamed into a loose french braid with little wisps around her pretty face. "Are you guys ready?"

Sienna nodded, sucking in a long, slow breath through her nose. She'd fixed up her red hair to billow out like Dakota's often did, even curling up her bangs to give them nineties-level volume. She fixed her makeup to look more alive than she had earlier, but she still felt bare with only her mascara and blush. After trying on six different outfits, she'd settled on a denim dress that hit just below her knees and belted around her waist. At Alex's urging, she wore her boots, and Dakota's eyes lit up when she noticed.

"Is this okay?" Sienna asked nervously, feeling like she should have tried to dress up to the same standard as the mayor, but Dakota nodded enthusiastically.

"It's perfect." She looked to Alex, who wore a flowing chiffon skirt in burnt yellow with a white lacy tank top that she tucked in. "You both look great. I'm sorry we don't have more men in this town for you." The comment was directed at Sienna, because she smiled slyly when she added to Alex, "Although, you seem to have caught Jesse's attention. He's such a sweetheart."

Alex blushed. "I mean, we're just friends. There's nothing going on between us."

"Mmhmm," Dakota hummed as she took a step back to allow them a path to exit. "Maybe you can convince him to get some of his friends to move out here." She unlocked her car as Sienna closed the motel room door, balking a little at the sleek black Cadillac that beeped. Dakota caught her surprise and laughed. "Like it?"

"I haven't seen a car in three weeks."

"That's so sad when you say it like that," Dakota mumbled, pulling open the driver's door to slide in. She turned on the car, running the air and turning down the radio as Alex and Sienna slid in after her.

They drove in silence for a few minutes, heading toward the main road that leads away from Lonewood. Before they could get there, though, Dakota turned right to take them past a bunch of beautiful homes made of dark brick. They all looked different, with little ornaments in the gardens and flags planted by the doors. Not a single one looked like it belonged in the old west.

"Welcome to my town," Dakota said quietly, looking over at Sienna. "We're more than just Main Street."

"I don't really know what I was expecting, but," Sienna looked up as they passed by a stunning three story home with a balcony lining the third floor and massive picture windows along the lower two. "It wasn't this."

Dakota hummed to herself as the school came into view, a white building with two levels and "Lonewood School" written across the side in burnt red paint. Sienna realized that this was the school. Not the high school, but *the* school. Every child, from kindergarten to senior year, learned right here in this one building. She wondered if they even had enough kids to fill every grade.

As they got out of the car, Sienna took in the sight of metal chairs lined up outside the school and a little wooden podium in the front. Many of the chairs were already filled with people dressed up, dressed down, looking like they came straight from the farm. Everyone talked amongst themselves, making Sienna feel even more like an outsider.

She took a deep breath and followed Dakota, smiling sweetly as everyone greeted their mayor excitedly. When she reached Leah and Wayne, Dakota gave them a big hug, and to Sienna's surprise, Leah hugged her and Alex, too. "Thank you for coming."

"Of course, we wouldn't miss it," Alex said with more certainty than Sienna could have mustered. Alex looked around, seeing Jesse stand and wave to get her attention. She looked down at Sienna and asked quietly, "Would you be okay if I sat with him?"

"Dakota asked us to come with her."

"I don't mind. I won't be offended," Dakota assured Alex, but Sienna's eyes pleaded her sister not to leave her alone.

Alex grinned though, and took off towards the young cowboy instead of staying by Sienna's side. When she reached him, he gave her a tight hug, then looked her up and down with a wonder-filled smile. Even from across the aisle of chairs, Sienna could see he was telling Alex how beautiful she looked. Alex looked down, kicking at the grass a little, but she had a cute, shy little smile on her lips as her cheeks turned pink. Sienna sighed, happy that Alex had found a friend. Seemingly one who wouldn't upend their lives this time.

Turning to see where they'd be sitting, Sienna realized the sheriff was nowhere to be found. Dakota looked slightly alarmed at his absence, and she waved over Skylar as she wandered past them.

"Where's Gentry?"

Skylar drew her brows, looking down the road away from the school. "I assumed he was with you."

Dakota pursed her lips, pulling out her phone and placing it to her ear as she put up a finger to tell Sienna she'd be back in a minute. Sienna turned to Skylar, noticing the woman was wearing a short baby blue dress with combat boots. She smiled, but it didn't quite reach her eyes. "How's it going?"

"Going good, going good," Sienna muttered. "My sister abandoned me for Jesse, so feeling a little awkward. Don't wanna be the third wheel with Dakota and the sheriff."

"They're siblings..."

"Oh, I'm aware, but I'm still clearly the third wheel," Sienna reiterated as she watched Dakota shove her phone back in the pocket of her dress. She turned to Skylar and asked, "Do you want to sit with us?"

"Sure." She didn't say anything else, but Dakota beamed at them when she returned and explained, "He's on his way. We'll take a seat, it'll start soon." Dakota led them to the third row on the right, then gestured for

Sienna and Skylar to go in first. "I'm actually giving out a scholarship on behalf of the town, so I need to sit on the end. Can you leave a spot for Gentry?"

Sienna nodded, then turned to see Skylar had already situated herself in the fourth seat, meaning Sienna could sit next to Dakota or Skylar, but either way, she'd be stuck next to the sheriff. She steeled her jaw and took a seat beside Skylar, knowing he'd be grumpier than usual if she placed herself between him and Dakota.

She played with the chain of her necklace, toying with the sapphire pendant as she watched Dakota get up to talk to somebody Sienna didn't know. Looking over her right shoulder, she saw Jesse and Alex talking near the back, with Alex flailing her hands around wildly as she told him a story. He watched her with genuine interest before laughing brightly at whatever she'd said, but suddenly he looked over her shoulder, causing Alex to turn and Sienna to follow their gaze towards the road to see Gentry galloping towards them.

Domino slowed to a stop, causing dust to flare up around him as he whinnied loudly. A couple of people whooped loudly and called greetings to Gentry as he hopped off his horse, but all he responded with was a weak wave. He looked breathless as he walked Domino over to a small fence around the parking lot, tying him up before meandering back towards the crowd.

"Why the hell did he ride his horse here?" Sienna asked Skylar, who looked at her in surprise.

"He rides Domino everywhere."

"Like, I get that, but why here? I thought this was a nice event?"

"No, I mean he rides Domino everywhere because he refuses to drive." Skylar looked back at Gentry nervously to make sure he wasn't approaching them. She lowered her voice and leaned in close to Sienna to explain, "He won't get near a car since the accident."

Sienna looked back at Gentry as he shook Wyane's hand, then turned to another young man to give him a big hug. It was the first time Sienna had ever seen the sheriff act so friendly. Skylar leaned forward a little, getting Sienna's attention. "What do you know? About Kenzie?"

"Dakota said she was her sister, and that she died a couple years ago." Skylar nodded a little, so Sienna asked, "What happened?"

Skylar looked back at Gentry, then around to make sure nobody else was listening. "She was a teacher. She loved the kids and the kids wanted to do theater, and music, and sports. So, she negotiated a deal with the state for the kids to do extracurriculars in the neighboring towns. She drove to Bismarck to sign paperwork after Christmas, so the kids could start being integrated for the spring semester, but she didn't make it back. Her car hit a patch of ice and skid off the road and into a ditch."

Sienna felt her heart ache, imagining how awful it must have been. Sienna fiddled with her necklace some more, dropping her gaze.

Skylar's voice was strained as she added in a whisper, "I read the accident report when I moved back. If someone had found her sooner she would have made it, but she was on the side of the road for at least two hours before anyone found her."

If she hadn't been alone, she'd still be alive.

Sienna could practically hear what Skylar was insinuating. It made sense to Sienna now. Dakota's determination. Gentry's cold nature. And Kenzie had died trying to do something nice for the kids in this town. It was no wonder Dakota wanted them to come back and live here, her sister had given her life so they could have a better life in Lonewood. And it would die out anyway if nobody had kids of their own to raise here and go to the school. It would all be for nothing.

Dakota had told Gentry he was standing in the way of what Kenzie wanted. If Sienna helped Dakota bring business to Lonewood, she'd be taking up Kenzie's cause, too.

There was a grunt as Gentry settled in beside Sienna, but when she slowly looked over her shoulder, she found him massaging his eyebrows. He didn't seem to notice her, because he looked sad and resigned. Whatever mask of excitement he'd worn while greeting the principal fell apart once he'd taken a seat.

"Hey, Sheriff," Skylar greeted cheerfully, and Sienna could have smacked her for drawing attention to them. Gentry looked up to greet Skylar, then did a double take when he realized who sat between them. His brows furrowed and his jaw clenched. Sienna dropped her hands into her lap, lowering her gaze. She didn't want to upset him more, but she wasn't about to move.

"What is she doing here?" His question was directed at Skylar. He didn't even have the decency to address Sienna directly.

Skylar draped her arm over the back of her chair so she could face Gentry and Sienna, telling him calmly, "Dakota invited her and Alex. She asked if I'd sit with them. Would you like us to move?"

From the corner of her eye, Sienna saw Gentry's gaze fall on her. He stared at her for a long moment and she finally looked up at him. Letting out a loud sigh, Sienna stood to leave, but he grumbled, "You can stay. I'm just in a bad mood."

At thirty-three years old, Sienna would have assumed the man could get his 'mood' under control, but considering what had happened to him and his family, she let it slide. If Kenzie was a teacher, being here at the school was probably hard for him.

She slowly sat back down, placing her hands back in her lap. If she fiddled with her necklace any more she was gonna break it. She looked over at Skylar, who gave her a tiny, firm nod. Assuring Sienna she had her back.

Sienna smiled back until Dakota took a seat, breathless from all her conversing. She turned to Gentry and wiped the dust off of his shirt. "You made it with seven minutes to spare."

"I didn't want to come."

"You have to come, it's what we do," Dakota chastised him, looking past her brother to Sienna. She looked like she was trying to hold it together. She threw her arm around her brother's broad shoulders and gave him a tight squeeze, even though she could barely reach his other side. "The ceremony will last thirty minutes tops, then we get food and you can head to the bar if you want. Or if you'd rather, you can head home and I'll take the first shift."

"No, I'll do it," Gentry grumbled, pulling off his hat to rub his forehead as he scrunched his eyes closed. "I have a headache."

Sienna opened her purse and pulled out a little bottle of ibuprofen she'd bought after getting thrown from Cheyanne. It seemed like a cruel joke that she was offering them to the man who caused her accident, but it would definitely win brownie points with his sister. She held out the bottle and he stared at it, looking like he wanted to say no, but had no good reason not to take them.

He tentatively plucked the bottle from Sienna. "Thanks." He popped two pills into his mouth and handed the bottle back. He twisted his mouth slightly, like he was going to say something else, but settled into a bored stare at the empty stage instead.

When the principal took to the stage, everyone cheered loudly, like he was about to star in some sort of show. Sienna looked back in an effort to find Alex, but she was seated somewhere behind the mass of people. Wayne waved at everyone and Sienna leaned to the left to see the four graduates standing off to the side of the stage. Two boys and two girls bounced on their heels as they waited for graduation to start. They looked so full of life and excitement. They were ready to leave Lonewood in their rearview mirror.

"Do you need a booster seat?"

Sienna glared up at Gentry, but he just raised his brows questioningly. "What?" she hissed, not wanting to interrupt the ceremony. She hadn't realized that she'd leaned a little too far into his space, except he was practically pressed up against Dakota, who ignored her brother skillfully, as if he were still an annoying child who would get them both in trouble if she intervened.

Gentry placed his index and middle fingers firmly onto Sienna's shoulder and gently pushed her away from him, repeating slowly, "Do you... need a... booster seat? Because you're too short to see without climbing into my lap?"

"Shh!" Dakota finally shushed, glaring over at him. He grunted and settled back into his seat, glaring ahead. Sienna glanced behind them, noticing a small woman with tanned skin and midnight-black hair trying to hold back a laugh, meaning she'd clearly seen their interaction. Her fingers were laced between those of a stocky man to her left, and when he raised her hand to kiss it, Sienna saw the shining wedding band on her finger.

"If you don't care to watch, why'd you even come?"

It took everything in Sienna not to strangle him then and there. She turned to Gentry with cold emerald eyes, and found Dakota glaring at him from his other side. He stared ahead though, pretending to be invested in what was happening ahead of them. Sienna leaned back in her chair, watching as the principal introduced all of the seniors and passed out their diplomas. After they'd all gotten roaring cheers from the audience, Sienna spared a quick look at Gentry, seeing him smiling.

But then Dakota got up, and his smile fell. His mouth twitched a little, and he shifted uncomfortably in his chair. He watched the mayor take to the stage, then dropped his head to look at his phone.

Sparing a quick look around, Sienna realized several of the people were watching him instead of the mayor, and she looked to Skylar questioningly. Skylar gave the slightest shake of her head, telling Sienna she wasn't going to explain. Not now, not here.

Dakota beamed at everyone, but her gaze never once got near her brother. "We are so excited to have four seniors graduating this year! And because of that, on behalf of the town, we wanted to award each of you a thousand dollar scholarship."

Sienna finally understood the gravity of her situation. This could have been her, but Landon Maddox had allowed Alex some borrowed time. Sienna should have lost her sister too. She might have ended up determined to continue on Alex's legacy like Dakota or she might have ended up broken-hearted and closed off like Gentry. They dealt with their grief in very different ways, but Sienna was struck by how lucky she was that she didn't have to grieve at all.

She'd been so angry about losing her life, her job, and her boyfriend, but she could have lost so much more.

So, because she was lucky and he wasn't, Sienna opened up her purse, grabbed a small box of sugar cubes and sat them on Gentry's thigh to distract him. He stared down at them, then at her. "What are these?" he whispered quietly, respecting Dakota enough not to draw attention away from her speech.

"I've been feeding your horse snacks every day and I found these are his favorite."

It was a lie, and Skylar knew that, but she slapped her hand across her mouth to keep from laughing. Instead, a muffled snort came out, and the man beside her turned to shush her. She dropped her hand and stared ahead, but it was clear her eyes were watering from trying not to laugh.

Gentry, though, wasn't amused and his voice wasn't hushed anymore when he blurted, "You're shitting me."

Sienna shrugged, leaning back in her chair and crossing one leg over the other, bumping into Gentry's jeans with the underside of her dirty boot. "Guess you'll never know." He wiped the dirt off his black jeans aggressively while he scowled.

He clapped when everyone else did, but it was clear his thoughts weren't on Dakota as he leaned over and whispered, "You better be kidding, or I swear I'll-"

"I have never fed Domino anything," Sienna confessed, and he relaxed just a bit, taking her words as truth. "But I did hear those are his favorite, so I bought some so I could feed him when you aren't around."

Dakota took a seat again, smiling over at them until she realized her brother was glaring at Sienna. She hissed under her breath, "What the hell happened now?"

Gentry ignored her though, shoving the sugar cubes into his pocket. "Leave my horse alone."

"I make no promises. I adore him," Sienna teased back as the four graduates stood on the stage once more. She glanced up at Gentry, then back to the stage with a smirk. "I have two more boxes at home."

The graduates threw their hats in the air and everyone stood and cheered, including Sienna. Gentry grunted as he stood beside her, clapping slowly and glaring down at her every once in a while. Before everyone could scatter, though, one of the graduates ran up to the microphone and called, "Jasmine! Is it summer?"

Everyone under the age of thirty turned to the woman with the tanned skin and the dark hair behind them. She smiled, and yelled back, "It's officially summer!"

The applause and screaming that erupted was deafening and Sienna looked around in confusion, which caused Gentry to laugh. The noise was so foreign coming from him it was almost more startling than whatever was happening around them. "Welcome to Lonewood, Miss Jade."

He snuck past his sister, only to be tackled by the two senior boys in a tight hug that he returned without hesitation. Sienna shook her head and looked at Skylar, who just raised her hands in front of her chest. "I told you to leave him alone. If you want to poke the bear, that's on you."

"Agitating him is the most fun I've had since moving here," Sienna told Skylar. It was a wicked feeling, but it was the truth. It was clear she couldn't avoid the sheriff, but that didn't mean they had to get along. "So what do we do now?"

"Head over to the saloon for the reception, then if you feel like taking a walk on the wild side, Jasmine says summer's arrived."

"What does that mean?" Sienna asked loudly as people started talking over each other.

"It means you're gonna get free a dinner and then you can either align yourself with the old timers or the youngins," Skylar called back. She laughed at her own joke, then looked down at her watch. "I offered to watch the station so everyone else could party. I'll catch you soon, okay?"

"Hopefully not too soon," Sienna droned, and Skylar snorted, understanding what she meant. It wouldn't surprise Sienna if the sheriff arrested her just for the hell of it. The woman disappeared into the crowd to go to work, and Alex bounded up in her place with Jesse in tow.

"So, Jesse asked if I'd go with him to the reception and then the afterparty at Jazzy's. Are you okay hanging with Skylar and Dakota for the night?"

Sienna really didn't want Alex to abandon her, but she looked so happy and hopeful and Sienna wasn't feeling nearly that optimistic about tonight. "Skylar has to work, so I'll probably just head back to the motel."

"What? Really? You aren't gonna come to the reception at least?" Alex asked sadly. Sienna shot her an annoyed look, unsure what her sister wanted from her. Alex tilted her head and said, "Don't be a killjoy. At least come for free a dinner. You can hang with us if you don't want to hang with Dakota. Although considering you've been desperately trying to impress her, I feel like avoiding her will send a conflicting message."

"It's not Dakota I'm trying to avoid," Sienna droned.

Alex snorted. "Come with us, then. Jesse's gonna drive us back to his place, then we'll walk from there."

"I'll be okay. You two go and I'll see you there." Sienna didn't want to intrude on Alex's time with Jesse, seeing as they appeared to be getting along so well. Sienna wouldn't be surprised if Alex didn't come back to the motel tonight.

As Jesse and Alex left, Sienna turned around to scan the mass of people lingering at the graduation. She recognized almost everyone, but didn't feel comfortable inserting herself into any of their conversations.

Two months ago, she and Mason had attended a gala thrown by his company. She'd been dressed in a six hundred dollar gown and a jeweled necklace that would have made the Heart of the Ocean jealous. Mason had led her around every cocktail table, introducing her to all his rich and powerful friends. Every new person they met congratulated Mason on finding such a stunning woman.

She didn't feel stunning anymore. Mason clearly didn't think so. If he did, he would have chosen her. Sienna had been so sure he would choose her forever, but she was wrong.

Gazing around, she noticed Domino standing unattended near the parking lot fence. She'd annoyed the sheriff enough already, but Domino seemed like better company than all the excited people who didn't know her.

"I had sugar cubes but the sheriff took 'em," Sienna told Domino as she approached. She leaned against the fence a good six feet away and he took a few steps closer, but couldn't reach her. "I know! I want to give you scratchies too, but he says no. Have a talk with him and then maybe I can give you sugar cubes and scratchies." She looked at Domino longingly. Maybe once they moved out of the motel Sienna could get a cat or a dog, or even a fish. Probably not a horse, but she wouldn't argue if the opportunity arose. She just wanted something to care for, and something to love her unconditionally. Above everything, she wanted something she could talk to about her secrets and her fears without worrying about getting plucked from this life and dropped into another one.

"I'd be angry that you're talking to my horse, except you look so pathetic that I almost feel sorry for you."

Sienna leaned forward to see Gentry approaching from the other side of Domino. He dug his nails deep into the horse's coat, and Domino started leaning towards Gentry for more attention. The man walked around to the other side, so he was in between his horse and the nuisance that was Sienna.

"I'm nowhere near him," Sienna deadpanned.

"Yeah, that makes it that much sadder. It's like he doesn't want you around either."

"Why are you such an ass?" Sienna scrunched her eyes closed as she leaned against the fence and groaned, "You know, my sister wanted to move here, not me. I'm doing this for her."

She heard Domino make a rumbling sound, something deep and soft and happy. Sienna opened her eyes to see Gentry holding out a handful of sugar cubes for Domino, but he was watching Sienna.

He looked frustrated. Domino reached out his lips to brush against Gentry's arm, testing for more sugar. Gentry released a sigh and held out the box. "Do you wanna feed him?"

Sienna perked up at that. Taking a few steps closer, she plucked the box from Gentry's hand and grabbed three sugar cubes before closing the box and dropping it into her open purse.

"Do you know how to feed him?"

Sienna stared up at him blankly. "I'm not stupid."

"So is that a no? Because if he takes your fingers off while I'm standing here Dakota is going to kill me."

Smirking, Sienna shrugged. "Maybe that would be worth losing my fingers for."

Gentry snorted, shaking his head and holding out his hand to show her. "Palm flat. Don't curl your fingers. As long as you do that, he'll use his lips, not his teeth and you'll be fine."

She did as he told her, holding out her flat palm for the horse to devour the sugar, then continued running his lips over her palm as she giggled. She reached up and stroked his face, tracing the pad of her thumb just below his blue eye. "What kind of horse is he?"

"He's a Paint."

"Was he wild like Bandit?"

Gentry shook his head, reaching up to scratch between Domino's ears. "No, he was bred. He was an expensive horse. I got him when he was a baby and raised him." Domino leaned his weight into Gentry, swinging his head for attention. "He's my best friend."

"That's kind of sad that your best friend is a horse," Sienna whispered with a teasing smile. Gentry grunted and untied Domino from the fence, preparing to leave. "Hey! I was kidding! He's really sweet. You two really care about each other."

He mounted Domino and shifted in the saddle. "Don't pretend like you understand. I don't expect you to, and it's insulting that you think I'd believe you. I'm not nearly as ignorant as you think I am."

Sienna balked at that, and Gentry kicked Domino's sides to take off sprinting, causing dirt to flare up around Sienna. She coughed and waved her hand in front of her face. Just when she thought they were getting somewhere, he reverted into an asshole again.

"Sooo, I see you and my brother are starting to get along." Dakota's voice was sickeningly sweet with a hint of hopefulness in there. When Sienna turned to her, wiping the dust off of her denim dress, Dakota sighed. "Maybe a little bit?"

"Why does it matter anyway?"

"Because I like you, and I think we could be good friends," Dakota admitted gently. "It would be easier if he liked you, too."

Sienna pushed back her hair, feeling little clumps of dirt stuck in it. She tossed her mass of curls to the side and attempted to pick them out until Dakota reached over to help. She grabbed a couple bits of gravel and flung them away, then wiped off Sienna's sleeves. "Some people just don't jive. You and I," Sienna gestured between herself and Dakota, "we are on the same wavelength. We see a problem and we want to fix it. He wants to wallow in whatever he's got going for him, and that's his prerogative, but I don't need to be a part of that."

Dakota nodded to herself, her mouth pulling up on the right side in a sad smile. "I understand. You and I can still be friends though, right?"

"I mean, I'm assuming you have friends here..."

"I'd like to consider you one, too. As you said, I think our ideals align, and I'm excited to hear what you think after Memorial Day. I want the place to be as full of life all year as it is today." She paused, watching the graduates all pile into the back of someone's pickup truck, hooting and hollering as a couple of the returning kids climbed in with them. "Don't you see it? What we could be if they stay? If we stop looking to the past and start looking to the future, they could run Lonewood, and people their age would want to come. I need you to help me convince them to come back."

"Why don't you just convince them not to go away in the first place?" Sienna blurted. She understood that getting a college education was important, but it seemed counter productive to support their efforts to leave in hopes they'd come back.

"I don't wanna clip their wings. I want them to go see the world and then decide they want to come home, not force them to." Dakota watched them drive away, smoothing her hand over her braid. "We want them to have every possible choice, and to have something worth choosing over everything else."

That was a tall order for a little town. If Sienna was one of those graduates, she'd leave and never look back. If she'd grown up here, and ended up in Manhattan, she'd never step foot in this place again. Dakota was naive to think she could create that out of her town, but Sienna smiled at the notion that it didn't hurt to try.

Chapter 17

JESSE LED ALEX INTO the saloon, and she gasped as she looked around. The tables had been covered in white linens and there were framed photos of the graduates on each one. A buffet was set up along the bar, but there was a little space at the end where Maude could still give out drinks. The stage had fairy lights hung from the edge and a microphone set up in the center.

"When I was a kid, I always wanted to perform here," Jesse said quietly. Alex looked at him, and he ducked his head bashfully. "Not as a showgirl, obviously, but I thought I'd make a pretty good song and dance man. Better than a cowboy if I'm being honest."

"Why don't you?" Alex asked softly.

"Because that's not what they do here. If I want a job in Lonewood, I can either sling beers, run trail rides, man one of the shops, or become a cowboy. I didn't major in theater to do the other three, so I'm Cowboy Jesse."

Alex looked at the stage, then to the man beside her. "Have you talked to Maude? Maybe you could be part of the show?"

"Nobody wants to watch one man dance, trust me," Jesse chuckled. He'd left his cowboy hat at home, leaving his thick hair free for Alex to admire. "I do sing, but Bill's wife has that on lockdown." Jesse grimaced a little, and Alex tried to hold in her laughter. "I don't mind being a cowboy. I just need something to put on my resume so I can do theater somewhere else."

"It's hard. Trust me, I know. I was a dancer for years..." Alex caught herself, realizing she couldn't share too much of her past with him. "But it wasn't fulfilling- not like I wanted it to be. So I dragged Sienna out here to try something new. Thought maybe there'd be a place for me, but I don't know if there is. I don't think the saloon girls would take too kindly to me. I'd blow 'em out of the water."

"It wouldn't take much," Jesse whispered and they laughed together. He dropped his hand to take Alex's and sucked in a sharp breath, then met her eyes. "If your sister gets around to making some changes, maybe we'll get up on that stage after all."

Alex followed his gaze to the front of the room, imagining herself on the stage. She'd been such a small fish in the biggest ocean of the world. Here she'd be a blue whale in a pond. She could be the brightest star to ever shine in Lonewood, and she knew she shouldn't try, but she wanted to. She missed performing. It felt like a bit of her heart was on that stage, but she wasn't allowed to claim it.

Jesse leaned around her to see her eyes, asking softly, "Are you okay?"

"Yeah, I just miss it." She felt like being honest. It was easy to be honest with Jesse. She looked away from the stage and smiled. "One day at a time though. I'm excited to be here, especially now that I've met you." He blushed a little at her confession, so Alex continued, "I like spending time with you, and I hope Sienna finds somebody to spend time with, too. Between you and me," Alex looked towards the door, making sure none of the people pouring in were her sister, "I'm getting a little tired of being her everything. I love her, don't get me wrong, but I want to be my own person. I think this plan she's got with the mayor will be a good distraction. It'll allow me the freedom to really figure out who I am. Do you ever feel like... like you don't know who you are? Because you've spent so much time playing other people and being who others want you to be that you aren't sure what's real underneath?"

"Yes," Jesse said so quietly it was almost a gasp. He nodded and took Alex's hand firmly in his. "Maybe we could figure it out together." Alex grinned down at their entwined hands, feeling safe for the first time in a long time.

"I'd like that."

Sienna and Dakota arrived soon after, and since the sheriff was nowhere to be found, Sienna was beaming and following Dakota around, allowing the mayor to introduce her to everyone who would talk to them. Eventually, they found their way through the buffet, and took a seat with Alex and Jesse, who had long finished eating.

"You having fun?" Alex prodded as she leaned over to Sienna.

"Surprisingly, yes." Sienna picked up her fork, poking at her roast beef before stabbing it to take a bite. As she chewed through her food, she asked, "You already eat?"

"Yeah, while you were schmoozing," Alex teased, leaning in close and laughing. She looked back at Jesse, then around the packed saloon. "I wanna dance," Alex murmured to herself, then caught that she'd said the words aloud when Jesse raised his brows to her. "I miss it! This place feels so alive for the first time since we've moved here... it makes me want to dance again."

Sienna chewed through her food, then gently bumped Dakota's arm to get her attention. "Do you ever have dancing here? It would make a great dance hall."

Dakota shook her head. "Not that I ever remember."

"Is it a *Footloose* kind of situation? No dancing allowed in Lonewood?"

Chuckling, Dakota refuted Sienna's question. "No, it's not that. Preston and Ruth used to throw barn dances out at the Circle W, but not recently. The only dancing we do these days is up on stage."

Jesse bumped shoulders with Alex, leaning in closely to explain, "It's the official first day of summer, which means everyone is heading to Jazzy's after dinner for a real party."

"The *young* people are heading to Jazzy's. I'll be heading to bed. The reception here will probably last till around ten or eleven." Dakota smiled sweetly and waved at a passing couple.

Alex looked at her phone, finding it only six o'clock. "What time will people head over there?"

"Probably around seven or eight," Dakota said quickly, then turned around to have a full conversation with the visiting family of one of the graduates.

Clearing her throat, Alex stood. "I think I'm gonna get something to drink. Do you want anything?" she asked Jesse, then turned to Sienna who shook her head to say no. Jesse stood and gestured for Alex to lead the way to the bar.

When they arrived, though, Maude beamed at Alex and called, "Are you having a fun evening?"

"I am! Everyone is so excited to be here!" Alex called back. She looked up at Jesse and he yelled over the clinking of glasses, "Could I get a rum and coke?"

Maude nodded, making his drink quickly before setting it up on the bar. Jesse looked at Alex expectedly, but Maude sat her glass beside his. She gave her a wink, then looked up at Jesse. "You take good care of my girl, you hear me?"

"Of course," Jesse said softly as Alex leaned into his side. "She wants to dance though, so we might need to head out soon."

Alex stared at him with wide eyes. She couldn't believe he'd told Maude that. Alex had built a good rapport with the woman and didn't want to offend her, but Maude gave a laugh from behind the bar. Her eyes sparkled mischievously as she looked from Alex to Jesse. "If she wants to dance, then dance. Don't disappoint the lady."

The pair looked to Maude curiously, and she lifted up the bar to sneak under it. She started shuffling past the people towards the stage, and Alex felt the heat in her cheeks rising. She bolted after her with Jesse on her tail. "Maude! That's not- that's not what I meant-"

"I see the look in your eyes when you watch everyone else perform," Maude told Alex when she reached the little set of stairs leading up onto the stage. She started to climb the first few steps and Alex grabbed her wrist. When Maude looked back at her, she shook her head rapidly, but Maude reached down and cupped her chin. "I think it's time you stop watching everyone else do the things you love."

Against Alex's wishes, Maude strode onto the stage. Alex clenched her fist to her mouth as Jesse stood behind her, waiting to see what the woman would say. When Maude got to the microphone, she tapped it to get everyone's attention. "Is everybody having a good time tonight?"

The room erupted in cheers and Alex felt her blood run cold as she realized what Maude was about to do. She looked back at Jesse and he looked equally as startled, frozen at the base of the stairs.

Maude looked down at Alex with a sympathetic smile, then turned towards the crowded room again. "I'm sure those of you who've been in town the past couple of weeks have noticed we have a couple of new faces. Now my girl Alex comes from a performance background in California. I've heard she's a pretty good dancer, but I guess the question is whether or not we want to find out?" Screaming and whooping were the answers to Maude's question and Alex looked over to see Sienna's eyes as wide as saucers. She shook her head a little, but Alex shrugged and mouthed 'I didn't mean to' as Maude gestured to her. "Everyone give a round of applause for Alex and Jesse!"

"We've never danced together!" Jesse croaked as Beau and Kitty motioned for them to go up onto the stage. Maude moved the microphone over to an old CD player in the corner.

Alex whipped around to face Jesse, seeing terror in his eyes. "You know how to dance, right?"

"Little bit."

"Little bit? Okay, well, you lead and I'll follow," Alex said through the breath she ripped into her lungs. An up-tempo country song started playing and Jesse grabbed her right hand with his left and yanked her towards him, spinning her around him as the song got under way.

Her eyes widened as he grabbed her and led her across the floor, and she started laughing as she kept up with his steps. When Jesse realized she knew what she was doing, he twirled her out to the crowd so she could dance on her own. She grabbed her chiffon skirt and yanked it up so she wouldn't step on it, doing a high kick that would make a Rockette proud. When she returned to Jesse, he spun her out just to pull her back in and dip her on his knee so she could kick her boot in the air as the song came to a close.

The whole saloon erupted into cheers and Alex felt something spark in her soul that had been missing for a long time, even in Manhattan.

It had been so long since she'd danced like this. There was no pressure. No need for recognition, feedback, or a paycheck. Alex was just dancing because she loved it. She laughed loudly, her voice echoing over the music as it got closer to the end.

Jesse led her farther back to the stage, twirling her again before sliding her through his long legs to skid on her knees towards the edge of the stage. She threw her hands up, beaming as everyone jumped to their feet to applaud. Her chest heaved as she looked to the stairs, seeing Maude applauding her with a proud expression. Jesse helped her up, then gestured for her to take a bow as he clapped, and she returned the gesture before allowing him to lead her in a run off the stage.

"I can't believe we did that!" Alex laughed as she threw her arms around Jesse's neck at the base of the stairs. She pulled away and grabbed his cheeks, seeing he was as exhausted as she was. "You said you knew a little."

"Well, I knew a little that you might know," he admitted. "I didn't think you'd know how to swing dance."

"Honestly, me neither, but you were a great lead," she answered, placing her hand on his chest as she panted. She turned to Maude, shaking her head. "I'm both incredibly angry at you but also so, so thankful you made us do that."

Maude smiled knowingly, patting Jesse on the back. "You're welcome to dance at my place anytime, kid. And you," she pointed at Alex, "we're gonna have a talk once we get past Memorial Day. I might be switching up a few acts. That is, if you two are interested in doing that again."

"We can do more than that!" Jesse exclaimed happily, leaning his chin against Alex's temple. Maude gave a nod and wandered away as Sienna practically jogged over to them.

Alex assumed she'd get an earful for garnering so much attention, but she didn't care. She was living again. Every strained breath reminded her of how much she loved performing and how desperately she wanted to do it again.

When Sienna opened her mouth, Alex cut her off, "I'm not gonna stop. I can't. Please don't tell me to stop."

Sienna looked surprised, pulling her head back in alarm. "I was going to say I had no idea you could dance like that. You were amazing!" Alex laughed and pulled her big sister in for a hug. She hadn't been this happy in years. When Sienna pulled away though, she did lean up and whisper, "Let's just make sure you don't draw too much attention, okay?"

"Definitely not." Alex whispered back. Her chest rose and fell as she looked towards their table, seeing several people swarming Dakota, including Hank, Bill, and his wife. They didn't look pleased. She glanced up at Jesse and muttered under her breath, "Maybe we should go. I think we've made enough of an impression tonight."

Jesse turned to see what she was looking at, then sucked in a sharp breath. "Yeah, maybe we should. But I'd love to get a little more dancing in if you're up for it. Jazzy's?"

"Sure! Why the hell not?" Alex laughed, then looked at Sienna, grabbing her hand. "You wanna come?"

"I'm gonna stay here for a bit, then I think I'll check it out since I've heard so much about it!" Sienna answered. She nodded, giving Alex's hand a supportive squeeze. "I'm really proud of you."

Alex felt like her heart could explode, but that could be from lack of oxygen. "Thank you, that means a lot."

It meant everything to Alex that Sienna was supportive. It gave her hope that maybe they could have a happy life here after all. After saying goodbye to Sienna, Alex allowed Jesse to run her through the saloon and down the stairs before they slowed down.

She laughed brightly as she twirled down Main Street, causing Jesse to beam at her proudly. He grabbed her hand and held it tight, then guided her down the dirt road towards the promise of pulsing lights, pounding music, and just maybe, something more.

Chapter 18

ALEX'S PERFORMANCE WITH JESSE reverberated through the saloon. The graduates and their college friends made their exit soon after, cheering and yelling over each other as they left to head over to Jazzy's. The volume of the saloon went down by half, and when Sienna looked around, she realized she was suddenly the youngest person in the room.

"She's impressive," Hank told Maude gruffly as the saloon owner wiped down the bar where the buffet had been sitting for the past few hours. "Too modern, though. Too *Californian.*"

Bill leaned past his brother, already on his fourth beer of the night. "Doesn't fit into the show. Don't be getting any ideas, Maude."

Sienna swallowed, ducking her head to stare at her red-painted nails. She was sitting a few seats down at the bar nursing a glass of red wine and she didn't want them to realize she was there.

Alex had done nothing wrong, performing for the hell of it because it was fun, but it was enough to send these people into a frenzy. If they realized what Sienna wanted to do... she'd be chased right out of town.

Maude tossed her cloth to the corner of the bartop, leaning on the clean wood to get closer to Hank, Bill, and Bill's wife Linda, whose lip quivered like she was gonna cry. "I've had lots of ideas over the years, Mr. Cassidy, but until recently I haven't had the opportunity to consider them. Memorial Day is next weekend, and if we don't draw a crowd, we're gonna need to make a change. I can't keep paying you all if nobody's watching." She pointed towards the doors to the saloon, which had been propped open to let the cool evening air keep the temperature down in the crowded old building. "That girl would draw a crowd. Did you hear how the young people cheered for her? I wish I could say they cheer for you all like that, but they don't."

"What're ya gonna do? Fire us?" Hank sneered darkly, but Sienna saw Maude pour herself a shot of fireball and down it before rinsing out the shot glass. "Maude?"

"I heard ya," she snapped back as she turned off the water. "Nobody's getting fired. We're a family. But this family might need to grow. Who do you think is gonna run this place when we're gone, Hank? Or are you gonna live forever?"

Hank grunted, slamming his whiskey glass on the bar top. "Maybe."

"No, you won't. If we don't get some fresh blood in here, this all goes away."

"But what about my act?" Linda asked sadly, and Sienna's heart broke for her. She imagined her sister giving her life to one place, giving everything her body, voice, and soul had to offer, only to be cast aside.

But a month ago, Broadway cast aside Alex for a lot less. Her sister was good at what she did, and Sienna wondered if she could make a bigger difference here than she could in New York. It would all come down to what Maude decided to do.

Dakota climbed onto the barstool beside Sienna, drawing the attention of the three actors and Maude. Their conversation ended abruptly, and Sienna raised her wine glass in a weak greeting. Hank huffed at her, but Bill managed a gentle smile and asked, "How are you enjoying your first summer evening, Miss Jade?"

Sienna looked around as the festivities began to die down. The saloon had been full of life for a brief moment, but was fading back to its prior state. As the tablecloths were pulled off the splintering tables, and the fairy lights were taken down off the stage, Sienna felt her heart ache for what could be. "I'm excited to see what next weekend brings. Tonight was really eye opening."

"Well, the kids bring a lot of energy," Maude chuckled, taking Sienna's glass when she finished her wine. "You want another?"

"No thank you, I'm okay." Sienna was ready to go. Sparing a look over at Dakota, she could see the young mayor was tired, too. Her amber eyes looked weary, beginning to droop a little. She'd done quite a bit of drinking, but the alcohol only made her uncharacteristically quiet. "You doing alright?"

"Tired. Getting old," Dakota laughed humorlessly. She gave Sienna a sad smile and bumped her shoulder with her own. "How old are you?"

"Excuse me?"

"How old are you? I'm curious." Dakota's words slurred, but her voice was still as gentle and genuine as always. She chuckled, pulling a fifty dollar bill out of her pocket and slamming it on the bar. "I know it's not polite to ask, but I figured we've reached the point where it's okay. Besides, you aren't old enough to be offended by it."

Sienna wasn't offended by the question, just curious where it had come from. "I'm twenty-nine. I'll be thirty in October."

Dakota rocked forward and backward, as if her whole body nodded instead of her head. "You're young to be so successful."

"I wouldn't say I'm successful-"

"You said you owned your own marketing firm. To own and lose your own business before thirty is definitely successful. I'm excited to see what you'll do next."

Sienna was, too. She was excited to see what she'd do once she left Dakota's little town and made a life for herself out in the world again. This was a small stepping stone on the path back to the real world. She couldn't have her life back in Manhattan, but that didn't mean she couldn't reforge herself somewhere else after starting here.

Dakota groaned as she stretched her arms above her head, arching her back until she sighed happily. "I'm heading home. Are you okay making it back by yourself? Or are you heading over to Jazzy's?"

"I feel like I need to check this place out," Sienna admitted. The redhead fluffed her deflated bangs and asked Dakota, "Do you want me to walk you home first?"

The mayor waved her off, laughing to herself. "No. I'm fine. I live across from my office, so I'm only five minutes away."

Sienna crawled off the stool, then reached into her bag and pulled out a ten, placing it on the counter. Maude took it and shoved it into her apron, giving Sienna a little smile before turning back to her actors. Back to their conversation about Alex.

She turned to Dakota and asked, "Where is Jazzy's?"

Dakota tossed her chin towards the door, as if there was another way out. "Head out the doors, down Main Street. When you get to the cafe, take a right and go across the street. Not towards the motel, but towards the residential area. You'll know it when you find it."

"Sounds good. Have a nice night. Thank you for inviting us," Sienna told the mayor, and Dakota pulled her in a one-armed hug to say goodbye.

The sun had finally set and the air was cool as Sienna wandered Main Street towards Jazzy's. Once she turned the corner past the Lonewood Cafe, she saw a small parking lot was filled with a dozen vehicles, packed so tightly together Sienna wasn't sure how they'd get out. The music was glaringly clear now - pop music with a deep bass that thumped the dark bricks of the old building. This was clearly a bar, which confused Sienna considering many of the people who'd flocked here were definitely under twenty-one.

When she approached the entrance, Sienna caught a glimpse of a blonde woman making out with a man near the door. Upon closer inspection, it was Jewel from the diner, and the man holding her by the ass was definitely her ex-boyfriend. Apparently Brenda was right about them getting back together.

Sienna pushed open the door to get past the distracted young couple. Inside, the music was impossibly loud, but Sienna saw at least a dozen people dancing at the base of a small stage. There was a drum set and a guitar stand, but no live band at the moment. Nobody seemed to mind as they ground against each other, laughing loudly.

In the center of the dance floor were Alex and Jesse, almost a decade older than the people around them. But Alex threw her arms in the air and swayed to the music with the biggest smile Sienna had seen in years.

It brought a sad smile to Sienna's face. She was happy that Alex was happy. That she'd found something in this little place that she loved. That she found somebody who cared enough to dance with her. Sienna couldn't even remember the last time she'd gone to see Alex dance in one of her shows. She'd been too busy with her own life.

Noticing the bar at the far left wall, Sienna slid past a couple of people laughing with drinks in hand. When she reached the bar, she looked to her right, realizing the girl beside her was one of the graduates from earlier. She slapped a bright red ticket on the counter and was handed a large glass of beer.

Sienna raised her finger, wanting to ask the girl how old she was, but she sipped the foam from the top to keep from spilling it as she situated herself between two other young women.

"Umm," Sienna started, sparing a quick glance at the woman behind the bar before pointing at the girl. "I'm not sure if I should say anything, but that girl is definitely not twenty-one. She graduated high school today-"

"I know." Sienna whipped around, realizing the woman pouring beers was the woman who'd been seated behind her at graduation. The woman with tanned skin and midnight black hair pulled back into a smooth braid that reached past the waistband of her tight jeans. She raised her brows to Sienna, as if asking what the problem was.

Sienna cocked her head, looking over at the red ticket that the woman grabbed and paperclipped to a driver's license that she had behind the bar. "You IDed her."

"Of course I IDed her, I own this bar. I know who I serve," the woman answered casually, not the least bit alarmed about what Sienna was accusing her of. She held out her hand for Sienna to shake, introducing herself. "Jasmine Lee. I run this place with my husband Bobby." She tossed her head towards a man farther down the bar, and Sienna recognized him from earlier. Jasmine smiled as she stepped back, studying Sienna's apprehensive expression. "You wanna call the cops? Be my guest," Jasmine said, grabbing a beer bottle from beneath the bar and setting it out. "Be a doll and drop this off for the sheriff, will you?"

The woman pointed across the bar to a small table near the door. Sienna hadn't even seen it when she entered, but sitting in the dark corner with his hat tipped low and his eyes glued to his phone was Gentry.

Sienna grabbed the beer and shot Jasmine a dirty look, stomping over to the sheriff before slamming the bottle on his table. He looked up at her slowly, blinking a little before grabbing the bottle and taking a long swig. They stared at each other for what felt like an hour before he greeted, "Miss Jade."

"So you're aware that this bar is serving underage kids?"

Gentry groaned a little and kicked the chair beside him so it moved away from the table. He gestured to it, inviting Sienna to sit. She ran her tongue along the front of her teeth, wanting nothing less than to keep him company. When she glared over her shoulder, he chuckled. "You're stubborn as an old milk cow. You can be all pissy and tell Skylar something she already knows or you can take a seat and let me answer your questions."

She narrowed her eyes at him, then slowly sat in the chair beside him. She was stiff, looking around nervously until she remembered that *she* couldn't get in trouble because she was literally with the head of the police department.

"So here's the deal," Gentry started, dangling the lip of his beer bottle between his fingers. "Binge drinking is a big thing out here in the midwest. There's not a lot to do. These kids, they're gonna drink. Nothing I do is gonna stop that. So I can either throw them all in jail or I can make sure they drink responsibly."

Although she understood what he was trying to get at, she wasn't impressed. This wasn't like someone letting their teenager try wine at the family dinner table, or even an older sibling buying a case of beer for someone underage; this was a licensed facility breaking a million codes. "So, like, I get that they're gonna drink, but why here? Why do you let them serve alcohol to kids?"

"First off, these aren't kids." Gentry gestured around the crowded bar. "Nobody's allowed in unless they are eighteen. We have a system. The summer they graduate high school, if they're eighteen, they get one ticket. One ticket for one drink. They give their license to Jasmine and use their voucher for whatever they want. Once they're nineteen, they get two tickets. At twenty, they're allowed three tickets, and if anybody's caught giving tickets or alcohol to somebody else, they don't get their license back until they leave for college at the end of the summer."

Gentry tipped back his beer, finishing it off and scooting the bottle to the edge of the table. His voice dropped a little, and he leaned in ever so slightly so she could still hear him. His breath smelled like beer, but his skin smelled like cologne. Sienna felt her breath hitch being this close, but she leaned in anyway so he could say whatever he wanted without having to yell above the music. "I know we could get in huge shit for what we're doing here, but if it saves their lives, it's a price I'll pay. They don't get to leave with their license without seeing me first. If I think they aren't safe to drive, they don't leave."

Sienna leaned back, needing some space from the man. The look in his eyes was softer than she was used to, and she was quick to blame the alcohol before considering that this meant a lot to him. She sighed and yelled, "How long have you been doing this?"

"Four or five years now!" Gentry yelled back as the music somehow became louder. He looked at the stage with an annoyed expression, then added, "It seems to be working! We haven't lost a single one of our kids to drunk driving, either here or when they're away at school. I'd rather they learn their limits somewhere safe, ya know?"

Alex must have caught a glimpse of her sister, because she charged over, leaving Jesse to dance in the mosh pit that was forming. "You came! Isn't this place wild?"

"Yeah, wild is a good way to describe it!" Sienna yelled back, already feeling her voice becoming hoarse. She wondered if Alex realized she was drinking among minors, or if she even cared. "You having fun?"

"So much fun!" Alex called back. She looked to Gentry, then back to Sienna with a surprised expression. "You wanna come dance?"

"I'm actually okay. Might get a drink. I think I owe the owner an apology," she called, her voice dropping a little as she cringed in embarrassment.

Gentry stood, pushing his hat back a little to see better. "Don't worry, I'll take care of it. What do you two want? It's on me."

Sienna stared up at him in shock, but his smirk told her he enjoyed her confusion. "Literally anything that isn't beer!"

"So water, got it." Gentry turned to Alex. "And you?"

"Just water for me is fine!"

"What? Are you kidding me? You drink alcohol like water in a desert," Sienna teased. She didn't understand why Alex looked so uncomfortable. "What is it?"

Alex turned to Gentry, smiling weakly as she shrugged a little. "I don't drink anymore. Not like I used to."

He looked between the sisters, seeming to realize something was off, but he just said loudly, "No shame in being sober. It's nice you can have this much fun without a lick of alcohol."

He turned to get their drinks and Alex looked down at Sienna. Her mouth was open, but she couldn't quite find the words to say. Finally, she clamped her mouth shut and looked up, then back around, then to Sienna with teary eyes. "I think we should go."

"What's happening?" Sienna stood abruptly, grabbing Alex's shoulders. "What's wrong?"

"The last time I got drunk, I ruined our lives."

Sienna moved her hands from her sister's shoulders to her cheeks, using her thumbs to smear away the tears that fell. From an outside perspective, the others probably thought Alex was a little too drunk and emotional, and paid her no mind. Knowing why she was sober broke Sienna's heart.

"I didn't realize that's why you weren't drinking." Sienna pulled Alex to her chest, and her sister started crying harder.

When she pulled away, Sienna realized Gentry was behind them with a glass of water for each of them. He looked worried, and normally Sienna would have said something snappy about it, but he was worried about her sister. So was she.

She took the water and thanked him quietly, downing it as her eyes scanned the dance floor. Sienna saw Jesse look over at her, and when he saw that she wasn't her normal smiley self, he came over to check on her, too.

"Do you wanna go?" Sienna asked. She wanted to ask if this place reminded Alex of the bar she went to that night with Landon, but she couldn't ask that in front of Gentry. She glared up at him to tell him to give them some space, but she heard her little sister say no.

When Sienna looked back over to Alex, the taller woman was wiping her own tears and straightening up. "No, I think I should stay. A little bit longer."

Sienna gave a slow nod, showing she wasn't so sure about her sister's decision. "If you decide you want to go, you tell me, okay?"

"I want to dance just a little bit longer."

Sienna smiled at that, and Jesse appeared and grabbed Alex's hand. He looked at her worriedly but she assured him she was fine. With one last brave smile to Sienna, Alex and Jesse were back out to the dance floor.

Gentry fell hard into his seat, grunting as his weight hit the chair. Much like his sister, he looked tired, but he still watched over the bar and the young people within it. Sienna sat back down with him, taking a slow sip of her water to find it was definitely vodka. She coughed a little, swallowing it before looking a little closer and seeing carbonated bubbles. She scowled up at Gentry and he looked at her blankly, then deadpanned, "You said literally anything that wasn't beer. So I got you a vodka Sprite."

She was torn between being angry that he didn't warn her and being grateful that he'd actually taken the time to ask for something she might like. She decided on a happy medium and slid the glass closer to her and snapped, "Thanks."

He sighed and leaned back in his chair, pulling out his phone again. His expression was melancholy, but every time someone would greet him he'd give them a gentle smile before going back to what he was looking at. The light of the cell phone cast a glow over his face, allowing Sienna a good look at his Roman nose and sharp jaw that stayed defined even when he wasn't clenching it for once. Sienna realized she'd never noticed the smaller features of his face, probably because she'd always been too intimidated by his massive figure looming over her.

Sitting beside him though, Sienna allowed herself the chance to really study him. Gentry was, factually speaking, handsome. If she'd met him in Manhattan, and he hadn't opened his mouth to insult her somehow, she would have chosen him out of a lineup of men without question. If it wasn't for his sharp, cruel wit and his cold heart, Sienna would have found him attractive. But no amount of good looks could make up for how he'd treated her. He'd taken every chance to insult her, tease her, and try to cause her physical harm without laying a hand on her. She quickly shook away the fleeting idea of being close to this man.

"Sheriff," Maddie slurred as she stumbled over to the table with her arm around Jolene's shoulder. "I think- I think we should go home."

"Oh yeah? How'd you get here?" Gentry challenged, looking between the two girls with a firm smile.

Jolene spoke up, her words clear, "I drove us. She's a lightweight. Clearly."

Gentry pointed up at Jolene, staring at her with sharp brown eyes. "You text me when you're both home safe, got it?"

"Of course. See you tomorrow," Jolene said sweetly as Maddie sprinted out the door with her hand to her mouth. Jolene rolled her eyes and went over to the bar, and Gentry gave Jasmine a thumbs up, so she handed Jolene Maddie's license with two green tickets paperclipped to it.

"We color code the tickets. They keep the same one all summer, so we know there's no funny business. The green tickets are for the nineteen year olds, red for eighteen, and blue for twenty. Makes it easy to keep track of."

"I'm more concerned over that girl having your number," Sienna shot back with a raised brow.

Gentry chuckled, watching as Jolene opened the door, and the faint sound of vomiting came from outside, followed by a couple of guys groaning in disgust. "My number is on the back of the tickets. They send a text so I know they got home. If I don't get one in thirty minutes, I'll go look for 'em myself."

"I don't remember seeing Domino."

"He's at the stable," Gentry said casually. "He doesn't like the loud music. I'll just walk."

Sienna let out a little scoff, shaking her head lightly. "Doesn't like the loud music, but the gunshots don't seem to bother him."

Gentry smirked at that, but didn't say anything about it. This would have been a good time for a genuine apology, but none came. They sat in silence, not even looking at each other, for forty-five minutes until the door to Jazzy's was pushed open and a petite blonde with fluffy hair and sideswept bangs came rushing through the door.

One of the girls on the dancefloor gasped loudly and yelled, "Annie!" and everyone cheered before half the bar sprinted over to tackle the panting girl in a series of hugs.

"I'm so sorry I'm late," she exclaimed, her voice honey-sweet with the slightest drawl. She gave one-armed hugs to everyone until finally she turned to Gentry with a breathless smile.

The look he gave this girl was something Sienna couldn't quite pin down. She had to be at least ten, if not more, years younger than him, but he looked at her like she was the only star in the night sky. He stood and she scrambled over to him, wrapping him in a tight hug that he returned, squeezing her shoulders so hard Sienna worried he might snap her spine.

When he pulled away, he looked her up and down, holding her hand and twirling her to get a good look at her. "Look at how pretty you've gotten! How's school been?"

"It's been great! I was the romantic lead in our spring musical," she said dramatically before bursting out into giggles. "It was so awkward but I've learned so much. It's good to be home though."

Her gaze fell on Sienna, and she had the most beautiful baby blue eyes Sienna had ever seen. She looked up at Gentry with unmistakable surprise and he quickly cleared his throat and introduced them. "This is Miss Jade. She and her sister moved here from California a couple weeks ago."

"Sienna," she corrected as she shook the blonde's hand. "It's nice to meet you."

"It's nice to meet you, too. I'm Annie." She looked up at Gentry, raising her brows to ask a silent question. When Gentry didn't answer it with words, she changed the subject. "How's Cheyanne been? Have you found anybody to ride her while I was away?"

"Nobody important," Gentry grunted, and Sienna scowled at the insult. "She misses you."

Annie's smile flickered sad and she murmured, "I miss her, too." She quickly brightened up again, much more skilled at switching her emotions than Gentry.

The young woman squeezed Gentry's hands, then looked around before yelling up at him, "I got into the Medora Musical." The smile that grew on his face was the biggest one Sienna had ever seen, and she almost wanted to disappear so they could have this conversation alone.

"That's amazing! Annie, that's so great!" Gentry pulled her in for another hug, then pushed her away to look at her again. "When do you leave? Are you just here for the night? They start next weekend, right?"

Sienna realized Annie's smile wasn't as big as Gentry's, but she wasn't prepared for the way his whole demeanor crashed when Annie admitted, "I turned them down."

He furrowed his brows, shaking his head in disbelief. "No. No you didn't. Annie-"

"Listen, it's not going anywhere. Lonewood needs me this year, not Medora."

"You've wanted to be in that musical for as long as I've known you."

"And I still do! I will. Maybe next year, but this year..." she trailed off, biting her lips together as she looked around the room. "Dad said things aren't great here. He said I should try to come home, at least one more time."

Gentry shook his head, pulling off his hat to push down his sweaty hair. He looked heartbroken. Annie smiled though, assuring him, "It's okay. I just wanted to prove I could do it. And I can. Next year. Okay?" When he didn't answer, she poked his shoulder with a sly grin. "You can make it up to me... My boyfriend is coming out for the Fourth of July. Think you could hook him up with some tickets? So we could drink together?"

Gentry scoffed, shooting Annie a warning look that she didn't shrink from. "This is a Lonewood thing. We don't extend it to visitors."

The little blonde stuck out her lower lip in an obvious pout and clasped her hands together dramatically. "Please, Gentry. I really like him. Pull some strings for me, please."

"Does he treat you well?"

"Yes, he treats me like a queen," Annie answered with a proud smile. Gentry grunted, sparing Sienna an annoyed look before turning back to Annie, who twirled her soft hair around her finger. That wasn't the only thing she had wrapped around her little finger.

"Fine. But I expect you out on Cheyanne everyday while you're here."

"Deal," Annie shook his hand, then turned to Sienna. "So, you're from California? What brings you to Lonewood?"

"I, uh, well, my sister was an actress. She was going through a rough patch between roles and we heard about this place from one of our friends. She wanted to check it out, so I'm here, too."

Annie's eyes lit up and she beamed, her straight teeth sparkling in the awful lights overhead. "Your sister is an actress? In Hollywood?"

"I mean, not Hollywood, but in California. She's more of a dancer, but she's done all sorts of theater work. She's hoping maybe Maude will find something for her to do." She chose not to mention the little display Alex made at the saloon earlier.

"Could you introduce us? I'd love to meet her." Annie looked up at Gentry, but his brows had drawn into their usual scowl. His eyes met Annie's for a minute and he tossed his sharp nose in the direction of Alex and Jesse. Annie gave him a quick side hug, then turned to Sienna with a beaming grin. "It was nice to meet you, Sienna. I'll see you around town!"

They watched as Annie slipped through the crowd, occasionally hugging people who hadn't greeted her upon arrival. When she reached Alex and Jesse, she thrust her hand out to introduce herself. Her confidence was radiant, as if she'd learned it from the mayor herself.

"So, who is Annie, exactly?" Sienna asked Gentry, deciding it was better to not get any ideas without asking. She'd made that mistake once already.

He grunted, leaning his back against the doorframe of the exit. "She graduated the year before last. Theater major. She was really close with Kenzie." He slammed his mouth shut, steeling his jaw.

"I'm sorry."

He scoffed, shaking his head and massaging his temples. "Yeah, me too. Excuse me." He stepped around Sienna to escape farther into the bar before disappearing under a restroom sign.

With Alex preoccupied with Annie and Jesse, and Gentry clearly not wanting company, Sienna snuck out the door to head back to the motel alone.

Chapter 19

As Memorial Day loomed before Lonewood, Sienna prepared to get some honest opinions from their guests when they arrived. She'd been scribbling ideas in her notebook for the past four days and had finally crafted a survey to pass out at the end of the weekend.

"Alright," Sienna started as she appeared in the bathroom doorway. "On a scale of one to ten, how would you rate your overall experience at Lonewood?"

Alex looked startled by the question as she looked up to meet her sister's gaze in the mirror. She spit out her toothpaste before she answered, "Uh, a seven?"

"I'll take a seven." Sienna marked it down. "Okay, how likely would you be to recommend Lonewood to a friend?"

"A... five?"

Sienna scoffed and mumbled, "I'd say, like a three or four."

"Are these surveys going to actually get opinions? Or just make everyone in town feel bad?"

"We're getting to it," Sienna told her sharply, pushing a chunk of hair behind her ear. "What could we offer to enhance your experience in Lonewood?"

Alex's hand froze mid-sweep of her blush to consider this. After a moment she continued brushing the pink color across her cheekbones. "A pizza parlor. And a petting zoo."

Sienna tilted her head to the side, then looked back to her survey. "Weird, but okay."

"The town needs more food options. I was gonna say steakhouse but I feel like a pizza parlor would be a more realistic start." Alex shrugged, then swept mascara over her lashes. "Also I feel like there should be more animals around here than just the horses."

"Because you like animals, but hate horses?"

"I don't hate horses," Alex clarified, "I'm just scared of them."

Sienna flipped to the next page, taking a deep breath and asked, "What would you say could be done better in Lonewood?"

Alex groaned and walked towards the doorway, forcing Sienna to let her through. She sat on her bed and looked up at Sienna with a forlorn expression. "Honestly, I don't know where to start."

"Me neither," Sienna sighed, closing her notebook. "But that's why I'm asking for opinions. I have ten rating questions and five open ended ones. We'll see what the people say. Kennedy is expecting twelve rooms to be booked."

As far as Sienna knew, there hadn't been anyone else in town since the weekend they arrived. It was weird to have three rooms rented out in the off season, but it was weirder that nobody had arrived since. Sienna wondered if one or both of the groups had been sent by the US Marshals to ease Sienna and Alex into their new home.

"I'm gonna go to the office and type these up. How many should I print?" Sienna asked as she grabbed her purse. Alex shrugged, looking through some photos she'd taken of her and Jesse at Jazzy's on Sunday night. It was cute that Alex had found someone nice to spend her time with, but Jesse wouldn't have a job if Lonewood ran out of money due to lack of business. "Hello? Earth to Alex?"

"Maybe like twenty. That way you can hand out surveys if there are day guests," she answered without looking up from the photo she was setting as her phone background.

"Thank you!" Sienna chirped. She fluffed her thick bangs before turning back to Alex. "I think I'll head to the diner for breakfast. You wanna come?"

Alex looked up at that, twisting her lips thoughtfully for a moment. "Naw. I'm okay. You enjoy, though. I'll meet up with you later.

Sienna wasn't expecting her sister to reject her offer, but she forced a smile and nodded. "Sounds good." She glanced around, looking for something to wear over her white lace top.

The motel room was a mess, their stuff strewn everywhere. Sienna tip-toed over their laundry, wincing a bit at the realization most of it was *hers*. Scarlett had never been this unorganized, but Sienna didn't really care anymore.

She reached down and scooped up an embroidered jean jacket that Alex had bought from Kennedy at the apparel shop last week. It had been discarded away from the dirty clothes, so Sienna decided it was safe to borrow.

"That's my jacket," Alex whined as Sienna tugged it over her blouse.

"Mine today, love you, bye!"

After printing twenty surveys at the front office, Sienna practically sprinted around the motel to get a glimpse of Main Street. According to Kennedy, two parties were scheduled to check in the night before, so Sienna was ready to catch their experience from the start.

Kitty was sweeping the porch of her shop wearing a long denim skirt and an embroidered top. She waved as Sienna passed by, but didn't say anything. That was a first from her.

One of the recent graduates flipped the sign to the apparel shop to read "Open", then propped open the doors. A few moments later, her friend did the same with the sign of the sweet's shop, opening the store, but leaving the door closed to keep it cool inside. Sienna still hadn't visited, but the smell that emanated from the building was heavenly. Even with the doors closed, the smell of fresh caramel wafted from inside, calling to Sienna as her stomach growled.

Sparing a look down Main towards the saloon, Sienna noticed Domino tied up to his hitching post at the sheriff's station and decided to pay him a visit. She had a sneaking suspicion Sheriff Gentry wouldn't be in the 'mood' to deal with Sienna during their big weekend.

"Hey, handsome," Sienna cooed as she approached, catching Domino's blue eyes. She reached into her purse and pulled out a box of sugar cubes, dumping a couple into her palm before holding them out for him to devour. While he nibbled on the treat, Sienna reached up and scratched behind the ears with her other hand. "Today's the day. Alex and I get to finally experience Lonewood at its finest. Now I know, I know... it's been fine the whole time we've been here, but now it'll be busy." He finished the sugar as she scratched his neck and got a little closer to lean her head against his side lightly. "I'm nervous. I don't know why. I'm not doing anything, but... I'm nervous."

She leaned away grabbing the bottom of Domino's halter to pull down his face and kiss his nose. "Thanks for being a great listener. I'll sneak you some more sugar on Tuesday, okay?"

The horse bumped into Sienna and she laughed, shaking her head as she gave him one last deep scratch behind the ears. She smiled to herself as she wiped the dust off of her jacket, not bothering to look if Gentry had seen her with his horse. If he'd seen her, he hadn't bothered her, and she didn't feel like verbally sparring with the sheriff this morning.

That wasn't the impression either of them wanted to make to their guests.

When she pulled open the door to the Lonewood Cafe and the little bell announced her arrival, everyone looked towards her excitedly. When they realized it was just Sienna, the staff and the few locals having breakfast all grumbled and went back to their conversations.

"Thanks! I appreciate your warm welcome!" Sienna called out teasingly, causing Brenda to laugh. She gestured towards the counter, and Sienna climbed onto a stool. She'd never sat here before. She'd never come without Alex before.

"Where's your other half?" Brenda asked as she sat down a coffee mug and began pouring Sienna a cup. She followed it up with two little cups of cream, knowing the way Sienna liked it without her having to ask.

"She decided to stay at the hotel this morning," Sienna answered, sliding her finger across the spotless white countertop. "I wanted to see if anything exciting was happening."

Brenda turned towards the kitchen window, grabbing a warm caramel roll and placing it in front of Sienna. She opened her purse to pull out some money, but Brenda shook her head. "On the house for you, Sweetie."

Sienna looked up from under her lashes. She'd put on three coats of mascara, giving her the appearance of big green doe eyes. Her bangs danced right over her neatly trimmed eyebrows, and she played with them absentmindedly as she pursed her lips, shaking her head to silently chastise Brenda. "You're not gonna make any money giving food away."

"Well, sometimes I like to spoil the people I like." Brenda winked at Sienna, then waved at whoever came in through the door. Sienna turned around to see Dakota glide through the door with Gentry right behind her.

Dakota's rhinestone-covered red boots clicked across the tile towards the counter. Her heeled boots added at least two inches of height, which made her almost as tall as her brother. She wore a sleeveless jean jacket over a red blouse, and skinny jeans tucked into her boots.

While Dakota looked like a Cowgirl Barbie, Gentry looked like an idiot. His badge was displayed prominently on his suede vest, which matched the worn out chaps belted over his jeans. The expression on his face told Sienna he knew he looked like a rodeo clown and that he would probably kick his jingling spur up her ass if she said anything about it.

"Good morning!" Dakota greeted Brenda with a bright smile as she sat beside Sienna. "Two coffees please."

"To go?" Brenda asked.

"No, for here, please." Dakota looked out the picture windows facing Main Street. She sucked in a long, shaky breath and clasped her hands together on the counter. She watched Brenda disappear into the kitchen, clicking her tongue until she realized her brother hadn't taken a seat. She looked over at him and asked, "You just gonna stand there?"

He grunted, looking away from Sienna and Dakota with a look of pure disdain. "These chaps are too damn tight to sit in."

Sienna ducked her head to hide her smirk, placing her lips onto the edge of her mug and averting her eyes. She could feel Gentry's cold gaze on her, but if she didn't steal a glance, he'd have no reason to bother her. He could be mad at his sister, who most likely told him to dress the part for their first big weekend of the summer.

It must have been frustrating being asked to dress up like an old western sheriff when he went through the work to go into actual law enforcement. Perhaps, it could be argued, Gentry Wyatt didn't know any better. He'd grown up here, and knew what he was getting into when he joined the police force. However, most people don't go through the rigorous training to be a cop, only to be shoved into too-tight chaps and a ridiculous outfit so they could wander down the street and take pictures with tourists. But he'd do it for his sister. Honestly, Sienna would probably do anything Dakota asked, too.

"Stop fidgeting, you're making me anxious," Gentry griped from the other side of Dakota. Sienna lifted her eyes to see the blonde adjusting her blouse, causing the tassels on her jean jacket to sway as she squirmed on her stool.

She shot her little brother a dirty look, then grabbed her mug to take a long drink of her coffee. Sienna hadn't even realized Brenda had dropped it off. "I can't help it. What if nobody comes?"

"They'll come."

"What if they don't? We need business. There's not enough money coming in."

"Well, isn't that what she's here for?" Gentry raised his mug towards Sienna, and her brows shot up in response. He groaned a little as he finally leaned against the stool. Despite herself, Sienna did notice that the chaps were too tight- squeezing his muscled thighs and pulling against the denim between his legs in a way that left little to the imagination. Sienna quickly shifted her attention to scarfing her caramel roll, desperately trying to think of anything else.

Gentry hummed a little as he leaned his elbow on the counter, and Sienna swore he did it on purpose, because when she glanced over at him, he was smirking at her. "You said you could bring in business with your marketing talents. Isn't that right, Miss Jade?"

Sienna looked from Gentry to Dakota, seeing her brows drawn with worry. "Do you still believe you can fill the motel by the Fourth?"

Gentry scoffed, rolling his eyes, and looking away from the women to stare out the window. "She's not a miracle worker."

"Yes, I do." Sienna glared at him. "If I have support and resources, I can turn this summer around. The motel only has a hundred rooms, we can easily do that in a month. If I have my way, we'll need to build another motel by Labor Day."

"Big talker, aren't ya?" Gentry challenged. He kept his gaze trained on Sienna as he sipped his coffee. The door opened and a couple with a toddler and a baby in the woman's arms came walking in. Dakota sat up straight, but Gentry didn't bother to move. He spared the family a quick glance, then turned back to Sienna with a wicked smile playing on his lips. "You confident enough in your abilities to make a little wager?"

"Gentry, no," his sister hissed under her breath.

"Why not?" Gentry asked, flicking up the brim of his cowboy hat so he could see the women better. "She claims she can bring so much business we won't be able to handle it. I'd like to see her try, wouldn't you?"

Sienna pursed her lips, watching as Brenda led the little family to the booth by the window. The toddler kept looking over at Gentry, probably thinking the cowboy was cool. The child didn't understand that he was actually an asshole.

But Sienna *was* confident in her abilities. She'd been dreaming up options and plans for Lonewood over the past three weeks, and she believed she could turn the town around. Although, if the sheriff kept trying to block her efforts, nothing would get done.

"What did you have in mind?"

"You have five weeks to fill the motel. Every room with paying customers."

"Alex and I pay-"

"I wasn't finished," Gentry cut her off. He pushed away from the stool, groaning a little as he stepped around his sister to face the redhead. He loomed over her with a devious grin, casting a shadow with his broad shoulders as she sat inches from his chest. She tilted her head back to see his face, causing her ponytail to reach the counter behind her. Once he had her full attention, Gentry continued, "If you don't achieve your goal, you leave. You can go alone or take your sister, but we'd actually miss her. But you pack your bags on July 5th and I never have to lay my eyes on your smug face again."

"And what's in it for me? If I can do it?"

"What do you want?"

"I want you to do whatever I ask of you for the rest of the summer. No questions, no complaints. If I can fill the motel by the Fourth, you spend every day until Labor Day following every order I give."

Gentry hooked his thumbs into his belt loops on either side of his belt buckle. His mouth twitched as he considered Sienna's offer. If Sienna had the sheriff's full support, the rest of the town would follow. And she'd have the satisfaction of knowing she had him at her beck and call.

"Gentry, this is stupid," Dakota said quietly.

Sienna didn't look away from the sheriff, even as his sister asked him not to make the bet. She wasn't going to back down, but if he did, she'd breathe easy for five weeks knowing even if she failed, she'd still have a place to live. What would Bridget say if she got run out of town? Would WitSec even care, or would they just let her go on her merry way and make her life somewhere off their radar? They didn't need Sienna to testify, they needed Alex, so if Sienna fell off the face of the Earth, it wouldn't really matter to the government.

The door to the diner opened again. From the corner of her eye, Sienna saw it was an older couple who greeted Colleen by name. She swallowed hard, waiting to hear what Gentry would say.

Say you won't do it, you big idiot.

His lips curled up into a smile and he raised his chin, looking down his nose at Sienna. To her horror, he held out his hand for her to shake. "You've got yourself a deal, Miss Jade."

It was on her now. She should tell him no, but before her mind could catch up, she grabbed his large, calloused hand and shook it. "Deal."

Chapter 20

"BILL CASSIDY. I DIDN'T think I'd see you round these parts again."

Hank's fingers ghosted over his gun as Bill stood between him and the saloon. One of the dancing girls was tied up to the outer porch, wiggling against the old rope as Bill twisted his mustache and grinned maniacally.

"Don't do it, Hank!"

"I gotta do it. For you. For the town." Hank pulled out his gun, but Bill was faster, pulling his gun from the holster and shooting first. Hank stumbled back a step, but not before getting a shot at Bill. Hank gripped his shoulder, deciding the hit he took wasn't lethal, but Bill fell forward dramatically and didn't move, playing dead.

Hank pushed himself to his feet, clutching his arm, even though he'd originally pretended to be hit in the shoulder. He stumbled over to the dancing girl and pulled the rope lightly, causing it to fall around her. She grabbed his face, then called dramatically, "Oh, Hank! You've saved the town!"

"Part of me thinks I should fail on purpose so I can leave this place in five weeks," Sienna droned under her breath. Alex tilted her head to look at her sister and Sienna huffed, "This is really bad."

Alex kicked at the dirt, watching the people around them. At least a dozen families had arrived since Friday morning, all dressed in their western finest. They watched the show on Saturday afternoon with smirks on their faces, glancing amongst each other with expressions that read as humored, but not engaged. This place was fun to make fun of.

"I think you might just wanna pack your bags now. Or beg Gentry to let you out of the bet. It was stupid. This place doesn't stand a chance."

"Don't say that," Sienna whispered weakly as the crowd dissipated. She massaged the bridge of her nose and groaned. "Maybe I'll get lost in the wilderness and never have to face my failure."

Alex didn't seem to appreciate Sienna's comment, side eyeing her as they turned to follow the crowd back down Main Street. "At least you know Lyle won't put you back on Cheyanne again. Are you nervous?"

"Not really. I'm excited to see the Badlands." Dakota had invited Sienna to join her on the big trail ride they'd booked. Every horse that was Lyle's was rented, and the mayor was ecstatic. Seeing as this was the last thing in Lonewood Sienna had yet to experience, she agreed to join. She needed something to pick up her spirits and unlike Alex, she actually did want to get back up on a horse again.

But a sunset trail ride had attracted quite a crowd. Although the entertainment felt a little stale, everybody Sienna had encountered seemed to be looking forward to the ride.

From what Sienna had gathered, everyone who arrived for Memorial Day had visited Lonewood before. Through her eavesdropping, Sienna heard them talking about how things hadn't 'changed since last year' and how 'this used to be better' but they all agreed that they were excited to go riding through the Badlands.

Alex met up with Jesse at the diner, giving Sienna a dramatic salute to wish her luck on her trail ride. Sienna rolled her eyes and started up the road towards Lonewood Ranch. It was still warm and the sun wouldn't set for another two hours. Dakota asked her to meet her at the stables at six, so she had about twenty minutes to make the long trek up the road.

When she made it up the hill and under the iron sign, Sienna saw Annie riding Cheyanne around the corral. The horse bucked a little, but her rider hunkered low to stay on her back, pulling back on the reins in an effort to get her to stop.

"What's wrong, Cheyanne?" Annie asked softly. Sienna leaned against the fence, watching the woman try to soothe the anxious horse. Cheyanne began to back up, tossing her head as she whinnied loudly. Sienna looked to her right to see Lyle inside the corral, watching Annie nervously. The blonde appeared unphased though as called to Lyle, "I don't know what's wrong with her."

"She's never gone six months without being ridden. She basically needs to be broken again."

Sienna saw the worry for the first time in Annie's eyes. Cheyanne started to rear up, and the young woman leaned forward, pressing all of her weight against the Buckskin's neck in an effort to stay on her back. The horse settled down, then snapped her head to the side, ripping the reins from Annie's hands. Cheyanne felt the moment her rider lost control and bucked, but Annie clamped onto the saddle horn as Lyle ran forward to intervene.

Once he had a grip on the reins, Annie dismounted quickly, backing away from Cheyanne as the horse continued to circle around Lyle. Even from a distance, Sienna could see how stiff Annie was. She seemed frustrated. "I don't know if I can ride her."

Lyle swallowed hard, causing his Adam's apple to bob. He struggled to keep his grip on Cheyanne, but managed to drag her towards the fence behind Annie. Sienna stiffened when they saw her, but she just waved weakly. Annie returned the gesture, then pushed her bangs away from her face. She reached up and grabbed Cheyanne's reins from Lyle, and the horse finally followed her without hesitation.

"What's happening with her?"

Annie smiled sadly at Sienna, then leaned her temple against Cheyanne's neck. "I don't know. Maybe it's me; maybe I'm rusty. I don't ride a lot of horses in Grand Forks." She rubbed Cheyanne's nose, and the horse snorted, but leaned against Annie anyway. "See, now you're being friendly! You tried to buck me off, you bitch!"

Sienna smiled as the young woman teased the horse. She reached forward to scratch Cheyanne's nose, but she flung her head up, knocking her hand away. "Well, she likes you more than me. She dumped me on my ass."

This seemed to surprise Annie, because she pulled away from Cheyanne to gape at her. "He let you ride her?"

"Lyle did. The sheriff shot off his gun to startle her and I fell off."

"Hmm," Annie hummed. "You have the time?"

"Almost six."

The young woman sighed and yanked down Cheyanne's halter to lean her forehead against the horse's. "You can't do this right now. I need you to be good."

Sienna leaned her chin on her forearms against the railing. She watched Annie with intrigue, wondering what Cheyanne was thinking. "Does she understand you?"

"Probably not, but she's intuitive. She can probably tell I'm nervous."

"Why are you nervous?"

Annie shrugged. "I don't know. Just feels like it might be the end of an era. I don't wanna let anybody down, but this place isn't my dream anymore. I gave up a lot to be here this summer, and it'll probably be my last one." She watched as Cheyanne looked over her shoulder, flipping her tail to swat away a bug. "I don't know what's gonna happen to Cheyanne. I get that Gentry doesn't wanna sell her, but he won't let anybody ride her either. She's confused, and she's unhappy. It's gonna be hard either way, but-"

She suddenly realized she was talking about something a little too personal with someone she didn't know. If Annie realized how Gentry felt about Sienna, she'd probably be embarrassed, but she just shrugged it off and scratched under Cheyanne's chin. "You ready to be good? And we can go see your family?"

Sienna pushed away from the fence as Annie turned Cheyanne around to walk the corral some more. The tourists were beginning to arrive, but Dakota was nowhere to be found.

For the next twenty minutes, Lyle and Annie led people around the back of the barn to help them up onto the horses, then once everyone was up, they worked together to give them a tutorial of how to ride around the corral. Sienna watched patiently, surprised Lyle didn't make her do it, too. She wanted to get back up on the horse and was anxious to see these Badlands everybody talked so highly of.

They'd been beautiful from the road, but she imagined they were stunning riding through them.

Just before six-thirty, the sound of hooves on the dirt road caught Sienna's attention, and she looked up to see Dakota riding Domino towards them. When she reached the stable, she dismounted effortlessly and walked him over to Sienna and Lyle.

"Wasn't sure if you had a plan for her, but I got Bandit all set up for you to ride," Lyle explained as he gestured to Sienna. Bandit was already tied to the gate, standing there patiently as he waited for someone to ride him. Sienna understood that if all of Lyle's horses had been rented out that meant that she'd have to ride somebody's personal horse. She assumed there'd be someone like Kitty, or Hank, or even Kennedy and Trevor who would loan Sienna a horse for the evening, but she wasn't expecting Dakota to lead Domino over to the mounting block.

She gestured to Domino, as if her plan was obvious. "She can ride him."

"Do you want me to be murdered?" Sienna blurted. She looked at Lyle, whose face began to turn scarlet as he shook his head vigorously.

"That's a bad idea."

Dakota shrugged as she scratched Domino's nose. He draped his head up and over the fence to sniff Sienna, and she rubbed the side of his face lovingly.

"Where does the sheriff think his horse is?" Sienna asked before pressing a light kiss to the side of Domino's face.

"He thinks I'm riding Domino because Bandit needs a shoe replaced," Dakota answered easily. She winked at Sienna and gestured to the splattered horse. "I won't tell if you don't."

Sienna pushed through the gate and climbed up on the mounting block, gripping the saddle horn as Lyle helped her swing up and over the massive horse. Domino shifted as she settled into the saddle and Sienna smiled, imagining he was used to someone heavier riding him. Maybe he'd be thankful for her. He was big, much wider than Cheyanne had been, but when she gave a slight kick of her heels, he walked forward slowly, bobbing his head a little as he fell in line with the other horses.

Annie looked surprised to see Sienna riding Domino, but she didn't say anything as she rode along the line of riders. Cheyanne trotted smoothly, wanting to run. Lyle mounted a tall black horse, then rode to the front as Annie situated herself in the back with Dakota and Sienna.

"Alright, is everyone ready to go?" Lyle called, and several of the visitors whooped excitedly. Lyle opened the gate, and turned his horse around, leading the group in a slow gait towards the national park.

Sienna bobbed along with Domino as they made their way up a sloping hill. The grass was a dusty shade of green, and sparse. There were hardly any trees, and where there were, they were small and sad looking.

But then they made it over the hill and Lyle stopped the group so everyone could pull out their phones to take pictures.

As far as Sienna could see were those beautiful multicolored hills. Every sweeping hill and jagged cliff showed off layers of different colored rock, from bright scoria to subtle tan to black streaks that looked like a trail of coal. A wide river cut through the landscape, carving its way through the Badlands while little pockets of deep green trees created a stark contrast to the short grass that filled the spaces between hills.

It took her breath away. Sienna looked over at Dakota, but the mayor sat straight in her saddle, unfazed as she gazed over the horizon. When she finally looked over at Sienna's wonder-struck expression, she smiled. "Do you like it?"

"It's so beautiful," she gasped out. She'd never seen space like this. A place where, as far as her eye could see, there were no buildings, no people. No bustling life. In this indescribable place, time stood still, and for a brief moment Sienna was allowed to be a part of it.

In the distance, dark flecks dotted the grasslands, moving ever so slightly. Wild animals. Alex's book had shown people riding through herds of bison, and she knew there were wild horses here. She was struck by the realization that this place was truly untamed, unlike anywhere she'd ever visited.

Cheyanne snorted as she and Annie paced along the line of people, asking if anyone wanted photos. When she reached Sienna and Dakota, the mayor handed Annie her phone, but gestured towards Sienna with a tilt of her head. "I have plenty of photos, but you should take one of her. Before the wonder fades away."

Knowing Gentry would throw a fit if there was evidence she'd ridden his horse, Sienna began shaking her head to tell Annie no, but the blonde held up the camera anyway and chirped, "Smile!"

Sienna gave a soft smile, shy and nervous, then quickly turned back to face the Badlands. She didn't want to waste a minute of time looking at the camera when she could be looking at this view.

Even the clouds were stark white and fluffy, like they weren't even real as they hung in a baby blue sky. There was no potential here for Sienna to enhance. It was already perfect.

"Ya know, people like to visit the Badlands, because they are unique. It's something different from the rest of the state. But every once in a while, people really fall in love with this place. Teddy Roosevelt did. He credited his time here to being the reason he'd go on to become president. He saw something here, something special. He made it his home."

Home. Sienna hadn't really thought of Lonewood as her home. This was the town she'd been placed in, plucked away from the home she loved to suffer and hide here. It had been a month and neither she nor Alex had made any attempt to find a permanent residence. It was easier to believe their time here would be brief if they continued living in the run-down Tumbleweed Motel.

But Sienna would consider herself lucky to call this place home. If she could pack up her suitcase and live in the Badlands she would. It made her feel small and unimportant in the most beautiful of ways. It wasn't like living in a city where she was a nobody in a crowd of nobodies. Here, Sienna was just part of the view, part of the painting across this beautiful, wild place. For the first time in a long time, Sienna didn't feel the need to prove herself. She just enjoyed this moment in this place. She didn't need anything more.

"Kenzie loved this view," Dakota said quietly. From the corner of her eye, Sienna saw Dakota suck in a sharp breath. Sienna didn't think she was meant to hear the woman's sad words. It was a memory for Dakota, and Dakota alone.

The group began to move, walking slowly down the hill into the belly of the Badlands. Sienna looked back at Dakota as she turned Domino, finding the woman still staring at the horizon. Sienna didn't know what to say to comfort her, so she didn't say anything at all.

"Are you happy here, Sienna?"

She was surprised by Dakota's question. When Domino took a sharp step down the cliff, Sienna whipped around to ground herself against the saddle horn, focusing on where they were going. Domino moved easily down the trail, but Sienna clenched her thighs against his sides anyway to keep her balance on the sharp decline. Once they reached the bottom of the valley and the land was flat and easy for the horses to walk through, Sienna looked over her shoulder at Dakota again. Her hair billowed over her shoulders, flyaway strands of deep red blocking her view. "Yeah, I guess."

Dakota nodded, looking up past Sienna. Near the middle of the group, Annie rode off to the right, answering questions as Cheyanne easily stepped through the grass away from the beaten path. Cheyanne picked up the pace on her own, and Annie let it happen, allowing the horse to move up a couple of people before slowing her down to the same pace as everyone else.

Sienna wondered if Dakota would ask her to elaborate on her answer about being happy. It wasn't that Sienna was miserable. This place was fine enough. Most of the people were nice. She didn't feel fulfilled, but that could change.

She wasn't sure what she missed about New York. She couldn't quite pinpoint what made her love that life so much, because she didn't have many friends to miss, and she sure as hell didn't miss Mason. She missed her job, but she could work anywhere. She had Alex with her here. As they wandered through the Badlands, Sienna started to wonder if she was ever truly happy with her life, or just happy that her life felt like it was going somewhere. It shouldn't be so difficult to pick out something she missed.

They rode in silence, through the valleys and over the hills until they got to the top of one of the bluffs near where they'd started. To the west, the sky was stunning orange with streaks of pink and blue and purple. The fading light caused the river to glitter like diamonds. The colors of the Badlands came alive as night threatened to fall. Dakota pointed to the east, though, and Sienna looked to see a group of wild horses sprinting down the hills towards the river. They were all different colors, ranging from solid brown to speckled to splotched like Domino.

She held his reins a little tighter, but he didn't even move. He was unfazed by the wild herd, but Sienna was fascinated. A couple horses brought up the rear, leaping down the rocks until they caught up with the rest to get a drink.

Dakota stayed put as Lyle led the group of tourists past her and Sienna, taking them back to the stable so they could head to the saloon for the evening's entertainment. Annie and Cheyanne trotted after the group, but she paused near Dakota and Sienna to look back at the sunset. "It's stunning, isn't it? There's nothing in the world like a North Dakota sunset."

Sienna had to agree. She'd traveled far and as often as work would allow, but there was something peaceful here that she hadn't found anywhere else. It was like the sky was happier here, more at home, and it showed its most beautiful colors to those who ventured into the wilds of this magical place.

Bandit nickered and Sienna looked over, surprised to find Dakota taking her photo with the sunset behind her. When she looked at the photo, she smiled sadly and shoved her phone back into her pocket. "I'll send you the photos when I get home tonight." Sienna nodded, looking back again. She could watch this every night if she had the opportunity.

By the time Annie, Dakota, and Sienna reached the stables, the sun had finally dipped below the hills and plunged the area into darkness. Annie dismounted first, hopping down easily before towing Cheyanne back into the barn. Dakota lingered on Bandit a moment, rubbing his neck as she watched the tourists laugh and talk on their way back towards town.

"What if we had some sort of transportation to get them up here?" Sienna blurted. Dakota turned to her, and Sienna stammered, "Or- or maybe we could start the rides in town? They could all meet at the saloon and ride through town on their way out."

"Then we'd have a dozen riderless horses in town," Dakota chuckled and Sienna blushed. These people weren't used to tossing ideas around in a meeting room. She needed to put her pitch to paper before she started spouting off ideas. She pulled the reins a little to get Domino over to the mounting block, knowing she'd need help getting down. Lyle and Annie were long gone, but Sienna swallowed hard when she realized Gentry was leaning against the fence.

She looked back at Dakota, who didn't seem alarmed. She dismounted Bandit and led him by the reins over to Domino, grabbing his halter and guiding him over to the mounting block for Sienna to get off. "It's not a bad idea by any means. Might take a little bit of brainstorming, but it adds more to the experience. Plus, then they don't have to hike all the way up here."

"What's she on about?" Gentry grunted. Sienna watched him, feeling like a mouse waiting to be devoured by a hawk. His forearms were draped across the fence, and when Domino got close enough, he grabbed the reins from his sister. Sienna was frozen in fear as she stared down at the sheriff, but he just groaned a little and motioned for her to hurry up. "I don't have all night. Let's get a move on."

"You aren't mad?"

"I'm not mad at you," he answered darkly. Dakota just shrugged, walking through the open gate to take Bandit back to his stall. Sienna felt like she'd been abandoned with a wolf. Gentry came around the gate, still holding Domino's reins lightly, then stared up at Sienna with a bored expression. She was waiting for him to rip her head off, but his fury never came.

Instead, his brows furrowed, almost as if he was in pain, and he sighed loudly. Domino knocked his chest into Gentry, causing that smile he reserved for his best friend to return as he reached up to scratch Domino's face.

Sienna managed to get her left foot out of the stirrup, then looked down at the small mounting block, preparing to swing herself over and hopefully land on it without breaking her leg. She was shaky as she pushed her weight on her right leg, not used to the swift momentum needed to get up and down off the horses easily.

She was just about to try to dismount when Gentry's hand landed on her right thigh, causing her to plop back down into the saddle. She stared down at him with wide eyes, wondering why the hell he'd put his hand on her, but he looked up at her with an equally confused expression.

"Why aren't you using the platform?"

"What platform?" Sienna asked. Gentry grabbed Domino's reins and led them around to the back of the stable. There, pressed up against the back wall of the building, was a long wooden platform about four feet off the ground. It was clearly meant to help people on and off the horses. This was where Lyle and Annie had taken their guests, but Lyle had conveniently forgotten to mention it to Sienna. "Oh."

Gentry chuckled as he guided Domino to the platform, and Sienna easily swung her leg over and landed on the wooden surface with a grateful sigh. She managed to wiggle her right foot out of the stirrup, feeling her legs ache from an hour and a half in the saddle.

"Thanks," she said quietly as Gentry turned Domino around to leave. He looked over his shoulder at her, and she wanted to ask him what was running through his head. He waited for her to climb down the steps of the platform, then walked slowly beside her until she reached the gate. He'd been too quiet, and his gaze hadn't nearly been threatening enough, meaning something was off. "So..."

"So?" he asked back, standing in place. He was waiting for her to leave.

Looking down the road to town, Sienna knew she'd be safe making the ten minute walk, but it was dark, and her instincts told her she shouldn't go alone. Although she didn't particularly enjoy Gentry's company, he'd probably know what to do if she encountered a coyote, or a rattlesnake, or a bison. She looked back at him, trying to decide how to word her request without seeming incompetent or desperate, but then Dakota's voice called from just outside the stable doors.

"Bandit is put up for the night. You wanna come down to the saloon for the show or hit the hay early?" She smiled at Sienna, ignoring Gentry completely. It wasn't very clear if this invite was for the both of them or just Sienna.

"I'm kind of tired to be honest. I know I should go to the show to get some feedback, but I really just want to take a long bath and go to bed."

"Alex will be there. She'll let you know if anything interesting happens," Dakota said. She looked up at her brother, then reached over and gave Domino a scratch under the chin. "Have a good night."

Sienna assumed she was talking to her, so she nodded and started walking away, but Dakota kept step with her as they wandered under the sign. Realizing Dakota was bidding goodnight to Gentry and not her, she looked over her shoulder, seeing Gentry lock the gate and walk Domino farther out into the corral. "What's he up to?"

"Whatever he wants," Dakota laughed. She slipped her hair over her shoulder and sighed. "I might be his sister and his boss, but I'm not his keeper. What he does at the end of the day is none of my concern."

It was an odd answer considering how close the two were, but Sienna realized it maybe wasn't that Dakota didn't know where he was going, but rather she didn't feel the need to share it.

"I actually wanted to talk to you about something... kinda personal? I guess?"

Sienna's head snapped up to Dakota and she raised her brow. "Okay?"

Dakota pulled out her cell phone, checking it quickly before shoving it back into her jeans pocket. She looked ahead thoughtfully, as if considering her words carefully. "I know that you've got a lot of ideas on how to fix up my town. I, for one, will be helping you achieve your goal by the Fourth, but Gentry will probably be standing in your way." She paused, fidgeting a little as they walked side by side. "You said he'd have to do anything and everything you asked of him. I guess I just wanted to see what you meant by that?"

Sienna stopped walking, cheeks beginning to color themselves like her hair. She looked at Dakota in horror as she registered what the woman was insinuating. That she had made the bargain in an attempt to get close to him. To go out with him, to *sleep* with him. Sienna began to feel her heart racing as embarrassment spread through her veins.

She shook her head and gasped, "I was thinking of making him paint some shit around town or lead kids around on pony rides with Domino. I don't want him for me. Oh no. No no no- nope." She shoved her fingers through the roots of her hair at her scalp, looking down at the ground before an awful thought popped into her head. She snapped her eyes closed, wincing as she asked, "Is that what he thinks?"

The sound of boots on gravel told Sienna the other woman had continued walking and Sienna had to jog to catch up with her long strides. When she reached Dakota, the blonde answered, "We actually haven't talked about it. I've been busy. He's been busy. He hasn't brought it up, but that was my immediate thought, so I figured I should clear it up with you before bringing it up to him. We'd hate to have any more misconceptions about his love life, wouldn't we?" She smirked and Sienna grimaced. She'd never live down thinking Dakota and Gentry were sleeping together.

"I just want him to stay out of my way," Sienna confessed as they approached the motel. "I'm really excited to see what we could do here, but nothing is going to change unless I have everyone's trust. I've been trying to earn it."

"I know you have. And we do trust you. Even Gentry, he just doesn't want to admit it."

Dakota lingered for a moment, seeing if Sienna had anything more to say. She wanted to say that she'd rather have her neck slit than spend time with Gentry, but that was both a little too on the nose considering their situation with Landon, and yet a little bit of a lie. The lie part she wasn't ready to fully admit to herself, though. "By Tuesday morning the crowd should clear out. I'm leaving surveys in the motel rooms to get people's opinions. Could we maybe call a town hall or something? And talk about the results?"

"Yeah," Dakota replied, "I'll set something up."

Taking that as her cue to leave, Sienna started down the dirt path towards the motel, but Dakota's airy voice called to her, "Do you want me to talk to Gentry? About the parameters of your bargain? Or would you rather do it once he loses?"

Sienna smiled to herself, then turned. "You go ahead and tell him not to get any fun ideas. I'd sooner sleep with Hank than him."

"Oh, that'll definitely get your point across."

"I figured it would," Sienna laughed. It felt good to laugh. She hoped she'd do it more often here. "Thanks for a great evening, Dakota."

Sienna made her way back to the motel alone, unlocking the door and flipping on the dim light. Her body ached, but not in the same way it had after being thrown off Cheyanne. Her legs were stretched out from riding Domino, but it was worth it. That view, that horse, that sunset... it was all worth it.

She turned on the faucet to the tub, running her fingers under it as it got as hot as it could go. While it filled, she pulled her mass of loose curls up onto her head and tied it back with a headband before unbuttoning her shirt. As she shimmied out of the tight button-up, she caught a glimpse of herself in the mirror, and looked down to her jeans. There, on her right thigh, was a very large, dusty handprint.

Her stomach flipped a little as she unbuttoned her jeans and thrust them to the ground, kicking them away with a huff. If she thought about Gentry grabbing her leg to keep her from falling, she'd start thinking about what Dakota said, and then her mind would run away to all the possible things Gentry had been thinking when they were alone at the stables. What he thought she was thinking while they were alone at the stables.

Perhaps he was trying to gauge her reaction, thinking she'd made her bet because she was attracted to him. A normal person- someone who thought about interpersonal relationships instead of job advancements- would have read her end of the bargain the same way Dakota did. And Sheriff Gentry definitely thought highly enough of himself to think she'd want him, too.

That couldn't be farther from the truth though, but Sienna was too blinded by her desire to prove herself to stop and think about what she was doing. Where she'd seen a way to keep an obstacle out of play, Gentry probably saw a woman who wanted to flirt with him. And that realization led Sienna to believe he either really thought she'd fail or he wanted her to want him, which was somehow more insulting than wanting her to fail.

Either way, Sienna had put her foot in her mouth with that deal, and people in this incredibly small town would start to talk. Sienna had wanted to grow her reputation as a business woman, not as a woman who did business in an effort to get close to some guy. She'd never been so embarrassed.

So since it was early, and most of the town was at the saloon, Sienna decided it was appropriate to let out all of her frustrations by screaming into the night as she soaked her aches away in scalding hot bath water.

Chapter 21

By Monday night, Lonewood was a ghost town once more. On Tuesday, Dakota arranged a town hall over lunch. Everyone who worked in the town, from the returning college students to Maude and her senior-most actors, were summoned to the saloon.

The feeling in the air was one of excitement and dread. Sienna could feel the tension building as Bill, Hank, and their families took a seat next to the stage, looking ready to fight for their way of life. Even sweet, even-tempered Kitty looked like she was ready to start a screaming match with anyone who dared suggest changes she didn't like.

Annie entered with the other college kids, but Kennedy quickly caught her and began asking about school. Annie looked over her shoulder at her friends, clearly wanting to align herself with them instead of the motel owner.

The divide between the young people who'd recently graduated or returned from college and the older folks who lived and worked here year round was obvious.

Kitty was loyal to her parents, even if maybe she would rather align with her new friends. Sienna and Alex had always gotten along well with Kitty. When her family wasn't around, she greeted them with the biggest toothy grin, but lately when Hank or Bill were near she greeted them with a firm, inhospitable nod.

Kennedy wanted business, but she wasn't about to burn bridges to get it. She was probably the closest to being on the fence as Sienna would find with the year-round locals. If she could sway Kennedy and Trevor to make updates to the motel, they'd be well on their way to creating a better vacation destination. Even if the entertainment was sub-par, if the beds were comfortable, people might still come just to see the Badlands.

Skylar was ready for any change Sienna could make, but silently. She wasn't about to stick her neck out for a woman who was the very embodiment of why the people didn't like her: someone who thought the world outside Lonewood was somehow better.

As the chairs began to fill, Dakota stood by the door with her hands clasped in front of her stomach. She greeted everyone cordially, but it was clear she was more tense than normal. Sienna stayed by her side, beaming at everyone who greeted her and hoping to appear friendly, trustworthy... someone these people could trust with their future.

"So," Dakota said through her teeth as she smiled, "are you ready for this?"

"Ready as I'll ever be," Sienna admitted, pushing her hair behind her ear. "I left surveys in the motel rooms. We definitely got some feedback."

"Is it bad?"

"It's not great."

Dakota's chest rose and fell as she took a deep breath. She looked down at Sienna and smiled weakly. "Well, maybe this is the wake up call we need."

Sienna's eyelids dropped as she breathed in through her nose. She imagined she was in Manhattan about to give a presentation to her boss. She'd blow it out of the water and go home to tell Alex and celebrate with Mason and-

"So, have you packed your bags yet, Miss Jade?"

Her eyelashes fluttered as she let out a slow, frustrated breath. She looked to her right, seeing Gentry leaning around Dakota to stare down at Sienna with a condescending smile. He adjusted his hat as he looked over his shoulder to greet Colleen, then turned back to Sienna and asked, "After witnessing one of our busiest weekends, do you still believe you can fill that motel?"

She pursed her lips, glaring up at Gentry. She opened her mouth to snap back, but Dakota grabbed her shoulders and guided her towards the stage. "Ignore him. He's just proud. He doesn't want to lose, and he doesn't want to admit that our town needs help."

Sienna grabbed her long skirt to hold it up as she ascended the stairs. She walked over to the microphone, taking a deep breath as she looked at the people sitting below. Alex gave her two quick thumbs up until Gentry took a seat right in front of her, front and center where he could intimidate Sienna with his judgemental stare and smug grin.

Her hands shook as she reached for the microphone, causing everyone to stop talking and stare at her. "Hi everybody. Most of you know me, but if you don't, I'm Sienna Jade. I moved here from California with my sister last month. I..." She looked at Dakota, whose face was paler than normal as she wrung her hands together nervously at the side of the stage. "I used to work in marketing, before the move. At the request of Mayor Wyatt, I got some feedback from our visitors this past weekend about ways we could improve their experience. With everyone's support, I think I could come up with some ideas to bring in more business for all of you."

She saw Hank's jaw tic as he leaned against the table. He leaned close to Bill, saying something that his brother nodded in agreement with. Annie was seated towards the back with the other college students, watching Sienna intently while Maddie, Jewel, and Jolene gossiped behind their hands. Kennedy's brows rose curiously as her husband held her hand tightly. Jasmine, the woman who ran the bar, leaned against the far wall by the back doors, not even bothering to take a seat.

"So, what did they say?" Maude called from the table in the middle where she sat with three of her dancing girls, Joe from the general store, and Doctor Thompson. Maude motioned with her hand for Sienna to continue. "What did they say about their experience?"

Sienna sighed, dreading this part. She pulled out the surveys she'd packed into her purse and unfolded the heap. She took a deep breath, and read off the first one. "Lonewood has been a staple for our family for fifty years. My grandparents brought my parents here, and my parents brought me, and now as a young mom, I'm bringing my kids." The faces lit up around the room and Sienna cleared her throat and gritted her teeth, knowing what she'd say next would bring that positivity crashing down. "Although I love bringing my family here, the town has gone downhill in the past decade. The lodging leaves a lot to be desired, there's virtually no food options, and there's so little to do that we did everything we wanted within two hours. Although we love seeing the same actors year after year, it would be nice to see something new."

"That's just one person's opinion!" Hank yelled aggressively, and Sienna had to remind herself that these weren't even her opinions.

"Now, now, let the lady speak, Hank," Gentry practically purred with his velveteen voice, causing a couple people to snicker at his mocking tone. "I'm curious to know what this big city marketing manager thinks of our hokey little town." His eyes sparkled mischievously, excited to see Sienna fail, but she wouldn't give him the satisfaction of running her out of town without a fight.

Steeling her nerves, she grabbed another survey and read aloud, "Although we've always loved visiting Lonewood, the spirit of the town seems to be dying. The only thing that continues to amaze are the Badlands themselves. Considering we can get the same Badlands with a better experience in Medora, we'll probably take two trips there next summer instead of spending one weekend in Lonewood." She flipped to another survey, not bothering to look up. "With nothing to do but watch the same cast of old folks perform outdated cowboy routines, one motel that's barely being held together by the seams, and a diner that has the same options as a local rest stop, the only part of our weekend we'll gush about is our trail ride. The best part about going to Lonewood is getting on a horse and riding right out of it."

Sienna finally raised her gaze, finding the people silent. Even Gentry's smug grin had been wiped off his face, as if she'd slapped him instead of reading people's opinions of his town. Hank swallowed hard and Maude took a deep, shaky breath and nodded. Kennedy looked to be about in tears, while Bill and Linda held hands while gazing up at Sienna with a melancholy expression.

Alex didn't look surprised. Jesse had his arm draped around her shoulders, mouth drawn to the side thoughtfully. Sienna would have focused on them if the sheriff wasn't sitting directly in front of them, blocking them from Sienna's view. He looked guilty, as if his taunting words were the cause of her cruel reviews. As if he made those people say such horrible things about his home.

Sparing a look at Dakota, Sienna found her gazing down. Sienna shook her head and looked back to the crowd. "Your visitors have given up on Lonewood, but I haven't. This place has potential. You all have potential, I've seen it! If you want people to come back, you need to change what you offer and how you operate. I know it isn't what you want to hear, especially from me." She looked past the sheriff to Alex, and her little sister gave an encouraging nod. "I came out here because my sister wanted a change. This isn't what I'm used to, but I can help if you want me to. If you don't, I'll leave. I'll pack my bags and leave, just like I said I would." Sienna looked directly at Gentry, and he stiffened. He looked down at his hands to avoid her gaze, but from the corner of her eye, Sienna saw Dakota watching her brother.

This was Sienna's moment to make the pitch. She understood that the bet with Gentry didn't mean anything compared to the livelihood of the people in front of her. If she failed, she'd figure out what came next. But if this town didn't change, eventually the people who so desperately tried to keep it afloat would have to leave, too.

"It's not that I don't appreciate what you're all trying to do here, you're just stuck in a simpler time. I love how close you all are- this town feels like a big family. You care about each other and you make sacrifices for one another, but nothing is going to get better if you aren't willing to change. Your visitors could love Lonewood. They could love Colleen's caramel rolls and Lyle's trail rides through the Badlands. They could love spending their evenings here in the saloon, but they'll never know how wonderful you all are if they don't come. We could make Lonewood a huge success, but it would take a lot of hard work."

"How exactly would you suggest we do that?" A voice called out from the back. Everyone turned around, seeing Jasmine with her brows raised, waiting to hear Sienna's idea.

What she was about to say would be the dividing factor among the town, but Sienna had to do it. There was no way around the truth: "We'd need to update everything. The entertainment, the town's offerings, the town itself. A lot would have to change. You all have the potential to create something really special, you just have to be willing to make sacrifices to bring in business again."

When she looked over to Dakota, she saw the corner of her mouth pulled up in a hopeful grin. The crowd spoke quietly amongst themselves, but Hank stood up and called to Sienna with his deep, gravelly voice, "Our way of life is centered around what we do and we've been doing it this way for decades. Who do you think you are coming in here to try and fix something that isn't broken?"

"You really think this town isn't broken?"

Sienna looked past Hank to see Annie standing at her table. Everyone watched her stride towards Hank, glaring darkly. He stammered a little, clearly understanding that the people around him thought highly of the young blonde. "This is our home, Annie. Your family has lived here for generations. If we change, what'll happen to your parents and brother?"

"They'll continue selling cattle, but Owen's kids will have to drive thirty minutes to school, because Lonewood won't have one. It won't have a general store, it won't have a diner, and it sure as hell won't have this saloon, because it'll all go out of business."

Even from the stage, Sienna could see Annie's nostrils flaring as she stood up to the older man. She placed her hands firmly on her hips and waited for him to challenge her, but it was Bill who stood up next to his brother to plead with the young woman. "Annie, what Miss Jade is suggesting could cost us our jobs-"

"In the real world actors don't continue to act if they are no longer performing up to par," Annie shot back. Sienna caught a glimpse of Alex as she stiffened, knowing from experience it was true.

Bill narrowed his eyes and crossed his arms, huffing, "You're saying we're bad?"

"I'm saying that if you want us to keep coming back summer after summer we should get a chance to do more than wait tables and take people out on trail rides. When was the last time Maude held auditions for new actors and dancers? When was the last time we had a script, or a schedule, or even a plan? What Miss Jade is suggesting could change the way people look at Lonewood. When I tell people I'm from here, they laugh. They *laugh* at us, because we're a joke. I'm proud of my home, and I want people to take it seriously."

"We didn't have problems with the young people until that Kenzie Wyatt started trying to change everything," Hank muttered under his breath.

His comment caused the crowd to explode.

The younger people in the back stood up and booed him as Annie took a couple bold steps towards him, fist raised as Bill placed himself between her and his brother. Kennedy swallowed and turned to Skylar, who watched the chaos unfold with a neutral expression.

"Keep her name out of your mouth, Hank." The cold tone belonging to Jasmine sent shivers down Sienna's spine. Everyone turned to her, quieting a little as she approached Hank. "These kids deserve the opportunity to go out and make their own lives. If they come back, that's wonderful, but we have to respect their decision if they don't. Why would they want to come back if we aren't willing to create a good life for them?"

"They should have to play their part, the way we did!" Kitty spat, then immediately shrunk back, as if she realized people might think she had a spine.

Jasmine chuckled and draped her arm around Annie's shoulders. "Ya know, our girl Annie got into the Medora Musical this summer. She turned it down so she could come back home and play her part. She made a sacrifice for this town, but we aren't willing to give her a shot at performing here? She's good. We all know she's good. We let that boy Jesse come and play second fiddle to Hank, but God forbid we let one of our own become more than the rancher's daughter. Kenzie would be ashamed of you. All of you. She dedicated her life to the youth of this town, and she died trying to do something nice for them. You know Braxton couldn't afford college if it weren't for his football scholarship? He wouldn't even be playing football if it weren't for Kenzie. And Annie would have never fallen in love with the arts, which would be a damn shame, because she's great at it. You lit the spark and Kenzie gave them the opportunity to grow it. But these kids come back and you put out their fire. You work them like pack mules, then grumble and groan when they don't want to come back?"

She looked over at Dakota and the two shared a long look. It was sad, and it said so much without a single word. The photo in the back of Kitty's book was these two and Kenzie Wyatt, meaning they'd lost their third. Sienna wondered if they were still close. She hadn't seen them interact since her arrival.

Maude, who had been listening intently to Jasmine, Annie, and Hank argue, turned to Sienna and asked, "If you were me, what would you do?"

Everyone's eyes found Sienna again, and she wished she could sink through the stage and disappear. She sucked in a sharp breath, not prepared to have everyone look to her for more answers after going at each other's throats. "Honestly, I'd update your entertainment. Build a new show. Maybe hold auditions, switch the cast around. Your visitors want something new. That's the easiest place to start."

Maude nodded, chewing through her thoughts until her gaze fell on Alex and Jesse. "I'll consider it."

"What else would you suggest? For the town?" Kennedy raised her hand slightly as she spoke up, her voice small and timid. Her eyes showed panic that her business was on the chopping block.

"Well," Sienna started, "We could start renovating the motel. Start with whatever we can do for cheap and as we earn more money, do bigger fixes. You only have a hundred rooms, there's no reason they couldn't be luxury suites. If they were nice enough you could charge two to three hundred dollars a night."

Kennedy looked at Trevor with wide, excited eyes, then back up to Sienna as Trevor asked, "You really think we could charge two hundred dollars a night?"

"I mean, with some serious upgrades to the current rooms, but yes. Easily." Sienna looked over at Kitty, seeing her bottom lip between her teeth. She wanted to be excited. She wanted to prosper, too, but she was too afraid to go against her dad and uncle. Sienna gave a little nod and turned to Dakota, who was looking up at her with hope in her big amber eyes. "I think we could turn this place around. It doesn't need to lose its spirit, or its identity." She paused, knowing she needed to bring it home now, while she had what little support she had. "I think Lonewood is really special. I know its mayor thinks so. I'd like to show the rest of the world what you all have to offer here."

Dakota stepped up onto the stage with Sienna and the shorter woman took a step back. "So here's the question, are we ready to try? Try to bring in business and make our home the best it can be? Or should we continue struggling to get by and hope for the best? Let me see a show of hands who is in support of some changes."

The young people- the newly graduated seniors and the returning college kids, all raised their hands above their heads. Annie raised hers, as did Jasmine, Skylar, Doctor Thompson, Kennedy, Trevor, and Lyle. Looking around nervously, Kitty slowly raised her hand, and Beau did the same. Jesse raised his hand as Alex nodded at Sienna, silently telling her she'd done a great job.

Hank, Bill, and Linda stared in surprise as the other three saloon girls tentatively raised their hands, followed by Brenda and Colleen from the diner. Maude raised hers last, but did so proudly, assured of her decision.

But Dakota's gaze, along with most of the room's, was on its sheriff. Gentry tilted his head, staring up at Sienna instead of Dakota with those sharp russet brown eyes. When he spoke, his voice was quiet, but stern. "We don't need another Kenzie."

Dakota looked devastated. The hands around the room began to fall slowly. Sienna strode forward though, determined not to let this momentum die. "I won't be another Kenzie. I'm here to offer my services, nothing more. I'm not trying to replace anybody, step on any toes, or take up anybody's agenda. We took a chance on this little town. This is our home now and I can help it thrive. And if not, I'll leave, as promised. What do you have to lose?"

His eyes narrowed, but his lips curved up into a taunting smile. He gave a slight nod and said, "Alright. Then go ahead and try."

Annie let out a loud whoop and the young people stood abruptly and made a beeline for the door, as if Gentry's blessing was the last word.

Everyone else stood slower, but left just the same, except for Annie, who ran up to the stage with a radiant smile.

"I can't believe we're doing this. We're revamping the town," Annie exclaimed up at Sienna. She followed Dakota down the stairs before being tackled by Alex, who squeezed her so tight her back cracked.

"I am so proud of you," she said when she pulled away, still holding Sienna by the arms. "I think we could put together something really exciting, and we can hold auditions and have it up and running by the Fourth. I know we can. You focus on you, and I'll focus on Maude, okay?"

Sienna nodded, overwhelmed by it all. Dakota was talking to Gentry, who stared past his sister to the redhead taking over his town. Annie quickly began chatting with Alex, asking her if she would help with the reworked acts.

As Sienna made her way to the bar for a drink of water, Doctor Thompson intercepted her. "That was quite impressive, Miss Jade. I never thought I'd see the day these people would agree to changing... well, any of it."

"We're gonna try a few things. See what happens," Sienna told him as she pushed her hair away from her face. She fanned herself, wishing the saloon wasn't so stuffy. Better air conditioning would definitely be on her list of projects. "I'm excited to get back to work. I've got a lot of ideas."

"I'm excited to see what you accomplish," Doctor Thompson told her gently. "If you have any free time, I'd love to hear more about your plans for Lonewood. Maybe over dinner? Somewhere a little nicer than the diner, I assure you."

Sienna felt her cheeks heat up even more as the doctor's words settled in. "I'm flattered, Doctor Thompson, but-"

"You can call me Brad. We aren't really that formal here in Lonewood." His dress slacks and leather shoes disagreed with his statement, but Sienna didn't point that out. He pulled a card out of his shirt pocket and handed it to Sienna. "Please give me a call when you're free. I'll see you soon."

She looked down at the business card reading *Brad Thompson, MD* as he left. The back side listed hours for walk-ins to the clinic, and beneath that were much shorter hours for hair cuts. Reservations not needed.

"Shoulda known you'd have Brad climbing into your bed already."

Gentry's smooth voice startled Sienna as she snapped her head up to find him looming over her shoulder. She glared up at him as she shoved Brad's card into her jean's pocket. "Excuse me?"

"Doctor Thompson seems quite taken with you, but then again he'll sleep with anything that'll spread her legs come summertime, so I'm not too surprised. You, though, I thought would be a little more particular, seeing as you're so particular about everything else in this town."

Sienna glared at Gentry, furious that he'd think she was trying to sleep with Brad. "First of all, you don't know me. You don't know anything about me, except that I have ideas to stop your town from falling off the face of the Earth. Secondly, I didn't make plans to go out with him. He just gave me a business card for the clinic in case we needed anything."

Gentry gave her a look that said he'd overheard their conversation and wasn't impressed with Sienna's attempts to downplay Brad's advances. She groaned loudly in response.

"I'm here to work, sheriff. Not fraternize with the local men. So don't you worry your jealous little mind about my intentions with Brad, or anybody for that matter. The only man I'll have the displeasure of seeing on a regular basis is *you*, which almost makes me want to lose our stupid bet just so I don't have to look at your scowl anymore."

Gentry's eyes widened in surprise as his smile grew hungry, excited. He let out a low, dark chuckle that rumbled from his chest and made Sienna go back over all the word vomit she'd spewed. She'd called him jealous.

Oh no.

Gentry leaned in close to whisper in her ear, causing the hairs on the back of her neck to stand up. "Miss Jade, I want to make one thing irrevocably clear: I wouldn't be with you if you were the last woman on Earth. You think so highly of yourself? That I might be jealous that Brad would want you? He'd take anyone, you aren't special. But maybe if you got a good lay you wouldn't have such a stick up your ass. He is a doctor after all, he could probably help you with that. At least you've got his office hours now."

He pulled away quickly, turning to leave without looking back. Sienna sat there, stunned, with her jaw hung open as Alex approached. Sienna hadn't even realized her sister was still here.

"What the hell just happened?" Alex whispered. There was nobody left in the saloon except Maude, who watched them with a sly, knowing smile on her face.

Sienna clenched her teeth, holding back the urge to growl at the intolerable man. "I'm going to fill that motel by the Fourth of July if it kills me."

Chapter 22

The day after the town hall, Maude Rivers finally offered Alex a job.

"You want me to help you design the new acts?" Alex asked as Maude led her towards the stage. Instead of going up the stairs, though, Maude led the younger woman into a back room that turned out to be Maude's office. The walls were covered in old playbills, leading Alex to realize Maude hadn't always lived in Lonewood, and that she hadn't come to run the saloon by chance. The framed photos on the walls were of her in touring companies. She'd been an actress once, too.

Maude caught her staring at one of the photos as she took a seat at her desk. "I was a dancer in *Carousel*. That was one of my favorite tours." She paused, her eyes on the far wall as her mind wandered somewhere long ago. She smiled and looked up at Alex. "I love what I do here, but I never thought I'd see the day when somebody had the guts to stand up to the Cassidy brothers. They've been running the show for as long as I can remember. Every critique I've given for the past thirty years has fallen on deaf ears. But now- now they know their time is up, and if they wanna stick around, they're gonna have to put in some work. But I need help. I can't do this alone. I'm too old for it. I run the bar by myself, and if this place gets as much traffic as your sister wants, I'm gonna need a helping hand. I'd rather place the talent in the hands of someone younger and I can continue doing what I know best."

"But this is your place," Alex said quietly, not wanting to take over Maude's hard work. "I can't just come in and change what you've done."

"You can, and you will. And we'll all be better off for it." Maude said sternly as Alex took a seat across from her. "I want you to be my partner in this process. It's been a long time since I've held auditions, but you're young. I'm sure you've had some recently."

Alex nodded, feeling her cheeks heat up as memories of Broadway came flooding back. "We'll need to advertise that we're holding auditions. We'll see what kind of talent is interested, then build a show around it. I think we should find a way to incorporate the visitors. Like, they can join the villain's gang to rob the bank, or become deputies to stop them. We need charismatic people who could lead that kind of show. I'm not sure Hank and Bill could pull it off."

"I think we can all agree we're tired of Hank and Bill yelling at each other several times a day to no audience. We'll find something for them to do, but I'm not sure how many of the young people will show up. Except for Miss Annie, who is bound and determined to prove Kenzie's death wasn't in vain, the others aren't really actors as far as I know. I'm not sure we'll have much for choices."

"Well," Alex said with a shrug, "we won't know until we try."

The next day, Alex taped up the casting call to the glass door of the diner when she went over for brunch. She took a step back, admiring it until she felt somebody hovering behind her. She turned to see Gentry staring down at the notice with an annoyed expression.

"You can't just post things on public property."

"I'm not Sienna. Go bother her, I got permission to put this up here."

"By who?"

"By Brenda."

He huffed, crossing his arms as he stared at the sign. He looked like he wanted to argue, but the sheriff didn't get under Alex's skin like he did Sienna's. She watched Gentry for a minute, then asked, "Why do you hate my sister?"

He didn't answer. Instead, he stepped around Alex and grabbed the metal handle to open the door, but she stayed blocking it, so he couldn't get in without answering her question or hitting her with the door.

With a groan, he responded, "I don't hate your sister. She's just aggravating. Uptight. Arrogant. Insubordinate. Shall I go on?" Alex scowled, so he added, "I don't find you to be any of those things. Is one of you adopted?"

"Very funny. I'll tell her you said hi, and that you miss her."

"Tell her the past few days I haven't seen her have been the best I've had all month."

Alex snorted and took a step away from the door so he could enter. "I'm sure she's felt the same."

Two days later, Alex sat beside Maude at a table in the saloon. Alex had asked Maude if they could do interviews before auditions to get an idea of what the people were looking to do and what their skills were. Maude's answer was, "Whatever you think is best. I trust you."

Alex was very aware that she'd never been in charge of anything this big in her entire life. Her parents couldn't even trust her with a goldfish, and Maude was trusting her with the town's life blood.

They each had a notebook and pen sitting in front of them and a chair set up across the table for the interviewee. Alex did that thing Sienna always did to calm her nerves: breathed in through her nose, then out through her lips. Over and over again until Maude said, "Don't be so nervous. I'm sure you'll be disappointed. Your hopes are way too high."

That definitely wasn't the spirit they were going for.

Alex waited with bated breath as her phone showed two o'clock, and the door was pushed open to reveal Annie and Jesse on the other side. Alex let out her breath as Jesse jogged over to her, leaning down to give her a hug where she sat.

"I wanted to be the first to audition, but somebody was already waiting at the door," Jesse teased as he nodded towards Annie.

The little blonde thrust forward her headshot, and Alex flipped it over, seeing her acting credits on the back. She smiled up at Jesse and murmured, "Let us talk to Annie first, then we'll see you second. Would you mind watching the door and letting anyone else know that they can come in once somebody comes out?"

"Of course." Jesse leaned down and pressed a chaste kiss to Alex's cheek, causing her to blush. She was waiting for him to make a move and give her a real kiss, but he hadn't been bold enough yet. It was both infuriating and endearing that he was so shy and polite, but Alex needed someone like Jesse in her life. Not only did he make her feel safe and cared for, but he made her be patient, because good things came to those who waited, not those who wandered drunk through the streets looking for a man they'd just met.

As Jesse disappeared through the doors, Alex and Maude turned their attention to Annie. The young woman, who Alex believed was now twenty years old, sat with her back straight and her hands in her lap. Her blue eyes flitted between Alex and Maude, waiting for one of them to speak. She was taking this seriously and wanted it badly. Annie could be the worst actress on the face of the earth, but Alex would find a role for her to play in Lonewood's new story. She'd shown up, ready to fight for what she wanted, and that needed to be rewarded. It would go miles with the other young people if they gave Annie a shot at her dream.

"I know you're studying theater out at UND, but tell us what your strengths are, and how you believe you could be an asset to our show?" Maude said as she rested her clasped hands on the table, leaning against her forearms.

Annie didn't miss a beat, smiling and saying, "I've been taking voice, dance, and acting classes at UND, so I feel very well rounded and suitable for anything really. Of course I'm an avid rider, so if need be I can perform on horseback, but I would love to work here in the saloon as a singer and dancer."

"If you had to pick one, which would you pick?"

A hard and unnecessary choice, Alex thought, but perhaps Maude was more curious than anything. Annie gave a slow nod, not prepared for this question. "I guess, my strong suit would be singing. It comes most naturally to me, but that doesn't mean I don't excel at all three."

Maude nodded, making notes on her notepad before looking over at Alex. "What questions do you have for Annie?"

"What styles of dance have you taken?"

"Tap, Jazz, Ballet, Contemporary. And I learned how to swing dance when I was very young, so I've been doing that socially for years."

Alex was surprised, and she quickly jotted down Annie's answer before asking, "You said singing is what comes most natural to you, what vocal part do you sing?"

"I'm a soprano. I prefer to sing soprano two, but I can hit all the higher notes if need be."

"Why do you want to perform?" Maude asked quietly. Alex stiffened, feeling that it was a loaded question.

Annie slowly inhaled, fiddling with a ring on her thumb. "I always loved to sing and dance, but never thought I could do it as a career. When I was able to join the drama department in Dickinson, I realized I was pretty good. I've excelled at school, but this is my home. I want my family and friends to see what I've learned- what I can do. And I want to make a difference here... it's what she would have wanted."

Alex assumed the 'she' Annie was referring to was Kenzie Wyatt, because her eyes were beginning to water and she wiped under them quickly before raising her chin and smiling through the tears. Clearly Annie and Kenzie were very close, and Annie was greatly affected by her death. It seemed like a lot of them were.

"Would you sing for us?" Alex asked, changing the subject. Annie nodded vigorously and stood, straightening up and waiting for further direction. Alex leaned back in her seat, appreciative of how professional the young actress was. "Sing whatever you want. Whatever shows you off best."

As she began to sing a slow country song, Alex felt shivers run down her arms at the soft, controlled tone the young woman had. There was power in her voice, especially as the notes slid higher, but she never lost her pitch. She sang for a minute or so before ending her song, looking at Alex hopefully.

If she could dance half as good as she could sing, she'd be on Broadway by the time she was Alex's age.

"Thank you. You're wonderful," Alex told her honestly. She looked over at Maude, who gave a firm nod, so Alex said to Annie, "We'll have a list of everyone we want tomorrow. You should expect to be on it. We'll find a place for you for sure."

"Thank you," Annie choked out. She gave an awkward little curtsy before jogging towards the door. When she opened it though, Jesse strode through with a big smile on his face. Annie paused, studying the young man as he looked at Alex.

"I think you'll be pleasantly surprised by the turnout."

Alex and Maude shared a look and Alex got up to check, followed closely by the older woman. She popped open the door, seeing the boardwalk of the saloon packed with people ready to audition. The two recently graduated senior girls were there, as were Jewel, Maddie, and Jolene. Even Colton was standing near Jewel with one hand in his pocket and the other holding up a monologue he was working on memorizing.

Most surprising though, was Bill and Beau, who looked both nervous and excited. When Bill saw Maude, he guided his future son-in-law up to her and said firmly, "He wants to audition, and, if he's any good, I'd like him to take over my part. So it can run in the family."

Maude blinked a couple of times, truly surprised for the first time since Alex had met her. "Aren't you gonna audition?"

Bill shook his head, clamping his hand on Beau's shoulder. "I'm tired of falling dead on my face every day. I'ma see how he handles it, so he knows what it'll feel like if he hurts my Kitty. If this makes him happy, it'll make my little girl happy, too. That's all I want, really."

Alex grinned at that, then motioned towards the doors. They had a long day of auditions ahead of them, and a new story for Lonewood to forge.

By five o'clock, Maude and Alex were weeding through their notes in preparation for casting their new show.

Maude had been dumbfounded by how enthusiastic the young people were about auditioning. The thing that stunned them both was that Hank didn't show up at all.

Whether he had silently quit, or was expecting to continue his act by himself, he hadn't shown up, called, or given word with his younger brother. Bill informed Maude that he was ready to retire from acting, and that his wife Linda felt the same. The other three saloon girls followed Bill's lead, but Alex wasn't sure their intentions had been as pure as his. Perhaps they'd quit to force Maude's hand, not anticipating such a turnout of fresh blood.

Either way, both Maude and Alex were pleased with their options.

Now, though, the problem was a cast of people only around for the summer. Alex was nervous that they wouldn't have enough people to keep the place afloat once the college kids left, but they'd cross that bridge when they came to it. For now, she'd focus on bringing in summer business, and maybe others would move to town full time to be a part of what they were creating.

"So, building from the basics out, I think Jesse should take over as the main deputy," Alex said as she wrote his name at the top of her list, followed by 'Deputy' next to it. Maude reclined in her chair, watching Alex as she took notes. "Since Gentry's around a lot, I think we should just say he's the sheriff. He can be Jesse's absent boss, and Jesse can be our lead protagonist. A young deputy trying to earn his stripes while the sheriff is busy tending to other affairs. What do you think?"

"I think it makes sense narratively, but also allows the sheriff the freedom to do what he needs to. Hank always called himself the sheriff and the old man who Gentry took over from never left the office, so it wasn't an issue. Gentry's out and about a lot, though, so I think including him in the story makes sense, even if he doesn't do anything."

Alex nodded, writing Gentry's name on her list with a little asterisk. She didn't expect him to do much except ride up and down the street like he always did. That was good enough for her. "Beau's a big guy. He's got the look, kind of like Bill did. I think he'd be a great villain and Kitty could be his secret lover. All she has to do is only talk to people who are on his side, while keeping up appearances for everyone else. Little details, but it makes all the difference."

Maude chuckled, nodding to herself as she stared at her framed playbills. "Not a lot going on in that pretty little head of hers, but I think she could manage that. That way, if they're seen together, the story stays intact."

"I'll lead the dancing girls. Maddie, Jewel, and Jolene want to stick together, and they've got decent enough rhythm. During the day they can walk around town, talk to people in character. Colton claims he can ride-

"But Jewel made that weird face when he said it, so I'm gonna need to see it before I trust him with any big horse work," Maude interrupted, looking over at Alex. "The two girls who just graduated can walk around and talk to people too. If Colton can ride, I say we make him another deputy. If he can't, he can just follow Jewel around like the sad puppy he is."

Grinning, Alex jotted down all their notes until Maude asked, "What about Annie?"

Through all the auditions, Alex thought long and hard about Annie. The girl had too much talent to be stuck here in Lonewood. She needed a role that would help her shine the way she deserved. "Annie's tough. I want to give her something weighty to do, but I'm not sure what."

"She's a singer, Alex. Let her sing. She can be the saloon headliner, and she can walk around and stay in character all day."

"But she needs something better than that. She's too good to just be a singer..." Alex tapped her fingers against Maude's desk, spotting a playbill for Annie Get Your Gun. "Plot twist. Jesse is a deputy who wants to be a song and dance man. Annie is a saloon singer who's actually the best shot in town."

Maude followed Alex's gaze to the playbill, chuckling a little to herself. "Miss Annie doesn't know how to shoot."

"But she knows how to ride. She could save the day. It's a dramatic turn for somebody who has the skills to show off. All she needs to do is learn how to shoot blanks safely and she could be our town hero. It's a modern take on every old western. Make the girl the one who saves everybody in the end."

"So if Annie gets the heroic turn in the end, Jesse will have to take a different one. Maybe a romantic one... with one of the dancers who he's attached at the hip to."

Alex blushed at what Maude was insinuating, but it wasn't a bad idea. "He comes to the saloon every night. He dances with her... me."

"Mmhmm, everybody loves a good romance. Especially a cowboy love story. There's something sexy about the rugged outdoorsman and the naughty saloon girl, don't you think?" Maude laughed at herself before studying Alex quietly. "Are you two an item?"

"Not officially."

"Well, why don't you talk to him about this idea before you make any personal decisions. You can play lovers and see how it fits."

"Maude!" Alex squawked, her cheeks turning beet red beneath her wisps of blonde hair. She'd been waiting for Jesse to make a move, but he moved at the speed of a shy turtle. Alex was patient, though, so she wouldn't push him. Jesse would come around if and when he wanted to. "Should we start making calls?"

"I think we should. If we start rehearsals tomorrow, we could put together a small show by Friday. I'm sure your sister would appreciate that."

Alex scoffed. Sienna was all about the deadlines.

"Why don't you run your ideas past Jesse. I'll take care of everything else." Maude stood and gestured towards the door, not-so-subtly telling Alex it was time to go. "Let him know rehearsal starts tomorrow at ten sharp."

The corner of Alex's mouth pulled up as she texted Jesse to ask him to meet her at the diner. Once she hit send, she looked to Maude and assured her, "We'll be here."

By the time Alex wandered over to the Lonewood Cafe, Jesse was already seated in one of the booths waiting for her. Alex saw him through the big windows and swallowed down her nerves, reminding herself that he was her friend. They were actors. Professionals. They weren't school kids like Jewel and Colton. They could work together and keep this level of decorum and camaraderie that they'd built over the past month.

Alex blew air through her lips as she walked around the building towards the door. She really liked Jesse. She liked how comfortable she was around him. They didn't know each other super well, but she enjoyed his company. If anything, he was a great friend, but she was nervous how their dynamic could change with this new storyline. With Sienna pouring herself into her new project, Alex really only had Jesse to keep her company. She didn't want to make things awkward between them, but there needed to be some sort of romance in their play, otherwise it would lack depth.

Even as her mind ran through all the horrific outcomes of this conversation, Alex's long legs took her over to Jesse's booth. He beamed up at her as she slid in across from him, and he held his hands out for her to take. She realized she was shaking as she placed her palms in his.

"Hey you, what's up?" Jesse asked gently, clearly sensing something was off. He clutched her hands a little tighter, rubbing her knuckles with his thumb. When she didn't answer, he said quietly, "Talk to me, Alex, what is it?"

"I like you," she blurted. His brows shot up in surprise and she started rambling, "I like you a lot. Maybe it's because we flirted when you thought I was a tourist and then you were so sweet and awkward when you realized I wasn't, or maybe it's because you're always the first person to greet me and ask about my day, and it's probably also because when we danced, I felt really, really happy. I haven't felt that happy in a long time and it's because I liked dancing with you. I like being with you, and I've been hurt before, and I'm scared to tell you that Maude and I want you and I to act opposite each other and I don't want to make anything weird between us, but I think..." She paused, taking a breath. "I think that ship has sailed."

Jesse stared wide-eyed at Alex for a moment, then leaned across the table to press his lips against hers. Alex met his kiss instinctually, reaching across the table to grab his cheeks. He pushed her hair back and she smiled, giggling as he pulled away and kissed her cheek.

"I like you, too. I didn't want to be too forward. I know the move hasn't exactly been easy and I didn't want to complicate things. But I like you, too." Jesse scooped her hand off the table and held it tightly. Alex realized he was shaking a little bit now, too. "Now, what was it you said about us acting opposite each other?"

Alex stepped out of the booth and slid in beside Jesse, sliding her hand into his and leaning her cheek against his shoulder. "So, we're gonna make you a dancing cowboy. A deputy, who tries to win over the saloon girl, which is me. And while I distract you," Alex leaned up and kissed his lips quickly, "Annie will swoop in and save the day. And you and I will live happily ever after... well, not us, but-"

"I know what you meant," Jesse said quietly as he rested his chin on Alex's head. She'd never been with a man this gentle. She'd always gone for guys who were bold and commanding, but Alex appreciated that Jesse just let her be. It was a nice change of pace.

Everything about this life was a nice change of pace.

She leaned away to smile at him and he kissed her softly until they were interrupted by Brenda clearing her throat. The pair looked up at her, and Alex felt her skin begin to heat up in embarrassment. Brenda had a smug expression as she stood above them with her pad and pen in hand. "It's about time."

Chapter 23

While Alex ran auditions for Lonewood's new entertainment, Sienna focused on bringing in visitors to see them perform.

Dakota paced behind Sienna, muttering, "I don't know where to begin."

"Well, that's what I'm here for," Sienna assured without looking up from the computer. After several days of tweaking, the website was ready to be relaunched, promising a new experience in Lonewood.

Now they had to make sure they delivered on their promises.

Sienna let out a heavy sigh as she clicked the button for the site to go live, then leaned back in Dakota's desk chair. "Alex assured me she'll have some semblance of a show ready by Friday, so we just gotta get people to show up. We need to update the motel. That's our first priority, then we'll go from there. You said you found someone to run the photo studio?"

"Yeah, Miss Rose. She isn't available all the time, but she said she'd be happy to help dress everyone up for portraits for two or three hours on the weekends. I figured it's better than nothing." Dakota settled into the chair across from Sienna and asked, "What else can I do?"

For the past three days Dakota had done everything Sienna needed. She drove to Dickinson to pick up the new curtains Sienna ordered for the motel rooms, as well as a hundred rooms worth of cleaning supplies. She'd allowed Sienna full use of her computer and office, even going as far as to let Sienna clutter her desk with pages and pages of notes she'd compiled over the past couple of weeks. She'd kept Sienna company as she spent hours and too much of Lonewood's humble budget on advertising, but Dakota was *still* asking what more she could do to help.

Sienna grinned, already knowing what she was going to request this time. "Well... I was hoping you'd go riding with me to get some updated photos of the Badlands for the website. Not that I don't love the ones you took of me, but I need some without me in them. I definitely don't need my photo plastered all over the internet."

Because Landon Maddox could find it and come here to kill my sister.

"I'd be happy to take you riding," Dakota told her, but the lilt of her voice told Sienna she had more to say. "But if you want some good photos, you should take Gentry. He's really good."

"At what? Making people disappear?" Sienna scoffed. "Because that's what'll happen if he and I go anywhere together."

"No, he's a good photographer," Dakota laughed. She smiled to herself, lost in her own thoughts for a moment. "But you're right, I'm less likely to let you fall off the side of a cliff, so we'll plan something soon... May I?" She gestured to her computer and Sienna quickly stood to give Dakota her chair. She clicked the mouse, eyes scanning the computer screen as she spoke with Sienna. "I know the photos we had on the site were fine, but I think I've got some that'll be even better."

"Are they Gentry's photos?" Sienna droned, already having a pretty good idea of what Dakota was going to show her.

"Maybe"

"The website doesn't need new photos," Sienna grumbled as she watched over Dakota's shoulder. She saw the blonde click a folder and bring up hundreds of small thumbnails.

Sliding the chair from the desk, Dakota gestured to the screen proudly. "I know you two don't get along, but he's really good. It's not like he'll ever know."

Sienna took Dakota's spot in the chair and pulled herself closer to the desk. "That's what you said about me riding Domino."

A tiny snort escaped Dakota as she stepped away, giving Sienna space to look through the photos. She clicked on the first one, bringing to life a stunning picture of the Badlands with storm clouds overhead. She moved to the next, seeing the same scene from a different angle, but a herd of wild horses galloped through the grass as lightning struck one of the hills in the distance. Sienna's mouth fell open in surprise as she scrolled through the photos, seeing beautiful images of the Badlands capped with snow, bison shuffling through the deep banks of white fluff with ice stuck to their fur. And sunset pictures, with the magnificent sky and the clouds that looked too perfect to be real. Pinks and purples and oranges blended together to make the photos look like paintings, because nothing on this earth should be that beautiful.

"These are stunning," Sienna said softly, flipping through the photos until they turned into ones of Lonewood: a photo focused on Bill shot from behind Hank, giving their poorly planned standoff an epic feel, Maude sweeping the porch of the saloon, and finally, a photo of all of Main Street taken from the motel. Horses were tied up in front of several of the buildings, and in front of the bank at the far end of the photo, the smoke from Hank's gun hung in the air.

Sienna looked up at Dakota, seeing her beaming proudly. "I hate that Gentry took them."

"Eh." Dakota shrugged her shoulders. "Someday you two will look back and laugh at all this. He's warming up to you."

Shaking her head, Sienna sighed. The photos *were* beautiful. Better than anything she could ever take. It would be enough to pique interest, and the people scrolling through wouldn't ever realize what a pain in the ass the man behind the camera was. Just because Gentry aggravated Sienna didn't mean he was good for nothing.

"I'm gonna swap out some of the old pictures for these," Sienna explained, but she couldn't keep the exhaustion from her voice. "Shouldn't take more than an hour, but you can go if you want."

Dakota sat in the opposite chair again, getting comfortable. "If you're working, so am I."

"You really don't have to stay-"

"You're doing all of this for my town. I'm more than happy to help in any way I can, even if it's just keeping you company." Dakota watched Sienna thoughtfully before saying, "You could have just as easily lived here for a while, kept your head down, and left without really giving it a chance. Why did you? Give it a chance?"

Sienna considered this for a moment. Part of her wanted to prove to herself she could rebuild her life, and helping to save an entire town seemed like a project worthy of someone who'd almost reached the top.

But part of her just wanted to do something nice for these people, because they were nice to her and Alex. They'd been welcomed into Lonewood with open arms by almost everyone, and Sienna could help them make a better life for themselves. It felt wrong to not try after everything they'd done to make her and Alex feel at home.

"I guess, I wound up here by accident," she said slowly, "and I realized a lot of good people were trying really hard to make something work that wasn't going to. I know how badly you want your town to survive and I think I can help. I want to do my part, because you're all so good to us."

Nobody back home had been this good to us.

Sienna wondered if any of her coworkers back home missed her. She wasn't sure anyone was even sad that she was gone. With her out of the way, someone else would get the promotion she'd worked for. Someone else would get the life she'd fought so hard for and Sienna wondered for the first time if people were *happy* she was gone.

She wasn't sure she had any real friends who would have mourned her back in Manhattan, but Sienna had found a true friend in Dakota. She wouldn't take her for granted.

Dakota looked touched by Sienna's words. She gave a little nod before motioning to her computer. "Why don't we call it a night? The website isn't going anywhere and tomorrow's gonna be a long day." Dakota grimaced a little, asking sheepishly, "Are you sure you don't need me to help at the motel tomorrow?"

"I'm positive. You've done more than enough." Sienna saved a couple of her favorite photos to the desktop. She wouldn't admit it, but she'd be sending a couple of these to herself next time she was in the office.

By nine the next morning, Sienna was at the front office asking Kennedy and Trevor for the keys to the motel rooms so she could start replacing curtains and cleaning the windows.

"Do you think anybody else would be willing to help?" Sienna questioned as she poured water into a bucket of soap. With one hundred and twelve rooms to clean, it would take hours, if not days. She at least wanted the curtains changed and the windows cleaned. She'd figure out the next project by Monday.

Kennedy shrugged, unlocking the first door and propping it open with a foot stopper. Trevor pulled up a small step ladder so Sienna could reach the top of the window outside while he helped his wife put up new curtains in the room.

"Most of the young people are working with Maude and your sister. You could always ask Dakota if she and Gentry would help?"

"I'd rather drown myself in this bucket of bubbles," Sienna mumbled to herself, and Trevor snorted, but his wife didn't seem to catch it. "Dakota has a meeting later. I don't wanna bother her," Sienna called a little louder as she reached up to scrub the top of the window, letting the foamy water drip down the glass.

She wiped from the top to the bottom, already seeing a difference. Inside, Kennedy and Trevor worked to rid the window of the dirty curtains and hang up thick, deep red drapes. Already the rooms looked homier. The red gave a warmer feel as opposed to the thin white curtains that looked cheap.

Kennedy and Trevor moved around to the outside to see how it looked, and Trevor nodded in approval. "These are really nice. Thank you for doing this."

"Of course! Thank you for being willing to let me have some input." They'd given her the go ahead to do whatever she wanted with the rooms. To buy whatever she thought would work well and to tell them what she needed. Sienna was used to being given some free rein, but never full control over such a big project. It just reminded her how high the stakes were for her to succeed.

"I'll give Kitty a call, see if she's free since Beau is working for Maude now. Maybe Lyle has some time to stop by. This would go a lot faster with a few more hands." Kennedy watched as Sienna grabbed a dry rag, wiping down the window till it was spotless. Only ninety-nine more to go. Kennedy raised a brow and hummed, "I think you should call Dakota.

She's never that busy. They have lunch every day before Gentry goes back to the station. She'll be free around one."

Every day since Sienna met Dakota, she had a meeting over lunch. Sienna hadn't really considered who Dakota was always so prompt to meet, but she should have guessed it was Gentry. "What is their deal? I get that they're siblings, but they are weirdly close."

Kennedy and Trevor shared a look, and the man cleared his throat as he grabbed the wet rag and moved around to the inside of the motel room to clean the other side of the window. Sienna watched him, waiting for one of them to answer, but nobody spoke until the window was cleaned and dried, shining in the June sunshine.

"She feels bad," Kennedy said softly. She tilted her head, watching her husband as he locked up the room and used a different key to unlock the next one. He climbed the step ladder, perfectly content to do Sienna's work if it meant he didn't have to be a part of this conversation. Kennedy shot him a look and told Sienna, "I don't know what she's told you and it's not my place to talk about it. Dakota is protective over him after what happened with Kenzie. I'll say that much, but if you want to know more you're gonna have to ask her."

Sienna nodded. Everything always came back to Kenzie. She understood that losing their sibling could make them closer, but she didn't understand why Dakota would feel bad about it.

"You two gonna gab or are you gonna help?" Trevor teased and Kennedy swatted his backside, causing him to laugh. He finished wiping down the window and moved into the room to hang the next set of curtains, leaving Sienna to ponder his wife's words. Kennedy smiled weakly and Sienna pulled out her phone to ask if Dakota wanted to help them after lunch.

As Kennedy predicted, Dakota was more than happy to stop by after her lunch meeting and help until it was done. Lyle and Trevor were able to install the curtains in a little over three hours, and Kitty, Kennedy and Sienna followed behind them washing the windows.

At exactly 1:10, Dakota sauntered up to the motel in a pair of short shorts and a tank top with her hair piled up on top of her head. She looked down the row of motel rooms, clearly impressed with what they'd accomplished. "They already look so good! What can I do?"

"We've got another thirty windows to wash," Sienna explained as she hopped down off the step ladder, wiping her hands on her jeans. "If there's time, I'd love to do the mirrors in the bathrooms, give 'em a really good shine."

Dakota looked past Sienna at the motel doors, nodding absentmindedly. "We can start on that if you'd like? Or finish the windows, whatever you need."

Sienna narrowed her gaze at Dakota, placing her hands firmly on her hips. "Who's we?"

The mayor smirked and shoved her hands in her back pockets, looking over her shoulder at the parking lot. Sienna wiped her forehead with the back of her hand, not in the mood to deal with the ever-present sheriff. Instead, though, after a few moments, Alex came bounding down the road with Jesse, followed by Annie and the other college kids.

"What's this? Thought you guys were practicing?" Sienna asked Alex and her sister shrugged, sharing a knowing look with Dakota.

"Well, we can practice anywhere. Tell us what to do and we can practice while we work."

Kennedy handed Alex a bottle of Windex and a couple dry rags. Alex led Jesse, Annie, and Jolene towards one end of the motel while Maddie, Jewel, and Colton started towards the other end to work their way towards the middle.

Dakota waited for directions from Sienna, but she was too overwhelmed to speak. "I can't believe they all showed up to help."

"Why wouldn't they? We all gotta pitch in if we want this to work," Dakota said, raising her chin proudly. "Now what else can we get fixed up?"

Sienna tilted her head to the side to look at Kennedy, and the woman blushed. "The water heaters could use some work. When the motel is full hardly anyone gets hot water. And the outlets aren't in the best of condition. We don't have time to go through every room every time so we only know something is wrong when somebody says something."

"I can call in a plumber to take a look at the water heaters. Then I'll start tightening the outlets. Let's get a night light or something to test them and make note of what doesn't work. If we need to hire an electrician we can do that, too." Dakota pulled out her phone to call a plumber and Kennedy quickly scampered after her with her hand up, trying to get her attention.

"We don't have money for a plumber-"

"The city will pay for it. Don't worry about it," Dakota assured her, then smiled into the phone as the plumber picked up.

Kennedy turned to Sienna with her jaw slack, looking both thankful and overwhelmed. "We've struggled every year since we bought this place. Do you really think this summer could be different?"

Sienna nodded, wanting so badly to make it happen for Kennedy and Trevor. "Yes, I do. I'm gonna do whatever it takes to fill this motel. Even if I have to scrub the windows every week."

They both laughed at that as Dakota returned. She shoved her phone in her pocket and turned to Kennedy. "Plumber will be here tomorrow morning. He thinks he'll be able to have the water heaters working before check-in at three. We're gonna keep moving along with the cleaning and making sure everything works, okay? You and Trevor take a break. We've got this." She turned to Sienna and pointed at her warningly. "And you, too. Let me know if you think of anything else we can have ready for tomorrow."

"But-"

"No buts. Take a break. Take a cold shower. They'll all be hot by this time tomorrow."

That sounded nice, actually. Sienna had been scrubbing windows for hours. Her fingers were pruney from the soapy water and her fingernails were brittle. She'd love nothing more than to take a cold shower, paint her nails, and take a nap.

"Are you sure?"

"I'm positive," Dakota assured her. A little smile played on her lips as she gestured towards Sienna and Alex's motel room.

She didn't need to be told twice. Sienna shuffled her way to her little home, unlocking the door and letting herself in. She padlocked the door, then leaned against it and closed her eyes. The room was cold, a stark contrast to the dry heat outside.

The new drapes were thick enough to block out the sun, creating a dark little haven for her to rest in. Sienna pulled off her sweat-covered tank top and discarded it on the floor before shimmying out of her jeans and flopping into her bed in her sports bra and underwear. She needed a shower because she smelled horrible, but Sienna could shower after she napped.

Laughter echoed from outside, and Sienna smiled a little when she recognized her sister's voice. She could hear Alex and Jesse chatting outside the door as the knob began to wiggle, and Sienna flinched, knowing she should let her sister in but wanting to stay in bed. The wiggling stopped, though, and she heard Alex tell Jesse she'd come back later for whatever she wanted to get.

Music began blasting from somebody's car, making it less peaceful, but no more difficult to rest. Sienna smiled to herself, imagining everyone having fun while they fixed up the motel. The smallest, deepest part of her wanted to join her sister and her friends, but sleep won out, and Sienna let the sound of music and laughter lull her to sleep.

Chapter 24

To Sienna's surprise, people came to visit Lonewood that Friday and a few more families arrived on Saturday. Once those families left, a couple more trickled in on Monday and Tuesday. At any given point, there weren't more than fifteen to twenty people visiting the town, but they seemed impressed by what they found. And if their steady increase in business was any indication, people were telling their friends.

While having breakfast at the diner, Sienna overheard one older woman telling her family that she was surprised at how nice the new motel rooms were, as if the new curtains somehow made the beds shriek and whine a little less. At least the water stayed hot.

Later that day, as Sienna drank a cup of coffee on the porch of the mayor's office, she watched a family following Jesse around until Beau appeared from the bank holding a bag of fake money in one hand and a gun in the other. The children shrieked and ran behind Jesse, but the deputy shot Beau, causing the larger man to fall and drop the money. The paper cash and coins fell everywhere, and the kids collected some of it before Jesse asked if they'd help him return it to the bank while he arrested the bad guy.

That evening at the saloon, Alex teased and flirted her way through the crowd while the young college girls kicked up their frilly skirts and giggled whenever Alex would make a man blush. Jesse watched silently with a beer in his hand, raising his brow questioningly whenever Alex would throw him a wink or a wave. The crowd ate it up, but when Annie leaned against the wall near the stage with her guitar in hand, everyone fell silent.

She was a headliner. That was clear from the first line she sang. Sienna understood why Alex wanted her to be both saloon singer and gun-slinging hero, because her smile was electric and her voice was like honey. Soon, once they'd found their footing, this girl would be the face of Lonewood.

Already, videos of her singing were beginning to hit social media, along with Jesse and Beau's scuffle on Main Street. Sienna posted in the bio of their Instagram for people to tag Lonewood for a chance to be featured, and suddenly people were calling and asking if this was "the Lonewood with the blonde country singer".

Dakota was thrilled. She floated through town, helping where she could since the businesses had more visitors than they knew what to do with. Brenda had two of the four former saloon girls working at the diner to pick up the extra slack, while Bill and his wife helped Kitty in the store now that Beau was a professional actor. The ice cream shop was run by the two recently graduated boys and Leah since school was out for the summer, while recent grads Chloe and Dana sold western wear next door. The town was all hands on deck, everyone doing their part to help, except for one incredibly stubborn sheriff who sat in his station all day, ignoring everyone's efforts.

At least that left Domino unattended.

One morning after breakfast, Sienna approached the Paint with a big grin, holding out a handful of sugar cubes for him to eat. "It's so busy, right? Kennedy says about a third of the rooms are booked, which means we're getting there." Sienna brushed her fingers across the side of his neck while his lips gobbled up all the sugar in her palm. "To be honest, I'm surprised, but... I don't know if we'll fill the motel by the Fourth."

Domino tossed his head, flicking his tail to get some bugs away. Sienna knew he couldn't understand her, but she liked talking to him. She could usually sit in silence with her thoughts, but since moving to Lonewood, the quiet drove her mad. Or maybe she was lonely since Alex spent so much of her time with Jesse, starting to find his bed more comfortable than her own. Sienna didn't like coming home to that empty motel room, but she wouldn't mention it to Alex and risk making her feel bad. Sienna would choose the comfier bed too if she had the option.

"I might have to leave. Might being the key word. I don't think the sheriff actually has the power to run me out of town, but... I should have never made that bet. But I'm really proud of everything we've accomplished. Everyone's working so hard. Most everybody. Your owner is a stick in the mud. I'm sorry you have to deal with him. Maybe if I have to leave town, I'll steal you away and we can ride off into the sunset... would you like that?"

She looked over her shoulder when she heard the slight crunch of boots smushing dirt behind her, finding Alex watching the exchange wearily. "Why are you talking to the horse?"

She was dressed in her finest saloon garb, with the ruched skirt and purple corset top that made her breasts look plumper than they actually were. Her blonde hair was pulled back in a sweeping updo with only a few curled tendrils around her face. She watched Sienna with a patient, albeit uncomfortable, expression. Even after seven weeks in Lonewood, the horses made Alex uneasy. Especially Domino, who was bigger than the others with those piercing blue eyes that followed Alex around, as if he understood that she was scared of him.

Sienna stroked his face as he stared at Alex. "I'm gonna miss him if I leave. I'm taking every opportunity to spend time with him in case I never see him again."

Alex rolled her eyes and crossed her arms, causing the corset to push her breasts up even more somehow. Sienna chortled. "Save those for Jesse."

With a huff, Alex turned her nose up in the air as she moved her hands to her hips. "I was just going to say that you aren't going anywhere. Bet or no bet you aren't leaving me. This is our home now. You aren't going to abandon me here."

"Tell that to the sheriff," Sienna huffed. She pulled away from Domino to hold his halter in both hands, lowering her voice to mock Gentry. "I'm the sheriff and this is my town and I'm gonna run that good-for-nothing Miss Jade out of Lonewood if it's the last thing I do."

Alex covered her mouth to hold back her laughter. She leaned her head to look away then quickly stood up straight and smacked Sienna's arm to get her attention.

She lowered her voice and leaned in close to Domino. "I love you. I wish I could take you out riding again so you weren't standing around by yourself all day."

"Sienna," Alex hissed warningly.

"No, go on. Tell me your plans to run away with my horse. It's romantic."

Sienna stood a little straighter and slowly turned towards the mayor's office to find Gentry leaning against the railing. His brows were raised, as if baiting her to continue, but his lips were curved up into the wolfish smile that made Sienna's skin prickle.

He wore the full uniform every day now: chaps, spurs, and all. He used his index finger to push the brim of his hat up a little so he could see her better.

"How long have you been standing there?"

"About thirty seconds, but I've been sitting on the bench the whole time. You city folk should learn to take a look around before going about your business."

Cheeks beginning to heat up, Sienna took a step closer to the porch and snarled, "You are insufferable."

Gentry nodded, accepting the insult casually. He groaned as he stood straight, stretching his back before sauntering down the steps. His spurs jingled as he approached, but Sienna held her ground.

A small group of people had formed, clearly thinking this part is the show.

When he was hovering over her, the smell of dust and cologne suffocating Sienna, he said, "You know theft is cause for arrest."

Sienna scrunched her face, unsure what the hell he was going on about now. "I didn't steal anything."

Gentry pulled out his phone, typed on it slowly, then played a clip of her voice saying, "I'll steal you away and we can ride off into the sunset."

"You were recording me? Without my knowledge? Pretty sure that's legitimately illegal," Sienna spat. She shoved him in the chest with her pointer and middle finger, but he was solid as rock. He didn't even flinch. "If I say I'm gonna rob a bank and don't, I've still done nothing wrong.

You can't arrest me for wanting to save poor Domino from spending his life with *you*."

Suddenly Gentry's firm grip was locked onto her wrist as he spun her around, pinning her hand behind her back before grabbing the other. She scoffed in disbelief, looking over her shoulder as he shoved her towards the outside jail cell. "You can't be serious!"

"It's my town, my rules, right?" He sounded like he was trying not to laugh as he shifted both of Sienna's small wrists into one of his big hands so he could use the other to unlock and open the jail cell.

Sienna would go to her grave before she admitted to anyone that she found it sexy the way he handled her so easily. She'd been deprived of any kind of physical touch since arriving in Lonewood and having the sheriff hold her hostage made her heart pound excitedly.

Then the moment he pushed her into the cell and released his grip, Sienna came back to her senses and whipped around to glare at him. "Gentry, let me out!"

"This is part of the experience! You said you were planning to rob the bank, so I caught you, because I'm the sheriff. All just part of the show, right?" He let out a true laugh this time and Sienna groaned.

"I did not say that. Not even a little bit."

"Eh, selective hearing," Gentry muttered to himself as he turned the key to lock her in. She ducked her head a little when she realized people were taking pictures. At first, embarrassment filled her for being part of the spectacle, but then she remembered they were supposed to be hiding.

"Gentry, please." Her voice dropped to just above a whisper, scared and desperate. For a moment the sheriff's gaze lightened, as if he understood something was really wrong, but as quickly as that sympathy came, it vanished and he huffed.

"Leave Domino alone." He turned to Alex and smirked, dangling the oversized keys in front of her. "I'll leave the keys so you can let her out when you see fit."

Sienna realized he'd had his fun and Alex put her hand out for the keys, but instead of handing them over, he clipped them to Domino's halter.

Knowing full well Alex was too scared to get them off, he turned to Sienna with a grin and gestured to his horse. "Your sister's in charge now. Hope she finds you more tolerable than I do."

"This isn't funny."

He snorted before letting out a dry laugh and pointing to himself. "Then why am I laughing?"

"Because you're a sadistic asshole," Sienna hissed under her breath so their small audience couldn't hear. She reached for her phone in her back pocket, threatening, "Dakota is going to be livid-" Her hand reached her pocket and realized it was flat against her butt. She gasped and glared at Gentry when she saw him holding her cell phone. "You pick-pocketed me?"

"My deputy Jesse says there's a ring of... unsavory individuals running around town. Can't have you calling in the reinforcements."

"This isn't a game, let me out!" Sienna snapped. "You aren't an actor, you're law enforcement, and you can't just arrest people for fun-"

"Oh, quit your barking."

"I'm not a dog," Sienna practically yelled, which only made him smile brighter. She huffed and stuck her nose in the air. "Dakota will have your head when she finds out! Your lunch meeting is within the hour, right?"

"She's actually meeting a friend in Belfield, so it'll probably be two or three before she comes back. Sorry." Gentry turned to leave as Sienna shook the bars. Even though the jail was meant for show, there was still no breaking out, at least to her knowledge.

"What about Skylar? She actually knows how to be a cop, so she'll definitely have words for you about this."

"She's visiting her uncle. I believe he lives out in Jamestown so she'll be back Friday." Gentry looked down at Sienna's phone, reading the screen before informing her, "It's Tuesday so you'll see her in about three days."

Sienna slammed her palms against the bars while Alex groaned, "Let her out. We know you can't arrest people for no reason, you could lose your job."

Gentry turned his attention to Alex, seeming to size her up for a moment. "I thought my role in your storyline is that I'm the sheriff? If I see people doing things wrong, I should lock them up, right? That's the whole thing about improv, it isn't planned. This..." He gestured towards Sienna, "This just feels right. And the audience loves when we throw people in jail. It'll bring in more business for you."

Alex opened her mouth to argue but she didn't get any words out quick enough before the sheriff lumbered up the steps to the station. A young woman in her early twenties called out to Gentry, "Can you arrest me next?"

Gentry let out a snort as he eyed the woman over his shoulder, but didn't respond, clearly annoyed.

When his brown eyes found Sienna, though, they crinkled in delight, not anger. He was playing a game with her. She was not having fun.

"Gentry!"

The door to the sheriff's station slammed closed and Sienna groaned loudly. "Great, just great. He's gonna get away with it, too."

"Were you feeding Domino sugar cubes again?"

Sienna huffed, leaning against the bars and pouting. "Maybe."

Alex looked towards the horse, his electric blue eyes watching her wearily. "He scares me."

"He's the sweetest, you can do this. Just grab his bridle and unhook the keys." Alex swallowed and shuffled a step towards Domino, and luckily the horse didn't move. Sienna continued to encourage her sister, "That's it. Nice and slow."

When Alex's hand was close to Domino, he flung his head up, causing the keys to jingle and Alex to shriek and dart away. Sienna stared blankly at her sister, annoyed that Gentry had found this small, cruel way to torture them together. "Are you serious? He's like a big dog, you aren't afraid of dogs."

"Dogs can't crush me," Alex mumbled as she tried again, but she made Domino as nervous as he made her, and he blew air through his lips, causing her to freeze.

Sienna sighed and rubbed her eyebrows. "Do you have your phone? I can call Dakota and ask her to swing by once she's back in town." She pursed her lips, not wanting the mayor to rush back home, but wanting her to control her little brother. Clearly he was bored, otherwise he'd have something better to do than eavesdrop on Sienna and Alex.

If Sienna won their bet, she had a laundry list of projects that would keep him busy.

"My phone is back at the saloon." Alex gestured to her tight dress, as if to prove she didn't have room to keep it on her person. It was true, if her waist was any smaller, she'd snap in half, and if she shoved her phone into her corset, she'd flash some children. "I can run and get it? Or see if Jesse has a key- I know Hank's been holding his set hostage so I'm not sure if Beau or Jesse has the keys today. If anything they can grab the key off Domino."

"If you wouldn't mind, I'd prefer not to spend my afternoon in prison," Sienna grumbled, looking over to meet Domino's eyes. She didn't understand how such a beautiful creature could belong to such a horrible man.

Alex left to find her boyfriend, leaving Sienna to suffer alone. She turned around and leaned her back against the bars, trying to avoid the prying eyes of the people who walked by.

She wished she had her phone so she could tell how long she'd been there. It felt like an eternity before Alex returned with a guilty expression on her face. "Neither Beau nor Jesse have keys."

"Okay, can they come get the key from Domino?"

"They said they aren't getting involved in your drama with the sheriff."

Sienna rolled her eyes and groaned loudly. "Cowards," she mumbled bitterly. "How do they not have keys? How are they supposed to get in and out of the jail?"

Alex kicked her boot against the dirt, grinding her molars together. She played with her layered skirt for a minute, then muttered quietly, "Apparently Gentry is getting a new trick lock put on the jail to make it easier for them to use for shows." Sienna took a step back, studying the lock for any sign of how to get out until Alex added, "Beau said Gentry took the keys to have them swapped out for Friday."

Sienna narrowed her eyes. "It's Tuesday."

"He told them not to use it until the new lock was installed on Thursday."

"That bastard knew nobody else had keys."

Alex shrugged, a smirk playing on her lips. "He's smart. It's a shame you two don't get along, because he could be pretty helpful if you put his ingenuity to good use."

Sienna clenched her jaw, feeling the heat in her cheeks rise at the idea of working with Gentry Wyatt. "I'd rather rot in this jail cell for the rest of my life."

Alex chuckled lowly, looking around before leaning in close to whisper, "You were never this feisty in New York. I like this side of you, it's fun."

"I'm glad you're enjoying yourself," Sienna snapped, crossing her arms and glaring up at Alex. The younger woman shrugged and swished her skirt a little, trying to hide her grin.

Although Sienna didn't enjoy being trapped in the jail cell, at least she had a front row seat for the entertainment. Jesse rode up and down the street on one of Lyle's horses, tipping his hat at the ladies and asking the men if they'd seen any unsavory characters around. Once he passed by, Beau would appear and talk to the people Jesse had just spoken to, telling them if they kept him hidden, he'd give them a cut of whatever he stole from the bank. Even from the jail cell, Sienna could see Alex leaning against one of the wooden beams on the saloon porch. When Jesse came riding back down the street, she shifted her corset before hiking up her skirt, causing several men to laugh and whistle until Jesse dismounted to talk to her. He stood below her as she leaned over the balcony, flirting so quietly that none of the guests could hear, but the loving gazes they gave each other were honest. They clearly truly cared for each other, and Sienna was happy for her sister, if not a little jealous.

It was hard to tell how much of their relationship was real and an act, but it read well either way. Sienna was so invested in watching Jesse bid her sister goodbye that she almost missed Dakota walking by.

The blonde did a double take, blinking as her jaw dropped open before furrowing her brows and growling, "What did he do?"

"He hooked the keys to Domino. Alex was too afraid to get them."

Dakota turned around and quickly unclipped the keys, mumbling something along the lines of the sheriff being 'immature' and 'on thin ice' before firmly telling Sienna she was sorry.

Now free from her public imprisonment, Sienna's fury burned like a bonfire as she stormed past Dakota towards the sheriff's office. She was vaguely aware of the mayor chasing after her as she stomped up the stairs and flung open the door, finding Gentry sitting with his boots up on his desk, reclining in his chair as if he'd been waiting for her.

He chuckled when he saw her red cheeks, motioning up and down as she approached him with her nostrils flaring. "You look like a tomato."

"Give me my phone. Now."

"Did you get a sunburn? The cell is like five feet deep, you could have stood under the roof."

Sienna slammed her hand on his desk, causing the framed photo to shake a little. He put his feet down and adjusted it, his humorous expression falling a little as he stared up at her with furrowed brows. She scoffed, "Don't look at me like you're so offended. Give me my damn phone!"

"Alright! Alright..." Gentry pulled it out of his pocket and handed it over. Sienna used the hem of her blouse to wipe the screen, glaring at the man as he leaned his forearms on his desk and looked past Sienna at his sister. "Hi Dakota."

"Gentry, what the hell?"

"She was feeding Domino again. She's gonna make him sick," Gentry told Dakota firmly, but Sienna paused her cleaning for a moment to look at him, worried she might actually hurt the horse. Gentry caught her guilt and smiled broadly. "Serves you right, messing with a man's horse. If I need to call in a vet, you're footing the bill." He shook his head at Dakota, as if he couldn't believe Sienna could be so reckless. As if he hadn't silently allowed her to feed his horse sugar cubes for the past three weeks before today. "City riff raff who doesn't belong in our town."

Sienna snorted and unlocked her phone to check her messages, occasionally shooting Gentry an annoyed look as Dakota berated him for speaking to Sienna that way. Gentry leaned back in his chair, smiling up at his sister without a hint of remorse as she told him she expected better from him and that she didn't want to make this a bigger deal, but if he didn't stop bothering Sienna she'd have to take action.

"What's gotten into you lately?" Dakota finally asked, her tone a mix of confusion and exhaustion. "You never used to be so mean." The hurt frown on Gentry's face sombered them both, and Sienna took a few steps away to give them some privacy. He looked up at her when he caught the movement, twisting his lips thoughtfully as he breathed through his nose.

Sienna thought for a minute he was going to apologize, but instead he said, "Maybe she should learn not to take everything so seriously. She's into the immersive experience thing, I thought she should try it out!"

"How on God's green Earth did you become sheriff? You are a child!" Sienna yelled back, causing him to chuckle and lean back in his chair.

"Me? You're, what? Like twelve?"

Sienna scoffed, shaking her head and rolling her eyes up at the ceiling as she ran her tongue along her teeth in frustration. "I'm almost thirty." Gentry nodded, making a big show of raking his eyes up and down her body. She placed her hands on her hips and asked, "Didn't your mother teach you any manners? Or did she give up after Dakota because you're so hopeless?"

Gentry gestured to Sienna, looking at Dakota with a hurt expression that clearly wasn't real. "You think I'm the mean one? Do you hear the way she's talking to me?"

Dakota opened her mouth to interject, but Sienna smacked her hand against his desk and shouted, "I can't stand you! You are such a pain in my ass!"

Without missing a beat, Gentry's hurt expression melted into a sly grin. He leaned his head a little, giving Sienna another once over before biting back with raised brows, "What ass?"

Sienna clenched her hands into fists. She narrowed her eyes at the man, but he just waited for her to respond to his insult. He wanted her to spar with him, but she wasn't going to give him that satisfaction.

Turning on her heels, Sienna strode out of the sheriff's station without another word. She didn't stop until she was at the hitching post, swiftly untying the rope holding Domino to the wooden pole. She snatched the rope and turned Domino around, leading him a few feet from the building.

Domino blocked Sienna's view of the sheriff's station, but she heard the door close and Gentry's panicked voice asking, "What the hell are you doing?"

Sienna wound up her arm and smacked Domino on the ass as hard as she could, causing him to startle and sprint down Main Street. Dust wafted around her as Gentry sprinted down the stairs, pulling his hat off to push his hair away from his face. He was already panting as he turned to the woman, but she swung around and pointed up at him. "I've already done my time in your stupid jail, so you better go fetch him if you're so worried about him."

He did that snort thing as he turned away, the one that he must have picked up from spending more time with Domino than with other humans. No wonder Domino was his best friend, no person with half a brain would spend time with Gentry Wyatt.

Dakota appeared beside her as Gentry jogged after his horse, causing enough of a stir that everyone on Main Street turned to watch. Their gazes followed him for a moment, then turned to the source of the commotion to find Sienna.

She swallowed, pushing her fluffy hair back and turning to Dakota. "I'm not sorry for what I did."

"I'm not mad," she said softly, surprise evident in her voice. "You've got some nerve, though."

Sienna looked in the direction Gentry had gone, smiling to herself as she crossed her arms over her chest, feeling triumphant after her little victory. "Well, I don't give up that easily."

Chapter 25

"Business has been booming since Beau became the town's new desperado," Kitty exclaimed as she added a few more Lonewood books to the display at the checkout counter. "He tells all the guests that his woman owns the Shoppe at Rattlesnake Bend. He tells them this is where he hides his loot." She giggled, pushing a chunk of hair behind her ear as she nodded at a customer who was leaving. "Thanks for stopping by!"

Sienna grinned at Kitty from where she'd planted herself behind the checkout counter, using her finger to hold the book open to the page she'd been reading. An older woman came up to the counter with matching necklaces for the two teenage girls accompanying her.

"How have you been enjoying your stay?" Sienna asked as she rang her up.

"I've been coming to Lonewood for years, and this is the best it's been in a long time. Whoever they've got running this place is doing a phenomenal job." The woman passed the necklaces to the girls, then leaned over to Sienna and whispered with a grin, "The cowboys are definitely cuter than years past. The girls love 'em."

Sienna smiled at that as they left. She felt a sense of pride knowing she'd caused that. She was the one who had brought life back to Lonewood. As far as she could tell, everyone, from the tourists to the locals, were appreciative of her efforts.

Next weekend was the Fourth of July, and the interest in Lonewood had been growing steadily. She was so close to her goal that she could taste it. They just needed a big draw to pique enough interest for the holiday weekend. Sienna was doing her research for ideas.

Kitty led a father and his young son to the counter to ring up the stuffed bison they'd picked out. Sienna stepped aside, taking her book with her. She flipped through the pages, stopping at the photo of cattle stampeding down Main Street. "Do we still do this? The cattle drive thing?"

"Yeah, Preston and Owen need to move the cattle from the ranch west of the town to a plot they rent on the east side. Usually they do it late July, early August."

That could be an interesting draw. "Could they do it earlier?"

Kitty shrugged as she handed the man his receipt and passed the toy to the child. "You'd have to call Preston. Or have Annie talk to him, it's her dad."

Sienna raised her brow at that. "Annie's dad is the cattle rancher?"

"Yeah, he and her older brother run the Circle W together. I don't know how strict they stick to their schedule, but you should talk to Annie. She's living out there while she's here." Kitty looked over Sienna's shoulder at the photo, then snatched the book and put it back in the display. "I've been meaning to talk to you and Alex. Beau and I are getting married at the end of July."

"Aww, congratulations! How are you feeling?"

"Excited! Nervous... Busy..." Kitty trailed off, looking towards the door as it opened and another couple wandered in. "But I'm moving into Beau's house. I currently live above the shop," she pointed above them, "so I need to rent it out. I was wondering if you and Alex would be interested? After all the work you two have put in, I wanted to offer it to you guys first before I listed it."

Sienna looked up, not having realized Kitty lived above the shop. The thought of leaving the Tumbleweed Motel was bittersweet, because the beds were still uncomfortable and it wasn't enough space for two adult women, but moving into Kitty's apartment made everything feel more real. It felt like they weren't staying in Lonewood for a little while. They were truly making it their home.

"Do you want to check it out? Lemme just close up the shop and I can take you up for a tour. There's a set of stairs on the side of the building, so we won't bother you if we're working here. It's pretty spacious for just me, but Beau's house is bigger. We'll need the space for the babies."

Eyes bursting wide, Sienna looked down at Kitty's stomach quickly and blurted, "Are you pregnant?"

"Well, no, not yet," Kitty giggled, as if it were obvious. "But once we've tied the knot, I'm expecting a little one within the year." She snuck around Sienna to turn the sign on the door around, telling everyone outside they were closed. The couple perusing her stock looked up, but she called, "Take your time, we'll head out whenever you're finished!"

Once the couple purchased their magnets and left, Kitty led Sienna out the main door and around the corner. Sienna realized she'd never looked closely, because the staircase leading up to the second level wasn't hidden by any means, but it was out of the way enough to be subtle. They climbed the creaky stairs to the apartment and Kitty held open the door for Sienna to enter.

The walls of the apartment were stark white, and her kitchen furniture was shiny black. White marble countertops popped against the black cabinets, but there were little pops of red everywhere, including a teapot on the shiny stovetop.

Beyond the kitchen was the living room, where a black leather sectional sat around a flatscreen television. There were still framed photos hanging on the walls above the television, but the bookshelf against the far wall had already been cleared out to move.

"Your home is stunning, Kitty." Sienna ran her fingertips along the back of the couch. The leather was smooth, relatively new and unscathed. A red throw blanket was draped over the top. It was soft and heavy, making Sienna want to curl up and take a nap. She looked at Kitty, seeing the woman looking hopeful. "Are you sure you want to rent it out?"

"Yes, very much so. Beau and I could really use the extra money. We'd sell it, but we don't want just anybody living above the store..." She paused, then quickly stammered, "Not that we wouldn't sell it to you two! I just assumed you'd rather not purchase an apartment. I figured you and Alex wouldn't want to live together forever."

Sienna laughed, looking down the hallway towards the bedrooms. "You're right. We've lived together for as long as I can remember, but eventually we're gonna need our own space."

Eventually one or both of us will leave Lonewood.

"I was thinking five hundred dollars a month. I know it's a lot, but-"

"Wait, what did you say?" Sienna asked, thinking she hadn't heard Kitty right.

Kitty raised her brows and repeated, "Would you be okay paying five hundred a month? If that's too much we can figure something out." She gestured towards the bedrooms, leading Sienna farther into the apartment. "Let me show you the bedrooms and bathroom before you decide."

Sienna's jaw went slack as she let Kitty lead her towards the bedrooms. First she popped open the first door on the left, showing a beautiful bathroom with a large shower and a separate garden tub and double sinks.

"The master bedroom is across the hall." Kitty popped open the door beside the bathroom and Sienna saw the spare bedroom was bigger than their motel room. When Kitty whipped around and opened up the door to the master, Sienna's breath was stolen away.

Thick, velvet curtains in lush purple draped around a large window overlooking the Badlands. Kitty had a king-sized bed and a walk in closet, and still enough room for a small desk in the corner.

"I'll sell you whatever furniture you want. Beau already has everything so I'm pretty much willing to part with all of it," Kitty said softly. "I want to ask for two thousand for all the furniture, but I know it's a lot."

"I'll take it." Kitty looked at her in surprise and Sienna nodded vigorously. "We'll take the apartment. Five hundred a month is a steal and I'll give you three thousand for whatever furniture you want to sell." She looked out the window, wanting to move the desk so she could see out while she worked. She turned around to Kitty and added, "If you need more money a month, we can do six hundred."

She shook her head, dismissing the idea quickly. "Absolutely not, that's highway robbery! Five hundred a month, but I will take the three thousand for the furniture if you're offering."

"Deal." Sienna placed her hands to her mouth, staring around the bedroom in excitement. She should have consulted Alex first, but honestly, she'd move here by herself if Alex didn't want to. "When will you move in with Beau?"

Kitty bobbed her head from right to left, looking up as she considered her answer. "I'll start moving my stuff after the Fourth, so I should be out by the tenth. Is that okay?"

"That's perfect. Thank you so much." Sienna walked out of the bedroom and back into the living room, startling a little when a small black and white cat darted in front of her.

"Sorry! She's friendly, I promise," Kitty assured Sienna as she scooped up the cat. "I'll deep clean all the furniture before I move. I'm kind of a clean freak."

Looking around the spotless apartment, Sienna could see that. The details were sharp, clean, and modern. She didn't know the Kitty that had designed this home, but she wanted to. "I love the black and white with the red details."

"I do, too. Beau's place is more rustic, which is kind of annoying, but I'll make it work with a few tweaks here and there." She smiled to herself as she opened up a cabinet, peeking up at the dinnerware before sighing. "We'll get all new stuff from the wedding, so I'll leave all that too. Sorry to dump so much on you."

"Please do not apologize, I haven't owned a dish in almost two months," Sienna chuckled. "I really appreciate this. I'll get the money for you after the Fourth?"

Kitty nodded, twisting her teapot ever so slightly so it sat perfectly straight on the stove. "Sounds like a plan to me. I'll get the extra keys from Beau and my dad so they'll be ready for you and Alex. But for now," she looked at her phone and pursed her lips, "I 'spose it's time to go back to work. I'm sure you've got work to do, too. Especially if you want to catch Annie before tonight's show."

Looking at her own phone, Sienna saw it was already four o'clock. If she wanted to talk to Annie she'd have to get to the saloon quickly before she had to get ready for the evening show. She said goodbye to Kitty and let herself out as the blonde locked up, taking the stairs two at a time before reaching the porch.

Sienna groaned a little when she saw Gentry and Jesse trotting by on their way to the stables. Jesse greeted Sienna with a tip of his hat and kept riding, but Gentry slowed to a stop and beamed at her. "Miss Jade."

"Sheriff Gentry," Sienna bit back. She tilted her head to the side, pushing her hair away from her face as she glared up at the man from beneath her eyelashes. Her emerald eyes slid from Gentry to Jesse and back. "Your partner is leaving you."

"I'm sure I can find my way." He grunted as he dismounted Domino, stretching out his back with a low groan. "I thought I'd check in. See how packing is going since you'll be leaving town next week."

She met Gentry at the bottom of the steps, crossing her arms and smiling up at him. "I have such a long list of things for you to do. The walkways need to be redone, the diner needs a new coat of paint... we're gonna need to expand the motel for all the business I'm bringing in." She looked towards the saloon, then back up at the sheriff. "Now if you'll excuse me, I have more important things to do than be harassed by you."

Sienna turned on her heel and took a few steps towards the saloon, but Gentry snatched her wrist and tugged her back harshly. She yelped as she crashed into his chest, but when she tried to push away, she found his arms wrapped tightly around her.

"What do you think you're-"

The unmistakable sound of rattling came from the direction of the saloon and Sienna looked to where Gentry gestured down at the ground with his nose. The brownish-gray rattlesnake had its head raised, tongue slipping out as its tail moved rapidly, a warning to stay away. Sienna's foot must have been inches from stepping on it before Gentry pulled her back.

The snake slithered back under the porch and Sienna breathed out weakly, still pressed up against Gentry's chest, "We gotta get rid of the rattlesnakes at Rattlesnake Bend."

Her whole body quivered from how tense she was and she shifted uneasily as she stared at the porch. Gentry chuckled, releasing his grip on her. "I'm guessing you'll add that to the list of things for me to do?"

"I mean, you'd be a lot less trouble to me pumped full of venom," Sienna deadpanned, but there wasn't any malice in her voice. She massaged her aching wrist, torn between being angry that he'd hurt her and being thankful he'd stopped her from getting hurt even worse. She looked up at him and sighed, "Thanks. I'm honestly surprised you didn't let me step on it."

He watched her massage her wrist for a moment, lips pursed slightly as if in thought. When he finally spoke, his voice was soft- a little sad. "You really think I'd let you get bit by a rattlesnake?"

"You shot your gun so Cheyanne would buck me off."

"Yeah, but-"

Sienna shook her head, cutting him off, "I could have been really hurt that day. You've been nothing but horrible to me since I moved here, why should I think any different now? You've made it abundantly clear you want me gone."

Gentry's brown eyes softened as he stammered, "I- I don't want you dead."

"Coulda fooled me," Sienna grumbled, looking down at the ground before starting towards the saloon again. "Thanks for surprising me, I guess."

"Sienna, wait." Gentry reached out and grabbed her again, but the contact caused her wrist to sting painfully. She grimaced as her palm wrapped around Gentry's fingers and he retracted his hand when he realized that he'd been the one to cause her pain. He swallowed hard and looked over her shoulder down Main Street, then back down to her with worry. "I'm sorry."

"For hurting my wrist or making my life a living hell?"

"For both?" Gentry offered with a weak smile. If he was trying to make amends, he was doing a decent job of it. Maybe he'd stopped to taunt her originally, but if he hadn't, she'd be praying Doctor Thompson had antivenom in his barbershop medical practice.

Sienna nodded a little, looking down at her wrist. Maybe she could use this encounter to her advantage. "I was going to the saloon to talk to Annie. Kitty says her dad does the big cattle drive thing every summer and I wanted to see if it was something they could do early. Like next weekend for the Fourth."

Gentry bobbed his head slowly, thinking about her idea. "It wouldn't be ideal, but they might be up for it. The people always love seeing the cattle run through town. It's a hell of a clean up after though. Dakota was saying something about having some sort of block party?"

"Yeah, we thought we could do games and activities and stuff for the Fourth. Have the actors walk around and interact with people, raise a little extra money, it could be fun." Sienna massaged her wrist, wondering if he'd dislocated it. He'd snapped her back pretty hard, but she had to remind herself that her aching wrist hurt a hell of a lot less than a snake bite would have. "Thank you for saving me."

"Contrary to what you believe, Miss Jade, I don't hate you." Gentry shoved his hands into his pockets, looking over at Domino as the horse stood by obediently. "You're a pain in my ass. I think you're entitled and bossy, but you are doing a lot to help this town, so I guess you aren't so terrible."

Sienna laughed, shaking her head and sighing as she shoved her hands through her hair at her scalp. Her bangs had gotten long and she'd been pushing them to the side, but they often fell in her eyes and annoyed her. This was one of those moments she was thankful for something to fuss with though, because the abrupt change in dynamic between herself and the sheriff made her anxious. She didn't necessarily want him to be rude to her, but she'd become accustomed to their verbal sparring. That had been fun and this worry wasn't.

"Thanks, I guess."

"I still don't want you feeding Domino sugar cubes every day. Unless you want to clean up his shit."

She smiled, shaking her head. "No, I'd rather not." Sienna reached out and pet Domino's nose, and he took a step towards her to get closer for more affection. Gentry grunted and rolled his eyes, leaning in to whisper to the horse, "Traitor."

This was the first time Sienna saw what Dakota saw in her little brother. Beneath all the grumbling, complaining, and harassing, Gentry wasn't a bad man. He was witty, clearly very smart, and kind when it suited him. Dakota hoped that Sienna and Gentry could be friends, and this was the first time Sienna actually believed it could happen someday.

"I'm sorry I hurt your wrist, but you should watch where you're going. Especially around a place called Rattlesnake Bend," Gentry scolded as he thrust his boot into the stirrup before hoisting himself up and over Domino. He ripped the reins to the side, forcing the horse away from Sienna so she couldn't pet him anymore. "Maybe if you hobble on over to Doctor Thompson's office he'll kiss it better for you."

And the Gentry Sienna knew was back.

She scowled up at him and he grinned back, giving her a wink as he kicked Domino's sides to send him tearing down the road towards the stables, leaving Sienna coughing in a cloud of dust.

Huffing, she wiped the dirt and grime off her teal shirt and shuffled her way across the street. Her wrist wasn't in horrible condition by any means, but behind Gentry's teasing was a suggestion that she'd actually take.

Brad's practice was nestled between the Portrait Studio and the mayor's office. It was a two-story building that probably had white siding when it was built, but the sun and dirt had painted it a worn shade of gray over the years. Like most of the businesses, it had a small set of stairs leading up to a porch, and Sienna began to wonder what other creatures dwelled beneath all the town's buildings.

She knocked on the old glass window of the door and waited to see if Brad would answer. A minute or two went by without a sign of anybody, so she twisted the doorknob and found it open, allowing her the chance to peek inside.

"Hello?" Sienna called as she took a step inside. It smelled old, like wood and dust, and Sienna felt like she'd stepped back in time. In the middle of the room was a brown leather barber's chair. It appeared to be both for hair cutting and examinations, because there was a little metal cart with an amalgamation of supplies. Although the hair cutting shears were real, the medical supplies looked glued to the table for decoration.

Suddenly Brad appeared from the back room, looking worried when he realized it was Sienna. "What happened? Are you okay?"

"I'm here to see the doctor, but I'm not dead, so I'd say I'm okay." She laughed, trying to lighten the mood a little. Brad swept across the room to her and she held out her hand for him to examine her wrist. "I think it might be dislocated."

"Let's go in the back and I'll take a closer look." Brad led her through the swinging doors into the back room, and Sienna gawked at how different his real examination room was. He chuckled at her wonder and gestured for her to climb up onto the examination table. "I do hair cuts and BandAids over there. If there's any real issues that need to be addressed, I'd rather it be done in a professional setting. The showmanship isn't nearly as important to me as the rest of the town."

Sienna smiled as he carefully bent her wrist, rubbing his thumb over it to look for any signs of serious damage. "I appreciate that, honestly. I love the theming, and I know the tourists do, too, but some things are better done using modern methods."

He smiled up at her, holding her wrist in one hand while using the other to massage it. "I can do X-rays but I don't think you need them. It's just bruised." Sienna relaxed at that, but the doctor still didn't drop her hand. "What happened, anyway?"

She blushed a little as her mind rewound the moment Gentry caught her and pulled her to his chest. At the time, she was so startled by the action that she hadn't actually dwelled on the fact that he'd held her in his arms, instinctively protective until the threat was gone. Any sane person would yell and bolt the other way, but he was more worried about her getting hurt than himself.

"I, uh-" As far as she knew, nobody else witnessed the interaction between herself and Gentry. Nosy people in a town this small would see it as a sort of meet-cute, and Dakota was right, Sienna didn't want any other misconceptions about his love life. "I don't know, I think I twisted it weird helping Kitty carry some stuff around the store today. It's just been achy."

The doctor didn't seem to buy her explanation, but he didn't push it. Instead he gently placed her hand in her lap and took a seat on a chair next to the examination table. "It's really nice how much you've done to help these people. I can tell they really appreciate it."

These people. It was a very different tone from what everyone else used. Sienna suddenly realized that Brad wasn't from Lonewood either, because he didn't talk about its citizens as old friends, but as patients and customers. "You aren't from here, are you?"

"No," he chuckled, "I'm from South Dakota actually. But I visited Lonewood as a kid, and once I got my Doctorate I was looking for work and saw they were looking for a physician. I hadn't meant to stay forever, but this place sucks you in. Being a big fish in a puddle has its perks, though. I'm sure you understand."

Although he hadn't meant it as rude, the comment made Sienna uncomfortable. When she arrived, she had considered herself better than the people of Lonewood. Bitter that she'd lost her perfect life in New York, Sienna had reveled in her superiority, but over the past few weeks she'd grown to love everyone here. Hearing Brad call this town a puddle made her stomach twist.

"I wouldn't say I'm a big fish, I-"

"You and your sister single handedly brought in business this summer," Brad interjected. "I've lived here over ten years and I've never seen it this busy. It's been three weeks, but the smallest of tweaks and changes have turned this entire town around. That has to feel good, to look around and know it's all because of you."

It did, but admitting that aloud didn't feel great.

Brad sensed her hesitation and studied her for a moment. "My offer for dinner still stands. I know you're busy, but I hope you'll make some time soon. I'd really like to get to know you better. I think we have a lot in common."

Sienna knew they were similar in a lot of ways. They were outsiders who believed Lonewood needed them, but they didn't necessarily need Lonewood. Sienna could have lived quietly, taken up knitting or some other lonely hobby, and avoided the world after losing everything. But she needed to work. She *needed* to do her job, and seeing her hard work paying off did feel good.

It might be nice to have somebody to talk to who understood that it was okay to be proud. And if she was being honest, she was lonely.

Though the idea of letting someone in again after Mason gave Sienna pause. She wasn't lonely enough to get hurt again and she wasn't selfish enough to use Brad if she wasn't ready to open up.

"Maybe after the Fourth," Sienna conceded, not wanting to be rude. Brad gave a little nod, accepting her answer. The look on his face said he wasn't about to give up, though.

"Whenever you're ready, I'll be waiting."

He walked her through the showroom and out the main door, holding it open for her as she carefully walked down the stairs. She took the time to look around and make sure there were no snakes or other critters lurking before suddenly raising her head to say, "I saw a rattlesnake over by Kitty's store. What happens if somebody gets bitten?"

Brad's lips drew into a thin line and he glared across the street. "We'll need to have them removed. I've told them it's too risky with the increase in business. I've got some antivenom, but if the bite is bad enough, they'd need to be sent to a bigger hospital. Depending on how long it took the ambulance to get here and back...I don't think it would end well."

Sienna paled at the realization that they were too far away to reach a hospital in time. She looked down at her wrist, cradling it with her other hand. She hated that she owed the sheriff a debt, but if he hadn't been there, Sienna would be laying in the middle of the road screaming in pain until Kitty eventually heard her and came down, or until some tourist wandered by and realized what had happened.

"I'll talk to the mayor. They'll be gone by the Fourth."

Brad gave a little nod to say goodbye as he closed the door and Sienna looked up the road towards the stables, thinking maybe she owed the sheriff another thanks for saving her life.

Chapter 26

When the first of July rolled around, Sienna and Alex were awoken by the sound of frantic knocking on their motel room door. Sienna groaned loudly as she rolled out of bed. She popped open the door enough to see who was there, then swung it wider when she realized it was Kennedy. "Is everything okay?"

The woman nodded, trying to contain the very clear excitement that played on her features. "I have an awful question for you… do you two think you could spend the weekend somewhere else?"

"That kinda is an awful question after waking us up," Sienna yawned. She pulled her heap of messy hair over her shoulder and stretched out her back, finally starting to feel awake. "What's wrong?"

Kennedy's smile burst through her entire face and she let out a little laugh as she explained, "I got a couple more email requests for rooms last night. I need to rent out your room because there aren't any others left."

Her words slowly registered in Sienna until she gasped, "The motel is booked?"

"Completely. Even if I rent out your room, I'll still have to turn a few people away."

"We did it. We filled the motel. We filled the motel!" Sienna squealed happily as she pulled Kennedy into a tight hug. She yelled over her shoulder at Alex, "Get up and start packing! Kennedy needs the room!"

Alex moaned and shoved her face into her pillow. "I heard you the first time."

"I feel horrible asking you guys to give up your space, but we've upped the prices for the holiday weekend and-"

"Don't feel bad! Not even a little bit!" Sienna told Kennedy as she started fluttering around the room picking up their belongings. "We'll find a place to crash for the weekend. We'll be out by noon. When are they coming?"

"Most of the guests are coming in tonight," Kennedy explained slowly as she took a step into their room, looking around. It was a mess, but the sisters had been living here for almost eight weeks. It would be nice to go to an actual home for a few days. "You're welcome to stay with Trevor and I if you don't have anywhere else to go. By Tuesday morning the motel should be mostly cleared out again."

Sienna grabbed the pillow from Alex and smacked her in the back with it in an effort to stir her, but the younger woman just yelped and buried her face in the mattress, causing the springs to creak loudly. Sienna looked back at Kennedy and said, "I'll let you know. I have to tell Dakota that we filled the motel. We have so much to do before Monday."

With the holiday falling on a Monday, it allowed people a long weekend to travel. Hearing the motel was booked fully lit Sienna on fire, and she threw her stuff haphazardly into her suitcase as her sister tried to sleep in. "Alex, get up! We've got stuff to do!"

"You get ready and I'll sleep in. I'll be out by noon, just like you promised," Alex yawned, not bothering to flip over and greet Kennedy properly. Alex had settled into the casual, friendly small-town life swimmingly.

Sienna rolled her eyes and turned to Kennedy. "Let me get packed and ready and after breakfast I'll let you know if we need a place to crash. Thank you for everything."

"No, thank you for everything," Kennedy answered with a beaming smile. Sienna had never seen the quiet woman smile so brightly. "We've never sold out every room. Never once since we bought the motel. If this continues, it's going to change our lives."

Sienna only had to ensure their success lasted. No pressure. "I'll do my best."

"You always do." Kennedy saw herself out, sparing a quick look at Alex with a knowing smirk before closing the door.

Within the hour, Sienna was charging into the Lonewood Cafe by herself. She strode up to the mayor and her brother, who were sitting at the counter talking quietly until she arrived. She tapped Dakota on the shoulder, causing the blonde to look up at her in surprise. "Good morning!"

"Weird question, you don't have a couch Alex and I could crash on this weekend, do you?" Sienna turned to Gentry with a wicked grin when he eyed her suspiciously. "Kennedy needs to rent out our room because the motel is fully booked."

The sheriff blinked a couple times, then looked away from Sienna with his brows drawn. "Huh."

Dakota, though, shrieked and slid off her stool to envelope Sienna in a hug. "You did it! I can't believe this!" Everyone in the small diner turned to their excitable mayor as she yelled to the room, "She filled the motel! We're sold out for the weekend!" She pointed proudly at Sienna as a few people whooped and clapped, causing Sienna to blush.

"Congrats," Gentry grunted. He didn't even look at Sienna, which made her prouder than any of the applause. She leaned against the counter between his stool and Dakota's, and he finally looked up at her and sighed, "I guess I'm at your service."

"Don't sound so down about it," Sienna teased, then dropped her voice and added seriously, "I owe you for getting them to move up the cattle drive. And for the other thing."

He nodded a little, looking over his shoulder to make sure nobody else was listening. Dakota had wandered off to talk to a couple of tourists who were caught up in the excitement. She gushed about their planned activities for the weekend, from the cattle drive tomorrow morning to the block party on Monday afternoon and every offering in between. Dakota was so proud she was practically glowing, but her brother looked like he had a rain cloud over his head.

"How's your wrist?"

"It's fine." She rubbed it instinctively. "Just a little bruised, but it doesn't really hurt anymore."

"I'm sorry."

"Don't be." Sienna groaned a little before murmuring reluctantly, "I… appreciate you." She pretended to retch, as if the confession pained her, and Gentry smiled. She smiled back and Dakota slipped up onto her stool and leaned around her, watching the two of them curiously. "What's going on here?"

Sienna quickly pushed away from the counter to stand away from them as Gentry looked back at the kitchen with his signature frown. "Nothing," he mumbled, but Dakota raised a curious brow at his change of demeanor. She turned to Sienna, silently asking for her explanation but Sienna shook her head and repeated, "Nothing."

"Hmm." Dakota hummed to herself as she raised her coffee mug to her lips, bright eyes darting between Gentry and Sienna. She sat the mug down and sighed, reaching into her tight jeans pocket to grab her wallet. "I have a lot of work to do before tomorrow. If we're expecting three to four hundred extra people for the cattle drive we're gonna need to set up a perimeter. It gets a little crazy."

"What can I do?" Sienna asked, always ready to dive in. The more she had her hands in, the more she could keep this town on the track she envisioned.

Gentry tilted his head to shoot Dakota a knowing look and the mayor looked to Sienna with a sympathetic smile. "You should just enjoy it! It's an interesting experience. The cattle are just gonna run down Main Street and be herded to the other end of town. It smells, there's lots of dirt and dust, and then all the cowboys have to clean up after the animals. It isn't glamorous by any means, but it's cool to see. They have around four hundred head of cattle, so it's a pretty big event. Takes a lot of hands to get it done right."

"So, don't get run over," Gentry said bluntly as he turned around to lean on the counter. He leaned back on his elbows, looking unimpressed by Sienna's continued presence. She thought he'd better get used to it since she wasn't going anywhere. He scoffed at her clean, intricate cowboy boots. "I'd hate for you to ruin your shoes."

"Listen, at least I'm trying to be helpful, unlike somebody else," she snapped at Gentry, losing her patience. Sienna wondered if Dakota would think less of her if she taped her brother's mouth shut for the rest of the summer.

He rolled his eyes dramatically, making a big show of his annoyance. "Congratulations. You're anal about your work and need to stick your nose in everything. I stay out of the way. I do my job, which is making sure all these people you've brought in stay safe."

"Oh please, I've yet to see you do any law enforcing since I moved here. The only person you've arrested is me and it was for giving your horse sugar cubes."

"Sorry my town is safe. Maybe it means I'm doing something right," Gentry bit back until Dakota reached over and covered his mouth with her hand, giving a firm shake of her head before turning her frustrated expression on Sienna.

"Enough of that. You two are going to get along this weekend. It's important for all of us, and it's something we've worked hard for. I don't want to make a spectacle over you two bickering." Dakota fluffed out her big curls before pulling down her red blouse, causing more of her cleavage to show.

Gentry slid from his stool to stand, looking out the big windows at Main Street. It wasn't even ten and the street was already bustling with people looking for things to see and do. A large group climbed the steps to the apparel store, ready to drop a bunch of money to dress the part for their holiday.

The sheriff pulled off his hat, pushing back his hair before asking Dakota, "You want me to go back for the chaps?"

She smirked, giving a firm nod. "Yes, please."

"Fine," he grumbled and put his hat back on his head. "But coffee's on you this morning."

She told him he had a deal as he left, then smiled at Sienna. "What can I get you? You want a coffee? Caramel roll to go? I 'spose you need to pack so you can move out of the motel for the weekend." She beamed, remembering what Sienna had initially asked her. "I have a couple of spare bedrooms, so you and Alex are welcome to stay as long as you need to. It's the least I can do."

"We'll be gone by Tuesday morning, I promise," Sienna assured her as she took a seat at the counter. Brenda looked up at her, raising her brows to ask what she wanted without even opening her mouth. "Caramel roll and coffee please! Black. I'm gonna need it black today." She barely finished her order before Brenda had the caramel roll in front of her and was pouring coffee into a fresh mug. She took Gentry's away, dumping out the liquid before setting the mug behind the counter.

Sienna started shoveling the roll into her mouth before washing it down with coffee. Dakota got up to leave, but Sienna sat up and raised her hand to get her attention. "Alex and I are moving into Kitty's place! She's renting out the apartment above the shop!"

Looking back at Sienna, there was surprise on Dakota's face. She considered what Sienna had said, then nodded slowly as she began to grin. "Putting down some roots, huh?"

"I guess so," Sienna answered quietly, understanding the gravity of her statement. "I'm not gonna lie, it's kind of scary. Makes this all feel more real."

"Well, we're happy to have you for as long as you'll stay. Lonewood is better because you two are in it."

Sienna smiled to herself, thankful that Lonewood appreciated her and her sister. She didn't think she would ever belong here, but recently she'd found herself thinking about what Dakota had asked her weeks ago: if Sienna was happy here. At the time, Sienna hadn't been so sure, but the truth was, in a surprising, weird way, Sienna was truly happy in Lonewood, North Dakota.

At noon on the dot, Dakota drove up to the motel in her sleek car, rolling down her window to call, "So I hear I'm only getting one of you for the weekend? What's up with that?"

Alex flinched as Sienna shot her a dark look. "By the time I got back from breakfast, Alex had already made other plans."

"Sorry! Jesse offered for me to stay with him and I said yes! It's gonna be busy for us and he lives near the saloon. It just makes sense."

"Hmm," Dakota hummed as Sienna slid into her passenger's seat. "I dunno, Sienna, sounds like Jesse's more fun than us."

Red blossomed on Alex's cheeks as she closed her door. Sienna hid her snort behind a fake cough. "Yeah, apparently."

After dropping Alex off at Jesse's small mobile home, Dakota pulled into the driveway of a beautiful two-story house down the street. Sienna was stunned that the woman lived here by herself, but she was clearly well paid as the mayor. Her house was made of beautiful red bricks and had a little porch out front with a swing next to the front door.

"You're not allergic to dogs, are you?" Dakota asked quickly when they approached the front door. "I should have asked before."

"Nope, I'm good. I love dogs."

"Okay, good, cuz they're gonna love you," Dakota warned as she popped open the door. Two dogs came sprinting towards them, barking loudly as Dakota shoved her way inside. "Hey! Hey, get down, be good!"

The smaller of the two, clearly a border collie, jumped up on Sienna and tried to lick her face as she laughed. The larger one looked like some sort of a mutt with its short brown and gray fur. They sat obediently when Dakota told them to. "Thank you!" Dakota told them before huffing at the black and white dog that panted up at Sienna with its paws on her chest. "Get down!"

"They're okay," Sienna murmured softly as she smoothed down the soft fur on the dog's head. "They're sweet."

"This is Tilly. She was a horrible failure as a farm dog so it was either me or the wilderness." Dakota laughed dryly, but Sienna couldn't tell if she was joking or not. Dakota pointed at the dog sitting obediently at Dakota's feet, looking up at her with sad eyes, as if begging to get affection from their visitor, too. "That's Buster. He's an Australian cattle dog. He was the runt of the litter and I've had him since he was a baby." She clicked her tongue and Buster sat up, panting with his tongue hanging out. "Good boy," Dakota told him as she walked past to lead Sienna farther into her home. "Make yourself at home! Spare bedroom is upstairs on the left. My room is on the right. The guest bathroom is next to the living room down here on the main floor, but there's towels and soap and stuff so help yourself to whatever you need."

Sienna followed Dakota around the kitchen, and Tilly never left her side. She reached down to scratch the dog's head, and the border collie licked her fingers. Dakota noticed and frowned. "Tilly!" The dog didn't even look at her, so she sighed, "She's such a ding dong. Border collies are supposed to be smart, but she apparently didn't get that memo."

Tilly finally left Sienna and wandered over to her water bowl, taking a long drink before running into the living room and catapulting herself onto the couch. Buster followed slowly, hopping up and curling into a ball to nap while his owner welcomed their guest.

"So, make sure you don't wear anything too fancy for tomorrow. We'll do the cattle run around eleven, then at noon I want to do a cookout at the stables so we can get the visitors away from clean up on Main Street. We can do horse rides for the kids along with lunch, but it'll be a long day of sweating outside for all of us." Dakota must have felt her phone vibrate in her back pocket, because she jolted a little and pulled it out to check. "Apparently people are trying to do walk-ins at the Portrait Studio. I gotta go deal with Miss Rose, but feel free to hang out for a while. I'll be back in a bit to get ready for the show tonight."

After all this time, Sienna was impressed that Dakota still made time to go to the show. Although she did it to support the citizens of her town, her presence didn't go unnoticed by their visitors, who loved chatting with the charismatic mayor whenever she was out and about.

It was almost humorous when Gentry would escort her around town with his grumpy expression and lack of conversation. He was a perfect foil for his older sister, either by choice or by personality. The longer Sienna knew them, the more apparent it became that Dakota was the face of the town, but Gentry was the backbone, and they liked it that way.

In recent days, the mysterious third Wyatt had rarely been mentioned. Sienna wondered how she fit in with Dakota and Gentry. From what she'd gathered, Kenzie sounded more like Dakota, someone vibrant and loved. The town's perception of Kenzie was a far cry from the bitter, quiet cowboy who rode his horse up and down the street without more than a tip of a hat to those he passed by.

"I've gotta run, but I'll see you later?" Dakota asked, snapping Sienna out of her thoughts.

"Of course! Thanks again for letting me stay here."

The door clicked closed and Sienna glanced around the house, noting it was devoid of photos or art. Sienna assumed Dakota's home would be decked out in memories, but the walls and counters were bare, as if she had one foot out the door just like Sienna.

She took a seat on the couch and Tilly draped her snout over her thigh. The lack of photos didn't bother Sienna nearly as much as the realization that she didn't really know Dakota. Although she considered the mayor one of her closest friends, they didn't talk about their pasts often. Sienna couldn't, so she tried not to bring up any personal anecdotes, and in response, neither had Dakota.

Sienna didn't leave behind a lot of close friends in Manhattan. She didn't stop working long enough to let people in, but she wanted Dakota to know who she truly was. First though, Sienna had to figure it out for herself.

Chapter 27

THE NEXT MORNING, JESSE, Beau, Lyle, and Gentry went barreling down Main Street on their horses, kicking up dust and catching the attention of all their visitors. Maude watched from her porch with Sienna as they swerved past her saloon, heading away from town to the Circle W.

"So they'll herd them right past here, up towards the stables and off to pasture?"

"Yes ma'am. Owen and Preston will ride along the sides with the dogs, making sure the cattle go where they should. Gentry and Lyle will help where they can, but Beau and Jesse are more for show. They'll bring up the back. Annie woulda been more helpful, but her dad didn't want her getting hurt." Maude shrugged, pushing her thick, hairsprayed locks away from her cheek.

Sienna looked in the direction the men had gone, feeling a pinch of worry in her chest. "Is it dangerous?"

"Anytime you're dealing with large groups of animals it's dangerous. But as long as none of your tourists wander into the road they should be fine."

"Humph." Sienna crossed her arms and leaned against the wooden pillar. She was excited to display this twice-a-year event for their biggest crowd in years, but if anything went wrong, they'd be a viral disaster. She trusted the ranchers, and even Gentry and Lyle to a certain degree, but if Alex's boyfriend found a way to mess this up, Sienna would hate him more than Landon.

Sienna glanced over her shoulder when Annie and Alex appeared from the main doors, already dressed in their corsets and ruffled skirts. Annie studied Sienna curiously, seeming to sense her unease because she asked, "What's up?"

"Just nervous I guess."

"It's fine. We do this every year. There's nothing to worry about." Annie waved her off, fiddling with the boning of her deep red corset. "My boyfriend's coming in today. I'm nervous to see what he thinks of Lonewood..."

"He's gonna love it because you're here," Alex told her as she bumped her hip against Annie's. She turned to her sister, studying her worn jeans and sleeveless plaid shirt. "You're looking incredibly casual. It's weird."

"I was told it was gonna be dirty, so I didn't feel like looking nice," Sienna grumbled. She'd worn tinted sunscreen and blush, but aside from that her face was bare. She'd pulled her red waves into two loose pigtails that flowed over her shoulders, making her look young and country. She shrugged. "Besides, nobody's looking at me. I'll take some photos, make a few Instagram posts, make sure the people know not to go into the road... but that's the extent of my duties today. Dakota says I should 'take a break and enjoy it'." Sienna used air quotes around the words, knowing she'd enjoy happy customers. The cows she wouldn't find that interesting.

Alex snorted, leaning against the railing as the tourists began to line the street. "I'd like to see that. You? Taking a break? I don't think so."

Sienna didn't feel like being mocked by her sister and her coworkers, so she started down the stairs to the street. She had to find Dakota and make sure everything was under control. "Not today, but you never know what tomorrow will bring."

Alex pulled out a baby blue handkerchief from her purple corset and waved it at Sienna, pretending to cry as her sister left. Sienna could hear Annie laughing boisterously until Maude shooed them back inside, telling them not to get their dresses dirty during the cattle run.

The truth was, Sienna was exhausted. The first two weeks of June only saw crowds during the weekend, but they'd been going strong for almost three weeks straight at this point. Nobody had gotten a day off, and there weren't enough people to switch out for shifts. Dakota had brought up concerns about burning out their talent and workers, but Sienna was determined to get through this weekend. They could figure out something else on Tuesday.

She'd never imagined when she first walked down the street of Lonewood that she'd see this many people lining the boardwalks. Even the photo in Alex's book paled in comparison to the crowd gathering today. Hundreds and hundreds of people dressed in their country finest, tapping away on their phones as they waited for the event to begin. Sienna saw Dakota walking along the crowd near the diner, and she chuckled when she realized the mayor had a bullhorn.

"Good morning, how's everybody doing today?" She was answered by cheers and yelling from all around, causing her brilliant smile to grow. "Great, glad to hear it. I'm Mayor Wyatt and I wanted to welcome you here to Lonewood for our annual summer cattle drive! Now just a couple of warnings before we begin since I've gotten word the cattle are on the move, meaning they'll be here soon!" More cheers erupted and she looked around, motioning for them to cheer louder. She laughed and said, "I'm glad you're all excited, but we want everybody to be safe, because these are big animals and there are *a lot* of them. About four hundred cattle are gonna come stampeding down this road, so it's incredibly important that we stay on the boardwalk. You can cheer and take photos, make as much commotion as you want, but we need to make sure we aren't in the road. So where are we gonna stay?"

"Outta the road!"

Dakota laughed loudly, giving a thumbs up to everybody with her free hand as she let the bullhorn rest at her side. She pulled the horn back up to her mouth and continued, "Exactly, you guys are amazing! So we're gonna stay out of the road and stay put until the cattle have all moved on to the greener pastures beyond the stables. Then we're all gonna follow behind them for a cookout catered by the Lonewood Cafe. We can't wait to see you all there!"

The tourists hooted and hollered as she strode quickly down the road towards her office, collecting Sienna along the way. "Now we just gotta hold tight till it's over. Then lunch." Dakota hummed happily to herself at the thought of food. Cecily, who had already found her place on the bench, smiled up at her boss and Sienna in greeting before looking back at her phone.

Sienna was glowing as she looked around Main Street, seeing all her efforts paying off in the most spectacular way. Suddenly, her attention was drawn away by a camera crew setting up at the courthouse across the street. Her stomach dropped and she whipped around to lean against the railing so her back was to the camera crew. "Who's that?"

"They sent the news station out from Bismarck to cover the run, meaning we're in the big leagues now."

Nodding slowly, Sienna pulled out her phone to text Alex. Showing up on social media was already risky enough, but being on the state-wide news station wasn't just irresponsible, it was dangerous.

Keep an eye out for the camera crew.

A high pitched whistle was heard in the distance, followed by barking and thundering like Sienna had never heard before. She turned to her left, seeing the dust before the cattle wafting beyond the saloon.

As the noise grew closer, Skylar patrolled the edge of the street, keeping an eye on everyone to make sure they were out of the way. When her gaze fell on Sienna, she tipped her head in a silent greeting before making an overexaggerated look towards the camera crew, as if warning Sienna to be careful. She smiled back grimly, telling Skylar she saw them too.

The sound of hooves on the gravel grew in time with the chattering of the people anxiously waiting. Suddenly, a small black and white dog that looked like Tilly came sprinting around the side of the saloon, swerving and cutting tightly as the first wave of cattle came into view.

From her place on Dakota's office porch, Sienna watched as several dozen cows came running from around the side of the saloon. Mostly black, but some brown and a few with slight markings, the herd surged forward towards the cheering people. Sparing a look down Main Street, Sienna saw that even Brenda, Colleen, and Kitty were cheering on the animals as they made their trek across town.

Two men Sienna hadn't met before rode slowly alongside the first wave of cattle, whistling to the border collies who worked to keep them moving in the right direction. Sienna understood the older man to be Preston,

Annie's dad, and the younger man was his eldest son Owen, who co-owned the ranch. They rode with an ease that could only be achieved after years in the saddle. The two true cowboys of Lonewood.

Lyle appeared around the corner on his black horse, keeping an eye on the cattle from the far side of the street. Jesse rode behind him, looking stiff as he watched all the animals running down the street. Without taking her gaze off the cattle, Sienna muttered to Dakota, "Maude said Jesse and Beau would bring up the rear. What does it mean if he's been moved up here with Lyle?"

Dakota shrugged, raising her head a little to see behind the herd. "I dunno. Maybe something happened towards the back and they needed to move him. I'm not too worried about it. They've got this under control."

Despite Sienna's worry, Dakota appeared to be right. Although Jesse looked nervous, Lyle, Preston, and Owen had focused, but not alarmed, expressions as they rode alongside the cattle. Once the first wave got close to the motel, Owen kicked his horse, picking up the pace to block the cattle and send them running towards the hills beyond the stables. Lyle followed suit, causing the cattle to moo loudly as the last of them made their way past the saloon.

At the back of the herd, Beau and Gentry rode slowly, talking to each other as they kept their gazes on the cows. Sienna scoffed when she realized that Gentry had somehow weaseled his way into Jesse's easy job of bringing up the rear, forcing the young, inexperienced actor into the fray.

"Typical," Sienna muttered under her breath. Dakota raised her brows curiously and Sienna shook her head, but suddenly their attention was broken by a large bull from the back picking up speed towards the boardwalk.

Several of the tourists screamed as it neared them in front of the sheriff's station, and Sienna panicked as she saw all her hard work about to go out the window, but the black behemoth didn't have a chance to reach them before being cut off by Domino. Gentry put himself and his horse between the bull and the people, yelling at the bull to move on before looking over at Dakota and Sienna with a cocky smirk. Sienna rolled her eyes and he winked at her, then kicked Domino to send him galloping after the rest of the herd, moving way faster than necessary to show off.

When Sienna glanced over at Dakota, she realized the blonde was looking at her and not the cattle drive, or even the tourists who were pouring into the streets to follow them towards the stables. Sienna furrowed her brows and asked, "What?"

The corner of Dakota's mouth tipped up as she gazed after the cattle. "Nothing."

Sienna didn't buy it, but she didn't press it either. Her heart was pounding from the almost disaster of the bull charging the people, but her cheeks were hot for a reason she couldn't quite comprehend. Despite the fluttering in her stomach, Sienna wouldn't allow herself to consider that *Gentry* caused her to blush.

She watched as the crowd began to clear, all of the locals leading the charge towards the cookout, except for the few unfortunate souls who were nominated to work as clean up crew for all the smushed cow patties left in the street.

The camera crew began moving their set up and Sienna realized they were coming towards her and Dakota.

"I'm gonna head to the stables, see you there?" Sienna's voice was shaky as she looked between Dakota and the news reporter who was waving to get their attention.

"Oh, I was hoping maybe you'd do an interview explaining all the work you've done for the town..." Dakota's smile dropped when she saw Sienna's terrified eyes. She reached out for Sienna's arm, finding her shaking. "Are you okay?"

From across the road, Sienna met Skylar's wide, nervous eyes. The small woman mouthed 'Don't do it' as she shook her head slowly. If Bridget saw this, they'd be removed.

"I think I'm overheated to be honest," Sienna lied. At least she knew with her heavy breathing and flushed face it would look like a valid excuse. Dakota looked truly concerned, completely blocking out the news crew as Sienna added quietly, "I think I need to go lay down for a bit. Then I'll come to the cookout after?"

"That's totally fine! Do you want me to come with you?"

"I'll be okay, I'll see you soon." Sienna pushed open the door to Dakota's office, making a beeline for the back door that led to the residential street. Once away from everyone, Sienna breathed heavily, feeling the full weight of what could happen if she ended up on the news.

She was thankful that Alex picked up on the first ring when she called. "Hey, Alex! There's a camera crew here to film the festivities."

"Yeah, I noticed," Alex deadpanned on the other end. Sienna could hear laughing and realized she was in the saloon with the other girls. Her voice dropped and she asked, "What should we do?"

"I told Dakota I was overheated. I'm heading back to her place now. Do you wanna meet me? Or see if Jesse will take you to his place? I think the news crew will go to the first part of the cookout, but we should be good to go in an hour or so."

A heavy sigh answered from the other end. "I know you meant to do a good thing bringing in all this business, but what did you think was gonna happen?"

It was a valid question, but Sienna didn't want to admit that she cared more about her job than their safety. "I guess I didn't think they'd send a news crew. It's from the capital, meaning it could go national. There's not a lot of chance Landon sees it, but I don't wanna risk it."

"Then maybe you shouldn't have turned Lonewood into the next Dollywood." There was a pause before Sienna heard muffled voices on the other end. When Alex came back, she sounded strained. "I'm gonna hang out here and do some work. I'll see if Jesse can bring me back some food. Does that work?"

Sienna nodded, even though her sister couldn't see her. "Yeah. I'll stay at Dakota's house till dinner then. I love you."

"I love you, too."

The line clicked and Sienna blew through her lips, staring down at her phone. Alex was upset. It was warranted, but Sienna hadn't actually expected Lonewood to be such a big hit. This whole time she'd been very adamant about not being in front of the camera, but today spooked her.

It reminded her that all of this could be ripped away if they made a wrong step.

"Let me guess, you finally remembered you're in WitSec?"

Sienna jolted as she spun around to face Skylar, seeing the woman standing outside the sheriff's station with her brows raised in question. Sienna panted and grabbed her chest, still wound up from her close encounter with the film crew. "What are you doing here?"

"I came to check on you. I saw what happened with Dakota and I wanted to make sure you were okay. I heard your call with your sister."

Sienna swallowed, sliding her phone into her back pocket. "So you were eavesdropping?"

"I didn't want to interrupt your conversation," Skylar corrected. She fiddled with her belt buckle, looking over her shoulder at the buildings separating them from Main Street. After a moment she turned back to Sienna and asked, "Are you okay?"

The deputy wasn't allowed to know why they'd been sent to Lonewood, but she knew they were here for a reason. Being broadcasted on television, even if it was just North Dakota news, could help whoever they were hiding from find them.

Sienna ran her fingers through one of her pigtails, feeling her eyes well up a little with tears. She told herself she wasn't going to cry, but she was exhausted, and now she was scared, too. "This was my job before. I was really good at it, but I could do my work and stay invisible. I expected that to be the same here. I publicize the town but I don't need any credit for it. I, uh... it kind of scared me, when I realized they might want to interview me."

"I bet," Skylar said softly. "You've done a wonderful job. I've never seen Lonewood this busy. But maybe it's time you take a step back and let nature run its course. Take a break, Sienna. Everyone in this town needs a break right about now, especially you. If Lonewood keeps up this trajectory, more news crews are gonna come looking for the story of whoever turned this place around."

It was a hard pill to swallow- that Sienna could make Lonewood bigger, better, busier. But if she did, it could cost her and Alex their new home, just as they were starting to belong. Being sent somewhere else wouldn't be the end of the world for Sienna, but Alex would be devastated. She loved this little town and its people. She loved that she got to act again, even if she'd never see her name in lights. She danced with so much spirit that she hardly touched the ground, and as much as Sienna wanted the world to see it, she knew they couldn't have it both ways.

"Why don't you get some rest. Cool down a bit, then come when you're ready. If you need anything give me a call. I won't tell Bridget about your near miss."

One of the things they'd explained during their time at the facility was that people in Witness Protection would have monthly check-ins with their agent, but Sienna had yet to speak to Bridget. To her knowledge, neither had Alex, but it occurred to her now that it wasn't necessary because of Bridget's inside man. Skylar had been sending updates quietly, something harder for Landon to track. It was smart, but Sienna and Alex couldn't control the narrative this way. Bridget got her truth from Skylar, however Skylar saw it.

Although seeing as Bridget hadn't swept in to relocate them, Skylar must not have been too worried.

"Thanks," Sienna answered quietly. "I'll talk to you soon."

Once Skylar left, the residential section of Lonewood felt hauntingly empty. Sienna looked around for some sign of life, but the houses were quiet, a clear sign that everybody was at the cookout. Although she'd wanted to be alone, she didn't like the feeling of being *entirely* alone.

A shiver ran down her spine as she imagined a man she'd never met sneaking up behind her, grabbing her mouth, and slitting her throat. There'd be nobody around to hear her cry or scream. They'd find her as a heap of blood and bones on the ground in the middle of the street.

She wondered if Skylar would even be surprised, and if they'd get Alex out in time to save her life.

During the time Sienna had spent in Lonewood, she'd never felt unsafe. She'd been surrounded by decent, rugged people who knew how to take care of themselves and their town, and she'd felt a part of it. But walking this street alone reminded Sienna that they were hiding, and she wasn't doing a great job of it.

She jogged to Dakota's door, looking over her shoulder as she dug the key out of her small purse. She unlocked the door and closed it quickly, closing her eyes and breathing through her nose until the sound of excited barking broke her out of her fears.

Tilly jumped up on Sienna, trying to lick at her face as Buster circled her excitedly. He barked his greeting as she reached behind herself to padlock the door. "Hey guys! Hi!" Sienna knelt down, allowing the dog to give her slobbery kisses. She felt safe again as she threw her arms around the border collie's neck, squeezing Tilly as she ran her tongue up the side of her cheek excitedly. Buster lingered nearby, his tail thumping against Sienna's side as he waited for his turn to get attention.

Sienna leaned away from Tilly to kiss Buster's head, then groaned as she got to her feet. "C'mon guys, let's go."

She led the dogs further into Dakota's home, wanting to shower off the thin layer of dust covering her skin before crawling into bed for a nap. If the dogs decided to cuddle in bed with her while she slept, Sienna wouldn't be opposed.

Right as Sienna's fingers ghosted over the knob to the guest bathroom, the door flung open from the other side. She yelped and stumbled back a step, grabbing her chest as she tried to catch her breath, but the thing she registered first was that the dogs were unalarmed.

That was because Gentry stood in the doorway of the bathroom with a towel around his waist. His cheeks began turning deep red as he gaped down at Sienna in shock and embarrassment. The muscles in his shoulders tightened, and his chest heaved when he sucked in a sharp, surprised gasp. "Why aren't you at the cookout?"

"Why are you in Dakota's house?" Sienna gasped back, finally finding it in her to meet his eyes, and only his eyes. "I'm staying here. I wanted to shower."

"Okay." That was all he had to say apparently. Sienna clenched her jaw, narrowing her eyes at the man ahead of her. Behind him the bathroom was steamy, meaning he'd been there for a while. The idea of climbing into the still-wet shower made Sienna's stomach drop. An irrational train of thought, but it felt wrong to be naked in a shower that still had the man's water going down the drain. It felt almost as wrong as her intense desire to drop her gaze over the taut, wet skin of his bare chest.

He raised his brows, as if asking what she was waiting for and she gestured to the doorway. "You gonna just stand there? Or are you gonna let me use the restroom?"

Now Gentry seemed to understand that he was perpetuating this awkward encounter and he shifted away from the doorway to allow Sienna entrance. His gaze dropped to Buster, who panted up at him patiently while Tilly barked at him. "Stop that," he mumbled, his strained voice annoyed. She jumped up and he took a step back, his fist clenching the towel tighter around his waist as she tried to paw him. "Absolutely not. Sit down."

"Don't be mean to her," Sienna snapped, and he glared darkly at her. Sienna didn't shrink from him though, instead adding, "Why the hell are you here? Don't you have your own home?"

"I live out of town. Sometimes I stop by here if I'm in a hurry. I didn't realize anyone would be here, otherwise I would have kept my distance." He looked her up and down, and Sienna fought the urge to do the same to him. "You look nice."

Sienna bit her tongue to hold in her gasp. She wasn't in the mood for his insults. Maybe after a shower and a nap, but not right now. "Go to hell."

He seemed surprised by her response, brows raising high. He used the hand not clenching his towel to push his wet hair away from his forehead, his mouth twitching a little like he wanted to say something. Sienna was about to slam the bathroom door closed when his velvet voice stopped her. "I was being sincere."

She tightened her grip on the door, releasing a ragged breath before turning her gaze up at Gentry's face. His mouth tugged up in an attempt at a smile, as if trying to prove he'd been telling the truth. Sienna was caught between telling him she didn't care and he could go to hell anyway, and telling him he was the most handsome man she'd ever seen.

Gentry Wyatt made her feel something she wasn't used to, and she hated it. She hated that she felt it and she especially hated that she felt it for him. Sienna would never, even if her life depended on it, admit it out loud, but she knew what the feeling was. She was... attracted... to him. To this horrible, awful man who tortured her every chance he got, but damn it if he wasn't handsome. It was cruel that he was Dakota's brother, and that he always seemed to be around. A selfish, conniving, handsome distraction from Sienna's efforts.

She scowled up at him from under her lashes, deciding to forgo the shower in favor of locking herself in the guest bedroom. She *knew* he wouldn't bother her there. "You know what, I'm just gonna take a nap. See you later."

Sienna pushed past him, accidentally bumping into his arm as she bolted past. She was so tired she could hardly think straight, but the thought that repeated over and over in her head was *Don't*. Don't look at him, don't think about him, don't even consider, for half a second, that there could be something there. There wasn't. There wouldn't be.

Sienna didn't want to find that spark that Alex spoke so lovingly of. She didn't want to find someone who set her soul on fire, she didn't want to find someone to love. Sienna wasn't foolish enough to entertain the idea that the sheriff could have feelings for her, but the idea that she was developing feelings at all was terrifying. The last time she'd let herself feel anything, he hadn't chosen her. Mason hadn't chosen her, even though she thought they were going to be together forever. Sienna wasn't ready to let anyone else in yet, especially someone she knew would hurt her in the end.

The slam of the bedroom door echoed through the house, and Sienna held back the urge to cry. She flopped onto the guest bed and wrapped her arms around the pillow to bury her face into it. A tear slipped from her eye as she sniffled. Sienna had rarely cried since she'd been in Lonewood. She'd been so determined to prove herself useful that she hadn't stopped to sit with her feelings.

Now those feelings of loss, and fear, and rejection came pouring over her like a wave, threatening to drown her. She'd filled the motel, she'd brought business to Lonewood. Now that she'd done her job, though, she had to make a life here. She had to find happiness here, but finding extracurriculars beyond her job was terrifying.

It had always been about her job and about her future. Even with Mason, the man she'd planned on marrying, they pushed each other to work harder and achieve more. Their relationship was more of a business partnership, and once she wasn't useful to his goals he abandoned her.

There was a soft knock at the door, and Sienna stiffened. She didn't want to talk to Gentry, but yelling at him to go away was childish, and he'd mock her for it later, so she sat up and wiped the tears from under her eyes and cleared her throat.

When she slowly opened the door, Sienna found Gentry dressed in jeans and a black t-shirt. He looked so casual she hardly recognized him. It was a far cry from the chaps and vest he'd been wearing atop Domino at the cattle drive, and Sienna wanted to ask if he had clothes here at his sister's house. She raked her eyes over him obviously, hoping he'd catch her hint and explain without her having to ask.

Gentry's soft, borderline-worried brown eyes watched her study him, but he didn't address the outfit change. "Are you okay? I didn't mean to upset you."

"Everything isn't always about you," Sienna spat, feeling her jaw quiver a little. Of course he'd be self-absorbed enough to think this was about *him*. "I'm just tired. I've been working hard and I haven't been sleeping well. I want to be alone."

He looked hurt, but he just nodded and stepped a little to the side, allowing Tilly to sprint through his legs into the bedroom. "Does that count for her? She's a needy thing, but I'll chase her out if you wanna be alone."

Sienna looked over at the dog with a fond smile, already loving Tilly like she was her own pet. "No. I like her company. She doesn't try to run me out of town." She turned her ire back to Gentry and he sighed, massaging the bridge of his nose. He looked as exhausted as Sienna felt.

"I'm trying to make amends. I thought you were going to come up in here and change everything and... well, you did, but everybody seems really happy. I should be happy they are happy, I just struggle with change, okay? Even good change is hard." Gentry shoved his hands roughly in his pockets and looked down at Buster, who looked between him and Sienna, as if trying to decide who he wanted to follow around. "I was gonna hang out here for a while, but I don't want to make you uncomfortable. Do you want anything from the cookout? I can send some food back with Dakota. I'm sure she'll come running when she realizes I ran into you."

"You don't have to leave," Sienna looked down at Buster, catching the dog's attention. "I'm just crabby, but you can stay. Not here with me obviously, but you can do whatever you were gonna do."

A little smile played on his lips as he gestured over his shoulder. "I was just gonna watch some tv. Drink Dakota's beer and enjoy the air conditioning for a while. It's hot outside."

He wasn't wrong. Although there was no humidity, the summer sun was still sweltering this time of day, and the sheriff's uniform wasn't exactly lightweight. Sienna couldn't blame the man for wanting to enjoy some AC. Dakota would probably be missing him, though. "You aren't going to the cookout?"

"I figured I'd catch the end of it," Gentry answered with a shrug. "If you want to rest for a while, we could go together?"

Sienna blinked a couple times, then ran her tongue over the front of her teeth beneath her lips. She wasn't sure what his angle was, but he'd been too nice. Amends or not, she was still wary of his intentions. "You want to go to the cookout... with me?"

"Well, you want to sleep and I want to watch tv and eventually we'll both need food, so I figured maybe you'd like some company instead of walking the half mile by yourself." When Sienna crossed her arms and narrowed her eyes, he placed his hands in front of his chest, his smile turning coy. "You're right though, we'd hate for people to think we get along. It would ruin my image."

She scoffed and rolled her eyes. "Yeah, you'd hate for people to think you actually care. Or, God forbid, like spending time with me."

His eyes crinkled at that and he took a step back, understanding the conversation was done. His broad smile was genuine and there was laughter in his voice when he said, "God forbid." He gave a little bow of his head before he left. "I'll make sure I'm gone by the time you wake up."

Sienna watched him go, feeling her stomach twist in knots as her eyes traveled down the muscles of his back that strained against his shirt. She shook her head and quickly snapped the door closed, deciding Tilly was the only company in this house worth sharing her bed with.

Chapter 28

Sienna slept until the sun had dipped low in the sky. When she finally climbed out of bed, she wiped off her arms, feeling the dust from earlier crusted into her sweat.

Tilly stayed by her side as she tiptoed out of the bedroom, looking around to make sure she was alone. Gentry had kept his word and was long gone by the time she emerged, allowing Sienna to relax as she quietly snuck down the stairs. Buster popped his head up from the couch, then jumped down and followed Sienna towards the bathroom.

Before she could lock herself in for a shower, though, the front door opened and Sienna cursed to herself as Tilly and Buster took off running and barking.

"Sienna?"

Sienna gave up on her shower again and met Dakota in the kitchen, finding the woman unloading a bag full of leftovers. "Did you bring dinner?"

"Well, I know you didn't get lunch and it's almost eight, so I figured you might be hungry." Dakota popped open a container and Sienna almost sighed at how good it smelled. Dakota dished up a plate and put it in the microwave as Sienna watched, thankful her friend was willing to mother her a little. She was too tired to take care of herself.

But then Dakota whipped around and leaned forward over the counter to watch Sienna carefully with a sly grin. "I heard you ran into my brother getting out of the shower."

It took everything in Sienna not to turn and run away. She took a deep breath, grimacing as Dakota continued to wait for her answer. "I didn't know he was here."

"I didn't either, but he has a key. I'm sorry about that." Dakota didn't sound sorry. She sounded amused. She smiled brightly and leaned her cheek against her palm. "Are you two finally getting along?"

"I guess."

"Good! I'm so glad." Dakota straightened when the microwave beeped and grabbed Sienna's plate. It was piled with two massive pieces of steak and a baked potato, carrots, and beans cooked underneath it. Sienna was practically salivating from the heavenly smell, remembering that all she'd eaten since yesterday was the coffee she downed this morning.

"He was worried about you, you know. Said you looked a little shaken." Sienna's dark gaze lifted to stare at Dakota. She didn't want to talk about Gentry. Not now, not ever.

Dakota realized this and cleared her throat before changing the subject. "Are you feeling better?"

Sienna scarfed her food, hungrier than she wanted to admit. The food was delicious, and she regretted missing the event. She felt even worse that Alex had to miss it, too. "Yeah, I'm okay. I'm sorry I sketched out, I think everything we've been working on kept me going and going and I crashed. I'm so exhausted."

Dakota nodded rapidly, telling Sienna it was okay. "I'm glad you got to rest. Everything went great. The guests are happy. The saloon should be a full house tonight. I just wanted to make sure you were okay. Gentry was worried about-"

"I'm fine. I feel so much better after a nap. I don't need his worry. It's not like he actually cares." Sienna didn't mean for it to come off as sharp as it did, but she didn't want to talk about Gentry or her absence from the day. She wanted to eat this delicious food and mentally prepare for Monday's events. It would be the crown jewel of her efforts, and she wanted it to go off without a hitch.

Although Sienna had made it clear she didn't want to talk about Gentry, Dakota smirked as she watched Sienna eat, and it became apparent that she *did* want to talk about why her brother irked her houseguest. "I gotta know, what is it about him that bothers you so much?"

"Aside from him being an asshole for the past two months?"

"He's trying. At least I hope he's trying, I asked him very specifically," Dakota grumbled. "I know he can be... difficult... at times, but he's sweet. He cares about this town a lot, and he was only busting your chops to make sure your intentions were good."

Sienna shoved a chunk of meat into her mouth and moaned at the flavor. If she'd gone to the cookout instead of sleeping, she could have not only avoided this conversation but eaten as much of this food as her stomach could handle.

She wondered how Dakota kept her stunning figure. She looked like an athlete: tall, muscular, and lean. With her bright eyes and perfect smile, she'd be intimidatingly beautiful if it weren't for her naturally kind demeanor.

It was a curious thing that the woman could be so open, yet so closed off. Sienna wasn't sure how she *knew* Dakota, but didn't know anything about her. Perhaps, like her brother, she was an onion who needed to be peeled back layer by layer. Gentry seemed to hide a kind soul beneath his tough, judgemental exterior. Sienna wondered if Dakota was the opposite: a woman who held everyone close with false trust, but kept her true feelings and intentions close to her chest. Only a woman could be so deceiving, so impressive. Sienna wanted to believe that Dakota was simpler, truly good to her core, but she wouldn't know until she dug a little deeper.

"What's your deal with your brother?" Sienna asked bluntly, deciding not to beat around the bush any longer. Dakota leaned back in surprise, furrowing her brows as Sienna elaborated on her question. "You two are impossibly close. Like, I initially thought you two were sleeping together, and I told myself that was because I didn't know either of you, but now that I do I'm even more confused. You're attached at the hip, but it feels a little... one sided."

"What do you mean by that?" Dakota's tone was cold and defensive. Sienna had never heard her speak to anybody like that, even Gentry.

Nobody in Lonewood batted an eye at the siblings' closeness, but it unnerved Sienna. She wanted to tread lightly with her words, but she needed to understand what everybody else seemed to. "You just seem very interested in his business, but he doesn't seem too worried about you. I guess I don't understand why you're always trying to make sure Alex and I don't have problems with him. He's an adult, he doesn't need help making friends. Well, maybe a little, but only because he's so boorish."

"It's my fault." Her lower lip quivered a little and she sucked in a shaky breath, trying not to cry. Sienna felt frozen in place as she waited for Dakota to elaborate and she watched the woman's facade crack and fall away as she confessed, "It's my fault that Kenzie died. I was supposed to go with her, but at the last moment I told her I couldn't. If I'd been there she might still be alive. I'm part of the reason she's gone and I feel horrible, so I make sure he's okay. I'm sure it comes across as weird and overbearing. I know he thinks so, but I can't just walk away. Because last time I did that- I just need to make sure he's okay."

Oh.

"I'm really sorry. I shouldn't have asked."

"No, it's fine," Dakota assured her, wiping tears from beneath her eyes. "She was my best friend- Kenzie. I adored her, almost as much as he did." She chuckled and Sienna furrowed her brows at the comment.

Dakota watched her for a moment, her eyes sparkling mischievously. She didn't speak for a few seconds, as if considering her next words carefully. "We did everything together, the three of us. And Jasmine- us girls lived together in college so we were inseparable."

The photo from Alex's book of the three women flashed through Sienna's mind and she nodded. She wondered if Jasmine felt some sort of resentment towards Dakota. It would explain why the third member of their trio didn't seem interested in socializing with the mayor, but didn't mind Gentry hanging around her bar.

"Was she the youngest? Of you three?" Sienna dared to ask and Dakota looked at her with wide eyes, but quickly blinked away whatever she was thinking and stared out the window with her jaw tight. Sienna quickly shook her head, picking up her empty plate to rinse it at the sink. "Nevermind. I'm sorry to bring it up. It's none of my business."

"It's not that..." Dakota trailed off, then forced a smile that didn't quite reach her eyes. She joined Sienna at the sink and took her plate, watching the water spray as she spoke. "She was younger than me, but older than Gentry. They were closer in age, so... but at college us girls lived together. We got really close then." She pulled her heap of hair over her shoulder, then placed Sienna's plate in the dishwasher.

"She had spirit. She wanted to be a teacher, and she wanted the people of Lonewood to believe there was more to life outside of here. That's why she pushed to get the kids into extracurriculars. She loved theater, and in turn, taught Annie to love theater. Annie was a junior and had no experience with acting, and Kenzie wasn't going to let her go to college like that, so she went to Bismarck to file a permit for our kids to go to the neighboring towns for sports and the arts. Her car slid off the road on the way back, but she filed what she needed to, so that spring the kids were invited to do Track and Field, Baseball, Theater, Choir, and Basketball at other schools."

Dakota sniffled, smiling through her tears. "Annie was so good that she went to UND on a Theater scholarship. She probably wouldn't have even gone to college if it wasn't for Kenzie, and she knows it, so we're very protective of her. We're protective of all of them."

"I'm so sorry for your loss," Sienna breathed out, feeling a guilty weight in her own stomach. That was the secret the mayor kept behind her mask. She was riddled with so much guilt that she felt the need to keep the town afloat. If she'd gone with Kenzie, she might not be doing it alone. "I'm glad you didn't go, though, as awful as it probably sounds. I'm really thankful that I got to meet you."

She laughed through the tears that flowed from her amber eyes, wiping them as she nodded. "I'm really thankful I got to meet you, too. You remind me of her a little bit. Which I'm sure you don't wanna hear, but it's definitely a compliment. I think, deep down, that's why Gentry doesn't want to open up to you. Because he sees her in you, and that's hard. But whether you mean to or not, you're bringing life back to this town.

It's something she wanted, so you're carrying on her legacy. I will follow wherever you lead, because I owe her that. I owe all of them that."

Sienna pulled Dakota in for a hug. She clutched Sienna tightly, like she hadn't been comforted in a long time. Sienna didn't know how to admit it, but she needed it too. And because Dakota had been vulnerable and told Sienna a hard truth, Sienna decided to tell her something vaguely true. "I wasn't actually sick earlier," she confessed quietly. "I was scared to be on camera because we're hiding from somebody."

Dakota pulled away roughly at that, looking down at Sienna in alarm as she kept her tight grip on her shoulders. "What?"

"Alex was in an abusive relationship. He was emotionally manipulative and things got really bad. She broke it off and he wasn't happy, so we left California to put some space between them. I panicked today because I don't want to risk him seeing us. I wouldn't put it past him to come here and try to reconcile, but I can't let her get back into that relationship again. She has a good life here. She has a good thing going with Jesse, even if it feels a little soon. It's casual I guess." Sienna laughed, because deep down she knew her little sister didn't do casual flings. She never would have dated Jesse back home, but he was exactly what she needed here. "I want her to be happy."

The blonde woman nodded to herself, chewing the inside of her cheek as she studied Sienna with newfound interest and pity. "You moved here for your sister? You gave up your life in California to make sure she was okay?"

It made Sienna sound like a saint, instead of the whining bitch who'd begrudgingly came with Alex because staying behind wasn't an option. She could stay and die, go off on her own, or stay with her sister. She'd chosen the least of the evils, but what she'd told Dakota was mostly true. Landon and Alex didn't have a relationship, but he was certainly emotionally manipulative. She was in a bad spot and they did leave to put some space between them. It did feel abusive, because if she'd stayed, she would have been killed. But Sienna felt horrible that Dakota somehow thought Sienna had done this to protect Alex. She hadn't been that selfless, but with time and space between her and the life she'd been forced to abandon, Sienna knew she would do anything to protect her little sister, just like Dakota was trying to protect her brother.

If Sienna didn't protect Alex, she could end up dead like Kenzie, and she could live with the same festering guilt that Dakota did.

"She's all I have left," Sienna admitted truthfully. "If she's happy and safe, I'll be okay wherever I am."

Dakota tapped her fingertips on the counter top for a moment before moving to the pantry to get treats for Tilly and Buster. "So Alex left an abusive relationship. She won't find that with Jesse, he doesn't have it in him. He's a good man, and he'll take good care of her." There was a pause, a silent question, but when Sienna didn't say anything, Dakota asked, "What about you? Are you lonely?"

Sienna shrugged. "Nope. I'm busy. My ex wasn't great either. Not abusive by any means, but we... I wanted him to come. Here. I wanted us to do this together. Thought there'd be a ring in my future, but he said his job was more important, so he declined. Then I had a choice to either stay with him or come with Alex and I broke it off."

Not exactly the truth, but it gave Sienna a little win. Dakota would never know.

"I'm sorry, that sucks," Dakota placed her hands on her hips. "You need a cowboy. Good men. Loyal, hard working. Great in bed. We'll find you somebody who's gonna make you forget he ever did you wrong."

A snort escaped Sienna's nose before she could stop it, but she embraced the moment and shook her head, causing her crumpled pigtails to whip back and forth. "I'm pretty sure the only eligible cowboy in this town under the age of fifty has been swept up by my little sister. No offense to him, but I'm not going out with Hank."

Dakota laughed loudly, the sound startling Tilly from her spot by her feet. "Jesus, no! Not Hank! There's tons of guys here who are single."

"Well, then why don't you date them?"

"Because I grew up with them," Dakota deadpanned. "Or I've already slept with them and it didn't work out."

Fair point. Sienna chuckled and shook her head, taking a seat at the table to rest her feet. She tossed her arm over the back of the chair, torn between wanting to gossip about who Dakota slept with and wanting to avoid this conversation all together.

She couldn't remember the last time she'd had girl talk. Even with Alex, it was always about work, or about her established relationship with Mason, which didn't quite feel the same. Sienna didn't exactly have a solid group of girl friends in Manhattan, because any time she wasn't working she spent with Mason and Alex.

Then Sienna remembered she already had one interested party in Lonewood, and he was no cowboy. "Doctor Thompson actually asked me out. I haven't said yes, but he's been very patient." He was polite enough, handsome, and successful. He was different from the other men here, and that was a quality that intrigued Sienna.

Dakota didn't seem impressed, though. "Oh, Brad. Yeah, he's quite persistent when he wants something." She tisked her tongue before sighing, "At least you'd enjoy a nice dinner and a good roll in the hay if that's what you're looking for."

"Do you know this from gossip or experience?"

She hesitated, squishing her face and groaning, "Experience."

Sienna put her finger up, telling Dakota to wait as she shook her head firmly and said. "No. Absolutely not."

"I mean, don't *not* go out with him on my account. We never dated. Just went out... twice I think. The sex wasn't worth suffering through a third date."

The food she'd just scarfed roiled in Sienna's stomach at Dakota's words. "Why do you say that?"

Dakota chuckled and pulled a beer out of the fridge. She offered it to Sienna, but she shook her head, so Dakota popped the cap off for herself before sitting across from her. "Brad isn't looking for a long-term love, he's looking for a good time. Nothing wrong with that. I'm honestly the same way. I doubt I'll ever get married and that doesn't bother me. But he's... he thinks he's important, because he's a doctor. Because he doesn't buy into our town bullshit. He's too good for our make-believe and pretend, so he presents himself as a classier option."

"That alone makes me want to say no," Sienna murmured, but she didn't sound as determined as she wanted to. A small part of her thought Brad could be a good partner for her in Lonewood. They probably had a lot in common and Sienna didn't feel like she had much in common with anyone else.

Dakota caught the waver in Sienna's voice and smiled softly. "If you want to go out with him, you should! Worst case he'll get you out of Lonewood for the evening and he's not a bad conversationalist by any means. He claims I bored him, but in reality I wasn't interested in anything more than sex. Gentry woulda pummeled him to a pulp, and we need him as the town's physician, so that's where our fling ended."

Sienna pursed her lips, unsure a man's company was worth potentially straining her friendship with Dakota. "I don't sleep with my friend's exes."

"Then it's a good thing he and I aren't exes," Dakota laughed. "But I'm glad we're friends. If you're interested in Brad, you should let him take you to dinner. Maybe you're what he needs to settle down. All it takes is the right person to change everything, you know?"

And sometimes, all it takes is the wrong person to ruin everything.

"Speaking of changing everything," Dakota started, her tone a warning that she was about to change the subject. "I talked to Maude at the cookout, and she agrees that we've done much better than we could have imagined. Our crowds are borderline uncontrollable and there's a lot of work to be done around town. So I asked Kennedy to stop booking Mondays through Thursdays. We want to make Lonewood a weekend experience. People come Friday afternoon and they leave Sunday evening or Monday morning. That'll give us the weekdays to recuperate and really overhaul anything that needs updating."

Sienna blinked, running through this idea in her head. Losing four days worth of income would be disastrous to their bottom line. It wouldn't turn people away, per se, but it would definitely be a hit to their progress.

"Sienna, everyone is tired. Including you," Dakota told her slowly. Sienna winced, knowing she'd proven Dakota's point by sleeping the entire day away. "And there's a lot to be done. Kennedy and Trevor actually have money to update the rooms. We can redo the walkways, paint the buildings, really update the spots that need it. But it's hard to do that while there are visitors here. There aren't enough of us to entertain and do updates, and we don't, and won't, have the money to hire a team to do it. This will be good for everyone. It can be even more immersive for our visitors. That's what they want."

It was like a new pathway opened up before Sienna. Instead of thinking about how much money and business they'd lose, she channeled her focus into what more they could offer. They could charge more for updated rooms. They could open new food options and come up with more activities that change every weekend. If people came Friday and left Monday they'd have an immersive, cohesive experience that lasted several days, something not offered anywhere else. "This could be big. It could change the way people look at Lonewood."

"And it could change the way the people in Lonewood think of their home." Dakota sounded so hopeful that Sienna realized what this was really about. This was another incentive for the kids to come back. For them to stay. A home where they lived in the old west three days a week and lived in their sleepy hometown the other four. It was a compromise between the old way of thinking and the modern world the young people so desperately wanted to be a part of.

Sienna agreed. "Yeah. I think this could be great. I'm assuming we're booked through next weekend?"

"Yeah, Kennedy said she'd adjust availability tonight," Dakota explained quietly, her mind somewhere else. Dakota sighed and stretched her arms above her head. "I'm tired. I'm gonna get some sleep, and tomorrow we'll start preparing for Monday. The college kids have some fun ideas, so I'm gonna let them run the activities, but I want you to be in charge of tickets. I figured you'd like that more than wandering around getting in people's photos, plus then you can gauge how they're enjoying it. Think you can handle it?"

"Of course, actually sounds relaxing,"

"I'll find somebody to help you so you aren't alone." Sienna raised her brow and Dakota scoffed, offended that Sienna would insinuate she'd pick someone she wouldn't appreciate. "I'll pick someone good, I promise."

Chapter 29

J ULY WAS SCORCHING IN Lonewood, North Dakota. Sienna's phone showed the temperature as 95 degrees, and when she peeked out the window of her bedroom in Dakota's house, she saw there wasn't a cloud in the sky.

So, knowing she'd spend the entire day out in the sun selling tickets at the Fourth of July festival, Sienna donned a pair of tiny jean shorts and a white halter top with her detailed cowboy boots. She swept her hair up into a high ponytail to get it off her neck and slathered herself in sunscreen, but when she stepped outside, she knew it wasn't going to help much.

She was roasting in the summer sun as she followed Dakota through her office and onto Main Street. Lyle and Annie led a group of tourists on horseback down the road from the saloon towards the Badlands for a morning trail ride and Sienna furrowed her brows when she realized a man was riding Bandit.

"A couple of us gave Lyle permission to use our horses so they could do a bigger ride today," Dakota explained. "If we stay this busy, we'll need to expand the stables, maybe even hire some help for Lyle." She waved at a couple of kids that ran by towards the saloon. "Maude's hosting an all-you-can-eat brunch, which will help clear out Main Street so we can prepare for the festival- carnival thing."

A handful of the college kids were already working on Main Street, setting up booths and games for their visitors to play. Maddie and Jewel set up a series of games near the courthouse, such as corn hole and hoseshoes, while Jolene helped Colton set up a couple of carnival games at some booths they'd built over the past week. Kennedy and Trevor helped haul out some of Kitty's wares to sell at an outdoor kiosk, including a bunch of Fourth of July items she'd brought back from a trip to Bismarck last week.

Preston, Owen, and Owen's wife Heidi had brought in a pair of tiny black and white calves who were currently being bottle fed by the woman as her husband used a hose to fill a water trough in the pen they'd erected to act as a petting zoo. They'd brought in goats, sheep, a couple of pigs, and an emu that caused Sienna to cock her head.

"Where the hell did we get an emu?"

Dakota shrugged, "Honestly, it's better not to ask questions."

Gentry appeared from behind them, carrying a large folding table in one arm and a black cash box in the other. He dropped the table on its side, letting it lean against his leg as he wiped his hand on his jeans. "Where d'ya wanna set up?"

"Near the entrance to Main Street coming from the motel." Dakota pointed towards the diner and Gentry hoisted the table and moved it to where Dakota directed. Sienna smiled as she looked back at the busy street, already smelling the caramel apples and popcorn they were making fresh from the sweets shop. Sienna hoped she could sneak away from the ticket counter long enough to get some snacks, because everything smelled heavenly. She also wouldn't complain if she got to cuddle all the animals in the petting zoo.

By the time she caught up with Gentry and Dakota, the table was set up and Dakota was smoothing a red, white, and blue tablecloth over it to make it look nicer while Gentry supervised with his hands on his hips. He glanced over at Sienna, nodding a little as he surveyed the preparations. "Should be a nice afternoon and evening. Let's just hope nothing catches on fire."

"Are we doing fireworks?" Sienna asked, having been told that wasn't an option due to the surrounding brush and wooden buildings.

Dakota shook her head, pursing her lips. "No, but we have sparklers. It'll be fine." She smacked Gentry's chest and said, "Don't be a downer. It's gonna go great."

The sheriff looked down at Sienna, staring at her outfit and hair before giving a slow nod of approval. His smile said he was amused, though. "You look festive."

"It's hot. I wore the lightest thing I could find," she muttered as she smoothed down her white shirt. It wasn't sheer by any means, but it was tight enough to cling to her stomach, so she lightly tucked it into her shorts and looked back up at Gentry. Apparently Dakota hadn't asked him to dress for the occasion, because he wore a navy t-shirt with his jeans and boots. Instead of a cowboy hat, he wore an old gray baseball cap that might have had a logo on the front at some point before being worn away. Sienna chuckled. "What, no chaps and spurs? Do we not need a sheriff on Independence Day?"

He snorted, yanking his head back while he stared down at her as if she'd offended him greatly. "Excuse you. I'm allowed to have a day off every once in a while. I don't work seven days a week."

"Coulda fooled me."

"Well," Gentry said quickly, gesturing to his sister as her smile grew all the way to her bright eyes. "I would have preferred to spend my day off actually celebrating the Fourth, but I've been wrangled into helping the mayor. Which means not only do I have to work on my day off, but I have to spend it working with you."

Sienna turned on Dakota so fast the blonde took a step back, placing her hands up in front of her chest. "Hey! You said you were getting along. You'll do great talking to the people and getting a good sense of how their trip is going and he'll be back up. A quiet, stoic presence to make sure there's no funny business." She turned to her brother and gestured towards the carnival games and activities being set up along the street. "Besides, I figured you'd rather do this than help little kids throw darts or be part of the kissing booth!"

"I'm sure all the women will be devastated to see you aren't available," Sienna hissed up at him, but she couldn't stop the smile from spreading at his annoyed expression. She smacked him hard on the back, but he didn't so much as flinch at the contact. "We'll have fun, won't we?"

He raised a brow, clearly not believing Sienna, but he shrugged and sighed anyway. "Yeah, it'll be fine."

Dakota clapped her hands together and released a long breath. "Good. Glad to hear it. I'll let you two get set up. It's two dollars per ticket, and one ticket gets them one turn at anything. The petting zoo closes at seven-thirty, so once it gets a little later, warn people, okay?"

"Yes ma'am." Gentry gave a half-hearted salute and doubled back to the diner to collect a couple of chairs. When Sienna turned back to Dakota, she saw the blonde wink before walking away, and Sienna wondered if Dakota was trying to set Sienna up with Gentry. As much as Dakota seemed to care about her brother, she clearly didn't know his taste in women very well if she thought he'd ever consider Sienna as a viable girlfriend. And Sienna would rather have her eyes pecked out by that emu than go on a date with Gentry Wyatt.

When he returned with two chairs, Sienna took a seat and pulled out her phone, snapping a few photos of Main Street as setup finished. She quickly edited her favorite and posted it to Instagram, writing that their Fourth of July Celebration was about to begin. She answered a few people's comments until she heard Gentry drop himself into the chair beside her.

She stiffened when he looked over her shoulder, watching her work. Turning to look at him, he met her gaze with an easy expression, even though their noses were less than a foot away from each other. "Can I help you?"

He stayed put, not pulling away at her sharp tone. "Just wanted to see what you're doing. I'm not on social media, but clearly whatever you're doing is working. I'm curious."

He was too close. His deep brown eyes were too alluring and his expression was too soft. His large, relaxed body was inches from pressing into hers. She didn't believe he wanted her to close the gap between them, but it would be so easy. Sienna swallowed hard and shook her head. She didn't want to play this game with him. She didn't want to play this game with anyone.

His brows furrowed as he finally leaned away, breaking the spell between them. "What is it?"

"We can't-"

"Can I purchase some tickets? Or is it too early?"

Sienna was jarred from her conversation with Gentry by a mother and her two little boys who were bobbing up and down excitedly. They looked at Sienna with big blue eyes as they waited for their mother to get them tickets to run off and enjoy the festivities. The littler child tugged on his mother's t-shirt and whispered, "Can I go to the petting zoo?"

"Of course! How many would you like?" Sienna chirped as she opened the cash box and pulled out a roll of red tickets. After the mom handed Sienna thirty dollars, she passed back fifteen tickets and the kids took off sprinting towards the petting zoo. Their mother trailed behind as her boys handed off their tickets to Heidi and were allowed entry to see the animals.

"Alright, out with it, what's wrong?" Gentry leaned forward on his elbow to see Sienna, forcing himself into her view.

"Nothing is wrong!" Sienna yelped, turning from Gentry to smile at a passing couple who handed her ten dollars. She gave them their tickets before passing over the ten dollar bill for Gentry to put away.

He snatched it from her hand and put it in the box, snapping the lid roughly before leaning back in his chair with his arms crossed. "It's gonna be a long day if you don't tell me what's bothering you. Is it Saturday? What happened at Dakota's?"

"No."

"Then what is it?"

"Nothing is wrong," Sienna snarled through gritted teeth. "What's wrong is you not focusing on the task at hand. We have a job to do, let's worry about that. There's no issues between us, but there will be if you keep bothering me."

Gentry chuckled airily, shaking his head in disbelief. "Always about the job, isn't it? I thought you were starting to get it, but you haven't changed a bit."

Sienna's blood ran cold at his words, and it took everything in her not to smack him for it. "How dare you? You don't know anything about me. You don't know how hard I worked to get to where I am-"

"It doesn't matter. None of it matters. Success, money- it doesn't matter." Gentry swallowed, pulling the brim of his baseball cap down a little more. He clamped his mouth shut, nostrils flaring as he stared ahead. "One day you could wake up and everything you worked for could be wiped away."

"Yeah, I'm aware," Sienna muttered. Everything she had worked for had been wiped away by the actions of somebody else. She couldn't do anything to salvage her hopes and dreams, except to start over....

Sienna suddenly realized what Gentry was referring to, though, and guilt coursed through her veins. One day he'd lost somebody important to him, and Sienna's words made her look even more like a spoiled brat than before. "Gentry, I'm-"

Another family approached them for tickets and Sienna plastered on a smile and finished the transaction while Gentry simmered beside her with his arms crossed over his chest and an ugly scowl on his face. It would be easier to stay silent and put their tense conversation to rest, but Sienna felt bad for upsetting him. He'd actually lost someone. She was fortunate that she couldn't relate to that.

When the family left, Sienna glanced at the man, finding his russet eyes fixed on the games ahead. Jewel was kneeling down to help a small child throw a ball at a tower of metal milk bottles, while Colton leaned against the side of the booth with a doting smile. Even from halfway down the road, Sienna could see how smitten he was, and she felt a pang in her own chest.

A year ago, Mason took her to the Hamptons for a beach weekend. They'd lounged around an infinity pool overlooking the ocean, while a butler served them drinks and charcuterie along the pool's edge at sunset. They'd talked about their aspirations and dreams, and each one of those had been about promotions, big homes, and lavish vacations. They hadn't spoken about marriage, not even once, but they'd made those plans together. It had seemed obvious at the time that they would realize those dreams together.

Sienna realized now those plans they'd made could happen with anyone. Mason didn't need *her*. Maybe he was happier with her gone-one less expensive distraction from his job he loved so much. If she really stopped and thought about it, she was happier without him, too.

"I'm sorry." Sienna's voice softened as she dropped her head, feeling guilty for upsetting Gentry. Sweat dripped from her temple and she wiped it away quickly, then turned to look Gentry in the eye. "I can't imagine what you've been through, and I shouldn't have blown you off. I've been pouring myself into my work because I left some things- some people- back home, and I've been having a hard time with that. But I haven't gone through anything like you and Dakota."

Her words must have struck a chord with Gentry, because he shifted a little to face her, giving her his full attention. "I didn't realize."

Sienna chuckled, blinking as she squinted her eyes in the sun. She should have brought sunglasses or a hat. "Just means I did a good job hiding it. And staying busy, which was my intention."

"How did you and Alex end up in Lonewood?"

She wondered if Dakota had told Gentry about Alex's abusive boyfriend, or if he was trying to figure Sienna out for himself since she'd started opening up. Either way, Sienna knew better than to tell a different story, and blowing off his curiosity would only make her look more suspicious. "Alex needed a change after getting out of a bad relationship. I didn't want her to leave town alone, so here I am. One of Skylar's friends told us about Lonewood, and it seemed like a decent enough place to start over. Somewhere we could dissapear. It's... uh, a little different than I anticipated." Sienna chuckled and Gentry smiled sadly. "I'm sorry I came in and changed your town. Your sister kinda cornered me, and I wanted to get back to work. It was a good offer and with my skill set I knew I could do a good job, but I know you haven't exactly been supportive."

He grunted, turning a little to watch Main Street fill with more people checking out the festivities. The trail ride would return within the hour, meaning what little solitude they had wouldn't last long, but once the event was in full swing, they'd have some quiet once they'd sold tickets to everyone. Sienna assumed some of these early parties would be back for more sooner rather than later.

"That reminds me, I guess I'm at your beck and call for the rest of the summer," Gentry mumbled, pulling the brim of his hat a little lower so Sienna couldn't see his eyes. She could see his little grin though. "What'll your first task be for me?"

Sienna looked around the celebration, smiling to herself at the possibilities. After a long moment of considering her options, Gentry added without any sort of prompting, "I draw the line at sleeping with you."

She glared at him darkly. He slowly lifted the brim of his hat, gazing back at her with crinkled eyes and a playful smirk. Sienna shook her head, hating her traitorous stomach that flipped at the fleeting thought of Gentry's mouth attacking hers. "Absolutely not. First of all, no. Second of all, I'm far too professional to waste such a lucrative deal on personal matters. Except maybe making you watch the ticket stand so I can visit the petting zoo."

He laughed at that, nodding as his chest shook with his laughter. "That I can do." He tossed his head towards the petting zoo where a horde of children were terrorizing the goats and pigs while a young woman petted one of the calves gently. "Big animal person, huh?"

"You know, I didn't think I was until I moved here," Sienna chuckled. "I guess I like that they listen. And sometimes it's nice to have something to hold. It's never that simple with people, you know?"

They gazed at each other for a moment, and Sienna felt her cheeks heat up. She probably sounded foolish, but she meant every word. Finally, Gentry nodded a little and murmured, "I get it. My best friend is a horse, remember?"

"Which is funny, because Dakota says you're her best friend."

"Well, Dakota can be a bit overbearing," Gentry grumbled. "She means well, though. She's a good sister, just... a little overprotective at times. I think she forgets that I can take care of myself."

Sienna leaned her elbow on the table, resting her cheek on her knuckles. Her inner thoughts tumbled out before she could consider the ramifications of it, "I think she's trying to set us up."

"Oh, she definitely is," Gentry laughed, and Sienna's body went rigid. Her eyes slid over to him, waiting for him to elaborate on his thoughts about the matter. He sighed, shaking his head. "I'm sorry about her. She knows better. Aside from us butting heads like a couple of bulls, I'm not looking for any sort of relationship."

The way Gentry let her down easy made Sienna cringe, because she didn't want him to think she was interested. She wasn't. "Good, glad we're on the same page."

"Besides, Brad's already made his intentions of taking you out abundantly clear." Gentry eyed Sienna curiously as her cheeks burned red.

"What do you mean?"

"He was at Jazzy's last night. Give that man a couple of drinks and he'll tell you whatever's on his mind." Sienna gaped at Gentry as he chuckled. "He made it very clear he didn't want me moving in on his woman."

"He *said* that?"

"Well, I read between the lines. He said he hoped you'd call him back soon, but he said it directly to me." Gentry's all-too-pleased smirk couldn't be contained, his ego boosted to an eleven. The only guy in town Sienna would consider dating thought *Gentry* was the man he had to watch out for.

Sienna wanted to go crawl under the porch with the rattlesnakes and die somewhere Lonewood's infuriating men couldn't find her.

Gentry bumped her with his elbow to get her attention. "You're looking a little pink."

When she looked at him, his gaze was gentler, a bit curious. Had the look come from anyone else, Sienna would have thought it was fondness, but that wasn't applicable for her and Gentry. Sienna pressed her fingers against her cheeks, feeling how hot they were, but it was from embarrassment, not sunburn. "I should have worn a hat," she mumbled, trying to deflect the truth.

Suddenly, Gentry pulled off his old baseball cap and placed it firmly over Sienna's ponytail to cover her head. He yanked down the brim and she tilted her head to look at him. "There," he told her as he scanned her face with a soft gaze. "Much better."

Her eyes widened a little when she felt it. That feeling, the one Alex always talked about. It was the spark, and Sienna had never felt anything like it. Her whole body felt like it was buzzing with electricity and she started praying for a power outage.

"If you two can stop staring into each other's eyes, I'd like to buy some tickets please."

Sienna and Gentry whipped around to see Jasmine hovering over them with a twenty dollar bill outstretched for one of them to take. Sienna breathed a sigh of relief at the distraction, willing the color in her face to go down as she took the money while Gentry snapped off ten tickets and handed them over to the woman. Jasmine split the tickets in half and handed them over to a pair of twin boys who looked to be about ten standing right behind her.

"How's it going?" Gentry asked casually, placing his forearms on the table to lean forward, squinting up at Jasmine. "How're the boys?"

"They're fine," Jasmine answered sharply, shooting Sienna a cold look. Sienna raised her brows to question it. She'd spoken to Jasmine Lee exactly once, and although accusing her of illegal activity in her bar wasn't exactly a great interaction, she assumed Jasmine had realized Sienna had gotten over her initial judgments. Judging by the way she looked at Sienna like an annoying gnat, perhaps she hadn't. Jasmine offered Gentry a sweet smile, an obvious show that she didn't mind *him*. "They're excited to play games and get sparklers later. How are you? Keeping busy I see."

"Yeah, I think it's going well." Gentry gestured down Main Street.

He raised his hand to shield his eyes from the sun when he looked back at Jasmine, and her dark eyes spared a lazy look at Sienna wearing his hat. She knew exactly what had happened, because she scoffed playfully, "Looks like you need a hat, Buddy."

Sienna quickly snatched the cap off her head and handed it back to Gentry without looking at him, using her free hand to smooth down her high ponytail. Stupid hat. Stupid smile. Stupid spark. She blinked her eyes quickly, adjusting to the bright sun overhead. It took longer than she expected for Gentry to take his hat back and pull it over his head.

He leaned back so he could look up at Jasmine, raising his brows high. Sienna was surprised to hear the bite in his voice when he asked, "Better?"

"Much," she answered. Her gaze was cruel when it slid to Sienna before addressing Gentry again. "I'll see you tonight at the bar."

She turned to leave and Sienna saw her husband following their sons towards a darts game. The dark-haired woman didn't turn around, but she walked with her chin high as if she owned the place. She was intimidating in her quiet confidence. She was different from Dakota in so many ways, but this had been her friend once. Sienna couldn't imagine the two together now.

"I'm gonna use the restroom really quick. Think you can hold down the fort while I'm gone?" Sienna asked, needing to get away from him. Dakota was trying to set them up. Brad seemed to think something was going on between them. Jasmine clearly wasn't happy that they were spending time together. The last thing Sienna needed was for people to think something was going on when it wasn't.

She pushed back from the table to stand, but when she looked down, Gentry was pulling out his wallet from his jeans. "What are you doing?"

He pulled out two dollar bills and put them in the cash box, then ripped off a single ticket and handed it up to Sienna. She took it tentatively, staring at it as if it was something more precious than a scrap of red paper. "So you can go to the petting zoo before the animals get tired of the kids harassing them."

Sienna smiled a little, clutching the ticket in her palm. "Thanks. I'll be back soon."

"Take your time," Gentry told her softly. "I'll be fine here."

After using the restroom at Dakota's quiet office, Sienna made her way over to the petting zoo. She didn't spare a look back at the ticket table as she handed off her ticket to Owen. He pulled open the gate and ushered her in, and she had to catch herself from tripping over a pig who smashed into her legs.

She laughed and stepped around it, then squatted down to scratch her long fingernails through the fur of one of the goats until a calf mooing stole her attention away. She walked over to the calves and rubbed one of their necks as she knelt and cooed, "Hi cutie. Look at you, aren't you adorable?"

"Almost as cute as you."

Sienna looked up to see Brad leaning against the fence, watching her play with the animals. Her cheeks flushed with embarrassment, but she didn't stop running her fingernails through the calf's fur. "Hi. I didn't know you were coming."

He gestured around and explained, "I mean, I heard all the commotion and wanted to see how your big Fourth of July celebration was going. Also I need to be around when a small child inevitably stabs somebody with a dart or catches themselves on fire with a sparkler later." Sienna wasn't amused that he was mocking her efforts, but he chuckled at her miffed expression. "It's a shame we aren't having any fireworks, but you are quite the firecracker in that outfit."

She adjusted her top, suddenly aware that he was standing over her and had quite the view of her cleavage. "Thank you," she managed, even if she didn't mean it. She stood, but her fingers continued to scratch the little black and white calf. It took a moment to shake off how uncomfortable she was, but when she found her voice again, she fired back, "I hear you were talking about me at the bar last night."

Brad shrugged, seemingly unworried by her accusation. "Just making sure to stake my claim." He looked her up and down and she froze, her fingers stopping their scratching to hold the calf's neck, as if it could protect her. His lips twitched up into a small smile. "You're a beautiful woman, Sienna. Any man would be lucky to spend time with you, so you gotta forgive me for wanting everyone to know I'm interested. Although, seeing as you'd rather spend time with the goats and pigs than Sheriff Wyatt, I don't think I have to worry about sharing your attention." His gaze darkened and he scoffed, "I don't blame you, he can be a bit rough around the edges for a woman like you."

What the hell is that supposed to mean?

"Well," Sienna reached her hand under the calf's chin to scratch its neck, "I wanted to come to the petting zoo so he bought me a ticket. I figured I shouldn't waste his money. I'm incredibly polite."

Her answer surprised Brad, and she thought maybe he heard the frustration in her voice for the first time, because he stood straighter and furrowed his brows. Sparing a look at the ticket table where Gentry still sat, Brad hummed deep in his throat. "He's just playing nice to appease the mayor. I wouldn't get too attached. He doesn't let anybody in."

"I have no intention of getting attached. We can hardly stand each other, but that is none of your business. You don't even know me."

If you did, you'd know that I'd rather be here with the cows and pigs than with you.

Sienna was tired of Brad's condescending words and sleazy compliments. She was about to tell him not to bother asking her out again, but when she opened her mouth to speak, he interrupted, "I want to get to know you. I'm sorry I'm doing a bad job of it, but let me try to get to know you my way."

From the corner of her eye, Sienna saw Alex walking down Main Street hand in hand with Jesse. She watched Sienna, and Sienna swore there was worry in her eyes. Or maybe it was disappointment. Brad Thompson was the type of man Sienna would choose ten out of ten times in Manhattan, even if he was a sleazebag. He had money, stature, and a stable, important job. He could take her out to nice restaurants and buy her expensive things. He could be the perfect replacement for Mason, but Alex had never liked Mason. She thought he wasn't good enough for Sienna, but Sienna had been happy. She didn't know any better.

Sienna met Brad's gaze, torn between giving in to her loneliness and saying yes or trusting her gut and rejecting him. Perhaps the truth would pacify him enough to buy her time: "To be honest, Brad, I left a serious relationship before moving here. It was really hard and I'm not emotionally available right now. I'm sorry."

Her answer seemed to surprise the doctor, because his brows shot up and he stammered, "I understand. To be transparent, I'm not necessarily looking for anything serious..."

It was as Dakota said, he was looking for a good time, but Sienna was too invested in making this summer a success for the town to let anyone distract her. "I'll reach out when I have time," she told Brad firmly before leaving the petting zoo to go back to the ticket table.

The afternoon sun finally began to dwindle into the evening until all the businesses lining Main Street turned on their exterior lights to illuminate the festivities still going strong. Around eight-thirty, Sienna noticed Lyle, Jolene, and Annie appear from inside the saloon. Lyle carried an old guitar, Jolene had a painted fiddle, and Annie brought out a cordless microphone. Four hundred people turned to her expectedly, and she beamed in return. "How's everybody doing tonight?" The crowd cheered in response and Annie looked over her shoulder to see Jolene tuning her fiddle. Once she had it placed on her shoulder, she gave Annie a little nod, and the blonde looked back at the crowd and asked, "Would y'all mind if we did a few songs to kick off the evening?

From the corner of her eye, she saw Gentry's expression light up. They'd spent most of the afternoon selling tickets in comfortable silence, but as the sun set and the people started shuffling towards the saloon, it appeared time for them to close up shop. The games and activities were done, and the party would now begin.

Gentry closed the cash box and stood, nodding towards the mayor's office. "I'll pass this off to Dakota. Maude will open up the bar for drinks, and then there'll probably be dancing if you're into that sort of thing."

"Do you think I'm into that sort of thing?" Sienna teased and the man shrugged, his large shoulders pulling against the thin fabric of his t-shirt.

"Not really, but I didn't want to assume." Gentry nodded towards the crowd as Lyle strummed his guitar and Annie began singing with a soft twang to her airy voice. Gentry wore a contented smile, as if Annie was singing a lullaby and not some modern hit from the country radio station. He suddenly looked down at Sienna and smirked. "I'd suggest you ask Brad to dance, but I doubt he'd engage in such a low-brow activity with the rest of us country bumpkins."

Sienna rolled her eyes, eliciting a small laugh from the sheriff. "What is it with you two, anyway? Is it because of what happened with him and Dakota?"

Gentry froze, gaze hardening as he stared at Sienna. "Did- what happened between him and Dakota?"

She choked on her own breath and started coughing, looking away for something, anything to take her away from this conversation. She thought she could pass out from embarrassment, but unfortunately she continued to be conscious and had to stammer her way out of her mistake. "I thought you- oh my gosh, I-"

"I'm just kidding, I know they slept together."

Sienna smacked Gentry's stomach, causing him to laugh loudly, brighter than she'd ever heard. His smile lit up his eyes beneath his baseball cap and Sienna felt that damn spark in her chest again. She glared at him, furious that he'd elicited this feeling in her. "You're such an ass."

He chuckled as he started towards the mayor's office, then hesitated, almost as if he didn't want to go. Sienna thought they both knew he should. "Go enjoy yourself, Miss Jade. You've earned it. I look forward to seeing what torture awaits me now that you've won our bet."

As he disappeared into the building, Sienna moved towards the saloon to watch everyone dance and sing along with Annie and the band.

Standing on the outskirts alone, she thought of Mason, and how he would hate this party. He'd hate this place and belittle these people. He'd probably hate who Sienna was slowly becoming, but she didn't hate any of it.

Through the crowd, Sienna could see Jesse spinning Alex around as she laughed. Her purple skirt flared out as he twirled her, and the crowd cheered as she spun another three or four times before returning back to him. Even from down the street, Sienna could see her sister's joy as she jumped into Jesse's arms, and he lifted her up and spun her quickly before setting her down.

She shuffled past Colton and Jewel, the former pulling the girl close by the waist while Jewel winked at Maddie. Maddie, in turn, took that as her cue to leave and Sienna followed suit. Instead of following Maddie into the crowd, though, Sienna snuck between the sheriff's station and the mayor's office, walking the thin pathway past the hitching post towards Dakota's house.

The fiddle and the guitar weaved together with Annie's singing over the excited crowd behind Sienna. She imagined Alex having the time of her life, but Sienna wanted some peace and quiet. She would rather be riding through the Badlands than partying the night away.

She closed her eyes and imagined the sunset over the rolling hills. Wild, open grasslands as far as she could see. A herd of wild horses in the distance. A coyote singing the sun to sleep as she swayed along with her horse's footsteps. Sienna would rather be there.

The sound of soft, hushed talking broke Sienna from her daydream and she leaned around the corner of the mayor's office, catching a glimpse of Gentry and Dakota sitting on the back porch, each of them holding a beer in their hand. Sienna pressed her back against the building, swearing under her breath that her plans for a quiet night had been ruined. She didn't want to sneak around the long way and she didn't know how she could get to Dakota's house without her suspecting Sienna had walked by her office.

She was about to sneak back to the party when Gentry's deep growl froze her in her tracks. "You're on thin ice, Dakota. You need to back off."

"Oh, C'mon! You like her, I can see it. Everyone can see it-"

"No," he said quietly, and Sienna felt her stomach drop at how frustrated he sounded. "She's gonna get hurt, and that's gonna be on you. I've made my intentions clear. You know- you *know* I'm not ready for any kind of relationship. You gotta stop this." Sienna's lip quivered a little as she held her breath, not trusting herself to keep quiet enough to remain unnoticed. She felt a dull ache in her chest when Gentry mumbled, "I'm trying to be friendly, because I know that's what you need from me, but I'm also trying to keep my distance, because that's what I want. Nothing is going to happen between Sienna and I. You need to stop forcing us together. You're only making things worse."

Sienna turned to leave, not wanting to hear any more. This didn't change anything. It only confirmed what she knew, and it strengthened her resolve to leave. Leave this exact spot, leave Lonewood and its people, and leave this life she hadn't asked for.

Being rejected by a man she wanted would be hard, but being rejected by a man she loathed was somehow worse.

She made her way back to the saloon as Annie continued to sing. The crowd was getting rowdier as the booze began to flow. Alex, sober as the day she was born, saw Sienna and jogged over to her, wrapping her in a tight hug and swaying side to side. "Isn't this amazing? I can't believe how busy it is! I'm so proud of you!"

"Thanks," Sienna mumbled. She looked over at Jesse as he arrived at Alex's side. Sienna didn't want to ruin her sister's evening, but she asked, "I hate to ask this, but could I maybe crash at your place? I misplaced my key for Dakota's and I don't want to bother her until tomorrow morning."

It was clear that Alex didn't buy her excuse, because she tilted her head ever-so-slightly, causing her blonde hair to topple over her shoulders. Jesse, though, nodded enthusiastically. "Yeah, of course! Are you ready to turn in now? I'll give you my key and you can just leave the front door open. Nobody's gonna bother you."

He fished through his jeans pocket for his key and handed it over. Alex leaned against him, placing one hand on his chest and wrapping the other arm around his waist as she watched Sienna with wary green eyes "You okay?"

"Yeah! I'm just tired. It's been a big weekend! I'm ready for a good night's sleep and tomorrow I'll be back to work."

Alex gave a little nod, the corner of her mouth tugging up into a smile. "Okay. We'll see you later. Love you."

"I love you, too. Thanks, Jesse." Sienna gave them a weak wave with the key in her hand. Jesse tugged on Alex's hand, pulling her back into the mass of people to dance some more. For years, Alex had suffered her failures alone. It only seemed fair now Sienna would be the one alone while her little sister danced the night away with the man of her dreams.

Chapter 30

On July tenth, Beau and Jesse drove what few belongings Kitty wanted to take with her to Beau's house, and Kitty handed off the keys to Sienna and Alex.

"Welcome home," she said with a smile as she gestured around the apartment. Alex immediately took her suitcase to the guest bedroom, surprising Sienna.

When she returned, she shoved her hands in her pockets and shrugged. "I'm gonna be spending a lot of time at Jesse's house, so I figured you might as well have the master."

"Thank you. I appreciate that." Sienna took her suitcase to her new room, leaving Kitty and Alex to talk about the former's impending nuptials.

Her room was as she remembered it, with the sweeping view of the Badlands out the window. Sienna stared into the distance, wanting to be there so badly. She hadn't been for a ride in ages, but starting tomorrow they wouldn't have visitors during the week. It would give her time to plan, dream, and ride.

Unfortunately, it would also give her time to dwell on why she'd started missing Dakota's brother.

She hadn't seen Gentry since the Fourth of July. Dakota hadn't spoken about him either, which Sienna found odd. Sienna had met with Dakota every day, but only once did she have a lunch meeting, meaning Gentry was avoiding her, too.

Sienna hadn't expected to miss Gentry's scowl and bad attitude, but Lonewood felt a little duller without the antagonistic sheriff harassing her every time he laid eyes on her. To make matters worse, he'd let her see him happy on the Fourth of July. He'd laughed and smiled and managed to melt a bit of the tension between them by treating Sienna like a person instead of an adversary.

She'd started to think of him as a friend until he told his sister he wanted to stay as far away as possible.

"Hey Sienna!"

All she wanted to do was unpack and lounge around her new home, but Sienna followed the sound of her sister's voice anyway. She found Alex leaning against the counter with a cup of coffee between her palms while Kitty looked over at Sienna with a big smile. "I wanted to invite you two to my bachelorette party! They're kind of a huge deal in town and I wanted to make sure you guys knew about it!"

"I, uh, we didn't." Sienna looked to Alex, who shook her head. "What are you doing? We'd love to join!"

Kitty's whole face lit up with excitement. "Great! Well, we're having a girl's trip down to the river. We'll float around and drink for hours in the sunshine and if we're too drunk at the end of the night to drive home we'll sleep under the stars. It's gonna be a lot of fun."

"No boys?" Alex teased and Kitty gave a firm shake of her head. Alex snapped, feigning disappointment. "How will the men survive without us?"

"We're about to find out. Tomorrow! We'll pick you up at eight. Pack your swimsuits and something comfortable! And some Advil for the next day." Kitty bid them both goodbye, leaving Sienna to finally enjoy her new home. She shared a look with Alex, and she raised her mug in a toast.

"To our home."

"Yeah, our home."

By eight-thirty the next morning, Alex and Sienna were piled into Trevor's pickup alongside Dakota. Kennedy drove and Kitty rode shotgun, but to Sienna's surprise, Skylar followed behind with Annie, Jewel, and Maddie in her car.

"Is anyone not coming?"

"Maude and the old saloon hens!" Kennedy shouted and Kitty threw her hands in the air and whooped loudly, causing Dakota to laugh. "Jolene and Cecily will be following behind with the boat. We've got the town's supply of booze, so we know where all the young people wanna be."

Dakota leaned her head against the window, watching as they passed by the Lonewood sign. They drove for about a half hour before Kennedy pulled off the main road. Gravel turned into a grassy path down a hill that led to a wide river along a muddy bank.

Kennedy parked the truck and climbed out in a hurry as Skylar pulled up beside her. The cop beamed as she looked around, wearing a black crop top and jean shorts with her boots. When Sienna followed Alex out of the truck, she was struck with the same awe as Skylar at the place around them.

The river reflected the clear blue sky above as it wove its way through the Badlands in the July sun. The water wasn't clear, but it looked refreshing as it ran through a red clay bank. Sienna couldn't remember the last time she went swimming. The idea of floating down the river with her sister and her friends with a drink in her hand made her feel free.

Kennedy opened the box of the truck and Sienna peeked around the corner of it, catching a glimpse of a dozen cases of wine, beer, and cider. "You really did steal the whole town's supply of alcohol."

"Bachelorette parties are serious business in Lonewood. We didn't steal anything, we bought it," Kennedy laughed as she handed a case of wine coolers over to Dakota.

Annie and Jewel began hauling the beer and cider over to the beach blanket Maddie laid out. Alex began using a pump to blow up some of the inner tubes with Kitty while Skyler guided Jolene to back up the pickup hauling the speedboat into the water.

Once the boat was off the trailer, Cecily climbed out and helped to steady the boat while Skylar tied it to a nearby rock. Sienna jogged over and grabbed the side to help. "What can I do?"

Skylar looked to Cecily, who in turn nodded towards Kennedy and Dakota. "Ask them."

When Sienna turned around, she ran into Annie holding a box. Sienna looked down, seeing a handful of cell phones and car keys. "What is this?"

"Bachelorette rules," Annie chirped with a grin. Dakota came up beside her and slung her arm over the young blonde's shoulders as she explained, "No phones for the women. No keys for the men. That way they can't leave town to get into any trouble and we can't drunk text anybody we're gonna regret."

Sienna pulled out her phone, looking at the lock screen photo of her and Alex in front of the saloon. Alex was in her purple dress with the proudest grin on her face, while Sienna smiled softly, head tilted towards her sister's shoulder. She put her phone in the box as Kennedy furrowed her brows, reaching in and pulling out a key that clearly didn't belong to a car.

"This is my house key."

"Guess Trevor's having a sleepover tonight," Kitty cooed. She held up the full bottle of champagne to her lips and took a long drink before cheering at the top of her lungs. "I'm getting married!"

She took her bottle of wine and climbed into the boat, causing Skylar to chuckle. She turned around with her lips around the mouth of the bottle, and Jewel called, "Save it for the wedding night, Kitty!"

"Jesus," Sienna mumbled to Alex as her younger sister laughed loudly. Alex grabbed a bottle of water for herself and a mini bottle of wine for Sienna. "Don't be a party pooper. Drink. Eat. Have fun."

Sienna watched as Alex climbed into the boat with Kitty, Kennedy, and Skyler while Jewel, Maddie, and Jolene ran into the water together. Their laughter echoed as they dipped below the surface to wet their hair, and Maddie reached up into the boat for Skylar to hand her a couple of beers. Dakota grabbed an inner tube to float in, looking back at Sienna questioningly. "You comin'?"

"Yeah, in a minute." Sienna downed her wine, then grabbed a big bottle. She smirked as she ripped off the cork and raised it to her lips, holding it tightly by the neck. Scarlett would never, ever have acted like this, but Sienna Jade could. Letting go of her inhibitions, she ripped her blouse over her head with one hand. She discarded it, then sat down her bottle just long enough to shove down her jean shorts to reveal her deep red bikini underneath.

"Damn, Sienna!" Kitty screamed back, holding onto the edge of the boat. The other women shushed her as she raised her bottle in the air and shimmied, calling back, "C'mon hot stuff! Let's get shit faced!"

"And that is why we now learn how to drink responsibly in Lonewood," Annie laughed quietly as she slipped past Sienna carrying a bag full of chips. She looked Sienna up and down, giving an approving nod. "You are smoking though."

Sienna looked down, taking in the view her friends saw. Her strappy bikini top did little to hide her cleavage, pulling her breasts together and hiking them up. It wasn't something she would have picked for herself, but Bridget didn't know that when she bought their things. She hadn't thought much of it at the time, having assumed she'd never wear it. But now she was here, with her sister and friends, and she could have a little fun without worrying what everyone thought of her.

For the first time in a long time, Sienna let herself go.

By the time dinner rolled around, Sienna wasn't sure whose lap she was laying in. From the blonde hair, it could have been Dakota or Annie, but Alex had been there at some point too. Alex had been the one to get her to drink water. Kitty was the one actively trying to get her to drink more wine.

Skylar plucked a grape from its stem and popped it into her mouth, watching the mystery blonde stroking Sienna's hair across her lap. She turned to Kitty and said, "Thank you for inviting me. It means a lot to be included. I sometimes feel like an outsider."

Kitty bobbed her head side to side, and Sienna leaned a little to catch her booze-fueled expression. "To be honest, for a long time you were one."

"Kitty!"

"No, it's true," Kitty slurred. "You left. You were so happy to leave and forget about us for a really long time, and then you came back and you acted like you were better than us. It wasn't our fault that your mom-"

"Watch yourself, Kitty," Dakota warned, but Skylar waved her off.

"No, it's fine. It was the truth. I was bitter, and I'm sorry. I'm sorry I took it out on all of you. I didn't need to stay after Mom died, but I did. I wanted to leave for a long time, but... I don't know if I want to leave anymore." She finished her beer and set it aside, groaning a little as she shifted. "I'm sad I've been missing out on these bachelorette parties."

"You weren't around for Kennedy's?" Cecily asked and Skylar shook her head.

"No, I was in New York."

Sienna flinched, remembering New York. The stroking of her hair turned to scratching, and she realized it was Alex holding her, because she understood what she was feeling. Sienna sat up, taking a water and drinking it. She'd better sober up before she said something she regretted.

"Ahh, that's right." Kennedy said softly. "Who came after me? Umm... oh! What about-"

"And on that note, Kitty! Tell us about your wedding!" Dakota said bluntly, ending the conversation.

Kitty looked taken aback by Dakota's rude tone and Kennedy's eyes were like saucers. She stammered, "Dee, I didn't-"

"It's fine!" She yelped a little too loudly. She clenched her jaw through her strained smile, exhaling loudly through her nose. "I just don't wanna talk about it."

Through her haze, Sienna saw Dakota look at Annie, as if a silent conversation passed between them, and the young woman straightened up and said, "So, Alex, you and Jesse still doing good?"

She nodded, surprise written across her face that the conversation had turned towards her. "Yeah! Yeah, we're doing good. Taking things slow, but it's going great. I really like him."

"He any good in the sack? He's like the only man in town none of us have banged."

"Kitty!" Kennedy hissed and Kitty laughed.

"What? It's not like we don't get around before we settle down. Remember when I went to prom with Trevor and Dakota went with Beau?" Kitty leaned back, taking a swig of her wine and sighing loudly. "Jasmine asked Gentry, right?"

"Asked? No- no they went together," Kennedy corrected with a little laugh, raising her beer bottle towards Annie's horrified expression. "I know, weird right? Dakota was not pleased."

She shook her head, rolling her eyes. "No, I was not amused that my best friend asked my little brother to prom. Everyone knows what prom is for."

Kitty let out a laugh that sounded like a wheeze and even Skylar chuckled when Sienna turned to her. "Asking someone to prom is basically like asking for a no-strings attached one night stand. At least it was when we were all in school. I'm a couple years older than them, and my date isn't in town anymore, so don't ask."

Sienna felt her stomach churn, imagining the raven- haired woman in bed with Gentry. She didn't understand why the image bothered her so much. "Did they?" Sienna asked quietly, unsure why she sounded so sad. She blinked, furrowing her brows to focus her mind as she clarified, "Did they sleep together?"

"Absolutely not," Dakota spat. "Nope, I put an end to that idea before it even started."

"But Jasmine liked him. She always liked him," Kennedy said softly, almost as if to herself and not the rest of them. Maddie and Jewel leaned forward, elbows on their knees as they waited for Kennedy to spill some more gossip about the sheriff and the bar owner. Kennedy looked at them with a knowing smile, then turned to Dakota. "How the three of you stayed friends as long as you did is mind boggling."

Sienna watched Dakota, but she wasn't upset by Kennedy's words. She shrugged. "None of my business."

"So Sienna." Jolene draped her elbow over the side of the boat, leaning her head to the side as she grinned slyly. She looked at her two best friends, and they looked hungry for whatever Jolene was gonna ask her. "You got your eye on anybody in town?"

Sienna shook her head, flapping her hand in their direction as she groaned dramatically. "Nope. Doctor Thompson keeps asking me out, but I'm too busy to date."

Kennedy shook her head, looking over at Cecily as Kitty cooed, "She's trying to steal your man, Cecily!"

"He is *not* my man."

"Well, you can have him," Sienna mumbled.

Dakota snorted into her bottle, but Cecily kept her attention on Sienna. "Word is he only has eyes for you. Apparently he tells everyone who'll listen he wants you. We've been on and off for a long time, but this is the first time he's been this invested in somebody else."

"I don't think we're a good fit," Sienna confessed, barely above a whisper. "I don't want to go out with him."

"Why? You got your eye on somebody else?" Jolene taunted, her friends laughing as she tipped back her beer.

"Shut up, Jolene." The whole boat of women turned to look at Annie in surprise.

"You know, I assumed this bachelorette party would be a bit more fun."

Everyone shifted to see Colton sitting on a tall, white horse by the bank, causing the girls to squeal as Jewel turned beet red. Dakota stared up at him blankly and sighed, "No boys allowed, Colton. Bachelorette party rules."

He dismounted and led the horse to the bank to get a drink from the river. "There's been so much change around here recently, maybe the bachelorette rules need to change, too."

"Go to him!" Maddie hissed in Jewel's ear and the young woman pulled off her cover up and dove off the side of the boat to swim towards the young man. He dropped the reins and sprinted into the water, splashing his way towards his girl until she reached him. She jumped into his arms and wrapped her legs around his waist as he kissed her deeply while her friends cheered.

Sienna leaned her cheek against Alex's shoulder, watching the moment with a content smile. That kind of foolish young love wouldn't last, but it was beautiful tonight. The way she looked at him, the way he whispered to her and made her giggle, it was cute.

Suddenly, though, Trevor, Jesse, and Lyle came riding up on their own horses, sliding to a stop at the bank and causing the horses to neigh. Kennedy stood at the sight of her husband, calling out, "What the hell?"

"Sorry babe, I was locked out. Plus, the groom is dead set on crashing the bachelorette party."

Beau rode up next on a massive black horse, but he didn't stop at the riverbank. Instead, he pushed his horse straight into the water and Kitty shrieked, jumping off the boat in her white one-piece swimsuit to meet her groom. When she reached him, she climbed onto the horse behind him and he turned them around, riding out of the water and past the other men. "Sorry to end the bachelorette party, but I believe it's my turn with the lady."

"Does she at least want her clothes?" Dakota droned.

"She won't be needing them," Beau called back, looking at Kitty while all the men whooped. Beau winked at Kitty's girls and kicked his horse's sides, sending them riding away in a cloud of dust.

Sienna raised her brows, looking over at Alex. "So, I guess the party's over?"

"Oh, we're just getting started," Lyle called back. Trevor looked over at him and shook his head in embarrassment. "What? I thought we were partying?"

"Lyle, why are you even here? You don't have a girl," Jesse mumbled under his breath.

Lyle looked around at Jesse, Trevor, and Colton, then over his shoulder, as if looking for somebody else.

"Ya know," Alex called back, leaning against the boat. "We've been sunbathing on this boat for hours. Maybe you boys wanna go for a swim?" She winked and Jesse quickly dismounted and pulled his shirt over his head, smiling shyly when the other men cheered for him. He pushed down his jeans and stepped through the muddy bottom of the river until he reached the boat floating in the shallow water. When he reached them, Alex leaned down and kissed him deeply.

"Get a room!" Cecily yelled at them and Alex pulled away just to leap up and over the boat and into the water with Jesse.

Trevor and Lyle followed suit, but Kennedy chose not to leave the boat, instead beckoning her husband to join her in the front. Maddie and Jolene bailed out, opting to float around while Annie found a discarded inner tube nearby. Lyle climbed into the boat behind Trevor, taking a now-empty seat between Dakota and Sienna.

"I can't believe you boys crashed her bachelorette party. We have traditions," Dakota whined, but Lyle just shrugged and draped his arm behind her. Sienna raised her brow and Dakota motioned between them, "We go way back."

"We're cousins, so don't get any ideas," Lyle added.

"Sienna is single though," Dakota told Lyle quickly and Sienna stared at her with livid green eyes. Dakota shrugged and grabbed another cider from the cooler on the floor. "What? Aren't you? I mean, you aren't if Brad has anything to say about it, but... where is Brad? Did you not invite him?" Dakota teased Lyle and the man shook his head firmly.

"I mean, word might have traveled, but he wasn't explicitly invited. If he wants to come, he knows where to find us."

Sienna grimaced, placing her hands over her bare stomach. She felt self-conscious at the idea of Brad seeing her like this. She was also suddenly very aware that she was still in a scandalous bikini. "I, uh, I think I'm gonna go for a swim."

"You sober enough to swim?" Dakota asked and Sienna nodded. "Okay... be careful," Dakota called as Sienna climbed up and over the back of the boat to stand on the board. She sat down and slid herself in, letting it lap around her neck as she treaded water.

The water was nice. It was warm, and the clay at the bottom was slimy between her toes when she'd occasionally kick it. It wasn't the beach in Mexico by any means, but it was fun. Like a little piece of paradise in the middle of nowhere. Sienna leaned back, closing her eyes and letting the sun hit her cheeks as she floated, letting the real world fade away for a brief moment.

Chapter 31

Jesse and Alex were nowhere to be found, having snuck away for some time alone. Sienna kept looking over her shoulder, worried Brad might still show up. If he did, one of two things- possibly both- would occur. He'd laugh at her for getting drunk and a little sunburnt on a boat in a dirty river. Or, and this was more likely, he'd take one look at her breasts spilling out of her top and the curve of her ass in her tight bottoms and make a move right then and there.

Neither scenario was good for Sienna, so she kept close to the boat, assuming she'd hear about his arrival before she saw him.

There was a slight gasp from Annie as the sound of hooves approached, then stopped. Lyle called out, "I didn't think you were comin!" and Sienna swore under her breath. She ducked behind the boat, letting it shield her from the group. Maybe she could steal a horse and sneak away undetected the way Jesse and Alex had. Maybe she could ride that horse to a different life, and they'd all assume she drowned. It was a tipsy, morbid thought, but Sienna enjoyed it more than the thought of Brad's hands all over her mostly-naked body.

She wrapped her arms around herself, feeling stupid for letting herself be so uninhibited. It was embarrassing, but she'd been assured that there'd be no men at this bachelorette party. They'd stolen all the car keys, but the bastards managed to find a way to them anyway.

Even if it was romantic as hell the way Colton and Beau rode up for their girls, Sienna was bitter that the horses had betrayed her this way.

The boat shifted a little to the side, and Sienna looked up to see Dakota leaning over the edge talking to somebody. Sienna realized the only person who was worse to encounter than Brad was Gentry. She started to swim towards the shore, thinking maybe she could get to her discarded clothes before any of the men got a really good look at her.

She was almost to the edge of the boat when Dakota's voice called her name and she stopped and turned around. Dakota raised a questioning brow and Sienna shook her hands in front of her chest frantically and mouthed, 'I'm not here', hoping Dakota would understand that she wanted to get away. She waved Sienna off before sitting back down to continue her conversation with Lyle.

Now that nobody was paying attention to her, Sienna made a break for the shore, digging her feet into the clay as she got closer. It became increasingly difficult to get out of the river, but she persisted until she finally was able to reach the blanket where she'd left her stuff hours earlier. She grabbed her jean shorts first, hastily pulling them over her hips until a voice from behind her asked, "Where are you going?"

Sienna swore under her breath as her whole body went rigid. She turned to see Gentry standing behind her, dripping wet and looking concerned. Sienna swallowed and told him the truth. "I knew it was either you or Brad. I don't want to see Brad and you don't want to see me, so I figured I'd make a break for it and go literally anywhere else."

Gentry seemed surprised by her answer, but he also seemed uncomfortable standing on the bank in nothing but his swim trunks. The way he shifted his bare feet in the clay told Sienna he wanted to get back in the water, but his desire to know why she was running outweighed his own discomfort.

"Why wouldn't I want to see you?"

Well now Sienna had to confess she'd overheard his conversation with Dakota on the Fourth, but enough time had passed for him to get over it. "You told your sister you wanted to put some distance between us. I assumed that's why you haven't been around."

His eyes flitted around beneath furrowed brows as he tried to remember whatever conversation he'd had with Dakota. When it came to him, he looked angry and snapped, "Did she tell you that?"

"No. I overheard it." Sienna wasn't going to let him turn his ire on Dakota. Sure, she was nosy and liked to butt into other peoples' business, but she hadn't mentioned Gentry all week, not even once. "I was walking by and heard you two talking on the back porch."

"What did you hear?"

"That you wanted Dakota to stop forcing us together. That you were only friendly because that's what she wanted but you want space."

He shook his head as his whole body deflated. Broad shoulders hunched as he sighed. "I told you I wasn't in a place for a relationship, but I do consider you a friend. I told Dakota I wanted space because I didn't want her to make you uncomfortable and I haven't been around because a pipe burst in my house and I've been dealing with that for almost a week." Sienna thought he looked hurt that she'd thought he didn't want to see her. The truth was, thinking he wanted to avoid her broke her heart.

"I just assumed you'd finally put your foot down about working with me." Sienna wrapped her arms around her stomach as a breeze hit her wet skin. The motion drew Gentry's gaze down, and his eyes widened slightly. Sienna sucked in a breath when she realized this was the first time he'd really looked at her body, because he'd been too concerned to ogle her. A true gentleman hidden somewhere beneath all of the layers Sienna was slowly peeling back. "I was sad," she confessed quietly, "because as much as I hate to admit it, I do consider you a good friend. I like fighting with you."

Gentry laughed and Sienna smiled weakly, but it was a real smile. It felt like the tension between them lifted and she loosened her grip around her stomach.

"I like fighting with you, too." He took a deep breath, puffing out his chest as he placed his hands on his hips. The college girls giggled from the water, and Sienna leaned past Gentry to see Colton dunking Jewel under, which she didn't appreciate because she splashed him angrily when she resurfaced.

Gentry looked back to Sienna though and smiled wickedly. She furrowed her brows, unsure what was going through his head. "What?"

His answer was to quickly grab Sienna by the waist and hurl her over his shoulder. She shrieked as she was lifted from the ground, suddenly hanging over Gentry's muscled back as he carried her back into the river.

Before she knew it, he'd splashed deep enough to shove Sienna off of him, sending her face first into the water. She emerged a moment later with a gasp, whipping around with a guttural growl to find the man. When her gaze reached him, he was laughing at her, water lapping at his collarbone. "I take it back. You are the worst!"

"There she is!" Gentry yelled back, smacking his palm against the water to send it flying into Sienna's face. She lunged towards him, seeing red from being manhandled and dropped like a sack of potatoes. When she reached him, she grabbed his shoulders and tried to push him back into the water, but he was like a boulder in her grasp, smooth and unmovable as he laughed at her futile efforts. "You know, for such a small woman, you've sure got a lot of fight in you."

"I'm not small! You're a giant," she seethed, her chest rising and falling as she struggled to catch her breath. She splashed him and he placed his hand on the top of her head and dunked her easily, causing her to sputter when she came back up. "Gentry!"

Her back knocked against the side of the boat and Gentry reached out for her forearm and gently pulled her away from it. The contact jolted Sienna back to reality, and she looked around to make sure nobody was watching them play. The college girls were talking with Colton, and the sound of Dakota's voice behind her told Sienna she was deep in conversation and not watching her brother's every move for once. Annie, though, floated in a tube nearby, and she was watching them curiously.

Sienna understood that Annie and Gentry were close, and her expression was unreadable. Sienna thought she looked sad, but maybe it was bittersweet. It wasn't out of the realm of possibility that Annie had feelings for Gentry, because it was clear how much she cared about him.

"What is it?" he asked softly.

"Nothing," she lied, "I think I'm still a little tipsy and definitely sunburned." She chuckled, then realized he was still holding her arm. She looked down at his hand and he did the same, but didn't let go.

When she looked up, Gentry was watching her, gauging her reaction. He sucked in a sharp breath and let go, looking up at the boat as he said, "I'm too sober. You want another drink?"

"Yeah, umm, a wine cooler?"

"That's a baby drink, but okay."

Sienna snorted as he leaned up into the boat, asking Dakota for the drinks. The muscles in his back stretched and his biceps bulged as he worked to keep himself up. Sienna allowed herself this one indulgence, then looked up at the sky thoughtfully when he began to turn back around. "What time is it anyway?"

"Like seven thirty-ish. Nights still young."

"Are we really going to stay out on this river when it gets dark?" Sienna questioned incredulously as he handed over her drink. She might be letting loose but she wasn't about to put herself in danger. Although, she wasn't sure much could scare her if he was around.

He shrugged. "You scared of the dark?"

"No, it just seems a little unsafe to be floating down a river at night."

"Night swimming is the best kind of swimming," Gentry teased. He chugged his beer, then reached up and handed it to Dakota before receiving another one. Sienna opened her mouth to ask, but he cut her off by saying, "I told you I was too sober. Gotta catch up."

Sienna smiled down at her can, running her thumb along the rim. "This is my last one, I think."

"Why?" Gentry whined, feigning disappointment. "You're telling me a California girl can't hold her cheap wine?"

She scoffed, rolling her eyes as she shook her head. A chunk of soaked hair fell in front of her eye and Gentry reached forward to move it.

That's when she saw it. Dakota told Gentry that everyone could see that he liked her, but Sienna didn't believe it. But there was a fondness in his eyes as he moved that bit of red hair from her cheek that was undeniable. He felt the spark, too.

And just like Sienna had panicked at the notion on the Fourth of July, Gentry seemed to do the same now. He quickly pulled back his hand and cleared his throat, looking up at the clouds with squinty eyes. "We probably should have checked the weather. Looks like it could storm."

Sienna looked up at the dark clouds in the distance. She'd been enjoying herself too much to spare the sky a long glance. "Well, all the phones were taken away as part of Bachelorette tradition, so..."

"Yeah, I figured. I'll see what Trevor wants to do. We could probably squeeze in another hour and head out before sundown. If it starts looking really bad I'll take Domino and a couple of the horses back early. The guys can ride back with you all."

Because Gentry didn't do cars. Because of what happened with Kenzie. Suddenly, Sienna remembered that the man beside her was broken and hurting, and that he needed a friend. They could be good friends, even if they sometimes felt that spark between them. They both wanted to bury it, so it was fine. It was fine.

She nodded. "I can ride back with you, if you want? I don't mind and honestly I think I've had enough time in the river for one day."

As hard as it was to admit to herself, the past ten minutes with Gentry had been the best part.

"You sure?" Gentry finished his second beer, but clung to the glass bottle. "I can do it alone. I don't want you to cut you day short-"

"Do you want me to come?" Sienna asked him bluntly. "If you don't, I won't, but I don't mind. If you don't want my company, you can be honest, but don't beat around the bush. Tell me what you want, because I don't care either way."

"Come with me," Gentry blurted, and he seemed almost surprised by his own answer. He blinked a couple times, and when he spoke again his voice sounded rougher, as if he'd diverted from the role he was meant to play and remembered he was supposed to be acting. "You're always looking at the horses like you wanna ride, but you're too busy to do something for yourself. Plus, it'll be one less horse for me to lead back myself."

"And you'll get to spend time with your favorite Californian," Sienna teased, testing him to see how he'd react to a little light flirting. Just because they wanted to bury the spark didn't mean they couldn't have fun with it.

"More like my favorite nuisance," Gentry corrected and Sienna beamed at him. He plucked her half-finished wine cooler from her hand and handed it up to Dakota with his beer bottle. "Sienna is gonna help me take the horses back. You got enough room for the guys in the cars?"

"With Kitty and Sienna gone, yeah. We'll make it work." Dakota looked past Gentry to Sienna, then back to her brother. "You want me to come, too? Offer a little more help? It's five horses."

Sienna waited for Gentry to answer, glad Dakota pressed the question. Sienna wondered if he would jump at the chance to avoid being alone with Sienna, but he shook his head and told his sister they'd be fine. Sienna was surprised.

Dakota's smile was restrained, but her eyes twinkled with mischief as she bid Gentry and Sienna goodbye. Sienna looked around one last time as they left the river, then called out, "Can somebody please make sure my sister makes it home in one piece? Wherever she is?"

"I'm sure Jesse's got her!" Lyle called back, but Sienna wouldn't put it past Alex and Jesse to do something stupid and get themselves in trouble.

She pulled her blouse back over her soaked torso, groaning a little at the feeling of wet denim between her thighs. She glared over at Gentry and hissed, "I can't believe you took me into the water with my jeans on."

He rolled his eyes as he clipped Lyle's horse to Domino with a long lead. "Don't be a baby. You're fine. You'll be dry by the time we get back, it's a good hour ride."

Sienna looked up at the sky, unsure if they'd make it home before the heavens opened up. As if to answer her silent question, Gentry added, "We'll be fine. I promise. If you aren't comfortable you can head back with the others."

"No, I wanna ride. You're right, I haven't had the chance and I miss it."

He gave a little nod at her explanation, then secured Jesse and Trevor's horses to Colton's white one. Gentry squirmed a little as he walked, and Sienna held back her giggle behind her palm. He wasn't any happier about wearing long jeans over his soaked swim trunks than she was. Sienna worked to pull her wet hair up into a messy bun again, getting the strands out of her face to ride. She unbuttoned the top button of her blouse to get some breeze, but reconsidered it when she caught Gentry watching her.

"You gonna go see Doctor Thompson when we get home?"

"Shut up!" Sienna snapped back. "No, I'm just trying to get some air. I'm all sticky and gross."

Gentry shrugged. "You look like you've spent a day at the river. Nothing wrong with it." He nodded towards Domino and said, "C'mon. Let's get moving."

She took a few tentative steps towards his horse, reaching out to pet Domino's nose while Gentry waited by the stirrups. She realized he was waiting to help her mount. "You want me to ride him?"

"You have before. He likes you. He'll be good."

"But don't you want to ride him?"

"I mean, I do, but I ride him every day." Gentry smiled a little as Sienna reached her foot up to catch the stirrup. Gentry grabbed her hips tightly as she clenched the horn with her right hand. "One, two, three." He hoisted her up as she pulled against the saddle, getting her leg up and over easily with his help. Gentry came around to the other side and situated her left foot in the stirrup, then rested his hand on her knee as he looked up at her. "You good?"

"Yeah, I'm good," Sienna assured him. He gave a slight nod and walked over to Colton's white horse, mounting it easily and looking back at Sienna. She motioned for him to lead the way, and he started up the trail towards the road.

Sienna looked back over her shoulder, noting that Dakota, Skylar, and Annie were watching her. Skylar looked a little alarmed, but Dakota looked almost bored, as if whatever was happening between Sienna and Gentry couldn't bother her. Perhaps there had been more to their conversation than Sienna had caught.

Annie, though, gave Sienna an encouraging nod and a thumbs up. The bittersweet smile looked genuine now, and it made Sienna's stomach clench. There wasn't anything between her and Gentry, even if they felt the spark, even if they enjoyed each other's company. They didn't want each other, and that was okay. Even if everyone else thought it was something that needed to be fixed or furthered, Sienna was happy with their friendship.

"So, you had fun with all the girls?" Gentry called after riding in silence for a while. He looked over his shoulder, swaying with the horse as they rode. Sienna wished she could get closer to talk, but with him towing two horses and her towing one, it wasn't an option.

"Yeah! Everyone was great. It was a fun afternoon. I... I'm not usually that wild, though." Sienna chuckled, scratching the still-wet hair at her scalp where her ponytail pulled. "I'm normally a bit more put together, so it was weird letting my guard down. But it was fun. I'd do it again. I was promised no boys though, otherwise I wouldn't have gone so hard."

Gentry smiled to himself as he turned back around, but he yelled loud enough for her to hear, "What difference does us arriving make? You can be all wild and crazy with the girls but not with the guys?"

"Well, yes. Exactly." Sienna drew her lips into a thin line as they moved alongside the road. The sun was beginning to dip, and the sky was turning pink, like it was blushing after giving away too much of itself over the course of the day. Sienna could relate. "It's one thing to lounge around with my tits hanging out with my sister and friends, but when men are involved it suddenly feels a little trashy."

"I think you're thinking way too hard about this whole thing. Besides, literally all of the men who showed up have wives or girlfriends except Lyle and I, so it's not like anybody was looking."

Sienna didn't believe that nobody was looking, because Gentry would have had to be blind to not notice how little she was wearing while he had her draped over his shoulder. Maybe he was being polite, but it didn't make her feel any less self conscious. "I'm not that kind of woman, though. If I was back home, and my parents saw me acting like I did today...And my coworkers? They'd judge me and they'd never let me forget it. They'd look down on me, and say I wasn't taking anything seriously. I have to be perfect all the time, and it's exhausting."

When Gentry looked over his shoulder at her, there was pity in his eyes. Sienna had never expressed to anyone that she felt like she had to be perfect.

The need was always there, in the back of her mind, reminding her that failure wasn't an option. She couldn't misstep and risk falling backwards.

"You don't have to be perfect here, Sienna," he told her gently, pulling the reins so his horse would slow down a little, allowing her and Domino to catch up. There were two horses between them, but she felt like she could breathe a little easier when she wasn't so far behind. "You're more than enough for this town. Too good for it, actually. You can let yourself go here, and we won't judge you. If anyone does, they can deal with Dakota and I."

Sienna didn't know if she'd ever had a friend say they'd have her back the way Gentry just promised. She wasn't sure she deserved it, or what she'd done to earn such loyalty from him, but she was thankful for it. Her lip wobbled a little bit as she nodded a silent thank you. He seemed to understand, because he just nodded back and turned to look ahead as they got closer to Lonewood. They rode in silence the rest of the way home.

When they reached the town's edge, Sienna released a heavy sigh of relief. This was the longest she'd been away from the town since moving here, and she was happy to be home. She was sunburnt, tipsy, and sore from riding for the past hour. All she wanted was to climb into her bathtub, soak, and plan for the weekend ahead.

Gentry led them to the Shoppe at Rattlesnake Bend, and Sienna raised her brow when he dismounted and walked over to her. She gestured to the road leading to the stables and asked, "Aren't we taking the horses back?"

"I'm taking the horses back. This is as far as you go." Gentry scratched Domino's neck and the horse snorted in response. When Gentry looked up at Sienna, he looked tired. "Just try to dismount normally, I'll help you down. I won't let you fall."

Sienna snorted, chuckling, "You've been awfully nice today. Maybe you've been lulling me into a false sense of security."

She shifted her right boot in the stirrup so only her toe was pushing against it, then swung her left leg up and over Domino's back. She started moving to the ground faster than was comfortable, but Gentry's strong hands caught her waist and helped her down easily. She grabbed the saddle to keep her balance, looking over her shoulder at him as he continued to hold her. "Thank you."

"You're welcome."

Sienna looked up the stairs towards her apartment over the shop. "I wish I had my phone so I knew when everyone would be home."

"Alex will bring it. Don't worry too much about it." He nodded up the stairs. "I'm not leaving till I know you're inside. If you're locked out I guess I'll be watching you sleep on the porch until the party animals get back."

She smirked at him as she climbed the stairs to the second story. She pushed aside a little planter by the door and pulled out the spare key, unlocking the door before calling down, "I'm in. Have a good night."

"You too, Miss Jade. Thanks for the help." Gentry mounted Domino and grabbed the reins of the white horse to lead them all back to the stables. Sienna watched as he rode away for a few moments before sighing to herself as she closed the door.

Chapter 32

"I have no clue what to wear to this thing."

Alex looked up from her place on Sienna's bed, finding her older sister still shuffling through the closet for a dress suitable to wear to Kitty and Beau's wedding.

"I'm sure anything will be fine. I doubt anyone will be very fancy," Alex told her softly. She had curled her blonde hair up in ringlets and pulled it into a beautiful updo, leaving her signature tendrils to dance along her cheek bones. Sienna's hair was reaching an almost untamable length, but Alex had helped her style it into a heap at the back of her neck before securing it with a rhinestone covered clip.

Sienna huffed as she pulled out a simple maroon dress with little flutter sleeves and a plunging neckline. She'd found it in the depths of the sale rack a couple weeks ago when she checked in on the store in town. "Is this too much?"

Alex smiled softly at the dress, noting how it almost matched the color of Sienna's hair. "I think it's beautiful."

"Not too booby?"

"Naw. Nobody's gonna be looking at you long enough to notice. It's Kitty's day." Alex stood as Sienna laid the dress on her bed and shuffled into the bathroom to finish her makeup. "You want some help?"

She popped her head out of the bathroom and nodded eagerly. Alex beamed as she followed Sienna into her master bathroom and gestured for her to take a seat on the little stool Kitty had left.

Tentatively popping open Sienna's eyeshadow, Alex began working on her sister's makeup while Sienna sat frozen with her eyes lightly closed. This had been a tradition between them for years. Alex had become accustomed to preparing Sienna for big events when Sienna wanted a look beyond her skill set. It had been a long time since Sienna needed her in this way.

A feeling like lead in her gut caused Alex to shiver as happy memories of laughter and light conversation shifted into the memory of preparing Sienna for what she assumed would be a proposal. Alex grimaced when she realized that was the last time they were in their home together in Manhattan.

When she pulled away to make sure the eyelids matched, Sienna opened her eyes and noticed Alex's devastated expression. "What is it?"

"Last time I did your makeup I ruined our lives."

She really didn't want to cry. She'd put a lot of work into her own makeup and didn't want to redo it all. So Alex sniffled and picked up Sienna's liquid liner to focus on her work, but her older sister grabbed her hand to stop her.

"Hey," she said softly, meeting Alex's watery eyes, "you didn't ruin our lives. To be honest, I think you might have saved them."

Alex shook her head, trying to banish the tears that so desperately wanted to fall. They hadn't spoken about the events that brought them here in a really long time and she hadn't meant to bring it up- but every once in a while the smallest things would remind Alex why they were in Lonewood. She just couldn't shake the feeling they were still living on borrowed time.

"Please don't say that. I know what I cost you-"

"I'm basically a marketing director. For a whole town. I think I'm doing just fine," Sienna assured Alex. "I know you're not on Broadway, but you're performing and you're so, so loved here. You're amazing and you're finally getting the recognition you deserve. And you've got Jesse! In a couple of years maybe we'll be planning one of these for you."

Alex sniffled at the idea as a small grin tugged at her lips. She picked up the eyeliner to begin again. Sienna closed her eyes and Alex felt her smile drop at the realization that Jesse didn't really know her. At least, he didn't know who she used to be. Whoever Alexandra Jacobs was had long been buried and any dreams of her wedding day pushed to the back of her mind past the memory of Landon in that dark alleyway

But life would go on. If it wasn't Jesse, it would be someone else. Alex didn't believe she'd be alone forever. She certainly didn't believe Sienna would. Alex could see the rest of her life in Lonewood, but Sienna would move on eventually. Maybe in time she'd move on to a bigger city with more men and jobs to choose from. Perhaps, if there was time and space between the Landon incident and the woman who caused it, then their parents could be a part of Sienna's life again. Alex wasn't sure it would ever be safe to see them herself.

"It's hard to imagine getting married... It'll be sad walking down the aisle without Dad. Getting ready without Mom. It makes me feel bad."

Once her eyeliner had dried, Sienna slowly opened her eyes to gaze at her sister seriously. "I'd walk you down the aisle. And I'd help you get ready. I know nothing moving forward will be like we planned, but we'll have each other. I promise."

"I deserve what I'll have, but you don't. Mom and Dad don't. Because of me, Mom will never marry you off in a lavish event that rivaled their own wedding." Alex hid her own feelings of inadequacy behind the jest, knowing well who the favorite daughter was and always had been. She steadied her hand against Sienna's cheek to fix the details of her eyeshadow as the redhead let out a frustrated hum.

"Thank God, honestly. I never really wanted a big production but I know Mom did. Mason would've, too. A big party paid for by our parents to make him seem more important to his coworkers? He would have cared more about impressing our guests than who the bride was..."

Alex knew she shouldn't grin, but she couldn't help it. When Sienna opened her eyes again, Alex was trying to hold back a full-on smile. "What are you smiling about?"

Brushing contour to sharpen Sienna's round cheeks, Alex admitted, "I always assumed you wanted that too. For all the reasons you just said. I'm glad you're different, though."

Sienna looked in the mirror as Alex prepared to apply blush to her cheeks. "Me too, honestly." A moment of comfortable silence passed between them before Sienna said, "I'm sorry Jesse had to go out of town. I'm sure this would be more fun with him here."

"I mean, he's great, but you aren't a bad date by any means," Alex teased as she swiped a fresh brush through Sienna's highlighter. She carefully brushed a strip of subtle shimmer down the length of Sienna's nose. "Besides, if you take me, you can't go with Brad, so it's really you making the sacrifices for me here. I know you're devastated."

"So heartbroken I don't think I'll ever recover." Alex gestured for Sienna to look in the mirror. She smiled before turning up to her little sister. "Thank you. It's beautiful."

Alex shrugged and started packing Sienna's makeup up. "It was a hobby once. Don't wear a ton here. Doesn't go with the theming."

"Well I appreciate you using your talents on me. And I've missed this time together." Sienna grabbed Alex's hand before she could skitter away. "I'm thankful that we get to be here together. It's complicated at times but I'm really glad I came with you. I love you."

"I love you, too," Alex answered softly. Sienna's words, and the earnestness behind them, lifted some of the weight from her heart. "I'm happy you're happy, and that you feel fulfilled here." She paused, smirking as she considered how Sienna would react to her next words. "Now we just have to find *you* a man."

As expected, Sienna's walls flew up and she scowled at her sister. "There are no eligible men in this town. I'm perfectly content by myself."

"You and the sheriff seem to be getting along well."

"Just because he hasn't tried to kill me lately doesn't mean we're getting along," Sienna grumbled, but Alex knew better. While she and Jesse were stealing some alone time on the river, Sienna had gone back with Gentry. Alone. Just the two of them. Dakota admitted to Alex she'd offered to join but Gentry turned her down and Sienna didn't protest.

But Alex knew not to press Sienna about it. She'd deny the chemistry between them until she was blue in the face, so there was no use bothering her about it. Instead, Alex just shrugged and grabbed the dress from Sienna's bed. "Well, you better get dressed. If you're trying to stay single, showing up in your underwear isn't going to get the result you want. Plus, then the sheriff will arrest you for public indecency and you'll have to spend more time with him."

Sienna swiped the dress and locked herself in the bathroom to change. Not because she didn't want Alex to see her naked. No, it was clear to Alex that Sienna needed a moment to calm the blush that raged on her cheeks at the thought of Gentry Wyatt hauling her to jail.

Alex would turn pink at the idea of being handcuffed by such a handsome cowboy, too.

The little white church on the hill with the Badlands beyond looked like something out of a movie. It was small, but clearly big enough to house a couple small rooms aside from the sanctuary. Alex hadn't been to church in a long time, but the sight of it brought her a comfort she wasn't expecting.

She believed in God. That said, she hadn't done a lot of praying the past couple of years. Not until she saw a man's life end before her eyes and a murderer threaten hers. Now Alex prayed silently as she stared at the ceiling before falling asleep at night, pleading God to keep her and her sister safe.

So far He hadn't let them down.

A small horde of people stood outside the doors, chatting amongst themselves as Sienna and Alex approached. When Maude saw the sisters, a brilliant smile broke across her features and she quickly enveloped Alex in a tight hug. "You two made it! We weren't sure if you'd come!"

Sienna and Alex shared a look before Alex asked quietly, "Why wouldn't we come?

Maude's smile softened a little. "Well, weddings are rare here. Everyone in town comes to show our love and support. Being here means you're a part of Lonewood now. You're one of us."

From the corner of her eye, Alex saw Sienna swallow hard. Sienna wanted more out of life than what Lonewood could offer. Hearing that she belonged here likely had the opposite effect than it was meant to- it didn't comfort her, it made her feel trapped.

Alex, though, felt an ease she hadn't felt in a long time at the statement. She wanted to belong here. She was cared for and accepted. She was good enough. It had been a long time since Alex had felt like she was good enough.

"I 'spose, I don't want to keep you from your friends." Maude gestured through the doors propped open. Alex saw Dakota chatting excitedly with Cecily while Gentry sat in the pew next to her, gazing up at his sister and secretary. He spared a quick glance at Annie to his right, but the singer was engaged in her conversation with Jolene and Maddie, too busy with her friends to notice the sheriff clearly wanted someone to talk to.

Alex knew just the person to keep him occupied.

Bidding Maude goodbye, Alex grabbed Sienna's wrist and led her into the church. As they passed the last pew, Brad stood quickly to get their attention, bringing Sienna to a grinding halt.

"You look... wow. That dress is stunning," Brad told Sienna as he stared her up and down. Alex narrowed her gaze when the man's eyes snagged on her older sister's breasts, but he recovered by reaching out for her hand and giving it a little squeeze. "You're breathtaking, Sienna."

"Thank you," she said softly. Her words weren't strained, per se, but they weren't effortless by any means. From somebody else it would have been a nice compliment, but Brad looked a little too hungry for Alex's taste. Part of her worried Sienna would give Brad a real chance, if only to convince herself there wasn't anything happening with Gentry.

Brad turned to Alex and nodded in greeting. "You look beautiful as well, Alex."

"Thanks," she deadpanned, then took another step towards the Wyatts. "We better get going, it looks like it's gonna start soon."

Before Brad could suggest Sienna sit with him, Alex was practically dragging her sister towards the mayor. Sienna stumbled a little in her wedges and hissed, "What's the matter with you?"

"He stared at your tits like he wanted to drown in them."

"You're the one who told me it wasn't too booby!" Sienna whined under her breath as they reached Dakota. Sienna straightened up and smoothed down her dress as Dakota turned to them with her million-dollar smile.

While Sienna and Dakota exchanged their usual pleasantries before getting to business, Alex surveyed the pew before tossing her hand up in greeting to Annie. "Hi! Do you mind if we join you?"

Annie blinked rapidly, startled by Alex's abrupt appearance and request. She shared a look with Gentry, who didn't look too pleased at the prospect, but Annie stammered, "Uh, sure? We can make room."

Alex bolted into the pew, accidentally bumping into Gentry's knees as she tried to shimmy past his long legs. She plopped down next to Annie and grinned, then turned to look up at Sienna expectedly.

Her sister looked as displeased as the sheriff.

"What are you doing?"

"I asked if we could join them," Alex answered innocently. Sienna narrowed her eyes. With a groan, Alex gestured to the front of the church when Beau came to stand and wait for Kitty. "It's about to start. Take a seat."

Sienna looked down at Gentry, clearly seeing what Alex's plan was. Unless she wanted to go sit with somebody else, she'd be sandwiched between her sister and him. For a brief moment, Alex panicked when Sienna looked towards the back of the church, as if considering going to sit with Brad. When she turned back to Alex, she mumbled, "I don't think there's enough room."

"We'll make room!" Annie told her before pressing herself closer to Jolene. She shot Annie a warning stare, but quickly surveyed the situation and smirked before whispering something to Maddie. They shifted closer to Jewel and Colton, cramming the couple together at the opposite end. Clearly Alex wasn't the only one who wanted to see what would happen if Sienna and Gentry were forced together.

Sienna finally looked down at Gentry and barked, "Can I get in please?"

He gestured to the small empty spot between himself and Alex. "Be my guest."

"Are you going to make me climb over you?" Sienna bit back and Gentry rolled his eyes and turned to the side to allow her passage past his legs. Once she was seated, they shared a bored stare for a moment, each waiting for the other to say something. After neither of them gave in, Sienna turned to Alex.

There was a fire burning in her green eyes that excited her little sister. Sure, Alex would have preferred Sienna not be upset with her, but she wouldn't be upset if Gentry didn't *matter* to her. The best part was, while Sienna glared at her, Gentry turned his body to watch Alex from over Sienna's head. It was like he had her back, ready to stand behind her in whatever choice she made to reprimand Alex for her scheming. He looked almost protective looming over the little redhead, and Alex felt a pang in her chest at the realization that Sienna would be *safe* with Gentry. Even if they were just friends, he wouldn't let anybody harm her.

The organ began to play loudly and Dakota quickly ducked into the pew so she was out of the aisle when Bill walked Kitty down. Everyone stood to watch as Kitty practically floated towards a beaming Beau.

Once they reached the altar, everyone took their seats. It became clear that Sienna was right about there not being enough room, because Gentry had to scoot closer to Sienna so his sister could sit beside him, and even then, Dakota was crammed up against the side of the pew.

Sienna shifted a little, trying to get comfortable shoved up against Gentry's broad shoulder. He looked annoyed at her squirming as he stared ahead and finally placed his left arm on the seat back behind Dakota, freeing up a little more space.

He raised his brow as if to ask if that was better and Sienna mouthed 'thank you' before looping her right arm through Alex's so she could lean into her sister and put some space between herself and Gentry. Alex leaned her head against Sienna's, smiling softly as they watched the ceremony.

It was long. Bill made a speech when he gave Kitty away. Hank felt the need to stand up and give a short, albeit heartfelt speech to his niece after his brother finished. Lyle played two songs on the organ, one of which Kitty and Beau spent just smiling at each other for almost four minutes.

When they finally started saying their vows, Alex caught a glimpse of movement from the corner of her eye. She glanced down at Sienna, seeing Gentry's right hand resting on the spot where their legs were pressed together.

At first glance, it looked like he'd just dropped his hand on his own leg and the edge had drifted a little too close to Sienna. But then Alex caught the way his pinkie finger drifted across Sienna's thigh. He dragged it back and forth across the soft fabric of her dress. It was subtle, but it was definitely a caress.

Alex held her breath as she waited for Sienna to react, but the only thing she did was let out the softest little sigh.

Perhaps Gentry caught it too, because he shifted his hand ever so slightly so all of his fingertips could ghost across her knee. That caused Sienna to stiffen, as if she finally registered who was touching her. Alex was only vaguely aware that her friends were getting married as Gentry leaned down and murmured in Sienna's ear, "You look beautiful in this dress."

The air was sucked from Alex's lungs at the comment. She felt like she was in a dream. There was no way this was reality.

Before Sienna could respond, Gentry leaned down and whispered even quieter, "I'm sure Brad would prefer it on his floor after getting such a good view of what's underneath."

Alex clamped her jaw closed tightly to keep from chortling as Sienna ripped her arm from Alex's so she could cover her chest while she moved to swat Gentry with her opposite hand. He caught it and lowered her hand quickly into her lap, keeping his gaze ahead as Dakota glanced up at him.

A little grin played on Gentry's lips as the pastor told Beau he could kiss his bride.

Everyone erupted into applause and cheers as they jumped to their feet, but through the excitement Alex saw Gentry drop Sienna's hand when they stood. He hadn't let go of her, and she hadn't pulled away.

Getting along, indeed.

Chapter 33

After Kitty and Beau's wedding, Lonewood began to get its footing as a weekend-long experience. Kennedy and Trevor greeted all the guests on Friday, getting them their rooms and telling them they'd heard rumors about a desperado making his way through town. They told the visitors to keep an eye out, and report any suspicious activity to Deputy Jesse. While around town, they'd be approached by Beau, offering them a cut if they join his gang, while also being welcomed by the reluctant cowboy Jesse, who wanted to spend his days at the saloon with his girl, one of the dancers in the nightly show. The show's star, Annie, wanted to be more than a saloon girl, and sang about it as she poured drinks and danced around the stage with the other women.

Sunday afternoon was the culmination of it all, where those who joined Beau would face off against those who joined Jesse in an epic standoff with laser guns that alerted the other person if they'd been shot. A little violent, but the people adored it. Country laser tag is what they called it, and Sienna shrugged off the tagline because when Jesse was sent off to rescue Alex, and Annie stepped up to defeat Beau, the crowd would go wild to see the little blonde girl save the day.

If they left Sunday evening, they got a full experience. If they stayed until Monday morning, they were treated to Alex and Jesse finally getting to sing and dance the night away at the saloon, and an all they could eat and drink dinner show with the whole cast of Lonewood's residents. Even the sheriff would make an appearance in his chaps and spurs, telling Annie she did a good job. Sienna knew he meant every word, and Annie's eyes often glistened when she thanked him quietly.

They were a hit. And as that last weekend of July came to a close, Sienna began her laundry list of things to do before the college kids left. As much money as they were making, they would need a little more to spruce up the town if they wanted to keep this going year round.

"An auction?" Alex asked incredulously as she applied her fake lashes in the saloon's dressing room on Sunday evening. This would be Alex's last show for the week, and then she'd be allowed a day or two of rest before being roped into helping her sister with whatever their next project would be.

"Yes, an auction," Sienna answered slowly. "I know it sounds a little weird."

"Cliche."

"But the people love cliches. The whole town is cliche." Sienna gestured around the old fashioned dressing room to prove her point. She could already hear the tables beginning to fill in the saloon and knew she didn't have much time. "I just gotta figure out what to auction off. Experiences could be fun, right? Private trail rides, themed portraits around the town... maybe dinner with some of the cowboys, people love that kinda thing."

Alex turned around to face her sister, giving a firm shake of her head. "I'm not letting you auction off my boyfriend!"

"It's for dinner, c'mon! He's the main player, and he's adorable. You can even be all jealous about it and it can play into the storyline." Sienna pulled a piece of hair away from Alex's cheek as she swept blush over her cheekbones. "Kennedy says we need about ten thousand dollars to upgrade the mattresses, and those aren't even great mattresses, but they are better than the squeaky ones. We need five thousand to redo all the boardwalks, which are rotting away, so that's a necessity, or we could expand the stable and buy new horses, but that'll cost at least a hundred grand."

"We aren't going to raise anywhere near that kind of money," Alex deadpanned as she stood and adjusted her corset. "We could auction off a date with everyone in the damn town and not get that kind of money. Auction off yourself, don't involve me and my boyfriend."

"Jesse already said yes if you're okay with it."

"Well," Alex huffed, grinding her teeth together in frustration. "Fine. He can do it. But I'm not doing it."

"That's okay! We're not letting strange men take out the college girls either, so I'm not expecting you to." The auction hadn't been Sienna's idea, but rather Dakota's, and the first thing that came to Sienna's mind was who and what they couldn't auction away. Dakota had laughed and suggested they auction off dates with some of the actors and single men. Although Sienna had teased that her brother would be a hot commodity, Dakota vehemently disagreed, shutting down Gentry's involvement before Sienna even had the chance to ask him.

So Lyle, Jesse, and even Brad agreed to take part, with Lyle also agreeing to guide half a dozen private trail rides through the Badlands. Sienna suggested they offer the old fashioned photo shoots around town, and although Miss Rose hadn't been enthusiastic about the idea, she did agree to let her son take the equipment out of the studio to do the sessions if Sienna insisted. Brenda and Colleen had been baking nonstop to auction off baked goods, while Kitty set up some gift baskets with items from her shop and the apparel store to auction off. By having the auction Friday afternoon, it allowed their visitors to bid on things they could do or use during their trip. Even if they only raised a couple hundred dollars, it would help fix the wooden boards that were rotting along Main Street.

They'd raised three thousand dollars from their Fourth of July carnival, and with a bit more, Sienna could start really sprucing this place up. It would take a long time to make a profit in Lonewood, which meant Sienna and Dakota had to scrape together every penny they could. If they didn't update Lonewood, it would become a one summer wonder, and next year people would be disappointed that they offered nothing new. Even if the fall and winter seasons were slow, they could work on projects and make Lonewood bigger and better come next summer.

By then, perhaps Sienna would have prospects elsewhere, and could leave Lonewood in the capable hands of its mayor and her new friends. Hopefully Landon would be locked away, Alex would be safe, and both of them could forge ahead with new lives. Although, as the weeks rolled by, Sienna began to wonder if Alex would ever leave Lonewood. Sienna always assumed she'd settle down first, but Alex was perfectly content with Jesse. Although their relationship was young, Sienna wouldn't be surprised if he was the one for her.

"Alright, I'm on," Alex said quickly as she fixed her lipstick line one more time. She turned to Sienna and raised her finger. "One date. At the diner. No kissing, no going anywhere else. Deal?"

"Make it the saloon. It needs to be nicer than the diner."

"Fine, saloon, but Maude is here keeping an eye on the whole thing."

"Deal. Break a leg." Sienna pulled Alex in for a quick hug, then let the dancer take the stage.

Alone in the dressing room, Sienna was able to study the bright bulbs that illuminated mirrors along the walls. Small stools sat at each one, along with photos, stickers, and water bottles left by the girls. Sienna walked by each of them, looking at the pictures of the college girls laughing together and Jewel and Colton when they were younger. At the farthest station, there was a small framed five by five photo with Annie hugging Kenzie Wyatt tightly around the middle as she beamed at the camera.

"Miss Jade," Maude called, startling Sienna. She whipped around to see the older woman, then quickly sat the photo back on Annie's dresser. She opened her mouth to apologize for snooping as Maude looked down at the photo, but Maude explained softly, "Whether you like it or not, you're a part of that woman's story. She might be gone, but you follow in her footsteps in more ways than you realize. It's hard for people to look at you and not see her."

Sienna looked down, focusing on buttoning and unbuttoning the cuff of her long sleeve. The dressing room was hot from all the lights, but she shivered anyway. She didn't want to be Kenzie Wyatt. She wasn't sure if she really wanted to be Sienna Jade, but she didn't really want to be Scarlett Jacobs either. She'd changed too much for that.

"You know," Maude leaned against the dresser beside Annie's looking at the far wall as she spoke, "people are gonna look up to you the way they looked up to Kenzie. I hear the girls talk with Alex. They ask her about California, and about the places you two have traveled. Having you here makes them feel like the world is coming to Lonewood, and that they don't have to leave to be a part of it. Even if this turns out to be one wild summer where we became something great, if our profits and popularity fall, even if you leave- people are gonna remember all the good you did for this town."

Sienna felt her eyes begin to well. "I don't know if I want that. I just want to do what I love. I love to imagine making things amazing. I love to take something and fill it with life and possibilities." Her voice dropped to a murmur as she stared into the mirror, then caught a glimpse of Annie and Kenzie on the table. She picked up the photo again, sighing. "It's not fair that I have to walk in the shadow of someone I never met. I don't get it... I don't see what similarities there are-"

"Maybe not now, but you will." Maude smiled sadly, taking the photo from Sienna's hand and putting it back on the dresser. "Kenzie loved so fiercely with all of her heart. She would have done and given anything for the people she cared about."

"Okay?" Sienna wasn't sure why Maude was telling her this, but the woman said it with so much earnestness that Sienna backed up a step. She watched as Maude nodded, as if making a decision about something she was keeping to herself.

"Don't worry about the opinions of the dead, Miss Jade. Nor the opinions of the living. Kenzie may be gone, but whatever happens to everything she left behind is up to you."

That wasn't ominous at all.

Maude gestured towards the set of swinging doors that closed off the dressing room from the hallway. She tilted her head as a bit of a signal to leave, and Sienna didn't wait for a verbal one. She had an auction to plan, and whatever the hell Maude had just told her to mull over. She could have sworn the woman chuckled as she snuck out the doors.

As she walked down Main Street towards Dakota's office, Sienna pulled out her phone to text her sister.

Sienna

Maude just went all Yoda on me. Not gonna lie, I'm a little shook.

She held her phone as she walked through the crowd of people rushing to the saloon to catch the show. After a few minutes, she felt it buzz and lifted it to read:

Alex

Yeah, she goes Yoda on me pretty much every day.
That's why I'm wiser than you now.

Sienna groaned as she shoved her phone in her pocket. She'd never understand why the people in this town were so dramatic.

Chapter 34

FRIDAY MORNING BROUGHT THE usual activities for Kennedy and Trevor, but Sienna had slipped them a script change to inform their arriving guests of the auction happening at two. It would occur at the steps of the court house, a beautiful building that didn't get much attention from the locals or the tourists. It seemed like the perfect backdrop for their first annual Lonewood auction, an event that might happen every weekend if it was a success and never again if it was a disaster.

"Okay, so everybody knows who's giving what, right?" Sienna asked, looking around at the small group of locals who were participating. "Lyle?"

"A private guided tour for up to four people through the national park lasting up to five hours, including lunch." He droned through his speech, unenthusiastic but at least he said it right.

Sienna turned to Brenda, who shrugged. "We're giving a coupon for free caramel rolls for life."

"That I might bid on," Sienna said to herself before glancing right towards Dakota. "Miss Rose says her son will do the photo shoot?"

"Yeah, he's around here somewhere," Dakota answered as she waved her hand to gesture to Main Street in general.

Sienna nodded, then smiled at Lyle, Jesse, and Brad. "And of course our handsome cowboys... and doctor."

"Not handsome doctor?" Brad teased, but Sienna just stared at him blankly, then looked back at her page. Lyle let out a loud 'ohhh!" while Jesse looked at Alex with wide eyes. Brad didn't seem amused, but didn't say anything about it. He just raised his chin and smiled proudly, cooing, "Anything for you, Sienna."

Lyle slammed his mouth closed and Alex rolled her eyes, but Sienna kept her composure and flipped to the next page as Dakota took over.

"Thank you all for all your hard work. With the college kids leaving in two weeks, we don't have a lot of time left to really stick the landing of this new process. Whatever money we raise today is going towards fixing up the boardwalks around town. It's gonna be a long one next week, so we'll need all hands on deck," Dakota told her townspeople. She smiled and added, "I can't say enough how much I appreciate all of you. I know this summer has been different, but it's been a good different. Everyone thinks so."

"Except Hank. Haven't seen him in a month aside from the wedding," Beau mumbled and Kitty elbowed him in the gut. Bill just shrugged, seemingly not worried about his brother's whereabouts.

Sienna looked at her watch, seeing they had about two hours to finish setting up before the auction would begin. "Joe is gonna be the auctioneer?" she asked Dakota, and the woman nodded. "And you'll be here to announce the items?"

"We've got this Sienna. You can sit and enjoy it with everyone else. Even bid on the caramel rolls if you want." Dakota placed her hand on Sienna's shoulder to assure her, but Sienna huffed worriedly.

"I could-"

"Nope. We got this. You and Alex can sit in the crowd and enjoy. Tell Alex she is more than welcome to drive up the bids for Jesse, but if she can't pay, she can't win."

Sienna bobbed her head side to side before smiling. "Understood."

By the time the auction was about to begin, the chairs were filled with people. Granted, many of them were locals who wanted to see how this went down, but it was still a phenomenal crowd. Sienna snapped a photo for their Instagram, posting it while her sister ground her molars together anxiously.

"You're fine. You can spare him for one evening."

"Easy for you to say, you aren't auctioning off your boyfriend," Alex grumbled. She raised her brows and elbowed Sienna as Dakota and Grocer Joe took the stage to start the auction. Sienna followed Alex's gaze, though, and found her looking to the left of the stage, where Gentry leaned against a pillar, chewing on a piece of straw out the corner of his mouth. His hat was pulled low over his brow as he looked down at his phone. He wore his too-tight chaps and shiny spurs, and a long sleeved cream shirt beneath his worn vest. Sienna pulled out her phone to text him, keeping an eye on him as she did so.

Sienna

> You look ridiculous. What are you doing?

"We'll start the bidding at fifty dollars."

She saw the smirk grow across his lips around the stalk, but he didn't raise his head to see her. Instead, he slowly typed on his phone until Sienna felt hers vibrate in her palm.

Sheriff

> You don't like the look?

Sienna

> Why are you chewing on straw like a hick? You're the sheriff, not the town drunk.

She saw his chest shake with a laugh and he began to type back, excruciatingly slow.

Joe smashed his gavel against the podium and pointed at a man two rows ahead of Sienna. "Sold for seventy-five dollars!" Gentry's response distracted her before she could register what had been sold.

Sheriff

> It's theming

Sienna

> It's ridiculous.

Grocer Joe pointed out at the crowd, waiting to hear anyone else bid for the private trail ride through the Badlands. Sienna tried to focus on what was happening, but she kept finding herself pulled towards the tall man standing off to the side from the stage.

Sienna watched as he plucked the straw from his lips and rolled it between his fingers for a moment before tossing it aside. He raised his head enough to meet Sienna's gaze, then looked down to his phone again.

Sheriff

Better?

Sienna

Much. Aren't you hot in all those layers? It's 100 degrees out.

Sheriff

Sweltering. But it's part of my job.

Sparing a glance at Alex, Sienna assumed she felt the same in her heavy costume. Even if she wasn't doing a show, Alex was always dressed the part during the weekend. Today she wore a heavy brown skirt with a white corset, but at least the light white top beneath the corset was sleeveless. Her hair was curled and stacked up on her head, and she wore a black embroidered choker around her neck, which emphasized the bob of her throat when Jesse came to stand beside Dakota to be auctioned off.

Her phone buzzed, drawing her attention away as Joe began the bidding on Alex's boyfriend.

Sheriff

I'm gonna stop by Dakota's place for a quick shower. You wanna join?

Sienna's stomach dropped as she gasped, drawing a glare from Alex. Sienna looked at her, then to the stage, then over to Gentry to stare at him incredulously as her jaw hung slack for a moment.

Sienna

You want me to shower with you?

Even from across the crowd, Sienna saw his eyes widen and his cheeks burn red as he typed back feverishly.

Alex raised her hand, yelling out one hundred dollars. Sienna looked at her in surprise, trying really hard to focus on what was happening with the auction instead of what Gentry had just asked her.

Sheriff

> Definitely not. Thought maybe you'd wanna come see the dogs. Tilly and Buster miss you.

She couldn't hold back the smile at his response.

"Sold! For two hundred dollars to the little brunette in the front."

Alex huffed as she crossed her arms and leaned back into her chair. She leaned over to Sienna and snapped, "What's got you so distracted? You missed the caramel roll auction."

"Nothing, sorry." Sienna mumbled as she placed her hand over her screen to shield it from Alex's view. Once Alex turned her attention back to the auction, Sienna picked up her phone again to respond.

Sienna

> That sounds really nice. I'll find you after.

From the corner of her eye, Sienna caught a glimpse of blue movement on the stage and looked up to see Dakota squatting down next to her brother. She was clearly frustrated, but Gentry looked up at her with an easy smile as she spoke quietly to him. Finally, she held out her hand and Gentry placed his phone in her palm. She shoved it into her jeans pocket as she stood and walked back over to Joe to announce the date with Brad they'd be auctioning off.

Gentry hooked his thumbs in his belt loops, looked up at Sienna and shrugged. She grimaced and mouthed 'I'm sorry', but he shook his head and mouthed 'Don't worry about it'. Sienna relaxed into her chair, pushing a chunk of hair behind her ear. Brad stood between Joe and Dakota, grinning out at the crowd. He was handsome according to the women immediately behind Sienna and Alex, and the sisters shared a look. They could have him.

When Joe began the bidding, one of the women behind them offered up seventy-five dollars, eliciting a surprised murmur from the crowd. Brad beamed, but then looked at Sienna, as if expecting her to bid on him. Alex had bid on her boyfriend, and had been visibly disappointed when she'd been outbid, and apparently Brad was expecting Sienna to do the same for him for some reason.

Despite her blowing him off relentlessly, Brad clearly had this idea that Sienna was his to lose. It brought back memories of Mason, who treated her like a pretty trophy to show off to his coworkers and friends. She was beautiful, successful, and worthy of him. Sienna hadn't realized that he didn't care about her happiness as much as he'd cared about her accomplishments and what they could accomplish together. She hadn't understood that Mason didn't love her as much as he loved having her on his arm.

Looking up at Brad on the stage, Sienna realized she couldn't go back to being somebody's prize.

A woman near the front bid one hundred and fifty dollars. Sienna stayed silent. When the woman behind her bid two hundred, Brad looked away from Sienna. He looked annoyed and Sienna told herself not to care. She glanced over at Gentry, who was smirking wickedly as he watched Brad's frustration grow. Another bid farther back came in for two-fifty, but the woman behind Sienna huffed and bid three hundred. The other two women didn't try to top her.

"Sold! For three hundred dollars to the blonde in the middle!" Joe called out and Brad gave a flirty smile to the woman behind Sienna. His eyes darkened a little when they landed on her and she flinched. One of these days she needed to tell him she wasn't interested. He was getting irritated coming to that conclusion on his own.

Joe gestured around at the crowd and called, "And that concludes our first annual Lonewood Auction!"

A woman in the front stood abruptly and yelled, "I'll give one hundred dollars to go out with the hot sheriff!" Her finger was pointed directly at Gentry.

Sienna's blood ran cold and she turned to him, seeing his face devoid of color. Dakota stepped up to the podium, explaining gently, "He's actually not-"

"I bid two-hundred dollars!" another woman called from Sienna's left and the first girl glared at her and said, "Three hundred!"

"He isn't a part of this-" Dakota stammered, but Joe held up his gavel and started auctioneering.

"We've got three hundred, do I hear four?"

"Four hundred!" A third woman laughed loudly, and the man sitting next to her turned to glare at her.

Gentry's whole body was stiff, as if someone was threatening his life. Dakota leaned close to Joe as he held his gavel to the crowd, but he turned to Dakota and shrugged, as if asking 'Why not?'

The rational part of Sienna said to let this play out and explain that he wasn't on the auctioning block. The *rational* part of Sienna said to tell him to suck it up and do it for the town, that taking a stranger to dinner wouldn't kill him. Instead, she stood up on wobbling legs and called, "Seven hundred dollars."

The whole crowd turned to look at her. Alex clenched her wrist so tight it hurt. There was a beat of silence as she stood there shaking, holding Joe's gaze until her eyes drifted to Gentry. He looked surprised. Sienna was surprised she'd done it, too.

An older woman sitting near the stage stood and turned around to face Sienna, staring her down in a challenge. "Eight hundred dollars."

A murmur ran through the crowd. Sienna swallowed, sparing a glance at Gentry and Dakota. The woman looked confused and her brother looked horrified, but Sienna opened her mouth to say anyway, "Eight-fifty."

The woman smiled, giving a little nod. Accepting Sienna's challenge. "Nine hundred."

"One thousand," Sienna bit back, sparing an angry glance at Joe to tell him to end the bidding. Dakota made a cut-it-out motion with her hand to her neck, shaking her head in an effort to tell Sienna to stop.

The other bidder looked to be in her early sixties with dull blonde hair swept back into a bun at the nape of her neck. She studied Sienna for a moment, then looked back at Gentry before gazing up at Grocer Joe as she said, "Two thousand dollars."

Joe looked to Sienna, but Dakota grabbed the gavel and smashed it violently against the podium. "Sold! To Miss Rose, apparently," she mumbled, flinging her hair out of her face. She panted, as if she was exhausted from watching the exchange, but she looked unusually nervous as she held the gaze of the winner.

Miss Rose was the woman who ran the portrait studio. She wasn't exactly warm to Sienna, but was always very polite. They'd never met, but spoke often, so Sienna hoped that she could use whatever professional rapport they had with one another to explain that she couldn't take Gentry out. For a variety of reasons, but mostly because he wouldn't want that. Sienna was confident that she knew him well enough to know he wouldn't want that.

As the crowd began to disperse, eyes followed Sienna as she approached Miss Rose. The woman was tall and proud, and when she noticed Sienna, her cat-like smile grew. "Miss Jade."

"Miss Rose! It's so nice to meet you in person!" Sienna wished her words came across more genuine, but what she was about to ask wasn't going to be fun. She'd do it for Gentry though. "I didn't realize that was you. I'm sorry I got a little... intense."

Miss Rose nodded, eyes roaming Sienna slowly, as if to size her up. "Yes, I noticed. I knew it was you the moment you spoke. I recognized your voice."

And you should have recognized mine, she seemed to say.

"Right. Yes, umm, about that-" Sienna clasped her palms together, pressing her index fingers to her lips as she began. "The man you've bid on wasn't supposed to be a part of this. He didn't agree to it, and-"

"I know Gentry Wyatt. And I'm very aware he wasn't supposed to be bid on, but seeing as you and the other women took your shot, I decided I could, too." She tilted her head, offering Sienna a condescending smile. "You aren't trying to get me to retract my offer, are you? That seems like a conflict of interest considering you were also trying to win time with him."

Sienna knew she didn't have a leg to stand on, and this woman knew who she was and that she was the one running the auction. As soon as she bid, she made the thing legitimate, but that hadn't been her intention. "I bid so he wouldn't have to go through with it. He's a good friend of mine and he's a really great guy. I know he would say yes if he has to, but I'm asking you to withdraw your offer for his sake."

"It's only dinner, Miss Jade. He's an adult, he could have spoken up, but he stood there and watched us volley back and forth without complaint. I've been meaning to talk to him for a while now and it seems like I've just bought my chance."

"Please," Sienna begged, darting around Miss Rose as she started to walk away. She might have decided the conversation was over, but Sienna wasn't done. "I know it's just dinner, but I didn't mean to start a bidding war. I just wanted to win so he wouldn't feel obligated to do anything he didn't want to. I'm asking you to reconsider."

Miss Rose gave a firm shake of her head. Sienna saw Dakota appear behind her, waiting to speak to the woman. Sienna's chest deflated as Miss Rose said, "You're very sweet, Miss Jade. I can see you care about Gentry, but he'll be okay. I promise."

Sienna nodded a little, feeling defeated as Miss Rose turned to speak with Dakota. The townspeople in the vicinity stared at Sienna, whispering amongst themselves. She cringed when she realized they were gossiping about her, and they only went silent when Gentry stormed her way.

She looked up at him with a weak smile, opening her mouth to apologize, but his frustration was clear when he hissed, "What the hell, Sienna! What were you thinking?"

"I'm so sorry that got so out of hand. I tried to talk to Miss Rose to get you out of it, but-"

"No, no, I don't need to get out of it." Gentry sighed loudly, dropping his head and massaging the bridge of his nose. She watched his shoulders fall a little. She hadn't meant to embarrass him. "I need to know why you tried to outbid my mother?"

Sienna blinked a couple times as her eyes grew wide. She sucked in a breath, her mind racing to catch up to what Gentry had just said. "She's your mom?"

Miss Rose appeared at his side, clearly having been listening to their conversation. She wrapped her arm around his middle to give him a squeeze. She smiled up at Gentry and teased, "So excited for our date."

He continued to stare at Sienna, but he mumbled to his mom, "You coulda just called."

She chuckled, and he draped his arm around her shoulder to hug her back for a moment. His eyes never left Sienna though. "Mom, this is Sienna. Sienna, this is my mom, Rose Wyatt."

"Oh, Miss Jade and I know each other very well," Rose said sweetly. Sienna waved awkwardly, wishing she could disappear. Especially when Rose added, "It was a valiant effort, Miss Jade, but you'll have to understand that I'm only looking out for my son."

"So was I," Sienna croaked. She tried not to consider what his mom thought about her and her intentions with her only son. If the town didn't think there was something going on between them before, they certainly did now.

When Sienna looked over her shoulder, she saw Brad glaring towards her and Gentry, jealousy burning clear in his rigid stance. The college girls spoke excitedly, occasionally looking over at her with wide, questioning eyes, while Annie spoke with Jesse and Alex near the stage. Everyone saw this as an effort to get a date with the sheriff, and she'd gone so far as to try and outbid his own mother. Sienna hadn't known that. Sienna thought she was saving Gentry from an awkward evening, but to the people in the town who knew who Rose was, it looked like Sienna was *really* desperate.

Needing to get away, go literally anywhere else but here, Sienna forced a bright smile and stood straighter as she faced the Wyatts. "I'm sorry for the confusion. It was nice to meet you officially, but I have some work to get to. Hopefully I'll see you around."

Rose softened a little when Gentry said, "You still wanna go see the dogs? I'm heading there now."

"No, that's okay. I'll stop by another time." Sienna wasn't going anywhere with Gentry. That would only fuel the nightmare that was beginning to unfurl around them. Maybe she could explain away the disaster at the auction as a misunderstanding, but she couldn't explain away going to Dakota's house together, just the two of them.

He nodded, smiling weakly. He looked a little disappointed, but resigned to her answer. They both understood that she'd meant well, but she'd messed up. "Well, we'll see you later then. Thanks for trying to look out for me. I do appreciate it, even if it made you look like an idiot."

Sienna knew he was trying to make her feel better by teasing her, but his mother glared up at him and smacked him in the stomach, hissing under her breath that that wasn't polite. He shrugged, then winked at Sienna, beaming at her as she started walking away. It eased her nerves a little, until she saw the way everyone stared at her as she retreated.

Chapter 35

"So, don't freak out," Alex started as Sienna leaned against the kitchen counter Sunday morning. Alex already had her base makeup on and her hair tied up in hot rollers. She was needed at the saloon by noon, and it was currently ten-thirty, meaning she'd been out way too late with Jesse the night before and had slept in. Sienna looked up at her from underneath her thick lashes, waiting for her to spill whatever was going to clearly bother her. "Everyone at the saloon is gossiping about you and Gentry."

Sienna tossed her head back and groaned, causing her waves to drape over the thin fabric of her soft violet blouse. "Of course they are. How could they not be? I bid a grand on a man who isn't my boyfriend. Story of the year, right here," she mumbled as she pressed the pads of her fingers to her temples, rubbing them gently. She'd been up all night budgeting for their planned repairs. Sleep had evaded her since Friday, because the judgemental gazes of everyone she knew in Lonewood lived in her mind every time she closed her eyes.

Luckily, nobody had reached out to press her about it. Dakota hadn't brought it up at work yesterday, and nobody else really had time to talk about it. The only person who'd mentioned the whole ordeal was Gentry, who texted late last night to tell her his date with his mom was delightful and that Sienna would never live it down. She was aware.

Alex handed Sienna a mug of fresh coffee without being asked, most likely because of the bags under her eyes. She'd tried to hide them beneath a light dusting of concealer, but Alex knew she hadn't been sleeping. "What's your plan for today?"

Sienna shrugged in response, sipping her coffee and letting the hot liquid coat her throat. "Tomorrow morning we'll get started ripping up the boardwalk, so today we'll probably just check which areas need to be fixed up first. Dakota said she'd call when she got an ETA on the supplies. Until then, I'll be working from home, avoiding everyone's thoughts about my non-existent love life."

"What would you have done if you had won?" Alex pressed gently, cautiously. Sienna shot her a dirty look, warning her not to hint at such a ridiculous notion as going on a date with Gentry.

"Would have been simple. I wouldn't have paid, and we wouldn't have done anything, and it would have been water under the bridge."

"The issue isn't that you bid, it's that you continued to bid," Alex told her and Sienna knew she was right. The first bid was a jump on purpose, meant to be too high for the tourists to match. But when Rose stared her down, as if challenging her loyalty to Gentry, Sienna began acting irrationally. She found herself doing that more and more recently.

Alex pushed away from the counter to continue getting ready, snatching her mug to take with her. "Have a good day at work," Sienna called after her. "Maybe don't stay out so late tonight, otherwise you won't wake up in time for tomorrow." Sienna winked to emphasize her words, reminding Alex that she'd be required to pitch in this week, too. Alex rolled her eyes and disappeared into her bedroom to change out of her yoga pants and into her costume.

Alone, Sienna scrolled through Lonewood's Instagram, checking on engagement of their posts and replying to comments. Around eleven, Sienna's phone began to ring, and she answered it quickly when she saw it was Dakota. "Hey, do we have an ETA for supply arrival?"

"No, not yet unfortunately," Dakota's chipper voice answered. "That's why I called, actually. Since we can't do much until tomorrow anyway, I want you to take a day off."

Sienna scoffed. She didn't do days off. At least not when there was work that could be done. "Why? We have plenty to do. Even if it's just being around and getting feedback, I think I need to be there."

"No, I want you to take the day off."

Sienna found this suspicious, and she tapped her fingernails against the counter anxiously as she asked Dakota why.

There was a pause, as if she was thinking, and Dakota spoke slowly when she answered, "As the mayor, it is in my best interests that I don't make you work today. Financially speaking."

"Dakota, what the hell is going on?"

"I just need you to be off, okay? I'll see you tomorrow morning, gotta go, bye!"

The line clicked and Sienna stared at her phone. "Alex? Is something happening today that I should know about?"

Alex appeared wearing her purple costume, her curls pulled back in a messy updo. Her white lace up boots were untied and she sat on the couch to secure them. "Not that I know of. Why?"

"Dakota told me not to come into work today."

"Maybe she wants you to take a break?" Alex suggested, then snorted. "Maybe she's sick of you."

"Thanks for that, I really appreciate it," Sienna mumbled back.

Sienna finished her coffee and rinsed out her mug before setting it upside down on the drying rack. She wiped her hands and looked through the living room to the big windows overlooking the Badlands. She always kept the curtains open, because seeing the multi-colored hills brightened Sienna's day. The sound of coyotes singing was her lullaby now, and the pull of the clear blue sky brought her out of bed in the morning. Sometimes, when she looked out the windows of her home, she forgot about work. She forgot about everything and just relaxed.

A knock broke Sienna from her daydream, and she looked at the door lazily as it continued. Alex popped up from the couch, practically floating to the door. She spun around to face Sienna, causing her skirt to flair out as she explained, "It's probably Jesse here to pick me up. He likes to walk me down Main Street to the saloon on Sunday mornings as part of the show."

It wasn't like Sienna needed an explanation for Jesse's presence, but she reminded herself to be happy for Alex. She'd worked hard, both as a person and as a performer, and she earned this happiness.

When Alex flung open the door though, she stammered, "Oh! Hi Gentry."

Sienna's brows drew in confusion as she came around the corner from the kitchen, finding Gentry standing in their doorway with a bouquet of wildflowers in his hand. He looked uncomfortable, his features hard and his chest quivering a little as he breathed heavily. When he saw Sienna, he sighed loudly and mumbled. "I'm here to ask you on a date."

"Excuse me?" she choked back, placing her hand on her hip. "What kind of stupid joke is this?"

Gentry looked from Alex to Sienna, his strained expression never lessening. "My mom said she'd pay the two thousand dollars she bid, but only if I ask you out on a date."

Sienna gaped at him, trying to come up with what she wanted to ask first. "I- why? I didn't think she liked me."

"She was testing you. She thinks you're great, and apparently you said all these nice things about me, and she told me that if I wanted her to donate money to the town, that I should ask you out on a date." He paused and thrust the flowers forward for Sienna to take so he didn't have to hold them anymore. "To clarify, she said I had to ask you, she never said that you had to say yes. You could end this right here and now by saying no."

That was the obvious choice. Sienna started to say no when Alex blurted, "If she says yes, where will you take her?"

Even though it was Alex who had spoken to him, his eyes didn't stray away from Sienna. He shrugged, softening a bit as she held his gaze. "I guess she'd have to say yes to find out."

Did he want her to say yes? He'd been very blunt about her option to say no, but just now he'd seemed almost hopeful that she might agree.

"What do you want to do?"

Gentry raised his brows at her question and shook his head. "That's not how this works. I asked you. You give the answer."

Sienna played with the petals of one of the flowers. They were soft and velvety. They reminded her of how he sounded when he teased her. She wondered if he'd do nothing but tease her if she said yes, and she wondered if that would comfort her or be a disappointment. "That's not fair," she said softly as she ran the edge of her finger over the petal again. "You come in here, asking me to do this thing that's meant to be for people who want to explore a relationship, and you don't even tell me what you want? My feelings are inconsequential to the money this town will get if you ask me out?"

"Your feelings are the only thing that matter to me. But I know what two thousand dollars could do for your work, and I know how much your work means to you. So I agreed to do this for you, even if it's kind of humiliating." The corner of his mouth pulled up into a shy, boyish grin. It was a look that resided often on Jesse's face, but on Gentry... it felt a little more sacred, like the sheriff was peeling back another layer of vulnerability. He was allowing Sienna to reject him, but she didn't think he wanted her to. She didn't want to.

Saying yes would mean allowing herself to trust the man standing in her doorway. Trusting him to not toy with her fragile emotions and trusting him to not embarrass her in front of everyone they knew. If she said yes, she'd have to protect his feelings, too.

"Okay." She clasped both her hands around the flowers and lowered them in front of her stomach, nodding through the bundle of nerves that was building in the pit of her gut behind the blossoms. "What time do you want to pick me up?"

"I'm here to pick you up right now," he told her, looking her over quickly before adding, "Maybe change the slippers for boots. We'll need them where we're going."

"What are you talking about? We're going now? Like, right now?" Sienna looked over at Alex, but her sister was holding her breath, looking between the two of them with unabashed glee. "Can I at least do my makeup? What should I wear?"

He stepped inside the threshold of their home, and everything felt a little smaller with him inside. "What you're wearing is perfect, just wear your boots. You don't need makeup, either. You look great." He wavered a little on the compliment, not because he wasn't sincere, but because he was nervous. He stayed by the doorway, holding still to keep from dragging mud through their entryway.

She quickly swept back into the kitchen, shuffling through the cabinets to find a vase to put the flowers in. She filled it with water from the sink, feeling her hands shake. She gently placed the flowers into the vase, then sat it on the edge of the counter where people could see it if they came in. She could already imagine everyone under the sun assuming they had been from Jesse to Alex. Nobody would bring Sienna flowers...

Except Gentry did.

Sienna held up a finger to tell him to wait a moment and walked towards her bedroom, trying hard to appear calm. When she got into her room, she realized Alex had followed her, and was shaking like a chihuahua in excitement.

"You two are finally going on a date!"

"Don't say it like it was some inevitable thing. We're just friends. The only reason he's doing it is because I got him into this mess." Sienna pulled her boots from the closet and tugged them over her socks. She darted into the bathroom, but Alex followed to continue harassing her.

"That's easier to tell yourself than to admit that there's something there and that you're excited."

Sienna shot Alex a dirty glare as the younger woman leaned against the doorway. She took this opportunity to fix her mascara and dust a little blush on her cheeks. She was about to put on more concealer when Alex taunted, "If you don't care, why are you trying to look so nice?"

"Because people are going to see us, and when they realize what's happening, they are going to stare." Sienna clenched her eyes closed, regretting saying yes. "Maybe we can tell them the truth: that we're only doing this so his mom will give money to the town. Which is kinda messed up, by the way, because her daughter is the mayor."

Alex shrugged, twirling a loose curl around her finger. "Maybe his mom is trying to get him out of his funk. You're a good friend, going on a date with you is harmless. Unless there's something there... a certain..."

"Don't say it."

"Spark?" Alex raised her brows, beaming from ear to ear with all her perfect teeth showing. Sienna shoved past her to get back to the living room, hearing her sister following behind. Gentry hadn't moved, but he smiled when he saw her, as if he was relieved she'd come back.

What did he expect, for her to climb out the window?

"Have fun you crazy kids! Not too much fun, though." Alex waved goodbye and Sienna subtly flipped her the bird when Gentry was turned the other way. Alex mouthed 'Have fun' anyway and shooed them out the front door.

He led Sienna down the steps to the porch, where Domino and Cheyanne were tied up to the hitching post. "Wait, are they for us?"

"Yeah. I figured if I was gonna take you out, I better do it right. So I planned something you might actually enjoy. We're going somewhere people aren't going to stare at us." He motioned towards Cheyanne, but Sienna stiffened when she saw the horse.

"I don't know if I should. Her and I... we aren't on the best terms."

Gentry snapped his head to look at Cheyanne, as if the horse had hurt his feelings. He flinched and rubbed the back of his neck. "I'm sorry. She's my horse though, and she's one of the best out on the trails. I'll be there to make sure she doesn't hurt you again."

Part of Sienna wanted to ask to ride Domino, but seeing the two horses side by side made it clear that Cheyanne was built for someone with a smaller stature. Sienna approached the horse, holding out her hand for Cheyanne to sniff. She blew air through her nostrils and swung her head around, and Sienna felt a little rejected.

Gentry suddenly reappeared beside Sienna and dumped a heap of grapes into her hand. She looked up at him in confusion and he nodded to Cheyanne. "She can have grapes?"

"They're better for her than all those sugar cubes you give Domino."

Smiling at that, Sienna held out her palm. She watched nervously as Cheyanne sniffed, then gobbled up the grapes, leaving a small trail of slime on Sienna's palm. She giggled and Gentry placed a few more in her hand. "See," Gentry said quietly near Sienna's ear, "now she's gonna like you."

"Is this how Annie won her over?"

"Maybe." Gentry motioned for Sienna to put her foot in the stirrup. Since Cheyanne was much smaller than Domino, she would be easier to mount, but he still helped hoist Sienna up and over her back anyway. He adjusted her stirrups, making sure she could ride easily before handing her the reins. "You ready?"

She nodded, trusting him. He swung himself up and over Domino and turned his horse around, leading Sienna towards the stables. Cheyanne picked up her pace to walk beside Domino, as if she knew where she belonged.

When they got to the stables, Lyle was waiting at the gate. He tipped his hat and opened it for them, allowing them to ride through before latching it tightly behind them. Sienna watched as the gate ahead of them slid open, welcoming them into the park.

"So," Sienna said as they passed through the gate, beginning their trek through the Badlands. "You told me when we first met that Gentry was your last name instead of your first. I thought you were just being an ass, which, obviously you were." He chuckled. "But your mom goes by Miss Rose. Even Dakota calls her that."

"Is there a question in there?"

"I guess I'm just wondering why? Why didn't you tell me you were Gentry Wyatt and why doesn't she go by Rose Wyatt? Dakota never once said it was her mother running the portrait studio, which, by the way, you're aware that she nominated you to do the outdoor session, right?"

With every step Cheyanne took, Sienna felt the side-to-side motion, but Gentry moved so easily with Domino that they could have been one being. It was fascinating to Sienna that Gentry could ride so confidently through such rough terrain without looking where he was going, because when he looked at her, he watched her like she might disappear.

"Well, once Dakota became mayor, we made the decision to let her be the public Wyatt. I don't really talk to the tourists, so they can call me by my first name, and Mom is retired, so she didn't care. At least she was retired until Dakota roped her into running the portrait studio. By next year it'll most likely be my problem."

"Dakota showed me some of your pictures. You're a great photographer."

"I used to enjoy it. Haven't done much recently." His voice dropped a little, but Sienna didn't want to make him unpack anything he didn't want to.

They started going down a sharp decline and Sienna stiffened, but Gentry looked back at her and called, "You okay?"

"Yeah, I'm fine. So what's your favorite color?"

He snorted, leaning back in the saddle to make the descent easier. "My favorite color?"

"Yeah." Sienna tried to mimic his stance, leaning back a little against Cheyanne as she got closer to the bottom of the hill. Once they were in the valley, Sienna gently urged her horse forward to ride beside Gentry instead of behind him. "We're on a date, aren't we? We should get to know each other."

"When was the last time you went on a date asking a man what his favorite color was? Kindergarten?" Gentry teased, causing Sienna to blush and look away. "Green, I guess. What's yours?"

"Purple." She peeked over at him, finding him staring ahead. He looked so content, as if the rest of the world didn't exist beyond him, his horse, and Sienna. Like the Badlands cast a spell over him, making his worries disappear. It was as if this thing happening between them felt easy.

"I hear you've traveled a lot. Where's your favorite place? Like, if you could be anywhere right now, where would you be?" Gentry lolled his head enough to look at her, a coy smile on his lips. His eyes followed her beneath messy hair smashed down by his black cowboy hat. Sienna wanted to push it out of his eyes to see them better, but quickly reminded herself that wasn't appropriate. Date or no date, they didn't have that kind of relationship.

She thought about his question for a moment. She knew what she wanted to say, but it wouldn't make sense for a Californian to say her favorite place was New York. It had been pretty easy to be honest in a lot of ways, but this was the first time Sienna felt like she needed to lie.

But she didn't want to. Not here, not when it was just the two of them. Lying in this place felt like a sin. "I don't know. I guess... I really liked New York. Alex loved visiting there. Being there feels like you're in the heart of the world. I loved the feeling." Sienna turned to her left, finding Gentry nodding thoughtfully. "What about you?"

"How about I just show you?"

Gentry turned Domino to the left, kicking his sides to pick up the pace as they started up another hill. Sienna followed behind, Cheyanne navigating her way up the hill easily. When they reached the top, Sienna looked around in wonder, able to see forever over the Badlands. The grass was thicker up here, and there was a single, twisted tree growing nearby. Gentry dismounted and led Domino over to the tree, tying him to one of the branches before doubling back for Sienna.

"This place is stunning!" Sienna gasped once she was on the ground. She took a few steps towards the edge of the hill, looking out over a massive herd of bison grazing below.

She spun around to see Gentry laying down a blanket on the grass. He wiped his hands on his jeans and grabbed a couple of packs from behind his saddle before gesturing for Sienna to sit. "This is my favorite place," he explained as she sat on the blanket, looking up at him as he slowly sat beside her, groaning a little as he did. "I like to come up here when I want to be alone. When I want to think and not have all the nosy people in Lonewood watching my every move."

"Yeah, I can see that," Sienna muttered quietly. She twisted a piece of her hair as he unpacked a bottle of wine and handed it over to her, followed by a corkscrew. She looked down at it, then back to him in surprise. "Did you have all of this packed? How did you know I'd say yes?"

He smirked as he pulled out a couple of containers of fruit, cheese, and crackers. "I took a leap of faith. And worst case I'd get wine drunk and eat all of it by myself. The horses can eat most of the fruit so I knew I'd have help." He winked and pulled out another container, popping it open and handing it over to Sienna as he took the wine bottle from her. "If you said no I was gonna leave this on your doorstep to make you feel guilty."

She gazed down at a caramel roll, absolutely drowning in caramel sauce and big enough to fill the entire container. It might have been the sweetest thing anybody had ever done for her. This guy wasn't her boyfriend, and they'd only known each other a couple months, but he'd brought her favorite food to a place he knew she'd be comfortable and happy. He listened and took note of Sienna's thoughts and feelings. Brad would've taken her to a fancy restaurant to flaunt his money and show her off, but Gentry had brought her somewhere she would enjoy because he *knew* her.

When Sienna looked up from the caramel roll, Gentry was holding out a fork with that shy, boyish smile again. It wasn't the same one he reserved for Domino. It was different, and special. She hoped it was a smile he'd reserve for her. "Thank you. For all of this, this is amazing."

"Well, to be honest, if I had to end up going on a date against my will, I'm glad it's with you." Gentry leaned against his hand, popping a strawberry into his mouth as he watched Sienna take a massive bite of her caramel roll. She ducked her head a little when she realized she'd taken too much, but Gentry didn't mock her for it. Instead, he took a swig of wine from the bottle and handed it over for her. He smeared some cheese on a cracker and chewed it for a minute, then said, "I haven't been on a date in a really long time, so I'm not exactly good at this sort of thing."

"Gentry, this is the nicest thing anyone's ever done for me. I really mean that." Sienna reached over and grabbed his hand, giving it a firm squeeze. His brown eyes met hers and she nodded to reinforce what she'd said. "I get that this date wasn't exactly your idea, but-"

"Please don't think I only did it for the money." Gentry turned over his hand to hold Sienna's. He was shaking a little and his breath hitched when she ran her thumb across his tanned skin. "I love spending time with you. Maybe I wouldn't have called it a date, but I don't mind doing this at all." He looked down at their entwined hands and smiled. "I don't mind this, either."

Sienna scooted a little closer to Gentry, watching him to see how he'd react. He let go of her hand and draped his arm around her shoulder. She leaned into him, trying not to be stiff as he stroked his thumb up and down her arm. The touch was innocent, but it sent shivers through Sienna's body. She felt that damn spark light between them like a match, and if they went any further, it would become a wildfire that could burn down Lonewood.

"You know, friends don't really do this sort of thing," she said slowly. His arm fell from her shoulders. She shifted to sit on her knees and face Gentry, but he leaned on his palm, looking up at her lazily. He raised his brows as if pretending he didn't understand, taunting her further. He was forcing her to make the first move or shut it down.

She rolled her eyes and dropped herself onto her ass, grabbing her caramel roll and shoveling it into her mouth. Gentry leaned back on his elbow, tossing another strawberry into his mouth as Sienna ignored him.

Finally, Gentry looked up at her with big puppy eyes. Sienna scowled, not wanting to fall for his efforts to get her to tell him her feelings. She'd have to face them first.

"So, if friends don't do this kind of thing, what does that make us?"

Sienna groaned loudly to show her frustration and he responded by popping another cracker into his mouth. His grin was heart-stopping and Sienna hated it. "You know what we are? We're friends with chemistry. It's the worst kind of friends, because it means that even if we don't want this, people are gonna think this should happen." She gestured between the two of them. The sound of a bird crying overhead caught her attention and she deflated a little, feeling her frustration fizzle away.

The vastness around them calmed her, as if she could let all her insecurities and worries fly away like that bird. The air was so clean that she could breathe easily, even if her heart was struggling to keep a steady pace.

Gentry looked thoughtful as he traced the pattern of the blanket they sat on. "It doesn't matter what anyone else wants."

"I know, but we're gonna keep hearing about it. It's my fault. The stupid bet, the stupid auction- half the town thinks I'm obsessed with you, which makes me look stupid because you've made it very clear you aren't interested-"

"Sienna," Gentry cut her off and she let out a deep breath. She looked everywhere but him. She watched Domino graze while Cheyanne looked across the Badlands. She followed the horse's gaze to a herd of wild horses in the distance. The bird in the sky had disappeared, but she searched for it anyway. Gentry grunted, annoyed she was avoiding him. "Sienna."

"What?"

"You don't look stupid." His voice was soft, as velvety as the flowers he'd brought her. It was enough to pull her gaze back to him. For a moment, they watched each other, scared to speak. This was dangerous territory. Whatever they said here would live between them forever, so they couldn't mess it up. Sienna wished they'd kept things light and fun, bickering and teasing as they always had. This type of vulnerable honesty was hard to swallow.

She ran her fingers through her hair, pulling the red strands up before letting them drop like a veil on her bare shoulders. She wanted to get up and pace around, but she didn't want to leave. Sienna considered hopping on Cheyanne and sprinting back to Lonewood, but she didn't want to run away. She just didn't want to say what he didn't want to hear.

Leaning over to play with a tuft of long, soft grass, Sienna's confession came out as barely above a whisper. "I've never felt this way before. I don't know what I'm doing and I'm scared. My last relationship was one of convenience, not passion." Her emerald eyes met his and she murmured, "There's something between us that's special, but that doesn't mean either of us are ready to act on it."

He nodded a little, accepting that she'd given more of herself than she was comfortable with. She'd rolled over and told him the truth, and it was up to him to admit whether or not he felt the same way. "I don't know if I'm ready for you, Sienna, but I want you. I want to see where this goes."

Sitting up, Gentry caressed Sienna's jaw, cradling it gently. He stroked her soft skin and she grabbed his hand to hold his palm against her cheek. When he smiled, she glanced at his mouth and licked her lips before looking back up to his eyes. If that didn't make her intentions clear, nothing would.

His breath hitched and he pressed his forehead to hers, breathing heavily as she cradled his face in her hands. "I want this. I really do, but you'll need to be patient with me. I'm not ready to- I'm gonna need time. I'm sorry."

"I'm not going anywhere," Sienna promised, running her thumb along his cheek. He leaned up and pressed a kiss to her forehead, lingering there a moment.

"Are you sure?" His words were muffled against her skin. She hummed as he placed a kiss to her temple before looking at her face.

"I'm positive."

He wrapped his arms around Sienna and pulled her close to his warm body. He wore a long sleeved button up like usual, but he'd rolled the sleeves to his elbows to get a little breeze. His body felt like fire against Sienna, but she leaned into the heat like she was freezing to death.

His cheek found its spot against her head, gazing at the Badlands ahead of them. Sienna shivered a little, and his responding chuckle rumbled through them both. "You okay?" She nodded and he reached over to grab the wine, holding it out for her. "Drink a little more, it'll ease your nerves."

"I'm not nervous."

"Really? 'Cause I'm terrified."

Sienna pulled away and swatted him, but he pulled her back with his strong arm, holding her easily against him. He sighed, and Sienna looked up at him. "So, just so we're on the same page... we aren't dating." He grimaced, guilt written across his face, so Sienna added, "But we're considering it. As a potential future relationship."

"I'd say that we're taking things slow. I don't have any other prospects, and I'm the one dragging my feet, so it comes down to what you want. If you want to keep your options open, I understand."

"There's nothing I want less than to keep my options open," Sienna grumbled and Gentry laughed, causing them both to shake as he held her like a vise.

"Aww, Brad is going to be heartbroken! He actually made a move, and you'd still choose little old me." He puffed out his chest proudly against Sienna's back, dropping his lips to murmur against her hair. "Either you really like me or he has a small dick."

He found himself hilarious, laughing against her as she rolled her eyes. This was the man she knew, the biggest pain in the ass in Lonewood. Sienna couldn't think of anybody else she'd rather spend her time with.

"You know I didn't sleep with Brad. I never even went out with him."

"I just like to assume it's small, but then again, Dakota did sleep with him twice-"

"How about we don't talk about Brad and your sister," Sienna groaned as she leaned against his chest.

He chuckled as he draped his chin over her shoulder, nuzzling her cheek with his nose. When Sienna agreed to go on a date with Gentry, she hadn't imagined in a million years that this is where it would lead. The sheriff practically melted against her, as if he'd never get another chance to hold her in his arms. Sienna felt her stomach flip when he pressed a kiss to her cheek. She turned to face him suddenly, silently pleading Gentry to kiss her with her wide, desperate eyes.

But the ragged breath he took told Sienna that was where he drew the line. She didn't understand what was so sacred about a simple kiss, but she didn't push him, didn't ask.

"I'm sorry," he whispered, pushing her hair behind her ear. She dropped her head, but he hooked his fingers under her chin so she had to look at him. "There's something I need to tell you before we go any farther, and if I kiss you now, I don't know if I'll be able to stop."

Her stomach dropped, worry flooding her entire body. As she wrapped her fingers around his hand, she realized she was shaking. It wasn't because Gentry had a secret, but because she did. She was in the Witness Protection Program. She was hiding here because a very dangerous man would kill her and her sister if he found them. He'd kill Gentry if he stood in the way. Whatever skeletons Gentry had in his closet couldn't be as bad as Landon Maddox.

She was about to tell him nothing could scare her off but he quickly said, "I don't want to talk about it today. Today I want to enjoy being with you. I want to hold you, and enjoy your company. I want you to ask me your weird first date questions and I want to hear you laugh. We can worry about everything else later, okay?"

Sienna nodded and grabbed a handful of grapes as she fell back against Gentry's chest, using him as a crutch as she ate her snack. She started to put a grape in her mouth, but Gentry reached around to pluck it from her hand and pop it in his mouth instead. She glared over her shoulder and he shrugged.

"I'm glad to know nothing is changing between us."

"Nothing?" Gentry teased as he hugged her tightly, squeezing her until she squirmed. "I don't remember doing this before."

She shook her head, smiling to herself as he pulled her tangled hair over her shoulder so it was out of his face. "I guess not. This one change I'll allow."

They would have to enjoy their time alone now, because once they got back to Lonewood, everything they knew would change. Dakota and Alex would lose their minds. They'd be the gossip of the town for weeks, and if it didn't work out, everyone would blame Sienna. To the citizens of Lonewood, Sheriff Gentry could do no wrong.

"So we're gonna take this slow, right? Are we also going to keep this quiet?" Sienna questioned under her breath.

"Personally, I think keeping this quiet could be for the best." Gentry ran his knuckles along her forearm gently. He kissed her shoulder and she sucked in a sharp breath. "I don't want you to think that I'm ashamed of you, because that couldn't be farther from the truth, but I have a lot of history in this town. I think we should keep this to ourselves until we're sure this is what we want."

"I couldn't agree more," Sienna told him quickly over her shoulder. He looked down at her with that boyish grin that he saved for her, and she felt her heart skip a beat. They sat there until the sun dipped below the horizon, stealing away a little time before Lonewood started missing them.

Chapter 36

Sienna came home from her date with Gentry Wyatt on cloud nine. When Alex got back from that Sunday evening's show, her sister was laying on her bed, staring at the ceiling with the biggest smile on her face.

Even if they'd just poked fun at each other for six hours, Sienna would have had the time of her life, because he challenged her. He didn't treat her like a glass trophy to show off, he treated Sienna like a sparring partner who could hold her own against him. Of course Sienna would like that. She didn't realize it, but that's what she needed.

Monday morning, Sienna was humming as she did her makeup, and she curled up her hair into voluminous waves. Her lips were cherry red, which matched the sweet button up sundress she wore. Although she'd been adamant about everyone pitching in with the boardwalk updates, clearly Sienna was more worried about looking cute than about being comfortable.

Alex couldn't wait to see her on her hands and knees in that cotton dress hammering wood into place. Although, if the date had gone as well as it appeared to, perhaps Gentry would be doing all the work for her.

Despite her sister looking like a knockout, Alex wore a baggy tank top and yoga pants out to the saloon where they'd begin work. It made sense to start there, seeing as the saloon was the focal point of the town. Bill rented some ladders that could reach the sign with the intention of repainting it, and even Hank came out of hiding with his thick workers gloves to help with the boards.

An older man Alex had never met arrived with Rose Wyatt, and when they saw Sienna, they beamed like they were meeting their daughter-in-law for the first time. "Miss Jade," Rose chirped proudly as she gestured to a tall, thin man standing beside her, "This is my husband Eli. This is Sienna Jade. She's the one who tried to outbid me at the auction."

"Which was an honest mistake," Sienna stammered, turning red as her hair. Alex chuckled and Sienna shot her a dirty look. She smiled at Eli, reaching out to shake his hand. "It's nice to meet you."

"Nice to meet you, too." He was quiet, reserved. Perhaps he was judging Sienna. She squirmed like he was. He turned to Alex and reached out to shake her hand as well. "You must be Alex. Gentry mentioned Miss Jade had a sister."

Alex nodded, trying to hold back a laugh at the notion that Gentry still referred to her sister as Miss Jade while calling her by her first name. Sienna didn't look amused. "Yes, younger sister. Does your son talk about us a lot?"

"I actually have to run, lots of work to do, but it was good to see you again Miss Rose... nice to meet you Mr. Wyatt." Sienna turned on the heels of her cowboy boots and strode towards the mayor's office to find Dakota. Alex, though, hung back with the older Wyatts for a few minutes. She was in no rush to start her hard labor.

"So you work at the saloon?" Rose asked gently, making casual conversation. Alex nodded and Rose continued, "How are you liking Lonewood? I'm sure it's a bit different than California. Where in California are you from?"

Nobody had asked them that. Alex had long assumed that nobody around here had ever been. She blinked, wracking her brain for the answer she was supposed to give. "Um, a little suburb of Anaheim. I got out of a pretty bad relationship and needed to put some space between him and I... it's weird, we ended up here based on a recommendation of a friend of Skylar's."

"Skylar's a sweet girl. Glad to have her back in town," Eli said, but his gaze was elsewhere. "Dakota asked me to help with the woodwork. It's a hobby of mine. Years ago I did all the headboards in the motel rooms and details on most of the buildings around town."

"That's awesome! It was beautiful, I remember noticing it when we lived in the motel." Rose raised her brow, and Alex elaborated, "We're living in Kitty's old apartment now. Figured it was time to put down some roots."

Rose and Eli shared a look, and Alex grinned to herself. The fact that she and Sienna were sticking around struck a chord with them. Whether it was good or bad, she didn't know, but these two clearly had an opinion about her sister. Alex knew both of their children did.

Suddenly, Dakota led Sienna down the steps of her office. Once again, Sienna looked terribly overdressed, because Dakota wore a sleeveless bodysuit tucked into skinny jeans, and her hair was pulled up into a messy ponytail on top of her head.

It was clear that something had been said between the women that made Sienna uncomfortable, because her cheeks were somehow redder than before, and Dakota was grinning so wide Alex could almost see her gums.

"I'm so glad you could come and help!" Dakota told her dad as she wrapped her arms around him in a big hug. When she backed away, she gestured towards Sienna, but Rose cut in with, "We've already met, no need to embarrass the poor girl more."

Sienna's cheeks would probably stay red for the rest of the day.

Dakota motioned for her dad to follow her towards Beau, Trevor, Colton, and the two newly graduated boys. They stood by the saloon, waiting for directions. Above them, Bill was carefully repainting the saloon sign while Hank held the ladder, doing the bare minimum while still being able to say he was helping.

After a few minutes of explaining, Dakota stood up straight and turned towards where Sienna, Rose, and Alex stood without speaking. Her brows furrowed as she called to no one in particular, "Where's Gentry?"

Their mother shrugged. "He wasn't at our place, I assumed he was here with you."

"Well, he's clearly not, and we need him."

Alex watched Sienna shrink back into her shoulders when Dakota's gaze fell on her, but she shook her head rapidly to say she hadn't seen him either and she didn't want them thinking she had. Dakota huffed and yelled back, "Well, if anyone sees him, tell him I'm gonna kick his ass for being late."

Alex studied Sienna's reaction, finding her older sister unusually fidgety. It wasn't like her to stand back and not stick her nose into the project, especially one she was spearheading. Alex began considering that Gentry had brainwashed her on their date and turned her into the perfect girlfriend, because she looked so sweet and dutiful blushing next to his mother.

If Sienna was just going to stand around looking all nervous and lovestruck, though, Alex was going to go inside.

"Jesse is helping Maude and the girls work on redoing the wood planks inside the saloon. If I'm not going to be of any assistance here, can I go help them?"

Sienna shot her a bored stare, but sighed and nodded. "Yeah, might as well. Dakota said she has a project for her mom and I, so I'll come get you if we need help with that."

As Alex took a few steps towards the saloon, the sound of thundering hooves froze her in place. She flinched a little as Gentry plowed towards them on Domino at full speed. He pulled back on the reins tightly, causing dust to rise up around him as he skidded to a stop.

He dismounted quickly as Dakota moved towards him, glaring from beneath her red cowboy hat. "You're late."

Blinking rapidly, Gentry looked at Dakota, then over to Sienna and his mom. When he saw them together, he ducked his head and cleared his throat, pulling off his hat to run his fingers through his hair. It was wet, like he'd just gotten out of the shower. Even from a good five feet away, Alex could smell his cologne, and his face was smooth. Freshly shaved.

Dakota crossed her arms as she waited for an explanation, but Gentry just grinned at his mom and Sienna, wrapping the former in a side hug. "How are you this morning?"

Rose coughed and waved her hand in the air to clear the still-lingering dust. "I was better before you made your grand entrance. Why are you late? You told your sister you'd be here."

Hearing Rose berate the sheriff over letting down the mayor might have been the funniest thing Alex had heard since she'd moved to Lonewood. Watching Gentry flinch at his mother's accusatory tone was adorable, especially when Dakota placed her hands on her hips and raised her chin proudly. An older sister who got her little brother scolded by mom.

"I slept through my alarm. Had to shower." He looked over at Sienna, and the corner of his mouth turned up in the cutest little grin Alex had ever seen on such a large man. "You look really nice."

Alex was right. Sienna's blush lived permanently on her cheeks today. "Thank you," she told him firmly, raising her head a little in an effort to look confident and less affected by the compliment. Alex wasn't sure why she bothered to hide it, everyone in this small circle of people knew they'd gone out yesterday.

"Hello?" Dakota snapped in front of Gentry's face and he threw a sharp glare her way. Dakota wasn't affected though. "We have a lot of work to do. Sienna wants all this done by Friday." Dakota gestured at the boardwalks lining both sides of the street before settling her wicked gaze on her brother. "You'd hate to let her down, wouldn't you? Seeing as you have to do everything she wants for the rest of the summer. Only a few weeks left."

Gentry rolled his eyes and Sienna smirked, then scratched her nose in an effort to hide it. "Don't be weird Dakota. I'll get the stupid boardwalk done. Just gimme a minute, okay?"

They stared at each other for a long moment, neither breaking until Rose called to her daughter, "Let's get to work on whatever this project is you want help with. Giving him a few minutes won't kill you."

Dakota side eyed her mother, then conceded, "Fine. Five minutes, then I'm putting your ass to work."

She started towards her office, collecting her mom on the way. They glanced at Sienna as they passed, but didn't say anything, instead leaving her with Gentry for his "five minutes".

With Dakota and Rose gone, the only person hanging around was Alex. Sienna jerked her head towards the saloon, telling Alex to leave so she could talk to Gentry alone. Alex raised her hands and backed away slowly, watching as Sienna turned her beaming grin up at the sheriff.

Watching her sister absolutely glow with joy washed away the last of Alex's guilt. Maybe she hadn't ruined Sienna's life after all. Maybe Alex had caused something good for her sister. She'd definitely found something good for herself.

When she reached the entrance to the saloon, she looked back one more time. Sienna was looking up at Gentry from under her lashes as he spoke quietly to her. Alex had never seen her sister look so blatantly smitten. It was like watching Sienna drop her mask like a heavy jacket. She was baring her soul to the man next to her and it was fascinating.

The inside of the saloon was bustling almost as much as the boardwalk outside. They'd ripped up all the flooring and were replacing it with new wooden panels. Jesse straightened up and waved when he saw Alex, and she beamed back at him. She passed by Jolene and Maddie, who were on their hands and knees shoving the new panels into place, while Annie, Jewel, and Maude were carefully replacing the wooden flooring of the stage.

"How are you?" Jesse asked after greeting Alex with a chaste kiss.

"I'm better now that I'm here with you."

While Jesse worked on snapping the panels into place, Alex looked at her phone quickly, seeing a news alert from Manhattan. She clicked on the link, furrowing her brows as an article appeared, detailing a man who'd been fished out of the East River. Beaten to a pulp, but now in Intensive Care. It was a miracle that Mason Cardoza was still alive.

Her heart stopped beating when she read his name. She grabbed her mouth and gasped. He had eighteen broken bones, a punctured lung, a severe concussion, and a slight cut along his neck. Like somebody had slit his throat, but only enough to leave a mark. A calling card. A warning.

"You okay?" Jesse asked softly and Alex sniffled, nodding as she shoved her phone in her back pocket. There was nothing she could do now. He was alive... he could have joined them. He could have been here right now, or somewhere else, but Mason chose to stay and risk his life. Alex couldn't blame herself for his decisions.

She needed to tell Sienna... but Sienna was moving on. Alex didn't know what would happen if she told her sister that Landon had gone after Mason. Selfishly, Alex didn't want her to know. She wanted to let Sienna live in this dreamland and not worry about what was happening back home. They couldn't do anything about it anyway.

Later that night, Alex washed off her makeup and crawled into Jesse's queen-sized bed in her underwear and one of his t-shirts. She crawled over to him and kissed him deeply, and he dug his fingers through her hair until she collapsed beside him, giggling.

He rolled over and sat up on his elbow, tracing her shoulder with his fingers and giving her goosebumps. He looked so content with his sleepy smile and lazy movements. Alex imagined spending the rest of her life like this, curled up in his arms. She'd never seen herself as the settle down type, but she was comfortable here, with him.

Until that news alert, it had almost felt like her life back in Manhattan had never existed. All the loss she'd felt had dwindled, and she felt like she was worth something for the first time in her adult life. Lonewood wasn't Broadway, but it didn't matter. Every night the crowd cheered and Alex got to dance with the man she loved. She was safe here, and she was happy.

But she was also scared. She wanted to tell the person beside her how much she loved and cared about him, but she couldn't share those things knowing she'd been lying to him. He didn't really know her, and she felt like a fraud for hiding this horrible, dangerous truth from the person she trusted the most.

Jesse draped his arm over Alex's shoulder and pulled her tight, nuzzling her nose with his. She sighed and ran her fingernail over his bare arm, tracing the muscles of his bicep as he closed his eyes to sleep. She watched him in the darkness, thinking about their future. Whether they liked it or not, business would dwindle when the summer ended. Even if they were open in the winter, they wouldn't be busy. There'd be less shows, meaning less work. It meant Alex wouldn't have as many distractions to ease her guilty conscience.

The rules were simple. Blend in, don't draw too much attention. Don't contact anyone from their old life. Don't tell anyone who they really were.

Alex clenched her eyes closed, imagining what would happen if she broke the rules. She'd be whisked away and have to start over. Alex Jade would die, as Alexandra Jacobs had. She'd never see Jesse or Maude again. She might never see Sienna again.

And that was assuming they didn't pull Sienna from Lonewood, too. The people in this town would understand that if Alex was on the run, so was her sister. Sienna would lose everything she'd found. She'd lose her job and her friends and whatever the hell she had with the sheriff. If Alex told Jesse the truth about her past, she could cost Sienna her future. But if Landon found her, and killed her, she wanted Jesse to know who he'd lost.

"Jesse?" Alex whispered, pressing her forehead to his. He hummed a little, a clear response to her questioning tone. Her breathing was shaky, but she asked, "Have you ever had to keep a secret? To protect somebody you care about?"

"Yeah."

"How do you live with that guilt?"

Jesse sat up, rubbing his eyes. "Where's this coming from?"

"Jesse, I love you."

He stared at her, eyes wide. His jaw hung open in surprise, but he closed it and gave her a single nod. She quickly stammered, "You don't have to say it back. We haven't been together that long, it's not like it's that serious, we haven't even slept together, but... I love you. And I want to be honest with you- about me." She needed to tell him something that was true. She wanted him to know her. "I'm not from California. I'm from New York. I was on Broadway." Jesse's eyes widened even more and Alex sputtered, feeling the breath evacuate her lungs as the truth came out. "I got in a mess with this guy. My sister and I had to leave, but I'm not who you think I am. But I want you to know me. I don't want to lie to you."

"Alex- I think I might be gay."

She slammed her mouth shut, blinking through the shock of what she'd just heard. "I don't understand..."

He nodded vigorously, clasping his hands together in front of his mouth as he took a deep breath. "Yeah. So, obviously I adore you. You're my best friend, and I do love you, so much. I- I just feel like something is wrong here, and I know it isn't you because you're wonderful." His breath turned shaky and his voice cracked when he admitted, "But I don't feel the same way about you. I want to. I wish I did. I never wanted you to know."

Alex felt her heart crack in her chest. Not because the man she was picturing her future with wasn't attracted to her but because he had no intention of telling her. "You can tell me anything. I would never judge you."

"Aren't you angry?"

She was heartbroken, but not angry. She wanted to tell him that, but he'd shared something hard with her. She couldn't punish him for being honest with her. It's what she'd wanted to do. "No. I'm just sad that you thought you couldn't tell me. And a little disappointed that you let it get this far if you weren't happy."

Jesse shook his head, grabbing Alex's hands. He was trembling. "I've loved every minute with you, Alex. Every single day with you has been the best. I'd marry you if you wanted, but I can't lie to you. I thought I could push away the things I feel, but I think I like... something else."

"Men? That's okay. You can like guys, it's not a big deal." Alex smiled weakly in an effort to comfort him, but Jesse looked ashamed. Her smile fell and she leaned forward, tilting up his chin to see him better. His eyes were watering, and she understood that this wasn't a secret he'd planned to keep from *her*. It was something he'd planned to keep from everyone, forever. "It's not okay here, is it?"

"If they found out I was gay I'd never hear the end of it. The guys would never look at me the same again. They'd be uncomfortable... I might lose my job." Jesse sucked in a harsh breath, holding back tears. "This isn't about me, this is about you. You told me something really personal but I want to be as honest with you as you are with me. And I want you to be happy. I didn't want to tell you- I shouldn't have told you." He wiped his hand down his face. His entire body was shaking, and Alex leaned over and threw her arm around him, pulling him close.

"How long have you known?"

Jesse leaned against Alex and she squeezed him, telling him she was there. "I don't know. I guess the closer we got I started thinking something was missing. I wanted to be intimate with you, but I couldn't bring myself to lead you on when I started thinking I was more attracted to men. I knew I couldn't act on anything and I'm so happy with you that I just figured I'd ignore it."

She groaned and flopped onto her back, covering her eyes with her arm. Jesse had done everything in his power to make sure *she* was happy. He felt like he had to hide his real feelings and their relationship was one of convenience...

It was just like Mason and Scarlett. It wasn't real.

He pulled her arm away and leaned down, kissing her cheek softly. "I'm so sorry, Alex. I shouldn't have told you. I don't want to lose you."

"Don't you dare apologize for being honest with me," Alex growled up at him. She felt like the world was crashing down on her, crushing her chest into the mattress. She felt angry and betrayed and hurt, but she was more upset that he thought he should hide his true feelings than admit that he liked men. She reached up and cupped his cheek. "I swear I won't tell anybody. Nobody has to know."

"They'll know something is wrong when we break up."

"Then we won't break up." Jesse stared at her in disbelief, but Alex was assured of her decision. He was the best friend she'd ever had. "I'm not gonna let you get hurt. I care about you too much."

He grabbed her wrist, pulling her hand to his lips. Even with his secret out, he instinctively wanted to kiss her, touch her. Alex wanted to unpack that a little more, but she had to assume that Jesse was still sorting through his feelings if he'd only started coming to this realization in the past few months. Right now, she was going to protect his heart, even if it broke hers.

"You could have somebody else," Jesse murmured.

"There is nobody else here. I'm okay." Alex confessed weakly. She was tired. She wanted to sleep, but she didn't know if she could. She knew she would run through every moment they'd spent together over the past several months, and weed through every memory to decide what was true and what was a lie. "Selfishly, I don't want to lose you either."

"I'm sorry."

"Stop apologizing. I'm proud of you. Being honest is really hard..." She tailed off, wanting to ask if Jesse would keep her secret. She knew telling Jesse the truth could cost Sienna the chance at love. She'd never considered it could unravel what she'd found for herself.

He laid down beside her, and she threw her arm around him, snuggling into his chest. It was safe, warm, and familiar. He wrapped his arm around her, too. "Tell me who you really are, and I'll never say it again. I swear on my life I'll never hurt you. Not again."

She swallowed, fluttering her eyelids to bat away her tears. "Alexandra Jacobs," she whispered.

He hummed and squeezed her tighter. "Beautiful, but I like Alex Jade better."

That made her smile, and she closed her eyes, letting the sound of his breathing lull her to sleep. "Me too."

Chapter 37

"So," Gentry started as he rode alongside Sienna, "Owen wants to throw a barn dance to celebrate such a successful summer before the college kids leave this weekend... Thursday night out at the Circle W."

Sienna swayed with Cheyanne as they walked slowly along the bank of the river. She faced ahead, but let her gaze drift to the left to look at Gentry from underneath the brown cowboy hat he'd loaned her. She was thankful for it now, because the sun was beating down on them at full force late in the afternoon. "And?"

"I'm gonna go. It's gonna be a lot of fun."

"Are you asking me to go? Or asking me not to go so nobody thinks we're there together?" Sienna wasn't in any hurry to publicize their relationship, if they could even call it that. She wouldn't even call them friends with benefits, because he hadn't even kissed her, but they were moving in the direction of exclusivity. They basically were exclusive: he clearly wasn't seeing anyone, and, despite Brad asking her to dinner again, Sienna wasn't interested in seeking out other prospects.

Gentry had been there when Brad casually mentioned the date he'd had with the girl from the auction. He said they had a wonderful time, but she wasn't Sienna. His gaze kept darting to Gentry, who watched from a distance with an easy, confident grin. Sienna wasn't sure if she was flattered that Gentry was so sure about them, or offended that he was so sure she'd reject Brad for him.

She'd politely told Brad that she was too busy working on end-of-the-season projects, but maybe another time they could go out. Gentry teased her, saying she was keeping her options open. She'd argued it would keep the town's people from thinking she was interested in their sheriff. After bidding a thousand dollars to take him on a date, most of the town assumed she was gunning for his attention, but luckily for Sienna, he wasn't great at hiding his emotions. It was clear that he was interested in her, too.

Sienna raised her brows expectantly as she waited for Gentry to answer her question. He pulled on the reins and Domino whinnied as he halted in place. He stomped his hooves and Sienna turned Cheyanne around to face them. The river sparkled beside them in the late summer sun, so Sienna dismounted to lead Cheyanne to the water.

While the horse drank, Sienna scratched her neck, giving her attention to the buckskin mare as Gentry kept his distance, deep in thought. She peered over Cheyanne's back at Gentry, watching as the man dismounted and led Domino towards a tree near the water. He tied him up, then doubled back and grabbed Cheyanne without a word to do the same while Sienna waited patiently. He'd talk when he was ready, and pressing him would get Sienna a sarcastic answer, not a real one.

Over the past week, Sienna and Gentry had kept their distance in public, but they'd stolen away moments like this where they could be alone. He'd brought her breakfast early in the morning before anyone would notice. She'd visited him at the sheriff's station in the afternoon, coming up with random things she needed to discuss with him in private. Today, after spending the morning replacing a hundred mattresses at the Tumbleweed Motel, a sweat-drenched Gentry snuck away to shower around two, and by three, he texted Sienna that Lyle wanted to meet her at the stables to talk about a potential schedule change for the trail rides. When she arrived, Gentry had Cheyanne and Domino already saddled up and waiting.

Now Sienna took a seat at the bank, pulling her boots and socks off and dipping her toes into the water while she waited. She rested her chin on her shoulder, watching Gentry intently as he sauntered back to her. She reached up and took his hand, gently tugging him down to sit beside her so she could lay her head against his arm.

He leaned back on his hands, sighing as he gazed across the river. "I want to take you to the dance." Gentry laughed and shook his head a little before tilting his chin down to look at Sienna. "Are we back in middle school?"

Sienna snorted through her nose, then bolted up to stare at Gentry in horror. She covered her mouth and nose with her hands as her cheeks turned red, embarrassed that she'd *snorted* in front of him. Mason would have given her a cold look to warn her he was unimpressed. Her mother would have dragged her into the restroom and berated her until there were tears in her eyes. But Gentry just chuckled and pulled her hand away from her face to kiss the pads of her fingers, banishing her embarrassment with his affection.

She wrapped her fingers around his and held them close to her chest, leaning forward to address him directly. "What will people say? If we show up together?"

"That we're in love?" Gentry teased and Sienna's already-nervous smile fell. Her panic must have been clear on her face because Gentry laughed loudly and pulled her close. He kissed her shoulder and whispered, "I'm teasing you. We're friends, Sienna. Everybody knows we're friends. We can go as two people who have fun together, and if anybody asks, Dakota told me I needed to ask you and you said yes before Brad got a chance."

"Are we just friends?" Sienna felt her stomach twist in knots at the idea. Part of her wanted him to confirm that they were just best friends, that they both needed whatever this mess was, but they weren't ready to be more. He was holding back and she didn't want to let anyone have her heart again. This could stay fun and mutually beneficial. They didn't have to ruin this with feelings and labels.

The other part of Sienna- the small, scared part of her- would shatter if Gentry told her this was just a fun game.

His eyes held a bit of worry as they studied her. Sienna held her breath, feeling her heart sink with every moment that passed without his answer. The birds gossiped about them as they fluttered overhead, and Domino nickered as he grazed beside Cheyanne, as if asking what Gentry was waiting for. Sienna started to turn away, but Gentry firmly placed his hand behind her head and pulled her forward to kiss her.

Sienna wasn't expecting it, and her eyes burst open in surprise as he pressed a little harder, then pulled away suddenly. He gaped at her, breathing heavily.

If he regretted the kiss, she hoped he wouldn't tell her. If he told her he felt nothing, she'd laugh it off, but secretly she'd want to try again, because as scared as she was to fall for him, she wasn't ready to give up on this feeling.

Her chest was tight as he stared at her. In reality, it was a couple seconds, but it felt like hours for Sienna.

"Gentry?"

Her voice seemed to startle him, and he shook his head a little to wake himself up from his daze. "I'm sorry, I shouldn't have- I mean…" His words trailed off and Sienna's heart sank. She felt her expression fall and told herself to keep her chin up. It was probably for the best.

But Gentry reached out and tucked a piece of hair behind Sienna's ear, ghosting his rough fingers across her skin. He traced the shell of her ear with his thumb absentmindedly as he stared at her lips.

"I should have asked. I'm sorry if I overstepped."

His words surprised Sienna. He wasn't upset about the kiss, he was upset about putting her in a position that might be uncomfortable. Mason never asked if she was comfortable having sex with him, even after realizing he'd be taking her virginity.

But here sat Gentry Wyatt, apologizing for the most innocent kiss Sienna had ever received. She'd worried that the spark between them would become a fire too dangerous and volatile to control, but she felt it light something worse inside her.

The spark became an ember, burning steadily and making her feel warm and fuzzy inside. Like a fire starting in a home she didn't want to leave. Gentry lit a feeling of comfort in her that was unfamiliar, because she considered, for the first time, that she wouldn't mind having him in her life forever.

The rational part of her said not to get too close. Because she could be ripped away or it could end badly, as her past relationship did. But her heart silenced her mind and told her clearly: *Let go.*

"Kiss me again?" Sienna whispered, making it clear it was a question and not an order. If she'd misunderstood and he truly regretted his actions, this was an out.

But he responded by pouncing on her, grabbing her face with both hands and kissing Sienna desperately, as if he hadn't kissed anyone in years.

Gentry held her jaw with one hand and moved his other one to cup the back of her head while his lips crashed against hers. She moaned a little, opening her mouth wider to deepen the kiss when Gentry tangled his left hand in her hair. She found herself wrapping her arms around his shoulders as she shifted to her knees, forcing him to lean his head back to continue kissing her. She knocked off his hat so she could run her fingers through his messy hair, tugging on it a little and causing him to chuckle.

"Sienna." Her name on his deep, desperate voice made her shake with anticipation. If he started stripping off all her clothes to have her here and now, she wouldn't stop him. Every rational thought vacated her mind when he bit her bottom lip a little. A sharp gasp left her throat and he released her mouth to pepper the column of her neck with faint kisses.

He slowly laid her down on her back in the sage-colored grass before pulling away to pant over her. The boyish grin he'd developed over the past week was nowhere to be found, replaced by a proud smirk as his eyes roamed Sienna's face and neck. For a moment, he forgot to be a gentleman, and his gaze dropped to the cleavage shown off by her low tank top.

Sienna grabbed the back of his neck and pulled him down for another kiss. She savored the feel of his soft lips against hers, and she let out a little whimper when he licked against her lips for entrance.

The sound was answered by a frustrated moan, and Gentry pushed away quickly. His brows furrowed and his jaw was set tightly as he raised his head to look at the Badlands behind Sienna. He looked disheartened, as if he'd lost the drive he possessed a moment ago. The desire still burned behind sadness though, and something Sienna couldn't quite pinpoint.

"Are you okay?"

Gentry let himself fall onto the grass beside Sienna to stare at the sky. He grabbed her hand and held it to his lips, clenching his eyes shut. "I'm sorry."

She rolled over to lean on her elbow so she could see the man beside her. Clenching his hand a little tighter, Sienna assured him with a quiet, soothing voice, "It's okay. Don't apologize."

"I owe you an explanation."

"You don't owe me anything." Sienna brushed back his hair, smiling when his grimace weakened a bit. He relaxed beneath her fingertips, but she didn't stop running her fingers through his shaggy strands. "Do you want to talk about it?"

He opened his eyes and sighed, "Not particularly."

Nodding, Sienna answered, "Then we don't need to. I just want to spend time with you." She pressed her palm to his chest and leaned against him, tracing lazy circles on his shirt. They wouldn't have the opportunity to spend the days lounging around much longer. Once all the college kids left, they would need to reconfigure the show, restaff the stores, and figure out how to keep business strong as the weather turned cold. Sienna dreaded the idea of massive heaps of snow in the middle of nowhere, but if she could snuggle up against Gentry's warm body she might just survive. "Are you nervous? For what happens next?"

"With us?" Gentry asked lightly. He stroked Sienna's hair, carefully pulling it up and letting it fall around her until she had a halo of red.

"I was thinking about the town, but... are you nervous about us?"

Gentry grunted and sat up, forcing Sienna to sit up with him. He took both of her hands in his and looked her in the eyes, baring into her soul with his intense gaze. "I don't move very fast. I need to make sure I'm ready for the kind of commitment you deserve, and that you understand what you're getting yourself into. I'm worried about you losing your patience, and if you do, I won't blame you. But I'm not afraid of what happens between us, as long as we're honest with each other."

Honesty. It was something Sienna couldn't give him. She wasn't allowed to. He could never know her past. He'd never know her mom's name or the street she grew up on. She could never tell Gentry who she really was, and she wondered if they could build any sort of future on lies she'd made up on a whim.

The cold, lifeless walls of the Marshals' facility felt like a lifetime ago. Scarlett Jacobs was a distant memory and the reason for their banishment from the real world was a horrible dream. Sienna felt a strange sort of guilt for pushing her old life away like an old box of clothes she forgot about.

If Gentry could know her, would he still like her? If he met the workaholic, would he still tease and play with her? If he took the soft-spoken, money-obsessed businesswoman out on a date, would he want to take her on another one?

Would the man beside her want her if she was Scarlett Jacobs, or had he fallen for Sienna Jade, the mask she'd begrudgingly donned to stay alive?

Sienna didn't want to wonder, she wanted to know. She just couldn't risk him learning the truth. If he knew her secret, it would put Gentry in danger, and Sienna couldn't bear the idea of him getting hurt because of her. She could enjoy this moment or dwell on how complicated it was until she ruined it for both of them. And they both needed each other in some capacity, whether it be friends, lovers, or somewhere in between.

"I think you're the best friend I've ever had. Nobody has ever cared enough to really get to know me, but you know me better than anybody." Sienna confessed, and she meant it. He knew who she was on such a personal level, deep inside where Sienna and Scarlett were the same person.

"I'm scared to fall for you," she told him softly. "It's different with you than it's ever been with anybody else. I don't think I've ever truly been in love- at least nobody's ever loved me."

"Well, I hate to break it to you, but if we keep going down this road, I don't think that'll be the case much longer."

He held out his hand and Sienna took it and allowed him to pull her back into his arms. She curled against him and rested her head on his shoulder, closing her eyes to imagine being in love with this man. Perhaps, if she thought a little less and followed her happy heart, she'd find out.

Chapter 38

On Monday after her ride with Gentry, Sienna spent her evening at the saloon with Alex and Maude, going over ideas for a reworked storyline for when Annie and the others left. Sienna could tell it was going to stretch the town thin without the college kids, and her dreams of being a year-round tourist destination began to dwindle at the realization.

They'd need new people to move into town to keep it at this level, or they'd need to go back to seasonal operation. Sienna wasn't ready to give up yet, but Maude only shrugged and told her she could be optimistic, but the old woman would be realistic, and plan on closing the saloon until at least the holidays. Alex stayed quiet for most of it, taking notes every once in a while. She looked pained at the idea of only operating seasonally, but they'd built their show around people they knew would leave. Perhaps they should have considered that they'd actually be successful, instead of desperately trying to survive the summer.

Tuesday found Sienna, Dakota, and a couple of the old saloon gals at the portrait studio with Miss Rose going through the costumes. Many needed mending after a busy summer, and some needed to be replaced entirely. Sienna and Dakota worked on a budget to purchase new outfits. Miss Rose informed them she wanted somebody else to run it next summer. That alone told Sienna the portrait studio wouldn't be open until next May at the earliest, and that was only if she could find somebody to operate it.

Dakota asked Sienna over for dinner that night, but when she arrived, it was Gentry standing in the kitchen. He pulled out Sienna's chair and served her home cooked steak with the nicest wine sold at the general store.

They'd talked for hours at the candlelit table until Dakota finally arrived home and shooed them out so she could get some rest.

By Wednesday, Sienna was on cloud nine. She'd laid awake most of the night, staring at the ceiling with a smile on her lips. Her only complaint was that Gentry wasn't lying there beside her. Even Alex looked at her like she was a lovestruck fool, an ironic twist of fate that wasn't lost on either of them.

"You're smitten," Alex said as Sienna sipped her coffee, looking out the window towards the Badlands. "Sienna."

She sat her coffee down and faced her sister, tapping the side of the ceramic mug impatiently. "Yes?"

Alex grinned widely, resting her elbows on the table as she leaned forward to get closer to Sienna. "You used to give me so much crap for running headfirst into a relationship and here you are... completely enamored with Sheriff Gentry. I can't say I blame you, it's just weird seeing you so affected by him."

Sienna pressed her palms to the hot mug, smiling down into it as she remembered Gentry's goodnight kiss twelve hours ago. He'd walked her up the stairs and waited while she unlocked the door, then kissed her in the doorway for a good five minutes before bidding her goodnight, mounting Domino, and sprinting off towards the stable.

"He's different. He's special." Sienna felt her heart clench and her eyes moved up to meet Alex's. "Am I moving too fast?"

"No, not for a normal person, just fast for you."

"He's a really good guy. I think we could have a good life together."

"I don't disagree," Alex told her slowly, and Sienna waited for the other shoe to drop. Finally, Alex lamented, "Don't you wish you could tell him the truth? About us? About why we're here?"

"Every damn day," Sienna choked out. "More than anything. I'm so scared that if he knew he'd run the other way. But on the other hand, if he knew... I think he'd protect me. I think he'd keep our secret." Sienna wanted to ask Alex if she could tell Gentry. She wanted Alex's blessing to be honest with him and pray that he'd understand and that it wouldn't change anything between them.

Alex reached across the counter and grabbed Sienna's wrist, whispering, "Then tell him." Sienna's eyes widened and Alex repeated, "Tell him the truth. Because I think he's the best thing to ever happen to you and I don't want you to be scared because you think he doesn't know you. Let him see all of you, and if we end up having to leave because of it, then at least we had a really great summer."

Sienna laughed and came around the counter, wrapping her little sister in a tight hug. "Thank you so much. I love you, Alex."

"I love you, too."

When Sienna left the apartment an hour later, Gentry was on his hands and knees in front of the apparel store, drilling holes into the boardwalk to replace the wooden railings they'd ripped up from the steps. Sienna approached quietly, then kicked his boot to get his attention. When he looked up at her in surprise, she thrust forward the lemonade she'd brought him.

"Thanks."

"You're welcome." She fanned herself with her hand, squinting up at the sky as she whined, "It's so hot."

"Wasn't too bad till you showed up."

Sienna's gaze snapped to Gentry, finding him laughing at his own joke. He sat down and leaned against the steps, staring up at Sienna as he sipped the lemonade. "You're cute when you're flustered, you know that?"

She could feel her cheeks heating up, and he pointed at her, as if to prove his point. "Keep hitting on me so blatantly and you're gonna start sounding like Brad."

Gentry drained his glass and handed it back, then picked up his drill to get back to work. "Well, we definitely don't want that. You better get a move on before I turn into a skeevy man-whore." He winked at her and she rolled her eyes, but wandered down the street towards the saloon anyway. She'd ask him if they could talk in private later.

While Gentry worked at the apparel shop, his father was hard at work carving intricate details into the door of the saloon. He had carefully carved the Badlands into the door, and upon closer inspection Sienna realized there were bison grazing at the base of the hills. She gasped a little, completely taken by his work. "It's beautiful. You're so talented."

Eli finished the bison he was carving and leaned away, wiping his brow with the back of hand. "Thank you. Haven't done anything this big in a long time." He looked up at her and smiled. "You've really done a number on my family, Miss Jade. You've got my wife and I out of retirement. My daughter is over the moon with how her town is doing, and my son adores you. I never thought I'd see him look so happy again after Kenzie passed."

Sienna ran her fingers through her hair, ducking her head. "I'm sorry for your loss."

The older Wyatt nodded a little and wiped his hands on his jeans, looking back at the door to study his work. "Never thought I'd have to bury my daughter-in-law. You hope they're gonna stick around to take care of your kids when you're gone. Gentry didn't speak to anybody for almost a..."

Whatever Eli was saying faded away as Sienna's mind continued to rewind his words over and over and over again until she finally blurted, "What did you say?"

He looked surprised, blinking a few times before repeating. "Gentry didn't talk to anybody for almost a year. He was devastated."

"No. Before that. I thought Kenzie was your daughter."

Eli shook his head slowly, grunting as he stood to face Sienna fully. "No, Kenzie was Gentry's wife. They were married six years when she passed."

Sienna felt her heart drop through her ribcage before cracking as if it hit the ground. "His... wife?"

"You didn't know?" Eli asked, looking over Sienna's shoulder at Main Street before stammering. "I assumed- I thought for sure he'd told you. He's crazy about you."

This was the thing he needed to tell her. The thing she told him she didn't want to talk about a week and a half ago. He was married. He had a wife. He had a wife for *six years* before she *died*. He was a widower. Sienna was flirting with some dead woman's husband.

"I gotta go."

She bolted down the stairs of the saloon, feeling her heart pounding as she sprinted farther away from Mr. Wyatt. Her boots dug into the dirt road as she passed the bank and the sheriff's station, not stopping as she approached the mayor's office.

When Sienna first learned about Kenzie Wyatt, she asked Dakota specifically if that was her sister. She'd told her yes. Perhaps Gentry had omitted some information, because he was working his way up to the truth, but Dakota had blatantly lied to Sienna's face.

Dakota knew what Sienna thought, she *knew*, and she continued to let Sienna think Kenzie was their sister anyway.

Before her mind could register where she was, Sienna was barging through the door of Dakota's office, where she found the blonde sitting at her desk. She looked up and smiled brightly, greeting Sienna with a "Hey!" before realizing Sienna was upset. Her smile fell and she asked with a pouty voice, "What's wrong?"

"You told me Kenzie was your sister."

Dakota gave a slow nod, but Sienna caught the way her pupils widened a little bit in realization. "She was."

Sienna scoffed, feeling her stomach drop as anger bubbled inside her. "So we're gonna do this? You're gonna pretend like you didn't lie to me? Why? What do you gain from not telling me the truth?"

"Did Gentry tell you?"

"No. He didn't," Sienna spat. She crossed her arms and looked up at the ceiling, feeling tears threatening to spill from her emerald eyes. "You both lied to me."

Dakota stood abruptly and strode around her desk to Sienna, but Sienna took a step back and put her finger up, telling Dakota to keep her distance. Her lip quivered as she said, "Please don't be mad at Gentry. I didn't want to tell you initially because I didn't really know you- But then he asked me not to."

"He's a widower, Dakota! He had a wife, don't you think I deserve to know that?"

"Does it make a difference?" Dakota asked darkly, becoming more defensive.

Sienna stood up a little straighter. She felt dizzy, like the world was falling out from under her feet. "Yes. It does. It does make a difference, because he already found the love of his life. I'm... I'm..."

Dakota took a step towards Sienna and looked down her nose at the shorter woman, clearly disappointed in her reaction. "You're the first woman he's given the time of day to since his wife was killed in a car wreck. You matter to him, and he didn't want you to look at him like he was broken."

"I wouldn't-.... I wouldn't have."

With a raise of one manicured eyebrow, Dakota challenged Sienna's claim. "Then why are you so upset? Are you upset because I lied, or are you upset because now you can't look at Gentry the same way again?"

Sienna wanted to tell her that she was upset that they'd lied to her, but it wasn't that simple. Even if Kenzie Wyatt was long buried, her spirit was alive and well in Lonewood. Sienna couldn't compete with the beloved teacher. Maybe she made Gentry happy when nobody else was around, but Sienna wasn't sure he was willing to face the scrutiny of his town. "I don't know. I need to think about it."

She turned to leave, but as her fingers wrapped around the doorknob, Dakota called out, "He was going to tell you. He's been waiting for the right time, but he's scared you won't want to see him anymore. I'm disappointed that he was right."

Her words broke Sienna's heart, but she was confused and overwhelmed. She knew she needed to talk to Gentry, but she needed to be alone. If she confronted Gentry now, she didn't know what would come out of her mouth, and Sienna wasn't willing to ruin what they had today.

She stormed out of Dakota's office, letting the tears stream down her cheeks. She told herself over and over again that she wasn't mad that Gentry had a wife, she was mad that he hadn't told her. But she knew better.

Gentry had been somebody's husband. Losing Kenzie was a horrible twist of fate, but that didn't change the fact that he'd chosen Kenzie to be the woman he spent forever with. He should have never had the chance to get to know Sienna.

As she walked across the street towards her apartment, Sienna's mind wandered to a life where Kenzie was still alive. She probably would have welcomed Sienna with open arms, and her doting husband would have more or less ignored the newcomer. The idea brought more tears to Sienna's eyes as she reached the porch of the store, and to her horror, Gentry was still working next door.

When he saw her, he stood quickly, concern written across his face. "What's wrong?"

"I'm sorry, I gotta go."

He chased after her as she took the stairs to the second floor of the building two at a time, but caught up with her by the time she fished her key out of her pocket. He ducked his head to try and get a better look at Sienna, but she shook her head as her quaking hand finally got the key into the lock.

"What happened?" Gentry asked worriedly. He tried to wrap his arms around Sienna's waist, but all she could think about when he held her was that, in a perfect world, he'd be holding somebody else. Sienna couldn't ignore the obvious fact that she would always be his second choice, because he'd already lost his first one.

The door finally unlocked and Sienna gasped for breath, turning around to look up at Gentry as she shoved the door open. She wanted to tell him she knew. She wanted to tell him she felt betrayed and angry. She wanted to tell him that she didn't want to see him anymore. She wanted to tell him that she was sorry she wasn't his wife.

But all that came out was, "I'm sorry."

The look on his face could only be described as heartbreak, but Sienna needed time. She knew better than to have this conversation before she could sort through her feelings about it. So she slammed the door in his face and darted to her bedroom. She locked her door and crashed her back against it, sliding down the wood to the plush carpet.

She couldn't imagine what it was like for Gentry to lose his wife. In a weird way, when she'd thought Kenzie was their sister, Sienna felt like she could relate to the Wyatts since her own sister's life was in danger. Now, though, Sienna tried to comprehend how lonely Gentry must have been.

He had to wake up every morning knowing he'd never get to see the love of his life again.

Sienna thought he kissed her like he hadn't kissed anybody in years. It was because he hadn't.

Her breath caught in her throat, and she coughed a little as she let out a humorless laugh. She'd broken through his pain and suffering. She'd found a way into his heart, and it meant something. It had to mean something if he hadn't let anyone else in since Kenzie died.

Through the sound of her own gasping for air, Sienna noticed her phone buzzing incessantly. She picked it up and saw that Gentry was calling her. He'd called her six times.

She ignored his call though, and dialed her sister instead. She needed to talk to Alex. After a couple of rings, she answered, and Sienna choked out, "Can you come home? I need you."

"What's wrong? Are you okay? I'll get Gentry-"

"No," Sienna said firmly. "No, I'm fine. I just need to talk to you. I need to talk to you alone."

There was a pause before Alex slowly answered, "Okay. I'll be home in ten."

Alex hung up first and Sienna let her phone drop, blowing air through her pursed lips. She should have asked Alex to pick up a bottle of wine. Or half a dozen.

Chapter 39

By the time Alex got home, Sienna had gotten out all her tears and was sitting on her bed, peeling off her nail polish into little peach shards. Her eyes were rimmed red, but all she said was, "They lied to me."

Alex listened while Sienna explained what had happened, and how betrayed she felt. It became clear as the hours rolled by that Sienna didn't just feel blindsided, she felt stupid. She said over and over again that she should have known.

But Alex would have never guessed that Kenzie had been Gentry's wife. For three and a half months, a whole town spoke highly of Kenzie Wyatt but never mentioned that she had left behind a husband. Either everyone in Lonewood was in on Dakota's ruse, or hiding the truth from Sienna and Alex was just a convenient consequence of being polite enough to not share Gentry's very personal business.

In hindsight, it was most likely a little of both. Moments that had felt off made sense now. Alex remembered Dakota's strange behavior at the bachelorette party when she'd snapped at Kennedy. She'd told her she didn't want to talk about 'it'. The bachelorette party Kennedy had alluded to was Kenzie's. Annie was in on it, too. She'd shut down Jolene when she started taunting Sienna, trying to get her to admit she liked Gentry. It was because if Sienna said yes, somebody might bring up Kenzie. Dakota and Annie had been working hard to make sure everybody in town kept their mouths shut.

It was easy to understand why Gentry wanted to tell Sienna himself. It was his story to tell, which was most likely why nobody else brought it up. Whether they were dating, friends, or strangers who happened to live in the same small town, it was Gentry's right to share his loss. Gossip was the town's favorite activity, but gossiping about the sheriff and his dead wife was a line everyone knew not to cross. The people in Lonewood cared about and protected one another. If somebody was going to get hurt in this situation, of course they'd protect Gentry over Sienna. He was their broken golden boy. Sienna was an outsider.

It was a shame that Gentry's own father let the truth slip before Gentry could be honest with Sienna. Clearly he'd been close to telling her if Eli thought she already knew. Maybe he would have told her at the dance, but the time for explaining himself had passed, and Sienna wasn't in the mood to listen.

Gentry Wyatt was a really good man, though. He treated Sienna well-at least over the past few weeks. He should have been honest about his past before they got close, but it wasn't like Sienna was being honest about hers. It was hypocritical, really, that she was upset about him withholding this from her.

Alex suspected this had more to do with Sienna's insecurities than Gentry and Dakota keeping the truth from her. Alex had seen the amount of texts and calls from Gentry. That man cared about Sienna, but she was scared that she couldn't live up to the woman everyone in town gushed about. Although nobody had let it slip that Kenzie had been Gentry's wife, they'd made it undeniably clear that she was irreplaceable. It was a hard act for Sienna to follow, and she'd already started down that road unknowingly.

Maybe after a good night's sleep Sienna would allow Gentry to explain himself.

It was almost ten the next morning when Sienna dragged herself out of bed. She spent a good thirty minutes in the shower, and another forty minutes locked in her bathroom getting ready for the day. When she emerged, she wore yoga pants and a flowy tank top. Her makeup was minimalist at best. She clearly didn't plan on leaving the apartment, for personal or work reasons.

She'd been ignoring Dakota's calls, too.

Since Sienna didn't feel like leaving the apartment, it allowed Alex to lounge around instead of busting her ass on one of Sienna's projects. It was a nice break, but Alex wished it was under better circumstances.

Around two, there was a knock on the door. Sienna didn't even look away from the tv at the sound, and Alex felt sick at how hollow her sister looked. She hadn't looked like this since their time in the safehouse.

It seemed like Sienna had moved on from being sad to being numb. Alex imagined she was trying to decide what she wanted to do: whether she wanted to hear Gentry out and attempt to patch things up or close herself off and focus on her work. Alex worried that Sienna might want to bolt, and the idea that her sister might want to leave Lonewood over this mess made her chest ache. Between Gentry, Jesse, and the end of the summer, maybe it was time for them both to move on.

But first, one of them had to answer the door.

"I'll get it," Alex said casually, trying to act normal. She prayed that it was Jesse, or even Kitty, because literally anybody else would be unwelcome.

When she swung open the door, she felt her stomach drop.

"Sienna, it's for you."

Alex looked over her shoulder as Sienna's eyes drifted towards the door, narrowing at the man who stood in the doorway. It was surprising that she stood to greet him, but her tone was cold when she finally addressed him.

"Brad." Her greeting was uncharacteristically short, and he looked surprised. She'd always been polite, even when rejecting him. "To what do I owe the pleasure?"

Brad cleared his throat, looking around the entryway and taking note of the paintings Kitty had left behind. "I've been told there's going to be a barn dance out at the Circle W. I've never gone in the past, but it's been a big summer, and I think there will be a good turnout. I'm assuming you'll go, and I was hoping you'd let me take you."

Alex felt queasy at how easy his offer was. It reminded her of Mason. This felt like a business offer instead of a date, and she half expected Sienna to say yes. Because she wasn't thinking clearly or because she wanted to hurt Gentry, or maybe because she didn't really care anymore. Alex waited with bated breath for Sienna to tell Brad she'd go, but she shook her head a little instead.

"I actually don't think I'm gonna go," Sienna admitted quietly. The venom in her voice was gone, replaced with melancholy. She seemed to catch herself, though, and smiled up at Brad the best she could. "I mean-maybe I'll make it? I'm not feeling well, but if I feel better I'll see you there?"

That was more like Sienna. A casual deflection. The hint of a possibility. Sienna was too scared to fight for what she wanted, but she was too hurt to say yes to a man she didn't want to spend time with. Alex was oddly proud.

Brad's brows shot up and he stammered, "Oh. I'm sorry you don't feel well. Do you need anything?"

"I think I'll be okay, I just need some rest."

Sienna truly did look sick. She was normally radiant but her sadness seemed to dull her entire being. She smiled weakly and Brad gave her a thorough once over. As a doctor, he was probably trying to figure out what ailed her. As a man interested in her, he was probably trying to figure out why she was pretending to be sick. "Okay," he finally said, "I hope I see you tonight." He gave a little wave as he saw himself out. At least he was smart enough to know when he wasn't welcome.

Alex locked the door behind him and looked back at Sienna. Her eyes fell to the floor as she let out a heavy sigh. "Should I have said yes?"

"Absolutely not," Alex snapped back. "No, you did the right thing. I would have told him a flat no."

Sienna's voice broke as she tried to speak, coming out more as a whimper. "Gentry and I didn't want people to realize we were seeing each other. That's why I haven't told Brad I'm not interested."

Another knock on the door caused Sienna to snap her head up. It took a moment, but her face contorted into a frustrated scowl. "If that's Brad again..."

"I'll handle it. Go to your room." Alex shooed Sienna away before storming over to the door.

She flung it open, prepared to tell Brad her sister wouldn't date him if he was the last man on Earth, but it was Gentry who stood on the other side. When he saw Alex, he sucked in a quick breath. "Hi."

He looked as wrecked as Sienna did.

His brows were drawn in worry, and his smile didn't quite reach his eyes. He swallowed as he held onto a bouquet of flowers, these ones more beautiful than the last. Alex noted that there were more purple flowers, which was almost certainly done on purpose because it was Sienna's favorite color.

"You were married," Alex blurted. She wanted to retract it as soon as it came out, because Gentry's expression crashed. It took a moment for him to regain his composure, but Alex noticed the hand holding the flowers was quivering.

"I was. For six years. She died in a car accident."

"Why am I hearing this from you before Sienna?" Alex asked boldly.

"I messed up, Alex." He lowered his head like a scolded dog, but his eyes met Alex's. "Can I see her?"

Alex wanted Sienna and Gentry to make up so badly, but she needed to put her sister's fragile feelings first. "I don't think that's a good idea right now. She was blindsided and she's hurting. She thought she knew you and Dakota, but now she's... she's sad."

"Please let me in."

She almost did. He sounded so desperate that Alex considered letting him in and locking him in Sienna's bedroom with her until they kissed and made up. His eyes were as pleading as his deep voice and Alex understood why Sienna was so worked up about him. Gentry was something special, but Sienna was too conflicted to make smart decisions at the moment.

So Alex shook her head. "I'm sorry, but no. I'll let her know you came by, and she'll call when she's ready to see you."

His whole body heaved as he sighed, but he nodded to show he understood. "Okay." He handed Alex the flowers and looked past her into the entryway one more time, hoping to catch a glimpse of Sienna. "We were supposed to go to the barn dance together. I know she doesn't wanna see me, but if she changes her mind, I'll be there."

Alex closed the door behind him, and Sienna came around the corner from the hallway leading to the bedrooms. Her bottom lip quivered and when she saw the flowers in Alex's hands she started bawling. Alex sat the flowers on the counter and wrapped Sienna in a firm embrace, resting her cheek on her head. "I'm so sorry, Sienna."

"I'm just so confused."

"I know. It's okay to be confused. You have really strong feelings for him," Alex murmured as she rubbed Sienna's back. "Do you want to come with Jesse and I to the dance tonight?"

Sienna pulled away and looked up at her sister. She looked torn. "I don't think I should."

"You don't have to decide now, but he's picking me up at seven. I know it'll be hard to face Dakota and Gentry, but if you aren't there, people will start to talk."

Sienna nodded a little, wiping her finger under her nose. "Yeah. You're right. I should probably make an appearance."

"And when you're ready to go, we'll go, okay? And you don't have to spend time with anyone you don't want to. Not Gentry, or Brad, or Dakota, or anybody. You can be my date and Jesse can be our third wheel. He and I are just going for show, too."

Sienna laughed at that and nodded. "Sounds good. Thanks, Alex." She locked herself in her room to get ready, leaving Alex in the kitchen staring at the flowers.

Chapter 40

THE WHITE BARN OUT at the Circle W clearly hadn't housed livestock in a long time, but it seemed to have found a second life as a reception hall. Crisply painted on the outside, rolling barn doors opened up into a massive space set up for partying. Thousands of white fairy lights were strung from the rafters around an old crystal chandelier, creating a soft, magical light in the old wooden building.

Along the left wall was a buffet of snacks and desserts where Maude was perched on a padded stool behind a permanent bar. The bar top was lined with liquor, and she was busy filling the cups of the laughing, boisterous Lonewood residents who lined up for her services. The right side of the room held several plush couches for socializing, but they sat empty as the moon began to rise. A wooden dance floor was placed in the center of the building, where half the town danced to the music of the live band situated on an elevated platform.

Annie beamed back at Jolene as the young woman played her fiddle with expert ease, all while Lyle tickled the keys of his keyboard without looking at what he was doing. Beau stood beside him, playing guitar while Annie sang her heart out like she wouldn't get another chance. A lot could happen between August and May, and this could very well be the last time they all played together. This could be the last time they were together in Lonewood at all.

When Alex saw everyone shuffling across the dance floor in a line dance, her entire countenance brightened. She stood a little straighter in her green maxi dress as her red-painted lips curved into a brilliant smile. She beamed at Jesse as he took her hand and gave it a little squeeze.

But her shoulders hunched when she remembered her sister, and Sienna grimaced when Alex whipped around to check on her with a worried expression.

"Go dance," Sienna told her softly. "I'll be okay."

There was no reason for both of them to be miserable. Alex fidgeted in her boots, playing with the long golden chain around her neck. She clearly wanted to go and dance, but she was worried about Sienna.

"Are you sure?"

"I'm positive, go." Sienna pointed towards the dance floor where the line dancing broke apart into swing dancing. Alex grabbed Jesse's wrist and bolted, as if her feet were in control instead of her mind.

Watching Alex dance eased the dull ache in Sienna's heart. Jesse spun her around several times in a row, causing Alex to laugh loudly above the music. As much as Sienna wanted to be sad that her own luck had turned sour, she felt worse for Alex. She loved Jesse so much, and she'd been so brave in realizing he couldn't return the affection she had for him. Even though there would never be true love between them, Alex stayed by his side, protecting him from the cruel world that could hurt him. It was the most selfless thing Sienna had ever seen, and it made her feel guilty about feeling sorry for herself.

But Alex and Jesse had each other, whether as friends or as something else, and they were happy. It could have been complicated, but they chose not to let it come between them. Sienna had run for the hills before she even gave Gentry the chance to explain himself.

The crowd cheered when Jesse dipped Alex, and Sienna clapped as the song came to an end. Everyone seemed to shuffle a little between songs, so Sienna took the opportunity to squeeze her way through the crowd towards the bar.

After a few minutes, she reached Maude and the older woman looked surprised to see her. "Miss Jade. I heard you weren't feeling well."

Apparently Brad had been drinking and blabbing again.

"Yeah, I wanted to see it though. This is really something." Sienna gestured around. She and Mason would frequent events where there'd be dancing, drinking, and socializing, but nothing held a candle to this.

Genuine joy hung in the air as the whole town partied together. It wasn't about schmoozing for a job or a donation. This was about being together before life changed for the fall.

Maude gave a little nod and pulled out a bottle of wine from beneath the bar. "You look stunning, by the way. You'll be beating off the men with a stick." She handed over the glass and Sienna thanked her quietly as she looked down. She'd found this white lace dress tucked in with the clothes Bridget bought her and decided this might be her last chance to wear it. At Alex's request, Sienna had allowed her sister to pull back the top chunk of her thick red hair with a soft white bow, the perfect accessory to the sweet little dress that flared a bit at her hips.

"Did you come here alone?" The surprise in Maude's voice made Sienna flinch.

"Yeah. I'm just making an appearance. I'll probably head out before they do." She nodded towards Alex and Jesse, who stood side by side as another line dance started up. Alex watched Jesse's boots as he taught her the steps, and she mimicked them perfectly.

Sienna shifted in her own cowboy boots, hoping she wouldn't garner too much attention. There were a few people in particular she was set on avoiding, but she hadn't seen any of them yet.

"During set up this evening, Heidi heard from Owen that Eli's in the doghouse for running his mouth. About what, nobody's heard." Maude raised a brow, questioning Sienna, but she just shrugged. "Hmm, I wondered if you'd heard something. I know you're close to their kids."

"Not as close as I thought," Sienna mumbled, tipping back her glass and setting it back on the bar. "How much do I owe you?"

"Nothing tonight, Hun. It's all free. I don't know what kind of parties you're used to in California, but this is about being together, not making money."

Sienna stiffened at that. It splintered her memories of galas in Manhattan, a clear reminder that this place was different. These people were different. Perhaps Sienna could never truly belong here. If she did, her best friends would have trusted her with the truth.

"Don't forget what I told you, Miss Jade. Whatever happens now is up to you."

Tears pricked at Sienna's eyes as she remembered their conversation in the dressing room. Maude had told her not to worry about the opinions of the dead, but Sienna hadn't understood the gravity of the statement at the time. She'd also told Sienna that Kenzie would have done or given anything for the people she loved. Maybe that was Maude's way of telling Sienna that Kenzie would have wanted her husband to be happy, even if she was gone.

"I just feel so bad."

"You feel bad about making somebody happy?" Maude challenged, and Sienna peered over her shoulder in the direction Maude was looking. She saw Dakota talking with Kitty and Bill. Behind them was Gentry with a beer in his hand. He searched the room with a pained expression, occasionally turning to Dakota to nod at whatever she was saying. Even Dakota looked uncomfortable, and Sienna wondered if she and Gentry were on bad terms. Just another thing for Sienna to feel bad about.

She turned back to find Maude giving her a knowing smile. "He's been looking around like that since he got here. I'd say he's waiting for somebody."

Sienna groaned and asked Maude to excuse her, sneaking her way to the far wall to watch everyone dance. She smiled at all the plaid skirts and cowboy hats that spun and shuffled across the dance floor with practiced ease. The stomping of boots became a beat that accompanied Jolene's fiddle, and Sienna found herself tapping along with it.

Cheers and laughter erupted nearby, causing Sienna to turn and see Dakota dragging Gentry onto the dance floor. A sad smile cracked his face as he begrudgingly allowed her to pull him into the center of the group to dance with her. Sienna grinned as Gentry swung his sister around, causing Dakota's deep blue dress to flare out as she stepped quickly to keep up with him.

Beau sat his guitar beside Lyle's keyboard and jumped off the stage to find his wife in the audience. He tugged Kitty onto the floor with their friends, pausing a moment and bobbing his head to find the beat before falling into step with everybody else. The blonde tossed her head back and laughed as they danced alongside Gentry, Dakota, Jesse, and Alex.

Annie laughed as Jolene and Lyle stopped playing at the end of the song. The musicians panted as they fought to catch their breath, beaming out at the crowd. Beau kissed Kitty quickly before bounding back up onto the stage to join them, pulling the guitar strap up and around his shoulder. Once he was ready, he gave Annie a nod and she turned back to the audience. "It's been an amazing summer. I think I speak on behalf of everyone that I never thought in a million years that our town could feel so alive. And I think we owe thanks to the two people who made it happen."

Sienna's eyes widened and she backed up a step, but inadvertently bumped into Hank, who chuckled and ushered her towards the stage. She dug her heels into the dance floor as everyone turned to look at her, and her cheeks burned when she saw Gentry's breath catch from the corner of her eye.

When she reached the stage, Alex slung her arm around Sienna's shoulder and squeezed. Annie motioned towards them and said, "Thank you both for everything. We couldn't have done any of this without you guys."

"Sure you could," Alex said quietly and Sienna smiled up at her, happy to let her speak on their behalf. "You just didn't know where to start." Sienna nodded in agreement, but the voice in her head whispered *"You'll be fine now without us"*.

"Before I leave, I was wondering if you'd maybe sing with me?" Annie asked Alex sweetly, leaning on the microphone stand as everyone cheered. Alex's eyes burst open in surprise as Jesse urged her to take the stage, and Sienna took a step back to allow her sister to take the spotlight, clapping as Alex looked around in terror. Alex wasn't a singer like Annie, but she could sing well, and Sienna knew everyone would be impressed.

When she climbed up on the stage to stand beside Annie, Alex leaned into the microphone and said, "Only if we slow things down a little bit."

"You got it," Annie replied, grabbing another microphone that Owen handed her. They huddled together with Jolene, Beau, and Lyle, allowing Sienna the opportunity to sneak away.

As the first slow, sweet notes of the fiddle began to play, someone caught Sienna's wrist lightly and she turned to see Brad looking down at her worriedly. He let go of her wrist and straightened up, but Sienna already knew what he was going to ask. "Could I have this dance?"

Sienna wanted to tell Brad that she was leaving, but he hadn't done anything wrong. It wasn't his fault that she'd been hurt by somebody else, and it wasn't his fault she'd been leading him on to protect the man who'd hurt her.

"Okay."

She tentatively placed her hand in Brad's and let him lead her back to the dance floor. Whispers surrounded them, but Brad held his head high, proud to finally have Sienna on his arm. She was uneasy with everyone's eyes on them, but he took it all in stride, holding onto Sienna as if she was a trophy he'd earned.

Annie and Alex watched with furrowed brows, not hiding their displeasure. Sienna looked away as Annie began to sing, unable to meet their disappointed stares.

Brad's grip on Sienna's waist tightened a little, and she swore she heard Alex's voice crack when she took over singing from Annie. When Brad ran his thumb over her arm, Sienna leaned her head against his chest, clenching her eyes closed. It would be over soon and then she could leave. Maybe she'd be long gone by the time Alex got home- vanished into the night and never to step foot in Lonewood again.

The music swelled as the chorus hit, and Sienna imagined she was anywhere else. She imagined sitting on that hill overlooking the Badlands. Laying by the river that sparkled in the summer sun. Riding Cheyanne somewhere far away where she could feel free.

She'd been really happy. She had opened up in ways she didn't think she ever could and discovered a version of herself she truly enjoyed. Sienna had started seeing what her life could be here, and she liked the future that laid before her when she was with Gentry. If she lost him, it would be entirely her fault. When he inevitably decided she was more trouble than she was worth, that would be entirely her fault, because she was too scared to help him heal from a horrible tragedy.

Sienna was selfish, and she realized that she'd been selfish for a really long time. She was so focused on her own goals that she didn't care about anybody else. If she was a good sister, she would've been more thankful that Alex was safe than angry she'd cost Sienna her career. If she was a good friend to Gentry, she would have given her condolences for losing his wife instead of locking him out of her life.

Suddenly, Brad stopped dancing and Sienna lifted her head, seeing Gentry standing in front of them with his hand outstretched to her. He ignored Brad, looking straight at Sienna as he asked, "May I cut in?"

Brad released his grip on Sienna as she nodded, feeling a weight lifted from her shoulders as she placed her hand in Gentry's. When his rough fingers wrapped around hers, Sienna felt like she'd come home.

He placed his hand firmly behind her back, silently telling Sienna he wasn't going to let her run. Her lip wobbled a little when he gave her that soft, boyish smile that she'd grown to love. For a moment, she forgot she'd been upset, and she smiled widely as he danced her around the floor to the second chorus of the song.

For those few moments, nobody else existed. Sienna didn't see the way Dakota beamed from behind her hands or the way Alex stopped singing mid-line to stare in happy surprise. She didn't notice how Jasmine's eyes narrowed, or when Brad stormed through the doors without looking back. All Sienna saw was the way Gentry looked at her like he had so much to say but couldn't find his words.

So he pulled her closer and she let out a little gasp, sliding her hand down to his chest. She could feel his heart pounding wildly beneath the black fabric of his embroidered shirt, but nothing else about his posture or expression gave away how he was feeling. Sienna swallowed and ducked her head, finally sparing a glance around. When she saw other couples had stopped dancing to watch them curiously, Sienna averted her gaze to stare at Gentry's chest. "Everybody's staring at us."

Gentry lifted her chin so she'd look up at him and told her softly, "I don't care."

Without warning, Gentry wrapped both of his arms around her to pull her flush against him, leaning his chin over her head as her arms instinctively wrapped around his torso. She felt him kiss her hair and she sighed, forgetting the rest of the world for a moment.

His body was so warm and relaxed that Sienna never wanted to leave the comfort of his arms, but as Annie and Alex finished the song in harmony, he let out a ragged breath and pulled away just enough look in her eyes. "Can we talk, please?"

She nodded, and Gentry took her hand and quickly led her towards the back of the barn before pushing open a small door to take them outside. The air was still hot, even for late August, but at least there was a little bit of a breeze. The moon was full and the lights on the exterior of the barn gave enough light for Gentry to lead them towards a fenced field where Domino was grazing.

Sienna cooed to the Paint as she approached, reaching out her hand for him to sniff before petting his face lovingly. She turned to Gentry, finding him watching her with his hands in his pockets.

"I didn't want you to find out from anybody else. I wanted to tell you so many times, but I didn't want anything to change between us."

She nodded, looking back to Domino as he leaned his large black and white head over the wooden rail to nudge against her. "I feel horrible that I didn't know."

Gentry stepped up beside her, leaning his elbow on the fence as he reached out to pet Domino with his other hand. "If you'd have known, would you have treated me differently?"

"Yes."

"That's why I didn't want you to know," Gentry told her firmly. He nodded away from the fence towards a fallen tree nearby and took a seat, motioning for her to join him. Sienna slowly sat, careful not to catch the delicate lace of her dress on the wood. Gentry rested his elbows on his knees and looked up at the moon. "You know the only thing worse than having someone you love die is having everyone you know look at you like you're the ghost. It's been three years and everyone in this town still treats me like I'm broken."

Sienna grabbed his hand to give him a comforting squeeze. He held it to his lips as he closed his eyes. "I never wanted to hurt you, Sienna. I liked the way we were together. I haven't had this much fun with anybody in a really long time. I thought if you knew you'd treat me differently, and when you found out yesterday I realized I was right."

"Dakota told me Kenzie was her sister. I assumed that meant she was yours, so imagine my surprise when your dad drops that she was his daughter-in-law." Sienna sat up a little straighter, but Gentry didn't release her hand. Instead, his eyes drifted to look at hers with a puppy dog look that made Sienna's chest clench. "Don't give me that look," she said softly. "I was hurt, Gentry. I thought I knew you."

"You do know me. You're the only person who I've gotten close to since Kenzie died." He let her hand drop onto his thigh, but continued to stroke her knuckles. "I know I should have told you sooner, but you gotta understand why I didn't. I just wanted you to judge me based on me, not based on what I lost. I didn't want to lose you after we'd gotten close- I've lost enough."

It was cruel how beautiful the night sky was for this conversation. With only the hazy light from the barn and the moon, the stars shone through in a way that Sienna had never seen. "I don't want to lose you either," she confessed. Her feelings weren't that simple though.

She grabbed both of his hands and shifted a little to face him on the tree, tucking one ankle under the other to steady herself in the mud below. "Listen," she started firmly, steeling her courage, "I think you're great, and I've had a really great time getting to know you, but-"

Gentry let out a humorless laugh, leaning back to look up at the sky as he groaned. "Right. Let me guess- the whole dead wife thing changes everything, right? Suddenly you're not comfortable being around me because I'm a widower."

"No! That's not it at all!"

His nostrils flared as he stared her down. "Then what is it? What's changed?"

She felt her eyes well up, and quickly swiped her fingers underneath her eyelashes to sweep the tears away. "I feel bad," she croaked. "You were somebody's husband, and I feel bad for wanting to be with you. It feels like I want something I'm not supposed to have."

Her words softened Gentry, and the corner of his mouth twisted up into a sad smile. "But the person I loved is gone. Don't I deserve to be happy again? Don't I deserve the chance to find love again, or do you think I should be alone for the rest of my life?"

"I'm scared that I'll never be able to live up to what you lost. I feel like I'm not good enough-"

"That's ridiculous," he cut her off and leaned forward to kiss her quickly, catching her off guard. "You're the best thing that's happened to me since Kenzie died. I wouldn't even consider being with you if I didn't know for certain that I felt something real. It's special, and it's rare. I didn't think I'd feel this way again, and I don't want you to give up on us. What can I do to prove that I'm not being careless with your heart?"

She blinked quickly, considering him. Considering the time they'd spent together and the life they could have if she stopped worrying about what could go wrong and trusted that Gentry hadn't hurt her on purpose. He'd let her get to know him without any preconceived notions, and she truly cared about the man she knew. Knowing he'd been loved wasn't so difficult. Knowing he'd had everything ripped out from under him was a harder pill to swallow.

As much as she wanted to say she wouldn't have thought differently of Gentry, she would have. She would have been more careful with him. She would have felt bad for him. Instead, they'd played together, laughed together, and dared to be vulnerable again with each other. He'd withheld the part of him that hurt and gave her everything that was good and happy.

She placed her hand against his cheek, stroking it softly as she whispered, "Are you sure you're ready for everyone to know about us?"

"We can be whatever you want, as long as I have you in my life. But if you want me, I'm yours. I can't lose you Sienna."

He held her hands tightly as he stood, pulling her up with him. He licked his bottom lip, looking back at the barn for a moment to make sure nobody was watching them. "If you've changed your mind, though, I have to accept that. I withheld the truth from you. I asked my sister and friends to lie to you. I'll accept the consequences of that, but I hope you'll still allow me to be a part of your life."

Sienna reached up and pushed a bit of his hair away from his face. She stroked his cheek gently, studying him before meeting his sad eyes. She was tired of seeing him sad.

"I want you. I want you in every way I can have you."

They clashed together wildly, his mouth on hers in an instant as he held her lower back with one hand and the back of her head with the other. She leaned up into him, grabbing the fabric of his shirt to keep him close while he lifted her boots from the ground. He ran his fingers through her hair, accidentally snagging her bow. She pulled back giggling as he tried to pull his hand free, leaning away to see what he was doing and slipping in the mud.

Gentry started going down, but Sienna didn't let go, falling on top of him next to the tree in the mud. She laughed loudly as the mud squelched beneath him. Then he rolled over, dumping her onto the ground beside him.

"My dress!" She twisted around to look down, smearing more mud all over the white lace. She glared at Gentry and he grimaced, but she placed her palm firmly in the mud and smeared it over his cheek as she dove forward for another kiss. He shifted to lean over her, causing her hair and back to slide further into the muck. His elbows dug into the earth on either side of Sienna as she smiled up at him with doting eyes. "You're really something, Gentry Wyatt."

His finger slid over her ribcage, drawing lines of mud over the delicate fabric of her ruined dress. He moved lower until the fabric ended and he reached the hem of her dress. Her breath hitched loudly when his calloused fingers stroked the soft skin of her thigh, and even in the darkness she could see his pupils grow. He grabbed her thigh as he kissed her, causing her to gasp into his mouth. "Really something, huh?" he taunted between kisses, enjoying the way she reacted to his hand on her leg.

Sienna pulled back, causing more mud to saturate her filthy hair. Her gaze narrowed and he laughed. He raised his brows, grinning through the filth that covered his handsome face. "See, nothing is different. You and me- we're still the same... you just know the worst thing that's ever happened to me now."

A pang of guilt hit Sienna like a freight train and she stammered, "I'm so sorry Gentry. I feel like I-"

"Shh, nope. None of that." He laid himself on top of her, smothering her while barely holding himself up by his elbows. She laughed, coughing a little until he pushed himself off of her. "I've had a lot of time to think about this over the past couple of months, especially this past week. I've prayed a lot for clarity, and to ease my guilt over moving on..."

He trailed off as his eyes glistened, and he sucked in a sharp breath and buried his fingers into Sienna's hair to anchor himself to her. She brushed her own fingers through his dirty hair, pulling out some chunks of mud and discarding them to the side. "Did you get what you were asking for?"

Gentry leaned down to kiss Sienna softly, barely brushing his lips against hers before he whispered, "Yes." He pulled away to look at Sienna seriously and she focused on what he was saying instead of how handsome he looked in the moonlight. "If the roles had been reversed, and I'd been the one who died, all I would want for Kenzie would be to find love again. I knew her better than I've ever known anybody, and I know that's what she'd want for me. I think she woulda liked you. Dakota loves you. You impressed my parents. I-" He paused, chuckling a little as he collected his words. "You make me want to live again, Sienna. I want you, and I want everyone to know it."

Sienna wiggled out from under Gentry and pushed herself up to lean back on her elbows. Almost every inch of skin was covered in mud, and her dress was ruined. She couldn't find it in her to be mad, though. "I'm not going back in there," she nodded towards the barn, then gestured to her dress, "People will get the wrong idea."

"That we went for a roll in the hay?"

"I mean, we did go for a roll in the mud, so..." Sienna winked at Gentry and he crawled forward to kiss her again, continuing to smear the mud caked onto her back as he pulled her close. She smiled at him, nuzzling her nose against his. "Jesse is going to have a cow when I drag all this mud into his car."

Gentry scoffed. "You really think I'm letting you go home with Jesse? No, Miss Jade, you're going home with me." She blinked, mouth opening in surprise and Gentry quickly stammered, "I mean, maybe not to my home. I'll take you to your home... Let's maybe not-"

"We can still take things slow. I get it now," Sienna told him gently. He pushed himself to his feet, flinging mud off his hands before reaching down to help Sienna back up. She slid a little, and he caught her, holding her to his chest. The butterflies in Sienna's stomach were disorienting as she gazed up at the man. "I'm not going anywhere, Gentry. I promise."

"Good, because you're mine."

Sienna's heart skipped a beat at that. She hoped he didn't notice the way her legs quivered as he led her to the fence to wait while he collected Domino from the field.

When he brought Domino over to Sienna, he helped her mount before locking the gate. Gentry pulled Sienna's feet out of the stirrups and tapped her lower back. "Scoot up."

She did as she was told and he grabbed the saddle around her to pull himself up and over Domino. He settled in behind Sienna, shoving her up against the saddle horn as his chest pressed against her back. She could feel his muscular thighs shifting as he got situated, and she was distinctly aware of him pressed against her. He ran his hand up and down her thigh as her dress rode up. "You comfy?"

"Not necessarily, but not complaining either."

Gentry smirked and kissed Sienna's head, then grabbed the reins with one hand and wrapped his opposite arm around Sienna's stomach. Then he kicked Domino's sides to send them walking slowly back to town.

Chapter 41

The next morning, the Lonewood Cafe was the sleepiest Sienna had ever seen. Most of the tables were full of the same local patrons who ate there like clockwork, but there was very little conversation happening between them.

Sienna looked around, catching a few pairs of eyes following her up to the counter. She brushed off the people's stares and addressed Brenda, "I take it the dance went pretty late."

The waitress smiled slyly as she pulled her pen out her apron to write down Sienna's order. "Haven't heard much except you and the sheriff disappeared part way through and didn't come back."

"Yeah, we needed to talk in private. I slipped and got my dress dirty so he took me home."

"Oh yeah? Did he stay?"

"Brenda!" Sienna looked around, finding a few more eyes on her than before. She lowered her voice and informed the nosy woman, "No, he did not stay. He dropped me off and went home. Said he had an early morning at the station."

"So should I send his coffee with you or the mayor?" Brenda questioned. She looked up at the wall clock and added, "I expect Dakota to arrive within the next two or three minutes. Heard you stormed in and out of her office Wednesday afternoon, so if you two are still at odds I suggest you make your decision quickly."

Sienna leaned her elbows on the counter and scratched at her scalp with her long fingernails. "Can I just get one coffee? For here. No creamer, I'm gonna need it black today."

She watched as Brenda poured her a mug of coffee, studying the liquid as it poured from the pot like it was the most fascinating thing in the diner. Sienna didn't want to inadvertently invite conversation with the meddlesome people who'd inevitably want to know what happened on the dance floor between her, Brad, and Gentry, as well as where they disappeared to for the rest of the night.

They'd bickered relentlessly for weeks and suddenly they were gazing doe-eyed at each other in front of everybody on the dance floor. Sienna wouldn't have thought anything of it before realizing that Kenzie Wyatt was the beloved *wife* of the man she was seeing. Now Sienna wasn't just a newcomer who brought change and success to Lonewood, she had mended their stoic sheriff's cold, broken heart.

The little bell above the door sounded and Brenda sat two to-go cups of coffee next to Sienna on the counter. "Looks like you missed your window."

Sienna looked up and over her right shoulder to see Dakota walk up and take a seat on the stool next to her. She took out a ten and handed it over to Brenda, then clasped her hands together on the counter and stared ahead. "So..."

"So..." Sienna pushed her hair behind her ear and turned to face Dakota fully. "I'm sorry about the other day. I'm sorry for how I reacted about the whole Kenzie thing. I get why you lied, I was just hurt and confused-"

"I'm sorry for lying to you." Dakota shot Brenda a warning look when she hovered a little too close. Turning back to Sienna, Dakota leaned forward and said quietly, "To be honest, I didn't think it would get this far. I assumed you'd find out sooner rather than later and by that time I could just brush it off as a miscommunication, but then you two got closer and Gentry made me promise not to tell you."

"I get it now, and I'm so sorry."

"No, *I'm* sorry," Dakota said again. She looked at the two coffee cups, turning one around slowly before asking, "What happened with you and Gentry last night?"

Sienna couldn't help the smile that bloomed at the memory of sitting under the stars with Gentry. A little gasp left Dakota and Sienna blushed as she met the mayor's eyes. "We talked. We want to give this a try."

Dakota nodded a little through her happy tears. "I'm really happy for you two. I'm so thankful he found you."

Sienna pulled her in for a tight hug. "And I'm really thankful to have you as a friend," Sienna told Dakota, her own eyes welling up. "I've never had really close friends."

"I think you were always meant to find us here. And now that you're here, I don't think we're ever gonna let you go," Dakota told her quietly. She patted Sienna's knee and slid off the stool to leave. She grabbed both coffee cups, then paused, and handed one to Sienna. "He's at the station. I'm sure he'd rather see you than me."

Sienna took the cup and watched Dakota go, feeling a weight lifted from her chest. When she spared a look around the diner though, she realized every person was staring at her in surprise. She cleared her throat, handed Brenda a five dollar bill, and carried Gentry's coffee out. The restaurant was silent as she walked out the door, and when she crossed in front of the big windows, she noticed a couple people still watching her curiously.

When she reached the sheriff's station, Cecily waved to her with a shocked expression, then bolted to her feet to guide Sienna towards Gentry's empty desk. It was as if Sienna had slipped into a predetermined role, and now that Cecily understood, she knew how to react to the new woman in Gentry's life.

"He's doing an interview in the back room. He should be done soon."

"An interview?" Sienna asked as she sat down the coffee cup. She turned towards the back of the station. She hadn't spent a ton of time here, but enough to know where Cecily was talking about. "For what? Another officer?"

"Yup," Cecily answered. She looked down the hall as well, giving a little nod and adding, "He's been a police officer in Mandan for about ten years, but he wants to move back home."

Sienna whipped back around so fast her hair flew around and whacked her in the face. She blew it away from her mouth and smiled. "There's people moving into town? He's from here?"

"Yeah, his name is Remington. We used to call him Dusty. He's Hank's son. He wasn't big on the whole cowboy thing, but seems like he's gotten past it since dear old dad isn't parading around Main Street anymore." Cecily took a seat back at her desk but kept her curious gaze on Sienna, as if waiting to see what she'd do here. She'd probably been expecting Dakota, but since she'd been at the dance last night, she probably had the same suspicions as everyone else about Sienna's intentions with Gentry. "His wife's really sweet. I've met her once or twice when they've come to visit. From what Dusty told Gentry it sounds like she's just looking for something easy to do for a while, maybe work in one of the shops. Having them around will definitely help fill the void of the college kids."

"I'm still stuck on Hank having a son," Sienna said under her breath. She looked towards the back room, wondering if Dakota would stick around or just leave Gentry's coffee and go. "Dakota told me he'd be here... Maybe I should have called first, though."

"You're fine. He won't care. They've been talking for almost an hour so they've got to be almost done. If Gentry says yes, we start filing the paperwork. Considering they went to school together, and seem to get along reasonably well, I'm assuming it'll be a yes."

Sienna wondered why he didn't tell her last night, but maybe he just didn't want to get her hopes up about having new people moving to town. This was what Dakota had hoped for. This was the true reason behind all of Sienna's hard work: creating a town not only worthy of their visitors but of the people who chose to live here.

Sienna took a seat at Gentry's desk, looking over all of his things. She wished she'd looked a little closer earlier. If she had, she might have realized the framed photo on his desk was of him, Dakota, and Kenzie. And if she'd looked a little closer, she'd have realized that his hand sat a little too low on her hip to be his sister, and that there was a beautiful wedding ring on her left hand.

The fact that he had this photo sitting out where everyone could see made Sienna feel stupid, but he'd never let her sit in his chair when she'd stopped by. The few times she'd been in here, she'd either come and gone quickly or he'd taken her to the back room to be alone.

But now there was another photo on Gentry's desk, propped against the framed one. Sienna smiled as her breath hitched, and she grabbed the photo to look at it closer. It was a photo of her on Domino from the trail ride she'd taken with Dakota months ago. The sunset was stunning, but the way it illuminated her red hair made her look like a fiery angel. Her big, surprised eyes looked at the camera, but there was a breathless smile on her lips. It was a nice photo of her, but the photo wasn't what made Sienna happy now, it was the fact that Gentry went out of his way to get it from Dakota and get it printed for his desk. She wondered if he'd brought it in this morning, or if he'd had it for a while now. Either way, Sienna fell a little harder for him at the sight of it.

The sound of men's voices accompanied the sound of the door opening and Sienna stood, clenching the back of Gentry's leather desk chair. She wanted to make it very clear that she'd been at his desk; that she'd seen his photos. Sienna didn't want there to be any more secrets between them.

Gentry's smile grew when he saw Sienna, and he quickened his pace to greet her with a kiss on the cheek. His hand slid easily along the waistband of her jean shorts to hold her at his side possessively. From the corner of her eye, Sienna saw Cecily gape at them as Gentry introduced her to Hank's son. "Sienna, this is Dusty. He's an old friend of mine from high school. Dusty, this is my girlfriend Sienna."

Sienna was surprised how easily the word 'girlfriend' came out, as if he'd called her that a thousand times. They hadn't exactly talked about it, but she assumed they were exclusive after last night... rightly so apparently.

Dusty looked as surprised by Gentry's words as Cecily, and he opened his mouth, then closed it, then finally smiled and thrust out his hand to Sienna. "It's nice to meet you."

"She moved here early this summer with her sister. She's a marketing director from California," Gentry told Dusty, the pride evident in his voice.

He squeezed her hip and looked down at her with a shit-eating grin. "It's her fault your dad got fired."

Sienna paled instantly and gasped at Gentry. "No it's not! He didn't- we- I…"

"It's really fine." Dusty didn't seem upset about his dad not being the town's leading man anymore, but the slight alarm on his face from when Gentry introduced her as his girlfriend hadn't quite fled yet. He scratched his scalp, furrowing his brows in thought. "I know I haven't been around much lately, but am I crazy in thinking you were married at some point?"

"Oh. Yeah." Gentry's hand dropped from Sienna's side and she shuffled back a step, allowing Gentry the space he needed to explain. She ducked her head, clutching her hands together in front of herself. From the corner of her eye, she saw Cecily's head snap down to pretend she wasn't listening.

Dusty seemed to catch that he'd brought up something sensitive, because his jaw tensed uncomfortably. Gentry rubbed the back of his neck and groaned a little, then reached back to catch Sienna's hand. An assurance that he was okay talking about this. "My wife died a few years back. It's been really hard, but this summer's changed a lot. This place is changing. It's coming back to life, and I finally am, too."

His words struck Sienna, and she rubbed her fingertips along his wrist as he held her other hand. She wanted to comfort him, but she didn't want to overstep a boundary.

Dusty gave a little nod and sighed, "I'm sorry for your loss, man. That's tough. That's really tough. But you look good. You look happy. The town seems to be doing great from what I hear. Everyone I know was out here this summer. It got me a little homesick, and with baby on the way, Gabby wants me to be a little more present. No offense, but y'all probably see less crime than Mandan."

"Well, we definitely see less arrests since we took the jail key from your father."

They both chuckled at that, and the sound eased Sienna's nerves. Gentry tugged her back to his side, not allowing her to hide their relationship any longer. "Well, I'd love to have you on the force. It's pretty sleepy, but if you find a house here in town you can basically work from home. As long as you swing around Main Street every now and then and make sure nobody's getting into trouble. We don't have a lot of it, but we do serve a lot of alcohol, and people drink beer like it's water when they don't have to drive."

Sienna patted Gentry's stomach, knowing he spent most of his summer evenings before they got together at Jasmine's bar. He'd been there keeping an eye on the college kids, but Sienna knew from talking to Dakota that he wasn't doing it without a beer in his hand. He shot her a look, as if he knew what she was alluding to, but she didn't break her easy expression. She enjoyed this playful, silent conversation between them. Perhaps it was because their relationship was so new and barely public, but Sienna liked the idea of saving their words for when they were alone.

"I have your paperwork ready whenever you're ready to fill it out," Cecily called from her desk. Dusty nodded and sauntered over to her, his steps heavy across the wooden floor, just like his father's.

While he began filling out his forms, Sienna held up Gentry's coffee and he finally released her hand to take a drink. "I see you're taking over Dakota's favorite morning pastime. She'll be devastated."

"For your information, she told me to bring this to you. Maybe she's sick of your face."

"Ha. You're funny," Gentry grunted back, taking another long drink as he watched Dusty fill out paperwork. "You smell delightful, by the way. What is that? Mud?"

Sienna glared up at him to find him holding back a laugh. "Is this how we're gonna be now?"

"This is how we've always been. Nothing's changing. Well, barely anything is changing." He leaned down and pecked her lips. "I'll be stealing a few more of those, but aside from that, you aren't getting off easy with me."

"You know, the weirdest part is that I'm not sure if I've missed this banter between us or if I'm missing the man who swept me off my feet last night."

A deep chuckle shook his chest beneath his worn leather vest. "Yeah, well, you'll be getting a little bit of both." He took another drink as he leaned on the edge of his desk, watching Dusty and Cecily thoughtfully. "You know, with an extra person around here, that'll free up a bit more time for me."

"Yeah?"

"Mhmm. I might get two days off for once. Means I have more time to spend with this new girlfriend of mine."

Sienna smiled at that as she plucked Gentry's coffee cup from his hand and took a quick drink. She wanted to suggest they go somewhere together, but they couldn't exactly ride Domino on a vacation. Sienna didn't know if Gentry would ever set foot in a vehicle again after what happened with Kenzie. She couldn't blame him, but it made it hard. He could never leave Lonewood. He'd effectively trapped himself here, and by association, her.

"You okay?" Gentry asked, the softness from the night prior returning to his voice. Sienna looked up at him and nodded, thrusting the cup back into his hand, as if taking it in the first place had crossed a line. His mouth pulled up on one side and he asked, "It's okay that I call you my girlfriend, right? I kinda thought after last night- I assumed you'd be okay with it."

"I'm honored," Sienna told him. "Nervous- a little wary of all the attention I'm suddenly getting, but honored."

"Don't think about anyone else. Their opinions don't matter. It's just you and me."

Maude's words came to Sienna's mind, and she understood what she'd been trying to tell her. The people of Lonewood would have a hard time seeing Gentry with somebody new, but it didn't matter as long as he and Sienna were happy. Kenzie would have wanted her husband to find happiness again, and eventually the town would accept that Sienna gave him that. All Sienna had to worry about was making sure she didn't ruin this.

"Okay," she whispered and Gentry stroked her hair away from her cheek before turning when Cecily called his name. Sienna grabbed his wrist and he looked back at her immediately, as if his secretary and newest employee weren't even there. "I'll see you later. Have a good day."

She leaned up to kiss him on the cheek, sparing another look at Cecily and Dusty as she made her way towards the door. When she reached it, she looked back to find Gentry still watching her with a lazy grin. A proud smirk more like it. She rolled her eyes and headed back to Dakota's office to work.

Chapter 42

On Sunday afternoon, Annie performed her last shootout with Beau to a packed Main Street. Although they would have loved to have kept her through Labor Day, she couldn't miss the first week of class, and the drive across the entire state was far too long to ask Annie to commute.

So after locking Beau in the fake jail, Annie passed off her key to Gentry with teary eyes and he embraced her as she cried to the applause of the townspeople who knew it was her last show. Alex and Jesse performed at the saloon alone that evening, because Jolene and Maddie had already left the night prior, and Colton and Jewel were packing up to head out after dinner.

Annie stuck around until the sun began to set, looking around the bustling Main Street with a forlorn look in her eye. Sienna approached her slowly, clearing her throat to get the young woman's attention. Annie turned around, then quickly wiped away the tears in her eyes and apologized. "Sorry. It's just always hard leaving home."

Sienna nodded, shoving her hands into the back pockets of her jean shorts. "I can imagine. You've had a big summer."

Annie threw her arms around Sienna's neck in a tight hug, startling the redhead. "Thanks for everything, Sienna. Thanks for convincing them to give us all a chance. This was the best summer of my life and it's because of you and Alex."

Sienna swayed back and forth as she told Annie, "I'm really gonna miss you. I hope you come back next summer, but if you have better offers, know we'll understand."

With a sniffle, Annie pulled away and admitted, "I'm sure I'll be back. This is home."

"You better only come back if you don't end up in Medora."

Sienna turned around at the sound of Gentry's voice, and he wrapped his arm around Sienna's shoulders lightly as he addressed Annie firmly. "If you get into that musical, you don't turn it down again, do you hear me?"

"But-"

"No buts. You gotta do it at least once, and if you turn it down for us, I swear I'll throw your ass in jail the day you show up," Gentry threatened, and Annie responded by raising her brows in worried surprise.

"That's a little much," Sienna mumbled in his ear, but he grinned at her warning. Annie smiled at the pair, looking between them and nodding. Gentry tossed his head up at her, asking, "You got something to say, kid?"

"I'm just really happy that you're happy."

Sienna wrapped her arms around Gentry's middle and gazed up at him lovingly. His smile grew and he bowed his head to Annie and thanked her. Since that morning at the station, Gentry had been incredibly open about his relationship with Sienna. When he saw her around town, he'd greet her with a kiss on the cheek, and when they spent time together, he held her hand no matter who was around.

Gentry let go of Sienna to hug Annie tightly, squeezing her until she pulled away with a laugh. "I 'spose. I better hit the road. The boyfriend's waiting for me in Bismarck to carpool back to Grand Forks." Gentry crossed his arms threateningly and Annie winked before turning to leave.

"If that boy breaks your heart-"

"He'll have Dad and Owen to deal with. He doesn't need to get any threats from you," Annie answered over her shoulder. Her eyes twinkled as she gave one last wave, then climbed into her car to leave town.

As they watched her drive away, Sienna rubbed Gentry's back and said, "I'm gonna miss her."

"Me too, but she's gonna be okay." He hooked his hand around Sienna's waist and pulled her close. "We're all gonna be okay."

The week leading up to Labor Day kept Sienna busier than she would have liked, but Gentry made a second office for himself out of Dakota's.

His sister made herself scarce while Gentry hovered over Sienna, massaging her shoulders as she finished up their summer marketing and updated their socials to reflect the changes to the entertainment. Every night he walked her home, though, and he spent a little longer in the doorway each time. Sienna hoped soon he'd come in and just stay.

The Friday of Labor Day weekend, Sienna ambled into the diner for lunch a little before noon. Brenda called a greeting from the kitchen and Sienna took a seat beside Skylar at the counter.

The deputy nodded her head in greeting as she chewed through her burger. She set it down and swallowed, then gestured to Sienna. "So you and the sheriff, huh? I didn't get a chance to congratulate you the other day. I gotta say I'm surprised, but I'm happy for you two."

"Thank you. I'm really happy." Sienna tucked a bit of red hair behind her ear and looked over her shoulder as Jasmine walked through the door. When Jasmine saw her, she motioned for her to come over with her finger and Sienna sucked in a sharp breath. "I'm being summoned. I'll see you later."

"Good luck, you're gonna need it," Skylar mumbled as she pushed her empty plate towards Brenda and slid off the stool to leave.

Sienna wandered over to the booth Jasmine had slid into and the other woman motioned for her to sit across from her. As Sienna slid in, she tipped her back the cowboy hat Gentry loaned her to see Jasmine better. With a shake of her head, Jasmine laughed humorlessly. "Look at you. A real cowgirl now, aren't ya?" Her dark eyes raked over Sienna, judging her without shame until she said, "You have no idea what you're doing here, do you?"

"What's that supposed to mean?"

"I'll give you this, Miss Jade, you are a great marketing director. Your work with Mayor Wyatt is commendable, but you've got to admit, you've done all you can here. Maybe it's time to move along."

Sienna's expression darkened and she leaned forward to stare down Jasmine. "How dare you!"

"How dare *you*. You come in here, acting like you're hot shit and we're nothing but a bunch of stupid country bumpkins. You didn't consider, not even for a moment, what would happen to the people here when you were done turning our town upside down." Jasmine composed herself, smoothing down her blouse as if she realized she'd gotten too sharp with the woman. She took a slow breath and offered a strained smile. "You've even got our men fighting over you."

"Oh please, if this is about Brad-"

Jasmine's laugh cut her off. She leaned forward on her forearms to get closer to Sienna and whispered, "You wanted to keep your options open, right? In case nothing happened with Gentry, you'd still have Brad waiting in the wings. But now look at you. You've got him wrapped around your little finger. I liked you, Sienna. You were driven and hardworking, and that's great for the town, but you're no Kenzie. You don't know who you're following up- who you're replacing in Gentry's life."

Sienna's cheeks began to redden as rage built up inside of her. Jasmine didn't know her. She hadn't bothered trying to get to know Sienna at all over the past four months. All she knew was that Sienna wasn't Kenzie. Sienna knew that. She was aware of it every single day she walked through Lonewood.

Tears began to well up in Sienna's eyes as Jasmine's smile darkened somehow, and she asked quietly, "Whose hat do you think you're wearing? Whose horse are you riding? Whose dreams are you bringing to life? You think Dakota hired you because she wanted change? No, she hired you because you could finish what Kenzie started. Kenzie would have wanted that, because she wanted what was best for this town, but she wouldn't have wanted you to sleep with her husband."

Sienna looked around the diner, realizing most of the people were eavesdropping on their conversation. When her gaze landed on Kennedy and Trevor, the small brunette ducked her head and looked away, but Trevor stared at his plate with wide eyes, trying really hard not to make eye contact. Sienna looked up pleadingly at Brenda, but the older woman turned away too, not wanting to be involved. Not wanting to stand up for her.

Jasmine wasn't through with Sienna, though. "I'm trying to protect you. I'm trying to save you from the heartache of losing someone who was never meant to be yours for the taking. Maybe you can keep his bed warm, but you can't replace what he lost. You can't salvage the life they planned together. That man buried his wife and unborn child; you think you can compete with that?"

The breath was knocked out of Sienna at Jasmine's words. She ripped off Kenzie's hat and smashed it on the table, scrambling to her feet as she snarled, "Your cruelty isn't going to bring your friend back, but I'm not going to sit here and be treated like this."

"I'm not trying to hurt you, Sienna. I just want you to understand the truth. If you keep going down this road... you're gonna thank me someday. For being the only person in this town who's truly honest with you."

Sparing another look around the diner, everyone looked away, as if they didn't want to meet Sienna's gaze. For months they were happy to follow Sienna's lead as she brought them business and popularity, but now that she was publicly dating Gentry, they were silent. She was an outsider, someone they were happy to praise and use for their own gains, but now that she was attached to one of their own, the people of Lonewood weren't so supportive. Maybe Jasmine was right- maybe Sienna had outstayed her welcome.

The world around Sienna was a blur as she left the Lonewood Cafe. She looked towards the saloon, wondering if she should try to talk to Alex. She spun around to look at her apartment, wondering if she should pack up her stuff and make plans to leave town. Clearly that's what Jasmine wanted, and maybe she wasn't the only one. The people Sienna thought were her friends couldn't even look at her.

Sienna was tired of feeling like she wasn't good enough. She was tired of walking in the footsteps of a dead woman. For a while, she thought she'd made a life for herself, but it was clear that she still didn't belong here. Maybe she never would.

Jasmine had dropped one little bit of knowledge Sienna hadn't learned yet. Another secret that Sienna wasn't trusted enough to know. If Jasmine was making up Kenzie being pregnant, she'd rot in hell. If she wasn't... Sienna wondered if anything anyone told her was the truth.

Her feet moved faster than her mind, which felt like it was being dragged through the mud to make a reasonable thought. Sienna wanted to run. She didn't know or care where she'd end up, but she needed to get away from Main Street. Later she'd tell Gentry what Jasmine had said. Later they'd talk this through, but for now... for now Sienna needed to be alone.

She moved up the hill towards the stables in a haze. Gentry had taught her how to saddle up Cheyanne so she could go riding whenever she wanted and right about now she wanted to get away as quickly as possible. Cheyanne could take her places nobody could find her until she wanted to be found.

Cheyanne watched Sienna warily as she tossed the saddle over her back, taking extra care to make sure the straps were tightened correctly. The stirrups were still in place from the last time they went riding, and the bridle was easy to clip on. Sienna led Cheyanne out of the stables about twenty minutes later, looking over her shoulder towards town before guiding her through the gate to the corral.

The gate at the far edge was closed. If Sienna wanted it opened, she could ask Lyle. He probably wouldn't ask questions, but then he might tell Gentry she'd gone riding alone.

The storm clouds hadn't moved as far as Sienna would have liked, meaning it could rain again in a few hours. Logically, Sienna shouldn't go out at all by herself. But she felt like she was being squeezed to death by the world around her. She needed to be alone and she needed the fresh air and open space and the freedom to be her own person for one damn minute. She was tired of playing Sienna Jade. She wanted to be whoever lived at her core.

She swung up and over Cheyanne, causing the horse to grunt as she backed up a step. "C'mon girl. I'm trusting you. Do you trust me?" Sienna stared ahead at the closed gate, wondering if Cheyanne could clear it. "I trust you."

Sienna kicked Cheyanne's sides, sending her sprinting towards the gate. Sienna didn't know if Cheyanne could jump at all, or if she'd slide to a stop and send Sienna flying into the rail. If she smashed into the rail at top speed, would she even survive? The darkest, most broken part of Sienna wondered if anyone would care.

Skylar had once told Sienna that everyone still treated her like an outsider. She understood now. Nothing she did, no amount of success she brought to the town, no amount of work she put into helping these people, nothing would matter. The last time the people in this town fell in love with an outsider, she died, so maybe it was easier to block everyone out and not get attached.

As Cheyanne neared the gate, Sienna slammed her eyes closed and leaned low, praying the horse would clear the fence. One moment her hooves were thundering on the ground and the next there was silence, and wind, and then a thud when they hit the ground again. Sienna opened her eyes to see them on the other side of the gate galloping into the Badlands.

She beamed and urged Cheyanne on as the wind whipped the horse's black hair into her face, "Let's get out of here."

The wind rushed through Sienna's loose, tangled hair, whipping it across her face as she leaned low against Cheyanne. She let the horse run where she wanted, flying over the ground at a speed Sienna had never ridden before. All of her thoughts faded away aside from the thudding of Cheyanne's hooves and the wind stinging her watery eyes.

She focused on the path ahead, not allowing her mind to wander back to where she'd come from. Cheyanne easily cleared a fallen tree and Sienna smiled at the brief feeling of weightlessness. Of being free. Free from the stress, and the lies, and the judgemental gazes that followed her around day after day for four months. For a moment, Sienna was just an extension of Cheyanne, able to join her as she ran through her home.

The sky darkened overhead, but Sienna ignored it. She wasn't ready to turn back. She wasn't ready to face her insecurities and prove everyone wrong. Right now, Sienna just wanted to ride.

Cheyanne's gait faltered a little and Sienna pulled the reins slightly, slowing the horse down to an easy walk. For a while, they continued moving at the slower speed until Sienna's heartbeat steadied, but when the thunder began to rumble in the distance, Cheyanne halted. Her ears twisted to listen and Sienna tightened her grip on the reins. "Whoa, Cheyanne. You're okay."

Lightning struck over the horizon and Cheyanne whinnied fearfully, backing up as the thunder cracked above them. Sienna clenched her legs tighter, trying to keep her balance as Cheyanne snorted and stomped the ground. "You're okay. You're okay."

Sienna watched as a curtain of rain spread towards them, and Sienna wished she hadn't left her hat with Jasmine. Right about now, she didn't care whose it had been, it would have kept her head dry.

The rain soaked Sienna instantly, drenching her to the bone through her skinny jeans and the sleeveless cotton blouse she wore. She looked up as the sky bellowed at them, black clouds spreading overhead across the Badlands. The beautiful colored hills looked muted, but Sienna could see movement in the distance. All of the wildlife knew to hide, but she'd been too caught up in her own thoughts to consider her own safety.

A bolt of lightning lit up the world around Sienna and Cheyanne reared up, kicking the air violently as Sienna clung to her for dear life. She managed to stay on Cheyanne as the horse settled on all four feet, but she bolted right out from under Sienna as she relaxed, causing her to fall off and land hard on her side.

Sienna groaned as she leaned on her elbow, watching as Cheyanne sprinted away. Tears slid down her cheeks as she carefully pushed herself to her hands and knees and crawled under the nearest tree in an effort to stay dry. She shivered as she looked up at the sky, then reached into her pocket to pull out her phone. The screen was cracked from where she landed on it, and it was so waterlogged it wouldn't turn on. She was lost and alone in the middle of nowhere, and nobody knew where she was.

Time slipped away as Sienna sat under the tree, wondering if and when somebody would find her. She was more likely to be found by coyotes or bison than by someone from Lonewood. When the rain stopped, she could try to figure out where she was and how to get home, but for the moment, Sienna leaned against the tree to hide beneath its branches, staring up at the dark sky as hail began to pound the earth, as if even God wanted to drive her out of Lonewood.

She heard thundering footsteps in the distance and leaned further against the tree, crying as she prayed whatever was out there didn't come near her. She didn't want to die. Not like this.

At least, she told herself, it was better than getting her throat slit.

As the hail rained down around her, she began to shake as the cold seeped into her skin. Without really thinking, Sienna gave into her desire to lay down on the dirt, curl one arm over her head and the other under, and drift off to sleep.

Chapter 43

Back in town, Jesse held a flimsy umbrella over Alex's head as they sprinted into the diner from the saloon. Once inside, she wiped off her corset and shook out her arms, trying to dry off a little before they ate. The diner was mostly quiet, most of the tourists seemed to be enjoying their rooms for the afternoon before venturing out to the saloon in the evening. It was about four o'clock and Alex didn't have a lot of time to get ready for the show, but she was starving.

"What can I get for ya?" Brenda called as Alex carefully swept her finger under her eye to clean the makeup line that smudged.

"The usual please," Alex said. To her left, she caught a glimpse of Gentry and Dakota by the window, looking out at the rain pummeling Main Street. At least the hail had stopped an hour ago. "I'll be right back," Alex told Jesse and he nodded, sliding onto a barstool to wait for his and Alex's dinner.

When Alex approached, Gentry looked up at her with furrowed brows. "Hey. Where's Sienna?"

Her heart plummeted. "I assumed she was with you. I haven't seen her since yesterday."

Gentry and Dakota shared a look, and the blonde pursed her lips thoughtfully. Her brother stood slowly and asked, "Was that the last you heard from her?"

"Yes. She texted around nine saying she was gonna find you. I haven't tried contacting her." Why would she? Alex assumed her older sister was safe with the overprotective sheriff, but clearly that wasn't the case. "She wasn't at home when I went back to change."

Gentry looked down at Dakota and she raised her hands in front of her chest. "I haven't heard from her since yesterday either."

"Shit," Alex mumbled, pushing back her damp curls. She looked outside, horrified that something bad had happened. These people didn't realize that she had a target on her back, and so did Sienna. Landon could have found them. Landon could have Sienna right now.

They looked over at Brenda as the woman came over to drop the check off with Dakota, wearing a look that said she knew something they didn't. "Miss Jade was here this morning. Jasmine had words with her." She pointed over her shoulder towards the direction of Jazzy's as she looked at Gentry with a sad expression. "She stormed out of here. Seemed pretty upset."

"What did Jasmine say to her?"

Brenda shook her head. "That is between you and Jasmine. I'm not about to get involved. We all know better than to get involved where the three of you are concerned."

Alex had to practically jog in her lace up boots to keep up with Gentry as he fled the diner, making a beeline for the bar across the street. Dakota chased after them with Jesse right behind her, but Alex was the first one to get through the door after Gentry started screaming at the bar owner, "What the hell did you say to her?"

The dark-haired woman scoffed and said coolly, "Nice to see you, too. Want a beer?"

"This isn't funny. What did you say to her-" Gentry's voice cut out and Alex saw where his gaze had landed. He stared at Jasmine's worn cowboy hat with a scowl. "That was Kenzie's."

"I'm aware. I bought it for her," Jasmine answered easily. She ran an old rag over the bartop, but her dark eyes stayed locked onto Gentry. "Why was some stranger wearing it?"

Gentry took a step closer but Dakota grabbed him by the shoulder to hold him back. "Sienna isn't a stranger, she's my girlfriend. And my wife's things are mine to give away to whoever I want."

"Jasmine, where is Sienna?" Dakota asked bluntly but Jasmine just laughed and tossed her long braid over her shoulder so it fell down her back.

She tossed the rag to the side and leaned her elbows on the bar, a slight smile playing on her lips. Alex wondered if she'd always been so cruel, or if her cold attitude was a result of her friend dying. She seemed to take the loss of Kenzie more personally than most. "You tricked that woman into doing your bidding. You *lied* to her for your own selfish reasons. I did Sienna a favor by doing the one thing you never could. I told her the truth."

Dakota's lower lip quivered and she dropped her arm from her brother, allowing him to surge forward to address Jasmine himself. "What did you tell her?"

Jasmine looked over at Alex with a mocking expression, pretending to feel sorry for her but not caring enough to sell it. "I told her maybe it was time to move along. She accomplished what she wanted to do, she brought business to Lonewood. Her work for the mayor is done. She's too talented for this place and clearly belongs somewhere else, so I got to thinking maybe she should leave before she got too attached."

Alex froze at that, knowing Sienna was enough of a flight risk already. Hearing Jasmine tell her she wasn't wanted and that she could, and should, leave may have pushed Sienna over the edge. She didn't want to come here in the first place, but she had succeeded against all odds. She was riding the high of her hard work and finding someone to love, but hearing from Gentry's close friend that she should leave would give Sienna doubts. Any worry Alex had that Landon had arrived dissipated when she realized Sienna hadn't been taken, she'd run away.

Gentry's whole body shook and Alex worried he might clear the bar and strangle the woman across from him. Her lazy, cold smile was a taunt, and it was clear that Gentry was trying hard to keep himself together. "Why would you tell her that? She matters to me, why do you want her to leave?"

Something akin to hurt flashed across Jasmine's face, but she gave a sharp shake of her head to dismiss the brief crack in her hard facade. "I don't want you to be alone, Gentry, but she isn't good for you. You really think she's gonna stay here? You think she's gonna settle down and have a family with you? Be what you've always wanted?" Jasmine sighed, shaking her head as she gazed at Gentry with a sad smile that made Alex squirm. "What would Kenzie say if she was here?"

"She'd tell her best friend that she'd want me to be happy!" Gentry yelled back, sounding desperate. He looked outside as thunder rumbled overhead, then looked back to Jasmine with a pleading expression. "Kenzie is gone. She's gone and she's not coming back. We all have to deal with that in our own ways, but you can't hurt Sienna to keep her from me. She deserves better than that."

"She doesn't even know who you are! You were somebody's husband, you were about to be a father. Don't you think she deserves to know what she was getting into?"

Alex's body went numb as Gentry stared at Jasmine with wide eyes and Dakota gasped a little. He swallowed and whispered, "How do you know about that?"

"Kenzie told me, because she was my best friend."

"Nobody knew. Only us and our parents," Dakota spat, clearly feeling betrayed. Alex realized that their loss was so much more than anyone had initially thought and if Jasmine told Sienna this... she'd feel lied to all over again.

"Did you tell Sienna?" Alex blurted. "Did you tell her that Kenzie was pregnant?"

Jasmine shrugged, not caring if she'd broken Sienna's heart. "Of course I did. Clearly neither of them were going to."

The sound of the bartop cracking echoed through the room when Gentry's fist slammed against it and he bellowed, "Where is she?"

"I didn't kidnap her. She left on her own, I don't know where she went." Jasmine rolled her eyes, but her gaze briefly fell to Gentry's clenched fist. "She looked like she was heading back to her place from the diner."

Alex looked up at Gentry as he backed away from the bar, pulling out his phone to call Sienna. Even Alex could hear that it didn't even ring. It wasn't on. "She wasn't home."

"Did she go to the stables?" Dakota asked and Gentry's face paled. He scrambled towards the door as he called another number, holding his phone close to his cheek so his hat would keep the rain from soaking it. Alex chased after him as he said loudly into the phone, "Are you home? Is Sienna there?"

He pushed his way back into the diner, holding the door open for Alex and Dakota to join him as Jesse brought up the rear. He leaned his phone against his shoulder and told Alex, "Lyle's checking the stables to see if Sienna's up there." He quickly brought his phone back to his ear when Lyle began talking, but Alex couldn't hear his answer. Gentry froze, eyes widening as he shoved his phone back into his pocket.

Before he could take off again, Alex grabbed his upper arm and asked, "What did he say?"

"He said Cheyanne is gone."

"You think Sienna went out riding in this?" Alex asked incredulously, gesturing to the storm raging outside. " I'm sure she's just laying low somewhere. We should check the motel, we should... I don't know, I just don't think she'd be that stupid."

"It's not stupid, it's what makes her happy," Gentry answered as he pulled his hat a little lower on his head, preparing to go back into the rain. "It wasn't this bad earlier. She probably went out before it started storming. I'm gonna find her."

Alex wanted to believe him, but if Sienna had taken off before the storm started that meant she was out in the Badlands on horseback during a hailstorm. She didn't want to think about what state Gentry would find Sienna in.

"You sure you wanna go out in this? We could call the rangers?" Dakota offered but Gentry shook his head.

"I'll find her faster. I know Sienna and I know Cheyanne. Besides, the rangers won't be able to move as fast as me. I gotta find her before something or someone else does."

He bolted from the diner and sprinted up the dirt road towards the stables. Alex felt tears well up in her eyes when she realized her sister could be dead.

Dakota slung her arm around Alex while Jesse rubbed her back comfortingly. "She's gonna be okay. He'll find her and save her. I know it."

"How can you be so sure?" Alex sniffled and Dakota looked out the window with a melancholy expression.

"Because last time he couldn't. He's not gonna make that mistake again."

Chapter 44

THE LAST THING SIENNA remembered was laying in the dirt, soaked to the bone in the freezing rain all alone. Which was why, when she started to stir, she became immediately aware that she'd been moved while she was unconscious.

She pried open her eyes to find herself in a large bed under a pile of blankets as the distant sound of wind continued to howl alongside the steady drum of the rain on a window. The pillow beneath her cheek was the softest thing she'd ever slept on, making it hard to convince herself to wake up. Sienna needed to figure out where she was and who had found her, but her entire body was sore from being thrown by Cheyanne again.

The room was dark, meaning Sienna couldn't gauge what time it was. Her hair was still wet, so she couldn't have been here too long, but her body felt heavy with sleep. Thick brown curtains shielded Sienna's view of her surroundings, but if she could get them open, she'd have a better idea of where she was and how long she'd been unconscious.

But the bed was so comfortable. She slowly sat up, leaning against her arm as she looked around the room. There was a dresser against the far wall near the closet, and through a doorway Sienna could see a corner tub in a private bathroom. A small pile of clothes was built up on the floor near the bathroom, and there were framed photos of the Badlands on the walls. This was clearly somebody's home, and whoever lived here had brought Sienna straight to their bed.

Her hand lazily fell across her thigh and she jolted when she realized it was bare. Sitting up straight, she looked down to see she was in a man's t-shirt with no pants. To her horror, she also realized her bra was gone too.

"Shit." Sienna scrambled out of bed, feet landing on a soft shag rug. She tiptoed over to the window, looking over her shoulder when she reached the curtains to make sure whoever had found her wasn't watching.

When she ripped open the curtains, she saw the sky was dark and starless, blocked by storm clouds that continued to dump rain onto the Earth. There was no sun trying to break through, meaning it had set for the evening, but even without any light the view was startling.

From Sienna's apartment, she could see the sprawling Badlands in the distance, but this home was settled within them. Nestled between a rare clump of trees, this house sat at the base of a large outcropping of rock less than fifty feet away. Although the rain found its way to the windows, Sienna realized the wind was far off, meaning the house was protected from its fury by the trees and hillside.

She looked around the room for her clothes, but they were gone. On foot, she wouldn't get very far, but it was better than being in a stranger's bed.

Outside the bedroom, Sienna could hear the faint sound of the television playing, meaning whoever found her had stuck around to be here when she woke up. She considered leaving through the window, but she knew well enough that wandering aimlessly half-naked through the wilderness would end up being a worse idea than facing whoever had found her. At least they hadn't tried to join her in bed.

Panic welled up in Sienna's chest as she considered the conversation she'd have to have with whoever brought her home, but suddenly, a familiar smell calmed her senses before she even registered what it was.

Cologne.

It was Gentry's cologne. He'd worn it every day since the moment they'd met and Sienna's eyes widened as she looked around with newfound interest. It wasn't out of the question that another man could wear the same cologne, but Gentry lived out of town. Not only that, but he often appeared to go riding by himself in the evenings when everyone else went back to Lonewood. He wasn't going riding, he was going home. This was Gentry's home.

Sienna slowly pushed open the bedroom door, finding it had been left slightly ajar. She shuffled across the wooden floor towards the sound of the television as she looked around. Much like Dakota's home, there weren't photos of people on the walls, but photos of the Badlands that Gentry had most likely taken himself. At least, until Sienna reached the living room, where a large photo of Gentry and Kenzie on their wedding day hung above a fireplace.

The crackling fire warmed the room as Gentry watched the television intently, eyes locked onto the screen in a way that told Sienna he wasn't watching it so much as thinking intently about something else. Sienna approached slowly, realizing he hadn't noticed her. He stayed deep in thought until she quietly said, "Gentry?"

His head snapped up and when he saw her he stood. Water dripped from his hair onto his damp clothes, and his hat sat on the mantle above the fireplace to dry. He hadn't even tried to change, but seeing as he was still damp, Sienna guessed they hadn't been here too long. His eyes held worry, but his stance was rigid, as if he was afraid to approach her. After staring at her for a few moments, though, his brows drew together and his deep voice mumbled, "What the hell were you thinking? You could have been killed."

Sienna scoffed, looking out the large windows of the living room. No witty retort came to mind as she stared at the sprawling field that the house sat near. Gentry had the most beautiful view of the most beautiful place Sienna had ever seen, and he'd been hiding it from everyone. Clearly he was a fan of hiding things from Sienna in particular.

"Would anyone have even cared? I'm surprised you even came looking for me. Jasmine made it pretty clear I wasn't welcome in Lonewood."

Sienna knew it was a childish response and expected Gentry to call her out on it. She wasn't struck so much by Jasmine's words, but by the idea that people she thought were her friends had only thought of her as a means to an end. Sienna knew Gentry didn't think of her that way though, and taking out her insecurities on him felt wrong. Especially when his glare fell into the saddest expression she'd ever seen.

"I cared. I was terrified that I wouldn't find you. I rode for three hours before I found you unconscious on the ground; I was so scared that you were dead." Gentry's arm twitched, but he clenched his fist and held it at his side. He was trying to keep it together, but his brown eyes held a fear Sienna had never seen in Gentry before. "This was why I didn't tell you about Kenzie and why I didn't want people to know you and I were together. Because people like Jasmine pull stupid shit like this. She manipulated you and you fell for it. You should have come to me the minute she said anything to you. You shouldn't have run off in the middle of a hailstorm."

"In my defense, it wasn't storming when I went out," Sienna countered, keeping her voice even despite Gentry's accusatory tone. She saw it for what it was: he was hurt that she'd put herself in danger instead of coming to him. So Sienna reached out for Gentry's hand, feeling it cold and clammy. "I needed to get some air. I needed to ride, and it got bad in a hurry and Cheyanne threw me. And I kinda just... gave up and went to sleep. I didn't think it through."

He shook his head, looking more angry than he did before. "Damn it, Sienna! I can't believe you thought you could just disappear and I wouldn't care..." His shaky voice trailed off, betraying his anger. When he spoke again, he sounded broken. "I thought you were better than this. I thought *we* were better than this. I thought you understood that I'm putting myself out there and it makes me feel like shit that you don't get how important you are to me."

"I'm sorry." Sienna clenched his hand tighter and he pulled her to his chest to hold her. "I'm sorry I'm not better at handling my emotions. I'm used to burying them because my job has always been more important than my feelings, but I want to be real with you, and Dakota, and the people in this town, and I don't know how."

Gentry's hand ran over her damp hair over and over again, assuring her that he was there. "Talk to *me*, tell *me* what's wrong. I was terrified, Sienna. I didn't know if I'd ever find you- I thought..."

He squeezed Sienna tighter and buried his face into her hair, sobbing softly as his hands grasped her back. She felt him trembling against her and rubbed his back to comfort him.

Jasmine had told her that she couldn't compete with the wife that Gentry lost, but Sienna hadn't considered that losing her could dig up that pain again. She didn't want to hurt Gentry, she just didn't want to get hurt herself. He'd thought he lost her, and she'd cracked open the part of him he'd tried to patch over all these years.

"I'm scared that this is a mistake. I don't want you to regret me," Sienna confessed, feeling her guilt and fear weigh her down.

Gentry just kissed her head in response. "I could never regret you, Sienna."

She smiled into him, letting herself relax in his arms as he rubbed her back. The rain from his clothes soaked through her t-shirt to her bare breasts and she shivered. She leaned back, looking down at the wet marks on the shirt that he'd clearly dressed her in while she'd been passed out. "Where are my clothes?"

Gentry chuckled darkly and ran his fingers along the hem of his t-shirt at her upper thigh. "They're in the wash. You were soaked, I didn't want you to get sick."

"So, you took off all my clothes?"

"It was going to happen eventually anyway."

"Gentry," Sienna warned and he leaned down to pepper kisses along her reddening cheek.

"Are you mad?" he mumbled against her temple. He was trying to ease her nerves, but he'd seen her naked after she'd run off like a child having a tantrum.

"No, I'm not mad. I'm just embarassed this happened."

"They should be done within the hour. I just put them in the dryer, so..." Gentry looked towards his bedroom as he trailed off and Sienna crossed her arms over her chest to shield herself from his view. When he turned back, he noticed that she was trying to hide and snorted. "Sweetheart, I changed you into the t-shirt and snaked your bra off from underneath. I didn't touch anything. I didn't see anything. Have a little faith in my chivalry. Trust me, I want you to be conscious when I get my eyes and hands on you."

Sienna shivered at the thought of Gentry's russet eyes raking over her naked body before running his calloused fingers over the curve of her breasts and between her legs. She blinked, bringing her mind back to reality and his smug gaze. He knew what she was thinking and was proud to elicit such dirty thoughts from her.

Gentry placed his hand on the small of Sienna's back and guided her into his kitchen. She took a seat at the counter of his island, gazing around at all the dark wood cabinets in an effort to distract herself from the heat forming between her thighs. "So this is your mysterious home." Gentry smiled to himself as he turned on the stove, then reached into the cabinet to pull out a couple cans of soup. Sienna leaned on the counter, watching as Gentry poured the soup into the pot. "Are we in the park?"

"Yup."

"How are you able to live here?"

"It's an inholding. The property was privately owned before the national park was created and I bought it a few years back. It's complicated, but legal."

Sienna nodded to herself, then carefully said, "I bet Kenzie loved it."

"She never got to see it. Not finished anyway," Gentry retorted, his voice sharp. He turned to Sienna since the food was cooking and leaned his elbows on the island to get closer to her. "We were staying with Dakota until it was finished. I almost sold it when she died, but we'd poured so much of ourselves into this place I couldn't bring myself to get rid of it."

He dropped his head, taking a long, ragged breath. Rubbing his hand over his mouth, he met Sienna's gaze and she smiled grimly. It wasn't a fun conversation by any means, but she'd listen politely anyway. Gentry knew this because he mumbled, "I want to tell you everything but I don't want to make you uncomfortable. You don't want to listen to me talk about the life I had with Kenzie and how it affected me. I want to be better for you than I've been with everyone else since she died."

"Was Kenzie pregnant?" Sienna asked slowly. Gentry nodded a little and Sienna reached across the counter to hold his hands. "I'm so sorry, Gentry. I can't imagine... I don't even know what to say."

"There isn't much to say, honestly." Gentry shrugged and stood tall, looking over his shoulder at the soup before pulling away from Sienna to stir it. "She was only about eight weeks along, not even showing yet. We told my parents and Dakota on Christmas morning and she left early the next day for Bismarck. She'd been working on filing some permits so the kids could go to the neighboring schools for theater and sports. Annie really wanted to do theater, and Kenzie wanted her to be able to start in the spring so she got at least one show under her belt before applying for college. She had to have the stuff filed before the first, so she took off for Bismarck alone."

Gentry paused, staring at the soup as his mind replayed the days leading up to Kenzie's death. "I got the call from the police at six that evening that they found her car. Autopsy showed she suffered minor injuries from the crash, but she was knocked unconscious and was bleeding. Things got worse and she was there by herself for hours. By the time they found her she was already gone."

Sienna's eyes began to well up with tears as she imagined Gentry getting the call that his wife had died. They had just started telling people they were starting a family and it was ripped away from him. It was all ripped away from him and Dakota and their parents as quickly as the news came.

Everything in Sienna told her that Jasmine was right. She couldn't compete with what he lost, but while Jasmine manipulated her into thinking about her own interests and fears, Sienna had forgotten to consider Gentry's. He'd opened his heart again after experiencing the worst thing that could ever happen to him, and he'd opened it to her. He'd considered a life with her, something he clearly hadn't considered with anybody else over the past couple of years. Sienna couldn't replace what he'd lost, but she could fill his life with happiness again. Maybe it wasn't about replacing Kenzie so much as allowing Gentry the pleasure of having someone again. It wasn't about loss, it was about love and healing and hope. It was about the two of them building a life from the ashes of what had been taken away from them unfairly, and in that aspect, they deserved each other.

Sienna understood, in ways Gentry could never know, what it felt like to have her life ripped out from under her. They'd both lost the future they thought they were heading towards, but maybe they could build a new one together.

So Sienna sniffled loudly, raising her head to the ceiling in an effort to hold back her tears. Gentry had been silent for a minute and she didn't know how he would react to what she wanted to say, so she started with, "Thank you for telling me. I'm so sorry for your loss, but I'm honored that you've allowed me to be a part of your life. I care about you more than I've ever cared about anybody."

He smiled at that, his eyes lighting up hopefully. Sienna pushed her tangled hair behind her ear and looked back at the photo of Gentry and Kenzie hanging above the fireplace. Jasmine tried to make Sienna feel bad for living Kenzie's life, but Kenzie had been incredibly fortunate to have such wonderful people in her world. They deserved to be happy. She would have wanted them to be happy. Sienna made Gentry happy, and Dakota happy, and the people in this town happy, and whether or not Jasmine or anyone else agreed, it was true, and it was a good thing.

"When Jasmine told me I should leave, I couldn't stand the thought of losing you, so I ran. I ran and honestly, I didn't care if nobody found me because if I couldn't have you I didn't even know why I'd want to come back at all. You're the best thing that's ever happened to me, and I'm so sorry that this came from you losing the love of your life. But if you can find it inside you to love again, I'd be willing to take whatever you have left."

Gentry pulled the pot off the stove and turned it off, then came around the island to stand in front of Sienna. He wedged himself between her knees and wiped away a stray tear that escaped her eye. "I want to spend the rest of my life with you. If you run, I'll chase you every time. I'm never gonna let you go, sweetheart."

Sienna leaned up to kiss Gentry deeply, holding the back of his neck as he reached behind her and hiked her up into his arms. She wrapped her bare legs around his waist as he situated his hands beneath her ass.

The soup was left on the stove as Gentry carried Sienna back into his bedroom. He sat her down on the mattress and stood in front of her at the foot of the bed. His eyes slowly moved from her bare legs, over the baggy t-shirt that draped across her waist, to her breasts that pushed against the soft fabric. His eyes lingered there for a moment, hungry and wanting, but he made no move.

Instead, he met Sienna's green eyes and murmured, "I built this bed for my wife and I. You're the first woman who's ever been in it, and if we do this, I'm planning to make you the last. If that isn't an option for you, tell me now. But if you can see a life with me, then I'm ready when you are."

It wasn't a proposal, but a bargain. Sienna understood that Gentry wasn't going to waste his time, be it with her or anybody else. By sleeping with him, Sienna was promising to try with him, and promising to stay. If she went to bed with him tonight, she'd spend the rest of her life in Lonewood.

Alex wasn't living her dream of Broadway by any means, but she was happy here. She was content, and she was safe. She was dancing and singing and acting and perhaps someday she'd find love in this slowly-growing town. Landon Maddox would never look here for them, and if he did, Gentry would end him.

The idea of spending the rest of her life in this house was intimidating, but she could see it. This was never Kenzie's home. Although it was initially built for her to share with Gentry and their family, that didn't come to pass. This could be Sienna's home, and she could be happy here.

"I'm not ready for marriage."

"Not yet or not ever?"

"Not yet, but I couldn't marry anyone else," Sienna admitted. Her smile grew and she laughed. "You've ruined me for all other men, Gentry. You're the best I'm ever gonna get. I want it to be you."

His grin matched hers as he puffed out his chest and took a step back. His hands started moving to undo his button-up shirt, but he never took his eyes off of the woman on his bed. Once his shirt was discarded on the floor, he ripped off his undershirt and started unbuckling his belt. Sienna bit her bottom lip as his jeans fell to the ground and he stepped out of them, stalking closer to her. He was still wet from the rain, and it made his muscles glisten. If Mason was handsome, Gentry was a Greek god.

"You think I've ruined you for all other men? Just wait until I'm done with you tonight."

Sienna's stomach clenched as he crawled over her, forcing her back onto the mattress. With one hand he slowly peeled her out of the t-shirt, revealing her body to him inch by inch before he gently tugged it off and tossed it back over his head. Sienna gasped when he nipped at the column of her neck, arching her back as her bare chest pressed against his. Her whole body quivered with anticipation as she imagined all the ways he'd ruin her before morning.

Chapter 45

When consciousness finally tugged Sienna from her slumber, she found herself tucked against Gentry's strong chest. He held her like a vise, arms wrapped around her bare shoulders to keep her flush against him. Moving ever so slightly, Sienna realized Gentry had his lips tucked against her head, as if he'd fallen asleep kissing her messy hair.

She wanted to stay there cuddled against Gentry forever, but Sienna had to use the bathroom. So she carefully peeled his large arm off and tiptoed to the bathroom, taking a deep breath as she closed the door.

Sienna had only slept with one man before Gentry. Alex was much more experienced, but everything Sienna knew about sex came from her time with Mason. She'd thought what they had was good, but now she understood that Mason never loved her. He was fond of her when they went out together and proud to show her off at work functions. He pleased her when it suited him and he took what he needed and they had fun for four years, but he'd never made love to her. Sienna understood what she'd been missing after her night with Gentry. She couldn't settle for anything less now.

Gentry held her like he may never get another chance, and sometime in the night Sienna realized she really loved him. She'd thought she loved Mason, but her feelings for him weren't even close to what she felt now. She loved Gentry in a way she hardly understood, but she knew she wanted to spend the rest of her life with him. She wanted him to make love to her every night and she wanted to wake up in his arms every morning and if she never worked or saw her family again she wouldn't complain because she had everything she needed now that she had him.

As she washed her hands, Sienna gazed at her reflection in the mirror and replayed the past twenty-four hours in her mind. She felt a clarity she hadn't known before, and a sense of calm washed over her when she realized this would be her home. This would be her house and her bed and her husband and her life. And that would be more than enough for Sienna Jade.

She turned off the faucet and crept back into the room, finding Gentry still sound asleep. He'd clutched Sienna's pillow in her absence, and she chuckled a little as she pulled back the covers to slide back into bed. When he didn't move, Sienna rubbed her fingertips from his shoulder down his arm and murmured, "Hey. Let me in."

A tiny smile formed on his lips and his eyelids fluttered open to look at her, and Sienna blushed as he stared at her naked body. "Good morning, gorgeous."

"Good morning," she answered. She raised her brow questioningly and asked, "You gonna let me come back to bed?"

"I don't know if I want to. The view's too nice."

"Mmhmm." She sat on top of his arm and he shifted over so she could lay back down. He threw his arm back over her stomach to pin her back against the mattress. Then he scooted himself further down the bed, resting his head on her bare chest with a sigh. Sienna shook her head a little and sighed, "You happy?"

"Very. I think we should stay in bed all day. Lonewood will be fine without us until tomorrow," Gentry teased. He squeezed her middle, nuzzling her breasts. Sienna began lazily brushing her fingers through his shaggy hair and he added, "What if we just stayed out here forever?"

"Don't tempt me. You literally built a home in my paradise." She pulled away to look down at him as he hummed against her skin. "I've traveled, Gentry. I've seen the most beautiful places in the world, but none of it compares to this."

She felt his mouth twitch against her in a smile, and he said softly, "I've never had any desire to leave. The farthest I've been is Minneapolis to see Kenzie's folks, but this is all I've ever known. I always knew in the back of my mind that there was something better out there, but if I didn't find it, I couldn't be sad about it."

"I'd love to travel to the ends of the earth with you, but only if we come home to this."

Gentry hummed and Sienna stroked his temple with her thumb. He threw his leg over her thighs and she chuckled when she realized he was hard. "Gentry."

"Sienna."

She smirked at him and he tilted his head to meet her eyes. His smile was lazy, like he wasn't awake enough to banter with the woman in his bed. Sienna was preparing for a morning similar to their night until her stomach rumbled loudly. She grimaced as Gentry pulled away, staring down at her with a teasing grin. "Ahhh, somebody's hungry."

"Well, you were going to feed me last night, but we got distracted..." Sienna shrugged a little, placing her hands on her stomach. Now that she was aware of it, her stomach ached a little. She hadn't eaten since early the day before and her nose felt a little stuffy from being out in the cold. Gentry would definitely be disappointed, but Sienna needed food. "Sorry."

He leaned down and kissed her lips, humming softly before pulling away. "Don't apologize. I'll feed you now if you let me eat you up later."

Sienna's cheeks burned red as Gentry rolled out of bed to get dressed. Hearing the growl in Gentry's usually velvet voice reminded Sienna that she'd slept with her best friend last night. The man who teased her relentlessly had spent the better part of last night inside her and made it very clear he had no intention of stopping anytime soon. Sienna hoped he'd save his dirty words for the times they were alone, but she doubted he would. She could already imagine him whispering sweet, salacious taunts in her ear in front of Dakota, Alex, and all of Lonewood just to turn her cherry red. That was the man she loved, and that was the man she was going to spend her life with. Sienna was sure of it now.

Gentry rifled through his drawers for fresh underwear and a shirt, but he pulled on his jeans from the night before. Sienna watched as he slowly buttoned up his brown shirt, facing the mirror and meeting her reflection.

Finally, he turned around with a sad smile. Sienna was worried something was wrong, but before she could ask he explained, "I'm sorry. It's just... I haven't done this since Kenzie-"

"It's okay. I know. Do what you have to do. I'm not gonna judge you, or blame you for needing some space to sort through your feelings."

"I didn't think about her. Not even once," he told Sienna quietly. She felt a pang in her chest at how conflicted he sounded, like he couldn't decide if that broke his heart or made him proud. "Part of me feels guilty, but I really loved last night. It was different, and it was great... It was easier before I started thinking about it."

Sienna nodded, imagining it was hard to be intimate with somebody new when Gentry thought he'd only ever sleep with his wife for the rest of his life. The little voice in the back of Sienna's head told her that she couldn't compete, but she wanted to try to fill the void in Gentry's life. She'd take whatever scraps he'd give her because they had something special. Maybe it wasn't better than what he had with Kenzie, but it was different and it mattered. She couldn't run away now.

"I'm gonna make some breakfast. You're welcome to look around. Borrow a shirt if you want, or wander around naked. I won't complain either way." Gentry cradled Sienna's jaw as he leaned down for a kiss, then swept out of the bedroom to make them something to eat.

At some point in the night, Gentry had closed the curtains, most likely to keep the sun from waking them up as opposed to giving them privacy. Sienna wasn't sure if the rain had stopped before they fell asleep or not, but she heard birds chirping outside now.

As she stood, she looked around for the t-shirt Gentry had discarded before realizing nobody could see her here. She'd never experienced true solitude before. Once upon a time, she would have hated the silence and the time that rolled by endlessly, but now she reveled in it. If she wanted to stay in bed until next week, Lonewood would survive. If she wanted to walk around Gentry's home naked, nobody would care. If Gentry made her scream until she lost her voice, nobody would complain. This little corner of the wilderness was Gentry's and it could be Sienna's too.

Last night, Gentry had told Sienna that if she slept with him she was promising to be his wife. The logical part of her mind told her to consider the ramifications of that promise, but for the first time in her life, Sienna listened to her heart instead of her head.

She had no regrets.

The sound of sizzling caught Sienna's attention and she reached down to scoop up Gentry's t-shirt. Gentry might enjoy the idea of her traipsing around his home with her tits out, but Sienna needed to eat before enticing him back to bed. Her growling stomach couldn't afford any more distractions.

Once dressed in his t-shirt, Sienna slowly made her way towards the kitchen. She looked a little closer at the photos framed along the walls, recognizing most of them as Gentry's.

"You're a really great photographer," Sienna called as she stared at a photo of a herd of wild horses sprinting across a flat plain. The photo was stunningly clear, meaning Gentry was most likely close enough to get the photo without using a zoom. "You ever show anyone your work?"

"Yeah," he called from around the corner, "Won a couple awards. Been in a couple magazines. It was my side-gig before I became sheriff. I used to have more time on my hands and Kenzie and I were out here all the time." Sienna turned the corner to find Gentry making omelets on the stove. He tossed a couple pieces of bread into his toaster and gestured towards the fridge with his head. "I've got milk and orange juice. I can make coffee if you want, but it tastes like shit."

Sienna laughed a little as she climbed up onto a stool at the island. "That explains why you're always at the diner." She leaned her chin against her knuckles and said, "You know, you could buy different coffee?"

He shrugged as he turned on another pan to fry up some bacon before grabbing the toast when it popped up with a ding. "This is what the general store sells. I can't exactly ride Domino to Dickinson, so my choices are limited."

"I'd drive to the town over to buy you coffee," Sienna told him softly.

Gentry's eyes met hers, but he didn't say anything right away. He filled a plate of food and passed it over to Sienna before turning back for his own breakfast. His silence was pointed, and Sienna wanted him to confess what he was thinking without her having to ask. Considering why he didn't drive, she had a guess his silence was reluctance to let Sienna behind the wheel of a car after losing Kenzie that way.

After serving himself, Gentry came around the island to sit beside Sienna, but he still didn't say anything as he ate. He stared at the far wall, but Sienna's gaze stayed trained on him, challenging him to share his thoughts with her. Finally, Sienna lost her patience and asked quietly, "What's on your mind, sheriff?"

He chuckled, leaning over to bump against her shoulder. "I guess it's weird thinking about you driving places to get things for me. Seems... a little counterproductive to the cause. I obviously have no right to tell you what to do and not do, but I'll admit the idea unnerves me a little." He took a bite of his eggs and chewed slowly, watching Sienna thoughtfully. "I don't need to leave Lonewood. I can get everything and everywhere I need to with Domino, but being with you makes that complicated. I'm assuming you won't want to be trapped here the rest of your life"

"I think that's a problem for tomorrow," Sienna told him with a little grin. She leaned forward to peck his lips. "I'm right where I want to be today."

Gentry leaned his forehead against Sienna's as he sighed. He gently rubbed her forearm with his fingertips as she rested her hands in her lap. "I don't want to share you," he grunted under his breath, "but Dakota said your sister is worried about you. I think I should take you back to town to see her."

"I could just call her. I need to borrow your phone though," Sienna suggested lightly. "We don't have to leave-"

"I think you need to rest," Gentry told her firmly as he finished his breakfast. He took their plates to the sink before leaning on the island across from Sienna. "You took quite a tumble and didn't get a lot of sleep..." His smile grew into a wolfish smirk. "If you rested at home this afternoon, I'd feel better about roughing you up again tonight."

Sienna scoffed and looked out the windows towards the open plains. "You think quite highly of yourself, don't you?"

"Well, if you didn't enjoy it, you're quite the actress. I totally thought your desperate moans for me were real."

"You are such an ass!" Sienna whined, hiding her face behind her hands so Gentry couldn't see how red she was turning. She peeled her fingers apart to peek through them, finding Gentry beaming at her proudly.

"I made you mewl like a kitten."

"I haven't had sex in five months!"

"I haven't had sex in almost four years," Gentry countered, but despite the sensitive nature of his comment, he couldn't wipe the toothy grin off his face. "I was worried I'd be a little rusty, but I still got it."

Sienna slid off the stool and strode towards the fireplace, sparing a glance at the photo of Gentry and Kenzie as she reached up for the hat he'd left on the mantle last night. She wondered if Kenzie put up with this boyish pride for all six years of their marriage, or if he was truly surprised and proud he could still please a woman after years of heartbroken celibacy.

When she turned back to Gentry, she found him stalking towards her slowly like a cat preparing to catch its prey. Sienna placed his hat on her head and looked up from under the large brim as he grabbed her waist to pull her close.

"It's a little big for you, sweetheart."

"Well, I doubt it'll fit you anymore, seeing how big your head's getting," Sienna teased back. Gentry tipped back the hat so he could see her better, then leaned down to capture her lips in a firm kiss. Sienna leaned all the way back to reach him easier, draping her arms over his shoulders to hold him tightly.

His hand slid down to her ass and she let out a little yelp when he squeezed, using his other hand to pull his hat off her head and toss it aside. He chuckled as he pulled away from the kiss to rest his chin on top of Sienna's head. "Thank you for waking me up again. I didn't think I ever would."

Sienna grimaced at the idea of Gentry living the rest of his life miserable and single. It was a crime that such a wonderful man lost his wife, and Sienna didn't take her new role in his life lightly. It was easy to tell herself that if she hadn't come into town that he would have found somebody else, but Sienna didn't know that. She didn't know if business would ever boom or if anyone new would ever move to town. It was incredibly likely that if Sienna and Alex hadn't been forced into Lonewood, Gentry Wyatt could have spent the rest of his life alone.

In a horrible, twisted way, Sienna was thankful for Landon Maddox. If it wasn't for him, she wouldn't have ended up here. Losing her old life was the best thing that ever happened to her, and now that she found Gentry, she wasn't ever going to let him go.

"I 'spose. We probably better head back," Sienna said and Gentry snorted. She looked up at him with drawn brows and asked, "What?"

"You 'spose? Your North Dakota is showing, Miss Jade. What would your friends in California say?"

She shook her head to dismiss the idea, not because she wasn't from California, but because it didn't matter. It would be an honor for Sienna Jade to fit in here with these people. They were a different caliber from everyone she'd ever known before.

Gentry grunted as he leaned down to scoop up his discarded hat to place on his own head. "C'mon. Let me grab your clothes from the laundry. If you want, you can pick out a new hat. Jasmine seems to have *acquired* your old one." He raised a brow questioningly, but Sienna didn't elaborate. She followed him to the small laundry room and he handed over her clothes. "I'll go get Domino saddled up while you change. If you wanna borrow something of Kenzie's, her stuff's in the closet. You can wear whatever you want, but if you aren't comfortable with that, I won't be offended. I know it's a little weird, but it's just sitting in my closet collecting dust so if you'd like anything of hers, go for it."

Once the front door closed, Sienna carefully pulled on yesterday's clothes, then peeked into Gentry's closet. It was massive, but there were only clothes hung on the left side. There was a small bin on the floor in the back of the mostly-empty closet. It was strikingly clear that this closet was designed to hold all of Kenzie's things, but it never saw its intended purpose.

Opening the storage bin, Sienna saw a stack of cowboy hats and a couple shirts folded neatly beneath them. Sienna pulled out the hats and looked through them, pausing when she found one at the bottom that was sun-worn leather with faded turquoise embroidery underneath the brim. She placed it on her head, feeling how it fit perfectly over her thick hair. Sienna could probably borrow this one thing and not feel horrible about it.

Once she'd pulled on her boots, she stepped through the front door and sucked in a long, deep breath. The air was cool and everything smelled like rain. Sienna wanted to go for a ride, but then she remembered that Cheyanne had taken off.

Sienna turned to her right, seeing a small stable attached to the side of the house. She walked forward slowly, not wanting to startle Gentry or Domino, but when she peeked inside the cracked-open door, she gasped. "You found her?"

Gentry turned around to look at Sienna in surprise, then over his shoulder to Cheyanne, who was eating hungrily out of a bucket of oats. "She was with you when I found you."

"But she ran after I fell- I don't remember her being there when I started falling asleep." Sienna dug her fingernails into Cheyanne's mane at the top of her head before leaning forward to kiss her face. "You came back for me?"

"Must've. I saw her standing under the tree and there you were." Gentry reached over to scratch Cheyanne. "Don't freak out," he started softly, causing Sienna's head to jolt up and he continued, "but she's hurt. She's favoring her back left foot, so you're not gonna be able to ride her for a while. I think she'll be okay, she just needs a little time."

Sienna's eyes welled up with tears and she threw her arms around Cheyanne's neck to cry against her. "I'm so sorry. I should have never taken you."

"She's gonna be okay, Sienna. I promise." Gentry pulled Sienna back and she sniffled, hating herself for getting Cheyanne hurt. Gentry leaned down and kissed her cheek, trying to assure Sienna that he wasn't upset, and that Cheyanne was gonna be just fine. He wouldn't be this calm if she wasn't.

After a moment, Sienna swallowed her guilt and Gentry used his finger to knock her hat brim down a little, distracting her and causing her to smile a little. "Nice hat."

"Is it okay?"

"Of course. Looks great on you." Gentry let go of Sienna to grab Domino and lead him out of his stall. "We'll leave Cheyanne here for now. Bring her back to town in a day or two. She'll be good as new soon."

"You promise?"

"I promise," Gentry assured her, grabbing Sienna's wrist so he could tug her over to Domino. Once she was settled in the saddle, Gentry guided Domino out of the stable and locked up, then swung up behind her and kicked Domino's sides to send them galloping over the plains towards Lonewood.

Chapter 46

"SHE'S FINE, ALEX. SHE'S with Gentry," Dakota assured the younger woman as they walked side by side down a crowded Main Street late Saturday morning.

Labor Day weekend brought droves of people wanting to experience the wonderful Lonewood before the weather turned cold and the kids went back to school. Although the college kids were gone, Jesse and Beau continued their act with practiced ease while Alex wandered the streets in her frilly costume and flirted her way through the tourists.

That was, until the sight of Mayor Wyatt caught her eye, because Dakota was the only person who'd heard anything about Sienna since yesterday morning. Dakota had called Alex around eight last night to tell her Gentry found Sienna. Alex assumed that meant he was bringing Sienna home, but Dakota told her that wouldn't be the case. Apparently Gentry had taken Sienna to *his* home, and he had no intention of bringing her back until *he* was ready.

Alex swished her ruched purple skirt as she walked, kicking at the dirt with her black lace up shoe. "Why isn't she answering her phone?"

"I don't know. Maybe her phone's dead, maybe it got damaged in the storm. Gentry said she was unconscious when he found her, but he didn't tell me much else. He said he found her knocked out under a tree and he was gonna take her to his place to rest. I'm sure if she wasn't okay he would have gotten a hold of us. No news is good news."

"Can't you call him?"

"I have. He's not answering," Dakota told her, flipping her blonde hair away from her face before smiling at a passing tourist. "I'll keep trying, but he's bad about checking his phone. I know he'd call if something was wrong, though."

That didn't bring her much comfort, but Alex knew Dakota was right. Gentry had called Dakota when he found Sienna and Dakota had called Alex right after. His lack of updates probably meant Sienna was fine and they were keeping each other busy. At least that's what Alex told herself, because imagining that Sienna hadn't woken up and Gentry was burying her somewhere out in the Badlands seemed a little out of character for the sheriff.

Dakota nodded towards Jesse and told Alex, "I'll find you as soon as I hear something. Try not to worry. We gotta get through this last weekend before we can rest. I'm actually jealous of Sienna. She's probably resting up at Gentry's house while the rest of us bust our asses one last time."

Alex offered the best smile she could muster as Dakota walked away, before turning her attention towards Jesse. He was currently talking to a group of kids, asking them to help him keep an eye out for Beau and his band of bandits. Alex took a couple bold steps towards him before one of the tourists bumped into her.

"I'm so sorry! I wasn't paying attention to where I was going."

"It's quite alright," Alex said honestly, brushing off her dress before straightening up. She managed to smile brightly and chirp as she faced him, "What brings a handsome man like you to Lonewood?"

"You did, Alexandra Jacobs," he said as a feline smile grew across his features.

Her eyes burst open and she pulled away roughly, but his hand jut out to grip her arm to pull her in close again. She quivered as he stared at her patiently, sending shivers down her spine as she held back the urge to scream and cry. If she did either of those things, he'd almost certainly kill her, and he was waiting for her to slip up and give him a reason to strike. "I think you've got the wrong person."

"Landon misses you," the man whispered and Alex choked out a sob. Her eyes darted around, but nobody seemed to realize anything was wrong. Alex tried to look over her shoulder for Jesse, but the man leaned close and spoke quickly in her ear, "The feds plan to extract you soon, because they think they're about to catch him. If you stay, and you keep your mouth shut, you can keep your life here a little longer. Tell them you won't testify and we can pretend this conversation never happened."

"You don't know what you're talking about," Alex gasped out. "I'm not who you think I am."

"Is there a problem here?"

Alex froze at the sound of Jesse's voice, but the man released her. He stared her down as she ran into Jesse's waiting arms, and he held her protectively as he studied the stranger. "Think about what I told you. This doesn't need to be difficult. It was nice to see you again."

Alex whimpered as Jesse surged forward. He hid Alex behind him as he confronted the man, "You need to leave."

"Jesse, don't." Where Jesse saw himself defending his friend, Alex knew he was playing a dangerous game with an adversary he greatly underestimated.

The man looked Jesse up and down with an unimpressed expression, but Jesse took another step forward and got up in his face. Alex felt her stomach drop in horror as Jesse ordered coldly, "Get the hell out of here, and don't approach my girl again."

"Watch your mouth," the man said evenly, unthreatened by the young cowboy. "You're out of your depth."

Alex grabbed Jesse's arm to try to pull him back, but Jesse shoved Landon's man hard against the chest and threatened, "If you ever show your face here again, I'll be the least of your worries."

"Does he know who you are?" The question was directed at Alex and she swallowed, wondering what difference it made to Landon. When she held his gaze, he sighed, "Alexandra, you know you can't stay if people know who you are..."

Jesse took a swing at the man, but he just rammed Jesse against the railing outside the mayor's office. A couple of people shrieked at the scuffle but others cheered and pulled out their phones, thinking it was part of the show. Jesse got one hit on Landon's enforcer as Alex pleaded with them to stop. Alex took a couple steps away, screaming for help until a gunshot rang out from behind her.

She looked back in horror to see Jesse stumble back onto the steps of Dakota's office, holding his left shoulder tightly as he gasped. Alex dropped to the ground beside him as he fell, pulling his hand away to see the blood pouring out from beneath his shirt at the same moment Landon's man bolted into the gathering crowd.

"What did I tell you boys about shooting outside my office?" Dakota asked incredulously as she burst through her office door, looking down at Alex and Jesse before her amber eyes widened in horror. She dropped to her knees as Jesse passed out against Alex's collarbone, continuing to lose blood from the bullet hole in his shoulder. Dakota shouted at Beau when he approached to see what had happened, "Get the doctor! Hurry!"

Tourists began screaming and running towards the saloon and the bank and the stores, realizing the gunfire that had just occurred wasn't part of the show. Beau began pounding on the door to the clinic, yelling for Brad. Alex felt her chest heave as she ducked her head and sobbed against Jesse's thick hair. Her world crumbled around her as she held her best friend, leaning back and whispering a prayer that he'd be okay.

Dakota ripped off a bit of thin fabric from the petticoat under Alex's dress, not caring if she ruined it. She pressed hard against the bullet wound in Jesse's shoulder to stop the bleeding, glaring up when she saw Cecily jog over from the sheriff's station. "Where the hell is everybody? Somebody brought a real gun here, we need to go after him! Who's on patrol?"

"I don't know- the boys went home a couple hours ago, but nobody came to take over for them."

"Who's supposed to be here right now?" Dakota yelled. "Why isn't there anybody around?"

"I haven't seen Gentry all morning. I assumed he was around. He's always around," Cecily stammered, backing away and looking around in fear. "I'll find Skylar... I'll find Dusty, I'll-!"

"Cecily, *go!*"

Alex began to sob as she leaned over Jesse. If Jesse died because of her, she'd never forgive herself. This was just the start. Landon would come to take her, and if anyone stood in his way, he'd kill them.

Everything was becoming foggy for Alex until she heard Brad yelp behind her, "Jesus! He's actually been shot?!"

Suddenly, Alex was pulled away from Jesse and tumbled back onto her ass, weeping as Dakota hugged her tightly. Through her tears, she saw Brad examining Jesse. He barked orders at Beau, but suddenly Dakota was murmuring against her ear as she stroked Alex's back, "What happened? Who did this?"

"I- I don't know. I don't know him, he just- he threatened me. He threatened- Jesse defended me and he shot him- he shot him and it's all my fault... he came here for me..." Alex wept against Dakota's shoulder, feeling the woman's hand still against her back.

Alex leaned away at the sound of a horse approaching and looked up in time to see Gentry and Sienna ride up empty Main Street on Domino together. Gentry looked around worriedly before practically leaping off the horse. When he got a good look at Jesse, his eyes widened and he stumbled back a step.

"What happened?"

"Where have you been?" Dakota hissed furiously. "We needed you."

"I'm sorry-"

"I'm gonna call for him to be airlifted out of here. We gotta get him to the hospital." Brad looked over at Gentry with wide, worried eyes and said, "This isn't from one of the guns we use here. We gotta find the shooter."

"Alex, why did he threaten you?"

Alex looked up at Dakota. The mayor was now standing above her with a nervousness that didn't seem to fit her bold personality. She was twitchy, shifting a little from foot to foot as she waited impatiently for an answer. Alex looked over at Sienna as she dismounted Domino, eyes wide as she surveyed the situation.

She knew.

"No. No, please. Tell me it's not true." Sienna begged as she ran to Alex and threw her arms around her. "What happened?" Sienna asked as she pulled away. She zeroed in on Alex and Alex alone, then whispered, "Was it him?"

"No. I've never seen that man before- but Landon sent him. He said if I didn't testify that I could stay, but- but he shot Jesse when he tried to defend me." Alex buried her face in the crook of Sienna's neck, weeping as her sister held her tightly. "I don't wanna go!"

Sienna stiffened. Alex swallowed down her fear and her pain and pulled away slowly, seeing the most heart-shattering expression on her sister's face. Sienna shook her head. "No. I'm not leaving." She scrambled back from Alex and tried to wrap her arms around Gentry but his whole frame was stiff as he stared down at her.

"What happened here?"

"Gentry, please-"

"Sienna, don't lie to me," Gentry's voice quivered and Sienna choked back a sob. Gentry held her cheeks between his palms and asked nervously, eyes darting between hers as he searched for answers. "What is Alex talking about?"

"I can't tell you here. If I tell you, I'll never see you again. It's not my fault. I didn't do anything wrong!" Her voice cracked as she cried, looking small and pathetic as she stared up at the sheriff. Gentry let go of her to rub his mouth roughly, looking around like he didn't know what he wanted to do. His sister cleared her throat.

Alex pushed herself to her feet to face Dakota, but the woman's amber eyes had never been so cold as she stared her down. "You don't seem surprised to be in this situation. Who the hell are you two?"

"Sienna told you the truth, I'm hiding from a man. I saw- I saw him kill somebody, and he knows that I saw, but he let me go. He's a really bad guy and they need me to lock him up," Alex explained weakly, sparing a glance at Sienna as tear marks stained her cheeks. There was no use lying anymore. They had to leave Lonewood, because Landon knew they were here. He'd come back for them sooner or later. "We're in Witness Protection so the government can keep us alive long enough to catch him."

Dakota's jaw tightened and she looked at Alex with a heartless stare. "You knowingly brought this danger to my town."

"We were hiding!"

"You were doing a shit job of it!" Dakota screamed and Alex took a few steps away to stand closer to Sienna and Gentry. Dakota followed her down the steps, driving her away from her office and Jesse and the life they'd come to love. She glared at Sienna and spat, "Seems a little counterproductive to bring business to the small town meant to hide you."

Sienna stammered as Gentry tightened his grip around her shoulder, "I did it because you needed me to. *You* asked me to-"

"You should have said no," Dakota cut her off, striding towards Sienna until she was looming over her. Sienna stared at her with a quivering lip, but Dakota's normally cheery voice was full of enough ice to freeze their veins. "I'm not mad that you hid the truth, Sienna. You brought attention to my town knowing you had a target on your back, and you didn't hesitate to drag my brother into your make-believe life, even after you knew what being with you meant to him. I'm not mad that you followed the government's directions and hid your identity, I'm mad that you didn't consider for a single damn second what your actions could mean for these people. Now that whoever you're hiding from knows you're here, what happens to all of us? What happens when he comes looking for you and Alex and the only person standing between him and you is my brother?"

Gentry grimaced at Dakota's words. He pulled away from Sienna to stand between her and his sister, raising his hands in an effort to placate Dakota. "Tensions are high. Let's just take a moment, we can figure something out-"

"No," Dakota glared daggers at him as she backed him towards her office, away from Sienna. "You're supposed to protect this town. If you won't, I will."

"I would never let anything happen to Gentry, or you, or anybody!" Sienna cried out, but Alex flinched, knowing she couldn't save them. She'd seen how merciless Landon Maddox was and nothing Sienna or Alex could do would save these people.

Except leave.

Sienna looked past Dakota to where Gentry now stood in front of Brad and Beau, who were trying to stop the bleeding from Jesse's shoulder. The sound of a chopper in the distance warned Alex that they were coming to take Jesse to the hospital, and she could see Dakota wasn't going to stick around and talk much longer. Gentry quickly collected Domino so he wouldn't spook, leading him closer to the sheriff's station to tie him up.

Sienna tried to bolt towards him, but Dakota grabbed her upper arm with an iron grip, ripping her back as she cried past the mayor, "Gentry, please… you gotta listen to me, I didn't lie to you!" He turned to look at her, listening as she wept. "What we have- what we've built- is real! I couldn't tell you because I didn't want you to get hurt, but you know me! You know me better than anybody and I don't wanna leave you-"

"Get the hell out of my town," Dakota growled darkly, shoving Sienna back with almost enough force to knock her over. Alex grabbed her sister's shoulders as Sienna ignored the mayor, focused on the sheriff standing behind Dakota with a look of shock on his face. When Sienna didn't make a move to leave, Dakota barked, "Leave, before I make you. I won't ask again."

"Dakota, don't-" Gentry started. He took a step towards his sister, giving Alex hope that he would fight for Sienna, but Dakota whirled on him and screamed, "I will not let you die for her! I will not lose *you*!" Gentry balked at her words, opening his mouth to argue, but Dakota cut him off, "She'll be the death of you if she stays. I won't let *anyone* hurt my family again. Not even her."

Gentry stayed silent until his sister turned around, then called to Sienna, "This isn't over, okay?"

"Please don't make us go," Sienna pleaded, finally looking away from Gentry to gaze up at Dakota with bleary eyes. She shook her head a little, gasping for air as her chest heaved. "I love him, Dakota. I love him and I don't want to leave him. I'd never put him in harm's way, you have to know that."

Dakota took one step closer, raising her hand enough to cause Sienna to flinch. Alex didn't believe the mayor would actually strike her sister, but there was a temper burning within Dakota that Alex hadn't realized was there. Dakota clenched her fist, holding it to her mouth for a minute before pointing towards the motel. Towards the edge of town.

"Let's pack our things," Alex told Sienna softly. "We gotta let Bridget know what's happened."

Wind began to swirl as the helicopter landed near the saloon, and the tourists and the locals came out in droves to see what was happening. Alex tugged on Sienna's wrist to lead her back to the apartment, but she ripped her hand away. "I'm not going anywhere with you."

Alex leaned close, trying to grab Sienna again, but her sister pushed her back. "Don't do this. This wasn't my fault," Alex choked out.

"It never is! It never is your fault, but I still pay for it!" Sienna sobbed as she looked towards where Gentry stood beside Domino, clenching his horse's bridle as the horse shifted uncomfortably at the loud sound of the helicopter landing. Sienna clamped her eyes closed, stopping the tears from continuing to drown her round cheeks. When she opened them, she scowled at Alex. "I don't care where you go, or what you do. Testify, go back to Bridget, run off with Landon for all I care... I don't give a shit anymore. I never want to see you again. You've taken *everything* that I've ever loved away from me. I can't let you ruin anything else."

"I'm sorry," Alex told her softly, her voice snatched away by the roar of the helicopter blades. She looked around, seeing everyone they'd known here watching them. Kitty, Kennedy, and Trevor watched from the porch of the apparel shop with shocked expressions. Brenda, Colleen, Hank, Bill, and his wife Linda had all come from the diner to see what the commotion was and watched with various levels of surprise. When Alex turned towards the saloon though, she saw Maude walking towards them slowly, horror and sadness written across her wrinkled features. When Alex met her gaze, she saw a resignation there, as if Maude realized everything they'd built together was gone.

From between the bank and the sheriff's station, Skylar came running, skidding to a stop when she saw who was at the center of the altercation. She looked around, seeing Gentry lingering near the station with a heartbroken look on his face, and Dakota standing between the women and her brother with her head held high. Skylar's head snapped towards the paramedics that sprinted towards Jesse and she gasped lightly when she realized who'd been injured. Finally, she looked back to Sienna and Alex and sighed.

It was time to go.

Sienna bolted towards Gentry again, but Dakota took a step to the left, cutting her off and shaking her head sharply. Sienna and Gentry met each other's eyes from across the street, and a silent conversation moved between them. Alex knew if she ended up never seeing Sienna again, this was how she'd remember her: desperate, broken, and finally having found love just to lose it. And it was all Alex's fault.

She watched Sienna walk away from her with her head lowered, determined not to meet anyone's eyes. Two hundred people watched her walk back to their apartment; but Alex gazed up as the helicopter carrying Jesse lifted off the ground, causing her messy blonde hair to whip around her face.

Her roots had grown out, but she never considered coloring it. She'd gained weight and lost muscle, but she preferred the person who looked back in the mirror. Alex liked who she'd become in every way. She liked her frilly costume and her painted lips and dancing the night away with Jesse. Alexandra Jacobs had never felt as happy and free as Alex Jade, and watching the helicopter fly away felt like watching that happiness flee with it.

But knowing Alex had cost Sienna her first chance at real love was worse. Alex would give her life if it meant Sienna could stay here with Gentry Wyatt, but it was too late. Even if Bridget and the Marshals allowed Sienna to remain in Lonewood, Dakota had made it abundantly clear that neither of them were welcome any longer. And Gentry hardly said a word to convince his sister otherwise.

There was nothing left to do here, Alex slowly stalked towards her apartment after Sienna to pack. She did her best to ignore everyone who watched her, but their eyes were like daggers, reminding Alex of the slit neck that ruined her life forever.

Chapter 47

SIENNA JADE DIDN'T PACK. There wasn't any reason to take anything with her, it wasn't like she had sentimental belongings here. She locked herself in her room and sobbed until she was numb. She didn't want to accept that she was losing everything she'd built here over the summer, but it was reality. She'd been avoiding reality for a long time, and it finally caught up with her.

Alex had tried to talk to her, but Sienna couldn't talk to her little sister right now. Everything in Sienna wanted to reach out to Gentry, but her phone was damaged beyond repair. If she let Alex in, she could borrow her sister's phone, but she didn't think Gentry would even answer.

She could apologize and plead with him to forgive her for withholding the truth, but the problem wasn't that Gentry was angry, but that Dakota was. Sienna thought Gentry looked hurt, but he wasn't angry. He was as devastated this happened as she was; she knew that much.

Maybe with time and space, Dakota and Gentry would understand that Sienna and Alex had never meant them any harm. Dakota had every right to be angry that Sienna had brought attention to their hiding place, but Sienna loved her brother. She loved Gentry in a way she'd never loved anyone, and she didn't want to give up on what they had. If she could just talk to him, they could figure something out, but if Dakota drove them out of town before Sienna had a chance, she'd never see him again.

Whether Sienna wanted to or not, she'd be plucked from Lonewood and sent somewhere else. The idea of starting over made Sienna sick. She'd given so much of her heart and soul to building up Lonewood that leaving it broke her heart. She didn't think she'd fall in love with this tiny North

Dakota town, but over the past couple months it had become her home. She'd choose it over Manhattan, Los Angeles, Paris, or Prague any day, and wherever they sent her next would feel empty in comparison.

She was vaguely aware of shuffling in the living room, and she realized somebody had knocked on their front door. Sienna didn't know who would dare to visit them, unless it was Dakota coming to escort them out of town herself.

After changing into a loose tank top and a clean pair of jeans, Sienna placed Kenzie's old embroidered hat on her dresser. Whoever came to check out the apartment after they left town would find it and probably return it to Gentry. Sienna hoped it would make it back to Gentry. She couldn't take anything more from him; she'd caused enough damage.

When Sienna peeked out her bedroom door, she heard hushed voices coming from the living room. She came around the corner to see Alex in a pair of yoga pants and a black t-shirt. Her packed suitcase sat beside her, but her showgirl dress was draped across the couch. Like Kenzie's hat, she was leaving it to be found. They were shedding the disguises Lonewood had offered them before leaving for good.

It was Skylar who had arrived, and who now leaned back against their kitchen counter with a tense expression. Her eyes darted between Sienna and Alex for a moment, seeming to take in the different ways they prepared to leave. Alex was taking her life with her, needing something to remember her brief time here. Sienna was leaving with nothing but the shirt on her back, because any reminder would only make the hurt last longer.

"I called Bridget," Alex croaked, and Sienna remembered she hadn't spoken to her sister since their fight on Main Street. Looking at the clock, she realized it had been almost two hours. Her green eyes were dull as she watched Alex, wondering if she wanted some sort of sign to continue. After a moment, Alex mumbled, "She's coming to get us."

"She texted and asked if I'd take y'all to Bismarck. She's worried your phone is compromised and wants to get you out of town before there's any more incidents. We gotta go now." Skylar forced a weak smile, but it didn't bring Sienna any comfort. "You ready to go?"

Sienna nodded, looking around one last time as Skylar led them towards the door. Her heart broke as she walked through the front door for the last time, remembering the times Gentry would walk her up and leave her with a kiss.

Whatever life was left in Sienna was snuffed out by the realization she'd spend forever dreaming of what could have been if she'd only gotten the chance to stay.

When she reached the dirt road, Sienna looked around, taking in Lonewood one last time. It was bustling, but there was an anxious feeling in the air. From where she stood, she could see Dusty and the night guys milling about in an effort to make the tourists feel safer. Gentry was nowhere to be found– Domino wasn't tied up outside the sheriff's station. Her heart sank further. Sienna had hoped to at least see Gentry one last time.

Kitty stood in front of her shop with Beau, and when they passed, she gave them both a firm nod. Sienna wanted to run into her arms and hug her, but Beau held her shoulder tightly, protectively. Sienna didn't blame him. She even understood: Sienna and Alex were a threat. They'd brought danger to their quiet little haven, and nobody would be safe again until they were gone.

"Thanks for everything," Sienna murmured as they passed Kitty and Beau, causing the former to soften. She followed Skylar towards the motel parking lot, feeling weird wearing her sneakers instead of her boots. Sienna's long hair was pulled up into a high ponytail to keep it out of her face, but right about now she wished she could hide behind her strands like a veil.

Kennedy and Trevor watched as they approached. Trevor stood behind Kennedy with his arms wrapped around her. He leaned his chin on her shoulder, looking disappointed. Kennedy looked frustrated and she gave Sienna a sad little wave when Skylar unlocked her car for Sienna and Alex to climb in.

Skylar popped open the trunk and climbed into the driver's seat next to Sienna while Alex loaded up her suitcase.. Sienna leaned her head against the window, eyes scanning Lonewood for Gentry or Dakota. She'd jump out of the car while it was moving if it meant she could say goodbye to the Wyatts.

But Gentry was nowhere to be seen as they drove down the road away from the Tumbleweed Motel. Before Sienna knew it, they were past the Lonewood sign and on the highway, and her life as Sienna Jade was in the rearview mirror.

"I'm sorry this happened," Skylar said softly as she focused on the road ahead. "And I'm sorry it ended the way it did."

"It is what it is. Time to get back to the real world." Sienna watched the endless expanse of grasslands roll by as they got farther and farther away from Lonewood. The sky was clear, but the sun didn't feel as bright. Sienna dreaded being ushered back into the Marshals' foxhole to be remade into somebody else again. For the first time in a really long time, she felt like Scarlett Jacobs. She'd long buried her name, her dreams, and her past, but now Scarlett emerged, sad and broken, to greet Sienna as she left her life behind.

She wondered who she'd have to become next.

They drove for almost an hour before Alex's phone began to ring in the pocket of her navy yoga pants. The Badlands had long given way to endless farmland on either side of the two lane highway, and the only signs of life were the barns and farmhouses that popped up every couple of miles.

Alex wiggled a little as she fished her phone out, then answered it with more cheer than Sienna could have mustered. "Hey Bridget!"

"Where the hell are you?" Bridget asked sharply through the phone. Sienna looked over her shoulder as Alex furrowed her brows and opened her mouth to answer, but Bridget's voice clearly stated, "I'm in Lonewood to collect you."

"Oh. Skylar said we were meeting you at the airport-"

"Here, let me talk to her, there must be some sort of misunderstanding," Skylar said casually as she reached behind her head to take the phone from Alex. Skylar rolled down her window as Alex passed it over, then chucked the phone out of the car. Sienna bolted up the same moment Skylar raised her left hand, a gun in her grip. "Good thing we left when we did, huh?"

Alex unbuckled her seatbelt to slide behind Sienna's seat as the older sister breathed heavily, staring at the gun that Skylar kept aimed at her even though her gaze stayed mostly on the road. "What are you doing?"

"I really hate Lonewood," Skylar said casually, as if they were old friends and she wasn't holding Sienna at gunpoint. She shrugged. "I've been trying to scrape together enough money to move after my mom died working for the sheriff's station, but nobody really gets paid well here. Then around the beginning of May, I get an intriguing phone call." She lolled her head enough to look at Alex with a lazy grin. "This guy- Landon Maddox- caught wind that his girl was being sent away in Witness Protection. He had an inside guy working for the Marshals feeding him updates, but then he heard Bridget Masterson was planning on sending her newest assets somewhere she could keep a closer eye on them. Maddox does a little research, finds out about me and calls with an offer I just can't refuse. He said if Bridget sent you two here, I was supposed to keep tabs on you. If I could keep you safe here until he was ready to get you, he'd pay me more money than I could ever earn working for Gentry."

"Bridget trusted you and you sold her out for money?" Alex sneered and Skylar rolled her eyes. She placed the gun back in the side of her door, then shot Sienna a warning look that told her not to get any ideas.

"I didn't sell Bridget out for money, I sold you two out for money. I didn't know you. I didn't care to. My job was to keep you in Lonewood until Landon was ready for you. If you stayed in Lonewood and didn't testify, the money would keep coming. That was the bargain. So, in my defense, I was helping Bridget with her cause. Everybody was happy until you went and told Jesse about why you were here."

Sienna turned around in her seat to stare at Alex with wide eyes. Skylar continued on, "I wasn't aware Landon was sending a guy today. But when Jesse basically told him that he knew why he was coming for you, he panicked, he shot him, Landon got called, then I got called...and now we're here."

"So if Jesse hadn't said anything..."

"Well, from what I've gathered, the feds are closing in on Maddox. Have been for a while." Skylar looked thoughtful as she stared down the endless road ahead. She looked almost relaxed, but Sienna started to wonder if Skylar had any intention of letting them leave her car alive. "Apparently they were so confident that they'd catch Landon that Bridget was gonna pull you two at the beginning of August. She changed her mind when Landon sent them a little message."

Skylar grabbed her phone from the center console of her car, occasionally looking down as she typed. Once she'd pulled up what she wanted, she handed the cell over to Sienna. "Landon couldn't give away that he knew you two were here, but he wanted to make sure you two didn't wanna leave."

A sob ripped from Sienna's throat as she read the article about Mason Cardoza, who had been fished from the river and beaten within an inch of his life. A slash across his neck, just enough to leave a scar, was the calling card of Landon Maddox. "Is he alive?" Sienna finally whispered, looking up at Skylar for confirmation. "Did he survive?"

"I don't know," she muttered. It was clear she didn't give a damn. "He was your boyfriend, right? Landon said something about you having an annoying boyfriend that his girl hated." Skylar looked over her shoulder at Alex and snorted, "He's a little cuckoo if you ask me. He's no Jesse, but he sure gets what he wants."

"What's that supposed to mean?"

"Means he wants you, so he'll have you, by any means necessary."

Skylar pulled off the highway onto a dirt road, causing the car to jolt as they fell off the smooth pavement. She swiped the cell phone from Sienna's hand and dropped it into the side of her door with her gun. Sienna looked out the window for any sign of where they were, so she could remember how to get out if they found a way to escape. Everything looked the same though. Tall, dry grass that stretched for miles and miles under clear blue sky.

"Where are you taking us?" Sienna asked sharply. "What's gonna happen now?"

"To you? No clue. But Landon's been dying to see your sister again. I'm sure he can't wait to steal her away."

Sienna's cheeks paled as she tried not to dwell on what Skylar was telling her. If she was lucky, Landon would leave her for dead. If she wasn't... thinking about it wasn't going to stop it from happening, so Sienna took a deep breath through pursed lips and let it out through her nose. She didn't want to draw attention, but it was becoming harder to keep her breath steady.

They slowed to a stop in front of an old, abandoned barn. Sienna stiffened when Skylar pushed open her door, grabbing her gun as Alex scrambled to get out. She'd locked them in and pointed the gun casually in Sienna's direction as she said, "From what I've gathered, you'll have a better time with Landon than you ever did in Lonewood. Just... don't piss him off. He's had a trying week."

The moment her door slammed closed, Sienna had unbuckled her seatbelt and was kneeling on her seat to look back at Alex. "Are you okay?"

"No! He's taking us! He's kidnapping us! I don't know what he wants..." Big tears rolled down Alex's cheeks as her chest heaved. "Do you think he's gonna kill us?"

"I don't know. It sounds like you should be safe, but seeing as Skylar's been working for Landon the whole time I don't know how much I trust her. We have to stay calm, Alex. Bridget knows we're missing."

Alex shook her head, dismissing the idea of being saved. "She doesn't know where we are. I don't know where we are. Skylar's too smart to be tracked-"

"Or they're confident we won't be around long enough for it to matter," Sienna grumbled as she sat back down. She watched as Skylar shoved open the barn door, and standing inside was a tall man with jet black hair. When his sharp gaze found Sienna, his smile grew, making him look even more menacing than he already did. She swallowed, trying to ease the dry, nervous lump in her throat. "Is that Landon?"

From her peripheral she could see Alex nodding slowly, but neither of them dared to look away. "Yeah. That's him."

"Whatever happens, I love you."

Alex reached forward and clenched Sienna's hand, her voice cracking as she answered, "I love you, too."

Landon swept over to them, opening up the backseat to let Alex out first. She cowered away from him, but to Sienna's surprise, he reached out his hand to help her. "Alexandra," he purred, "it's been a long time."

She nodded as she placed her hand in his, reluctantly accepting his help. At least at the moment he didn't seem too keen on killing them, so maybe if they stayed quiet and followed directions they'd make it out in one piece.

The man pulled Alex's arm through his once she was out of the car and held her hand against his bicep as he led her into the barn. She looked over her shoulder at Sienna, throat bobbing as she swallowed hard. It was almost harder to watch Landon treat Alex like his girlfriend than it would have been to watch him toss her around and threaten her life. This felt more sinister, more calculated, and Sienna realized that she and Alex hadn't been hiding from Landon, but rather kept somewhere he couldn't lose track of them. This had all been so he could have Alex when he was ready for her, and Sienna felt her stomach drop at what that meant for her.

Whether or not Sienna lived wasn't a concern for Landon Maddox. The only thing that could save her was Alex, and if Alex didn't play Landon's game, Sienna was a dead woman.

Suddenly the car door was ripped open and Skylar grabbed Sienna's arm, roughly tugging her to her feet and handcuffing Sienna's hands behind her back. "Still not sure what he's gonna wanna do with you." Sienna squirmed as she was led into the building, wanting to run and hide, but the gun attached to Skylar's hip told her to be smarter than that.

Once inside the dark, damp barn, Sienna was shoved into an old chair by Skylar. She looked over her shoulder to see two large, bearded men appear to cuff her hands to the metal frame, forcing her to stay in her seat. "Go to hell!" Sienna snarled, but Skylar chuckled as she untied the blue plaid bandana she'd been wearing around her neck. She rolled it up and pushed it into Sienna's mouth, tying it behind her head tightly to work as a gag.

Sienna glared up at her with fiery eyes, trying to swear through the fabric, but it cut off her words. Skylar sighed, "I so prefer you with your mouth shut. Listening to you and Gentry go at it day after day after day was tortuous. A couple of stubborn idiots. Maybe if you're good, I'll drop you back in Lonewood so Gentry can bury you next to Kenzie. It'll make grieving so much more convenient for him."

The dark-haired woman turned to Alex, who watched Skylar manhandle her sister with a terrified expression. Landon's hand rested lazily on her hip, as if Alex was his girlfriend and they were out somewhere together. As he ordered his men to prepare to leave, his fingers kneaded Alex's side and he looked down at her and chuckled, "I'm glad they fed you well. I was a little worried you wouldn't survive up here with all these hicks."

"So what's gonna happen to us now?" Alex asked meekly, and Landon smoothed a loose curl away from her cheek. She was ghostly pale, and Sienna felt her eyes well up at the thought of her sister laying lifeless in this dirty barn. Maybe he'd brought them here to kill them and leave them. If that were the case, Sienna hoped they'd do it quickly, and she hoped they'd kill her first. After everything she'd gone through, the least they could do would be to spare her from seeing her little sister murdered.

Landon pulled Alex a little closer, but she put her hands up defensively against his chest to keep the distance between them. He looked at her curiously, then grabbed her hands and pulled them down between them. "I don't think you understand the gravity of the situation, Love. When I encounter a pest, I crush them. Anybody else, I woulda killed them that night in the alley. But I like you Alexandra. I liked our night together and I'd like to have a few more. Maybe you can't look past what you saw that night, but with the right leverage, maybe you could try."

He nodded towards Sienna. She swallowed. Of course. She was the leverage.

As if to prove his point, Landon stalked away from Alex, pulling a knife out of his pocket. Sienna eyed it warily as he approached, seeing the blade sharp, but there was the slightest bit of red stained on it. Landon placed the knife against Sienna's skin, but didn't press. She held her breath, afraid any movement in her throat would cause him to slit it while he waited for Alex to say something. After a moment, he pulled the knife away and asked, "Do you understand how generous I'm being, Alexandra? I've kept your sister and parents alive. Your friends back home. The only person I laid a hand on was the pest *you* wanted to be rid of, and I didn't even kill him. I left him alive just to show you that I do care about you and your feelings."

"I almost wish you didn't." Alex snapped, then grabbed her mouth with both hands and let out a strained sob. While Skylar rolled her eyes at the woman's dramatics, Landon rushed to her and enveloped her in his arms like he was the one who always comforted her. Alex didn't return the sentiment, but she didn't push him away either. She was frozen in fear and confusion and dread. Finally, when he pulled away, she got out, "If I do what you want, you can't hurt her. You have to promise me."

"Alex, no!" Sienna's muffled voice yelled through the bandana, but Landon stroked Alex's cheek with more off-putting affection. Skylar said that Landon Maddox was insane, and Sienna could see it now. He'd made Alex the object of his obsession, and now he had her like putty in his hand.

"You come with me, wherever I go, for as long as I want you, and I won't touch a hair on your sister's head." Landon looked over at Skylar, and the woman shifted uncomfortably, as if realizing for the first time that she'd handed them over to a murderer. Landon chuckled to himself and wandered back over to Sienna, stroking her head while he studied her, sizing her up. His eyes lingered on her breasts beneath her t-shirt, nodding to himself before calling over his shoulder at Alex, "She can live with my employees. You can see her sometimes if you want. She'll be safe there."

Sienna's eyes widened when one of the burly men behind her chuckled deeply. Alex caught it too and looked up at Landon with her mouth open, like she wanted to say something but he cut her off. "I can't promise that we'll last forever, but I can promise you won't live to see tomorrow if you don't trust me now. You'll leave this barn with me or in a hundred pieces. I would much prefer the former, but I know you're a feisty one. That's why I couldn't stop thinking about you after that night at the bar. If you hadn't followed me... if you hadn't seen what I did, we could have had such a good life together. We still can. The choice is yours, Alexandra."

In a show of vulnerability that cracked Sienna's heart, Alex confessed quietly, "I'm scared."

"I know. I only ever wanted to make you smile, though. I want you to smile at me like you did the night we met... the way you smiled at that man you danced with over the summer. I want to make you that happy."

He'd been watching them. Watching the videos that were posted as the business in Lonewood continued to boom. Sienna did that. Sienna caused the people to flood the saloon and film her sister night after night and Landon sat somewhere alone imagining what it would be like when he had her again.

"We should get moving. Their contact knows they're missing and will probably call in reinforcements. Seeing as we've both burned our inside sources we better play it safe," Skylar told Landon sternly, but he just waved her off.

"We'll be gone within the hour, Miss Hyde. Once our plane lands and is refueled, I'll be taking Alexandra and you'll be taking your money. Not a moment before."

Neither of them mentioned who'd be taking Sienna.

Skylar huffed as two more men came through the door, each holding massive rifles. They pushed the sliding barn door closed until there was just enough room for a person to slip in and out.

Deep in her heart, Sienna hoped Gentry would come to save her. Too stubborn to let somebody more equipped handle it, and too brash to think better of it, Sienna could imagine him bursting in here with guns ablaze to save his girl. At least he would have done that yesterday.

Today, Sienna assumed the only person who might try to save them would be Bridget. Even if Bridget managed to find them in the middle of nowhere, she would be seriously outgunned, and would most likely lose her life in a futile effort to protect the sisters she'd inadvertently put in danger. Sienna couldn't be mad at Bridget for trusting one of her friends. She just didn't realize that Landon Maddox was always three steps ahead.

Chapter 48

"Why don't we go somewhere we can talk in private. I'd like to make some plans with you that they don't need to be privy to." Landon's gaze slid to Skylar and Sienna, then he snapped his fingers and the man who'd shot Jesse appeared with a duffle bag. Alex flinched when he got close to her, but Landon just took the bag and rubbed her forearm with his other hand. "I got you some things. I want you to go through everything and if you need something else we'll have it ready when we land."

Alex looked back at Sienna as Landon led her towards the far corner of the barn. Sienna's eyes were red from crying, and her jaw quivered as she breathed heavily through the gag. Alex was scared that they'd kill her as soon as she was out of the room, but if she was difficult, they wouldn't even wait that long. So she allowed Landon to lead her into an old storage room and close the door, giving them privacy to talk.

He unzipped the duffle bag and sat it on a dusty table. Alex noted there were horseshoes and hammers strewn about the tack room, but even though there were plenty of weapons to attempt to subdue Landon, she didn't actually believe she could if she tried. The man in front of her killed effortlessly, yet he was currently sitting on a little stool waiting for her to go through her clothes. It felt unnervingly domestic, like he'd bought her presents and couldn't wait to see if he'd impressed her.

Alex didn't look away as she approached the bag. Finally, she peered down at it for a brief moment, then looked back at Landon to find him watching her patiently. He gestured for her to look and she peeled the lips of the bag apart, finding dozens of expensive dresses packed neatly on top of one another.

She pulled out the first one and held it up to her chest, letting the long purple fabric fall to the ground and pool around her ankles. The thin straps had gold colored rings around them, giving them a Grecian look, and upon further inspection Alex realized the gold was real. Her eyes dropped back into the bag as she carefully set the dress aside, trying not to get it filthy. She picked up a black box and opened it, finding a thick gold chain with a giant amethyst pendant, along with a golden ring with a deep purple stone. A set to match the dress.

"Everything in there is of the highest quality. I loved the purple on you in the saloon show, and I thought you'd look stunning in that- walking along the beach in Mykonos. I thought we'd start there, then work our way through Spain and Italy in the fall. Christmas in Paris." Landon smiled softly, tilting his head as he watched Alex run her thumb over the purple stone. "We can run anywhere you want, Alexandra. Just because we're hiding doesn't mean we can't do everything you've ever dreamed of."

Alex looked back in the bag, finding a very skimpy bikini in bright yellow. She met Landon's eyes once more and he chuckled darkly. "I saw the dress you wore that night at the bar. You aren't afraid to show off your body, and I love that about you. I want to worship you, Alexandra. I'll treat you like a queen. Just say yes."

"If I say yes, what happens to Sienna?"

"I told you, my men will take good care of her-"

"Yeah, I've gathered that," Alex spat, "but I don't think she'd appreciate it. Let her go back to Lonewood. Let her have her life back and I'll come with you."

He laughed brightly, like she'd told him a funny joke. "Alexandra." He purred her name like it was his favorite word, but it made Alex sick. "I think Scarlett could use a lesson in humility, don't you? She hasn't been a very good big sister."

Alex reddened, remembering her complaints that night at the bar. "She's different now," Alex whispered. "We're both different. I want you to let her go, or else I won't go with you."

Landon sighed, stretching his right arm behind his neck as he stared up at the rafters. "You don't get to make demands, Love. Now put on something pretty, or I'll start chopping off your sister's fingers." He motioned towards the duffle. "The boys are gonna want her hands intact so I suggest you hurry."

Alex threw the purple dress into the duffle with a huff, then shuffled through it and pulled out a short black dress with long sleeves and a plunging neckline. She glared at Landon but he smirked at her expectantly. "I've waited a long time to see you naked."

"This isn't going to look great with my sports bra."

"You'll find undergarments in the bag as well." Landon leaned towards her and unzipped a side pouch, pulling out a sheer lacy bra and thong. Alex's skin paled when she saw what draped from Landon's finger, feeling her heart sink at the realization that she'd been reduced to Landon's dress-up doll. She pulled off her t-shirt and discarded it, then pushed down her yoga pants, keeping eye contact with Landon just so his dark eyes would stay off her body.

The corner of his mouth turned up into a smile as he got comfortable against the work table. His eyes finally broke away from Alex's when she stripped out of her underwear and sports bra, and she felt tears prick at her emerald eyes.

"Dry your eyes, Love. If you don't get dressed soon, I'll have to take you to the jet naked."

She quickly pulled the thong between her legs, letting out a little snarl when Landon's eyes dipped between her thighs. She quickly clasped the bra before roughly grabbing the black dress and pulling it over her head before tugging it down over her muscular thighs.

"Happy now?"

"Very," Landon told her as he stood and pulled her close with one hand while zipping up the duffel bag with the other. "You look stunning. Once we're on the jet we can go through more of your things. We'll be dropping off some of the baggage before we head abroad."

Sienna.

Alex watched as Landon pushed open the door to the main barn. She slowly emerged, feeling her breath hitch when she met Skylar's alarmed gaze and Sienna's horrified one.

Sienna looked broken, like they'd already drained the last bit of hope inside of her. Alex wished she could blame Landon or Skylar or the brutes who circled Sienna like she was their dinner, but she was the one to blame. Alex was the one who'd cost Sienna the life and man she loved. At least Alex would be treated to a life of luxury as payment for being Landon's pet, but Alex knew Sienna would be beaten and raped until she wished she was dead. From the look in her eyes, Alex wondered if she already wished she was.

Landon's men all eyed Alex curiously, but nobody spoke or made an effort to get close to her. When Landon reached Sienna, he grabbed her chin roughly and forced her to face Alex as she squirmed against the handcuffs holding her tight. "She's beautiful, isn't she?" Sienna's green eyes drifted up to glare darkly at Landon, but he ignored her, as if she was nothing more than something for him to lean on. "My God, I can't wait to get my hands on her."

Landon finally dropped his gaze to Sienna, seeing the fire in her eyes starting to flicker out. "You're a pretty little thing, too, but I've heard you're difficult. Skylar said you were difficult. And don't get me started on what Alexandra told me."

"Landon," Alex warned and he smiled sweetly at her, then put his hands up in front of his chest, as if to say he was sorry.

When he turned back to Sienna though, Alex saw his stance change. She realized that Landon had taken her complaints about her older sister to heart, and wanted to teach Sienna a lesson. When he met Alex, she was broken down and feeling inadequate while Scarlett soared through life with ease. Now, Landon Maddox was determined to prove that his girl was the most important woman in the room, even if it meant shattering her own sister.

"Next time I see you, I expect to see a little more submission," Landon told Sienna, his voice deep and threatening. Alex watched Sienna's confidence waver, but she didn't move as Landon leaned closer to whisper loud enough for the whole room to hear. "By the time the boys are done with you, I think you'll do anything I say."

Sienna's whole body shook as she whimpered, a sound that made Alex clamp her eyes closed. She couldn't watch this. She didn't want to be a part of this. It wasn't until Skylar's voice broke through the silence that she forced herself to come back to reality.

"Do you hear that?" Skylar asked, causing Landon to pull away from Sienna to look towards the doors. "Sounds like we've got company."

Chapter 49

"Get her up. Get ready to move out," Landon gestured to Sienna for one of his men to untie her from the chair. As soon as he was done, Alex darted away from Landon to kneel beside Sienna, keeping her eyes locked on Landon as he stalked towards the door to see who'd arrived.

Alex pulled down the gag and Sienna gasped for breath. "Thanks," she mumbled, glaring over at Skylar as she conversed with Landon. Sienna lowered her voice and asked, "Are you okay?"

"Yeah. He didn't touch me. It won't last though..." Alex and Sienna shared a look and Alex muttered, "I'm a lot more worried about you."

"That makes two of us," Sienna grumbled. If Alex had been forced into an expensive dress, Sienna would be lucky to stay in her undergarments. One of the bearded men watched her hungrily. She could hardly believe she'd somehow made it here from the safety of Gentry's bed just a few hours ago. "If you get a chance to run, you take it."

"I'm not leaving you."

"Listen, I'm as good as dead," Sienna whispered. She sighed and shrugged her shoulders, her hands still cuffed behind her back as she tried to give her little sister a brave smile. "I love you so much. You're in a better position than me, don't squander it if the opportunity arises-"

With a firm shake of her head, Alex cut Sienna off. "No. We're getting out of this together, or not at all."

Sienna swallowed hard, watching as Skylar listened intently to whatever Landon told her near the barn door. "Well, if I had to place bets, I'm guessing we aren't making it out at all. Somebody's here. Don't know if it's more of Landon's guys or someone trying to save us, but if they can't take us alive, they sure as hell aren't going to *leave* us alive."

"What do we do?"

"Wait," Sienna said. "We're gonna wait and see what happens. That's all we can do at the moment."

Skylar walked quickly back to the women and hoisted Sienna from her chair. "C'mon. It's time to go." Skylar led Sienna towards the door as Landon latched onto Alex's hand.

"Where are we going?"

"Don't worry about it, Love, our ride's almost here."

"You made a big mistake, Miss Hyde!" Everyone turned to see Hank standing across the barn with his fingers dancing over the gun in his holster. All of Landon's men pulled their guns on the man, but Skylar just threw her hand up to tell them not to shoot. Hank's gravelly, bellowing voice echoed through the barn. "Lonewood is supposed to protect their own."

Skylar rolled her eyes and dropped Sienna's hands so she could pull her own gun on Hank, not willing to let anyone *else* shoot him. "Thank God Dusty moved home so he can bury you. You've been eyeing that plot next to your wife for a while now, haven't ya?"

Sienna's stomach dropped at the threat. She'd never realized Hank was a widower. She watched Skylar take a cautious step forward and yell, "I don't believe for a second you're here alone! Where is he?"

Gentry.

"We told you, Skylar." Bill emerged from behind the wall with his gun already drawn. "We protect our own."

With a groan, Skylar aimed her gun and mumbled, "I'm really gonna enjoy this."

She shot Hank in the shoulder when he started for his gun, causing him to tumble back onto his ass as Bill began shooting at her wildly. Sienna was shoved roughly to the ground behind an old tractor's wheel while Alex was shoved behind Landon when his four men began shooting at Bill.

Unlike his brother, who was now groaning on the ground with his hand to his shoulder, Bill stayed hidden and only appeared to make a few badly aimed shots in their direction. Hank used his good arm to crawl slowly behind the cover of the barn wall, which was chipping away by the minute from all the gunfire coming from Landon and his guys.

Alex grabbed onto Sienna's shoulders as they watched Bill duck behind the wall for a long moment, presumably out of ammo. Landon motioned with his hand for his men to move towards the brothers, and Sienna clenched her jaw nervously as she waited for Bill and Hank to be murdered just out of sight.

Suddenly though, the sound of a gun discharging came from the other end of the barn, opposite where Bill and Hank were hiding. Three of the goons turned towards the new source of gunfire as they quickly retreated back to Landon and Skylar, while the fourth kept his gun trained towards Bill and Hank. Sienna leaned far around the large tractor wheel to see Beau appear from behind the wall to shoot towards them. At his knees knelt Lyle with a hunting rifle. The stableman aimed the weapon easily, clearly more comfortable with shooting than Sienna had ever given the man credit for.

"It's an ambush!" Skylar yelled, leaning against the tractor to refill her gun from her ammo belt. Her dark eyes darted towards the door, narrowing when she realized it appeared to be just the four men across the barn. She glared down at Alex and Sienna, then sneered, "Seems like the real sharpshooter didn't care enough to come. Lucky us."

Alex rubbed Sienna's back as she scowled at Skylar, but the comment stung almost as much as the reality of it. Gentry hadn't come to save her. At least somebody else had, but Beau, Lyle, and the Cassidy brothers wouldn't be a match for a team of trained mercenaries.

A loud yelp from across the barn meant somebody else had been shot, but Sienna couldn't see who it was. Bill, Lyle, and Beau were still shooting at them wildly, but even though Hank had taken a hit, none of Landon's men seemed to.

Skylar furrowed her brows and held up her hands, stepping around the tractor as she yelled. "Hold your fire!" When Landon's men ignored her, she looked over at him and he repeated her order. "You heard her, stop shooting!"

Landon and his men fell silent, but a few stray shots fired from the other side. Bill's eyes widened as he ducked around the wall again, and Beau carefully pulled Lyle's shoulder back so they'd both be out of view. Skylar laughed, "They're shooting blanks! They don't have real guns!"

A gunshot echoed through the silent barn and the burly man who had laughed at the idea of bedding Sienna fell dead to their right. Alex shrieked and ducked behind Sienna, seeing blood begin to drip from the man's shirt onto the dirt-covered floor. From the shadows, Maude appeared, cocking her shotgun to fire again.

"Maude!" Alex yelped happily, but Sienna shushed her as Landon grabbed Alex's shoulder to tug her away from view. Sienna leaned around the tire to try to see Maude, but Landon grabbed her hair at the nape of her neck and ripped her back, causing Sienna to cry out as she was slammed against the wall beside Alex.

Alex threw her arms around Sienna protectively, watching Landon in horror as he turned to face Maude. The old woman smiled broadly though as Landon's three remaining men and Skylar all drew their guns on her. "Nobody messes with my girls."

"You're gonna die, Maude. Reconsider what you're doing," Skylar warned, and Sienna heard a hint of worry in her voice. She slowly backed up, preparing to join the line again once the firefight started back up. "You can't stop us by yourself. We're gonna leave either way, the only question is whether or not you survive."

Hushed voices came from the corner where Lyle and Beau hid, and finally Lyle leaned forward with his hunting gun aimed at one of Landon's men. "Well if I'da known we'd all been deputized, this woulda been over already."

Landon yelled for them all to take cover as Lyle took aim. He took down the man who'd shot Jesse, then pulled back as the gunfire erupted again. Maude slipped back behind the wall with Bill, occasionally leaning out to make a well-timed shot.

Seeing the firefight going south, Landon grabbed Skylar and whipped her around to face him, drawing Sienna's attention away from their rescuers. "Take the sister. I'll take Alexandra. They'll finish this while we slip away."

Alex's eyes widened and she started to run, but Landon grabbed her easily, flinging her over his shoulder and carrying her towards the slightly open door as she screamed. Skylar yanked Sienna to her feet to follow, and the only reason Sienna didn't drag her heels was because she didn't trust Lyle or Maude not to shoot her by accident.

Sienna spared a look over her shoulder, meeting Beau's gaze with her panicked eyes. Just before she was pushed through the sliver of opening between the wall and the door, she saw him hold up what looked like a two-way radio.

Once outside, the late afternoon sun was blinding, disorienting Sienna after being trapped in the barn. She didn't know how long they'd been there, or how their friends found them, but the sun felt like a prison sentence. Inside the barn, Sienna and Alex had a chance of being rescued, but out in the open air, it was clear they were about to disappear forever.

After dropping Alex back to her feet, Landon pushed the door closed and locked it with a rotting wooden beam, effectively trapping his men inside. If Maude and Lyle were the only two with real weapons, there was still a chance they could be overpowered. And if by some miracle they managed to win, Sienna and Alex would be long gone anyway.

"Gimme your keys, we'll take your car," Landon ordered Skylar, but when he turned around to leave, they became aware of a gun cocking at the back of his head.

"Let them go."

Sienna turned to see Gentry standing at the corner of the building with the barrel of his gun pressed against Landon's head. His arms were shaking, but his gaze was unbreakable as he waited for Landon to surrender. His eyes bore into the other man, but his attention shifted swiftly when Skylar pushed Alex towards Landon and raised her gun to Sienna's temple. Gentry kept his aim on Landon, but he took one nervous step back as his deputy threatened Sienna, allowing Landon to get his hands on Alex again.

"Alright Maddox, here's how this is gonna work," Skylar started darkly, taking a few steps towards the car so she was between Gentry and their escape plan. "You're gonna take your girl and run, and I'll deal with him."

She smirked at Gentry, then called to Alex without looking as she squirmed in Landon's tight grip, "Everything your sister wants is standing right in front of her, Alex! You could give back the life you stole from her if you let Landon take you. She can be swept back to Lonewood in her sheriff's arms. Sure, you'll never see her again, but you'll know she's happy. It's much better than the alternative, isn't it?" Gentry swallowed as Skylar pressed the barrel of her gun harder against Sienna's skull, causing her to whimper. "Tell him to drop the gun, Alex. Because if Gentry shoots Landon, I'll shoot your sister."

"If you shoot her, I'll kill you," Gentry threatened, and Sienna's stomach churned. She believed his threat, but it wouldn't matter for them. Landon wouldn't kill Alex, but between Skylar and Landon, somebody was going to gun down the sheriff. If Landon got a chance to pull his gun, Gentry was as good as dead.

Skylar shook her head, negating his warning. "If you want her to live, you'll drop the gun. You let Landon and I go, I'll let you have Sienna. It's simple really. You can save yourself and get the girl, or you can seal your own death along with hers. Make your choice, *Sheriff Gentry*."

Her mocking tone sent shivers through Sienna, and she gasped when Skylar twisted the cold barrel against her skin. From the corner of her eye, she could see Skylar's finger resting casually on the trigger. Even if Gentry killed Skylar instead, Landon would shoot him in the back and disappear with Alex. There was no scenario where they all got out of this alive unless Gentry let Landon walk away.

"You are quite the negotiator, Miss Hyde." Landon chuckled darkly as he guided Alex past Skylar towards the car. Gentry kept his gun trained on Landon but his eyes kept darting back to Sienna, as if to make sure Skylar hadn't made any moves to shoot her unprovoked.

The sound of a branch snapping caught Landon's attention and he whipped around to the other side of the barn to see Bridget creeping towards them with her gun drawn.

In half a second, he'd pulled his gun and shot Bridget in the thigh, causing her to cry out as she fell. The muscles in Gentry's forearms tightened as he prepared to shoot Landon, but Skylar discharged her gun inches from Sienna's head, causing Gentry to turn towards them in horror.

Instinctively, he lunged towards Skylar before he realized she hadn't killed Sienna, but it was enough of a distraction for Landon to shuffle over to Bridget to make sure the woman was incapacitated.

He dragged Alex the few steps over to the freckled woman, kicking her gun out of her hand as she writhed in pain. "Nice to meet you Marshal Masterson. I'd finish you off myself, but I have a plane to catch."

Bridget's bleary eyes drifted up to him as he took a few steps away from her towards Skylar's car. Skylar used the hand not holding her gun to fish out her keys, letting go of Sienna for a moment, but she was too scared to run. She held Gentry's gaze, watching his chest rise and fall roughly as he studied her to make sure she was okay. With his weapon low, he couldn't raise it without being shot by either Landon or Skylar, and he couldn't risk the latter actually putting a bullet in Sienna's brain.

This morning, everything had been so simple. They'd woken up in each other's arms with the promise of forever. Sienna had realized she loved him, but she hadn't gotten the chance to tell him that. Now she didn't think she ever would, but if the desperate look in his brown eyes said anything, she thought he loved her too.

Skylar tossed her keys to Landon as he took another step away, but Gentry didn't move after him. Landon aimed his gun at Gentry, seeing the small-town sheriff as the only potential threat between him and his escape. "You've kept up your end of the bargain, Skylar. I'll transfer what you're owed if you survive." He shoved Alex into the passenger's seat before turning back to casually gesture his gun at Sienna. "Take care of her, will ya?"

He taunted Gentry by slowly walking around the car, never breaking eye contact. He'd slung his gun back into his belt loop, not seeing Gentry as much of a threat if Skylar still had Sienna at gunpoint. Landon started Skylar's car, and Sienna could see him laughing as he put it into reverse. It was too easy for him, and he almost seemed disappointed that Lonewood hadn't put up more of a fight.

"Stop him!" Sienna cried as Landon slammed the gas pedal of Skylar's car, causing them to skid into reverse. Gentry's back stiffened as Sienna yelled out again, "Gentry!" He finally spared a look at Sienna, seeing the tears streaming down her cheeks. Even if Skylar made good on her promise, and allowed her to go home safe and sound with Gentry, Sienna would never forgive herself for letting Alex be taken away just to keep her alive. She'd given up so much to protect Alex. She couldn't lose her now.

"Please save her!"

Sienna didn't expect him to honor her wishes, but after shifting uncomfortably for a few moments, Gentry bolted back around the side of the building where he'd come from. Skylar let out a heavy sigh as she grabbed a hold of Sienna and shoved her roughly against the side of the barn.

Her whole body ached. Between being thrown from Cheyanne and getting dragged around by Landon and Skylar, Sienna wanted to collapse. She'd been stiff for hours, waiting for the inevitable pain and darkness that followed. Dread froze her frame as she closed her eyes lightly, willing Skylar to let her go to save her own skin.

She rested her gun lazily against Sienna's collarbone and laughed a little. "Well, I did not expect that" She looked around for some other escape plan, seeing as she'd offered up the ride they were going to share with Landon. She paused thoughtfully when Gentry still didn't appear, then told Sienna, "He'll never catch her though. Not on Domino-"

The sound of sirens cut off Skylar's train of thought and she looked truly surprised as she whipped around to see a police car come flying around the side of the barn. She dropped her gun to her side as she shoved back her ebony hair, her whole body slumping a bit as she realized that Gentry might actually catch Landon. He might save Alex, and if he arrested Landon, she'd never see her money.

Without the money, Sienna knew Skylar would be running from the law with a target on her back. Anger blazed in her eyes as her dark gaze landed on Bridget. She stormed over to her old friend, dragging Sienna along beside her like a child's rag doll.

She shoved Sienna towards Bridget, and she tripped on the woman's calf, causing her to fall hard into the dirt on her side. Since her hands were bound, Sienna struggled to turn over, looking up to see Skylar's gun pointing down at her. "At least I'll have the satisfaction of knowing he won't have *you* to come back to. And that's assuming Landon doesn't finish him off first."

Bridget tried to reach for her gun, but Skylar kicked her in the side, causing Bridget to gasp for air. "Give me your keys," Skylar ordered, but Bridget just glowered up at her defiantly. She was too weak to put up a real fight, but she wouldn't give Skylar the satisfaction of knowing she'd given up.

Sienna watched in horror as Skylar sighed and leaned down to murmur in Bridget's ear, "I'm sorry it has to be this way. For what it's worth, I always did consider you my best friend."

As she stood again, Skylar blocked out the sun and Sienna clamped her eyes closed, saying a final prayer that Gentry saved Alex, and that they'd both know how much she loved them. She flinched when the shot fired, but there was a heavy thud against her leg and she opened her eyes to see Skylar's dark orbs staring at her lifelessly as blood leaked from her head.

Sienna jolted and looked up behind the dead woman, seeing the smoking gun in Dakota's hand. She staggered a little as she panted, "Nobody threatens my family."

She looked at Sienna with tears in her eyes and fell to her knees to fish the key to the cuffs out of Skylar's pocket. Her hands were shaking as she unclasped the handcuffs, then grasped Sienna in a desperate hug that the redhead returned thankfully.

"I'm so sorry!" Sienna sobbed into Dakota's shoulder.

"No, I'm sorry. I'm so sorry," Dakota hushed her, holding the back of her head tightly as she studied Sienna to make sure she wasn't hurt. "I shouldn't have sent you away- I made a mistake."

"I didn't mean to lie, I didn't have a choice."

"Guys, I've been shot." Sienna and Dakota looked down at Bridget as she grimaced, pushing down on her bleeding leg in a futile effort to stop the bleeding. Sienna grabbed her hand as Dakota stood and sprinted around the building, calling out for anybody who could help.

Bridget let out a hiss as Sienna pressed down on her leg, then groaned, "I'm sorry I entrusted you to a traitor. I didn't know."

Sienna let out a humorless laugh. "None of us did. Thanks for coming to save us."

"Well, you're half saved," she grunted as she attempted to sit up a little despite the bullet lodged in her muscular thigh. "You know, Skylar might not have been who I thought she was, but these people are the real deal. They really care about you guys."

"How did you even find us?"

"I put trackers in your suitcases," Bridget said, her voice breathy and laced in pain. "To be completely honest, I knew you two were a flight risk when I met you. You especially. I expected you to run for the hills within a couple weeks, so I wanted to track your whereabouts if you decided to disappear."

Sienna was about to respond when Dakota came running back leading Lyle and Beau as they helped a limping Brad stumble over to Bridget. Sienna balked when she saw him, unable to keep the surprise out of her voice, "Brad?"

"Came to save you. It's fine, so did Gentry, and we all know he's your favorite." Brad muttered. He looked down at Bridget and sighed. "I guess I can't complain about being grazed in the leg."

"At least the bullet isn't lodged inside you," She grunted and Lyle carefully knelt to help Brad down so he could take a closer look. Brad looked her up and down, smiling sweetly as he gently traced his thumb over the torn skin of her bloody leg. Bridget looked up as Hank ambled out with his good arm over Bill's shoulder, followed by Maude carrying her shotgun and Lyle's rifle. "How bad is it in there?"

"Worse than out here," Lyle mumbled, looking over his shoulder as the sound of sirens approached. His eyes widened a little and he questioned Bridget, "To clarify, we killed those people in self defense, right?"

Bridget shot Brad a dirty look when he put more pressure on the bullet wound, then asked Lyle, "Were you being shot at?"

"Yes."

"Then, yes, it was self defense." Her eyes drifted to Skylar, then up to Dakota, who shook like she was freezing. Sienna stood and wrapped her arm around the woman, but she stilled when Bridget added, "That's what happened out here. If I didn't shoot her, she would have killed both of us."

Dakota gave a little nod to thank Bridget as a swarm of cop cars arrived. Sienna hugged Dakota as they watched Hank come over and spit on Skylar. "Hank!"

"She shot me," was all he said before ambling away towards a pickup truck parked a little ways away. The injury to his arm was clearly not severe, because he seemed more grumbly about it than in actual pain.

Sienna smiled to herself as she realized how they'd all gotten here in the old pickup truck, but then she turned to Dakota in surprise. "Gentry drove here?"

Dakota nodded. "He was so scared he wasn't gonna make it in time." Sienna's lip began to quiver as several medics approached Brad and Bridget, while a couple of officers were asking Lyle, Beau, and Maude some questions about what happened inside. "Sienna." She looked up at Dakota to find her crying. "I'm really glad you're okay. I was so afraid you were gonna die because I didn't protect you... Gentry is gonna find her, okay? And if he doesn't find her today, he's never gonna stop looking for Alex, because he'd do anything for you. We both would."

The women crashed against each other in a desperate hug until a man cleared his throat. Sienna pulled away and recognized Detective Shields looking down at her. His smile was grim as he greeted, "Miss Jacobs."

"It's Miss Jade now," she told him quietly, not oblivious to the way Dakota perked up in surprise to hear her old name. Sienna felt her stomach drop as she told the man, "Landon took my sister."

The detective leaned around Sienna to see Bridget being helped to her feet. "You okay there, Marshal?"

"Never better," Bridget called weakly. She looked between Detective Shields and Sienna and Dakota. "Local law enforcement is going after Maddox. I gave him permission to stop him by any means necessary."

The man nodded, pursing his lips a little as he looked down the road. "Seems like this was quite a mess."

"Quite a mess is an understatement... but- we're hoping we can salvage it. Maybe we can get Alex back and get Maddox in handcuffs." Bridget looked at Dakota and Sienna and smiled weakly. "You think he can catch him?"

Dakota gave a slow nod. "If Gentry can't, nobody can."

Chapter 50

Between the dust from the gravel and the tears stinging her eyes, Alex couldn't even see that they'd finally made it onto the highway. When she felt the smooth asphalt under the tires, she looked over at Landon and begged, "Please don't kill her. Please, *please* don't let them kill my sister."

"Baby," he murmured, grabbing her hand, but she ripped it away violently. "I told her to take care of Scarlett."

"Yeah, well you made it sound like the 'shoot and bury' kind of take care of, not the 'make sure she's fed and sheltered' kind!"

Landon grinned and Alex wanted to strangle him. "You're cute when you're angry, you know that?"

"How dare you? Why didn't you just kill me when you had the chance?"

He shrugged and leaned his neck back against the headrest that was too short for him. "I told you. I liked you. I thought we had something."

Alex let out a ragged breath and mumbled to herself, "Yeah. A spark."

Landon began to slow the car down, apparently deciding they were far enough away from the rabble to make a clean getaway. He turned on the radio and Alex rolled her eyes, looking out the window as she crossed her arms. This wasn't a fun, cute road trip. Her best friend was in the hospital. Her friends were being shot at, Bridget had been left for dead, and if Alex was being honest with herself, she didn't think Skylar was a good enough person to spare Sienna. She'd probably shot her just to hurt Gentry, then put a bullet through his heart, too.

It wasn't easy for Alex to imagine the people she cared about dying, but in a morbid sort of way, telling herself they were gone made it a little easier to accept that she was too. She was a corpse walking through whatever short life Landon would offer her with a gun to her head. Maybe he'd put her out of her misery sooner rather than later.

The sound of sirens caught Alex's attention, but Landon just glanced up in his rearview mirror, as if the cops were nothing more than a random car riding his ass on the highway. What he saw bothered him though, because he slammed on the gas, sending them flying down the highway at ninety miles per hour.

"What are you doing? You're gonna kill us!" Alex screeched as she held the roof of the car with one hand and the dashboard with the other. Landon gritted his teeth and reached into the waistband of his pants to pull out his gun. He rolled down the window and Alex looked to her left to see Gentry driving up beside them.

When Landon fired his gun, Gentry hit the brakes, falling behind them in an instant before swerving directly behind them where he could chase them without being shot by Landon. Seeing the sheriff's plan, Landon cursed as he held the gun and the wheel with the same hand, but Alex grinned, looking over her shoulder as she watched Gentry drive with one hand while holding his gun with the other.

"I am not going down like this."

Landon hit the brakes in an effort to slam into Gentry, but Gentry's reflexes were too quick and he did the same, staying behind them as their speed dropped. Alex watched as Gentry steadied the wheel with his right hand, then raised his gun with his left towards their car. Alex realized the barrel was aimed low, not towards Landon's head, but towards the tires.

She slid her seat back as far as it could go, distracting Landon as Gentry shot out both of their rear tires in quick succession, causing the bumper of the car to drop to the ground and skid off the road. They slammed into the ditch, causing the airbags to go off and knock Alex back.

As she struggled to catch her breath, Alex looked to her left to see Gentry striding towards them with his gun outstretched, ready to take Landon into custody. Still disoriented from the crash, Landon reached for his own weapon, but Gentry ripped open the door at the same moment Alex reached for the gun.

Landon slid his finger against the trigger as Alex struggled with the barrel, shrieking as he tried to aim it at her. She managed to shove the gun up, discharging it through the roof of the car. Gentry took the distraction as a chance to grab the back of Landon's head and smash it violently against the dash to knock him unconscious.

For a long moment, Gentry stood with his gun aimed at Landon, waiting for the man to stir. The sound of screeching tires told Alex they had company, but she didn't let out her breath until Gentry looked away from Landon to ask, "Are you okay?"

"You're a really great driver."

"Yeah, well, I'll mark that down as two things I'm still good at." He panted as he took a step back, allowing a team of Marshals to unstrap Landon and take him into custody. Gentry came over to the other side of the car, tripping a little on shaky legs as he got to the passenger's door. When he opened it up for Alex, she sprung out and wrapped her arms around his neck. Tears flowed openly as he held her, and he stroked her back until she heard her sister shriek.

"Alex!"

Gentry released Alex just in time for Sienna to tackle her in a desperate hug. She swayed them back and forth as they cried, then finally pulled away to gasp, "I was so scared I'd never see you again!"

"I'm so sorry. I'm so sorry for everything!" Alex sobbed as she dove in for another hug, but Sienna shushed her.

"You're okay. We're both okay." Sienna paused and Alex realized she was looking at Gentry.

She took a step back, allowing Sienna the chance to greet him. Gentry pushed back his hair and looked away, nodding towards the line of cop cars that were arriving. "I'm assuming they'll want you."

"Gentry... I'm sorry." Sienna told him earnestly as she tentatively reached out for his hand. It felt like a lifetime had passed since they'd woken up in bed together earlier that day. The sun was setting now, and Sienna didn't want the daylight to go, because she knew he was right about her needing to leave. "I should have told you."

"It's okay. I understand why you couldn't," Gentry told her softly as he wrapped her in a tight hug. She nuzzled her head against his chest, wanting to stay buried here forever where she was safe and warm. After a couple of moments, Gentry leaned down and murmured into her hair, "You said something to my sister earlier today. Something about you loving me?"

When Sienna pulled back, he was giving her that boyish grin that made her heart melt. She wanted to tease him back, but she didn't have any fight left in her after today. So Sienna decided not to play games, but to be honest- something she hadn't been for a long time. "I love you, Gentry Wyatt. I love you more than I've ever loved anyone."

His smile grew and he answered, "I knew it." She gasped a little and he tossed his head back and laughed, still holding her tightly by the waist. "I love you, too. Whoever the hell you are."

"Scarlett Jacobs," she said softly. Her body buzzed with a weird feeling of excitement and nerves, as if she couldn't decide if she was ecstatic or scared that Gentry could know who she really was.

"Scarlett." His breath hitched a little and he shook his head as he looked out at the pink streaks that were overtaking the dark blue of the sky. "It's beautiful. It suits you." She thought he looked sad as he turned his gaze towards Alex, Dakota, and Detective Shields. Dakota and Alex listened intently as the detective spoke, and he had a grave look on his face that told Sienna it wasn't a pleasant conversation. Gentry let out a heavy sigh that drew Sienna's attention back to him. He looked so melancholy she felt like she could cry. Sienna wanted, more than anything, to tell Gentry they'd be together again. But she didn't know that. Neither of them could say for sure what would happen next.

He shifted, clearing his throat as he stared down at his boots. "I'm guessing I have a long night of paperwork ahead of me. And, as much as I don't want to accept it, I'm assuming you won't be around to go home with me after."

Sienna shook her head and a tear slipped from her eye. "No. They want us to go back to the safehouse until Landon is incarcerated and his ring has been dissolved. I don't know much more than that. Our handler was shot, then hit on by Brad, so it's been a pretty traumatizing evening for her."

Gentry snorted and pulled her back into his arms, as if he thought he could keep her if he just continued to hold her. "Will I ever see you again?"

"I hope so. My life will be nothing without you now."

"That's not true. You've got her." Gentry nodded towards Alex, who watched them hold each other with watery eyes and a quivering lower lip. She looked exhausted, and Sienna imagined she did too. She wanted nothing more than to take a long, hot bath and crawl into bed with the man beside her, but she'd be lucky if she even got the first thing. Sienna knew better than to hope for more time with Gentry after everything that happened.

"Miss Jacobs, it's time to go," Detective Shields called. Gentry loosened his grip on Sienna, but she didn't loosen hers. She wanted to hold him a moment longer.

Finally Dakota appeared to say goodbye and Sienna pulled away from Gentry to allow the blonde to wrap her in a tight hug. She squeezed Sienna tightly, any resentment she'd harbored earlier long burned away. "Please reach out if you can. I hope we see you soon."

The strained sound of her voice told Sienna that Dakota didn't believe they would meet again, but Sienna wasn't ready to consider that possibility yet. When Dakota pulled away, tears slid from her amber eyes down her cheeks. She gave a little nod as her breath caught, and she looked back at Gentry as she took a step out of the way for them to say goodbye.

Sienna just stood there and stared at Gentry, not knowing what to say. She tried to study every inch of him to store away in her memory. He shoved his hands in his pockets and tilted his head to the side, smiling sadly. "Maybe if you hadn't broken your phone you coulda taken a picture."

"It woulda lasted longer," Sienna finished his snarky remark before he could, nodding a little to herself. If he was trying to be brave, he was doing a better job of it than her. "I love you so much."

"I love you, too. I'll see you again soon. I promise."

Gentry leaned down to give Sienna a long, deep kiss until Dakota cleared her throat. Sienna pulled away, mouthing goodbye as she followed Alex into a van. She watched Dakota wrap her arms around Gentry's torso as he held Sienna's gaze until the door closed and took her perfect life away.

Chapter 51

SIENNA REMEMBERED BEING LOADED into a van like this months ago, but it might as well have been a different life.

Sienna wept for days. She stared at the blank walls and saw Lonewood. She saw Alex laughing as she high-kicked at the saloon. She saw Jesse and Beau doing their shootout in front of the bank and she saw Brad watching with a bored expression from the deck of his practice. She saw Brenda's smile as she served her caramel rolls and heard Kitty's laugh tinkling from the steps of her shop.

When Sienna tried to sleep, staring at the ceiling for hours, she imagined the beautiful woodwork of Dakota's desk and Domino tied up outside the sheriff's station waiting for her to sneak him sugar cubes. She remembered Gentry's home in the Badlands, and how she had just started to imagine it could be hers. And when dawn began to break somewhere outside the hidden compound, Sienna imagined his smile. If she never saw that smile again, she'd never feel alive again, even if her heart was still beating.

After a few weeks, Bridget appeared at their door. It was the first time they'd seen her since they'd left North Dakota, but she hobbled back to work early just so she could be the one to inform Alex it was time to testify.

Sienna sat in the courtroom with her parents when Alex stood up in front of the jury and confessed that she'd seen Landon Maddox kill a man, and that he'd attempted to kill a dozen others, including herself. Sienna had offered to testify, but Bridget said it wasn't needed. There was more than enough evidence to put the man behind bars for the rest of his life, and with his influence cut off at the head, his reign of terror would fizzle out and die.

But it wasn't dead yet. Bridget requested that Sienna and Alex remain in New York so they could be closely monitored. Apparently the Marshals were still deciding if they needed to go back into hiding or not. Either way, much to Sienna's heartbreak, Bridget told them they couldn't return to North Dakota.

At Sienna's request, Bridget sent word to Gentry and Dakota that they weren't able to keep contact with anyone from their time in hiding. Bridget hoped it wouldn't be a permanent thing, but at the moment it was the only way to ensure their friends in Lonewood would be safe while they finished off Landon's criminal network. If they wrote back, Bridget didn't tell Sienna, and that made her feel worse than she already did about the situation. They'd told each other they'd be together again, but with each passing day, Sienna wasn't so sure.

By December, Alex and Sienna were settled into a small Manhattan apartment across town from their old one. The Marshals kept close tabs on them from across the hall, but the sisters gave them little reason to worry. The outside world held nothing for them now.

On the walls hung framed photos of Alex with Jesse and the other actors that Sienna found on Instagram. She also hung up printed photos she'd found online of the Badlands, and realized a couple of them were Gentry's. She hung those in her bedroom so she could think of him when she laid alone in bed. Sienna imagined Gentry's arms around her every single night.

On December 23, Alex lounged on the couch watching tv while Sienna worked from the floor at her sister's feet. They had been told to lay low, so Sienna Jade dedicated her time to freelance marketing work under a fake name. Since the Marshals were giving them another round of stipends to hide out, she didn't really need the money, but it kept her busy.

Alex was bored out of her mind though. She would dance through their open living room in the mornings, practicing jazz, ballet, and tap. Thank goodness they were on the bottom floor, because they'd get complaints from here till tomorrow if they had neighbors downstairs. And even though they weren't supposed to have contact with anyone in Lonewood, Alex did call the Dickinson hospital every day until Jesse was released. From what Sienna gathered, she never spoke to Jesse directly, but just knowing he was okay was enough to ease her tremendous guilt.

The opening notes of some old Broadway song blared from the kitchen and Alex grunted as she got up to answer it. "Hey Bridget? How's it going?"

Sienna looked up from her laptop as Alex came around to stand in front of her. Alex furrowed her brows and handed Sienna the phone. "She said she needs to talk to both of us."

"Hello?" Sienna greeted casually as she sat her laptop to the side and turned Alex's phone on speaker.

"Hey, so... I've got some bad news for you and Alex."

Sienna's heart stopped and she swallowed hard. She clenched her jaw and met Alex's worried gaze before asking, "What is it?"

There was a slight groan from Bridget, and when she spoke her voice was strained. "I've really been pushing to get you guys released from WitSec. You've done enough, but my higher ups are worried that Landon isn't really gone. We aren't sure if his influence can ever really be cut off."

"What are you saying, Bridget?"

"They want to keep you in the program for your own safety. For the time being, they want to keep you here in New York so we can monitor you both closely, but there's talk of prepping you both to move again." Bridget sucked in a sharp breath and added quietly, "I asked about returning to Lonewood, but they won't sign off on it after what happened with Skylar. You've been outed to the public there, and the agency doesn't want to risk putting you or them in danger."

Tears began to well in Sienna's eyes. She blinked them away and nodded, trying to find her bravery. When she looked back at Alex, she realized her sister was watching her with a devastated expression. Alex had long accepted that she wasn't going back, but Sienna had thought of nothing else. This news was sad for Alex, but she felt sorry for Sienna, not herself.

"We understand," Sienna murmured, trying to keep her voice even. She wanted to scream and sob and ask what it would take to go home, but her life wasn't her own anymore. Whatever happened to Sienna was now in the hands of Bridget and the US Marshals. She should be thankful they allowed her to stay in New York for a while, where they could see their parents and have some semblance of familiarity.

But it wasn't good enough.

"I'm so sorry. I know-" Bridget paused and Sienna slammed her eyes closed, silently pleading the woman not to finish whatever she wanted to say. Her pity wouldn't bring Gentry back into her life. It wouldn't bring back Dakota and Jesse and all their friends. Bridget's pity couldn't bring the North Dakota sunsets to the shores of Manhattan, and they couldn't patch her broken heart.

"Can you do something for me, though?" Sienna croaked, and Alex snuggled up next to her and threw her arm around Sienna's shoulders. She laid her head against Sienna's and the older sister let out a shaky gasp when Bridget asked what she could do. "Can you find a way to tell Gentry Wyatt that I love him so much, and I'm so sorry."

"I'll make sure he gets the message," Bridget answered quietly and Sienna finally let out a sob as she curled into Alex. Her sister held her tightly as she wept, rubbing Sienna's back as she shushed her and told her it was gonna be okay.

They hadn't realized Bridget was still there until the Marshal said, "I'll call you guys after Christmas with an update. I'm sorry it's not better news, but I'm glad you get to see your parents tomorrow night."

Sienna held her hand tightly to her mouth to keep from wailing, so Alex spoke up in her place. "We really appreciate you clearing us to see them. It's been really good for us to spend time as a family."

"There's actually somebody else who reached out to see Sienna."

She sniffled and stared at the phone, brows furrowing as she considered who would want to see her. "I- I don't understand."

"It's complicated, but they've been persistent. I know you were hoping to be released by now, but that's not gonna happen for a while. That said, there's somebody here who wants to see you. If you're willing to see someone from your old life, I can set up a meeting."

Old life? As in, pre-Landon life? Or Lonewood life? Just because they couldn't go back to Lonewood didn't mean the people from North Dakota couldn't come here. Sienna looked to Alex, who shrugged and mouthed 'You won't know unless you go'.

"Yeah. That would be fine." Sienna rubbed the underside of her nose as she sniffled. She knew better than to get her hopes up, but she had to cling to any hope she could find. "Can I ask who it is?"

"I can't disclose that over the phone for security reasons," Bridget answered slowly and Sienna twisted her lips thoughtfully. Bridget took a deep breath and continued, "They told me they could be available whenever you are, so you tell me when you're ready to see somebody and I'll set it up."

Sienna wanted to believe the man she loved was here in Manhattan, but that wasn't Gentry. He might have gotten behind the wheel for her, but hopping on a plane and flying across the country for a woman he wasn't allowed to have contact with was too far out of his comfort zone. Imagining him waiting for her felt like a taunt from God, but Sienna wanted to believe it so badly.

"Set it up for tomorrow."

The next day, Sienna stood at the entrance to Central Park with her hands shoved into her pockets. She shuddered as a cold breeze blew through the skyscrapers towards the park, chilling her to the bone. The sky was gray, sad like the way she was feeling inside. She'd spent the night convincing herself it wasn't Gentry who wanted to see her, and set herself up to be disappointed.

Part of Sienna didn't want Gentry to be here. She wanted him to be home for Christmas with his sister and his parents and their friends. The last thing Sienna wanted was to get in the way of their family time.

If he was here, she might never let him leave. She'd skip dinner with her parents and use the empty apartment to show him just how much she loved him. They'd spend the next week curled up together, and maybe, if they got bored, she'd show him New York.

She'd take him to her favorite restaurants and her favorite shows. She'd show him where she used to work. Sienna could already imagine the snarky remarks he'd make when he saw Thomas and Co. He'd tease her to high heaven for who she used to be, but she'd just smile and shrug. Then they'd go home and make love and never be apart again and-

"Hey, Scarlett."

Her breath caught in her throat as her heart cracked, disappointment flooding her very being as she reminded herself she'd been prepared for this moment. Then she turned around and saw Mason.

Considering what the news reports said, Mason looked pretty good. She could hardly tell that this man had been beaten within an inch of his life and left for dead. Perhaps it was all the expensive clothing he had layered to stay warm, but aside from a slight scar on his neck, right above his Adam's apple, it was easy to ignore the fact that he had almost died because of Alex and Sienna.

"I heard what happened," Sienna said slowly, torn between wanting to hug him and wanting to walk away. She wasn't angry at him anymore, but she wasn't here for any sort of reconciliation, even as friends. That said, Sienna had no intention of being rude. "I'm sorry we dragged you into this mess. I'm thankful you're okay."

"I had no idea what kind of trouble you were in, Scarlett." He reached forward to clench her hands in his Italian leather gloves. She stared at their hands, feeling her disappointment begin to well up in her chest at the realization she'd never hold Gentry's hand again. "I made a mistake in not going with you. I realized too late what you meant to me."

She blinked rapidly as she snapped her head up to look at Mason, remembering that she had once thought they would get married. The idea seemed laughable now, even if she couldn't be with the man she loved. "I understand. It was a hard situation. You had to make a split- second decision, I don't blame you for the one you made."

"Going back to the office and telling everyone we'd broken up when I never even got to say goodbye was the hardest thing I've ever done," Mason explained and Sienna raised a brow at that. He could have said goodbye, but he chose not to, just like he chose not to acknowledge her judgmental expression. Sienna was insulted; he obviously assumed that she wouldn't call him out on it. He continued blabbering on, apparently thinking Sienna wanted to hear him grovel some more. "All of my colleagues kept saying

how surprised they were that we ended things because they were sure you were going to be my wife. I realized too late that I had given up the best I was ever going to have."

"What are you saying Mason?" She didn't want to listen to him ramble. She didn't want to listen to him tell her that he regretted not coming with her. She didn't regret his decision at all. If he'd come to Lonewood, she would have never gotten to know Gentry, and she would have never understood what it was like to love her best friend.

None of that mattered now. The life and love and the brief future Sienna had imagined with Gentry was gone and nothing Mason said could fix that. The same program that banished Sienna and Alex to Lonewood now deemed it too dangerous to return, and Sienna felt like she was screaming in a glass box but nobody could hear her. Nobody was going to break her out of this hell.

Mason pulled her close and wrapped his arm around her shoulder to keep her warm, falling back into old habits. It was as comforting as it was unnerving. "You lost your job. Everything you've worked for is gone. You lost your friends and your home and your life. And I let you lose me, too. I'm never going to let you go again, Scarlett. I want to spend my life with you. I'm aware that it's complicated, and I'm aware things won't be the same, but I want to make it up to you so you can have the life you worked for- so *we* can have the life we planned and-"

"I can't just go back to my old life, Mason," Sienna blurted. "I'm not allowed. I can't be Scarlett Jacobs anymore. She's dead. I'm not even sure I should be seen with you out in public; Bridget wasn't even able to tell me you were the one meeting me today. New York is a big city, but I can't go back to my old job and I can't show up as your old girlfriend. I just... I can't."

"Then we'll leave," Mason told her firmly. He shifted so he was looking straight at her, holding her hands tightly again. "I can transfer to another office. We can move, go somewhere nobody knows you. Chicago, LA, Seattle... we can make a new life. We can make a new start, you and me."

Sienna swallowed, wondering if the Marshals would approve this plan. She could start her own marketing firm. She and Mason could achieve everything they'd planned, just somewhere else. It wasn't what she wanted, but since that wasn't an option, perhaps this was worth considering. A consolation prize for losing the man she loved.

It wasn't that simple though.

"What about Alex?" Sienna pressed. "I don't think they want her to leave Manhattan."

Mason raised his brow in question. "After everything she's done, you still care what happens to her?"

Sienna clenched her jaw and ripped her hands from Mason's. "She's my sister."

"She ruined our lives!"

"No, she saved my life!" Sienna yelled, causing several people to stare. Mason made a 'quiet down' motion with his hands, but Sienna was livid. "No, you don't get to talk about my sister that way."

"You've never cared about her. She's always been a nuisance, now we have a reason to leave her and start our own lives! I can give you everything you need to pick yourself up from the bottom. Everything we dreamed, we can still have it, Scarlett-"

"Don't call me that, that isn't my name," Sienna snarled. He looked startled by her cruel tone, but Sienna wasn't the woman he thought he loved anymore. "Mason, I'm different now. I really cared about you, but we're never getting back together. I found a new life, and new friends, and I found someone who truly loves me for who I am. I didn't get it before, but I get it now. There are more important things than work and success. Maybe not to you, and that's okay, but to me... he's more important than anything you could offer me here in New York or anywhere else in the world."

And I need to get back to him.

"I gotta go," Sienna said to herself as she backed away from Mason. He looked dumbfounded. Too stunned to speak, he watched her with wide eyes as she left him for the last time. "I have to go home." She turned and shuffled through the snow towards her apartment.

Home. She needed to go home, she needed to get back to Lonewood. For once in her life, Sienna silenced the little voice that told her to follow directions. Nobody, not even the US Marshals, were going to keep her from the life she wanted. She was tired of being what everyone expected her to be, Sienna was going to be who she wanted. She wanted to be a little selfish, but more than that, she wanted to be there for Gentry. He'd let her in because he wanted her in his life, and she'd promised to try. So she was going to try. The rest of the world be damned, she was going to try to get back to him.

When she got back to her apartment, Sienna shoved open the door and ran straight to Alex's room. She pounded on the door until Alex answered with a towel wrapped around her chest, getting ready for the Christmas Eve dinner with their parents. When she saw Sienna's breathless expression, she blurted, "What the hell?"

"I'm going back," Sienna told her quickly. "I'm going back to Lonewood. It's where I belong. It's where the man I love is." Alex nodded, but her smile didn't quite reach her eyes.

"Sienna..." Alex trailed off quietly. "You know you can't."

"Yes I can. I don't care what anybody says, I'm getting back to him." Sienna wasn't sure where this bravery was coming from, but she knew she needed to go before she lost her nerve. "I don't want to lose him, Alex. He's worth it."

Alex didn't say anything for a minute, but when she finally spoke her voice was strained. "I'm not coming with you." Sienna straightened up, having not considered returning without her sister. Maybe not today, but Sienna assumed she'd follow when she could. Between the two of them, Sienna hadn't expected her sister to be the one too afraid to break the rules.

Alex led Sienna into her bedroom and quickly grabbed her bathrobe from her bathroom. She sat on her bed beside Sienna and grabbed her hands. "I'm so thankful that you found Gentry. He's really great, and I think you should be with him. But I don't have anybody waiting for me in Lonewood. If I come back, everyone will expect me to get back with Jesse, and I can't risk outing him. There's nothing there for me now, but that doesn't mean you shouldn't go."

"But we've always been together."

"I know, but I think... I think you're gonna be okay." Alex threw her arm around Sienna and pulled her in for a hug, the soft satin of her bathrobe scraping against the heavy material of Sienna's winter coat. "We had a really great summer. I wouldn't trade it for the world. But Bridget isn't sure we're safe, and I think I need to stay here in case they need me. They aren't asking us to stay to keep you here- it's to keep me here. I'll stay and you can go, and they won't chase after you. I'll be okay here. I've gotta figure some stuff out for myself."

"I understand." Sienna sniffled, then let out a sad laugh. "It's just hard to imagine being there without you."

"You'll be okay. If Bridget cuts us off, I'll find a way to keep in touch."

"Promise?"

"I promise."

Sienna held Alex for almost five minutes, not ready to go their separate ways. For twenty eight years they'd done everything together, but it was time for them both to be on their own for a while, even if it was hard to admit.

"Fly safe. Let me know when you land," Alex told Sienna as she stood. "Give Gentry and Dakota a big hug from me. And tell Jesse I love him, and that I'm sorry."

"I will. Tell mom and dad that I'm in love, and that I'm going back into hiding." She laughed, imagining the look of horror on her mother's face when Alex confessed that Sienna had not only run off, but disobeyed a direct order from the US Marshals. If Alex had done it, they wouldn't be surprised, but Sienna? She hoped she didn't give her mother a heart attack.

Sienna waved as she looked around, deciding there was nothing here she needed but her coat and her heart on her sleeve.

When she reached the airport, it took approximately seven minutes from the time she booked her flight to Bismarck for her phone to start ringing, Bridget's name flashing across the screen.

"Hey, what's up?" Sienna asked casually as she picked out a couple of snacks from the gift shop, pretending she wasn't going on the lam.

"Oh, not much. Just my asset booking an unauthorized flight to the one place I asked her specifically not to go."

There was a bite of annoyance in Bridget's voice that made Sienna grin, but there wasn't anger or even urgency. It didn't sound like the woman was planning on running after her. "That's weird. Who would do that?"

Sienna chuckled as she placed her licorice and water bottle on the counter, then flipped through her wad of cash to pay for it. The first thing she did after buying her ticket was to pull out as much money from her account as the ATM would allow. That alone would have been enough to flag her actions for the Marshals, but she wasn't about to risk them shutting down her cards before she booked her flights and rental car.

"Sienna, what are you doing?"

"Isn't it obvious? I'm going home." Sienna grabbed her licorice and water and wandered over to her gate. She was thankful there was a flight within the hour she was able to get onto. A middle seat towards the back was not ideal but the plane was about to board. Bridget couldn't stop her if she tried. Well, she probably *could*, but Sienna wasn't worth the trouble of getting airport security involved. "I'm sorry Bridget, but I can't stay here. I love him."

"You know, of the two of you, I didn't expect this from you," Bridget droned, sounding annoyed still, but not too worried. "What am I supposed to tell my boss? That I lost an asset? Again?"

Sienna flinched, knowing she was about to get Bridget in trouble, but she'd come too far to chicken out now. "I'm sorry. Tell them you tried to stop me but I was already gone."

"I'll do you one better. You're discharged from the program."

"I thought you couldn't do that-"

"I never said I couldn't, I said my bosses don't want to. I don't recommend it, but if you're already boarding a flight you clearly don't care," Bridget's voice lightened a little, like she was smiling. "I can't force you to stay in WitSec, Sienna. You're free to go, but Landon's guys are still out there. You'll be on your own."

Sienna heard them call for her to board her flight. If she got on that plane, there'd be nobody to stop Landon from finding her and killing her. But he'd been thwarted by Gentry Wyatt once. He'd be a fool to try again.

"Thank you for everything Bridget."

"I hope you find what you're looking for. Fly safe."

She ended the call and Sienna handed the woman at the gate her ticket. She scanned the code and handed the ticket back with a smile. "Enjoy your flight, Miss Jade."

<h1 style="text-align:center">Chapter 52</h1>

THERE WAS SNOW IN New York. Sienna didn't mind it, and she didn't even mind the cold, but she couldn't *stand* how freezing North Dakota was in winter. She'd be lying if she said she didn't consider getting back on the plane when it landed in Bismarck late on December 24, but she forged through the sliding glass doors of the tiny airport and drove her rental car to a hotel for the evening.

As much as she wanted to reach Gentry as quickly as possible, one look at all the snow and ice reminded Sienna of how he lost his wife, and that Gentry would be livid if Sienna drove these roads by herself in the middle of the night.

When morning came, though, there was a strange sort of calm. The few people staying in the hotel were cheerfully eating breakfast together, celebrating Christmas morning with their relatives. It tugged on Sienna's heartstrings, and she wondered if she shouldn't have waited until tomorrow to make this trek so she could spend Christmas with her own parents and sister.

But, no. She knew what she wanted for Christmas.

For three hours she drove down the snowy roads, knuckles clenched so hard they turned white against the wheel, until she saw the Lonewood sign. Her whole body relaxed as she pulled into the parking lot of the Tumbleweed Motel, surprised to see dozens of cars.

Sienna climbed out of the SUV she'd rented and looked around, realizing the wooden exterior of the motel had been varnished, and little green wreaths had been hung on every door.

Despite being covered in a heavy layer of snow, Main Street was bustling with people all bundled up in their coats and boots and scarves. Sienna gasped as Lyle steered a big sleigh pulled by four horses holding at least a dozen people sitting on hay bails. The smell of gingerbread and peppermint radiated from the newly rebranded Sweets Shop, while Brenda and Colleen scurried around the crowded diner behind the large glass windows.

Sienna shuffled her way towards the diner, pushing open the door and causing the little bell to ring. She wiped her boots off on the mat, then looked up to see the locals staring at her while the tourists continued to talk amongst themselves. After a few moments, even the tourists turned to look at the redhead with the rosy cheeks shivering in the doorway, waiting to see what was so special about her.

"You're back." It was Brenda who broke the silence, depositing her tray to scuttle over to Sienna and wrap her up in a hug. She grabbed her cheeks to hold her close, rambling as she studied Sienna. "My darling, you're skin and bones! Let me get you something to eat! How have you been? Where's your sister?"

"We're doing fine. She's back home." Brenda's smile fell a little at that, but Sienna added, "And now so am I."

Colleen appeared with a coffee in a to-go cup, which Brenda scowled at, but Colleen said quietly, "I doubt she came all this way for us."

Sienna spared a look around the diner, knowing that if the person she was looking for was here that he'd already have her in his arms.

Her gaze fell on Dusty and his wife, who held a baby dressed in a little red Christmas onesie. Sienna wandered over to them, lip quivering as she faced Hank. He huffed, staring up at her with a playfully upset expression. "Hank," Sienna said sweetly. "It's good to see you."

His grin grew and he slid out of the booth to wrap Sienna in a hug. "It's good to see you too, City Girl. I'm surprised to see you back in these parts."

"Well, there's somebody here I can't get in New York."

"New York? Thought you were from California?" Hank challenged, but Brenda hushed him from where she stood behind Sienna.

Sienna shrugged, the smooth fabric of her heavy jacket hitting her jaw. "Maybe later I'll have time to explain, but I'm actually looking for someone." Sienna's gaze drifted to Dusty. "You wouldn't happen to know where I could find your boss?"

"He's actually off this Christmas. I'm on patrol, can't you tell?" Dusty gestured towards the picture windows where he could watch everyone come and go from his wife's side. "I think he said something about Christmas dinner at Dakota's place. That's probably the best place to start."

Sienna bowed her head in thanks and gave Brenda another one-armed hug before heading back out into the cold with her coffee between her mittens.

Over the summer, the homes down the residential streets were silent and empty, but on Christmas afternoon they were full of life. She could see people watching football through open blinds and a couple of children playing with toys under the trees.

But when she found herself on Dakota's doorstep, Sienna froze. For the first time, Sienna considered that she was making a mistake. A lot could happen in four months. It wasn't like she called ahead to tell them she was coming, Sienna was literally arriving on Dakota's doorstep on Christmas morning. Gentry could have found somebody else or have moved on.

Summoning her bravery, Sienna knocked firmly on the door. She heard Tilly barking wildly inside, followed by the high pitched whine of Buster trying to be obedient but wanting to see who was at the door. When it swung open, Dakota's jaw dropped and she gasped.

"Hi," Sienna blurted, unsure what else to say. Dakota stared at her for a moment, then tackled her in a bear hug. Sienna held her tightly as Tilly jumped up at her, panting excitedly.

"Dakota? Who's at the door?"

Sienna's heart clenched at the sound of his voice. Dakota quickly shuffled her into the foyer and closed the door behind her, gesturing for Sienna to take off her coat. She slid out of it as Dakota ripped the beanie off her head then took her coat, allowing Sienna the chance to fix her hair just as Gentry stepped around the corner from the kitchen.

His eyes locked onto her in shock, and Sienna watched the breaths build up in his chest until he closed the space between them and leaned down to kiss her. She sighed into his mouth and he wrapped one arm around her waist and the other around her shoulders, holding her against him for dear life. He deepened the kiss as Sienna grabbed his cheeks, feeling the rough beard he'd grown over the past couple of months. His hair had gotten longer, and his skin was less tanned, but the way they melded together hadn't changed a bit.

Finally, Gentry pulled away, panting as he stared at her lovingly. "You're really here."

"I missed you so much." Sienna leaned up on her toes for another kiss. Gentry happily obliged, kissing her back desperately. When she pulled away again, she murmured, "They told me I couldn't come back to Lonewood, so I left Witness Protection. Bridget said if I don't want their help I'm free to do whatever I want."

He swallowed and pulled away, watching her as she stroked the back of his neck. "And what is it you want?"

"You, obviously." She laughed and he smiled, melting her heart. "I literally got on a plane with no luggage, no plan. I just knew I wanted to see you, and I spent the past day hoping you wanted to see me, too."

"Oh. Right, this is awkward…" Gentry trailed off teasingly as he pointed over his shoulder towards the kitchen, but he turned back to Sienna and kissed her quickly. "I've thought of nothing else but seeing you again. You better not be planning on leaving."

She shook her head. "Nope. I'm home for good. You're stuck with me now, Sheriff."

"Good," he huffed as he grabbed her backside and pulled her close. "Because I love you, and I'm going to marry you, and we're gonna live in my super great house out in the Badlands, and we're gonna ride through the plains every day, and I'm gonna make you scream until you lose your voice every night for the rest of your life."

"Gentry," his mother's dissaproving voice drawled, causing Sienna and Gentry to both look up and see his entire family watching them gush over each other. Dakota looked proud, but Rose looked unimpressed by her son's crude plans.

Sienna waved awkwardly. "Hi, Miss Rose."

"Hi, Sienna. Would you like to join us for dinner? Or will that get in the way of your plans?" Rose asked Gentry with a pointed look that made Sienna's cheeks turn red, but Gentry grinned proudly to make Sienna blush even more.

"Dinner would be nice," she admitted before Gentry could sweep her away. Rose, Eli, and finally Dakota disappeared into the kitchen to give them some privacy, and Sienna glared up at Gentry and hissed, "Seriously?"

"What? It's not like they don't know that we slept together."

"You told them we had sex?"

"Well, yeah, it was kind of a big deal," Gentry retorted back, unable to hide his smirk. Sienna rolled her eyes, then shook her head at him. "You wanted this. You came all the way from... wherever you're actually from, for this." He pointed to himself to emphasize his point. He looked like an excited child who got exactly what he asked for on Christmas, and he was going to be an absolute brat until he got to play with his new toy.

Sienna crossed her arms and stared up at Gentry in pretend resignation. "I guess I did, didn't I?" She couldn't contain her smile and leaned up to kiss his lips softly. "I love you."

"I love you too... Scarlett?" His voice lilted up a little in question and she shook her head, telling him no. "Sienna, then?" She nodded and he leaned his forehead against hers to still her. "I love you, Sienna. So much. I'm going to spend the rest of my life with you."

There it was, burning deep in her soul, that little spark that Gentry Wyatt lit inside her. She felt it smoldering stronger with every kiss and touch and Sienna Jade knew she'd finally found herself. She'd finally found home. It was the peace she felt in Gentry's arms, the love in Dakota's little town, and the wild spirit of the Badlands under the pink-streaked sunsets of North Dakota.